DAYBREAK ON NEWEDEN

Night-quiet, the two _____ unseen in the overlyi__ _____ nd-
spiders of the west____ _____ the
contracted victim, ra__ _____ his
chest and stabbed i_ _____ as
the Khaelian-made _____ line
from shoulder to mid-back, then slipped and fell in the rank
mud at his feet.

The Hoorka assassins stood over him. Gunnar lay face
down in the mud, and they knew he was waiting for the cold
violation of steel to pierce his body. But relays warned them
that morning had touched the Dawnrock with delicate
fingers. It would be so easy to kill Gunnar despite the
Hoorka code. No one was there to see . . .

Strong hands helped Gunnar to his feet, grunting with
the man's limp weight.

"Our admiration, Gunnar. Your life is your own once
more," the Hoorka said in a voice that masked his bitterness.
"You may go with the light."

ASSASSINS' DAWN

SLOW FALL TO DAWN

DANCE OF THE HAG

A QUIET OF STONE

STEPHEN LEIGH

DAW BOOKS, INC.
DONALD A. WOLLHEIM, FOUNDER
375 Hudson Street, New York, NY 10014
**ELIZABETH R. WOLLHEIM
SHEILA E. GILBERT
PUBLISHERS**
www.dawbooks.com

First Printing, May 2013
1 2 3 4 5 6 7 8 9

DAW TRADEMARK REGISTERED
U.S. PAT. AND TM. OFF. AND FOREIGN COUNTRIES
—MARCA REGISTRADA
HECHO EN U.S.A.

PRINTED IN THE U.S.A.

Introduction

THIS UNIVERSE ISN'T GOOD ENOUGH; I'M MAKING ANOTHER ONE

Way back (and at this point in my life, believe me, "way back" is the correct terminology) when I was first starting to devour adult science fiction, I became fascinated by the fabulous, intricate fictional universes created by the writers of the time: Asimov's "Foundation" stories, the "Mars" tales of Ray Bradbury, the ambiguously-linked future of many of the Heinlein novels, James Blish's "Cities in Flight" novels, E.E. Smith's "Lensman" series, and so on. When I eventually started writing my own fiction, those examples were still in my head, and so I created my own universe sandbox in which to play.

Now, I have to say that there's a significant issue with writing fiction set in some far-off future: no writer's *ever* going to be able to predict the technology of the far future, especially given the rapid increase in technological innovation. We're destined (almost always) to fall short of technological advances, and probably miss badly no matter how much we push the envelope. The technologies of our fictional future usually end up being invented long before that time arrives, or we totally miss new technologies that will arise after we wrote the story. At the time I'd read those Asimovian, Bradburian, and Heinleinian stories, I was already a few decades past when they'd been originally written and the technologies in those books had nearly all—except for the magical hyperdrive—been invented in the meantime, or been surpassed. Often, the technology of those universes was laughably outdated.

After all, if someone in the 1400s tried to imagine the technology of today, it's extremely unlikely that he or she would accurately predict or describe the world all of us inhabit. No matter what we like to think, humans aren't *good* at predicting what a world two or three or four centuries further along might be like. Heck, we're not really good at predicting what a world ten years from now will look like. Fiction written in the 1950s generally reflects 1950s sensibilities. Just watch the classic movie "Forbidden Planet" if you want to witness that—a spaceship from 22nd century Earth crewed by an exclusively white, exclusively male crew? The same applies to 1960s fiction, and 1970s, and 1980s, and so on. You see the time in which the stories were written echoed subtly in the background.

Unless . . . My "clever strategy" to avoid this problem was to postulate a total collapse of civilization, followed by a genuine "dark age" where most technology was lost (and lost in erratic fashion)—thus providing a convenient, built-in excuse for me when the reader's technology inevitably caught up with what I wrote in the Alliance stories. "Sure, the technology's outdated even now," I could tell my future reader. "Yes, I know that we already have superior technology, and it's only twenty years past when I initially wrote the story, but you see, there was this collapse, and that's why their technology is still behind ours . . ."

The "dark age" would explain the relatively small technological leaps from "now" to "then." Mind you, my "now" was the mid-1970s to the mid-1980s for the Alliance stories, and looking at those stories several decades later . . . well, just as with the old tales I'd read Way Back Then, technology has indeed already passed by my imagined future ones, and I can see where I entirely missed certain advances.

So you see, dear reader, before you read this book, I want to tell you that there was this collapse . . .

Remember that, and forgive the paltry limits of my imagination. One of the statements I often make to my writing classes, when talking about science fiction, is that the genre really *isn't* about the future. It's actually about the *present*— the present of the time in which the story was written—with the author holding up a funhouse mirror to the world he or she knows and thinking "What if *this* went on . . . ?" The imagined future is our reflection in that warped mirror, showing us a "present" stretched and taffy-pulled into a future.

Science fiction tells us far more about how we were at the time of the story than about any future generation.

Now that you have my excuse, let's get back to the history of the stories I wrote for the Alliance universe. Many of the first stories I wrote in that universe never sold—for good reason; I was still learning the craft. Mind you, *I* thought those newbie efforts were *tremendous* and I couldn't understand how the editors could be so blind as not to see the incredible genius of them. But . . . now when I scan the crumpled, mail-worn manuscripts lingering forlornly in their folders in my file cabinet, I can see why they never sold.

They *sucked*.

But I persevered through the barrage of rejection slips and even managed to learn a bit about the craft in the process, and eventually started selling a few of the tales, the majority of them still set in what I called the "Alliance" universe. In the end, I placed several short stories in that alternate history in the various magazines and anthologies.

And three novels, as well—and those three novels are what you're holding in your hand right now. Here's how the first one, SLOW FALL TO DAWN, came about . . .

Around 1976 or so, I read an article about the Hashshashin, an early band of assassins, which started me thinking about the concept of "ethical assassins"—murderers who would attempt an assassination, but would for philosophical reasons permit the victim a small chance of survival. I started putting together a world (yes, in the Alliance universe, which was nothing if not flexible) with these "ethical assassins," which I was calling the "Hoorka." I suddenly realized, as I starting planning and writing this tale, that this wasn't going to be a short story or novelette, but a full-fledged novel.

Characters and sub-plots and complications. Oh, my!

Honestly, I rather rapidly became lost in the book. One thing writing short stories hadn't prepared me for was how complicated novels are, how long they take to write, how difficult it is to hold the details in your head, and the amount of persistence and dedication required to complete them . . .

I panicked. Instead of finishing what I'd started, I eviscerated the book. I retained only the basic shell of the story and produced a novelette called "In Darkness Waiting." I sent the story (still bleeding from the massive surgery) to *Isaac Asimov's Science Fiction Magazine*, and Gardner Dozois, who was the Assistant Editor there at the time, liked it enough to send me revision notes and a promise to look at the story again once I'd revised it. I made changes and sent it back, and Gardner (or George Scithers, who was editor at the time) bought it. It appeared in the October 1977 issue. (If you're curious, it's reprinted in my ebook short story collection A RAIN OF PEBBLES, along with most of the other Alliance Universe stories)

I continued to write and occasionally sell short stories for the next few years, but I was realizing that if I ever wanted to have any shot at actually making writing a substantial part of my income, I had to overcome my trepidation and write novels.

Being the eminently lazy sort, I thought: "Why not start with the novel you've already planned out?" I'd been smart enough—which is honestly a rarity—not to actually trash the notes I'd made. I began to reconstruct the novel, gluing back onto the skeleton of "In Darkness Waiting" all the material and ideas I'd trimmed away, rewriting the story from the beginning.

Early in 1980 I had a pile of paper that somewhat resembled a novel, which I titled SLOW FALL TO DAWN. I also had no idea how to market the thing to agents. Here's where networking (of the pre–Facebook, Twitter, and Live-Journal variety, using letters and phone calls) came in.

Denise and I had begun attending the regional SF cons as well as the occasional Worldcon or big East Coast gathering. I'd met quite a few writers—most of them farther along in their career than me—and become good friends with some. I contacted a select few, asking if they knew of an agent they'd recommend I contact. George RR Martin suggested a relatively new agent he'd met, and was kind enough to say he'd send her a personal recommendation.

Just as good networking can lead to a "real" job, good networking can also lead to work in your writing career. People do tend to help other people whom they know and like.

I will point out before someone brings out the old cliché that "You see! It's all just about who you know!" that networking only works to a point. Getting an introduction to someone via a friend might crack open a door you thought locked, but your fiction still has to do the heavy lifting—and that's far more important. You can sell a novel without networking if it's well-written and compelling; you *can't* sell a poorly-written novel no matter how fantastic a network you have.

Fast-forward a few months. . . . The agent, after reading the novel, had agreed to represent me. At the time, I was running a bi-weekly RPG game—mostly AD&D but with lots of rule changes we'd made on our own. During the middle of one of our games late in 1980, the phone rang and Denise answered. She passed the phone over to me. "It's your agent," she said. She gave me an eyebrow-raised look as I took the phone.

"I have good news," the voice on the other end said. "Bantam's made an offer on your book . . ." I don't remember much of the rest of the night, except that I recall it involved more beer than usual and that I happily allowed the characters in the RPG to get away with far too much mayhem and treasure. Everyone went up a level or two.

I had sold my first book!

It did pretty well, too: had some good reviews, and *Locus* named it one of the Top Ten First Novels, and sales were good enough that my editor at Bantam wanted more books.

I realized that I wanted to follow the character arc of Gyll, my protagonist, through the rest of his story. I wanted to see what would happen if I took my ethical assassins and moved them *off* this peculiar little world of theirs and out into the greater Alliance.

Those speculations would lead to the sequel DANCE OF THE HAG as well as the concluding novel A QUIET OF STONE, the other two books that make up the omnibus edition you're holding.

Over the years, I've often wished I could get these books back into print. Now, thanks to Sheila Gilbert and the other good folks at DAW Books, that wish has become a reality.

I hope you enjoy the journey as much as I enjoyed writing it!

SLOW FALL TO DAWN

for DENISE—
she knows why,
but still enjoys being told

Chapter 1

PAUSE. And shiveringly inhale. The two Hoorka-kin gathered air for their complaining lungs. It had been a long run for Aldhelm and Sartas, far too long. Sweat varnished the skin under their nightcloaks, and their legs were cramped and sore. Still, the quarry was just ahead, and they could allow themselves only the briefest rest. Night-quiet, the two assassins advanced like shadows unseen in overlying murk; as deadly as the wind-spiders of the western tundra.

In but seventeen minutes, the photoreceptors on the dawnrock would signal Underasgard's dawn and the end of their hunt. They ran, the Hoorka.

Aldhelm signaled Sartas to a halt in the comforting darkness cast by a high porch. Somewhere just ahead, Gunnar—the contracted victim—was enmeshed in the thick metal pilings that held the houses above the early rains and the cold flood that inevitably followed. These were the tenements of Sterka, the most temporary sector of a city that had not been meant by its founders to survive more than half a century and was now well into its second hundred years. Wooden beams lent support to the time- and rust-weakened pillars of metal. Decay, an odor formed of river mud and rust, filled their nostrils. Aldhelm fought the inclination to cough in the fetid air.

It hadn't been an easy or lucky night for them.

The apprentices had done their work admirably. With six hours still to pass before the Underasgard dawn terminated the contract, Aldhelm and Sartas had taken up the trail within meters of Gunnar. They'd pursued him down the

Street of Ravines, scenting an easy kill and an early night; the Thane would be pleased, for this was politically an important assassination. The street was deserted, the only light coming from hoverlamps spaced at long intervals, and Gunnar was already winded. But as the Hoorka reached for their daggers, Gunnar suddenly lifted his head, cast a frightened yet oddly hopeful look behind him, and ducked into a cross street to his left. A moment later, the two Hoorka heard the sound that had caused Gunnar's optimism—the low-moaning chant of the Dead, a lassari sect. The Dead were the disenfranchised, the most depressed of the unguilded: the lassari. Their balm was ignorance, their unity hopelessness. Those of the Dead did nothing save to march and chant their melancholy mantras, accompanied by the scent of burning incense and finding catharsis in the act of marching. Their indifference to reality was legendary; the Dead paid no attention to pedestrians in their path, ignored the occasional assaults on peripheral members of their processions, and failed to notice their own members who would swoon and fall from exhaustion. They considered their lives already ended. Why should any lagging pain from the life they considered finished bother them? They marched to meet Hag Death, and took her foul embrace as they would that of a lover.

The Dead entered the Street of Ravines from the right of the cross street, and made a slow, agonizing turn toward the Hoorka. There were perhaps thirty of them, eyes closed as they chanted, their bodies—wrapped in simple cloth robes—filling the narrow street. Cursing, the Hoorka fought to make a passage through the press. The fuming censers filled their nostrils with acrid fumes, and around them the expressionless faces moved in the sibilant chanting, ignoring the Hoorka who pushed and shoved the unresisting Dead from their path. Aldhelm raised an open hand—the Dead One on his left was a young woman who looked as if she might have once been pretty—and pushed her away from him. Her eyes opened briefly, though she didn't look at him, and then she resumed her chanting, stumbling as she regained her balance.

And abruptly, they were through. The procession of Dead, unruffled, continued down the street, their chant echoing from the buildings to either side. Gunnar had disappeared. The Hoorka ran down the cross street, searching the alleyways that led off from the street. Dame Fate rewarded their diligence. Aldhelm motioned to Sartas, beckoning. He gave inward thanks to She of the Five Limbs for her favor, and moved into a narrow, dingy alley.

The moons were yet to rise, but a pallid lemon-light filtered through a greasy window high up on one wall of the bordering structures. The window gave but a wan and uncertain illumination, but with the light-enhancers the Hoorka wore, it was enough. They could see Gunnar, halfway up a pile of packing crates that had been thrown into the alley, blocking it. Gunnar hadn't yet seen the Hoorka, but in his haste to get by the crates, he sent them tumbling noisily to the ground. Sartas grinned at Aldhelm and loosened his vibro in its sheath. A victim so obviously frightened, so careless, was an easy kill.

But his very clumsiness saved Gunnar. The lighted window was suddenly flung open. Brilliant light washed over the alley, stabbing at the packing crates, the startled Gunnar, and the cobbled surface of the ground.

"Bastard!" a voice shouted, hoarsely. "Get away from those crates or I'll have your manhood!"

Gunnar whirled, losing his precarious balance and sending more crates to the ground. He slipped, tumbling halfway to earth, and in that instant saw the Hoorka, momentarily blinded by the sudden overload of the light-enhancers. Sartas flung his vibro: a wild throw, it came nowhere near Gunnar. And as the Hoorka recovered their vision and moved toward their victim, the window was slammed shut again with a final curse. In the time it took the Hoorka to regain sight once more, Gunnar scrambled over and through the labyrinth of crates and into the maze of streets beyond.

Sartas picked one of the cobblestones from the alley, hefted it, and sent it crashing through the window.

"May all your children be lassari," he shouted. "And if your pride is offended by my insult, see Sartas of the Hoorka. I'll give you satisfaction *and* an introduction to Hag Death."

Silence. After a moment, Sartas grinned. "He doesn't answer, Aldhelm. Too bad."

Aldhelm didn't share his companion's humor. "We have to find Gunnar, kin-brother. This is petty."

"Let's go, then."

They found Gunnar again more because the apprentices had done their preliminary work than through any skills of their own. Gunnar's mistress, Ricia Cuscratti, lived in the Burgh. As with most neighborhoods in Sterka, the rich lived in uncomfortable proximity to the poor, and m'Dame Cuscratti, a member of the Banker's Guild, was rich. The Hoorka, having little recourse, made their way to her dwelling after ascertaining that Gunnar had fled in that direction.

The Cuscratti house was large, set away from the street and buffered by a well-lit garden. Parti-colored hoverlamps flickered above the topiary and illuminated the skeleton of a small ippicator. The wall facing the street was translucent—colors melted and collided in abstract patterns while the shadows of figures moved in the rooms behind. Aldhelm and Sartas paused, taking refuge in the shadowed recesses of a run-down warehouse adjacent to the house.

"We could wait for him." Sartas's voice was heavy with his breathing.

Aldhelm, in darkness, shook his head. "There isn't that much time now. No, *if* he's there, he'll stay unless we set him running again. We'll have to go in."

"As you say." Sartas shrugged. "I'll want hot mead when we get back to the caverns. If Felling doesn't have the cooking fires lit, I'll use his bed for kindling."

It took no great skill to loose the hoverlamps from the magnetic field powering them. The lamps fell like stunned fireflies, and in darkness the garden gave more cover than they required. The flowing colors of the wall cast oddly-hued shadows from the trimmed shrubbery. Drifting patches of shade twisted like pastel vines over the street and into the houses beyond. Aldhelm and Sartas were quickly standing near the doorshield. Aldhelm rummaged in his nightcloak, found the random field generator, and began to adjust the device, searching for the frequency that would dilate the shield and let them pass. The mechanism hummed loudly in the quiet of the garden.

In the night silence, the Hoorka heard the footsteps many seconds before anyone came into view. The assassins slipped into deeper cover and watched four men approach the house from the street. The figures hesitated near the entrance to the garden, and the wall threw mad images dancing behind them, animating the sleeping hulks of buildings. The intruders made no attempt at stealth, nor did they bother with any subtlety when confronted by the obstacle of the doorshield. One of the four brought a fieldgun to bear. Phosphorescent sparks arced, spat angrily, and expired on the rich humus of the garden. The translucent wall rippled patterns of alarm: billows of purple-scarlet welled outward from the shield and spread across the face of the house, growing larger and more saturated with color. Somewhere inside, a disconsolate siren wailed mournfully and shadow-figures raced from front to back, away from the disturbance. The intruders — Aldhelm could see them clearly in the aching blue-white glare of the dying shield — wore cloaks not unlike the gray and black nightcloaks of the Hoorka-kin, but these were no Hoorka. He signaled to Sartas, using the hand code. *Vingi's people?*

In the depths of some fanciful bird of shrubbery, Sartas's hand moved in reply. *Probable.*

A flick of a hand, a flashing of palm. *We'll wait.*

The shield died in orange and white agony. Flame guttered and died, running fitfully up and down the perimeter of the opening as the door dilated. The four ran quickly past the smoking ruin and into the house, weapons ready. Aldhelm unsheathed his vibro.

Now. Aldhelm nodded to Sartas, and the two Hoorka swept past the wreckage of the shield.

They were in a reception room. An animo-painting swirled on the far wall and ornate floaters waited for occupants. Lifianstone pillars carved like vines climbed from floor to distant ceiling in a mockery of nature, curling and spreading when they reached the balcony that overlooked the room. Beyond the balcony, the Hoorka could hear the sounds of a struggle, and then the wall opposite the railings began to smoke as a line of blistering paint ran quickly across it in a ragged diagonal. A hand laser, then. The thought did little to comfort Aldhelm. Standing in the room, they were exposed to anyone caring to glance over the balcony rail.

Aldhelm moved to the staircase (carved mermen waved flippered hands at carved fish in a frozen ocean: the railing), and Sartas followed quickly. They ran quietly up the stairs.

"I don't like this. We're not armed or protected for a laser fight." Aldhelm glanced back at Sartas.

"*You* want to go back and explain all this to the Thane? This would be a cleaner death."

"He's going to be upset no matter what happens." Aldhelm exhaled deeply. "Dame Fate keeps playing Her hand against us tonight, and I don't like that."

Aldhelm crouched down and glanced around the corner at the top of the staircase. Nothing. "Fine," he said. "Let's find out who these fake guild-kin of ours are."

This floor of the house was built in a semi-circle around an interior garden redolent with tropical flowers. Across the open space, Aldhelm could see the focus of the fighting. The four cloaked men had taken shelter behind a convenient sculpture and were firing into a darkened archway that led farther back into the interior of the house. Someone was returning their fire with a projectile weapon. Aldhelm could hear the whine of shells and see chunks of masonry flying as the bullets struck the walls. The Hoorka began moving to one side of the battle.

"Damned clumsy people, these counterfeit Hoorka," muttered Sartas.

"They're not particularly alert. We could take them easily enough. Go around to the left. I think we can circle the garden and come out somewhere on the other side of that arch."

"They've enough firepower to destroy the house. Clumsy."

"Yah," Aldhelm agreed. "But let's stay out of their way. If we can get around them, maybe we can get to Gunnar first. I don't like the thought of someone's blood-feud interfering with our contract."

They had no chance. There was a sudden flurry of movement as three of the intruders rushed the archway while the other kept his laser activated and pointed at the corridor beyond. Then the three were past the arch and the sound of a physical struggle intensified. A high scream, like tearing velvet, rose and died. The last of the intruders ran through the archway. The Hoorka waited.

Nothing.

Aldhelm strode quickly across the garden, heedless of the painstakingly-arranged plants he was trampling underfoot, and Sartas followed. At the archway, they paused, peering inside cautiously. A purplish fog filled the corridor and wisped about the lamps set in the wall. A woman's body, wrapped in a gauzy dress, lay on her side, crumpled against the wall with an odd lack of blood. The intruders were gone. Aldhelm gestured to Sartas to stay, and went to examine the body. He turned it over gently—it was Ricia. He didn't need to check the pulse to know that she was in Hag Death's domain.

The Hoorka followed the path of the intruders through the house—the trail of a running battle. Here were charred draperies, there a vase overturned and broken. They passed through a series of bedrooms, an expansive dining area where a stray bolt had evidently hit a power circuit and dumped the table, set for dinner, onto the floor. Silver utensils littered the tiles, slivers of crockery crunched underfoot. They went through a kitchen, then were back outside again. And when they found themselves out of the grounds and back in the entangling clustering of houses, they came upon an apprentice Hoorka waiting for them, out of breath.

"The Thane sent me, sirrahs." A gasping intake of breath, fish-mouthed. "He has learned that Vingi (breath) has sent some of his guard (breath) force to kill Gunnar."

Aldhelm and Sartas glanced at each other, then Aldhelm grimaced and nodded. "So Vingi doesn't trust the task to Hoorka. Well, he's managed to foul it up for himself. We have to track Gunnar again."

The apprentice clutched his sides and crouched slightly. "I saw Gunnar leave this house as I came here," he said as he straightened. "He began moving toward the river, and he seemed to know the ground well. Vingi's guards—at least I assume the men I saw were of the Li-Gallant Vingi's guild—had a short meeting in the garden near the ippicator skeleton. They left in the direction of Vingi's keep."

Sartas shook his head at Aldhelm. "I told you they were incompetent." The Hoorka chuckled.

"The Thane won't be laughing if we fail to meet the contract." Aldhelm turned to the apprentice. "Tell the Thane that we've already had a problem with Vingi's guard. You can also tell him—but step back when you do so—that Gunnar is still alive. Then run, neh?"

The apprentice grinned and nodded. He bowed his

salutation to the Hoorka and was off. The sound of his running could be heard for some time in the sleeping city.

That had been hours ago. Now they were finally in sight of Gunnar again, having tracked him through the twisting streets. Aldhelm could see the man clearly. Gunnar was breathing heavily, his right arm extended as he leaned against the understructure of the tenements. His head was bowed, his knees were slightly bent. The muck of the river had caked his shoes — he'd been easy to follow since entering undercity.

The ooze glistened coldly with slats of blue-white light. The seams of the flooring overhead grinned with age. Aldhelm could hear the indistinct rise and fall of murmured conversation above him, punctuated unevenly with the breathing of Sartas and himself. A voice complained loudly of the abundance of sandmites as the Hoorka began moving.

The mud that had so clearly marked this stage of Gunnar's flight also aided him. Even Hoorka assassins, adept at silentstalk, were not immune to chance, as this night had amply proved. The river-filth sucked greedily at the soles of their boots, relinquishing them with a liquid protest. Gunnar's head snapped up: they were still thirty meters from him, under the next dwelling. The man ducked instinctively, and the Khaelian-made dagger only creased him, drawing a burning line from shoulder to mid-back before burying its ultra-hard point several millimeters into the metal pillar behind him. Even as Gunnar looked up, weighing the chances of grasping the dagger, it began to wriggle and loosen, the electronic devices in the dagger seeking to return to the homing pulse from the Hoorka. Gunnar floundered to his feet and ran, weaving from pillar to pillar.

(And Aldhelm cursed under his breath, reproaching the Goddess of Chaos for tipping the scales of chance so unequally, and praying that She of the Five would hold back the sun — dawn at Underasgard would give Gunnar his life.)

The Hoorka knew Gunnar would be praying to his own gods for the light, for Underasgard was but fifty kilometers distant and the sun would touch the dawnrock at much the same time as dawn here in the city of Sterka. Then — unmoved and uncaring, at least outwardly — the Hoorka would be bound to let the man live. Already the morning sky was luminous with that promise.

Aldhelm, knowing this, sought to end it quickly.

He loosed another dagger. It clattered from a pillar and, twirling, struck Gunnar handle foremost. Silver glimmered as the weapon turned and arced back to the Hoorka.

Pursuer and pursued ran, ignoring the banded pain that constricted their chests and stabbed in their lungs. Sartas threw: the dagger found a pillar at Gunnar's right, and the man feinted left and dove as another Hoorka blade fountained mud at his feet. Gunnar slipped, coating himself with umber goo, and regained his footing. The stench of decaying vegetation made him gag, and he slipped again, retching and struggling. Mud blinded him. He scrabbled frantically at his face.

The Hoorka stood over him. Gunnar lay in the mud, and Aldhelm watched the man flailing in panic, knowing Gunnar could feel the pressure of his gaze, knowing the man was waiting for the cold rape of a blade piercing his body, twisting deep into his entrails ...

But the relays had told them that morning had touched the dawnrock with its delicate fingers. Aldhelm looked about him. It would be so easy to kill Gunnar despite the Hoorka code. No one would see, and it might save future trouble with Li-Gallant Vingi. He sighed, glancing at Sartas, weighing the choices in his mind. Sartas shook his head, sensing Aldhelm's hesitation.

Dawn was a tepid light on a misty morning. They helped Gunnar to his feet, grunting with the man's limp weight.

"Come on, damnit. You can stand." Aldhelm's voice was neither ice nor fire, not devoid of emotion but rather so full of it that the individual nuances were indistinguishable with surfeit.

The Hoorka watched composure slowly return to Gunnar's drawn, haggard face. He wiped vainly at his soiled clothing, looking as if he were about to speak. But he lowered his eyes and looked at the ruin of his pants.

Aldhelm spoke again. "Our admiration, Gunnar. Your life is your own once more." His voice, without the inflections that might have turned it mocking and bitter, spoke of the ritualistic completion of a ceremony. "You may go with the light."

"Ricia's dead." Gunnar's voice was cracked and dry; his eyes were wild, puzzled.

"M'Dame Cuscratti was not killed by Hoorka. That is a matter of bloodfeud between yourself and another. You will bear the truth of that." For a moment, Aldhelm's eyes glinted angrily in the dawnlight, then he half-turned. "Make your way home. Your path is safe," he said. Aldhelm motioned to Sartas, and the assassins were gone, slipping into the twilight gloom of undercity.

Gunnar stood: dripping and covered with filth, gasping with tortured lungs, confused and thankful both. He glanced at the landscape around him, then stared at the ruddy arc of sun above the line of trees across the river. He breathed deeply and walked away.

The house stood well away from the river and its urban banks. Unlike the majority of Neweden buildings, this one disdained the pillared, flighty architecture, and squatted dourly on the earth, attended by a cluster of outbuildings. It straddled the crest of a low hill that was the first outcropping of the Dagorta Mountains, and it was similar to the other dwellings of this fertile land in that it too had ranks of gardens and trees shielding the Neweden soil from the sunstar. Sterka, the city, lay in the blue-tinged distance, just visible from the highest point of the rise: the city was a massive grouping of buildings, with the outlying burghs arrayed before it like a shield, a buffer against the wilderness. As a panorama, the view wasn't exceptional—the most common scenes of a hundred worlds of the Alliance were more pleasing aesthetically, and Neweden herself had better, but it satisfied those who normally dwelt here. It reeked of sylvan, pastoral quietness. Unassertive, it seemed strong.

Through this display of verdant order, a man moved, stumbling and slow. His hair was matted and gleaming with sweat, his tunic torn and coated with mud now dried and caked to a sienna lamination. He walked clumsily, drunkenly, nearly falling now and again, as if he weren't fully awake or aware of his surroundings. The sun glazed the air about him, and drone-beetles made desultory circles about his head, flying lazily away with every step. He raised his head to stare at the cluster of buildings on the rise, focusing his attention on the main house with its mirror walls reflecting the heat-wave of the guard shield around it. The windows were opaqued and empty. He stood, as the sun inched itself infinitesimally higher in the cloud-choked sky, and some animal hooted disconsolately in the nearby woods. Then he lowered his head and resumed his ambling, slow progress toward the crest.

He reached the guard shield and halted again. He stared at the house, his hand shielding his eyes from the reflected sun-glare as the walls threw back the image of his surroundings. Nothing moved, nothing acknowledged his arrival. Shrugging—dried mud fell from the sleeve of his tunic to the ground, revealing purple cloth—he placed his hand on the butler post and let it scan his fingerprints. The guard shield coalesced and drew back from the butler, leaving him room to pass through an opening defined by a sparking perimeter. He moved through and onto the manicured lawn beyond.

"A good morning, sirrah," the butler said as the shield collapsed back into position. The man didn't reply. After a pause, the post spoke again. "Sirrah Potok will be glad to see you."

"No doubt he told you to expect me." The man's voice was weary.

A moment's silence as the butler scanned its small memory. "I'm afraid not, sirrah. You, of course, are always welcome here. Should I inform the house?"

But he'd already moved on. The butler, uncaring, lapsed into silence.

He performed the same ritual at the door, placing his hands before the entry plate and allowing the mechanism to identify and clear him. The door dilated silently, and he was inside.

The room he entered was small and made even more claustrophobic with furniture and racks of books and microfiche. He sighed, taking in the familiarity, allowing himself to relax for the first time that day. The same flat paintings, the well-used and scarred malawood desk with flimsies scattered over it in a paper avalanche, the holotank stolid in isolated dominance in the center of the room, floaters arranged before it for an invisible audience: all of this evoked calm and comfort. Home.

From the meeting room just beyond the archway to his

right, he could hear the basso, garbled drone of filtered and shielded speech. He moved toward the sound, pushing open the intricately-carved doors.

"Gunnar!"

Potok, rotund and florid, his minister's garb in its habitual disarray, rose from his seat at the head of a long table. The four remaining people in the room looked up in surprise, glancing first at the astonished face of Potok and then following his eyes to where Gunnar stood, leaning against the door. Potok shook his head and one pudgy hand went to smooth non-existent hair. He spoke with obvious relief in his voice.

"Gunnar," he repeated. "I don't believe this. We thought—" he broke off his speech and came around the table. With a guttural obscenity, he took Gunnar's hand, then clasped him fully. Gunnar managed a wan smile.

"By all the ippicators in hell, man, you stink." Potok held Gunnar at arm's length and looked down at the mud that now smeared his own clothing. "Where've you been crawling?"

"I'd rather not think about it." Gunnar's grin wavered and died as the color drained from his face. He ignored the others in the room—guild-kin, all members of his own ruling guild—looking at Potok with eyes quickly moist and fragile. His gaze darted about, without seeing anything, from the table ringed with moisture from glasses to the faces staring at him to the empty, black windows. "Potok," he said, with discernable effort in his voice, "they killed Ricia. I saw it."

"Ricia? Who, the Hoorka?"

"No, some others." Gunnar remembered the Hoorka's eyes. *M'Dame Cuscratti was not killed by Hoorka,* he'd said. *You will bear the truth of that.* And Gunnar understood the implicit threat in those words. "I don't know who they were, unless that bastard Vingi sent them. They weren't Hoorka, at least I don't think so . . ." His voice trailed off as he seemed to notice the others for the first time. "Sirrahs Tuirrene, de Vegnes, Hollbrook, m'Dame Avina." He nodded to each in turn. "I'm sorry to have to bear such tidings to my kin. I, umm, don't . . ."

He turned back to Potok. "I'm just tired, too tired." He shook his head and took a slow breath. "I seem to have interrupted a meeting of the Guild Council. Have I disturbed something of importance?" Gunnar looked at m'Dame Avina, but she seemed intent on studying a chip on the side of her mocha cup.

"Gunnar?" Potok's voice brought Gunnar's head around sharply. "We were meeting to discuss the future of our guild, to elect a new kin-lord."

"You couldn't wait? You couldn't take the time to know that I'd been killed? Is that what you're saying, my friend?" Gunnar's voice held an edge that cut all of them.

"No one here thought you'd escape the Hoorka."

"You didn't seem upset when I decided to run rather than remain here. And had you elected the new head?" Scorn lashed them.

"We"—Potok glanced back at the others—"hadn't yet come to a decision."

"Then I'm sorry to have interrupted you with such alarming news." As if he could no longer sustain his anger, Gunnar slumped, leaning heavily against the wall. He closed his eyes for a long moment, then opened them again. "I have to rest. There's much we have to do. With Ricia gone"—the pain returned briefly to his face—"we have no contacts among the upper strata of Sterka. Discuss that, if you must plot and plan. And send someone to see Ricia's guild-kin and offer our support, to make sure that all the rites are performed for her, until I can see to it myself." He paused, and the room seemed to waver before him. "I need a bed," he said, simply.

"Upstairs. Your normal room." Gunnar, with Potok's help, took his leave. At the door to the bedroom, Gunnar paused and sighed. "My legs ache like hell." He shook his head, started a laugh tinged with hysteria, then shook his head again.

Potok opened the door for him and took his arm. "I *am* glad to see you again, Gunnar."

"Despite any thwarted ambitions?"

"You taught me ambition. If I've learned too well, you can only blame yourself. And with the Hoorka contract, it was easy to think of you as . . . dead." Potok shrugged. "The guild would have declared bloodfeud when the Hoorka revealed the signer of the contract. You would have had your revenge, and the gods would have been at rest."

"A small compensation, I suppose. And I did enjoy the guilt on your faces when I entered. Tell me, Potok, who had you elected?"

Potok stared at Gunnar, his eyes challenging. "Myself. But I step down gladly now that you're back." A pause. "Truthfully."

"I'll sleep easier for that knowledge." Gunnar nodded his thanks to Potok and closed the door.

On his way downstairs, Potok wondered if it had been sarcasm or merely weariness in Gunnar's voice.

Chapter 2

THE HOORKA-THANE was possessed by the closest approximation of rage any had ever seen in him. The Thane found himself very aware of Sondall-Cadhurst Cranmer, watching from a floater near the thermal duct behind the Thane. He knew the man, the little scholar, would be alternately fascinated and frightened by the outburst, and that he would be busily recording the new facets of the Thane's personality that this outrush of temper revealed.

That knowledge did nothing to quell the irritation. The Thane faced Aldhelm and Sartas, his face lined with emotion. "Gunnar simply escaped, you say. Unarmed. Alone." The words fell like hammer blows. "The two of you let him live until dawn. Two supposedly competent Hoorka let simple prey escape them?" The Thane's voice was laced with mock surprise that raked Aldhelm and Sartas. The Hoorka bore the outburst in obedient silence.

The Thane gestured with a fisted hand. "Do both of you need training in rudimentary exercises? I won't permit this, not now. I won't have Hoorka destroyed by incompetence. You, Aldhelm." In a swirling of nightcloak, the Thane turned and glared at him. "You're the best knife man of our kin. How could you have missed, how could you have allowed this to happen?"

Aldhelm and Sartas looked at the Thane, though neither one moved nor spoke. His last words came redundantly back at them, an echo from the far walls of the cavern in which they stood. Hoverlamps glistened from water-filmed rocks and ruddied their complexions, making deep hollows of their eyes. Underasgard. Hoorka-home. The caverns. Again the Thane was conscious of Cranmer watching from his vantage point, and he remembered that once the scholar had made the comparison between the Thane and the caverns: both cool, dark, and with hidden recesses you felt more than saw. And one more thing that he hadn't said. Old.

A vibroblade gleamed in the Thane's hand, the luminous tip describing short lines of brilliance in the atmosphere of the cavern—the Thane had brought them away from the well-lit rooms of the main caverns, not wanting to admonish the two Hoorka in public. Vibro held foremost, the Thane advanced upon them. They didn't flinch.

"Do the two of you realize what you've done? When I came to Neweden there were no Hoorka, only a band of petty thugs without kinship; lassari, no more respect than the processions of the Dead. I spent years setting up our guild, gaining us grudging respect, making this a group protected by the Neweden Assembly and tolerated by the Alliance. Idiots!"

The blade swept before their eyes. The following wind cut them coldly. Cranmer—the Thane saw him at the edge of his peripheral vision—jumped involuntarily, but the two Hoorka before the Thane stood in taut rigidity.

"The Li-Gallant Vingi himself signed that contract," the Thane continued. "Gunnar's death would have left the opposing Ruling Guild in shambles—and Vingi might have had total control of the Assembly. Don't you see the possibilities there? Fools!"

The Thane gesticulated violently and the vibro tip gashed Aldhelm's cheek. Blood, bright scarlet, ran freely, but Aldhelm didn't grimace or show pain beyond a narrowing of his eyes. The Thane cursed himself inwardly: he shouldn't have drawn blood then, shouldn't have let his anger at circumstances controlled by Dame Fate spill over into his relations with Hoorka-kin. *Are you getting so old and stupid?* Yet he refused to let any of this show on his face. He let the hand holding the vibro fall to his side.

"You're both out of rotation until further notice," he said. "You'll do apprentice work if that's all you're capable of. Aldhelm, do I need to see you work again?

"An elementary lesson, children. We're but one step removed from outlaw or lassari. No other world of the Alliance accepts us, and only this one backwater world allows us to work, due to its own code of bloodfeud. We're free *because* we have no loyalty to those in power—because the Neweden Assembly and the Alliance know that we follow our code. *My* code. We have no alliances: we can be trusted to side with no person or no cause. We're social carnivores feeding on death without caring what beast provides the meal. Do you see what the Li-Gallant will be thinking? We allowed Gunnar to escape because we've allied ourselves with him—that's his thought, if I know the man at all. To his mind, we've lost our adherence to the code. Bunglers!"

The Thane shoved the vibro back into its scabbard. The leather, blackened with age, showed much use. "Wipe your face, Aldhelm. I should have you both cast from the kin for last night. It's good that I know you both and have respect for your earlier work—and because I love you as guild-kin. It appeases my anger." Then his voice softened, though his dark eyes didn't.

"I know: because of my code, the victim has a chance of survival. I just wish it hadn't been *this* one. I wish She of the Five had looked a little more kindly on the Hoorka."

Aldhelm daubed at the blood on his cheek with the sleeve of his nightcloak while Sartas glanced quickly from his companion to the Thane.

"I've never seen Her so much against us. Gunnar could have stood against the entire kin." Aldhelm looked at the blood on his cloak, then at the Thane. "But I'll accept the blame for this, Thane. My dagger missed its target, and it shouldn't."

The Thane glanced at him, immersed in hidden guilt. Yah, he thought, it's not the fault of these two; it was Dame Fate's doing. But it's easier to chastise men than gods, and the anger/fear demanded release. He stroked his beard as the lamps coaxed red highlights from the graying hair. "Extra knife work for the two of you," he said finally. "At least you followed the dawn code. The Alliance might have had someone observing. I'll try to redeem our standing with the Li-Gallant, if I can. Go on, you must both be hungry and tired after a night's fruitless chasing. Get something from the kitchens, though neither of you deserve it."

The two Hoorka turned. As they were about to walk away, the Thane called to Aldhelm, prodded by his conscience. Aldhelm swiveled on his toes and looked back, his cerulean eyes cold.

"I didn't mean to cut you, Aldhelm. No one should draw the blood of kin, neh? I was angry, and I'm sorry for that."

Aldhelm shrugged. "I can understand your anger." Then, after a pause, "Thane." He nodded his head in leave.

"Truly, Aldhelm. My hand . . ." The Thane grappled briefly with the truth. ". . . slipped."

Aldhelm's eyebrows rose slightly. "I said I understand," he said, his voice flat.

"Rest well, then."

The two Hoorka walked away, the compacted earth under their feet making a gritty rasp. The memory of Aldhelm's chilly eyes remained with the Thane for a long time as he watched the nightcloaks blend with the darkness. *Was I that far out of control of myself?* He slammed a fist into his open hand.

"That won't do much good. It only makes your hand sore."

The Thane started and turned quickly, then straightened with a slight smile. The lines on his scarred face deepened. "Cranmer. I'd forgotten you were here."

"I'd wager you forgot more than that." Cranmer, a short, slight man by Neweden standards, indicated the passage down which Aldhelm and Sartas had gone. "I've never seen you that way, Thane. I don't think you intended to be so, ahh, cruel." Cranmer chose his words carefully, but censure rode lightly on the surface. An elfin figure in the twilight of the caverns, the small man blew on his cupped hands, holding them out above the thermal duct. "You almost warmed the cavern with your anger."

The Thane didn't reply. He took the tether of the hoverlamps and put them on the clips of his belt, slaving the lamps to him. Quickly-shifting wedges of light pursued themselves over the lines of his body, sending distorted shadows to fight on the creviced walls and ceiling of the cavern. Cranmer, grunting, rose from his seat on the floater and absently wiped at his pants before throwing his cloak around him, muffling himself to the chin. Underasgard stayed a constant but cool temperature in the regions where the Hoorka did not live, and even here it was comfortable for most Neweden natives. But Cranmer always felt chilled, used as he was to a more temperate offworld climate.

The Thane completed his gathering of hoverlamps. The brilliant globes arrayed themselves about him like attendant suns around a god. Held in the stressed magnetic fields of the tethers, they bobbed slightly, never quite at rest, giving everything they illuminated a shivering animation. In this shifting atmosphere, the Thane watched Cranmer pick up his recorder and walk toward him over the broken rock of the cave floor.

"You were making a record of all that? I'm not sure I'm pleased."

"It seemed rather important to the sociological aspects of Hoorka, and you did give me leave to record as I wished." Cranmer eyed the Thane, looking for irritation in that well-used face. The confrontation with Aldhelm and Sartas had shown him a new aspect of that personality he'd thought he knew so well. Still, he failed to detect anything but simple curiosity in the Thane's question.

"It looked as if it might have some bearing on my study of Hoorka," he continued. "The image won't be too good. The lamps are really too dim for this unit. It'll be rather grainy." The cloak around him moved and rippled as he put the recorder in a pocket.

The Thane made a noise that might have been affirmation. He looked about, waiting, as Cranmer sealed out any possible draft in his cloak.

"Would you care to see some of the inner sections of the caverns?" The Thane nodded his head to the gathered darkness to his right, and for the first time Cranmer saw a cleft between the rocks. He sighed, relinquishing the thought of his comfortable heater back in the Hoorka caverns. But it wasn't often that the Thane offered tours. "If you're willing. I've never gone further than this room."

The Thane nodded, knowing that the little man sensed that it wasn't simple courtesy that had moved the Thane to make this offer. He gave Cranmer two of the tethers and watched while the man strapped them to his waist, over his cloak.

"A Hoorka would put the tethers *under* the cloak. It won't affect the holding field, and the cloak, as you have it, will bind your movements."

Cranmer shook his head. Two shadow heads moved in sympathy. "It's warmer this way, and I'm not planning to do any fighting. Why else have a Hoorka with you, if not to do your fighting! And I'm *cold.*" He shivered, involuntarily.

The Thane laughed, and echoes rose to share his amusement. "Scholars."

"Fighters," Cranmer replied, and smiled back at him, glad that the Thane seemed to have recovered some of his humor. He nodded toward the passage. "You're the guide, then. Lead."

They began walking, satin night retreating before them, giving way softly and grudgingly and falling back into place behind them. The Underasgard caverns, a system not yet completely mapped, were judged to be among the largest cave systems in the Alliance. The Thane made his way easily through the tumbled rocks with the nonchalance of one who had been this way before. The smaller and less muscular Cranmer followed with more difficulty—unlike the inhabited sections of the Hoorka caverns, the floor here hadn't been cleared of rubble and ionized to a dustless, flat perfection. Cranmer picked his way slowly over the slippery rock. The dull clunking of stone against stone marked their progress. Milky-white clusters of mineral crystals splotched the gray-blue walls, a stone fungus. The narrow passageway opened out into a large room that the lamps failed to light fully, then narrowed again until the Thane was forced to stoop to avoid striking his head on the roof—Cranmer could walk upright. They slid over a scree of small pebbles and around a fractured slab of roofstone. Another room opened up before them, the lamps only dimly showing its perimeters. There the Thane stopped and pointed to a large recess under a projecting shelf of rock.

"I found this quite some time ago, but I've yet to show it to Hoorka-kin. I've questioned my reluctance to point it out, but I haven't any answers." The Thane laughed, more a modulated exhalation than amusement. "Count yourself privileged, neh?" He fumbled with a tether holder, turning the field off and holding the lamp globe in his hand. He opened the shutters wide and threw the ball toward the darkness of the shelf. The lamp bounced and rolled, wild shadows darting crazily. When it settled, they could see the white arch of an ippicator skeleton, the rib cage upright, the two left legs and three right ones sprawled out to either side, while the small neck and head had fallen and lay in disorder.

"It's huge." Cranmer's voice was but a whisper.

"The largest I've seen," said the Thane, pride in his voice. He left unspoken the obvious value of the skeleton. Ippicators were an extinct Neweden animal, and the only asymmetrical mammal yet discovered. Why they had developed the uneven arrangement of limbs was a question of great interest to paleontologists, but what mattered to Neweden was that the skeletons were rare and their bones could be polished to a vivid sheen—ippicator jewelry commanded a great price on the trade markets. This particular skeleton was, due to its size and condition, a thing of great potential wealth. The Thane, for his part, was determined that it would lie undisturbed.

Cranmer's stance and awed demeanor showed the impression the ippicator had made on him. The Thane smiled with pleasure. "I had it dated once: took a chip of bone and sent it to the Alliance labs in the Center. It's at least thirty thousand standards old. That makes it among the oldest ippicators found. And it's well-preserved. Those bones would hold a polish unlike any other."

The Thane settled himself on a rock and cupped his chin on his hands, staring at the skeleton. Cranmer fumbled in his cloak for his recorder, then hesitated. "You mind?" he asked.

The Thane shrugged. "As you like." He paused. "I like to imagine that beast, the most powerful of its kind—perhaps an object of awe among its fellows—realizing that his time has come and that he's no longer capable of ruling the ippicator world. So the beast dragged himself in here, through that passage"—the Thane pointed to a darkness on the far side of the room—"and lay down. It was better than simply growing older and weaker until some stronger challenger fought him and won. A good way to end things, still in control."

"Too melodramatic. More likely it wandered in here and the stupid beast couldn't find its way back out." Cranmer pursed his lips. "Not that *I* could make my way back to the Hoorka caverns alone. So this is your meditation spot, yah?"

"I suppose that's as good a description as possible."

"It bothers you that the Hoorka-thane can have doubts, like the rest of common humanity? My friend, you're one of a small group of violent people on a violent world, interesting only in that you've set up an organization with a moralistic rationale that passes for philosophy, and a religious understructure that is, at best, loosely bound. It's hardly a thing to make the Alliance rise or fall. You worry overmuch."

"And Sondall-Cadhurst Cranmer speaks strongly for a scholar here by the grace of the one he insults, and he has the arrogance of most Alliance people I've met." The Thane used the impersonal mode of insult, the one most likely to cause offense on Neweden, and the one least likely to affect Cranmer. He smiled, with a tint of self-effacing sadness. "I'm not angry, Cranmer. I understand what you're saying, but this small world is the one on which I've built Hoorka, and Hoorka—what it does and where it goes—is of primary importance to me. Like the rest of the kin, I've given it my primary allegiance. This is my family, and I owe it my loyalty. Hoorka owns me, not the Alliance."

"Are you having doubts as to your ability to deal with the problems of Hoorka?"

"I didn't say that." The Thane's voice was sharp in the quiet of the cavern.

"I apologize, then. I thought you might be hinting . . . ah, never mind." Cranmer pitched a small stone into the darkness. Together they listened to it rattle and stop. The echoes eddied, growing steadily weaker until they died. There was a long silence, then, as both men stared at the skeleton.

"I don't know my own mind anymore," the Thane said, finally. He rubbed a muscular thigh with his hand, then stretched his legs out in front of him. "I'm not growing any younger, certainly, and the Hoorka problems are becoming more complicated as we grow. I hope the code can hold us together, that Dame Fate lets us survive. I know we'll survive, if Hoorka-kin will let themselves be governed by the code."

"Then you're not thinking of finding some back cavern and crawling in to die?" Cranmer made a show of switching off his recorder and putting it back in his pocket. "I'm disappointed."

The Thane smiled, adding to Cranmer's laugh. "Disappointed that I don't react as my ippicator? No, the analogy's a poor one, anyway. Didn't you tell me that from all indications, the ippicator was most likely a herbivore? That doesn't sound like Hoorka-kin."

Cranmer snorted in derision. "Thane, I'm an archaeo-sociologist, not a digger into dead bones. But yes, I seem to recall that in one of my university classes back on Niffle-heim, I was told that the ippicator was a lowly grass-eater. I think so, at least."

The Thane waved his hand. "It doesn't matter."

Velvet silence settled in on them again, pressing down like a tangible substance. The Thane could hear Cranmer breathing and the whisper of cloth against flesh as he moved. When Cranmer spoke, the sound startled him with its loudness.

"Thane, what happened back there with Aldhelm and Sartas? I've never seen you succumb to your anger before. The Hoorka *must* fail to kill their victims at times—it's part of your code; Dame Fate has to have Her chance. Yes, it was the Li-Gallant's contract, but surely he'll understand what happened—and since the contract was unsuccessful, you won't be revealing who signed the contract. He's safe from retribution. Why were you so upset?"

"So I have to explain again?" The Thane swept to his feet. The hoverlamps followed him, and light flickered madly about the cavern. The bones of the ippicator danced in the moving light. It's *Vingi's* contract," the Thane said, his voice oddly quiet, "not some guild-feud jealousy or a personal feud. The Li-Gallant's contract. I don't want his paranoia affecting Hoorka. The Alliance has been watching us closely, even to the extent of giving us a contract in their sector of Sterka Port—and the Alliance is more important than Neweden, if I ever want Hoorka to go offworld. But Neweden—and Vingi—can foul that dream. That's the importance."

"Because you're afraid that this organization you've built has a faulty structure and can't survive a few questionings? Your protestations are surface, Thane. Something else had to drive you to lash out at your own kin when you knew they were blameless." Cranmer's voice was soft and he looked not at the Thane, but at the ippicator.

"*Damn* you, Cranmer!" The Thane's voice was suddenly hoarse with venom. Cranmer turned at the shout and saw the Thane's hand on the hilt of his vibro.

And as suddenly as it had flared, the anger drained away and his hand moved to his side, away from his weapon, though his eyes were still held in sharp lines of flesh. *He's right, old man. He's right, and that's why you're angry. Because he's pricked the core of your uncertainty. Because you always considered your emotions too well-hidden to be fathomed. Fool.* "You've had time to study Hoorka, scholar." He stressed the last word slightly too much. "What do you think?"

"*I* don't know. But I never get angry at my ignorance."

"Some things are too large to be angry with." The Thane watched Cranmer slowly relax as the smaller man realized that the irritation was gone from the Thane's voice. "I'm surprised you maintain your interest in us."

"I've been interested enough to have taken two extensions of my leave from Niffleheim Center."

The Thane shrugged. He watched Cranmer draw his cloak tighter around him, noting for the first time the man's growing discomfort from the cold of the room.

The Thane glanced a last time at the ippicator skeleton, shrugged again, and took a step toward the passage leading back to the Hoorka sector. "I'm tired of talk, and I've much to do back in Hoorka-home. If you've seen enough of our five-legged friend . . ."

"Thane, I'm willing to listen more, if that's what you need. The recorder's off, and I keep secrets."

"I wouldn't have shown you the ippicator if I hadn't been sure of your discretion." He shook his head and allowed his features to relax, his shoulders to sag. "No, I've tormented you with enough of my idiocy. But I thank you for the offer." A pause. "Friend."

Cranmer got to his feet. The Thane leading, they followed the sounds of their footsteps back to familiar ground.

Chapter 3

VINGI'S KEEP HUDDLED against the Port barrier, as if drawing comfort from its proximity to that demarcation line between Neweden and land that was officially Alliance territory. The keep was a massive building of local white stone. Turrets flowered unexpectedly from one side, while a row of thin caryatids masked the front facing the city. Like most Neweden estates, it had its gardens, though these were larger than most, with plants coaxed into geometric patterns around which the footpaths meandered. A brook threw foam as it made its way around the rocks lining its bed; ground birds preened in their iridescent plumage. As a symbol of Vingi's wealth and power, it was more than effective: a pretty but useless display. Vingi would starve were he reduced to eating the produce of his gardens. Still, it flaunted his success in the face of the poor world in which it stood.

The Thane, quite irrevocably, hated it.

The Hoorka felt the habitual disgust the keep grounds always engendered in him. Standing before the gates (real metal, not a shield: more ostentation and non-utility) he could see the great contrast between the keep and the rest of Sterka—and Sterka was the richest of Neweden's cities, thanks to the trade of the Port. The Thane, who had seen most of the other urban centers, knew that the Keep was far and away the most lavish display of wealth on Neweden, shadowing even the famous Temple of Khala built by the Guild of Artisans.

And like any Neweden native, he knew that the wealth of Vingi derived not from Vingi but from his kin-father, a brilliant but cruel ruler who had leeched money from kin and kinless without a thought and built a base of power none had assailed. Vingi—now Li-Gallant, as his kin-father had been before him—had inherited that man's cruelty but not his intelligence. It wasn't a pleasant combination.

But, the Thane mused as he showed his pass to the gate ward, Neweden seemed none the worse for it. Guilds still fought with guilds, and kinship of guilds mattered more than biological ancestry, and lassari were still poor and despised. Nothing had changed.

It took much time to breach the layers of officialdom that shielded Vingi from the common public. The Thane was handed from attendant to attendant; from the gate ward to a garden-steward to a bland receptionist who ushered him into a waiting room and left him to stare at undecorated walls for several minutes. Finally, a secretary opened the door and beckoned to the Thane to follow—by the badge on the woman's uniform, she'd been accepted into Vingi's ruling guild and was now due the full respect of a person with kin. He bowed to her politely and entered the Li-Gallant's office. The secretary bowed herself out.

The Li-Gallant was standing at a window, his back to the Thane. He said nothing in the way of salutation, but began speaking as if in the middle of a conversation.

"I failed to see a body at the gates this morning, Thane." Vingi continued looking at the garden. His ornate robes of office moved with his breathing.

The Thane, knowing it would irritate the Li-Gallant, seated himself in a floater near the desk that dominated the room. The Li-Gallant, hearing no answer to his statement, opaqued the window and turned to see the Thane already seated. He grimaced. Rings flared from his gold-banded and pudgy fingers. "I asked a question, Hoorka. I have kin, and I'll brook no insult from anyone. Speak, man."

The Thane didn't move, nor did his eyes flinch. He spoke with distillate calm. "There was no body to give you, Li-Gallant. Gunnar survived. He lived until our dawn. I can't put it any more simply for you, nor do I think I owe you any further explanation." A moment. "With all respect due kin, Li-Gallant."

Vingi backed away from the assassin, his face screaming undisguised anger, though his body sought to put the comforting bulwark of his desk between himself and the

Hoorka. The Thane's lassitude increased Vingi's nervousness, made his bladder ache to be emptied.

"You followed my orders?" The Li-Gallant seated himself.

"We followed the code. You've read the contract, Li-Gallant. The victim is given his chance. We're not murderers, not acting for our own kin in bloodfeud. We tilt the scales of life and death, but we don't presume to be gods, able to take life at whim. That is Her prerogative." The Thane bowed his head at the mention of She of the Five and watched Vingi expel an irritated breath. Good, he thought, Vingi's upset, and our failure is justified ethically. Let him try to bring us before the Assembly. For the first time, he had hopes of leaving the keep with Hoorka safe.

"I've no interest in the gods of your kin," the Li-Gallant said, "simply in results."

"Results are often in a god's control."

Vingi scowled. "What weapons did your people use?"

"Daggers from Khaelia. The Alliance brought them to us as payment for a contract a few months ago. Very effective."

"Obviously." Vingi waited for a reaction to his sarcasm and received none. He hurried to fill the silence. "Why didn't you use firearms? Lasers?"

"Li-Gallant, Gunnar had no bodyshield. The odds would have been over-balanced, and Dame Fate would have been angered. It isn't our intention to tamper with destinies. If a person dies by the Hoorka, then he wasn't meant for survival. If he lives, he was meant to live. The weak: they fall. The strong—perhaps they live. If that's cruel, it's no crueler than Dame Fate Herself." The Thane folded his hands on the gray-black cloth of his lap as his eyes glittered darkly, daring objection. He sounded bored, as if reciting a lesson to a child.

"I should have sent my own people." Vingi's right hand made a bejeweled fist that hovered indecisively over the marbled desk top. The fist was an impotent weapon, speaking of too much disuse to be a symbol of anything but wealth. The Thane's lips curled in a vestige of a smile that flickered for an instant and was gone.

"You sent your forces," he said. "They interfered with the two assassins and were in part to blame for Gunnar's escape. I wouldn't bring that up before the Assembly, Li-

Gallant, but let's not try to deceive ourselves here. You sent four killers of your own — and without declaring bloodfeud, which the Neweden Assembly might find interesting — and they failed. Accuse Hoorka, Li-Gallant, and Hoorka will speak the truth. Again, with no disrespect."

Vingi didn't deny the veracity of the Thane's words. The raised fist struck the desk with soft anger. Papers scattered there didn't move.

"Almost," he said.

"They killed Ricia Cuscratti, Gunnar's mistress, I believe." The Hoorka's voice seemed devoid of any emotion, but behind the words was contempt. "I understand that, as kin-lord of a competing guild, you've sent a tithing to defray the expense of the death rites. A gift. I hope it eased your conscience."

"M'Dame Cuscratti's death was unfortunate but almost unavoidable. She was harboring Gunnar." Vingi smiled. "And *if* those people responsible are ever found, my government will punish them. They'll pay the fine for accidental death."

"Ahh." *So he won't admit it, even privately.*

"I fail to see, in any event, what bearing that has on the failure of Hoorka."

"It caused the two Hoorka trailing Gunnar to lose several hours. Had, ahh, the person who sent the intruders more trust in the Hoorka, *you* might have had your death."

"I'm not interested in excuses."

"We've no need for excuses. The Hoorka had to deal with interference. It doesn't matter who caused it. But I intend to post notice of feud with the Assembly, should we find those responsible. So I wish your investigation success, neh?" The Thane waved a disparaging hand. "The Hoorka can also play the game of pretended ignorance."

Vingi shrugged. The cloth of his robes glistened with interwoven metallic strands. The Thane allowed himself another brief moment of amusement. Vingi compounded distrust on distrust. That fabric would turn back the sting of any hand weapon, and the Thane was certain that when he'd arrived he'd been surreptitiously searched: beamed and probed. He also knew that if he intended to kill the obese man before him, he wouldn't need any weapon other than his hands. The Li-Gallant didn't trust him — that was obvious, and it was disturbing. The Hoorka-guild was based on the precept that no Hoorka would kill unless threatened or contracted to do so. Never without warning, unlike the other guilds, who declared bloodfeud at the slightest provocation. Vingi's uncertainty in the face of that code was a bad omen.

The Thane decided to waste no more time. "You have our payment, I suppose?"

Vingi's face became a rictus, a snarl. "You demand a large price for small results."

"You know the code, and you declined to pay in advance." There was no apology in the Thane's voice. It lashed at the Li-Gallant with feigned nonchalance. Yet the Thane knew that this was a dangerous moment. He felt uncertainty in his tactics. *Do I doubt myself so much? Where is the vaunted confidence?*

"I've registered a complaint with the Neweden Assembly." There was a triumphant sneer on Vingi's face, a vestige of bravado. "The Alliance Regent, m'Dame d'Embry, has expressed her interest in this situation, and I felt it might aid her, as she has said that she would like answers to the questions I've raised."

"You play dangerously, Li-Gallant, if I may speak frankly. I wouldn't care to have a bloodfeud between your kin and mine, were I you. We are trained for fighting."

"You'll be notified when to appear, Thane. You must admit that circumstances—despite any protestations of interference from, ahh, outside sources—are suspicious. If the Hoorka are aligned with Gunnar's party, they're a danger to the stability of Neweden government. Surely you see that. No disrespect intended for Hoorka. I merely wish to have an account of that night."

"Do you intend to reveal that you signed the contract?"

The Li-Gallant laughed. "I'm not so foolish, Thane. And should it happen that Gunnar learns that I was the signer, it would simply add to the suspicions."

"It still wouldn't be wise or prudent to neglect our payment, Li-Gallant." The Thane stood abruptly, his nightcloak swirling. Vingi started, his eyes wide, and his hands disappeared below the surface of the desk. The Thane could see him fumbling for something unseen there.

"Should I think you were summoning your guards, Li-

Gallant, I might take it as a personal affront. I could easily appease my wounded dignity before they could enter." The Thane hoped he'd taken the right path, had gauged Vingi's fear correctly. If not—he thrust the apprehensions from him.

"I don't care for your threats, Hoorka," Vingi replied, but his hands were now still. "If we were in public . . ."

The Thane said nothing, waiting. In the silence, the sound of a muffled voice could be heard in Vingi's outer office, followed by a high, clear laugh. It held no threat.

The Li-Gallant brought his hands up and slid a pastel check across his desk. The Hoorka-thane smiled, his eyes openly laughing, and he leaned forward to take the payment.

"Our thanks, Li-Gallant."

The Thane walked easily through the streets: easily because the throngs parted before him with an apprehensive glance at the black and gray nightcloak of the Assassin's Guild. Gray and black: no colors, no loyalty except to Hoorka-kin. The aura of the deathgods hung about him, subtle and menacing, and none cared to taint themselves by approaching too closely to this impassive man. They were used to hardship and death—the people of Neweden, a ghetto world by any standard—but the Hoorka were hardened and deadly beyond the norm. Better they be avoided. That was the consensus.

The check from the Li-Gallant didn't give the Thane as much pleasure as he'd expected. He had anticipated Vingi's covert avoidance of payment, the hedging of an angered ruler. But Vingi's anger had been something beyond the measured and calculating displeasure of a kin's defense of offended pride, and it wasn't in the Li-Gallant's nature to let his ire fester long within himself. He'd exorcize the demon. How, and how would it affect Hoorka? The question nagged at him. Surely Vingi wouldn't be so foolish as to declare this a matter of bloodfeud between their guilds? Vingi's kin would die, and that would allow Gunnar's ruling guild access to vacant seats on the Assembly. No, something more devious.

The populace noised about him as the Thane passed through a market square. Carts loaded with produce were surrounded by shouting buyers while farmers bellowed vaguely-heard prices and boasted of the quality of their particular products. Someone brushed against the Thane's side and muttered a quick, overly-sincere apology as he darted back into the crowd. Here and there a few flashily-clothed Diplos — members of the Alliance Diplomatic Resources Team — made their way through the milling people, but even they, the aristocracy protected by the offworld power of the Alliance, gave the Thane wide berth. It was, after all, a Neweden jest that even the Dead would part to let a Hoorka pass.

The Thane walked slowly, letting the noise and bustle fade to the edges of his consciousness, thinking—

— the Li-Gallant wants Gunnar dead, and he wants to know whether the Hoorka have sided with his opposition. He'll find a way to determine if his paranoia is founded in truth or not. But how will he go about it, what can he do?

— and what bothers me? Once I would have reveled in a confrontation like this, would have enjoyed the knife-edge of tension. Now I'm simply tired and unsure — I'd avoid this if I could. Cranmer's thought: is it time to step aside? Should Aldhelm or Valdisa or someone else be Thane? No. No.

— it's a fine day. The sunstar shines, She of the Five smiles. But my frown puzzles these people. Do they think I'm contemplating my next contract, that I'm daydreaming of spilled blood and death? And how many of them, thinking my imagined thoughts distasteful, would still advise their kin to come to Hoorka to settle a bloodfeud with another guild?

— I should rest. I've been so tired lately. Perhaps Valdisa — but no, that relationship has passed. Too many complications—

He touched the pouch in which the check rode and smiled, forcibly evicting his pessimism. Passersby shook their heads at the evil omen.

The Hoorka smile only at death.

The Thane was nearly across the market square, in the bluish shadow cast by the spires of the Tri-Guild Church. Just ahead of him, a man shoved his way through the throngs before the Hoorka. The Hoorka could see the wake of the disturbance spreading as people scattered, and in a brief clear space he caught a brief glimpse of the problem. A man without a badge of kinship—a lassari, kin-less and status-less—was shoving aside those in front of him. Then the crowds closed in again, pushing. The Thane saw a blur of blue-and-yellow–tinted flesh as a woman was knocked to the pavement, though he couldn't tell if it were due to the manic lassari or the pressure of the crowd. He started to walk away at an angle to the welling struggling as a roar of wordless protest began to rise. He kept a scowl on his face, relying on that and the uniform of the Hoorka to make his way.

"Hoorka! I see you!" The shout came as the lassari thrust aside those nearest the Thane and entered the clear space about the Hoorka. The Thane continued walking, ignoring the man—he had a brief impression of frantic, dark eyes and a thin, wiry body clothed in dingy wraps—but the shout was repeated, imperious and commanding.

"Hoorka!"

The Thane halted and turned slowly. From the corner of his eyes he saw the crowd in the square moving to a safe distance from the confrontation, forming a rough circle about the two. The man was armed: the Thane could see the wavering orange fleck of a vibro tip in the man's right hand, and the Hoorka swept his nightcloak over his shoulder, out of the way of his arms.

"A problem, sirrah?" The honorific was a mockery in his voice. Lassari were not due the respect of those with kin, and his intonation made it clear that he was mocking the man. It was, however, a truism that an angered lassari made a dangerous enemy—they didn't have the worry of the safety of their fellow guild members. The Thane kept his eyes on the vibro arm, wary.

The lassari was breathing heavily, as if nervous or excited, and he shifted his weight from one foot to the other in a constant motion. The watching crowd moved a step farther back.

"Hoorka!" the man shouted a third time. "You've destroyed me. I might as well mumble chants with the Dead. No one talks to me, no one deals with me. Lassari, they say, and spit. Your fault." The words were slurred, and from the distance of two meters, the Thane could smell the spicy odor of lujisa. The man was an addict, then, and a thief, for only a rich man or a thief could afford the offworld drug. On Neweden, there were no rich lassari. It also meant that he was beyond reason, lost in the false logic of an interior world with few touchstones to the reality around him. Lujisa addicts had been known to attack strangers because of a sudden whim or fancy. Was this such an accidental encounter? The Thane wondered. Then: could Vingi have arranged this so quickly after our meeting?

The Thane stalled, saying anything that came to mind as he studied the man. "I don't know you. Hoorka-kin doesn't know you. You've mistaken me for another, perhaps? I have nothing to do with you, and I don't see you, lassari." He spoke tentatively, watching for any reactions his words had on the man.

"You DO!" The last word was a scream that echoed from the spires of the church. Birds took quick flight from the rooftops and settled down again slowly. The lassari spat on the pavement and shook his head as if annoyed by some insect. "The Hoorka wouldn't accept me as apprentice. You made me lassari." He scuffed at the ground. "You did it. You know me."

"I don't even see you. And Hoorka chooses its kin as it pleases." He waited, then spoke again. "I don't see you. You don't exist to me, lassari."

There seemed to be nothing else to do. The insult came grudgingly from his lips. The susurrus from the watching crowd held them, as aware as the Thane that there was nothing else he could do. The attack would come, or not: who could tell? Lujisa made for strange behavior, and until the lassari moved, he was trapped. The Thane moved his hand fractionally closer to his vibro.

And as if that action had triggered a reflex in the lassari, the man lunged without warning. The Thane, more out of instinct than intent, stepped back and to one side, his hands reaching for the attacker. The hum of the vibro dopplered past his ear, and the Thane chopped at the man as his momentum carried the lassari past the Hoorka. The lassari twisted in an effort to stop his fall and the Thane's blow caught him on the shoulder. The Thane pivoted to see the man roll and gain his feet—the crowd retreating frantically as the lassari came near them. The Thane watched the hand holding the vibro and the waist: his training—the training he'd in turn imparted to Hoorka-kin—had taught him that while a person may feint with any part of his body, the hips must go in the direction of movement. The Thane unsheathed and activated his vibro as the lassari regained his footing.

The man's next charge was unsubtle, lacking any pretense or grace. With a flick of his wrist, the Thane brought his nightcloak over the man's vibro arm as he cut at him with his own weapon. The lassari screamed in pain as the vibro tip gashed his side. He went limp, dropping his weapon. The Thane kicked it away as the man rolled on the ground, clutching his wounded side. The crowd moved in closer, drawn to the agony.

The Thane shut off his vibro and sheathed it. He was breathing heavily, tired far beyond the little effort he'd needed. He looked down at the moaning lassari. "I had no quarrel with you, no-kin-of-mine. And Hoorka do not kill unless paid to do so. Not even lassari." He let his cloak fall back around him, and the people moved to give him a corridor through the crowd. Trying not to show his weariness, the Thane walked away, his face forbidding comment.

As he passed from the square into the narrow back streets of Sterka, he found all the vague pleasure of the day gone. It was unusual enough for a Hoorka to be attacked, but this confrontation nagged at him with implications beyond the surface. Had Vingi, or even Gunnar, arranged it, as a way of avoiding a declaration of formal bloodfeud with the Hoorka? Had it been intentional and not simply an accident of timing and circumstance—a whim of Dame Fate?

Lastly—and it bothered the Thane that this seemed important—could he have avoided the fight, could he have eased himself away without knifing the man?

After all, what insult was there to the deranged maunderings of a lassari and lujisa addict?

The questions pounded at him, one with the throbbing in his chest and the troubling wheeze he could hear in his lungs.

He moved in his clear space through the streets. The sunstar sparked lazy motes of dust in the air. Birds foraged for crumbs in the central gutter of the street.

The Thane walked toward the city gates.

Chapter 4

"**A**T THE CORE OF the Hoorka philosophy, if that's what this, ahh, moral code with religion must be called, is a shrewd knowledge of Neweden mores and cultural patterns. The Hoorka exist through the practice of guild-kinship—Neweden's replacement for the biological, nuclear family—*and* the normal jealousies to which humans are prone. Now; no, make that: Since the advent of the Hoorka, there is an alternative offered Neweden. Rather than calling a formal bloodfeud between guilds and the possibility of carnage that that entails and by all the gods, that's a clumsy sentence. Umm, cancel and begin program, please.

"The Hoorka function as an alternative to the traditional method of settling conflicts: the bloodfeud. On Neweden, a bloodfeud may become a small-scale war, all perfectly legal. By contacting the Hoorka and signing their contract, a person can fulfill his duty to his kin or his gods for any insult, and still retain his life with his pride.

"The Hoorka price is high, but that fits in with their crude; no, make that"—(pause)—"*unsophisticated* variation on Social Darwinism: in essence, crude survival of the fit. They contend that wealth is an outgrowth of power and fitness—and yet the victim retains a chance of escaping this harsh justice, for the victim may have 'survival traits' that are not tied in with the accumulation of lucre. The odds are never overloaded in the favor of the Hoorka. If the victim isn't carrying a bodyshield, as an example, the Hoorka will decline to carry firearms or stings in carrying out the contract. This aspect of the code has had a corollary effect: most contracted victims decline to use such technologically-based defenses, relying instead upon speed and stealth."

Cranmer reached over the desk to switch off the voice-typer and then looked at the words he'd just written. "Anything particularly wrong with that, Thane? It's simply for my notes. What eventually gets put together for publication will be scattered with a more esoteric vocabulary so that the University people don't feel their intelligence is being insulted—if they can understand a concept too easily, they think it below their notice."

"You sound mildly bitter, scholar."

Cranmer leaned back in his floater and put his hands behind his head. He pursed his lips, eyes closed. "No, just realistic. I've been away from it long enough to have an objectivity about the drawbacks of my profession. I don't care for that much posturing and pretension in anyone but myself." He grinned. "And *that's* a normal human instinct."

The Thane had been standing near the shield that cut this—Cranmer's rooms—from the other caverns of Underasgard. Now he moved forward and sat on the bed. Above him, a lamp tinted gold threw light down on the crown of the Thane's head, so that every line of his face was accentuated. The Thane caught sight of himself in a mirror across the room, and he grimaced. He moved slightly, so that the light struck him at an angle, softening his face. He surreptitiously examined the results, hoping Cranmer hadn't noticed his vanity. "Wait until we Hoorka go offworld. You'll have to revise your paper."

Cranmer frowned. He leaned forward toward the Thane, his eyes questioning. "Thane, in the months I've spent with you, I've never hedged truths. If the Hoorka *do* go offworld—and I don't know that d'Embry's ever going to allow that—I think you're going to run into far more trouble remaining consistent than you realize. You'll be operating under totally different social structures, if nothing else. The code might have to be re-worked to some degree. You're set up for Neweden, not Niffleheim or Longago or Aris. This planet is the only one of which I'm aware that has such a hidebound caste system—the guilds—and *they* are what make the Hoorka code work."

"The code is sufficient." The Thane shook his head in disagreement. Light shifted across his face. "If we start tampering with our structure, making exceptions and addendums here and there, what will distinguish us from common criminals? No," he said emphatically, "I've thought of this before. I don't see where the structure of any other society will be so alien that the code would fail."

"I'm not suggesting that the code become fluid."

"That's good. Then perhaps you do understand Hoorka."

"Do the two of you do nothing but argue all day?" Both men turned to the doorshield to see Valdisa standing there, a gentle smile on her face, her hands on her hips in mock disgust. Short dark hair frothed the side of her thin, finely-featured face and neck. A nightcloak was clasped around her shoulders, masking her figure.

"Come in, m'Dame," the Thane said. She nodded. Her lithe, athletic body moved with a grace that the Thane remembered with pleasure and envy. She sat on the foot of the bed, near the Thane.

Cranmer had sat back in his floater again, half-reclining, his head staring at the ceiling. "I was informing our revered Thane that sometimes the creation has to transcend the creator—my old line, I realize—but all things are subject to modification, if they want to survive."

Valdisa laughed, a crystalline sound. "Not a philosophy that would appeal to him, neh?" She placed a cool hand briefly over the Thane's, then withdrew it. The Thane glanced at her; she smiled in return.

"Or to most Hoorka, I would hope." The Thane chuckled to show that he was jesting, but he was remembering Valdisa's hand. "Cranmer's simply caught up in a vision of the perfect thesis, neatly bound and impervious to logic."

"And life *isn't* definable in terms of a thesis, then? Gods, my colleagues will be profoundly disappointed to hear that. They'll mull it over for a year and then write a paper on it. Smash their entire concept of reality . . ." He thumped the voicetyper for emphasis. The three of them laughed. Cranmer looked from Valdisa to the Thane. He shoved the floater back from his desk and stretched his arms out, fingers interlocked. Joints cracked aridly, and Valdisa winced.

"I guess I should wander off and see who's on kitchen duty," Cranmer said. "Thinking's hard enough work for us sedentary types—and from the look on m'Dame Valdisa's face, she has business to discuss. Yah?"

Valdisa nodded, smiling. "And you should take some exercise. That's a flabby body you carry with you."

"Would I then stand a chance with you, m'Dame?" Cranmer struck a melodramatically romantic pose.

"Possibly, sirrah." Over-coyly.

"I'll see the two of you later, then." Cranmer, whistling a motet off-key, waved a hand at the two Hoorka as he left the room. Valdisa watched the doorshield close again behind him and turned to the Thane.

"I'll miss the little man when he leaves us," she said.

The Thane, looking at the papers neatly stacked beside the typer, nodded his head in agreement. "As will I. I need his objectivity, however galling it sometimes becomes."

"Well, he was right; I do have business to discuss with you." Valdisa pulled a flimsy from the breast pocket of her nightcloak. Paper crackled as she unfolded it. "You said to notify you when the next contract arrived. I just received one." She glanced at the document. "From a Jast Claswell of the Bard's Guild, to attempt the killing of an E. J. Dausset, of the Engineers."

The Thane sighed as he moved, stretching out a hand to take the flimsy from Valdisa. He moved so that the light from the hoverlamp fell full on the paper, putting him in shadow. "I know I'm due next in the rotation. Who was I to be teamed with?"

"D'Mannberg."

The Thane nodded and handed the contract back to Valdisa. As her eyes watched him, he walked a few steps toward the wall. He rested his hand on the cool rock, then turned back to her. "Move him back in the rotation and have Aldhelm posted to go with me." He wiped his hand, damp from the chill of the rock, absently on his cloak. He looked up to see surprise raise Valdisa's eyebrows, but she lowered her gaze at first contact and folded the flimsy slowly and deliberately. When she did speak, her voice and manner were carefully devoid of question or censure; because of that, it was obvious to the Thane that she was disturbed.

"Am I to give Aldhelm an explanation?"

The Thane shook his head. "No, I just want to cause our kin to think of the Gunnar mistake."

"Thane"—and now her voice spoke with soft, gentle reproach—"are you sure that's what you want to do? It won't help Aldhelm's mood. You haven't seen him today.

Your chastisement, his own guilt at having let Gunnar escape when he knew full well the importance of that contract, the knife-cut . . ."

"I didn't mean to cut him," the Thane interrupted. His voice was high and loud with hurried protest. *Calm, calm. Why do you allow yourself to become upset so quickly?*

"I know—and he knows, whether he cares to admit it or not." Valdisa's voice soothed him. She'd always been able to do so, when they'd been lovers, and since then as a friend. "But that doesn't mean a great deal. He's not an apprentice or a new Hoorka. He's the best of the kin. What happened the other night was Dame Fate's whim, not Hoorka clumsiness. You didn't need to make an example of him."

Two spots of color flared high on the Thane's cheeks. "I have my own thoughts. I'm doing what I think is right, and I *do* rule the Hoorka. If you'd like to change that, call for a vote by the kin." *Haughty, so haughty.* He hated himself for the way the last sentence had sounded, but it was too late. *Why do you always hurt her?*

Valdisa's hands described a helpless circle. She shook her head. "No, I can't agree with you. But I wouldn't say that anywhere but here, and if you insist, I'll go along with this." After a moment: "For what it's worth."

The Thane's expression softened as the ruddiness faded from his cheeks. He impulsively touched her hand, felt the calluses there, the broken fingernails.

"I appreciate that," he said. "I need the support, and Aldhelm would take the news better from you."

She shrugged, her eyes steady on his. She let her hand stay where it was. "I owe you that much."

Her forefinger stroked his palm and the Thane slowly let his hand fall back to his side. "That's all past. You owe me nothing."

"It's past only because you insist that it need to be so. I'd still sleep with you—and you haven't slept with any of the kin for some time. It needn't be me. A hint . . ." She smiled.

"You're too interested in other's affairs."

"They used to be partially mine, if you recall."

"And you know why I wanted to end it. It wasn't for my sake."

Valdisa's smile faded. She rose from the bed and moved over to Cranmer's floater, and idly toyed with his 'typer, running her fingers over the controls. She switched on the machine, listened to its mechanical humming, then turned it off again. "I understand your intentions, Thane. I *don't* understand the reasoning. The code encourages a certain promiscuity among Hoorka-kin if they haven't formed a relationship with a single person—and it helps, with our imbalance of men to women. But you don't forbid monogamous relationships. You couldn't. You wouldn't want to. I remember your jealousy when I slept with Bronton. I even enjoyed it. You were so mutely gentle and hurt. You should be so open with your kin more often, love."

"I don't want it said that you're on the Hoorka Council because you are the Thane's bed partner." ·

Valdisa flared with sudden anger. "I don't need your altruism *or* your protection. I can stand with my own abilities. I've told you that before. Let someone challenge me on the practice floor if they doubt my skills."

"This still makes it easier."

"For whom? You? Me?" Valdisa spread her hands wide, the folds of the nightcloak shifting fluidly. "If you can't handle the relationship, tell me. That would be easier. But don't make excuses. I want truth, not evasions." Her voice was dangerously gentle. "Damn you, I still care for you—it doesn't matter if that's no longer mutual. It doesn't change the feelings. But tell me the truth, kin to kin."

"I don't know myself any more. Damn it, Valdisa, we've had this argument before. It never does any good, and we go about for the next few days angry with ourselves because we've hurt one another. That's something I have no interest in doing." He paused, searching her eyes and drifting down to her set lips. "That's the truth."

"And I said I wouldn't bring it up again. I know." She pressed her lips together in a half-smile, a sad amusement. "I'm sorry. If you change your mind, you know where to find me. I'll go post the names for the Claswell contract. Aldhelm and yourself? You won't change that?"

"Neh. Aldhelm and myself." The Thane paused a moment, began to speak, then lapsed into silence.

"Go on." Valdisa touched his hand, her forefinger moving from the wrist to the back of his veined hand and back again.

"It's nothing," he said, his eyes watching the slow caress

of her finger. Then he looked up to see her watching. "I feel *old,* somehow, and I've never felt so uncertain before. And it's not age, but . . ." He shook his head. "I'm just tired of the intrigue, tired of the chase, the hunt. What was it Cranmer called us, an 'adolescent fantasy in a prepubescent world'? I'm weary of blood, and I keep looking for other solutions to our problems. And there don't seem to be any. Kin fight other kin, and kin always fight lassari, and Dame Fate laughs while Hag Death collects her due."

"You should hear yourself. Maudlin, love, maudlin."

"You should feel this way."

"Are you telling me you should step down as Thane?"

"No!" His denial was vigorous, and the vehemence startled even himself. "No," he repeated more gently. "Not yet, in any event. Post the names, would you?"

"As you wish." Valdisa rose, then stepped toward the Thane. She stopped an arm's length from him and touched his face with her hand. She traced the line of his cheekbone, the furrow running from nostril to mouth. "I'm not angry. I just see you changing. You don't seem as confident in yourself as you once did, and I worry for you. For Hoorka, and for you. Because I still care."

Her hand dropped, and she walked quickly to the doorshield, stepping through it before he could formulate a reply. The Thane sat on the bed for a long hour, steeping himself in frustration.

The domed roof of the Neweden Assembly Hall was set with stained-glass murals depicting the fall of Huard, works of art as famous for their beauty as for the difficulties involved in appeasing the seven major artisan's guilds. Each had wanted their guild commissioned for the work, and it was only through the determined efforts of the Assembly that the work had been done at all. Seven panes there were, and through each jeweled shafts of light fell in dusty pillars to the distant floor. Birds roosted in the gutters of the dome, spotting the murals with whitish droppings that were daily cleaned. Today, the birds' rest was disturbed by the faint sound of shouting voices below; bureaucratic strife and political dueling among the various guild-kin that composed the Assembly.

"The ruling guild of Sirrah Gunnar is at least concerned

with the welfare of those people on Neweden that haven't the advantages of the Li-Gallant."

Potok leaned forward at his desk, shouting across the length of the Assembly Hall to the high dais where Vingi sat behind a bank of viewscreens. A stylus, held between forefinger and thumb, stabbed the air in Vingi's direction, and if Potok seemed a trifle more theatrical than was his wont—as a trio of holocameras recorded the scene with cyclopian indifference, broadcasting the meeting to the Diplo Center a few blocks away—nobody remarked upon it. Assembly meetings were half-stage production, half-serious at best, and much was tolerated that would, in the streets, be cause for declaration of bloodfeud.

The session thus far had proved to be one of the more entertaining for those in a position to find the semi-functioning of their Assembly amusing—which were those few who didn't depend on it in some way for the stability of their lives. Neweden's government—by law a republic with an elected head, the Li-Gallant—was in practice an economic dictatorship with Vingi as ruler through his holding of the monetary reins of the planet, a ruler as his kin-father had been before him. It was not always an efficient system, but like all governments it worked occasionally.

There was a shout from the far side of the floor, another of the many guild representatives. "Haven't we heard enough rhetoric designed simply to slow down the functioning of this Assembly? Li-Gallant, I respectfully ask that Representative Potok—"

Potok shouted down the man—he had good lungs. *"And I have the floor,* honored representative. If you'll be so good as not to interrupt me, this body may well function more efficiently." He turned, slowly and with exaggerated pride, to face Vingi again. The sunlight from above sparked and flared over the glittering satin of his ceremonial robes: turquoise, the color of his guild, Gunnar's guild. What he had just said, uttered in public, would have caused the other party to demand satisfaction. But candor, and what might be rudeness in normal Neweden society, were tolerated here. Potok glared at the Li-Gallant and pressed his point.

"I ask again, Li-Gallant, for an investigation into the attempted murder of our party leader. You've evaded giving a direct answer or letting the matter come to a vote. I request that you speak your mind and enlighten us down on the floor as to your reasoning."

Vingi squinted into the bluish haze around him—the smoke filters in the room didn't seem to be working. He toyed with a stack of microfiche in front of him, checked one of the screens (a view of the hall outside: a bored guard was relating a story to another with extravagant and obscene gestures), and looked down at Potok. He bit on his lower lip in concentration.

"Representative Potok," he said languidly, his voice just this side of boredom, "Gunnar had been contracted to be killed by the Hoorka—as you well know—and the Hoorka are bound by their guild bylaws not to release the name involved in their unsuccessful attempts *and* to make public the signer of successful assassinations. I suggest you make your plea to Hoorka, and not the Assembly, if you are so interested in learning the identity—or perhaps you might advise Gunnar to run slower next time."

A roar of laughter rose from guild-members allied with Vingi, coupled with derisive boos from Gunnar's supporters.

"M'Dame Ricia Cuscratti was not killed by Hoorka," insisted Potok.

Vingi waved pudgy fingers in dismissal. "There is no proof of *that* beyond vague rumors; in any event, sirrah, m'Dame Cuscratti's murderers will be fined to the limits of the law should their identities come to light, and your guild-kin may demand bloodfeud if m'Dame Cuscratti's guild-kin do not insist upon preference. I fail to see the point of your persistence."

There was a murmuring of affirmation from the floor, a bee-hum that filled the hall with wordless clamor. Potok raised his eyes to the sun-brightened windows above him and waited for silence. The noise died slowly and incompletely.

"The attempted killing of Gunnar might well be a cause for bloodfeud between our guild and another," he continued. "And we have a right to know what lies behind the attempt, whether it was a personal insult or a matter for all of Gunnar's kin—my kin. If, for instance, a part of our government were trying to gain total control of this Assembly"—he paused significantly—"or attempting to consolidate what they already control, then the guilds would have a right to know."

A shout of contempt came from the left side of the hall, joined by a few other voices. "Sit down, Potok! You're interrupting—"

As Potok turned to deal with the hecklers, his own supporters voiced their own feelings at suitable volume. The contention rose, the voices growing steadily louder and more numerous as members of the ruling guilds joined in on one side or another. Potok, his chest heaving, struggled to be heard above them, facing Vingi and bellowing his complaints. Vingi sat watching the disturbance, then raised the gavel of office. He let the gavel fall and the amplified thud of wood on wood rang throughout the hall; a low, ringing note. The discussions faded slowly. Potok bowed to Vingi. "My thanks, Li-Gallant."

"I simply didn't care to see the hall in dissension, Representative. I wouldn't think it would behoove you to see it so, either. Will you yield the floor *now,* sirrah?"

Potok shook his head. He shuffled the papers on his desk, glancing up to the dais. "I do not. There are other questions I would like answered, if the Li-Gallant has no answer to the others I've asked. Our sources, for one, tell us that certain parties have been selling ippicator skeletons to offworld concerns without paying the proper tithes to the guild treasuries, and without the tax that is due Neweden. Is that true?"

"If your sources are reliable, but the government has heard nothing of this. I will investigate it personally. Does that satisfy you, sirrah?"

"I trust the report will be prompt, Li-Gallant, since ippicator skeletons are a finite resource, and once depleted cannot be restored. Another matter: our guild-kin in Illi say that their continent has not been receiving its entire stipend for food, and that lassari have actually starved in Illicata. The ore mines have provided ore for the factories, the fishermen have produced record catches, and the farmers of the Southern Plain have had adequate rainfall this season. How can they not be prospering? Yet the figures I have before me"—he waved a sheet of flimsies about—"show an interesting dichotomy. I would like to read these into the record . . ."

"The government of Neweden is not interested in fiction, Representative Potok. Your kin in Illi are not members of this Assembly by vote of the guilds. Representative Heenan of Illi *is*. I suggest you go over the figures with him and let us get on with more pressing business." Vingi turned deliberately away from Potok, his ringed fingers spitting light as they passed through a stray sunbeam. Again shouts of agreement and protest came from the floor. Potok screamed to be heard.

"I will not yield the floor until this Assembly listens to me!"

He was shouted down. Across the floor, representatives rose to their feet to be better heard. Several strident voices demanded the floor as members of contending guilds exchanged taunts and threats. The pounding of the gavel was heard and ignored, and Vingi shouted for order into a nearby microphone, his voice ragged with overamplification. The noise quieted somewhat, but did not die. Potok crossed his arms over his chest and faced the dais with a face gray with anger. "I demand to be heard, Li-Gallant."

"You've been heard for the last hour, sirrah. Will you yield?" Wearily, for Vingi was genuinely tired. His rump hurt, his right foot itched, and he was beginning to feel faint hunger.

"I will not. I have the floor. I intend to keep it until I receive some satisfaction. I'll talk all day if necessary. The leader of my guild has been nearly killed, and the current government ignores the people it supposedly serves."

"You needn't slander this Assembly in the hall, in open meeting." Vingi's voice boomed through the speakers, dwarfing that of Potok.

"Slander is sometimes truth," Potok said harshly, his voice showing the strain of constant shouting. Behind him, others of his guild clamored agreement. The holocameras filming the session moved from the over-righteous face of Potok to the thick features of Vingi.

The Li-Gallant's double chin trembled as he pointed to Potok with a forefinger. "You had better be prepared to back up such libel with facts, Representative, if only for the sake of your kin. Do you understand me, sirrah?" From the Li-Gallant, the honorific sounded like an insult. "We've heard more than enough of your vague references to troubles of which we're already fully aware. For the last time, will you yield the floor? There are others waiting to be heard, with problems perhaps more urgent than your own."

Shouts of "Sit down!" now alternated with yells of support for Potok, a cacophony that caused the birds on the dome to once more rise from their nests and flutter about. The gavel boomed unsuccessfully as Potok stood with his arms still folded, waiting for quiet to return. The tumult continued, the gavel booming repeatedly until it finally wore down the opposition. Vingi spoke as soon as he felt he could be heard.

"A final warning, Representative Potok. Sit down and yield the floor, or I'll be compelled to call for the sergeant-at-arms to remove you from the hall. I don't make that threat lightly, sirrah."

Potok took a prolonged sip from the glass of water on his desk, feeling the cool liquid soothe his ragged throat. He swallowed, taking his time and trying to gauge the growing ire of the Li-Gallant. Finally, he placed the glass carefully on his desk and shuffled his papers into order, holding them in one hand and raising them to the multi-colored windows above. "I cannot in conscience yield, Li-Gallant. There is importance in what I'm saying, and if the Assembly won't hear me willingly, then let it suffer."

He brought the papers down before him, cleared his throat, and began reading from the first sheet as once more the riotous clangor of protest rose. Potok continued reading, seemingly undisturbed, though his voice was no longer audible. Papers were scattered from a desk to the rear of the hall as two representatives argued furiously. Vingi didn't bother to use the gavel, but gestured to the guards behind him. They moved through the aisles toward Potok; he, seeing their approach, continued reading as the uproar raged about him. The guards reached him, and Potok threw the papers into the air in dramatic disgust as they forced him away from his desk, finally pinning his arms to his side and carrying him when he refused to walk before them. The papers fell, autumnal. They were trampled onto the hall floor underfoot as the guards bore Potok to the doors leading from the hall. The noise rose decibels louder, and the gavel rose and fell unheeded. The great doors of the hall opened and swallowed the trio of guards and Potok. Birds flew in uneasy circles outside the dome.

In her office in the Diplo Center, m'Dame d'Embry watched a holotank set temporarily in the center of her room. There, in miniature, the Assembly Hall teemed with furiously gesticulating figures and a dull, inarticulate roar filled the speakers under the 'tank. Stretching forth an orange-tinted arm to the controls on her desk, the Alliance Regent turned down the volume with a sharp movement of her wrist. She shook her head, lips pursed, and then turned to her own work.

A procession of the Dead walked outward from the Sterka Gates, into the roadway that hugged the hill ridges of the plain beyond. The fumes of their incense were smeared behind them by the easterly wind and their chanting—a dull and sibilant mantra—lulled the Neweden breeze into submission and put the sunstar to sleep. In darkness, they made their aimless, sorrowful way through the countryside; unseeing, uncaring.

A man in ragged clothing toppled in their midst, falling to the hard-packed surface of the road. The Dead ignored him, though the chant changed subtly into a praise for the presence of Hag Death. The man groaned in pain as he clutched his side. If the Dead that passed saw the blood from a vibro gash that stained his clothing, they took no notice.

What did it matter how Hag Death arranged to take a person? All would go to Her in time.

Chapter 5

IT WAS ANOTHER LOCAL and petty bloodfeud.

Jast Claswell, a wealthy kin of the Bard's Guild, wished to dispose of his wife's lover, a problem compounded by the fact that his wife had had the bad taste to choose a lover outside the guild. The problem was common enough on any world, and common on Neweden. Kinship made for further difficulties. Claswell, a native of the Illian continent, had contacted the Hoorka rather than demanding personal satisfaction. The Hoorka price was normally too high for such domestic vendettas, but Claswell had recently come into possession of a cache of ippicator skeletons and had sold them to an offworld trader without going through the normal Neweden channels, thus avoiding the heavy tax on ippicator relics. It meant that he had monies to use as he wished, and his wish was to kill the man that made him a cuckold.

The apprentices had offered the alternatives to the potential victim, Enus Dausset, but the man couldn't match the fee and thus negate the contract. Five hours before the Underasgard sunset, Dausset was given the traditional warning, and a dye containing a trace of radioactive material was splashed on his arm; it could not easily be washed off and would remain active for several hours, allowing the apprentices to track the man until the Hoorka assassins arrived. A watch was set around Dausset's home—it was midafternoon on that part of the Illian continent.

All this unfolded while the Thane and Aldhelm slept in Underasgard. For such routines, apprentices were sufficient.

An hour before the sun dropped behind the cliff fronting the main entrance to the Hoorka caverns, word came to

Underasgard that Dausset had purchased a hand laser from
a weapons store. Body shields were set out and the two
Hoorka awakened. Final reports drifted in as they prepared
to leave the caverns and fly to Illi. Dausset had secretly paid
a last visit to Caswell's wife (the Thane found himself ad-
miring the man's courage and/or foolishness in doing that).
Dausset had headed south from the city of Irast. Dausset
had turned west by south and fled toward the tumbled
ridges of the Twisted Hills. After the last report, rope and
heavy footgear were added to the assassin's equipment.

During the flight in the Hoorka-owned hovercraft, Aldhelm and the Thane confined their speech to generalities,
and when the craft landed near the edge of the Twisted
Hills, they simply unloaded their equipment and watched as
the aircraft blinked its landing lights in salute and left them.
Around the two, the hills were silvered in the light of Neweden's double moons, Gulltopp and Sleipnir. The night held
the chill of the approaching winter and both the Thane and
Aldhelm kept their nightcloaks wrapped tightly about them
as some protection against the breeze. A few night-stalkers
mewled and shrieked their various hunting cries to the cold
air, but otherwise the landscape was a barren panorama of
shattered rock and broken ground, the remnants of some
ancient cataclysm.

"What did that last report say?" The Thane scanned the
empty slopes, seeing nothing but the unmoving, scraggling
desert brush that clung precariously to the few pockets of
soil. The night, for all its briskness, was arid. The Thane's
throat was dry, as if the air had leached him of inner moisture. He cleared his throat in irritation. After the noise of
the flight, the silence was a palpable presence. His voice had
sounded dead and weak.

Aldhelm squinted into darkness and waited a long minute before he answered the Thane. "The apprentices swear
he's hidden himself in the foothills a few kilometers south
of here. I have the bearings." He swung his hand in the indicated direction, his nightcloak rustling. To the Thane, Aldhelm was a deeper darkness against the sky, his flesh
shadowed and his mouth concealed in the folds of his cloak.
Only his eyes and the crusted wound on his upper cheek
were clearly visible. That bothered the Thane—it briefly occurred to him that Aldhelm might be trying to make the

wound more conspicuous, knowing it would irritate the Thane—but the Thane was himself bundled in a similar fashion. *Your fears are taking over your logic. Stop trying to rationalize every small detail.*

The Thane checked the gear in the pouch of his night-cloak, loosened his vibro in its sheath, and checked the power of his bodyshield.

"Well, kin-brother," he said, "what do you suggest we do?" The Thane yawned and shivered.

"Go around the man. He expects us from the direction of the port in Irast, in all likelihood. It'll be simpler if we can come in unseen from the opposite direction. I doubt that he has any idea where our craft left us."

"Good." Even as he said it, the Thane knew that his response was wrong. It sounded patronizing and belittling; as the question, in essence, had been. It was a question the least schooled apprentice could have answered, and it spoke well of Aldhelm's forbearance that he even deigned to speak. And he spoke now with feeling.

"I'm not an apprentice or journeyman, Thane. I haven't your age or experience, but I've been your kin for some time, if you recall." Aldhelm's voice was haughty and righteously angry. The words cut into the Thane as if edged.

Aldhelm stared into the shadowed valleys of the hills. He scuffed his feet at the dirt in impatience, not looking at the Thane. "The night isn't eternal, Thane, and Hag Death waits Her due. Let's go."

"Not until we settle this. Speak your mind. We can spare the time, and I think it more important than the contract."

"This contract is less important than Gunnar's? What of your—our—code, Thane? Each contract is as important as the next."

"It was a poor choice of words." Wearily, but with impatience. "What bothers you, Aldhelm?"

"You don't know?" His voice sounded genuinely surprised. Aldhelm turned to face the Thane, eyes glinting in the darkness of his face. When he next spoke, his words were harsh and bitter, as if the taste of them burned his tongue. "Why did you pull me from the rotation? Wasn't it enough that I failed the Gunnar contract, or don't you think I'm capable of realizing the import of my mistake? Don't you think I chastised myself far more harshly than you ever could?"

Gulltopp, the smaller of the moons, was setting behind Aldhelm, and its brass-gold light shimmered around him and glazed the hills. "I came close to breaking the damned code, knowing the reactions to Gunnar's escape. I could have killed Gunnar, just seconds after dawn. But I held back—I have that much respect for what the code has done for my kin; I respect Dame Fate and She of the Five Limbs that much. But I should have followed my instincts. No one would have seen, no one but the Gods would have known. Not even you. If I were able to return to that moment . . ."

He paused, then continued with an agonized hurt in his voice that lashed at the Thane. "Do you have to give me further humiliation by treating me like some rank nouveau?" He uttered a short, caustic expletive as the edge of Gulltopp touched the peaks of the Twisted Hills.

The Thane met Aldhelm's gaze. Neither flinched or looked away.

"What did you expect?" asked the Thane. "I had to emphasize to all Hoorka-kin the precariousness of our position in this power struggle between the Li-Gallant and Gunnar. The fact that I'd found it necessary to discipline *you,* the most competent Hoorka I have, man or woman, will carry much weight. It's the most convincing evidence that we're innocent of conspiring with Gunnar. I don't want Hoorka involved in a bloodfeud between guilds, and I won't let us be dragged into the Assembly and outlawed. Anything such as that would jeopardize our chances of growing, of going offworld or escaping Neweden. Gunnar and Vingi will play their power games, and I won't let Hoorka be a pawn on that board." *So simplistic,* he thought. *The words don't even convince me. What can they do for Aldhelm except to convince him that I don't care for him; as a friend, as kin?*

Aldhelm spread his hands wide in the dying light of Gulltopp. "So I'm reduced to being an example in your textbook?" His words quivered with suppressed menace, and for the first time the Thane was aware of the other's sheer bulk, of his physical conditioning and sharper skills. In the Thane's younger days, he could have taken Aldhelm, or at least he flattered himself to think so, but now . . . He was no longer sure, and were there a physical confrontation, Aldhelm would most likely best the Thane. The realization did little to comfort the older man.

But Aldhelm suddenly swept his hand through the cold air in aimless, undirected disgust, breaking their locked gazes as he turned to stare moodily at the surrounding hills as if they were mocking strangers tittering at the Hoorka's overheard conversation.

The Thane placed a hand on Aldhelm's shoulder and forced the Hoorka to look at him. "Aldhelm, I've considered you to be my most likely successor, and I've considered you to be more than a simple kin-brother. You're the best of the kin, more accomplished than I ever was. But I'd throw you to Vingi's guards tied hand and foot if I thought it would save Hoorka. My life is Hoorka's. As is yours. I won't have us destroyed, no matter what sacrifice is demanded. Do you understand?" There was no sympathy there, no hint of the doubts he felt inside. The Thane spoke with an iron voice tempered and made steel, the voice he'd used in the past when he'd taken a ragged band of lassari and by force of personality and fighting prowess had turned them into the Hoorka—a voice he hadn't used in standards. The words echoed faintly among the stones of the hills.

Aldhelm glanced at the Thane's hand and brushed it away ungently. "I understand better than you may think," he said.

Aldhelm turned and began moving into the tortured land of the hills, the sparse night dew from the brush beading on the hem of his nightcloak as Gulltopp sank fully below the horizon. The light in the hills changed suddenly, becoming more bluish and cold, as only Sleipnir was left to wander among the stars. Aldhelm, one foot on a fallen boulder, suddenly thrust himself up and pivoted, facing the Thane again. "I understand your reasoning and your motives. As to your claim of friendship, I don't believe you capable of it. Nor would Valdisa, I think. You're too reserved a man for that, my kin-brother, too much in love with your creation. No, your love is reserved for a thing, not for people. You care for the words that bind Hoorka, not for the kin that form our guild, and your affection is cold and dry." He walked a few steps away from the Thane. "And I hope that disturbs you," he said to the rocky landscape before them.

The Thane, his thoughts a maelstrom both contradictory and painful, watched Aldhelm move away into the Hills, finally disappearing from sight around a cliff that held back the heights from the broken ground below. He listened to the quiet around him. Finally, with a violent start, he followed the path Aldhelm had taken.

Fulfillment of the contract was simple, routine.

The Thane wondered if he should not have left the task to the apprentices to hone their skills. They found Dausset sitting on a rock below a ledge not far into the hills, looking toward the glow on the horizon that bespoke the presence of Irast. The man's head moved slowly from side to side as he swept the plains for signs of movement, but he never looked to the slope behind him nor saw the two Hoorka suddenly appear against the sky and stare down at him from the heights. The barrel of his weapon glistened harshly in Sleipnir's light. Dausset coughed once, a sound startlingly loud in the night. The Thane and Aldhelm studied the man, and their sensors picked up the mark of the apprentices' dye on him. The Thane nodded to Aldhelm.

The younger Hoorka kicked a pebble downslope and, as Dausset turned toward the noise, threw his dagger with seeming nonchalance. It sped true. Dausset grunted in surprise, then crumpled without further outcry, the hand laser unused. Blood stained the rocks beneath him. Quite quickly, quite simply, it was over. The assassins made their way to where the body lay.

"Good work, Aldhelm."

Aldhelm disdained to reply.

The Thane shrugged. "Turn him over. I want to look at him."

"Doesn't the fourth code-line state that the Hoorka must show no concern for the victim, must consider him to be wed to Hag Death once the warning is given so we feel no pity?"

There was mockery in Aldhelm's voice. The Thane ignored it. "A minor quirk, that's all. I like to see their faces, to know how the souls I send to the gods appeared in this life." *No, that's not the truth. This sudden concern with appearances started only recently, when the faceless dead began crowding your dreams. Are you . . .* The Thane cut off the inner contention with a physical wrench. "Turn him over," he repeated, with self-irritation evident in his voice. He doubted that Aldhelm would notice the inward direction of his contempt.

Aldhelm shrugged and turned the body with his foot. Moonlight washed the contorted features of the man's face and outlined the edges of the death-rictus. A thick rivulet of blood trickled from the corner of his mouth and across his right cheek. Thin and unmuscular hands clasped his useless weapon. Dausset's was a common face, a crowd face: thin but not exceedingly so, eyes set a shade too close to a bony and inelegant nose. The Thane wondered what the woman had seen in him to violate her contract with a wealthy man. He reached down and turned off Aldhelm's vibro before pulling it from the wound. It came forth easily, with more blood following; bright, arterial blood. The Thane handed the blade to the Hoorka. Aldhelm plunged it once into the earth to cleanse it—feeding She of the Five Limbs—and placed it back in its sheath.

"Let's finish this."

They wrapped the body in an extra nightcloak and began the long trek back to Claswell's dwelling. The body, a limp weight, swung loosely between the two.

It was still early night when they passed the Irast city gates—two huge doors of black malawood swung to and secured, a symbolic defense. The taverns just inside the gates were full of drinking customers and the shops still had their display windows open to the streets, holos flaring above them in a visual cacophony. The lanes and pedestrian ways were crowded, but all moved aside for the Hoorka and their burden. Faces turned from the business of buying and selling, the more curious following for a time, though no one attempted to hinder them. No sane person would insult Hoorka-kin. Once they passed a band of jussar, young ruffians as yet unattached to any guild but too young to be termed lassari. Their bare chests glittered with fluorescent patterns and vibros hung conspicuously at their sides, but they, too, let the Hoorka pass. The assassins walked slowly, without speaking, their eyes glaring at the path ahead and not to the gathering crowd behind them. The people of Irast, after a curious stare, moved quickly aside.

When they finally deposited the body of Dausset at the gate of Claswell's home, they had attracted a sizable number of the denizens of Irastian nightlife. There were scat-

tered catcalls directed to the opaqued windows of the
Claswell manse; cries of amused derision, for Irast was a
small town and many were privy to this particular piece of
gossip. The crowd, rapidly growing larger and more pleased
with its attempts at wit, parted to let the assassins by as the
Hoorka turned to go, then closed in again. They clamored
excitedly around the corpse and hooted their contempt for
Claswell's cowardice in the face of cuckoldry. As they began
to pound at the gates and a ragged chorus began—a popular song with the words altered to suit the situation by some
quick mind in the crowd—the Hoorka left, as calm and un-
emotionally as they'd come.

(For is it not the sixth code-line that states that the signer of
a fulfilled contract be made a matter of public knowledge—
that the Hoorka will hide the identity of neither slayer nor
slain? For the Hoorka are but weapons in the hands of
another, and the murder will not lie before their conscience,
but that of the contractor. And it is also true that the contractor may himself become the subject of a Hoorka contract.
Revenge is a powerful emotion.)

The Thane and Aldhelm spoke of nothing but trivialities
during their return to Underasgard. After eating and bath-
ing, they retired to their rooms to sleep. The Thane's rest
was fitful. Specters without faces haunted his dreams. And
then there were faces: his own face, an old, old visage channeled and furrowed by too much time; he danced a macabre
arabesque with the swollen and malevolent mask of Vingi
in the dank caverns of the ippicator. Vingi laughed at the
odd appearance of the five-legged beast, mocking it as an
animal unfit to live, unsuited to its environment and unable
to cope with change. Then, together, they smashed the skeleton to broken dust. And in the darkness, he could hear the
giggling mirth of Hag Death.

The spires of the Port were gilded by the early sun. Far off on
the flattened expanse of earth that served as Neweden's link
to the worlds of the Alliance, ground vehicles bore the phallic
cylinders of storage units to the waiting freighters at the edge
of the landing field. To one side of the Port stood the buildings of Sterka—nearest the Port, the hostels, the bars, and
places of varied entertainment for the crews of the Alliance
ships coming in and out of Neweden. Across the field from

the city stood the ornate and intricate architecture of the Diplo Center. It was a varied if not beautiful scene by morning, and m'Dame d'Embry, the Alliance Regent of the Diplos on Neweden, gazed long at it before opaquing the window and turning back into her rooms.

She often compared Neweden to Niffleheim, and Neweden sometimes had the best of the comparison. Neweden had the rough grace of untitled and little-known regions to recommend it, a crude pastorality that the more urban and urbane worlds lacked. Crowded worlds and aesthetics that turned to dry dust in the eyes seemed to go together—it had been decades since she had been awed by the sight of Niffleheim's metallic surface.

The room had already taken the sleeping plate to the ceiling, where the plate functioned as a lighting unit. Music drifted in polyphonic eddies from the walls—a harpsichord concerto by Hagee, an obscure Terran composer—and a holo of d'Vellia's soundsculpture *Gehennah*, half-size, loomed in the corner nearest the comlink. In her dressing gown and without the bodytints that had once been fashionable (and which she still wore, unaware or simply uncaring that they were no longer in favor), her body reflected its age. The eyes were caught up in a finely-knit spiderweb of lines, her face had a patina of grayness, and when she moved it was with a certain sureness that is missing in a younger person's step, the kittenish ungainliness of youth. She didn't bother to treat her hair—it was dry and whitened. The flesh on her body had a laxness, a sag, as if it had once confined more bulk than she now possessed. But if d'Embry had lost physical fullness, she was compensated by an avid spirit; as if in leaving, the flesh had cast off and left behind the energy it once encompassed. The snared eyes were undimmed and lively, the gnarled hands strong and agile. She was a legend in Diplo circles, the grand-dame of Niffleheim, and she had resisted all well-meaning attempts to retire her from active duty with a fervor that had impressed, awed, and irritated the Niffleheim authorities. As a Diplo, she was effective; as a political in-fighter, without peer.

And she was nearing the end. Inside, she knew it. Perhaps another ten standards before the drugs, implants, and mechanical aids could no longer keep that body together. That gave her drive, and if she was occasionally brusque and quick, she attributed it—in her mind—to that fact. She had little time to waste on foolishness.

"Comlink," she said to the empty room.

"M'Dame?" The screen of the comlink flared and settled into a blue-gray background that flickered slightly. D'Embry moved to the mechanism and, running her hands across the keyboard there, pressed a button. Light surged and letters raced across the screen. "Neweden status bank," chimed the comlink in a neuter voice, echoing redundantly the words printed on the screen.

"Report from local time 21:30 to the present. I want an emphasis on governmental problems. Briefly. You know what I'm after."

The comlink voice changed to a woman's contralto, evidently that of a staff Diplo. "M'Dame, one moment please."

"Certainly." D'Embry tapped the carpet of the room with one bare foot, noticing that the carpet needed to be trimmed again—it had grown too high for her liking. She made a mental note to have the Maintenance Department groom the rug.

"Sorry for the delay, m'Dame. I note here that at 22:00, the Li-Gallant received a committee of guild-members sympathetic to his guild's rule." The woman's voice continued as an accompanying text appeared on the screen. "Topic of their discussion is unknown, but the conjecture is that it concerned consolidation of support after the Assembly meeting of yesterday afternoon. Query?"

"No." D'Embry's voice was dry, and she cleared her throat. "Continue, please."

"22:15. Gunnar and Potok were seen in the pastures of their guild holdings outside Sterka. They refused to speak to the news services. Query?"

"No. Give me a general update, quickly." She used a side panel of the comlink to order her breakfast, then asked the room to elevate a chair. She sat, then spoke as the woman on the link began to speak again. "Cancel that last request. My mind's already cluttered with enough useless facts for the day. What of the Hoorka?"

"We understand that they fulfilled a contract last night in Irast. A copy of the completed contract was sent to the Center from Underasgard in compliance with your request. Query?"

"Put the contract on visual, please." D'Embry scanned the contract without truly reading it. She glanced at the names of contractor and victim, her lips pursed in a moue of distaste, but the names were simply a random arrangement of letters that meant nothing to her. Her fingertips tapped the console of the comlink. The gray paint was worn to bare metal where her hands rested. "Negate," she said, and the screen cleared.

"Please come on visual yourself," she said. The screen flickered and then filled with the head and shoulders of a young woman, her hair short at the sides and long down her back in current fashion, her eyelids and lips touched with a faint scarlet sheen that seemed to burn with a tepid fire. "Ahh, Stanee," d'Embry said. "Good morning."

The face smiled. "Thank you, m'Dame. Anything else I can do for you?"

D'Embry waved the question away. "I hate the coldness of the words on the screen after a while, so you'll excuse the visual contact. I simply get an urge, now and again, to see to whom I'm talking. A whim, child, nothing more."

Stanee's smile remained fixed. It seemed the predominant feature of her face. "Certainly, m'Dame."

"Do you have the figures for Sterka last night?—not the gory facts that get attached to them in this barbaric place, just the figures. And I'll probably ask you to stop halfway through them, so don't be overly perturbed at your record-keeping being unappreciated."

Stanee looked down, below the camera's view. The head and shoulders on the screen moved as her fingers raced over controls. Without looking up, she began reading. "Sterka continent: killed by bloodfeud, three. Assaults, twenty. Incidents that might lead to guild conflicts, four reported . . ." The list went on, number after number sifted from the chaff of the night.

"Enough," d'Embry interrupted finally. She sigh-smiled and shook her head at Stanee. "Enough for now. Did it ever occur to you that this is a world with damnably little to recommend it—with the exception of ippicator skeletons and some pretty but unspectacular scenery? Ahh, never mind, never mind." She waved a hand in the air. "Just the normal morning grumpiness. Have a flimsy sent to my office to look over later, will you? You can cram into it all those boring details that I know you've been dying to give me, neh?"

Dutiful laughter. "Yes, m'Dame. Is that all?"

"For now. End," she said in a less personal tone of voice. The comlink cleared to a blank blue-gray. "Off." The screen darkened and went black as it eased into its niche in the wall, out of sight.

D'Embry went to the window and cleared it again. The sun had risen higher in the sky, pursued by high cumulus clouds, and the light had gone from the honey-thick yellow of the dawn to the whiter, more penetrating glare of full day. The buildings basked in warmth, throwing sharp-edged shadows across the plain of the Port. A freighter rose, its attitude jets throwing off hot gases to waver the air. The ship hovered low over the Port for a moment, and then arced into the Neweden morning, leaving a dirty trail that the wind wiped across the sky. In the city, dark specks of birds wheeled in alarm.

The Port was alive with workers and Alliance personnel beginning a new day. For them, another day of relative sameness. The daily problems came and went without ever being eliminated.

M'Dame d'Embry sighed deep within herself and slapped at the window controls. She watched the glass turn slowly smoky and then deep purple-black, inking out the view of the Port. She leaned against the wall in reverie for a moment or two, forcing her mind to come to full alertness. Finally, rather desultorily, she began to dress.

The sun warmed the soil of the hills, but the heat and light of the sunstar failed to disturb the cool night that lingered below ground. The caverns of Underasgard, eternally cloaked and ever-mild, paid little attention to the vagaries of the surface.

For Hoorka-kin, however, the rising sun heralded a Rites Day, a day full with the worship of their patron gods. Kin spoke quietly to one another, the kitchens served only cold bread and milk, and the apprentices were kept busy ensuring that all nightcloaks were pressed and clean. A hurried calm held the caverns, a busy laziness. The Hoorka gathered slowly in the Chamber, the largest of the caverns they inhabited, and took their seats before the High Altar.

The Thane, sitting to the utter rear of the Chamber, watched the assembly as if rapt. His mind, however, dwelt elsewhere. He was only marginally aware of Valdisa's warmth at his side, of Cranmer's fidgeting, of Aldhelm's curt greetings. He distantly nodded to the journeymen and apprentices as they entered. When the ponderous chords of the chant of praise rose, his lips mouthed the words and his voice sang, but he heard nothing.

"I love the feel of your body." Valdisa smiled, faint lines appearing at the corners of her mouth. Teasing, her eyes danced.

The Thane rolled over on his back so that her roving hands had access to all of him. His gaze moved from her face and down the lean tautness of Valdisa's body. He stroked the upper swell of her breasts softly, and smiled as her eyes closed.

"Damn you," she said, a velvet growl, and her hand found him. Laughing, they kissed. Still laughing, she straddled him.

The chanters had finished the descant. Ric d'Mannberg began a short reading from the annals of She of the Five Limbs, one of the more violent passages. His droning voice spoke of kin slaying kin, of disembowelments and cannibalism. The Thane woke from his reverie and found Cranmer engrossed in the account of She. "You find this fascinating, scholar?" he whispered.

Cranmer leaned toward the Thane, whispering in return. "Only in the sheer number of gods with which Neweden, for all her poverty, is, ahh, blessed with having. It's staggering. All the various guilds, and few of them sharing the same patrons . . . Neweden must have been a crowded world during the days of these gods."

"Until She of the Five Limbs banished most."

"For an ippicator, even one of such power, that must have been an amazing feat." Cranmer glanced at the Altar, where d'Mannberg had closed the book and nodded in salutation. "And I notice that your attention wanders, Thane. I'm curious—your true father was an offworlder by birth, and came to Neweden's religions as a convert. Do you believe, or is it simply convenient?"

"Do you have faith, Cranmer?"

"In gods? No."

"Too bad." The Thane leaned back in his seat, closing his

eyes again. D'Mannberg opened the Annals once more. His voice droned on.

His real parents, lassari, had brought the boy to Hoorka. The Thane had glared down at the thin, wiry child of . . . thirteen? And the boy had glared back, uncowed. The Thane had liked the defiance of the child and took the young Aldhelm as kin. The parents, over-grateful, and perhaps pleased to be rid of the extra mouth, had taken a quick leave. They had never again inquired after their son. He now had kin— parents were unimportant.

"Watch your opponent's hips," he'd said to the new apprentice one day, during a training session. "Other parts of the body may feint—the legs, the arms, the head, the eyes. But where the hips go, the body must follow."

Aldhelm shook his head. His hands toying with the hilt of his vibro, he'd stared at the Thane. "No, that seems wrong. I watch the hands and feet. They do the damage."

"You don't have four eyes to watch each."

"Two are sufficient."

Something in the boy's stubbornness and insistence touched a response in the Thane. He'd stripped and joined the youngster on the practice floor. "Defend yourself, then," he'd said. He circled the apprentice, watching the vibro and the hips. It took much longer than he'd anticipated—the Thane was slick with sweat when they'd finished—but he found the flaws in Aldhelm's defense, disarmed and pinned the boy to the floor of Underasgard. Still, he was impressed by Aldhelm's raw, untutored skill.

"You see," he said, getting to his feet and releasing the boy. "Had you watched me correctly, that would not have happened. In a fight, you'd have been very dead, boy, despite your thoughts on what to watch."

"I'll think about it, sirrah." That was as much admission as Aldhelm would give the Thane.

The dance to Hag Death had begun. Brilliant in scarlet robes and satin ribbons, blue hairplumes bobbing with movement, the dancers circled each other. Steel blades in their hands glinted in the lights. A sackbutt snorted a chorus, joined by a trio of recorders. There were two dancers of each sex, and their bare feet slapped the stones of Underasgard as they went through the ritualistic steps, a choreographed battle representing the strife between Dame Fate and the Hag. Blades flashed and met, clashing with a faint, bell-like ringing.

The bells for evening meals had just rung. Aldhelm had brought the Thane's dinner to him, dismissing the apprentice that usually performed that task. He sat the tray on the Thane's table, setting the controls to "warm" so that the meat remained hot. Fragrant vapors filled the room.

"Aldhelm?" the Thane said in some surprise. "Since when do you perform apprentice's tasks? You're nearly a full Hoorka."

"I had a favor to ask, a boon." His voice, usually so confident, was slow and unsure, halting.

"Ask, then."

A hesitation. "You'll sponsor me for my mastership in the Hoorka, be my kin-father?" Aldhelm said the words in a rush, the words falling over each other in their haste to leave his mouth. But his eyes—they held the Thane, and there was open affection there, and an unusual vulnerability that was foreign to Aldhelm.

Knowing what he was going to say, that openness hurt the Thane more than he thought possible.

"I've never sponsored any journeyman, Aldhelm." He said the words slowly, hoping that Aldhelm might reconsider and withdraw the request himself, and knowing that it wouldn't happen that way.

Aldhelm frowned. He looked down at the floor and then up to the Thane. "I realize that. That's why I've waited so long to ask." A vague smile touched his lips. "You've spoken well of me, and we like each other. I would like your sponsoring. It would mean much to me."

"I"—a pause—"can't."

Aldhelm was stoic. His stance was as erect as before, his body betraying no disappointment. Yet something had changed: his eyes were guarded now, and perhaps too moist.

The Thane hastened to explain. "If there were a journeyman I would take as kin-son, it would be you, Aldhelm. Truly. But I don't care to have the Hoorka become like other guilds, where the kin-son of the guild ruler inherits his father's position. The best Hoorka should always rule Hoorka, and all the kin should have some say in who governs them. If I were to name a son or daughter, it would be a statement, an indication of favoritism. It's easier if I simply avoid that."

The Thane stared at Aldhelm, but the young man simply gazed back at him, his eyes unreadable and untouchable. "Do you understand? Aldhelm, I don't wish to hurt you—as I said, were I to sponsor anyone . . ."

"I understand, Thane." Aldhelm shrugged and began to leave the room.

"Aldhelm . . ."

"Yah?" The Hoorka turned and faced the Thane.

"What of Bronton? He admires your skill as much as I, and he is well-liked among the kin. He would sponsor you, and it would be to your credit."

"Thank you for your concern, Thane." Again, the shrugging of shoulders. A smile came and vanished, tentative. "I'll ask him." And with that, Aldhelm turned and left.

The Thane stared at the tray of food on his table for long minutes before beginning to eat.

The dancers, in a flourish of weapons, left the dais. A journeywoman attired in saffron robes intoned the benediction. An audible sigh crossed the Chamber, and with a rustling of cloth, the Hoorka-kin rose and began to leave. The Thane stretched and rose as Cranmer and Valdisa stood beside him.

"He slept well, didn't he, Valdisa?" Cranmer placed his hands below his head in imitation of a pillow and closed his eyes.

"Our Thane?" Valdisa smiled. "He has an excuse, having taken the contract last night."

"Both of you are mistaken. I simply concentrate better with my eyes closed. Prayer, after all, is a mental effort. Neh, scholar?" The Thane yawned, involuntarily, then joined in with the laughter of the other two.

Chapter 6

A LARGE GATHERING HAD CROWDED *en masse* before the Assembly Hall after marching noisily from Tri-Unity Square. A few flat-signs proclaimed various guilds' support of one obscure issue or another, but the guards ranked on the steps to the Hall didn't bother to read them, being all too used to such displays. Protests of one variety or another were commonplace enough on Neweden since the advent of the All-Guild Assembly created by Li-Gallant Perrin, the current Li-Gallant's kin-father. The week before, it had been a group of ore farmers from Nean that had staged a minor riot in the capital city of that continent during the Li-Gallant's visit. Several demonstrators had been incarcerated, and more were injured in the fighting that came when the security people attempted to disperse them. It was not, however, an unusual occurrence except in the number of injuries.

Where guilds and pride were concerned, tempers flared easily but carefully—the offended person might be a better fighter than you. Most demonstrations were noisy but well-behaved. After their time of shouting and preening for the news services, the crowds faded and died, the people melting back into the streets.

So the guards watched with a bored and uninterested demeanor as the vanguard of the protestors edged to the base of the steps. A chant was shouted in ragged unison, though no words could be easily discerned. Two beats—a strong accent followed by a weaker one, then a pause—a waltz protest. The signs moved with the chant, upraised to the sunstar in the phosphorus zenith.

One guard fidgeted in his pockets, pulling forth a packet

of mildly intoxicating candies from the south coast. He offered one to the nearest companion.

The chant of the crowd waxed and ebbed, a tide-swell that moved in its own rhythm, a thousand-throated beast wailing distress to the silent facade of the Hall. Few details stood out in the Brownian motion of the protesters: a flash of iridescent cloth; a person near the front, taller by a head than his neighbors and further individualized by a spiked plant-pet growing like a living collar around his neck; the uneven summits of the signs pooling thin shadows on those below. The far edge of the crowd was not sharply defined, but faded into a perimeter consisting equally of interested but unmotivated spectators and those using the demonstration as an excuse for play—youngsters running happily through the legs of adults; streetkids, jussar.

Had it been like the hundred protests before it, this would have been a short-lived commingling that would have died quickly from the lack of response from the Hall and the failure of the Neweden news services to arrive (the holo networks had been prudently notified by the march's organizers, but knowing Vingi's present mood, had declined the offer).

But the former demonstrations didn't have the Nean "riot" and the furor of the Assembly meeting the day before. These gnawed at Vingi's thin tolerance for opposition. The guards had been sternly instructed to disperse and scatter any large gatherings before the Hall. Following those directions, they began walking slowly down the steps with their crowd-prods loose in their holders, but with a good-natured casualness designed to dispel any ill-feelings among the people.

It didn't work.

The guards pushed into the front ranks, shouting in voices almost inaudible to the bulk of the crowd to move on, that all gatherings had been forbidden for the immediate future, and to lodge their complaints via the more officially correct channels. The guards weren't gentle, nor were they particularly cruel—they were simply doing what they had been assigned to do. They pressed forward, and the amoebic crowd bent with the pressure, the people gathered at the contact point stepping backward into those behind them. The perimeter was moved back from the steps and then—forced by the wall of bodies behind them and the normal reaction of people hemmed into too small a space—stopped and pushed back against the guards. It became quickly and painfully obvious to those dutiful people that Vingi had overestimated the amount of co-operation they would receive, and that they should have called for disperser screens. It occurred to them that the aura of authority given them by their uniforms and guild-affiliation was a fragile thing and had deceived them into thinking themselves impervious to harm.

And then, quite suddenly, they had no time for thinking.

A guard went down (stumbled or pushed? It was a question that would remain unanswered when the incident was reviewed by the Li-Gallant) and the tone of the crowd-creature's voice changed. The timbre became deeper, more threatening. The tall man with the plant-covered neck strode through the tumult around the downed guard. He bent down, struggled against some unseen adversary, and emerged with a hand grasping a crowd-prod. He waved the instrument high, and cheers greeted his gesture of victory. Those nearest the guards, encouraged, began actively resisting. The guards pulled prods from their holders, using them liberally. Screams of genuine pain lanced the general din. The situation degenerated.

The focus of the disturbance wandered and swelled as members of various guilds found reason to fight with others. There was no single source—it was no longer even guards against the crowd, but an amalgamation of several small altercations with no definite boundaries. Combatants changed at whim.

When the edges of the riot had spread to the shield-barrier skirting Port property, the Alliance Diplos were sent out from the Center. M'Dame d'Embry had watched the fighting after being pulled from a staff meeting by a harried aide. She quickly ordered her people to stop any possible destruction of Alliance property. If the locals wanted to fight, excellent, but no Alliance holding would be harmed. The Diplo security forces used tanglefeet bombs and gas to stop the fighting and began dragging the participants away from the central melee. By the time reinforcements arrived for Vingi's harassed guards, the Diplos had settled the disturbance considerably. The Diplos withdrew back to the

Center, leaving the job of caring for the wounded and arresting the appropriate number of guild-members to Vingi's more interested hands.

In time, the last remnants of the crowd had departed— walking or carted—and the area before the Hall was left to the wind, which idly toyed with scraps of paper. Bored guards, the new shift, lounged against the pillars of the Hall, staring with unfocused eyes at the birds foraging for crumbs on the steps. A few representatives, officious and hurried, nodded to the guards as they entered the doors.

All in all, just another day.

The practice room of Underasgard was a long, meandering room of the caverns, wandering crookedly and lit primarily by two parallel strips of light-emitting fungi that receded— like a badly designed painting—in a shaky v of deep perspective. The muzzy, warm light from the fungi was heavily greenish. A few hoverlamps, filtered to compensate to some degree, were distributed around the room to offset the odd coloration. A moving person walked through varying shades and tints. Racks of practice weapons lined the walls, and if the choice of weaponry seemed antiquated, it was because the Thane felt that the art of epee, foil, and saber kept the Hoorka in better physical condition, and because the proliferation of shields against most projectile and beam weapons made the blades of the romantic eras once again useful. The floor of the cavern was softer and more resilient than the hard-packed seal of the living quarters. Sound dampeners dotted the ceiling at intervals. These were the most recent addition to the room, added because the din of mock fighting echoed terrifically through the caverns and disturbed the rest of any sleeping Hoorka.

A good number of the kin could generally be found here, either practicing, watching, or gathered in the rest area at one end of the room. This day was no exception.

The Thane, Valdisa, and Cranmer were standing near the central practice strip in a group of Hoorka that included Ric d'Mannberg. D'Mannberg had signed to use that strip for a long-vibro exercise. Aldhelm, who was to work with him, hadn't yet arrived.

Cranmer was carrying a camera—the tri-lensed apparatus of a portable holo. He adjusted a vernier, squinted into the eyepiece, and checked the room lighting. Somewhere inside the metal casing, a motor purred. Taking his eyes from the viewpiece, Cranmer stared critically at the lines marked on the floor of the cavern.

"Someday you're going to have to let me work against one of your apprentices," he said.

An undercurrent of laughter rippled through the Hoorka standing around him, dominated by d'Mannberg's booming chuckle. A heavy, massive man with blond-red hair and a thick beard, he looked perhaps more ponderous than dangerous. It was a deceptive appearance.

"Yah, laugh, you arrogant bastard." Cranmer turned to d'Mannberg, a comically stern frown on his face and his light tone leaching any possible sting from his words. "We scholars have our own attributes. I've a lot less flesh to move around, for one."

Stepping forward, he poked a finger into d'Mannberg's stomach. It was obvious by the sudden widening of his eyes that he was startled when his finger was repulsed by strong muscles—the gray-black folds of the Hoorka uniform were barely dented.

"You *could* always run between my legs and reach up, I suppose," d'Mannberg retorted into Cranmer's amazement. Cranmer's lack of stature led to many—too many, to Cranmer's view—comments about his shortness.

Cranmer gazed at his ineffectual forefinger, then stared appraisingly at d'Mannberg. "I doubt that it would do much good. Nothing to hold on to."

D'Mannberg winced.

"The scholar has a sting."

"At least I have *something*." As the Hoorka laughed, Cranmer shook his head, a grin on his face. "You understand," he observed at large, "it will be noted in my eventual paper that the Hoorka seem to find the crudest sort of humor appealing. Unsophisticated and rowdy, lacking taste and refinement, and indulging in gutter humor of the lowest variety. I can visualize a group of Hoorka sitting about the caverns, exchanging puns and sexual metaphors . . ."

"One must have some type of social intercourse," said Valdisa, smiling overmuch.

"Sirrahs and dames, can we get our minds attuned to business?" the Thane broke in roughly. He tempered the reproof in his voice with a mock shaking of his head, but the joking conversations died. The Thane nodded toward the door leading to the Hoorka living quarters. "Aldhelm is coming."

Watching Aldhelm walk toward them, the Thane felt indecision hammering at him. The unresolved conflict of the contract night lay like a barrier between them through which only the most innocuous comments could pass, a pall of caution. *How should I speak to him? What can dissolve that curtain?* The questions remained unanswered.

As Aldhelm came up to the group of Hoorka, he acknowledged the Thane's presence with the barest salutation. "Thane, Valdisa; how are you?"

As Valdisa said her hello, Aldhelm glanced about and noted Cranmer's recording gear and the Hoorka waiting to see the practice bout. "An oddly popular exercise," he said drily. "Are you ready, then, Ric?"

"Definitely." D'Mannberg stretched and grunted.

Aldhelm and d'Mannberg stripped to the waist. As Aldhelm straightened and threw his tunic to the ground, the Thane caught his eye. The two locked gazes, nearly glaring, until Aldhelm shook his head with a rough motion and broke the contact. Spectators began moving away from the practice strip and the Thane felt Valdisa shift position until she stood next to him. Her hand touched his thigh with a light, accidental brush held a fraction of a second too long. Suddenly sensitive to such things, the Thane could feel her warmth along his right side as he watched Cranmer film the preliminaries. He started, hesitantly, to put his arm around her shoulders, then changed his mind. He brushed his hair back.

Half-naked, Aldhelm was impressive: a wedge of a torso with sharply defined muscles and a firm abdomen. He moved as if he were all too well aware of his physical impression, striding carefully erect and with a certain equipoise that suggested he was expecting an assault from an unseen assailant. The Thane compared it mentally with his own self—that figure he examined critically and vainly in the mirror of his room. The Thane was beginning to lose the tone and vigor of his younger days, despite his constant exercising. *No,* he thought, *in all honesty I don't exercise as I once did. I can't summon the same enthusiasm for it.* He remembered a time when he would have been eager to face the challenge of an Aldhelm, but now ... He shook the thought away.

D'Mannberg and Aldhelm had exchanged their vibros, checking to see that each had been adjusted and locked to the practice setting. A half meter from the end of the grip to the tip, the long-vibro was a hybrid of sword and knife. Set correctly, they would sting but not cut. That was incentive enough to avoid being touched, for the welt it would leave behind was painful and slow to heal. Having checked the weapons, they returned them to each other and repeated the process: calibrate, twist the locking ring on the hilt until it clicked and moved forward, test against a fingertip—a mistake could easily cost flesh. D'Mannberg winced and shook his hand as the vibro slapped against his finger, eyes half-closed. The two Hoorka bowed to each other, and because the Thane was watching, to him. If the Thane noted that Aldhelm's bow was less deep than d'Mannberg's, he said nothing.

The combatants began to cautiously circle each other, hands outspread, bare feet hushing against the floor. As they moved, the varied color of the lights swept over them, faint washes glazing the flesh tones: green-white, then a pale purple. From another strip on the far end of the room, steel rapiers could be heard clashing with a faint ringing, but still louder was the hard breathing of Aldhelm and d'Mannberg, the low thrumming of their vibros, and the slithering of their feet on the packed earth.

D'Mannberg attacked first. A thick arm darted forward, quicker than one might have expected from the sheer mass it carried. Through a gauze of vermillion to decaying green: the vibros met with a protest of hissing rage and a few blue-white sparks that fell—a dying parabola—to the ground. Aldhelm quickly showed his superior strength. His parry combined with d'Mannberg's forward momentum to throw the larger man off-balance. D'Mannberg barely missed being nicked as he stumbled and recovered. Cranmer, filming from the side nearest them, suddenly found himself too near the combat and quickly moved backward. Laughter from the watching Hoorka pursued him. D'Mannberg, his eyes on Aldhelm, smiled ruefully in response to the amusement, thinking it directed toward his clumsy attempt to pass Aldhelm's guard. He shook his head in self-chastisement.

Aldhelm's grim expression never matched the light-hearted comments around him.

The Hoorka thrust quickly, and d'Mannberg barely had time to bring his vibro up. Their weapons shrieked agony as Aldhelm's free hand reached out and grasped d'Mannberg's vibro hand at the wrist. He twisted, viciously, and with a yelp of pain and surprise, d'Mannberg dropped his blade. Aldhelm kicked it aside as d'Mannberg shook free of Aldhelm's grip and backed away, holding the injured wrist.

(Murmured approval from the watchers. Valdisa leaned close to the Thane and whispered "That was a good move. He's quick, isn't he?" The Thane grunted assent as she pressed his hand with her fingertips.)

Sweat was beginning to bead on Aldhelm's skin. On his shoulders, the fungi-lights glistened wetly. D'Mannberg, his face radiating his disgust at being so easily caught, expelled an irritated breath and reached down casually for his fallen vibro. Aldhelm, a step away, thrust at the exposed chest, and the tip of the vibro touched d'Mannberg just below the rib-cage. The slap of vibro against flesh was loud in the caverns and d'Mannberg, shocked, bellowed his hurt. His fingers closed on air short of the vibro hilt; he rolled to the ground and kicked out with his legs. His left foot struck the forearm of Aldhelm's vibro arm. The weapon shivered and nearly dropped before Aldhelm could grasp it firmly again. His hand chopped at Aldhelm's leg, missing by millimeters.

"Aldhelm!" The admonishment came unbidden from the Thane, startling everyone—including himself—with its ve-hemence. The Hoorka-kin standing about added their own vague protest at Aldhelm's seeming disregard for practice etiquette. It was well and good to use any advantage when seriously threatened, but in practice the adversary had the right to recover a dropped weapon unless such a rule was stated beforehand. It saved people from unnecessary hurt. Aldhelm seemed too serious, too intent on showing his prowess and humbling d'Mannberg. *And it's my fault.* "Damn," said the Thane aloud.

The Thane's shout had turned Aldhelm, and in that moment d'Mannberg regained his footing. Shouting his anger, he rushed Aldhelm, getting his burly arms about the Hoorka's shoulders and bearing the smaller man down with sheer weight. On his knees, Aldhelm half-turned in d'Mannberg's hold and freed his vibro, bringing it around until it touched d'Mannberg's bicep. A yelp of pain: involuntary moisture filled d'Mannberg's eyes. He held on with desperation, but his grip had been weakened, allowing Aldhelm to turn to face him. Aldhelm lashed out with knee and vibro. His leg struck hard at d'Mannberg's thick waist, and d'Mannberg fought for breath, backing away from the threatening vibro. Sweat, rainbow-hued, rained on the floor. The hair of both men was matted to their heads, dark with moisture. D'Mannberg started forward to attack again, but his feet slid on the slick floor; in that instant, Aldhelm thrust his vibro and touched d'Mannberg's massive chest. D'Mannberg gulped for air, his eyes wide and pained. He flailed at Aldhelm, and this time struck his wrist— Aldhelm's vibro skidded across the strip. D'Mannberg struggled to rise and pursue his advantage.

A hand caught at Aldhelm's shoulder from behind as he reached for his fallen weapon, slipping once on the sweat and then gripping tightly. Aldhelm shook off the restraint with a violent motion and spun on his toes to face his new attacker—the Thane. Anger etched the lines of the older man's face even deeper. His lips were drawn back slightly from his teeth and his body was braced, the legs spread.

"Enough, Aldhelm." His voice lashed at the man. "You've managed to make your point, whatever it was supposed to be. Do you mind telling me what you're trying to prove that's worth a kin's pain?"

Aldhelm's vibro was held at his side, still activated. He stared at the Thane, a berserker rage in his eyes—dilated pupils, eyelids drawn far back. He blinked once, then again, and suddenly seemed to recognize the Hoorka ruler. His voice was almost too normal, too calm and even. "I'm a competent fighter, Thane—that's all I wished to show my kin. They needn't treat me as a nouveau or an apprentice."

"And you feel a need to demonstrate that? I'll admit it here before the rest of Hoorka, if it eases your childish temper. Or do you wish me to call a general meeting and stand up before the kin to say 'Aldhelm can fight, if he sometimes forgets to think'?" The Thane tapped a forefinger to his temple.

With the last words, Aldhelm's face moved as if struck. His hands clenched the vibro hilt convulsively.

"Let me defer to my elders then, Thane. I, the child, ask forgiveness and stand corrected. I don't think." Aldhelm spat out the words.

"Give me your vibro, then." The Thane held out his hand, and the light-fungi bathed it with an odd coloration. Glancing down, the Thane saw his palm as a dead and withered thing, devoid of power and impact, decaying and impotent. *It isn't working—this is all wrong. I should have let the others separate them and have sent Aldhelm off to cool his temper. Just let the incident go at that with nothing said. Too late, too late. You have to play this charade out now.*

Aldhelm glanced at the Thane's hand. "The vibro?" he asked. And he stared at the Thane in mute challenge, making no move to hand over the weapon.

Anger fought logic inside the Thane, anger allied with a need to prove his own competence to himself and sweep away the doubts that had come to bother him more of late. He glanced at Aldhelm, at the vibro, at the muscular body confronting him. It would be easy to simply stand there, hand out; Aldhelm would give in from the force of the Hoorka-kin watching at the Thane's back. The younger Hoorka was in the wrong and knew it—and it would be a strengthening of the Thane's authority. All he need do was wait.

But he couldn't wait.

Without a word, the Thane pulled his tunic over his head as a small, rational part of his mind shrilled alarm. He held the bunched cloth in his hand, then threw it at Aldhelm and leaped to follow. He heard Valdisa's voice crying wordlessly as he struck out at the man.

The Thane's attack knocked Aldhelm to the ground, the Hoorka still trying to free himself from the tunic. They fell in a tangle of limbs, the Thane with both hands on Aldhelm's knife arm. Aldhelm thrust the blinding cloth aside and levered himself with his powerful legs, driving and turning so that the Thane found himself below the other man, still holding desperately to the vibro hand.

By the Hag, he's strong. I've made a mistake. I can't take him. The realization came even as he brought his knees up in a reflex motion, searching for groin or stomach. But Aldhelm had anticipated that maneuver and had moved quickly to the left, his body braced against the pressure of the Thane's grip. The Thane let go his hold of Aldhelm. The sudden loss of support toppled Aldhelm. The Thane brought interlocked hands down between the man's shoulderblades and scrambled to his feet.

Too low. I hit him too low and too late.

Aldhelm regained his footing almost as quickly, but Valdisa and another of the Hoorka took him by the arms before he could move to attack the Thane once more. He glowered angrily, but didn't struggle.

"Let him go. Let him try to finish it." The Thane was breathing heavily, feeling weaker than he should for the amount of exertion. His mind still shouted its admonition, but the adrenalin—the excitement of the fight—had taken him. He felt he had to carry through this farce or face an unresolved problem. *But if you lose . . . No, I won't lose.* He nodded at Aldhelm. "You wanted this, kin. Let him go, Valdisa."

"Thane—"

"Let him go!" The voice was like the slap of a whip on flesh. She released Aldhelm. The Thane stooped and picked up d'Mannberg's vibro from the floor of the strip and checked the setting. "Come on then, Hoorka."

Aldhelm didn't move. The rage had gone from him, and his eyes searched the Thane. "You don't have to do this. You'll lose, Thane, and it will prove nothing." His voice was suddenly soft and penitent. "What do you demand of me? My apology to Ric? He has it." Aldhelm nodded to d'Mannberg. "My vibro? Here."

Aldhelm held his weapon out to the Thane, hilt foremost.

The cavern was silent, the Hoorka watching. Valdisa stirred, her voice low and pleading.

"Thane, take it."

"No!" He shouted the word. *I can't. Don't you see that?* "You wished to practice, Aldhelm. I need the exercise myself. Defend yourself, Hoorka."

They came together in the middle of the strip. Their hands locked, the vibros clashed once, then twice more before Aldhelm, grunting with the effort, threw the Thane back. The Thane stumbled, his ankle turning beneath him, and he swung his hands wide in an attempt to maintain equilibrium. Aldhelm did not hesitate to take the opening.

He came at the Thane as the older man strove to recover his balance. The Thane brought his vibro up a fraction of a second too late: in a flurry of sparks, he turned the blade, but the searing hiss of the vibro tip marked his side. He grimaced in pain as he parried and prepared to meet another thrust, but Aldhelm had moved back, waiting.

The Thane, his side aflame, saw that the Hoorka was holding his vibro too low and he thrust at the opening, coming in over Aldhelm's blade. He met flesh, and saw with satisfaction a red welt form high on Aldhelm's shoulder. He continued his attack, following his advantage as the excitement flowed more swiftly in his veins. His body seemed to have shed some of its years, shed even the weariness of a minute before. He thought, oddly at variance with his earlier pessimism, that he might have a chance. Aldhelm, yes, was stronger; still, experience . . .

Aldhelm backed and parried, the Thane following eagerly. Near the back line of the practice strip, Aldhelm kicked out with a foot, almost sending the Thane to the ground as his heel brushed the Thane's knee. Now it was the Thane who retreated as they circled, feinting and jabbing without making contact. The cavern floor was becoming slippery with their sweat, the footing uncertain and treacherous. A drop of perspiration burned its way into the Thane's left eye. He blinked it away. At the edge of his vision, he could see Cranmer filming, with Valdisa beside him, her face showing her concern.

Old man, old man, hurry this farce. The Thane's breathing was harsh and too quick, accompanied by a thin wheezing. He knew he must make a final move, win or lose, very soon. The euphoria had been false, the adrenalin weak. His body would all too soon succumb to the punishment.

Aldhelm thrust again, coming at the Thane with his arm extended. In deflecting the blade, the Thane felt a searing pull at his side where he'd been touched by Aldhelm's vibro, and knew that he could not retain his mobility much longer. Time would award Aldhelm victory. The Thane judged his distance, waited for the slightest relaxation in Aldhelm's defense. When he thought he saw the opening, he attacked.

Vibros snapped and snarled, clattering against each other. The Thane drove his other hand, fisted, toward Aldhelm's stomach as the younger Hoorka tried to twist away, his eyes wide with the vehemence of the Thane's attack. But the Thane's fist found its mark, though the blow was partially deflected by an instinctive shielding by Aldhelm's forearm. Aldhelm fought for breath, pushing back against the Thane as their vibros slid—with an aching, high-frequency squeal—along each other's lengths. The Thane felt more than saw the blades disengage. Too close to Aldhelm, he moved to parry the expected riposte. He found nothing.

Again Aldhelm's vibro burned him, this time slapping at the skin over his heart. He screamed in inarticulate agony as Aldhelm's open hand drove into his chin, thrusting him backward. The Thane fought for balance, arms flailing, and fell with one leg underneath him. He broke the fall with his elbows, but the breath was knocked from him. Aldhelm flicked off his vibro as the Thane struggled to breathe.

Aldhelm stared at the Thane with an unreadable emotion on his face. His mouth worked and he started to speak; he suddenly shook his head and threw his vibro to the ground away from the Thane. Limping slightly, a hand kneading his bruised shoulder, he turned from the Thane and walked away.

Chapter 7

A SINGLE SMEAR OF LIGHT.

Cranmer rubbed his hands over his eyes to clear them, not sure of what it was that he saw in the darkness before him. The rubbing only produced the blindness of retinal colors—a pulsing orange blob that slowly went purple. It was several moments before it faded and his eyes readjusted to the darkness. He peered into the cavern-night ahead of him as if trying to pierce a thick fog. His thumb fidgeted over the switch to his hoverlamps but he kept them unlit, waiting in the dark of Underasgard.

Yes, it was still there.

There were shifting colors—gold to yellow-green like the liquid shades of a late afternoon sun in summer, a light that was pierced by bars of black that seemed to enclose it. To one side was a darker silhouette like an irregular hill. It took a moment for Cranmer to synthesize the abstractness of the scene, and then it all fell into perspective. The light, a hoverlamp set on the ground; the bars, the skeleton of the ippicator; the hill, the hunched shoulder of the Thane covered with his nightcloak. The hoverlamp must have been set inside the body of the ippicator, oscillating slightly and giving out only a dim illumination, for the light died before reaching the walls of the cavern. Cranmer hesitated and started to turn back, not wanting to disturb the Thane's obvious meditation. In turning, his shoe scraped rock loudly, and the black shape of the Thane moved and rose.

"Thane?" Cranmer called out, resigning himself, and hoping that a knife was not on its way.

Shadows raced over rock as the hoverlamp inside the

ippicator flared into sudden brilliance, striping the distant roof with the distorted image of the skeleton.

"Cranmer? Damnit, man, identify yourself when you sneak up behind a person."

"Yah. You want a companion? If you don't care for company, sirrah, simply say so. I could always pretend I was looking for the kitchens and got lost."

The Thane shrugged, not seeming to take notice of Cranmer's attempt at levity. Cranmer took the shrug for assent. He switched on his lamps and moved over the broken ground toward the ippicator.

The Thane said nothing as the scholar approached. His eyes were fixed on the hoverlamp inside the skeleton, a shadow from the ribs across his eyes like a mask. Cranmer, amidst the noise of disturbed pebbles, came up to stand next to him. He stood there, shielding his eyes from the glare and glancing from the Hoorka to the ippicator. The Thane touched the control belt and the light dimmed once more and began to oscillate, like a caged, golden fire.

"It's cold here." Cranmer could think of no other overture to conversation, and he was sure it sounded as inane to the Thane as it did to his own ears. The Hoorka was obviously disconsolate and moody—it seemed part of the introspective man's nature, but Cranmer had never seen it so naked, without any attempt to mask the melancholia. Cranmer, after waiting what seemed an appropriate time for a reply to his comment and receiving none, sat on the stones next to the Thane. He could feel the chill of the rock through his clothing.

Cranmer made another attempt at conversation. "You know, after you showed me this skeleton, I went back to my rooms and checked with my data-link to Center. Seems the latest theory in favor states that the ippicator became extinct not before, but during the Settling. The Neweden Archives are in such poor shape that it can't be verified—the Interregnum did that to the records of a hundred worlds, I know . . . But evidently the ippicators couldn't compete with us or adapt well enough to survive. They had to be dying out long before the Settling, but there were reports of ippicator sightings in some of the wilder regions. I don't know . . . You would think that some of the Settlers would have made some effort to save the beast, if only for its physical appearance, if the theory is true."

The Thane grunted a monosyllabic reply.

Silence. The lamp flickered inside the ippicator.

"Valdisa received a new contract," Cranmer said.

Now the Thane moved. He seemed to note Cranmer for the first time. His head turned and dark eyes moved under the shadow of his brow. He stirred, stretching slightly. "She knows what to do with it," he said finally. "You didn't come back here just to tell me that." His voice was a challenge, a question.

"No. When I noticed you'd gone, I thought it'd be easier to speak with you back here, away from Hoorka-kin." Cranmer paused and the Thane looked back at the ippicator.

"Speak, then," he said, gruffly.

"You're probably not going to be pleased."

A shrug. "I'm not pleased with much at the moment."

"Anything I say is said as an outsider, I know. To the Hoorka-kin, I'm a lassari and an offworlder, but I *do* have an interest in and a liking for Hoorka. I don't want to see the kin destroyed any more than you would, and not simply for selfish reasons. Hoorka could die now, at this moment, and I'd simply incorporate that extinction into my eventual work. It wouldn't alter the interest in it that the academic community would have. But I wouldn't want to see that. Truly."

"Why do scholars have such a burning need to preamble their statements to death?"

"Because you don't seem to be taking criticism very well, and I want you to understand why I speak." Cranmer spoke sharply, mild irritation in his voice that awakened echoes in the rocks. He softened his voice. "Thane, I know I've no right to speak, which is why I'm being so circumspect, but I thought you'd be better able to listen to me than your kin. Quite simply and brutally, Thane, you've been stupid. You don't seem to think of yourself as guild-elder of the Hoorka, and what alarms me most is that you don't seem to care a great deal. Your decisions of late have been at best mediocre. You're putting crises aside rather than dealing with them."

Cranmer looked at the Thane's face, searching for a reaction.

Nothing.

"Your handling of Aldhelm . . ." Cranmer shook his head,

his hands cupping air. "You didn't do much to dispel anyone's uneasiness. Even if you'd beaten him, what good would it have done? I don't pretend to understand the subtleties of Neweden kinship, but even this violent world can't believe that a physical victory symbolizes the truth of intellectual assertions. Or do you think it does? What are you thinking?"

"My thoughts are my own." Curtly, without a glance.

"But your actions are Hoorka's. Do you remember that? Or do you just sit here feeling sorry for yourself?"

Now the Thane glared angrily at the smaller man, who looked back with a calmness he didn't feel. Then the Thane twisted his head away with a savage motion, his eyes intent once again on the ippicator. "I made Hoorka into the guild-kin it is. My father was lassari when he came here, but *I* made myself a niche in this society. My actions *should* be Hoorka's. Do you dispute that?"

"Yah, to a degree." Cranmer, feeling the heat of the Thane's gaze, hastened to explain. "I've told you my thoughts before. I don't say you should step down—though if this continues, that might well be my counsel. I suggest instead that you do something and quickly. Act more decisively. You endanger what you've built: you might bring it down with you, destroy all you've strived for."

"Is that the extent of your advice?"

Cranmer lifted one shoulder and let it fall. "I suppose."

"It's easy to see flaws, no matter how beautiful the gem that encloses them. Can you tell me how to cut and polish this stone to remove all the imperfections?"

"I can point out those imperfections as you work, and that's to your advantage. I suppose you know that your little fight with Aldhelm was a grave mistake."

The last words seemed to finally kindle the building wrath inside the Thane. With a whispering of cloth, the Hoorka leapt to his feet, the nightcloak swirling. Cranmer threw up his hands in instinctive defense.

"I don't *need* your advice," the Thane shouted, the words ringing in the cavern. "I don't care for your manufactured guilt, either. I can furnish enough of my own." And with a much-practiced motion, he drew and activated his vibro. Its humming filled Cranmer's ears. The Thane's arm drew back, poised for an instant, and then he threw the blade. It sped true.

With an arid crack, the vibro severed a rib from the ippicator's shoulder and lodged itself deeply in the animal's spine. The vibro's low hum died as dust settled to earth.

Cranmer found himself lying on his side, arms hugging himself. He sat up slowly, his breath loud and quick.

The Thane's shadow was huge on the cavern wall behind him as he stood, his hands at his side, his head down, the feet slightly spread. The Hoorka raised his head as with an effort, glancing at the weapon impaling the dead beast.

"You've said nothing I haven't thought myself, Cranmer." He strode over to the ippicator and pulled on the hilt of the vibro. It came loose easily. The Thane held the weapon in his hand for a moment, staring at the broken rib on the cavern floor. He put it back in its scabbard.

"Did I frighten you, scholar?" The Thane came over and sat next to Cranmer. His voice had an odd jocularity. "Good. I scare myself. I've done so many dumb things of late."

The Thane allowed a slight smile to lift the corners of his mouth. "And I become rather too maudlin and melodramatic, also," he continued. "No, I don't need your advice, my friend—I've counseled myself with the same words you've used, and perhaps more harshly than you might suspect."

"Have you thought of resigning as active head?"

For a moment, the anger returned to the Thane's face, creasing the forehead and inflaming the broken veins of his cheeks. Then it died, as quickly as it had come, as if there were no longer any internal fuel on which it could feed. "Yes," he answered. "But events are moving. The Hoorka are involved in a crisis that I can see forming, and I can't bring myself to trust anyone else. Aldhelm—yes, he's a leader and the kin would probably follow him if I gave them leave to do so, but he needs tempering or he'll break under the pressures. He's too quick to make his choices and he tends to see things in some two-value logic of his own devising; no shades or degrees, just Right and Wrong. And Valdisa—I'm afraid that I diffused her effectiveness by being her lover. The kin might think I've named her as my successor only because of my affection for her. Sartas—he's far too headstrong, too argumentative, and not all that well-liked. And myself . . ." He put his hands out, palms upward. Cranmer saw calluses there. "I suppose I have my own problems," the Thane said, "but *I made Hoorka*. It's my onus, my responsibility, and I need to make the decisions. If I fail, at least I can only blame myself for that failure."

"It adds unnecessary burdens to your mind. What of your gods? Can't you find consolation there, some guidance in your teachings?"

"Did you see priests at the ceremony, scholar?" The Thane smiled, almost sadly. "As head of the kin, I am the mediator between Hoorka and the gods. Whom can I go to when the gods don't answer? And I suspect that you are not a religious man, Cranmer. Do you think gods would interfere and guide my path?"

"No."

"And neither do I." The Thane spoke slowly, quietly. "Hoorka faces a challenge. I intend to see us through it. Afterwards, perhaps I'll consider your words and my own doubts."

"Now you sound sure of yourself once more."

The Thane shook his head. He looked at Cranmer with pained eyes. "I wish I were. I feel no different."

The Thane touched his belt and the lamp inside the ippicator died completely, the golden fire fading into the eternal night of Underasgard. The two men sat there for a time, listening to the silence around them.

Gunnar toyed with a Tarot deck, thumbing through the dog-eared and brilliantly-colored pieces of pasteboard. It was an old set, stained with use—most of which was not his—and not even holographic. The pictures stared back flatly, inked on the surface of the cards. He'd once had the deck appraised by a dealer in oddities at Sterka Port—the woman had found it to be worth more than he'd anticipated: the deck was over two centuries old, and from Terra itself. To maintain their value and their use (the Knight of Swords had once been folded in half and was in danger of tearing), he knew he should avoid handling them often or carrying them about; it wasn't advice he often followed.

The cards gave him pleasure, and he liked to imagine that he could feel an undercurrent of power in them. Gunnar wasn't so self-deceiving as to imagine that he could tap that power, but somewhere back in the deck's murky history a person of sensitivity had possessed them, and it pleased Gunnar to believe that he could detect the residue of that power hidden in the cards.

Gunnar held a card up to the sunlight that lanced across the room like a palpable shaft until it struck the far wall and was broken. Too-saturated colors just beginning to fade: they glistened and awakened in the light, the gilt and silver shimmering. Potok, from across the room, could see a little of the card's face — an old man sitting on an ornate throne, the arms of which ended in carved ram's heads. The man held an ankh-scepter in one hand and a globe in the other with a bleary and desolate mountain range hunched in the background under a lowering sky lanced by rays from a hidden star.

"A pretty card, neh?" said Gunnar. He flipped it around in the sunlight, enjoying the way reflections shot from the slick surface. He let the card slide to the desk at which he was seated, watching it fall with one hand cupping his chin. It landed face up.

"The Emperor," he said, "a card of leadership and temporal power, of logic besting emotion. Considering the time in which these cards were evidently manufactured, I've wondered if the old man isn't supposed to be the tyrant Huard. He looks like the old bastard, doesn't he?"

Gunnar picked up the card and shuffled it back into the deck. He stacked the cards carefully, then began laying them out in the Celtic mode, mumbling under his breath.

"I almost think you believe in those things." Potok moved forward. His figure — in robes of Assembly blue — eclipsed the window light, so that the room darkened with a premature twilight. Lamps throughout the room kindled themselves to compensate for the reduced illumination.

"They're here," said Gunnar. "How can I not believe in them?"

"You know what I meant."

Gunnar smiled. "At times, I almost find myself wanting to believe in a foreplanned future. That can be a comforting notion, knowing that the gods have set out everything beforehand. And the Hoorka, like our own guild, profess a belief in Dame Fate. Why couldn't there be a device in which we could see Her intent?"

"The Hoorka." Potok harrumphed. "You're so certain those Tarot can foretell the future?"

"The Tarot don't predict. They indicate possibilities. That's a subtle difference, kin-brother." One hand toyed with the cards, idly riffling the wear-softened edges. "They can suggest what will occur should all things remain the same. You can change the fortune if you heed their advice."

"Whatever." Potok waved an impatient hand.

"That's your trouble, Potok. You're too impatient."

Potok shrugged, his face revealing a mild irritation. "And what do you and your cards suggest for our future course of action?"

"I assume by that you mean what are we going to do with our dear Li-Gallant?"

"I do."

"I don't know." Again Gunnar smiled. "Haven't thought about it all that much, to be truthful." He leaned back in his chair and clasped his hands behind his head. "You are sure, then, that it was Vingi's contract that the Hoorka were working?"

"Who else would want you dead so badly? Have you insulted anyone other than him? And who else would be so cowardly not to declare bloodfeud and settle it face to face? Yes, I'm sure it was Vingi." Potok folded his arms across his chest. About him, dust-motes swirled in the sun. He stood in a field of golden pollen.

Gunnar chuckled at the image—had it been a muscular young person standing in the yellow warmth with righteous anger on his face, perhaps it wouldn't have seemed humorous. But it was Potok, short and pudgy. Gunnar laughed, and Potok's face took on an aspect of puzzlement.

"Sit down, man," said Gunnar, waving a hand toward a nearby floater. "You look too pompous standing there. Sit down. Let's not fool ourselves, my kin. My guild-kin were frightened enough of Vingi when the contract came—no one offered to come with me to protect me from Hoorka weapons. Your anger is odd in light of that."

Potok said nothing. He looked at Gunnar's smile, which no longer was a gesture of humor, but a deadly thing, sharp and menacing. Potok sat back in his floater, pursed his lips, then sat up abruptly once more.

"Gunnar, the Li-Gallant is confused. He half-believes that we've somehow managed to bribe the Hoorka to our side—at least this is what my sources in his guild tell me.

Despite Vingi's protestations to the contrary, the Hoorka would give Neweden security forces a problem. So Vingi's poised, ready to move either way but afraid to commit himself. He'd drag both our guild and the Hoorka into an Assembly trial and have us disbanded if he thought he could make his charges stand. We can use his doubts."

Gunnar nodded. "By using the Hoorka."

"By using their reputation. We might be able to force their hand."

Gunnar shook his head. "I don't know. The basic idea is appealing, but I don't know." His fingertips brushed the Tarot deck idly.

Potok leaned forward and reached out as if to pick up the cards, but Gunnar placed his hand over them. "If you don't mind," he said. "Superstition"—with a slight laugh—"says that no one else is supposed to handle your Tarot unless he's the subject of a reading."

"Give me a reading, then. For that matter, read your own fate and ease your doubts. We should grasp this situation while Vingi waits."

"You're sure it's necessary to approach the Hoorka?" Gunnar shivered, despite the sunlit warmth of the room. The Hoorka reputation exceeded the truth—their portrait was one of bloodthirsty killers happy only when in the act of slaughter theatrically macabre—but it was a truth that no guild enjoyed doing business with the assassins. And no guild had yet dared to risk bloodfeud with them. Gunnar didn't wish his own guild to be the one to perform that experiment. "It could be dangerous, Potok. Let me ask you, have you kept an edge on your fencing skills?"

"The Hoorka can't get involved in vendettas against other guilds. It would destroy them. They're safe."

"Tell me that after they've chased *you.*" Gunnar looked at Potok, who found the scene outside the window suddenly interesting. "Would a vendetta destroy the Hoorka? And would you care to take that chance, knowing that the result might be that you nestle in Hag Death's arms earlier than you wish?"

Potok glanced at the Tarot, then at Gunnar. "I'm here suggesting it, kin-brother."

"It might destroy the guild." Gunnar hesitated. "Brother," he added.

"I don't think so."

"It might destroy Hoorka."

"You'd care?"

Gunnar laughed. "Not at all." He began spreading out the cards. "Not at all," he repeated. "In fact, I might well enjoy that more than thwarting Vingi."

Gunnar plucked a card at random from the deck and turned it face up on the desk. On the painted surface, a horse strode, bearing a skeleton dressed in ancient armor and bearing a tattered banner. Below the apparition, people prostrated themselves. The skeleton grinned as the horse trampled them underneath.

The Li-Gallant Vingi was wearing a loose tunic and pants, all woven of a soft, bluish material showing the thinness of much use. Vingi wore this when he desired comfort rather than ostentation; in private, that was often. It was a uniform most of the guild-kin that formed his private staff saw often and were used to, but it tended to startle those whose image of the Li-Gallant was the public one.

The Domoraj, though head of the security force of Vingi's guild, was not one of the privileged few.

The Domoraj stared more than would be considered polite by the standards of kinship, taking in the frayed sleeves, the worn elbows, the stains that had gotten past the dirtshield and set in the fabric—a mustard-brown splotch putting a tentative pseudopod on Vingi's breast fascinated him. The Domoraj forced his eyes up past the clothing to the corpulent face. He set his lips, hoping that the Li-Gallant had missed his insubordination.

Vingi, however, was engrossed in a com-unit set on his desk and in an iced drink that resided—glass sides sweating—in one hand. The sea-green light of the com-unit washed over his face from below, giving his features an unnatural edging. Vingi sipped once at his drink, nodded thoughtfully at the screen, and flicked the unit's controls. The light slowly receded and Vingi's large, almost sorrowful eyes found the Domoraj.

"I just had a less than satisfactory report, sirrah," he said without preliminary. "It appears that Gunnar has gained some popularity since his escape from the Hoorka. Two previously unaligned guilds have given their Assembly votes to Gunnar's kin. The Weaver's Guild of Tellis has re-scinded their support of our guild and will send a represen-tative to the Assembly until they make a decision on which ruling guild will represent them. What does that suggest to you?"

The Domoraj shifted his position in his seat. Vingi's sud-den gaze bothered him—he was too used to the deference of the guild-kin under him.

"I'm a military man," he said. "I have no part in the gov-erning affairs of our kin, Li-Gallant. And I don't pretend to meddle in politics. I take my orders from you, sirrah. That's sufficient." It was temporizing, but he could think of noth-ing else to say.

Vingi shook his head. "No, kin-brother, that won't do. Every person living on Neweden dabbles in politics. It's im-possible not to take a stand unless one is lassari. There are no neutral guilds."

"There are the Hoorka."

"Yah, the Hoorka." Vingi sat his drink down on his desk and shook moisture from his hand. "The Hoorka," he re-peated. "What do you think of them, Domoraj? As a, ahh, 'military man'?"

"In what respect, Li-Gallant? They're excellently trained and very good at what they do . . ." He shrugged.

Vingi lifted an arm and plucked a loose thread from the sleeve of his tunic. For a few moments his attention was completely on that small task and he ignored the other man. Finally, he looked up again.

"A pity things must eventually wear out—and it is al-ways the favorites. But"—he changed the topic with an inflection—"I meant, do you think the Hoorka as apolitical as they claim to be? Yah, they have no voice in the Assem-bly and stay prominently distant from the constant blood-feuds of the guilds, but does that prove their neutrality in the affairs of Neweden?"

"I don't know." Simply.

Vingi nodded. He sighed. "*That* was not the answer I desired. Let me phrase it this way: Do you find it odd that Gunnar managed to escape?"

"I see your point, Li-Gallant." The Domoraj was care-fully neutral, his hands folded on his lap, his back stiff and not touching the back of his chair: a man as careful as his appearance. When he killed, he killed daintily, he killed with finesse and affected grace. "Victims *have* escaped the Hoorka before," he said. "It's essential to their existence — and at the risk of incurring your wrath, kin-brother, the men I sent — at *your* behest — to insure Gunnar's death did no better."

Vingi's face was briefly touched by anger. It trembled his chin. "And they were very clumsy to have killed m'Dame Cuscratti. You needn't remind me of such things. My point, however, is that none that have previously escaped the assassins have been so important or influential."

"The gods sometimes do smile on odd people." The Domoraj was also devout — it was a matter of some humor among his subordinates that the Domoraj spent as much time praying to the gods as sending others to their domain.

"Don't speak of Dame Fate's whims."

The Domoraj, unsure of his ground or perhaps simply shocked by the hint of blasphemy in his leader, waited in silence.

Vingi idly rubbed a forefinger over the lip of his glass. Outside his office, the two men could hear the hushing of a soft tread as a watchrobot passed along the hallway. Vingi leaned forward. "You have contacts, Domoraj. I want Gunnar killed, but I don't want to tie up our guild's resources with a formal bloodfeud."

"Is that wise, Li-Gallant? The other guilds —"

"— will not find out," the Li-Gallant finished. "Don't spout ethics to me, Domoraj. Dame Fate smiles on those who grasp their own lives. Find me a lassari that's competent enough to do the task. Then do a hypnofix on him so that he thinks he's acting of his own volition and can't be traced back to us if he should fail. That should suffice."

The Domoraj said nothing.

Vingi leaned back and took up his drink once more. "I'm not a person given to subtle tactics," he said. "It's been said that my bluntness indicates a lack of my kin-father's skill with such things. No" — he raised a hand as the Domoraj began the obligatory objection — "you needn't say anything. I have my ears, my sources of information. I might even be tempted to acknowledge it as a partial truth. Still, I see a simple solution, one that fits Neweden. If Gunnar falls to a lassari, the guilds will withdraw their support of his guild —

a man with kin that would fall to a lassari. Yah, that would indeed suffice. The guilds won't think Gunnar's organization strong enough, no matter who heads the guild."

The Domoraj watched as Vingi switched his com-unit on. The tide of sea-light rushed over him noiselessly. Vingi waved an impatient hand in dismissal.

"You have a task, guild-brother. See to it, and may Dame Fate guide your choice."

Chapter 8

A TRIANGLE OF MILKY LIGHT slashed across the viewscreen set in m'Dame d'Embry's desk. The light trailed across the front of the desk and across the grassed floor to a genesis at the window. There, the Neweden sun (she could never fall into the habit of referring to it in the Neweden way as the 'sunstar') glowered down at a new day. The glare made it difficult for her to see the screen; she moved so that her thin body blocked the distracting light. Her hand passed over a contact. The screen responded with an inner illumination of its own, caught in which were the head and shoulders of her secretary.

"Karl," she said immediately, "I want to speak to the Hoorka-thane. When you reach him, I'll take the call here." She switched off his "Yes, m'Dame," leaning back in her chair and allowing her body a moment of relaxation. She was all too aware of the fact that she seemed to need more of these interludes each standard. *Tired, getting old,* she thought. *Old.* Yet she still managed to retain her reputation as perhaps the most successful liaison for the Diplomatic Resources Team—the Diplos—*and* as the most crusty of them. She could remember all the forgotten, misplaced, and unwanted worlds she'd cajoled into some semblance of normalcy within the Alliance; picking up the shards of Huard's empire and the age of sundering that followed the tyrant's death. . . .

She shook her head. *Daydreaming again.* She rebuked herself inwardly. Waiting for the call from the Thane, she let her eyes wander about the office.

She allowed herself few luxuries. A holo of a d'Vellia soundsculpture always seemed to be present in her offices (the more persistent rumors among the staffers were that she had once had an affair with that temperamental sculptor), and an animo-painting by some anonymous artist went through random changes on the wall, a last remnant of a fad that had been popular many standards back. The only touch of richness was an etched ippicator bone—the ankle of the fifth leg, she would point out to curious visitors—which was a gift from the Li-Gallant Vingi. It was, perhaps, worth more than anything else in the room, a rare item that offworld collectors would pay much to acquire. Other than these, the room was unornamented. Even the viewscreen on the desk echoed the room—the lowest Diplo staffer had a holo comlink rather than a flat viewscreen. With reverse snobbery, d'Embry prided herself on her austerity.

Her reverie was broken by a sprinkling of lightning across the desk. On the viewscreen, random dots, prodded and cajoled, formed themselves into Karl's face.

"M'Dame, I have the Thane."

"I'm ready to speak with him, then." She leaned back in her chair, "and bring me a pot of tea when I've finished, please. Thank you, Karl."

"Yah, m'Dame." The screen dimmed and motes of bluish-white danced a hesitant ballet before giving way to the image of the Hoorka-thane. His lips moved, the last sparks of interference flitting across his scarred cheeks.

"M'Dame d'Embry." The Thane nodded. Beyond him, d'Embry could see stone walls and an apprentice Hoorka working on some indiscernible task, hunched over a bench. The complaining whine of a drill rasped the speaker.

"I'll be brief, Thane. Quite simply, there have been allegations passing through Sterka—rumors—that concern me. Most of them revolve around you and your organization's relationships with the, ahh, political aspirants, shall we say, of the Neweden Assembly."

As she spoke, she watched the face in the screen. The deep-set eyes narrowed, the lips set themselves in a thin line, a new ridge formed in the forehead as if he were holding back . . . anger? Irritation? Well, he could indulge in temper if he wished. "The Li-Gallant," she continued, "has asked me to withdraw my consideration of letting your guild operate offworld. He's also mentioned bringing the Hoorka forward in the Assembly."

D'Embry's hand reached out and found the smooth surface of the ippicator bone, the thin valleys of the carved lines. "Between the two of us, Thane, I don't think you need to concern yourself greatly with that latter threat. As I understand your people's odd social structure, he can't afford to invoke the wrath of Gunnar's guild in a bloodfeud. He'd lose face—or worse—unless conditions were ripe for such actions. But he *is* insistent, and he *is* the head of local government. I have told the Li-Gallant"—with the proper amount of emphasis on the word "told"—"that I will hold a brief, very informal meeting here at the Center in two local days."

Through this, the Thane had looked increasingly impatient, though he did not interrupt. He glanced frequently to one side of the screen, as if his interest lay elsewhere. "Is that an invitation for me to attend, m'Dame?"

For once, d'Embry found a disadvantage in simplicity. There were overtones in his resonant voice that were lost in the reproduction of the viewer, nuances that she wanted to read. Was he simply being offhandedly sarcastic or humorously flippant? No, not the last. The Thane didn't seem to be a man with humor: a dry, worn-out husk of a man. Had he ever laughed? she wondered.

"I hope you'll be there, Thane. The Li-Gallant and Potok will also attend. I frankly consider the entire business a waste of my time and I don't have a great deal of that commodity to squander, if you'll pardon my bluntness. But I *am* the Alliance Regent for Neweden"—she paused—"and the Li-Gallant did insist. I have neither the inclination nor the staff to undertake an investigation of the whole situation, and my people don't have enough feel for your guild-kinship structure to judge you fairly. Therefore I need the interested parties to outline their stands."

"Hoorka has no stance."

No, definitely no humor to him at all. He is, instead, quite comically serious.

"Even neutrality is a stance, Thane. And as I understand the guilds, only lassari can have true neutrality. A person with kin must be loyal to his kin. That is a stance."

The shoulders in the viewscreen rose in a minor shrug. "Is that all you wished to say, m'Dame?" In the voice of a hurried man, with the implication of a task waiting.

"You'll be here?"

"I will, if it serves Hoorka."

"Then that is all I need to say, Thane. Good day, sirrah."

The contact was broken, and before she could gather her thoughts to fit them into her impression of the Thane, the door dilated and Karl brought in a tray.

"Your tea, m'Dame?"

Its bittersweet aroma filled the room.

Night.

Violet scarves of clouds wrapped two spheres, one large and saffron and caught in the dark fingers of trees; the other smaller and cold, becalmed at zenith: Sleipnir and Gulltopp. Double shadows—one purple-tinged—clawed at the earth. It was quiet and watchfully peaceful, the landscape.

A distraction in the scene: a figure moved. It shushed aside scattered leaves of the nearly-spent autumn. A light-shunter moved patterns of elusive dark across his/her clothing and moonlight stuttered across shapes at its waist as it moved through knee-level grasses toward the house on the knoll. With the laughter of dry leaves, the wind flung clouds to the horizon and freed the moons. In the instant before the light-shunter reacted to the increased light and fuzzed the figure's outlines again, it could be seen more clearly.

She was a tall, almost emaciated woman. Her startled eyes looked upward at the sky's betrayal.

Near the interface of meadow grass and stately lawn, she paused. She looked up toward the house and the trees gathered at the crest of the hill, all dark against the moonlit sky. There were no signs of life or vigilance.

Good. This might be easier, then.

The windows of the house were polarized black, or the rooms beyond them were dark: she could not tell which. Either way, no one could easily see her. She went to her knees in the tall grass, checking the equipment hung on her belt. No signs of life, but already a detector was flashing its awareness of a warning field just ahead. She fumbled at a loop and unhooked a cylinder of black metal rimmed with switches. She flipped one, then another, watching a red light on the detector with intense eyes. It pulsed red, then an amber that burned and slowly died. She smiled into darkness, patted the cylinder, and replaced it at her side. She rose again to her feet.

The transition to lawn was more heard than seen—the light-shunter fogged her perception of the scene—as the tidal soughing of weeds gave way to the soft padding of low grass. She could feel her pants, wet from mid-thigh to ankle, clinging to her legs with cold dampness. But treated fabrics that resisted moisture also tended to be noisier when moving. A small thing, but it would be small things that kept her alive tonight.

She began to curve diagonally up the hill toward the side of the house, remembering the whispered advice given to her the night before in a Port bar near the Center. Her contact had taken her over toward the bio-pilot's alcove, away from the general commotion of the place. He had detailed the grounds and obstacles she might expect to meet; the entrances to the home and how they might be guarded. The information, if correct, was invaluable. If wrong . . . it meant little. She hated Gunnar, who had once refused her membership in his guild. She hated all he stood for, and if her contact knew of someone that would pay her to do this, all the better. The payment had been generous, at least the half she'd managed to get in advance. Last night had been more than pleasant. The euphoria still clung to her, diaphanous.

They'd gone together to his rooms, and she'd slept for a while. Yes, and she'd woken with a fierce passion against Gunnar. It remained, a backdrop, to the more gentle passions she felt that night.

She was aware of trouble before she could physically sense it. A momentary prickling shivered along her back. She crouched, rolled, and sought cover without thinking . . . but there was no cover on that hillside.

She heard, suddenly, the electric crackling of a sting, and her right side tingled with the near-miss—she'd been seen. She felt the beginning of panic. A scream rose in her throat, and she forced it down.

Her contact had told her—in his harsh, sibilant whisper— that Gunnar's house was not well-guarded, that she would have no trouble once past the shield. She'd been skeptical, even then, but the money he had shown her and the things the money had bought . . .

She rolled again, the opposite way, as she freed a hand laser from its holster and fired toward the house. She knew she had next to no chance of hitting someone, but hoped it would confuse the person with the sting long enough for her to run to the meadow grass and the small protection it would bring. Gunnar. She hated him and his guild all the more, and she felt keen frustration at being thwarted. The wash of emotion blunted the first onrushing of panic. She began to think again. She raked laser fire across the darkened front of the house, smelling the acrid fumes of burning paint.

There had been, first, the Stretcher: an innocuous-looking pill that had elongated her time sense. It had taken a week to yawn, a hour to raise glass to lips . . .

The sting barked again, and again it struck very near her. She abandoned stealth and ran.

. . . and the girl who'd been so co-operative once her palm had been crossed with silver. Her hands had been slick and smooth like malleable porcelain, her breasts small and girlish . . .

She switched direction at random, with little hope. The moons were bright, the light-shunter was poor camouflage, there was no place to hide and Dame Fate and Hag Death pursued her, their twin breaths hot on her neck.

. . . offworld foods she'd always wanted to taste simply because their names had been so exotic: cockatrice, day-diggers. And because she was lassari, there had been no money for such luxuries. . . .

The next shot found her. The grass was surprisingly soft as she fell. It caressed her. The shunter, broken, bathed her with bands of sparkling brilliance.

. . . and . . . and . . .

The body of a woman was found the next morning by a caravan of spice traders moving autowains toward Sterka and the Port. The night animals had gotten to the carcass—a not particularly pleasant sight—but the traders, a stoic guild, threw the body across the back of a wain. After all, if she were of kin, her guild would wish to give final rites, and might pay for the body. The cinnamon odor of the spice cloaked the smell of blood.

They found that the woman was well-known to denizens of the Port, and that she was lassari—a minor criminal record had made her face (what remained of it) familiar to the constabulary. They shrugged their collective shoulders, complimenting the traders on their generosity in bringing the body back and shaking their heads sorrowfully at the wasted effort.

Irritated that they had spent their time on a lassari, they left the body with the policing guild, who had the hospital nearby remove any useful parts and then dispose of what remained.

No one particularly mourned her death—and since murder is not always a crime in Neweden, no one bothered to look any further into the matter.

Hag Death was mollified.

The Thane lay on his bed. He pillowed his head with his hands, lying on his back, and stared at the reflections of a dim hoverlamp skittering across the bare rock of the ceiling. The top of his uniform lay discarded on the floor; glancing down, he could see the torso of a man still in fair shape, but the edges of the once sharply-defined musculature were being slowly eroded. A general blurring of tone, an indefinable sag—he sometimes wondered if it wasn't more emotional than physical. The Thane would find himself, now and then, staring into a mirror at the reflection of his profile, seeking assurance that the stomach was still relatively flat and the posture erect, trying to find in that shadow Thane the echo of his younger reality, that earlier Thane. Where was age, how did one see it? Was it a function of the hands, the face, the mind? Could it be captured and removed, could he rekindle the intensity?

It was distressing to him that only he of all Hoorka-kin could remember his father—his biological father—telling him tales of the long fall of Huard and how his father had been trained to kill Huard, part of a group of revolutionaries. Huard's suicide had destroyed that group's meaning and drive; his father's among them. He had wandered through the wreckage of a reeling empire, finally ending on Neweden to find himself a pariah, a social outcast without kin—and, as suddenly, as trade between worlds ended, with no way of leaving. The Thane could remember his father, who had been old when he was born, but it was a wavery face dimmed and filtered by distance. He had a holocube of the man somewhere, but it had been years since he'd looked at it, and kin do not honor their biological parents.

The chime of the doorward interrupted his thoughts. He considered rising to dress, then shrugged mentally, not caring to move.

"Come," he said. He sat up on an elbow and watched the doorshield waver and dilate. Valdisa stepped through, her eyes wide as she tried to adjust to the dimness. The Thane could see her clearly against the corridor lamps. Hers was a full, almost stocky figure that—while feminine and graceful—still carried a raw power. Auburn hair was glossed by the backlighting, a frothy, soft nimbus. Her legs were trim and muscular, her hands at her side. The stubby fingers opened and closed. She moved into the room hesitantly, glancing at the hoverlamp on the ceiling, and then to the bed. She stepped fully into the room and the doorshield irised shut behind her.

"Damned dark in here. You think this is a cave?"

"Cute."

"An old joke, neh?" Valdisa smiled.

"Yah. I can see you, anyway."

"So? What color are my palms? I'll bet you can't see that well." She held them out toward him. He saw a pair of dark islands, each with five peninsulas.

"Blue," he said. It seemed likely.

"Flesh. I washed the tint from them this evening—and the dye was orange, in any event. Have you ceased to notice my appearance at dinner, or are your eyes failing you? Either way, I'm not flattered."

The Thane hmmed a reply deep in his throat. He glanced down the length of his body and saw the roll of flesh at his waist. He stretched himself and finally lay back down so that the stomach was again smooth. His own vanity amused him, but he made no move to ignore it. "Did you come in here simply to be flattered?"

"I need reasons to see you?" she asked, lightly.

"I suppose not."

With that, the talk faltered. There was a moment of mutual embarrassment as Valdisa glanced nervously from the Thane to the hoverlamp. Then, hesitantly: "You haven't been much in evidence the last few days. Problems?" She waited, a beat. "As a friend, Thane." Her eyes pleaded with his.

"Problems," he conceded.

"The fight with Aldhelm?"

"Partially." He knew the curt replies were hurting her, but somehow couldn't bring himself to elaborate. He watched her standing in the center of the room, shifting her weight from one foot to the other, and he knew he could end her discomfiture with a word. He couldn't say it.

"Do you want to talk about it?" she asked finally.

"No."

"Talk sometimes helps."

"You really think it necessary? Talking won't make anything clearer, won't change situations."

"Maybe not, but it won't cloud things, either."

"Then talk." The Thane waved a hand and closed his eyes. Through the self-imposed darkness, he could hear her soft breathing, the rustling of cloth as she moved.

"You're letting everything that happens become some"—Valdisa hesitated, searching for words—"some magical symbol of vague doom. I don't even know what's most disturbing, your twisting of small events into auguries of great import, or the events themselves. The Hoorka are facing a real crisis. We need a real solution. And you seem content to let Dame Fate twist the threads into whatever pattern She desires."

"As She always will do. Hoorka has faced crises before, and come through them." He spoke with his eyes clamped shut. He didn't want to see the concern in her face.

"And it has always been your guidance that led us."

Valdisa came over to the bed and sat beside him. He felt the supporting field bounce slightly as it compensated for the increased weight. She touched his hand tentatively; then, when he didn't pull away, she let her hand rest there, covering his. All of the Thane's consciousness seemed concentrated there—he could feel the satiny texture of her palm and the roughness of the calluses gathered at the tip of each finger. Her hand was warm, with a trace of sweat, and his own hand seemed chill against hers: autumn and high summer. Still, he couldn't bring himself to look at her, though his eyes opened. He stared at the nether regions beyond the hoverlamp.

"Why these sudden hesitations?" she asked. "You can see what it's doing to the others." Her voice was gritty sand and fluffed cotton. "*You* made the fight with Aldhelm take on an importance beyond its true proportions. No Hoorka would expect you to defeat him in a fight at any other time—he's simply bigger, stronger, and more agile than you, and if that pricks your damned pride, I'm sorry. You insisted on turning it into a power play. If it *was* a symbol, you made it that way."

"It seemed necessary."

The Thane's voice rasped through his throat, rough and husky. But his eyes, finding her face, discovered it to be vulnerable and open with genuine empathy. His hand moved, a spasm, beneath hers.

"A reprimand . . ."

"Wouldn't have been enough," he finished for her. Then: "I don't know. Maybe you're right." Irritated, he moved his hand from under hers and gesticulated violently. The hoverlamp bobbed with the moving air as Valdisa moved back in surprise.

"I don't know any more," he shouted. "I find myself wondering about the morality of what I've built here, wondering whether I care to have my name forever linked with that of Hoorka . . . Valdisa, I'm tired. I find myself caring more about myself than for my kin."

"You've always masked yourself. I don't even know your family name."

"Does it matter on Neweden?" His eyes were pained. "They were lassari."

"I'd like to know."

"Hermond. Gyll Hermond." His voice dared her to comment.

Valdisa shrugged. "It's a name. What does it matter that Hermond isn't among the lists of the guilded?"

"It mattered. You've never been lassari—your family had kin. You wouldn't understand."

"Perhaps not, but I can still feel your pain, kin-brother."

The Thane shook his head. "I sit here and make excuses for all my problems. I'm getting very tired—and I'm not senile, not in my dotage, not even particularly old. I don't think I've lost any mental agility I once had. And making you feel guilty about my background is just another ploy on my part. I surround myself with sophistry and easy motivations." A pause. He ran his hand through graying hair. "I'm sorry, Valdisa. I truly am."

The Thane sat back against the rough stones of the wall, staring at the hoverlamp in the center of the room. Valdisa reached out to stroke his cheek with her hand. The undepilated stubble dragged at her skin, and she let the hand wander from cheek to shoulder. She moved close to him, the bed jiggling as it took her full weight. Shadows merged on rock. She forced him to look at her, her hands moving in mute comfort.

He didn't encourage her. He didn't resist.

Valdisa kissed his mouth, but his lips were unpliant; she could feel his muscles stiffen. Then, as suddenly, he relaxed, the tension sloughing from his body. His arms came around her, and he sigh-groaned as she clasped him. Her fingers searched for the fastener to her tunic, found it, and tugged.

Cloth fell away with a whisper.

His hands cupped her breasts, circled one nipple with a forefinger, and then felt the smoothness of her back. The Thane sighed. "I've missed you," he said in a harsh whisper. "I wouldn't let myself admit it, but I knew it inside."

"I would have come. Any time." Her voice was soft in his ear, and her hands roamed his body.

"I know. I don't know why—"

Valdisa stopped his voice with her mouth.

Chapter 9

TRI-GUILD CHURCH threw sharp-spiked shadows across the pavement of Market Square. The palpable darkness shivered as the crowds moved through it and lifted its borders onto their shoulders. Its keen edges and protrusions should have caught and impaled those walking below, but the best the shadows could do was impart a temporary chill, a premonition of unguessed doom.

McWilms entered the shade and immediately missed the sunstar—it was a chilly morning prescient with impending winter and snow. Though the sunstar lent a psychic warmth to the air, it seemed unable to warm the earth with its distant fires. Even the Hoorka uniform (with the red sleeve that signified his apprentice status: that would be gone soon, McWilms hoped) could only blunt the cutting edge of the cool wind. McWilms glanced at the spires of the church and shivered unreligiously. It was a massive building, ornate with flowering spires and graceless arches—he would be in its shadow for some minutes before entering the realm of the sunstar again. He cursed the builders for having chosen such an inconvenient site for their place of worship, then as abruptly asked She of the Five to protect him from his blasphemy.

McWilms did not mind hedging his skepticisms.

He moved through a welter of people, accepting the open area that seemed to move with him as part of the deference due him as a Hoorka. He had to admit that such things were aspects of being a Hoorka that thrilled him: the sense of grudging respect that other kin gave him, even as an apprentice. A young man with kin, such as himself, would under normal circumstances have far less status in Neweden society. But he was Hoorka, however lowly in that guild, and the fear of the Hoorka extended even to him. He had, now and again, deliberately sought out the more crowded streets of Sterka just to feel the aura of power that surrounded him; he would watch the people step—grudgingly—from his path. Fear laced with loathing would congeal their faces. It was ... pleasant.

Today was the height of autumn's Market Days, when the outlying farming guilds brought in their harvested bounty. The streams of people that normally used the square each day was doubled and trebled, swelled into rivers, joined into seas. The noise grew as the Days went on and buyers attempted to wheedle prices from impassive and unsympathetic growers. Modified chaos: Neweden locals found the Days to be pleasant diversions in their lives, offworlders shook their heads and mumbled—inaudibly—comments concerning backward societies and their engaging oddities.

McWilms, after broaching church-shadow and entering the morning sun once more, found the truth to be somewhere between the two poles. He had been sent on an errand by the Hoorka in charge of the kitchens, and could not tarry overlong to enjoy the sights for fear of that master's justifiably-famous wrath. McWilms found a fishmonger's stall and watched the haggling. He pretended not to notice that he stood in an anomaly: a small open space all his own.

Behind a counter stocked with frozen sea creatures, the monger was arguing vehemently with a woman concerning the quality of a spiny puffindle that, admittedly, appeared undernourished. The monger quoted a price; the woman, in a greenish pearl wrap, snorted derision. She offered the man half that price, prodding the puffindle's side with a forefinger to make her point. Vapor from the cooling circuits in the counter swirled between them.

McWilms stepped closer, shouldering through the crowd with less courtesy than the guild etiquette required and watching as anger turned to carefully-masked irritation on their faces. People moved away with controlled distaste; the monger looked up from behind his stall. His features revolved through an interesting gamut of emotions: anger at being interrupted during a sale, quick shock at seeing the young man was a Hoorka, and finally a gelid shielding of all facial contortions that left his face blandly amiable. He stepped back and to one side, wiping his hands nervously on his stained pants; he ignored the woman, who glanced at the Hoorka apprentice, shut her mouth sullenly, then went back to prodding the cold scales of the puffindle as if trying to awaken the fish from liquid dreams.

"What can I do for you, young sirrah?" The monger's voice was deferential, but everything about him, from the skittish eyes to the tapping fingers to the manner in which he stood under his slickcloth awning, spoke of impatience, or possibly unwillingness to deal with Hoorka.

An older Hoorka might have been amused or angry in turn with the man's attitude, but McWilms was unused to the subtleties in other kin's reactions to Hoorka. He didn't notice. He smiled.

"I'd like to buy all of your stock for my kin."

Eyebrows sought new heights on the monger's forehead, then clambered down once more. He closed his eyes in thought. "For my entire selection? I'd have to charge you 150C. And that's a fine price, too."

"For whom, sirrah? You? I didn't ask you to empty the oceans. I can offer you 75C." The Hoorka master Felling had given him 120C, but had threatened to double Mc-Wilms's work load if he came back with less than 15C of that amount. The master was known for his gruff manner and gentle ways, but McWilms intended to take no chance on his good humor.

The monger looked pained at the offer. (And behind and around him, McWilms could hear the mildest undercurrent of speech as the kin around him realized that the Hoorka intended to buy all of this monger's stock. The woman next to the apprentice stopped examining the puffindle to watch.)

"75C wouldn't pay my transportation costs here, much less the rest of my expenses. Sterka is an expensive city in which to stay during Market Days, sirrah."

"Other people are selling here." McWilms indicated the gaily-colored stalls around the square. "I could see if perhaps their overhead is lower than yours."

The monger cogitated. "For the Hoorka—a fine guild—I could go, perhaps, to 125C."

Too slowly, Mc Wilms started to turn away. The people

crowded near him stepped back into those behind them, startled.

"100C, then," the monger called out.

Mc Wilms stopped and turned around. "You'd deliver it to Underasgard?" he said over his shoulder, still poised to leave.

The pained look returned to the monger's face.

McWilms, hearing nothing, started to move away once more.

"I'll deliver, sirrah. For 105C."

McWilms stepped back to the counter. "That sounds acceptable," he said. The two finalized the arrangements and tabulated the fish the monger had brought. Scrip changed hands; as it did, people began moving away from the stall, going off to search for other mongers as it became obvious that the Hoorka deal had been completed. The pique on their faces was evident. Finally, McWilms put his purse back under his cloak and moved back into the crowds, walking in his inviolate space.

He went from the temporary stalls of the various mongers toward the street emptying into the square from the north, its taverns and small guildshops attracting a large share of the revelers. He had time, since he had completed his task earlier than Felling could have expected, and the sights were intriguing to a boy whose true family had lived in a rural district of Illi. Events moved at a quicker pace here in Sterka, and as a Hoorka-kin, he had the added thrill of fear/respect. The wares of the Market Days shouted for his attention. He could see, on a shop ledge protruding out into the walkways, a selection of offworld items imported by Alliance traders, a meatfruit ball with its scaly, yellowish rind, a pile of Bosich exoskeletons (spiked and brilliantly colored). The sculptor's guild had opened the doors to the studio adjoining the street; inside he saw apprentices polishing a huge lifianstone sculpture partially hidden in shadow—it seemed to be two men locked in a fervent embrace; one thin, the other stocky—and he heard the soft *tchunk* of a chisel striking the soft stone. From somewhere ahead, the breeze brought the yeasty aroma of bread, a free advertisement for a bakery. Sights, sounds, smells: Sterka abounded in them during Market Days. McWilms reveled in the sensory surfeit.

(Yet he hadn't noticed the person who watched his movements through the crowds. The man was dressed in the uniform of a guilded kin—a belt with a holographic buckle adorned his waist, but the hologram was shattered and the guild insignia that should have been visible was lost in a welter of varied images and depths—and the uniform was not of any familiar guild in Sterka. Not that this in itself was unusual during Market Days; travelers filled the city. The man received no second glances. A person, noting him, might think he came from the far south, for certainly no nearby guilds used such odd boot fasteners on their pants. That was as he wished it. As McWilms walked past him, the man abandoned his post by the silversmith shop and plunged into the crowd after the apprentice.)

McWilms was absorbed in the bustling of the Days. The sunstar spilled its warmth into the street as it hauled itself toward the tenuous pinnacle of the zenith. The apprentice had no mind for strife, and trusted the Hoorka-fear to keep others from hindering him. So he was unprepared to see a man suddenly stumble into the pocket of open space around him.

McWilms caught a brief, dizzy glimpse of blue-green eyes, clutching hands, and a broken holobuckle at the man's waist. Stubby fingers grasped at his clothing—heavily—and a booted foot caught his shins. McWilms stumbled backward, falling to the ground as the man caught his balance and plunged back into the crowded street. McWilms cursed and got to his feet (around him, he saw open smiles and—judiciously distant—a snickering from some onlooker). It was too late. The man was gone and the people standing around him were too closely packed to easily pursue the man. The apprentice dusted off his clothing, trying vainly to collect the shards of his wounded pride. He straightened his clothing where the man's fingers had clawed at him. Paper crackled under his belt.

McWilms pulled an envelope from where it had been stuffed between belt and uniform. He stared at it.

It was addressed, in a spidery hand, to the Thane.

"You've both seen the note. I'd like your thoughts on it."

The Thane looked at Aldhelm and Valdisa, seated in floaters in the Thane's room. Aldhelm held the slip of paper in his hand. He looked down at it, his eyes scanning the words once more, and shook his head.

"So Gunnar would like to meet you privately," he said. "I don't care for the idea, Thane. No matter that he says he has information that might interest us. You can't go to see him or have him come to Underasgard. Vingi wouldn't hesitate to consider that as more circumstantial evidence against us, and he'd drag us before the Assembly on a charge of illegal conspiracy. He couldn't win, of course, but the residual damage that the charge might do to Hoorka . . ." He shook his head again and held the note out to the Thane, who reached forward to take it from him. "We can't afford this, Thane. And believe me, Gunnar will be trying to extract a price. He's no better or more altruistic a man than the Li-Gallant."

"You're not at all curious about this 'substantial offer for the good of Hoorka' or"—his fingers scratched along the paper—"'information which may have the greatest import for you'?"

"I'm admittedly curious, Thane, but not enough to wish to compromise Hoorka," Aldhelm replied. "There are higher allegiances than curiosity."

The answer disturbed the Thane. He'd asked Aldhelm and Valdisa to come to his rooms, thinking that perhaps by taking Aldhelm into his confidence he could bridge some of the growing rift between them—and because he knew that Valdisa would understand that ploy and aid him. By the code, the Hoorka-thane was not bound to take advice from any other Hoorka unless he should call a full Council meeting. But advice was helpful—even if he had, for the most part, made his decision. If it would help the uneasy relationship between Aldhelm and himself, so much the better.

Except that it wouldn't work.

Aldhelm seemed only mildly concerned with Gunnar's sudden interest in the Hoorka, and was evidently disinclined to investigate this offer of his. But the Thane wished to know what prompted it. The challenge of the note tugged at him, as he knew Gunnar had intended it to do. It was full of enigmatic terseness.

No, he wouldn't let it endanger Hoorka, if that's what it came to; yes, Aldhelm was right about Vingi's probable reaction to any meeting between the two guild-heads. It would be a powerful alliance, that of the Hoorka and Gunnar's Ruling Guild. Vingi would be forced to deplete much of his resources and capital to defeat them should they join in actual treaty. Neweden might see a guild war to rival the Great Feud of the last century. If the Thane hadn't the vision of an offworld Hoorka-guild, hadn't the goal of making the assassins something more than a planetbound curiosity, it would be tempting.

Perhaps too tempting.

The possibilities were not attractive.

"I was thinking of possibly arranging the meeting, nonetheless," the Thane said. Aldhelm's face clouded over with the words; Valdisa, sitting cross-legged in her floater, tilted her head in surprise. The Thane hurried to continue.

"I've no intention of actually dealing with the man. I simply wish to know more about this proposal. And I'm most interested in knowing what information he claims to possess that would make us consider such a rash move as to consider a proposal from his guild. The information—it might be important to Hoorka."

"But most likely not," said Valdisa. She unlaced her legs and stretched them, folding her hands on her lap. The Thane could read those movements—she always tried to appear relaxed when her thoughts were actually in turmoil. It could fool those who knew her casually, but it worried the Thane. "I don't know if it's worth the risk, Thane. It's *Gunnar* that Vingi would prefer to eliminate, not Hoorka. If we can avoid angering the Li-Gallant any further, he'll leave us in peace. We've done nothing to anger him before now, despite his damned paranoia."

Aldhelm had turned to look at Valdisa as she spoke. Now he glanced back at the Thane, nodding his agreement. "M'Dame is right, Thane. Let Gunnar wonder why we failed to answer his note. And salve your curiosity with your kin."

So we must disagree again. Perhaps I should give in . . . "I have to disagree with the two of you on one point. Vingi *does* consider us a threat to his guild, if only because—now that the possibility has occurred to him—we will always be a potential enemy for his rivals to ally with. It was through us that Gunnar escaped"—with those words, Aldhelm's eyes narrowed—"and just his suspicions are enough. He would like to see us unguilded and hunted down like lassari criminals."

"Does that mean that you intend to see Gunnar?" Aldhelm shifted his weight in the floater, a preamble to rising.

I should give in. Their stand makes as much sense as mine. The Thane nodded in mute acknowledgment. He waited for angry words, for violent disagreement.

Nothing.

Aldhelm rose slowly from his floater. A finger ran idly from forehead to the tip of his nose, then finally curled around his chin. He stood, stretching. "I still think it unnecessary and possibly dangerous to Hoorka. But I don't think I can change your mind, Thane. At least I haven't been too successful at that recently. I trust you have the good sense to avoid the meeting being made public—that's the primary danger."

"I intend to take precautions." *Is it going to be this easy?*

Aldhelm shrugged. "Then there's nothing more to say. I hope you dredge the information from the man. Good day, Thane, Valdisa." He left the room, walking slowly. The door closed behind him with a sibilant hissing.

The Thane glanced at Valdisa, catching her profile as she looked at the door. She must have felt his eyes upon her, for she spoke without looking at the Thane.

"He's right. You know it, don't you? The potential doesn't match the danger involved."

"I don't agree," he said, more stiffly and formally than he'd intended. It hurt her visibly, and he cursed his social clumsiness.

"Then, as Aldhelm said, there's nothing more I can say."

"Valdisa, I'm sorry. I swear to She of the Five I am. I don't mean to trod all over your feelings."

"You never do. That's the problem."

She wouldn't smile.

The Thane had never met Gunnar before but had seen him—as had all Neweden—any number of times on Assembly holocasts. For all that, he had been prepared to see some vague difference in the man, some masked dichotomy between the image and the reality. Gunnar looked neither taller nor shorter, thinner nor more rotund than he did in the holotanks. He had the same affably neutral half-smile, the unsteady doe eyes, the bluffly handsome features and well-tended body of the holo-Gunnar. There was nothing about him to shock the senses and make the Thane realize that the man he was facing was alive and not simply another random arrangement of light and shade beamed in the holotank at Underasgard.

Their meeting seemed to be a clandestine cliché. They met in one of the narrow and dark alleys of the Dasta Borough of Sterka, a section of the city inhabited largely by lassari. The Thane had eschewed his Hoorka uniform, choosing instead a cloaked outfit of some silky material that felt strangely cool against his skin. Gunnar, waiting for them, was muffled in a dull wrap that twisted and knotted in an indecipherable pattern around his body. The Thane wondered how—if he ever removed the clothing—he would put it back on.

Sartas and d'Mannberg, several steps behind the Thane and in the clothing of lassari, stared into the semi-darkness around the Thane and Gunnar. Sartas held a wide-dispersion infrared beamer and both Hoorka wore night glasses. To them, the alley was a brilliant wash of scarlet and orange.

To the Thane, it was merely dim. A faint glimmer of city-light glazed the sky and sent down a weak glow. Sleipnir cast a harsh shadow ten meters or so up the sooty brick walls that lined the street. He could see, if not particularly well, the garbage wind-piled at the edges of the wall, the gritty earth of the unpaved ground, and the mortar falling in a brittle dust from between the bricks.

A chance meeting of strangers in a dismal landscape.

Gunnar spoke first. "I didn't really think you'd come, Thane." He smiled.

In the night, the Thane could sense that meaningless smile. Gunnar extended his left hand, palm up and the hand inclined slightly below horizontal—a greeting between kin of different guilds—a gesture of gratitude and mild deference. Should the thumb move any higher above horizontal, it would be demeaning for a man of Gunnar's stature; too low and the Hoorka would be insulted at the implication that Gunnar considered himself above him. Proper form dictated that the Thane should return the gesture, but he kept his hand at his side. Hoorka have no friends outside the guild: you may be contracted to kill them the next day.

"I almost stayed in Underasgard. My coming seems to be against everyone's better judgment," the Thane replied. His voice was dry and uncaring.

Gunnar withdrew his hand as it became apparent that the Thane would not return the gesture of peace. His smile flickered and returned. "So my own kin thought. *I* thought, though, that it might be to our mutual advantage. We seem to have a common enemy, Thane." Gunnar glanced about him, from the dirty walls to the two Hoorka standing behind the Thane. There, his eyes seemed to be snagged. He laughed, a short bark that skittered into moonlight and was shattered. "You don't need to fear me that greatly, Thane," he said. "There's no feud between our houses, our gods are at peace, and there are, I trust, no contracts on me."

"You can understand my caution. I wouldn't care to have the Li-Gallant become aware of this meeting, no matter how innocent it may be—nor do I think you'd find it to your liking either, neh? It would not only be the Hoorka that would come before the Assembly."

Again the laugh. "I have no doubts that he'd try to break my guild if he thought it would serve his own purposes."

(And the Thane remarked to himself: I don't trust this man, don't care for his light-hearted friendliness or his handsome face. Everything about him rings false and hollow . . .)

"Your information, Gunnar?"

Gunnar shook his head, the smile—it seemed to be an unvarying feature of his face—moving with him. He stuck his hands between folds of his clothing, putting all his weight on one foot: the pose of a relaxed man. "You're impatient, good sirrah. The information will come to you. But you must listen to my proposal first. I'm sure it will be neither startling nor unexpected to you. Look at the present situation on Neweden, and you can certainly see that we are in a position to lend each other considerable aid."

Silence from the Thane. In the middle distance, someone could be heard singing discordantly, while overhead the roar of a transport from Sterka Port shook mortar dust from the parapets above them.

The Thane stared at Gunnar, waiting.

The man continued his speech hurriedly, as if trying to get all the words out before the Thane turned and strode away. "My ruling guild has a small policing force, unlike that of Vingi. If we were to gain a majority in the Assembly, if I were Li-Gallant, we'd need a larger, far more efficient force. The Hoorka could provide the nucleus for that. And if you joined us now, well, Vingi's people simply aren't the trained professionals of the Hoorka. Should there be, say, a blood-feud between the guilds of Gunnar and Vingi—and should the Hoorka side with us—we might well be in a position afterward to amply reward our allies."

"Do you know that m'Dame d'Embry of the Alliance is considering letting the Hoorka continue our work off-world?"

Gunnar spread his hands wide, sweeping them toward the stars above them, pale through the miasma of Sleipnir's light. "Do you know the woman, sirrah? I think her influence with the Alliance is on the wane. Yah, she is well-known among the Diplos, but she's *here,* and Neweden is just another name to the Alliance rulers on Niffleheim. They've given her a token assignment where she can no longer bother them with her unorthodoxy. You think she'll actually be the key to letting the Hoorka go offworld?" Gunnar's smile became sad, his head shook. "I grant you, Thane, that the Alliance would be a huge arena in which the Hoorka could work, but Neweden is large enough, and you have the advantage of knowing *how* to work here. Would you pass up what would be almost certain success to chase a ghost?"

"Your specter or hers, what difference?" The Thane shrugged. "And hers more closely resembles my own."

"Ahh, so the Hoorka can sting with words as well as weapons. Yah, of course I'm chasing my own dreams. And I'll guarantee you that my ruling would be better for all Neweden. *And* for Hoorka."

"Every ruling guild says no differently."

"The Neweden bureaucracies need us to function, Thane. If there is no government providing a stable economy in which the guilds can operate, then there is no payment for Hoorka. Or do your people enjoy killing for its own excitement?"

The last statement was couched in a jocular tone that

belied its sarcasm. In another person, the Thane might have found it simply distasteful—with Gunnar, it was bald insult. The Thane eyed the man, wondering again how he'd managed to escape Aldhelm and Sartas. Dame Fate had most decidedly smiled on him, but She had a way of suddenly releasing those who relied too heavily on Her good favor, laughing as the unfortunate fell. The Thane would enjoy being there when that happened—he would enjoy it even more were he the instrument of the Dame's reprisal.

He wondered if Gunnar knew how close to Hag Death he was.

The Thane scuffed a foot against the gravel of the alley, deciding finally to ignore the insult and let Gunnar live. Aldhelm and Valdisa had been right, and the worst realization was that he'd suspected that all along. "Neweden's a violent world," he said finally. "You've never drawn blood?"

Gunnar shrugged. "What guild-kin hasn't done so at one point or another? I can defend myself in a feud, if that's your meaning."

"You found it . . . pleasant? Unpleasant?"

"Neither."

"The Hoorka do their job on a contract. They don't do it for pleasure. But it would give me great pleasure to slay a man who slighted my kin."

The Thane watched the smile on Gunnar's face fade. The man backed away from the Hoorka a step before the Thane waved a hand in dismissal.

"The Hoorka have no interest in your offer, sirrah," he said. "You know the Hoorka code. I intend to continue to follow it."

Gunnar stood as if poised for flight. Without the smile, his face looked naked, the lips a trifle too thin for the full cheeks and strong chin. Slowly, the man relaxed as the Hoorka made no move to harm him. "I had to make the effort, Thane. For my kin. You can understand that."

The Thane nodded slowly. "I can. And your information, so that I may feel that the evening wasn't totally wasted . . . ?"

"Vingi sent another assassin to our headquarters. A lassari."

"You're sure it was Vingi? Lassari have been known to be foolish." The Thane thought of the man that had attacked him in Market Square.

"Do you know of a lassari that could afford a light-shunter, or that would have 100C in her pocket? Look around us, Thane. This is where lassari live. Is this a rich district where a person can afford to have the equipment to foil my detectors?"

"If you have proof of your charges, then why haven't you gone to the Assembly with the complaint? It's illegal to involve lassari in a guild matter. Declare bloodfeud. Or don't you care for the excitement of killing?"

Gunnar ignored the irony. He looked up at the light-smeared sky, then back to the Thane. "You underestimate the resources of my guild. And what this might indicate is that Vingi already believes the Hoorka to have allied themselves with my kin. Why else send a lassari when the Hoorka are available? What's to prevent him from attacking the Hoorka in the same manner? The man's mad, sirrah. He no longer follows the dictates of Neweden society."

"I don't think his arrogance that blind. If he couldn't defeat *you,* then he'll have no chance against my kin."

Gunnar stared at the Thane. He shrugged, as if ridding himself of the thinly-veiled insult. "Granted. But it would still be a nuisance to you, would it not?"

The Thane wished himself back in Underasgard. The night had already depressed him more than he'd expected: the squalid surroundings, Gunnar's irritating self-confidence, a vague feeling of dismal failure—he wallowed in a gray ennui. The Thane stepped back, turning half away from Gunnar as the man suddenly stood erect and held a hand up to halt the Thane's retreat.

"Thane, I might be holding Hoorka's fate in my hands. The interested parties in this altercation have a meeting with the Regent d'Embry, if you recall. And I know that your men are flooding this alley with infrared light. What if I had the forethought to position a person on the roofs and film this little meeting?"

It was a measure of Gunnar's desperation that he used that ploy. If he had expected his words to frighten the Thane, to cow the assassin, he had seriously misjudged his mark. Already angered by Gunnar, the Thane put one hand beneath his flowing cape. His eyes grew cold, the lines of his face as deep as if etched in an ippicator bone. Sartas and d'Mannberg, sensing the tension, moved closer to their leader; the menace on their faces was open. Gunnar stepped backward once more, the mask of his face broken and fright written there.

"You'd find the Hoorka to be a strong enemy." The Thane fingered the hilt of his vibro. He spat on the ground. "You'd also delight Vingi by doing that. You'd spare him the expense of buying a contract for you. Or are you simply a fool?"

A direct insult was something that should provoke guild-kin into a feud. Words such as the Thane's were seldom tolerated. The Hoorka could see the muscles of Gunnar's body at war with each other, vacillating between anger and fright. The Thane found himself wishing the man would make a threatening move, so that he would have no qualms about ending the matter here. Sartas had a flat-camera with him and had been recording the meeting, for the Thane had anticipated Gunnar using a conveniently-edited tape of their meeting to blackmail Hoorka. It would be easy . . .

But Gunnar seemed to rein himself in. The smile made a weak return.

"Not a . . . *fool*, Thane." Gunnar stumbled over the word, emphasizing it. "Simply a man trying to further the influence of his kin. Something we would all do, neh? Neither of us can blame the other for doing so, can we? If I speak frankly to you, it's because of the importance of our actions. I mean no insult to Hoorka. And I"—he paused— "apologize for any insult." He bowed his head in submission.

The Thane remained silent, staring over his shoulder at Gunnar. Sleipnir peered over the lip of the buildings.

Gunnar cleared his throat, looking up again. "There's nothing for me to say, then. I think the Hoorka might have done well to consider my offer, but . . ." He shook his head. "Potok will be at the meeting as my representative. I refuse to face Vingi as an equal until this matter is settled. If you should change your mind, Thane, please inform Potok. He'll relay the news to me. Good night, and may Dame Fate smile on your kin."

And with an unhurried pace that the Thane admired despite himself, Gunnar strode past the Thane and the two assassins and into the maze of streets.

Chapter 10

AN ARMED ESCORT met the Thane at the entrance to Diplo Center.

It seemed an indication of the times—to his knowledge, the Alliance had always depended on automatic systems to guard themselves against attack and unwanted visitors. He might have been flattered to a degree if he thought that he was the only one accorded such treatment, but the Thane wasn't quite so vain. It seemed more likely that both Potok and Vingi had been met similarly. The Thane, deliberately late as a minor protest, followed the Diplo guards across a grassed lawn and into the yawning maw of the Center. The huge edifice swallowed them without effort. The Thane ignored the curious stares of those they passed in the lengthy corridors or moving the opposite way on the slidewalks. When the guards shuffled off the walk at an unmarked door, he nodded to them with mocking politeness. His muscles tense despite the show of calm, the Thane activated the door lock and stepped through.

There were three other people in the room, gathered about a wooden table in an otherwise barren room: Li-Gallant Vingi, Regent d'Embry, and Potok. The Thane bowed to d'Embry—he hoped she knew of the contract the Hoorka had completed for the last Alliance Regent. The Alliance shuffled Diplos so often that it was conceivable she might not know of her predecessor, and it had been to a young and too casual man that the Thane had first broached his dream of an offworld Hoorka guild. An obvious truism, he knew; but much was at stake here.

The Thane seated himself, ignoring the presence of both

the Li-Gallant and Potok, directing all his attention to the
Regent as the most important of the people in the room.

She appeared impatient. Her lips were tight and drawn
and her posture was rigid—she looked as if she might rise
and stalk off at any moment. One hand fondled a carved
medallion on a chain around her neck. From the sheen and
ivory brilliance of the jewelry, the Thane knew it to be a
polished ippicator bone, worth far more than its size might
indicate. He couldn't decide if her irritation was truth or a
sham, for he knew that the Diplos were trained in psycho-
logical subtleties and deception. That meant he couldn't
trust instinct here; she might be leading him. That bothered
him—the Hoorka preferred to be the manipulators.

The Thane examined his callused hands, waiting for
someone to speak.

It was Vingi who broke the uncomfortable silence, clearing his throat to gain their attention. "The Regent has asked
that this be a private meeting rather than a full Assembly
conference, a request I've bowed to, considering that this is
neither an official trial nor a registered complaint. Thane,
you recognize Representative Potok of Gunnar's ruling
guild? The Regent wished the opposition party to have
their representative here—"

"Hold, if you will, Li-Gallant."

The Regent spoke suddenly and coldly, her gaze drifting
past the others at the table and then boring into Vingi. The
pupils were gray, the Thane noticed, as frigid as the void.
For the first time since he'd entered the room, he allowed
himself to relax, if slightly. The Regent was obviously on no
side but her own. She seemed to hold a weary contempt for
the Li-Gallant's pomposity, and that could only be to Hoorka's advantage. "Everyone here is aware of the context for
the meeting," she continued. "I'm interested in one thing
only: the Assassins' Guild's credibility—and my ship lifts in
an hour for a conference on Aris. Leave your local squab-
bles for your Assembly. Please waste no more of my—our—
time with such things."

(Cold, always cold. Does it come from erecting an Alliance from the scattered ashes of Huard's long-dead empire? the Thane wondered. They all seemed like her, at least
to some degree, these people of the Diplomatic Resources
Team.)

Vingi accepted d'Embry's rebuff with a curt nod. He again cleared his throat. "To the point, then, m'Dame. Isn't it true, Thane, that Gunnar escaped from two Hoorka while totally unarmed and helpless? Doesn't that seem a trifle odd or suspiciously well-timed to you, with all respect to the whims of Dame Fate?"

The Thane glanced at d'Embry.

She shrugged and rested her chin on a cupped hand, while the other toyed with the ippicator medallion.

The Thane leaned back in his chair. "Gunnar escaped, Li-Gallant. That's hardly in dispute. And so did Geraint Sooms, and Erbin ca Dellia, and several others over the last several standards. You seem to forget, sirrah, that it's part of the Hoorka code that the victim retains a chance of escape. We contract only to attempt a fair assassination, and our efforts cease when the contract day expires. Gunnar was intelligent or favored enough by Dame Fate to elude my people. It was *not* conspiracy. Anyone can escape the Hoorka, should it be decreed by the gods that he should. You might escape yourself."

"Someone paid, Hoorka-Thane. Someone paid for death, not sophistry and rhetoric."

"The person who signed that contract should be advised that death is not for any man to buy. Hag Death makes a jealous lover." The Thane glanced at Potok, wondering what emotions were hidden behind that man's intent and serious stare. It was an ill-kept secret, the identity of the contractor for Gunnar, but it would be improper for any of those here to admit that, by Neweden morals. Yet the Thane admired Potok's reserve. He steepled his hands as he waited for Vingi's reply.

Unconcerned. Always appear unconcerned.

"You're dangerous if you've allied yourselves with Gunnar," said Vingi. "I make no pretext of enjoying the presence of members of his guild in the Assembly, nor do I conceal the pleasure I find in hearing that others of Neweden feel as I do"—this with a glare at Potok, huddled deep in the recesses of his chair as if seeking some hidden warmth—"since they only impede Neweden's progress to prosperity. I don't know who paid for the Gunnar contract, obviously, but the outcome disturbs me. That is why I must make certain of Hoorka's role."

Unexpectedly, d'Embry broke in, her voice low and steady. "Li-Gallant, you should recognize one thing. The *Alliance* will work with anyone holding the power of Neweden. It doesn't matter to us whether that is you, Gunnar, or any of the other scheming little ruling guilds that proliferate here. We're concerned only with aspects of Neweden that touch upon the Alliance: your exports, your payment for imports, the maintenance of the Port, and your representation on the Niffleheim Council. What is important here, I stress for the last time, is the possibility that the Hoorka have placed themselves in a compromising position of support for one or another of your guilds. If they wish to do so, it's entirely their choice. It would mean that they would be restricted to Neweden, but that is all—as far as the Alliance is concerned. We would have no further restriction for them.

"Your men fulfilled a contract for the Port authorities, if I recall correctly?" D'Embry's gaze slowly moved from the Li-Gallant to the Thane. He realized belatedly that the last question had been directed to him.

"We were paid to remove a saboteur. Your predecessor paid with offworld weaponry. The contract was successful, as I recall. Valdisa and d'Mannberg were the Hoorka-kin working that night. Yes, I remember."

The Thane watched the Regent's hand—tinted a faint blue as if numbed by cold—go from the medallion to the table. And then the Regent shifted positions in her chair, a slight movement, but so quick and sure that it startled the Thane. It was incongruous in comparison to her slow speech and deliberate gestures, not at all part of the carefully-nurtured image of an antagonistic older woman. It worried him—he wondered how else he'd underestimated her complexities. He'd made the mistake of thinking her two-dimensional, taking her aloofness as shallowness or—at best—indifference. He would have to revise that estimation.

And he realized that he'd missed part of her reply. ". . . considered allowing the Hoorka to accept offworld contracts, but this matter needs to be settled. There are other questions, of course. Can the Hoorka maintain cohesiveness on a larger scale? Perhaps you'll find you have to limit the contracts you accept, and in that case what would determine acceptance or non-acceptance? The whole question of your integrity would take on a new dimension. Can you maintain the para-military regimentation that seems to be the only thing between the Hoorka and chaos? What would happen when there is no guild structure in which to function? But these questions are to be answered when you are implanted offworld—*if* that happens—and obviously I can have no real glimmering of that final solution, and have no real interest in it. I won't be involved by then. So let us first settle this small problem. If the Hoorka can't function on one . . ." The Regent hesitated, and the Thane saw her swallow the next word. A derogatory adjective? And was that hesitation deliberate also? ". . . small world, then certainly they cannot deal with several." There was hauteur in that voice, the ingrained superiority of civilization to the rural, the backward.

Duel with her, then. Parry and riposte. But you're outclassed.

"Our kind aren't unknown historically, m'Dame, even on the homeworld. Are you familiar with the Thuggee of ancient India?"

"No. And our ancestors were once also barbarians. We've progressed beyond that stage, and no one should use them as an excuse." A pause. "Well, one would *hope* that we've passed beyond our old follies. But I'm not concerned with historical precedent. Your particular, ahh, commodity is useless if it becomes linked to a political cause."

Touché.

"If I may be allowed a moment," interjected Potok. He had been slumped deep in the yielding caress of his chair. He spoke from that same ultra-relaxed position, a body seemingly without skeletal support. "I'm closer to the problem in some ways than any of us here. It was, after all, the leader of my guild *and* my personal friend who was the target of this unknown contractor."

Looking at the Li-Gallant.

"It *is* one aspect of your code I would change, Thane," Potok continued, turning to the Thane. "Why not release the names of the unsuccessful contracts as well as those you complete?"

"The bolt that misses you in the dark can tell you nothing of its owner, sirrah. The code works, and I see no reason to change it. Nothing can be proved. I say Gunnar escaped us, as some contracted victims will do, and the Li-Gallant claims that we let him go free. We can argue the point all day, should we care to do so."

"That, at least, is true." Potok slid ever deeper into his chair. His chin rested on his chest. He seemed totally at ease with the room and the situation, and, because of that, certain of his position.

It suddenly seemed ludicrous to the Thane. *All of us,* he thought, *carrying on our pretexts of self-confidence, making sure that our posturings fit the image, that we stay in character. And how many of us are that sure of ourselves and not simply frightened actors? The Regent? Perhaps.*

Surely not myself.

Potok spoke again. "My only contribution to this meeting is to state that the Hoorka have not allied themselves with us. I'll state that under oath, if necessary. The truth is quite the contrary." His gaze flickered past the Thane. "Our records are open to Alliance scrutiny, m'Dame d'Embry— or to the Li-Gallant Vingi, if it will satisfy his curiosity. I've no love for the assassins—my kin-brother was almost killed—but they are fair. I'll grant them that much. Were I or Gunnar less scrupulous, I might be tempted to say that they *had* formed an agreement with us, simply because that would discredit them and possibly erase a future threat to my guild, especially when one considers that the contractor is evidently too cowardly to declare an open bloodfeud against Gunnar."

The Li-Gallant examined his sleeve.

"M'Dame, Neweden wouldn't allow the joining of our guilds," Potok continued. "We'd simply unite the other guilds against us and fall. Murder is too easy a solution here; it comes too quickly to our minds, perhaps because it is so simple. No, the Hoorka have nothing to do with us. My words should have some weight with you, Regent."

There were innuendos, shadows of meaning that colored Potok's words. The Thane felt helpless amid the possibilities. *Does he say those words hoping he won't be believed, since it's the obvious way for him to respond if he is allied with the Hoorka? Does he say it hoping that I'll feel indebted to him and Gunnar, and reconsider their offer? Or be less eager with a future contract? Is it simply that he can't miss the opportunity of contradicting and hindering the Li-Gallant?*

He shook his head slightly. Too many possibilities, too many directions.

He had lost any semblance of confidence. It had drained away.

"It does seem to have been an odd time for your kin to fail a contract, Thane, considering the stature of the victim," reiterated Vingi.

You're right, Li-Gallant. The thought roared in the Thane's head. *You're right. Perhaps there should have been no escape, even if it meant violation of the code.* (And further inside: *No, how can you think that?* It was a small voice.) "I would consider that, instead, evidence in our favor," the Thane said, speaking from habit while the inner fight raged. "Even realizing the consequences, we followed the code."

"And around we go again?" The Regent let disgust show in her voice. She turned to the Li-Gallant, the medallion on her neck catching the light softly and throwing it back into the room. "You mentioned that you had a thought for deciding this question, Li-Gallant?"

"I did, m'Dame."

Both the Thane and Potok looked at Vingi, the Thane with feigned nonchalance, Potok with the beginning of some faint alarm that dragged him from the depths of his chair.

The Regent stood, quickly. Her tunic swirled, then settled around her in an unruffled perfection. Light shimmered from the fabric, and the pale yellow-white of the ippicator bone was set like a jewel in the play of light. "Good. Then I'll waste no more time with these semantic games. Since you've managed to fritter away my morning inconclusively, Li-Gallant, I hope your plan bears ripened fruit. I shall be interested in the results." She stared at the Thane for a long moment as her hand went again to the ippicator medallion. "If the Hoorka can't be indicted, perhaps you and I will talk further, sirrah."

M'Dame d'Embry, in a rustling of glowcloth, left the room.

Neweden rested uneasily in the twilight. The sunstar, declining with haste from the western sky, laced the horizon with brilliant scarves of farewell—banded azure, green-

gold, and topaz bordered by brilliant orange—all drifting to
gray as the star became bloated and oblate, a gelatinous
mass easing its weight carefully onto the pricking spires of
distant hills. The ghost of Gulltopp had its entrance in the
east. Lights began to move in the streets as Neweden sought
to banish the tiresome onslaught of night.

For Eorl, it was time to return to Underasgard and its
eternal night.

Eorl had been visiting his true family—not that it ever
seemed to be a pleasant task. In the two standards since
he'd joined the Hoorka, they had yet to accept the fact that
he had no interest in becoming an artisan like his true-
mother (and she for her own part refused to see his lack of
talent). As for his true-father, non-guilded himself and
saved from the onus of being named lassari because of his
true-mother's affiliations (it was this very law that made it
preferable to marry within one's own guild)—his true-
father would sit and watch their arguments without comment, his eyes dulled by too much binda juice. She persisted
in viewing the Hoorka as a temporary affectation of her
true-son that would, given time and much argument, wither
and disappear like a discarded garment.

Such attachment to true-family came because both true-
parents-had been offworlders and did not entirely understand the rigors of guild-kinship. It was an onus Eorl had
borne through his childhood, having to endure the taunts of
Neweden children because Eorl lived with his true-parents
instead of at the guild commune. He had not enjoyed that,
and he did not enjoy the visits home.

And this day was no different from the others that preceded it. Eorl wondered why he persisted in taking the time.
It was a masochistic relationship; he succeeded only in ripping open the crusted skin over the old wounds and in reminding himself of how those wounds had once hurt.

The visits always started off well, a glow of optimism
born of distance. They'd avoid the sensitive topics with an
uneasy adroitness until all the neutral, dull subjects were
laid aside with a nearly audible sigh and someone (it was
almost always his mother) would ask about the Hoorka or
mention that someone had been assassinated by Hoorka-
kin. The voice would suddenly turn archly cruel—had Eorl
been involved in *that* killing?—and mention that it was a

fine thing for a person who could have joined a respectable guild to kill another person without personal enmity or a formally declared bloodfeud. And the argument would begin, until mingled pain and anger would drive him from their house.

No, it wasn't worth the effort. Eorl suddenly realized that he had subconsciously arrived at a decision. This had been the last visit. He wouldn't see them again.

The thoughts held remarkably little sting.

Shadows raced eastward from the closely-packed buildings, clawing their way up walls or pooling in exhaustion in the streets. Eorl was in Brentwood, a dilapidated section of Sterka with some houses dating back to the Settling. It was reputed—despite the evidence in the scant and spotty Neweden archives—that the first ship had set down here, on what was once a hilly forest. The styles of that fabled period tended toward tall structures with decorative and non-functional facades. Occasionally, one would see a bas-relief with fanciful representations of ippicators or mythical creatures. Grotesques perched menacingly above the street and leered down at the passers-by—across the street from him, Eorl watched one grotesque scamper along the roofline, point, and jeer insults at him. Despite his melancholia, Eorl smiled—not too many of the houses still functioned that well. He gestured at the imp with a fist and the creature fondled itself obscenely and ran to the far side of the building. For the most part, the friezes of Brentwood had cracked and fallen as the machinery failed, and grotesques stared stiffly from their last posture or leered up from the ground on which they'd fallen. Still, seen in evening's half-shadow, the area had a gothic character that called racial memories from long sleep. Old superstitions seemed to walk freely here—and Brentwood had more than its share of bizarre cults and odd happenings.

But a Hoorka could walk anywhere. The aura of the guild surrounded and protected him. The deathgods smiled on the assassins. They were safe.

The streets were nearly empty—it was too late in the day for the neighborhood crowds and too early for the night denizens. Up the narrow, winding street, Eorl saw a woman pushing a floater across the intersection. Heads grinned and frowned from the floater, several dozen of them—it was a startling moment before Eorl recognized the pallor of their faces as being native stone and the heads themselves as gargoyle carvings. A few youths lounged in a tavern doorway near him, speaking in the tortuously slow syllables of people on a time-stretcher. They scowled—too slowly—as the Hoorka passed; not unexpectedly, since Stretchers made most people irritable. By the time they decided to confront him (Stretchers also having been known to make the user foolishly brave) he had passed them. He glanced back to see one of the youths open his mouth and raise a fist. The air around him seemed heavy—the fist moved ponderously. A wirehead, stumbling by the youths and lost in his own reality, attracted their attention then, and Eorl looked away. The head-carting woman had passed through the intersection. He caught a brief glimpse of her blue dress before houses blocked her from view.

It was not the most pleasant of neighborhoods. Yet he'd grown up here, while his true-mother's guildhouse had been located in the interface between Brentwood and a richer neighborhood. He'd roamed these streets as a child and then again as the leader of a band of unruly jussar. And then the guildhouse had been moved; while his true-mother followed her kin, he'd offered himself to the Hoorka. They'd taken him.

He knew the area. He enjoyed its defiance of Neweden conventions.

Yet even the most familiar landscapes can hold a surprise.

As Eorl came to the intersection, he heard the low chant of a procession of the Dead. He shook his head in disgust— the mantra was coming from the street he wished to take. Eorl had no wish to waste time waiting for the procession to pass him, and the Dead had an annoying habit of blocking streets completely, knocking down those who stood in their way and weren't nimble enough to dodge. The chant was louder—they were moving toward him, then. Eorl cursed and turned westward.

He strode into molten sun, his shadow long behind him. He shrugged at his nightcloak, tugging it into place over his shoulders. This street was narrower than the last—he thought he could reach out and touch the buildings on either side.

Eorl scowled, anxious to be home in Underasgard and irritated at the delay caused by the Dead. Their wordless chant pursued him.

There was no transition. One moment he was walking, and the next he saw vague shapes run toward him as his mind shrieked alarm. They came at him from all sides; a flurry of fists and limbs moved in a wash of dying sun. Hands grasped the Hoorka from behind. Eorl went with the attack immediately, planting his feet and pushing backward as he sought the vibro sheathed at his waist. Something (hot? That was his first impression) sliced along his back, followed by a sluggish wetness that was surprisingly without pain. He found his vibro and slashed at the attacker behind him, feeling the comfortable resistance of blade meeting flesh.

(Thinking: *how deep is that back wound? How much time do I have?*)

A man's baritone yelped in pain, retreating as Eorl pivoted to meet the others. But his body failed to complete the turn. Sudden white agony arced across his waist and stomach—another vibro—and his face contorted. Eorl doubled over in torture. He tried to keep his footing, to hold the vibro out as a symbolic resistance as they closed in on him.

(*How many? Gods, I don't know. At least let one of them precede my soul when I stand before She of the Five let my blood stain their gods it HURTS . . .*)

Something blunt and hard struck him from the side and his kidneys screamed. He saw with terrible clarity a hand holding a whining vibro (scarlet in the last rays of the sunstar, shining), watched with open, amazed eyes as it plunged into his stomach. Thick and full blood welled over the hilt and down a long, deadly canyon as the hand wrenched the vibro to the side. Eorl felt himself falling, saw the street slant and then rise to meet him. There were more blows, more stabbings. In the end he no longer felt them, only heard the dulling sounds as the darkness deeper than the coming night closed in around him.

Then even the sounds were lost.

Chapter 11

"**W**E HAVE VERY LITTLE choice."

The eternal night of Underasgard: black cotton of darkness angry at being disturbed and held back by glow-torches guttering fitfully in their wall holders. And beyond where the torches glowed and people walked, the darkness spread its feather weight around rocks and slept.

In a room in the Hoorka section of the caverns sat the Hoorka: the Thane, Aldhelm, and a few others seated at a rough wooden table (made by a new apprentice whose true-father had been a carpenter. It was evident from the grinning joints between the boards that he had not inherited his true-father's craft). Cranmer, as always, sat unobtrusively to one side, watching the meters on his recording equipment as if his gaze would provide assurance that it would remain functioning. Mugs filled with newly-made mead sat like islands in gold-brown ringlets of condensation. A pitcher held more of the drink within easy reach—beads of the liquor ran from the spout to the base. The scent of honey freshened the air.

"We can assume that Vingi will sign a new contract for Gunnar." Aldhelm lifted his mug, sipped, wiped his lips, then set the mug down again. He wiped his hand on his thigh. "He'll give us our second chance to kill the man. This time, the Hoorka can't afford to fail."

"Even if success means abandoning the code?" asked Valdisa. "You assume too much there, Aldhelm." She shook her head. Ringlets of dark hair shivered in sympathy.

Aldhelm slapped at the table. The meaty *thwapp* of flesh against wood cracked loudly in the room; heads turned as liquid sloshed over the edge of mugs. "I'm assuming only that we're interested in surviving on Neweden."

"Yah, but to abandon the code isn't the way of survival."

The Thane's voice, quiet but emphatic, gave him the attention of the Hoorka Council. As he spoke, one finger stroked the lip of the mug in front of him. "If we violate the code," he continued, "we've lost our integrity—which is exactly the claim Vingi already makes against us. Everything we've set up, everything we've struggled to build, would be a sham. And we wouldn't survive it."

The last sentence was directed to Aldhelm. The Thane's eyes brushed past the scarred cheek of the younger Hoorka, where a red-brown scab marked the line of a vibro gash. Across the table from the Thane, Valdisa flashed him a quick smile. He returned it with a slight raising of his lips.

Aldhelm's arm slashed at the air. "The code *is* good for Hoorka. I don't dispute that. It works well enough for most contracts we deal with. But it has nearly failed us in the Gunnar/Vingi conflict. If it threatens to fail us again, we should be prepared to break those rules. Don't you see, my kin? We can break the code and live with whatever guilt that brings us, or we die. We'll accept whatever punishment She of the Five might send us. That's quite simple. The choice seems easy—now—to me. Thane, you remember your anger with Sartas and myself... I don't think you would have been too upset if we'd broken the code but killed Gunnar."

Yes, I remember. And he's right—I was more angry with the failure, and I had no right to be. "I remember, Aldhelm. But I also told you that I was glad you followed the code. I am not going to be swayed on that point—would Hag Death be pleased that you consider yourself her equal?"

"And if Gunnar would live, what then?" Aldhelm shook his head. "If the guilds ever thought we'd joined with another guild, we wouldn't have the people to answer all the declarations of bloodfeud."

A susurrus of argument filled the room as everyone tried to speak at once. The noise echoed through the cavern. In the end, it was Valdisa's clear voice that broke through and held.

"I see your reasoning, Aldhelm. I do. But I can't agree that what you suggest is the right course. The code may be an artificial set of rules created by the Thane, but even he doesn't hold himself free to break them or release himself from them. For good or ill, we've based our existence around them, structured the fabric of Hoorka about the code. Sometimes the created must transcend the creator."

(At his recording equipment, Cranmer started, hearing his own words to the Thane so closely paraphrased. Had she overheard that, he wondered, or was that simply her own ironic choice of words?)

"Transcend the creator, or simply destroy him?" A beat. Aldhelm sipped from his mug again. "And his creation with him. *And* all his kin."

Valdisa shook her head, exhaling loudly.

"Aldhelm, listen to me," the Thane said, fighting to rein in his increasing anger. *If I were stronger, this wouldn't be necessary. Once, standards ago, no meeting would have been needed or called. I wouldn't have explained myself to anyone, nor would they have asked—my kin would have followed without question. When did this vacillation start?* "Eorl was brutally murdered last night by a pack of cowards. No feud, no formal duel, no honor. Do you think it's because some unknown people don't like the code? No, I think it quite the opposite. It's symptomatic of our problem. We'll be beset on all sides if it ever becomes known that we've stepped aside from a rigidly neutral stance. Things such as Eorl's death might become commonplace. And the easiest way to insure that no other guild finds the Hoorka untrustworthy is simply never to sway from the code."

"Was it to retain our neutrality that you went to talk with Gunnar? Please, Thane, spare me your altruism." Aldhelm's voice held barely-controlled contempt. "Eorl's death may have been a chance accident. Look where it took place—Brentwood. I know we're all thinking of Gunnar and Vingi—but we'll pay the cost of Eorl's death when his murderers are found. My suggestion that the code be ignored wouldn't be common knowledge, not as long as kin can trust kin. Once, and then *only* if it becomes necessary, would we tamper with the code. No one would be shouting it through the streets of Sterka. It will save us more trouble. If Gunnar would live . . ."

"And if the Li-Gallant should want to kill another political rival, then what? Would we examine every contract with an eye for its possible effects on Hoorka and make *that* the determining factor as to whether a victim lives or dies?

Damnit, man, we're only a level above every lassari cut-throat in Neweden now, whether you care to admit the truth of that or not. Would you sink your kin back down to that level once more?" The last words were a shout as the Thane's temper at last broke through his control, thrashing and boiling.

Again, Aldhelm gestured violently. What had begun as a simple meeting seemed to have become a confrontation, a power struggle, and the other Hoorka watched in silence: interested spectators.

"No, I wouldn't drag us down, as you say." Aldhelm's voice now matched that of the Thane in volume. "I can agree with Valdisa on one point. The created *has* become more important than the creator. To insure its—*our*—safety, we have to *do* something rather than cower behind the sacred code. I'm sorry, Thane, but if Vingi feels that he has proof to link us to Gunnar, no matter how circumstantial or ambiguous that proof is, he'll not only have the Assembly outlaw us, but he'll have every assassin hunted down and executed. Your Regent d'Embry won't lift a hand to stop him—she won't interfere with local politics unless she stands to gain something by it."

"What does that matter, Aldhelm?" The Thane shook his head. "The Alliance has nothing to do with the contract."

"The Alliance can sit and wait to see if we're what we claim to be."

"And you counsel us to become something else."

"I want us to live. Look at the facts, Thane!" Aldhelm struck the table with fisted violence and rose to his feet.

(And what of the vaunted Hoorka composure, the icy calm that is supposed to distinguish the Hoorka from other guild-kin? Remember that the thirty-first code-line states that one shows his inner faces only to Hoorka-kin. One can let occasion dictate manners, and one can be honest with kin.)

Aldhelm stalked across the room. His voice was suddenly low and tense with emotion. "Whatever the Li-Gallant's contract is, we fulfill it. That's my advice, and I know others here would agree." His index finger pointed at each of the Hoorka around the table in turn. "The Thane can't sleep with all of us."

The Thane's chair scraped against the floor as he stood

in fury, his hand on the hilt of his vibro. He unsheathed the
weapon. But Valdisa was on her feet, also, before the low
hum of the Thane's vibro began.

"Sit down, Thane," she said. Her voice brooked no argument, though the Thane remained standing, holding his activated vibro as he stared at Aldhelm. Valdisa strode across
the room to Aldhelm; she held her own blade, real-steel and
nearly as sharp as a vibro, point foremost in her hand.
Standing before the impassive Hoorka, her dagger touched
cloth a few centimeters below his waist.

"You're not so good as to be untouchable, Hoorka." She
spat out the words, her face twisted by emotion. "I can take
you, and I think you realize that. If you'd care to chance
your luck, just inform me and I'll arrange a meeting for our
duel. Otherwise, watch your tongue—it seems to be discon-
nected from your mind. I *demand*"—her knife jabbed at
him, pricking his skin lightly—"an apology for that last in-
ference; or you'll give me satisfaction in a more physical
way. Your choice, no-kin-of-mine."

Their eyes met and locked, and it was Aldhelm who
looked away first.

Aldhelm stepped back from the woman, glancing down
at her knife hand and the unwavering tip of her blade. He
looked at the table, to where the Thane stood, one hand still
on the hilt of his vibro, though the weapon was now in its
sheath once more.

Aldhelm's voice was hesitant. "I spoke too quickly . . . I
let my passion for Hoorka . . ." He shook his head. "Valdisa,
Thane, you have my apology. My kin should feel sorrow for
my outburst."

"I appreciate your fervor," said the Thane, "but if you
say such a thing again in my hearing, you would do well to
look to your blade."

"I spoke without thinking, Thane, as Valdisa pointed
out." He nodded to her. "But I still hold by the rest. Thane,
you're floundering. You chastised Sartas and myself for failing to kill Gunnar, but you won't listen to me when I suggest that your chastisement was right, and that we should
indeed slay the man. Do you simply enjoy contradicting me,
or don't you know your own mind? We'll have another contract for Gunnar, if we know Vingi at all. If we—you—
choose wrongly, then the Hoorka will die and become

lassari scum. You've had my counsel. Make your decision as you will."

And with that, the Hoorka turned to bow to Valdisa—her face still contorted with anger—and walked from the council room.

The closing of the door reverberated in the caverns.

That night.

Sleep never really came to the Thane. He hovered in a twilight landscape between sleep and waking, worry and oblivion; drifting back and forth on some tidal flow he couldn't control and prey to the misshapen creatures that lurked there. His thoughts were formless and chaotic, as elusive as the chimera of sleep that he chased: a gossamer wisp. The Hoorka lay on his bed, eyes closed to the gray roof of Underasgard, trying to keep his restlessness from waking Valdisa, who slept beside him.

Visitors from the formless dark came:

He saw the vibro arcing toward Aldhelm's face, moving with an aching slowness and haloed with silver reflections as if seen through a flawed and cloudy glass. Though he tried, he couldn't hold it back or turn it aside. The blade cut into flesh, leaving a gash that grinned white and bloodless for a moment before—like lava from a fault—the blood welled and flowed. He dropped the blade as the blood stained the side of Aldhelm's face. He could only mutter, over and over, that he was sorry. Very sorry.

He was sorry that he remained so unsure, so uneasy in his role as Thane. The remainder of the Council meeting had gone badly, destroyed by the acrimony between Aldhelm and himself. The ghost of the younger Hoorka had remained in the room, casting a pall over the talking. Only Valdisa seemed sure of her stand; she defended the code against the hesitant questions of the others while the Thane half-listened, lost in selfish brooding. The others . . . they didn't know how he felt. Could it be that it *is* necessary to sacrifice the principles that were their foundation? Could it be that survival depended on knowing when to set aside rules? No, please . . . no. If he felt he had a choice, he might choose to simply flee from it all.

The Thane, an ippicator, ran alongside a stream. Green foliage was crushed under his five hoofs, the earth turning black as they pitted the turf. He could sense it, deep within him: the Changing, the day the world would alter itself. The sky was heavy with feeling. Even as he raised his head to look, the clouds dropped the seedlings—the Breathers of Flame—and they descended to sit heavily on the hills above the river: the Change-bringers. He ran along the river, nostrils flaring as he breathed the scent of . . . something new, something fresh. He knew: this would change him, and his fellow ippicators knew it also; as he ran to the Change-bringers, others of his kind joined him. The thundering of their hooves shook the earth, sent birds into screaming flight, battered the trees. But the mud along the riverbank was treacherous. He fell, mewling his sorrow at not being able to see the Change. The muddy waters closed over his head as he bellowed in anger to the bright seedlings on the hill. Water filled his lungs, choking him . . .

The Thane looked into the waters of the river and saw that he wore the face of his true-father. The face was young—and *he* was young once more, just dismissed from the task force that had gleefully joined in the rebellion that followed the suicide-death of the dictator Huard. All his life he'd been trained and honed for that one task—to assassinate that hated despot—and now the madman had taken that life purpose away from him with one stroke of his knife. Chaos, his mentors had always said, is to be preferred to ordered tyranny, to routine tortures, to the rape and plundering of worlds for the satisfaction of one man's twisted whims. If chaos must follow Huard's death, then let there be chaos. But Huard had given no one that choice between order and chaos. He'd removed himself suddenly and without warning: the years, the indoctrination, the education, the training, the fanaticism—all were wasted, meaningless. Nowhere to go, nothing to do. He'd watched five of his teachers immolate themselves on a huge pyre, feeling that their earthly task was now finished. They, at least, had seemed pleased. Everyone with any power or ambition now greedily tried to snatch up their portion of Huard's riches. Garbage pickers. He'd drifted, a trained killer with no reason to kill, a weapon without a target. And he'd eventually come to Neweden, a nowhere world. Yet still a world that could tolerate him only because he was unguilded, lassari, and Neweden would take no special notice of him for that reason. Young, sure, proud—filled with channeled arrogance. Pride that Neweden slowly leached from him. He lived with a lassari woman already cowed from birth, and they had a son. To that son, he gave the knowledge, the training he'd had. On Neweden, if nowhere else, that would be a boon beyond imagination.

The young man had become much like Aldhelm. Aldhelm wasn't of the original Hoorka, who'd been little more than a motley set of half-criminal lassari. Most of those the Thane had originally gathered to him were gone now, dead or drifted away when they found that the code prevented them from grasping the power or riches they wanted. The Thane had been strong, he had been stubborn, he'd listened to no one but himself. Like Aldhelm.

(The Thane, restless, rubbed his eyes with knuckled hands. His movement stopped the dreams for a moment. He touched Valdisa, felt her breasts and idly stroked a nipple until it swelled and hardened. He drew his legs up, cuddling with her spoon-fashion. He closed his eyes: the dreams had waited in the dark for him.)

Chaos *had* followed Huard's death, long decades in which worlds were sometimes out of reach, with no contact from the other worlds of humanity. Colonies were sometimes forgotten, sometimes lost. But the Alliance had come, loosely re-structuring the order of human space, allowing a proliferation of variety but placing the rein of order on chaos. Like all governments, it worked sometimes.

Sometime, he knew, he would have to retire and pass on the figurative scepter. But there had always been one more thing to do, one more minor crisis to settle that, when ended, had engendered another. Now came a major cusp, and he was left with uncertainty and the onus of leadership. He had even lost his name somewhere along that path he'd followed and he was left with nothing but a name/title that was heavy with responsibility and—yes—vanity: Thane. He wanted the burden. He didn't want it.

He did.

Possibly.

In time, he slept, and the dreams left him.

And the next morning . . .

. The annoying whine of the doorbuzzer woke the Thane.

Valdisa, head pillowed against his arm, stirred next to him. "Yah?" he said, tasting the raw settlings of last night's mead in his mouth. He kept his eyes closed.

"A new contract, Thane, with payment enclosed." The doorshield muffled the voice. It sounded dark and distant.

"From whom?" He opened his eyes to see Valdisa staring at him with sleep-rimed eyes. She smiled, closed her eyes again, and snuggled next to him. From beyond the doorshield, he could hear the rustling of parchment, the tearing of a seal.

"It's from the Li-Gallant Vingi, sirrah."

"He's giving us another chance at Gunnar, then?"

Silence freighted with affirmation.

"The Hoorka-thane is here, m'Dame."

"Send him in."

"Yes, Regent."

The desk worker turned from the holo, glanced at the Thane, and pointed to a door across the lobby of the Center. In the high, vaulted ceiling, a glittering spheroid rotated slowly, sending winking lights across the walls and floor.

"Take that corridor, sirrah," he said. "Then enter the third door on your left." The Diplo, halfway through his directions, bent his head to sort through the microfiches on his desk. Varied lights from the receiver set into the desk swirled across his features. He didn't look up again, seemingly forgetting the Thane as the Hoorka, his face set in a scowl, turned and walked to the indicated corridor.

As he walked, he felt resentment building. The cool, impersonal efficiency of the Alliance irritated him like an annoying sound just below the threshold of hearing, sandpapering the bone just behind the ear. Walking into the Diplo Center was to walk out of Neweden's social structure and all that it implied. It took an effort to restrain himself from simply cursing and walking out again, except that he was afraid that such a grandiloquent gesture would be wasted on these people. They simply didn't care. *Hoorka do not beg,* he thought, but he was here not to beg, only to ask advice. He—and his world—simply weren't used to the cumbersome machinery that cocooned a sophisticated society: the words were Cranmer's, from one of the innumerable long talks that had filled their time together. They struck truth. Neweden had been too long isolated from the mainstream of human culture. Enough generations had passed for them to become used to their slower pace, for customs to diverge. Enough time for them to feel resentment tinged with envy at having to confront that sophistication once more.

The Thane counted doors: one, two (with the image of a mother reaching out loving hands toward him—Nordic model, indeterminate features, and not well-crafted), three—there a doorshield dilated, and he turned to stride through.

The Regent's office was not the mirror of his dream image. No, the room was too spartan, an arid oasis in the verdant desert of the Center. The ostentatious splendor was missing—the lack of it caused him disappointment rather than satisfaction, for it made it more difficult to maintain his scorn for Alliance practices. There was an animopainting on one wall and a soundsculpture in a corner. The desk (from behind which the Regent motioned for him to enter) was stripped of any bureaucratic clutter. An inverted d'Embry stared from the varnished surface. She waved a yellow-tinted hand at the only other piece of furniture in the room, a hump-chair extruded from the floor.

"Please be seated, Thane."

He took the chair, feeling it move beneath him as it adjusted to his size. D'Embry folded her hands and rested her chin on them. "What can I do for Hoorka?" she asked, her voice as antiseptic as the room. The Thane realized now, having seen the environment in which she chose to live, that what he had taken for haughtiness was simply the manner of a busy and rather reclusive person. This office wasn't built for visitors, wasn't designed to accommodate anyone other than the woman who normally occupied it. The knowledge didn't relieve him. It was easier to dislike a cultural set than an individual.

"I assume you're aware of the new contract for Gunnar," he said without preamble.

A faint smile ghosted across the Regent's face. "My sources *have* mentioned it to me—and they've told me who signed that contract. Since there is no one else present but you and me, I don't feel any compunction to have it remain a pretended secret between us. I'm afraid I find the Li-

Gallant rather unimaginative. I'd expected—and, I confess, hoped for—a more devious form of testing the Hoorka. I certainly could have devised a better method."

The Thane ignored the last sentence. If it were an attempt at humor, he didn't find it amusing; if it were the truth, he didn't care for her honesty. "Gunnar hasn't the finances to void this contract, no matter who has signed it."

"So you won't admit that the Li-Gallant is the signer? Ah, well. I do realize that what you say about Gunnar's finances is true. His guild is growing in popularity, but popularity, even on Neweden, doesn't guarantee wealth. He's not backed by the right guilds yet, especially since Ricia Cuscratti was killed and her guild withdrew their proxy vote from him. And that reminds me to ask a question. Does it bother the Hoorka that you are essentially working for the rich? It's a point of interest to myself and the Alliance."

The Thane forced his face to show nothing. He made his words sound as icily removed as the Regent's. "In most societies, wealth is a sign of power, real or acquired through other means. Those endowed with survival traits will survive, and money makes survival easier. That's one answer. And remember that we only attempt the assassination. Gunnar can—and did, in fact—escape us. And that's also survival, in a rude and perhaps crueler form. It's real, nonetheless. We've no desire to anger the gods concerned with the timing of a person's life. We are not images of Hag Death, and Dame Fate is our mentor."

"You don't find that philosophy rather simplistic?"

"I leave judgment on such things to scholars like Sondall-Cadhurst Cranmer. The code works, and Neweden accepts it as fitting into their structure. Surely you'll read Cranmer's treatise on the Hoorka, when he finishes it."

"I will." Flatly. Her chin rose from her clasped hands and sank again. Her tunic folded around her neck as she moved, and the Thane caught a glimpse of the ippicator medallion in the hollow of her throat. "It seems cruel," she said.

"The 45th code-line states that the Hoorka will not accept more than two contracts for the life of any one individual."

"Ahh, a change in the code?"

The Thane searched the voice for sarcasm and found none. "An addendum to the code, m'Dame." He spoke carefully, choosing his words. "The code is a growing entity. We've no intention of serving as a policing force for the rich *or* the poor. We endeavor only to be fair—and to survive." *There. Is that what the bitch wants to hear?*

The Regent shook her head. She used little of the current fashion—above the long and narrow neck, only the earlobes were dashed with color: yellow-white beneath the sandy-white hair. "And what of competition? If Neweden can live with one Assassin's Guild, why not two, four, ten?"

The Thane shook his head. "No one else could offer our training, our expertise—and still be content to let the victim live. Neweden won't accept an Assassin's Guild that guarantees death. That would break our concepts of honor, and anger the gods besides. The Hoorka bend that concept, but not dangerously. We fail in perhaps 15% of our contracts, but we *do* fail, and we refuse to overload the odds in our favor. So you see, m'Dame, I don't expect competition. If it comes, we'll deal with it then."

The Regent leaned back in her chair. "The Hoorka are interesting, if nothing else. I'll be honest with you, Thane. I don't think you'd survive for long offworld. Neweden is too precise and sheltered an environment, and that's what nurtures your organization. I think you'd be swamped with complexities once you step from this rural place."

"I would like the opportunity to make that experiment."

The Regent seemed to ignore his words. Her hand brushed the medallion underneath the fabric of her tunic, then lightly swept through the hair behind her neck. "There are a thousand problems I can foresee, one of the largest of which is whether the Alliance cares to have murder—and it *is* murder, however you dress and disguise it—walking the streets of other worlds. However, it's not really for me to decide. The ultimate choice will be given to the individual world governments, once the Diplos make the decision to allow the Hoorka to leave Neweden. And I must be honest with you and tell you that we've had inquiries as to when the Hoorka might be available. There is work for you offworld; for a time, at least."

Abruptly, she smiled, a spring thaw. For a brief moment, the Thane had a glimpse of the person behind the efficient mask she wore, and then it was gone. D'Embry was her removed self again. "You'd have to be carefully policed, Thane, always under scrutiny to be sure of your fairness. Taint the Hoorka name at *all*, and you become nothing more than hired killers—and you can find those on any world, with guaranteed results, also. Shorn of your nice little sophistries concerning survival and chance and the gods, you're nothing."

She sat forward, obviously waiting for some reaction from him. Her eyes wandered from the Thane to the sound-sculpture to the animo, the points that defined the space of her office. He heard the sound of her feet whisking against the grass-carpet, a restless rhythm. The Thane knew, suddenly, that she would say nothing else of any importance, and the irritation he'd felt since walking into the Center grew stronger. Valdisa had cautioned him that this meeting with the Regent would solve nothing, but he'd insisted on arranging it. He railed at himself inwardly. He'd thought he could tell the Regent of the internal conflict that Hoorka faced, make her aware of the way Aldhelm felt and perhaps gain Alliance support for being open and honest, but no . . . She was already unsure of Hoorka and the idea of their working offworld, and any admission of doubt in Hoorka's ranks would mean that they would be confined to Neweden forever. No, he couldn't tell her. Yes, he'd nearly made another error in judgment. *How can I call myself Thane? I should return to the old name and stop this nonsense. The weariness would go away.* And yet he knew he couldn't do that. His pride would wrestle the guilt and strangle it. It was *his* organization—he'd built it and it was only fitting that, if it were to be destroyed, he would be the agent of that destruction.

None of the arguments convinced him.

He felt only doubt.

"If Gunnar dies, what will that prove to you, m'Dame?" His control was faltering. He could feel his voice beginning to rise in pitch and vehemence, and he could do nothing to stop it. Restless, he stood and walked over to the animo-painting, touching the surface with one tentative finger. It felt oily and slick, but his fingertip was dry when he pulled it away. Illusion. He turned to face the Regent.

"If Gunnar died, would that prove Hoorka's innocence?" he asked. "If he lives, would that signify guilt? Is that to be the measure of our judgment?"

M'Dame d'Embry barked a short and unamused laugh. Her feet slapped at the floor. "If he dies," she replied, "it would seem to me that you have no ties with Gunnar—or that your instinct for survival is higher than any artificial loyalty to his guild. Have you ever met the man, incidentally?"

For a brief second, the Thane wondered if she knew of his encounter with Gunnar. But she went on. "It would be quite a coincidence if he lives, given the odds. Doesn't that make sense to you?"

"I've had others say much the same." Thinking of Aldhelm.

"That I can understand." The Regent pressed a contact underneath her desk. The wall to her left depolarized and a lemon wash of sunlight flooded the room. The Port basked in afternoon sun. Both the Thane and the Regent looked at the scene: Neweden metropolitan pastoral. The Thane looked away first.

"It's still possible Gunnar may escape, m'Dame. Dame Fate smiled on him once before, and may again. His odds remain the same as the last contract, and he escaped us then."

"Which is what began this entire uproar. Are you warning me to expect him to slip past you once more?"

"The victim always has his chance."

"Even Gunnar? When the Li-Gallant will be very angry?"

"Yah."

"That is good, I suppose." Unconcerned, she watched the bustling disorder of the Port outside. Then, as if she was suddenly reminded of something: "Would you care for tea or breakfast? I've yet to eat today." Again, she smiled at him, but this smile had the plasticity of a professional tool, a rehearsed gesture.

"M'Dame, all I wish to know is whether you'll give consideration to our request to be allowed offworld—*if* the Hoorka can prove our innocence to your satisfaction."

"And if the answer would be, ahh, no?" She turned to him, the smile still on her face. The Thane suddenly remembered where he'd seen its twin, on the face of Gunnar.

He chose his words with care, speaking slowly. "Then the Hoorka would be compelled to do whatever best suits them for their continued existence on Neweden. I won't allow the Hoorka to die, m'Dame."

D'Embry nodded, but her mind seemed elsewhere. "Thane, I promise you only that we will be watching this very carefully."

"But you'll watch?"

The Regent nodded her head. She looked once more at the scene revealed in her window.

"Nothing is certain in this world, Thane. Huard thought his empire would last centuries—it died with him. I once thought that I would be satisfied with the span of years given to me." She turned back to him, and the smile had gone sad and genuine. "You may rest your mind on that one point, Thane. We will watch."

Chapter 12

IT WAS PERHAPS a measure of Gunnar's altruism that, when the contract was made known to him, he immediately sought refuge in solitude rather than remaining with his guild-kin.

Or—perhaps more likely—those kin, fearing for their own lives, simply refused to aid him and forced him to flee. The truth was never revealed afterward.

Whatever the reasons, it made the task simpler for the Hoorka. They had been forced to storm citadels of resistance before and it had always been costly in terms of lives, even those of Hoorka-kin. It didn't often happen—the Hoorka, by the code, would make no attempt to deliberately kill anyone but the contracted party. Neither would they do anything to endanger their own lives; if that meant others must die, then it would be so. It was, then, with a certain amount of relief on everyone's part that the news was received: Gunnar had fled—alone—to the forested ridges of the Dagorta Mountains. Stone could hide Gunnar, but stone wouldn't suffer from misdirected stings or a vibro gone amiss.

The report from the shadowing apprentices stated that Gunnar had carried with him neither weapons nor bodyshield. The Khaelian daggers were once again laid out for the use of the Thane and Aldhelm—for the Thane had once more changed the rotation of the Hoorka. It was true that the two Hoorka who owned that turn—Ric d'Mannberg and a young woman named Iduna—protested the change, but the Thane was adamant. He told the Hoorka council that the assassins would send their two best representatives. Privately, the speculation was that the order had been shuffled so that the Thane could have the advantage of Aldhelm's skill while keeping him under observation. After all, they said, wouldn't the two most accomplished and skillful kin have been Aldhelm and Valdisa?

It was not far past midnight when the Thane and Aldhelm caught up to the apprentices. One of the shadowers gave them a final report and traced on a map the trail Gunnar had taken and where he'd last been seen: he was a few kilometers away and, they said, showing signs of tiring. Another apprentice would be awaiting them not far ahead.

The Thane shrugged his nightcloak over his shoulders and stared into the rustling darkness that flowed under the trees. A cry from some nocturnal animal shrilled nearby, and starlight brushed a white-blue patina on the edges of the foliage. Sleipnir was just rising above the slopes but its light barely reached the clearing in which they stood, though the trees upslope cast futile long shadows into the valleys.

"Let's go, then," said the Thane. He turned to the apprentices and handed the map back to them with a nod. "We'll contact you if we need assistance with the body. Keep the flyer in the vicinity, in any case. It's been fueled, and the kitchens have provided a hot meal for you."

"Yah, Thane. Good luck to you both." The apprentices, in a shivering of darkness, left the clearing. The moon eased itself higher and the tops of the trees were touched with its brilliance.

Without a backward glance at Aldhelm, the Thane set off into the forest, closely followed by the other assassin. Both knew that nothing had been decided. Their ride to the foothills of the Dagortas had been silent, each of them content to think his own thoughts rather than dealing with pleasantries and inconsequential topics, all the while skirting the areas that caused pain. The Thane knew he should have spoken and tried to lance that wound before they were in the field, but he found himself unable to begin. He'd spent the flight staring at the moonlit landscape below. For punishment, Dame Fate now sent to him the specters of his own fear and guilt. They chased him, even as he pursued Gunnar.

The trail had been marked by the apprentices— luminous patches that adhered to the trees or glowed in the dirt.

The path meandered up and down the rough slopes, always leading deeper into the forest. It seemed obvious that Gunnar had planned this flight well. The cover was thick and abundant, and their quarry would be difficult to track down, since the code forbade their use of infrared devices when the victim was unarmed and unshielded. Ahead, if their map was accurate, the ground cover would thin out as the mountains began to rise in earnest to the heights—but there they would be forced into a slower pace because of the slopes.

The Hoorka said nothing. They used their energy only for pursuit and left their thoughts unvoiced. The Thane's apprehensions gave that silence no peace. He wondered what Aldhelm would do, and his mind provided him with frightening scenarios. He wondered whether he could really stop his kin-brother or whether he even wished to do so. For the first time in his memory, he could feel a situation controlling him, rather than the reverse. He hated that sense of frustration and blamed himself for its presence. He glanced back at Aldhelm, but the Hoorka seemed intent only on following the track of the apprentices—*his* harbored doubts, if any, seemed well-hidden. The Thane envied Aldhelm his seeming peace.

Three hours later, they came upon fresh traces of Gunnar's flight—a rudely trampled section of underbrush. The scent of broken milkpods was heavy in the area, and the whitish secretion from the plants slid stickily down the sides of the broken stalks. The remaining apprentice, McWilms, was waiting there for them. He leaned against a gnarled tree trunk, his breath labored and sweat from his open sleeves steaming in the night air—it was far too chilly for the summer attire: the Thane shivered in sympathy.

McWilms greeted them, then pointed to his left. "Gunnar's not far ahead. I was within sight of him not ten minutes ago. If you continue at your present pace, you'll catch up to him shortly. He seems tired, but he's not slowing as much as I'd expected. He's in good shape, sirrahs."

"Hag Death can chase a man beyond his normal limits. Is there anything else we should be aware of?" The Thane and Aldhelm both crouched down, stretching tired legs and regaining their breaths.

McWilms started to shake his head, then shrugged and

gave a sheepish grin. "Not really, Thane. I once thought I heard a movement behind me, and turned to see what I thought was a small globe in the air ..." He laughed in short, quick gasps. "But it was gone before I could even be certain I truly saw it. It was probably nothing: the moonlight, a reflection, fatigue and Sirrah Felling's bad cooking ..."

The Thane glanced at Aldhelm with apprehension, but the assassin didn't seem to be listening to the conversation. Aldhelm was staring upslope to the path Gunnar had taken. The Thane felt his stomach knot with sudden tension as possible implications occurred to him. *Hover-holos. The Alliance could be watching. She said they would.* Possibilities. He wished he could believe in McWilms's reflections.

Still, he said nothing of this to the others. They dismissed McWilms, the Hoorka rising to their feet as the apprentice took his leave.

They followed the spoor of a desperate man, now; a man who knew he was being followed and who left behind the detritus of panic: broken twigs, a fragment of neo-cloth impaled on thorns, a muddy slope furrowed by fingers grasping for holds. The forest thinned, the trees moving farther apart as if tired of each other's company. Moonlight dappled the ground as they crossed rock- and boulder-strewn fields carpeted with thick grasses that clutched at their nightcloaks as they passed. Twice, they caught a glimpse of a figure before them; each time it disappeared again, rounding a boulder-fall or passing a shoulder of a hill. Gunnar was moving with a certain confidence, keeping the Hoorka a constant distance behind him. They saw no indications that he was tiring now. The situation frustrated the Hoorka and profited Gunnar, for dawn was not far distant. Aldhelm cursed openly and exhorted the Thane to move faster. Their breaths were ragged and loud, misting in the early morning coolness.

"Aldhelm, can you see him?"

"No, Thane."

"Damn him." The Thane fingered the hilt of his vibro, stroking the well-used leather of the scabbard. He'd begun to wonder if there would come an opportunity to use the weapon tonight — and, if that were true, whether there would ever be another chance for Hoorka.

"He can't be too far ahead, Thane, and he'll have to rest soon. He can't keep up this pace." The last sentence had the intonations of a prayer.

"Nor can we."

Aldhelm looked back over his shoulder, standing a few meters up from the Thane. Sleipnir arced flame in his eyes. "Do we have a choice, Thane? You know what this contract means to Hoorka. If you can't keep pace with me, I'll go on alone."

"Aldhelm"—the Thane spoke wearily as he felt the old argument starting again—"remember the code. Please, kin-brother. We don't *have* to be this concerned about the victim. If he lives, he lives—it is Dame Fate's decree. It shouldn't matter to us." *No, but it does. You know that as well as Aldhelm. Why do you lie to Aldhelm when he knows that you don't believe your words any more than he does?*

"If Gunnar lives, we die. That's a decree I won't accept." Each of the last words was uttered in an explosion of breath, the syllables separated by silence. The grass beneath them rustled with harsh whispers. "We've gone over this point too many times, Thane. You can't deny that you think I'm right. Gunnar *has* to die tonight, no matter how that's accomplished. He's even helped us. Look around. There will be no witnesses here."

The Thane shook his head, refusing to acknowledge the truth of Aldhelm's words. Yet the Hoorka's reasoning had taken root in the uncertainty of his mind. "No," he began, half-heartedly.

"Yes!" Aldhelm cut in sharply. "You've become ... I don't know. Soft, perhaps. You're certainly not looking at this realistically. And I'm not the only Hoorka-kin who feels this way." Aldhelm spoke in almost a pleading tone, and with a touch of sympathy that hurt the Thane more than his former harshness.

Of course he speaks harshly—I was never gentle with him, but always masked affection with gruffness. I taught him, and can one blame the pupil for emulating the teacher?

The Thane stared at the rocks about them, not wanting to speak. No, he couldn't see any sign of the watching eyes that m'Dame d' Embry had hinted would be there; no, there was no sign of Gunnar. "And if the Alliance is watching?" he asked finally.

"It's a risk we have to take. She of the Five will watch for us." Aldhelm's voice softened, but his eyes were hard and unrelenting. "I've nothing but respect for what you've done in the past, Thane. Leave, if you don't want to be sullied by this, but Gunnar will die tonight."

So easy. It would be so easy to listen to those words and walk away. All I need do is acknowledge that I've lost and Aldhelm deserves to be Thane. And perhaps he does . . .

"We lose our integrity either way, Aldhelm." The Thane's voice was touched with a weariness beyond the physical. He continued the dispute more from duty than conviction.

"Would you have integrity or survival? You heard it said the other night—the created must transcend the creator. And his rules."

"Or is it simply that you don't trust those guidelines, Aldhelm? If so, *you* are the betrayer of your kin." The Thane scuffed his boots against the ground. Gravel rasped against leather. He was anxious to move on. The longer they delayed, the more chance Aldhelm would need to put his ideas into reality.

Aldhelm, perhaps sensing the Thane's thoughts, turned and walked away without answering the Thane's last comment. The Thane watched him go. He put his hands in the pockets of his nightcloak, shifting his weight from one leg to another. He looked at the ground, then at the dwindling back of his kin-brother.

Then, slowly, he followed.

It was nearing dawn when they finally saw Gunnar once more. The man was scrambling up a ridge many meters above them, a deeper darkness etched against a satin sky. Either he couldn't see the assassins below him— wrapped as they were in their nightcloaks—or he no longer cared. He glanced downward several times, but made no move to seek cover. He fought his way upward. The stillness carried the sound of falling pebbles to the Hoorka.

"We have to get closer, Aldhelm. The daggers won't reach him at this distance."

Aldhelm made no reply. He stared at the figure above him as if the intensity of his gaze could halt the man's flight. Then he swept his nightcloak over one shoulder and drew an instrument from his pack. It glistened metallically in the moonlight. The Thane recognized it with a chill—an aast, a weapon that did for sonics much what the laser does for light—and he knew the charade was over.

"Aldhelm, Gunnar has no shield. An aast . . ." And he knew that Aldhelm was aware of that, and that he was simply wasting his breath.

Aldhelm fitted the power pack into its sockets and aligned the sights. A high keening wail like distant death came from the shielding of the weapon—Hag Death's cry.

"The code, man—"

Aldhelm whirled, his nightcloak moving. "*Damn* your code!" His lips were drawn back from his teeth in a grimace. He turned and sighted down the barrel. Above them, Gunnar reached for a handhold.

"The Alliance, then!" The Thane's voice was loud with desperation, though his mind told him to let it go, to be silent and watch as his days as Thane ended. "Think, kinbrother. They might be watching. D'Embry told me, promised me . . ."

Aldhelm shouted. *"No!"* A screech, a scream; the word struck rock and echoed through the peaks nearby. Against the stars, Gunnar turned, startled.

"Aldhelm, the Regent will protect us if we follow the code. I feel that to be true."

"I can't believe that, Thane. I'm sorry." Aldhelm held the aast in position, waiting.

And, at once . . .

Gunnar stood, momentarily a silhouette against the night sky. Aldhelm's finger convulsed on the triggering mechanism and a banshee howling cleaved the heavens. The Thane tugged at his side and loosed a dagger.

Aldhelm fell, his cry of rage shocking the mountainside.

Gunnar scrabbled his way to the top of the ridge and over.

It was done.

Her gray eyes watched with bland interest, a cool amusement. Head and shoulders; her features floated in the holotank like a dismembered corpse, the ivory sheen of the ippicator medallion bright against her sallow skin.

"So, Thane, it is over?"

He shrugged. "Yah. And you saw the hunt, m'Dame?"

D'Embry nodded. "I just ran the film through a viewer

here—I assume that the one apprentice spoke to you of the hover-holos, since it did appear that he saw them. At that point, they were near Gunnar."

"He mentioned them." The Thane sat before the holo-tank, waiting. The call from the Regent d'Embry had been waiting when he'd returned to Underasgard. He supposed that he should be feeling apprehension and anxiety as he waited for her to speak, but he was too tired. He sat slump-shouldered in his chair. He felt surprisingly little at the moment. "And what of the film, m'Dame? How does it reflect on Hoorka?"

"Accurately. And interestingly." Her hand appeared at the bottom of the holotank, fingering the ippicator bone that hung there. Suddenly noticing her own gesture, she held the bone out to the Thane. "You Hoorka remind me of the ippicator, you know. An odd combination of features that doesn't seem viable, yet you exist."

"The ippicator died."

"So must we all, sirrah." She let the medallion drop against her throat once more. "That was close, Thane. Very close."

"You've made a decision, then?" He didn't care what the answer was. He swore by She of the Five that he didn't care.

"I have some contracts here for you to examine once you come to the Diplo Center again." She did not smile. "I'm not sure I approve at all personally, but I can't in conscience delay any longer. That news should cause rejoicing among the kin, neh?"

He should have felt vindication. He should have run shouting for Valdisa and his kin. Instead, he sat and stared at the mud on his boots.

Aldhelm awoke with the unsmiling face of the Thane hovering above him. Beyond the face he could see the fissured walls of Underasgard. He felt the coarse nap of a blanket against his arm, and to his ears came the faint sound of voices beyond the closed door of the room. Alive, then, he thought. Alive. He closed his eyes, inhaled, and opened them again.

The Thane was still there.

His face evidently echoed his surprise and relief at finding himself in other than the Hag's domains, for the Thane moved away and spoke.

"That's right, Aldhelm. You're back in the caverns. And you're still breathing. You may thank Dame Fate that I'm still capable of disabling a man without killing him."

With an effort, Aldhelm managed to struggle to a sitting position—the Thane, seated on a floater next to the bed, made no move to help him. Something tugged at Aldhelm's side and he grimaced at the sudden shock of pain. Burrs from the Dagorta underbrush dotted his clothing and the nightcloak laying across the foot of the bed. A med-kit weighted down his chest, the pinpricks of the IVs giving him a vague discomfort. His mouth was dry and stiff. His words rasped and scraped their way from his throat.

"The contract . . . ?"

The Thane shrugged. "Gunnar lives. Still."

"And the Li-Gallant Vingi?"

"As you might expect, he is rather perturbed. But he can do nothing. The Assembly will protect us. The other guilds were given a full report by the Diplos."

The Thane found himself reluctant to talk. Here was his revenge, and yet he was reticent to flaunt it in Aldhelm's face. He forced himself to continue. "The Alliance had been watching, as I said they might be. The Regent showed Vingi their record of the night, and distributed copies to other guilds, here in Sterka at least. Vingi is satisfied—publicly."

The Thane's gaze was like the sting of a weapon.

"I did what I thought best for Hoorka and my kin," Aldhelm said. "By She of the Five, I thought I was right."

"Really?" The Thane couldn't keep the sarcasm from his voice.

Before Aldhelm could reply, a young apprentice knocked at the door and entered the room, the light of the main caverns flooding in behind her. She bent her head in salutation. "Thane Valdisa has received a new contract, sirrah. She'd like you to see it."

"Tell the Thane I'll be there in a moment."

The apprentice bowed once more and left them. Silence threatened to smother them.

It was several moments before it was broken. "Thane Valdisa?" Aldhelm's voice was a fragile melding of melancholy and question.

"I—" A pause. "I dealt poorly with this whole situation. If I'd been a stronger leader, perhaps you wouldn't have had a dagger in you, perhaps Eorl wouldn't have been killed. And Valdisa is capable, perhaps not as good a knife-wielder as you, but she follows the code." The Thane shrugged. "So I'm no longer the Thane. I've taken up my true name once more: Gyll—though I've heard some refer to me as Ulthane. An emeritus title for the creator, neh?" He smiled, wanly.

Again, silence came between them. There was nothing to say. After a moment, the Thane nodded his leave to Aldhelm and left the chamber.

Cranmer was waiting for him outside. The scholar had evidently been repairing his voicetyper—ink stained his forehead. The Thane smiled at the sight, and Cranmer inclined his head toward Aldhelm's room.

"How is he?"

"Upset."

"I don't blame him, but he'll understand in time, Gyll. You did what you needed to do. Events bore you out." Cranmer's hand grasped the Hoorka's arm in affection and concern. "You saved Hoorka from extinction. Aldhelm would have destroyed your kin."

"I didn't do what I did to save Hoorka. I did it to stop Aldhelm. There's a difference. And I don't care for it."

Cranmer shrugged. "Possibly . . ." He shook his head. "In any event, Valdisa—I mean, *Thane* Valdisa—asked me to be sure that the apprentice delivered her message and didn't get waylaid in the kitchens."

"It was delivered. I'm going there now. You can do something for me, also."

"What, my friend? Clean the kitchens, launder your nightcloak?" He spoke with too much good humor.

"Find several apprentices and one large floater. You know where the ippicator skeleton sits in the caves. Collect the head and send it to m'Dame d'Embry. A gift to the Alliance from the Hoorka."

Cranmer whistled. "That's a princely gift, Ulthane. You of all people should realize what it's worth."

"It's a dead animal, scholar. Nothing more. It's worth nothing to Hoorka-kin. It belongs only to Neweden."

Cranmer hesitated, then nodded. He rubbed his hand over his forehead, smearing the ink. "As you wish, sirrah. I'll take care of it immediately, and I'll let Valdisa know that you're on your way to her. Talk to you later, neh?"

"I'll have all the time you'll need."

"Good." Cranmer walked away, an off-key whistling echoing in his wake.

Gyll leaned against a wall as his thoughts lashed at him. To hear another person called "Thane" had struck him more deeply than he wished to admit. At least he was still Hoorka, he reminded himself, still of the kin.

He hoped it would be enough.

DANCE OF THE HAG

FOR JOHN MASSARELLA
—who made the dance begin,
and who never saw the first one

Chapter 1

SHE HAD A NAME, but she would not let it enter her thoughts. It was archaic, a useless symbol of the past still clinging to her like an autumnal leaf, dead and lifeless—like an ippicator. Her existence belonged to the Dead now; the past was something she had forcibly torn from her mind. It had been a systematic pillaging, a harvest all of discarded chaff, pain and disappointment and too few joys—the onus of being lassari. Now she had no past to haunt her and no future to mock her with false hope. There was only the long and endless present and the companionship of her fellow Dead.

The Dead had no names and no kin. They were beyond the dull hurt of their lives. They had only themselves and the everpresent specter of Hag Death, leading them on their procession to Her. They gave no notice to anyone else.

Yet tonight she could almost feel the brush of the Hag's talons against her skin. The presence stirred the air, made her forget the wall between herself and the world Neweden. She could smell the miasma of decay, the sweetness of rotting flesh. The presence moved with familiarity in the land.

As if it was very secure in its domain.

Close, very close. It was as if Hag Death mocked her with Her gap-toothed grin, as if—turning quickly, gasping—she would see Her and the end of this life would come.

There are always endings.

The Dead were encamped on the plain of Kotta. Someone had found the ambition to start a small fire: it threw a wavering circle of yellow warmth across the dry grass. There was little food to be had; those of the Dead that still had the desire to feed themselves were now huddled about the blazing sticks, silently eating. The woman who had sensed the presence shook her head at them, then turned outward to the plain once more, snuffling like an animal. Yes, it was there, mingling with the odor of burnt meat and unwashed bodies (for why should the Dead, who counted themselves beyond the ken of life, care for hygiene?). It was a spice smell and the cool sweetness of rich earth: the spoor of the Hag wafted to her, elusive, on the northern breeze. She shook her head, lashing her neck with stringy, grease-matted strands of hair as she strove to capture the essence moving over Neweden. She concentrated on feeling that ethereal world that lay, a gossamer veil, over reality. This was a meditation she practiced while marching with the Dead, during the long days while they chanted the eternal mantra. She often saw visions through the marches. Once, even the face of Hag Death had appeared to her, and she had trembled at the thought that the Hag had come at last to claim her.

No—she berated herself, pushing the thoughts away—*the Hag would come in Her own time.* Now she must get beyond the aching of her hard-callused feet, the itching of her flaking scalp, the hard knot of hunger in her belly.

Yes. The sense of presence was still there, but she despaired of its coming nearer. She tugged at the ragged tunic falling down one shoulder, sniffing. She hunkered down on the earth, gasping handfuls of dirt and letting it fall back through her fingers. She stared at the darkness beyond the fire.

A star moved in the sky, from east to west.

She knew, suddenly, that this would be a full night for Neweden, an evening of unrest. The Hag would see to that: She was full of cold mirth and an uncaring amusement. The woman found herself hoping that the presence would turn to her. Then, perhaps, Hag Death would embrace her at last. *The Hag would pull her to Her sagging breasts, drooping blue-veined over her stomach. She would suckle the bitter milk of those paps as the taloned hands of the Hag tore open her skin, as if it were the husk of some insect. The empty body, bloody, would be disdainfully cast aside for the maggots, and Hag Death would draw out her naked soul and place the morsel in Her broken mouth.*

To join with the All-Dead. To be, finally, at peace.

Letting the last of the dirt fall from her hand, she lay down on the high grass. Around her, the Dead—perhaps thirty of them in this group—slept or chanted or simply sat. The stars veiled themselves in cloud. Sleipnir, rising, colored the horizon with milky blue-white.

She wondered again at the Hag's presence. Who would She touch? Who were they?

The city of Remeale sat on the edge of the Kotta Plain, near Arrowhead Bay's triangular mouth. It was a mining town, a dirty and poor city perched wanly by the ravaged hills, a spectator to the exhumation of the earth's riches. Sectors of Remeale were legendary for their filth and anarchy—"a lassari from Remeale" was a vile description for any person on Neweden, a vivid insult even if somewhat of a cliché— and those sectors were noted for their ability to supply anything anyone might want of an illicit sort. By day, Remeale was merely shabby; at night, it took on a filthy animation.

Here, two shapes moved in the black night, cloaked with rough capes dyed matte ebony and gray.

In this burrough, dying buildings leaned drunkenly toward each other, at times meeting in a decaying embrace above the narrow streets, trapping foul darkness below. The walkways, littered with the detritus of humanity, weren't wide enough to allow a groundcar passage; at various places, a person walking would find himself crowded by the houses on either side or need to duck beneath an obstruction half-seen in the night. Even with the daylight, some part of the evening remained, darkening the area, making it a twilight landscape viewed through a dingy gel.

The two intruders came to a brief halt in a doorway. The smaller of the specters leaned against a doorjamb that was many degrees from vertical.

"How close do you think we are, Ric?" The voice was a light contralto, pleasant even though roughened by whispering.

Light flared by the larger shape, which rapidly took on substance and form: a massive man enfolded in a cloak as dark as the streets around him, his face doubly hidden by a beard and longish blond hair glowing ruddily in the light of his handtorch. The light died as quickly as it had come, and he waited for his night vision to return.

"He's close, if the apprentices have done their work well—and remind me to tell Thane Valdísa to repair this damned map. The light's gone out in it, and I don't like using the handtorch. We've still hours left to the contract, though. Dawn's at 5:56:40, and it's barely one at Underasgard."

"Good." Iduna sighed and pushed herself erect. "Let's move, then. I want some time to do other things before sleeping."

"Need a partner?"

"Certainly." She touched his arm briefly, a quick caress. "Let's get this over with."

Masked again by night, the two Hoorka made their way down the tangle of streets, half-running and keeping to the sides of the walkways where shadows cloaked them. The Hoorka were rarely bothered by others, especially when on a contract, armed and alert, but they wanted no interference tonight. They turned at a corner where a hoverlamp sputtered fitfully and cast a dancing illumination over a sated wirehead sprawled in the intersection, his open eyes glazed and unfocused. He moved fitfully, spastic, as the Hoorka slipped past him.

They went by a large house where some celebration was evidently in progress. The Hoorka could hear conversation, music, and—once—a scream that held genuine terror, a ululation of horror. D'Mannberg paused a moment, listening for the repetition of the scream, but Iduna touched him on the shoulder, shaking her head. They began moving once more into the maze of tiny streets and claustrophobic alleys.

It was only a few minutes before they came to a small square where the buildings leaned away from each other to form a marketplace. Empty stalls sat in disordered ranks around the area; a few hoverlamps bobbed in their holding fields, throwing erratic shadows about the houses bordering the square. The Hoorka paused in the dark mouth of an archway leading into the marketplace, searching for any movement before they entered—Hoorka had been killed on contract before; that knowledge bred caution where the assassins suspected traps. It was, after all, the victim's right to escape in any way he could. Dame Fate had no special dispensation for Hoorka, and Hag Death did not care who

fell into Her maw. It was best to pray to She of the Five
Limbs, the goddess of the extinct ippicators and patron of
the Hoorka, and to be careful.

There was a man in the square.

They both saw him in the same instant. He sat on an
overturned crate on the far side of the market, staring dully
in their direction. The hoverlamps threw a gigantic shadow-
parody of him on the wall behind. At the foot of darkness,
he looked very small and fragile.

D'Mannberg squinted into the light. He nodded to Iduna
and the two assassins walked slowly into the open space,
drawing and activating their vibroblades. Their footsteps
were loud in the night stillness, and the vibros gave forth a
low humming that resonated and built, echoing from the
buildings. The man made no move to flee from them. He
watched the Hoorka approach, his face resigned and hopeless, his hands clenched between his knees. His head
dropped slowly as they came nearer to him, as if he were
unable to hold its weight any longer. By the time the
Hoorka stood before him, he was in a huddled crouch. They
knew he could feel their eyes on his back.

"Cade Gies, stand up." D'Mannberg's voice, though
pitched softly, sounded loud in the square, deep and ritualistic. Iduna, beside him, looked briefly at the walls flanking
the market. Heads had begun to appear at a few of the windows, curious people staring down at the tableau below
them. It didn't matter. The spectators didn't look as if they
intended to hinder the Hoorka in their task, and it was better entertainment than that offered by their holotanks.

Gies made no movement, still tucked against himself.
D'Mannberg, glancing at his companion and the silent witnesses around them (lips drawn back from his teeth in a
snarl of distaste at the watchers), put his hand on the man's
shoulder. He felt Gies shudder at the touch and move away
with a soft moan. The assassin tightened his grip on the
cloth and pulled. Gies came stiffly to his feet, hands balled
into impotent fists, his eyes closed and his head averted. He
waited, a thin, soft wailing escaping his clenched teeth.

"Cade Gies, your life has been claimed by Hag Death.
Dame Fate has severed the cords of your existence."
D'Mannberg's words were brittle with ritual, but then they
softened in pity/disgust as Gies suddenly jerked away from

the Hoorka and doubled up, retching dryly. D'Mannberg stared down at the frightened man. "We're not monsters, Gies. You're a slave of the Hag, but we can make your passage to Her easier. It needn't be painful or frightful." His voice was a whisper, harsh in darkness. Gies did not reply. Still hunched over, he spat once, then again, wiping his mouth with the back of his hand. His breathing was rapid, wheezing from his lungs.

"Look at us, Cade." Iduna's velvet voice seemed to calm him. Gies stood, slowly, his gaze sweeping over the onlookers, now leaning on their elbows in the windows. His broken stare finally came to rest on the Hoorka. He saw two pairs of oddly sympathetic eyes. The rest of their faces were masked in their nightcloaks.

"Death comes to each of us," Iduna said. "Even as an offworlder, you can understand that. Hag Death will have Her due. And we Hoorka are but instruments in Dame Fate's hands."

"They're not my gods." Gies's voice was a cracked whisper, his eyes as wild as an animal's, pleading with their moist softness.

"You're on Neweden, and those are the gods that rule here."

Gies shook his head. "I don't believe in gods."

"Then simply believe in death," d'Mannberg said. "You had your chance to escape us and you chose not to run—the apprentices explained your alternatives to you." D'Mannberg's voice struck at Gies as if it were a weapon. The man shuddered under the impact.

"You're going to murder me!" His last words were a frantic shout that echoed back to them from the surrounding walls.

"Not the Hoorka," d'Mannberg replied, very softly. "We're but weapons in another's hands. The guilt, if any, belongs to them."

"Who?" Gies demanded. His hands clutched at the assassin's nightcloak, and d'Mannberg backed away a step.

"I can't tell you."

"Tell me, if you have any compassion. I'm dead anyway—what difference would it make? Tell me, so that I can haunt her from my grave."

D'Mannberg glanced at Iduna, an exchange without

words. "I don't know who signed the contract, Gies. I would tell you if I knew, but I don't. I'm sorry."

Gies swayed softly, as if he might fall. D'Mannberg reached out to steady the man. "I can't tell you," he continued, "but your kin will know. All Neweden will know. Our code commands that all successful contracts be made public. You can be assured of that."

"It's not *fair!*" He ended with a wail. A few more windows dilated to reveal new spectators.

"The Hag is never fair." Iduna held out her hand to Gies. The man looked down, as if expecting to see a vibro held there. But the palm held only a small gelatin capsule.

"Take it, Gies. It'll make your passage to the Hag enjoyable." Iduna waited as Gies reached out with a tentative forefinger to touch the capsule. He had small hands, dainty hands—he had not seen much labor. His fingertips trembled, and he hesitated, looking at d'Mannberg.

"Consider the alternatives, man. Would you rather I used my vibro?" He held out the weapon to Gies. Its angry snarl was frighteningly loud to the man. Gies, his lips tightly clamped, shook his head.

"It doesn't matter," he said. "Oldin—she wants Neweden, and she'll take it as she's taken everything else." He grasped the capsule gently between thumb and forefinger—always with that slight aura of the effete—and held it for a moment near his mouth. "She'll destroy you, too. You'll see."

With a convulsive movement quite unlike his normal demeanor, he tilted his head back and swallowed.

"Soon?" he asked.

D'Mannberg nodded.

The two Hoorka moved back from Gies as he sat on the crate once more. Gies stared at the assassins, blinking slowly. He grinned, abruptly, then giggled, a sound that, reverberating, became a full manic laugh. D'Mannberg glanced about the market: they were still watching, the silent ones, leaning forward now as if they wanted to be closer to the moment of this pathetic man's death, as if the Hag might momentarily become visible as She came to collect the proffered soul. D'Mannberg knew that this night would fill the next morning's conversations.

Gies was still laughing when his body found that it could

no longer support itself. He fell backwards to the ground
and rolled onto his side, his legs doubled up, fetal. He took
a deep, rattling breath that began to dissolve into hilarity,
then was suddenly still.

Silence wrapped the square as the Hoorka switched off
their vibros.

Iduna took a spare nightcloak from her pouch, handed
one end to d'Mannberg, and together they covered the
body. The onlookers slowly began to withdraw, the windows
going opaque as they returned to more private diversions.
Distantly, they could hear a complaining voice and loud
music beginning in mid-bar.

"At least this is over," d'Mannberg commented. He
hefted the body of Gies across his shoulders, grunting with
the weight.

He was wrong in that. It was just beginning.

"You're just reflecting your own doubts, Gyll. The meeting
wasn't run that badly, no matter how you view it. Bachier's
challenge couldn't have been anticipated. I thought Thane
Valdisa handled herself well."

"To a point, Cranmer. I saw her, I know what I would
have done in her place, a few months ago. Bachier wouldn't
have been cut by kin then. Gods, man, I have a good deal of
affection for Valdisa, both as a friend and a lover, but I can
see that she shouldn't have been so abrupt with kin. They're
all proud people. Leadership doesn't have to mean heavy-
handedness."

"And it's always easier to criticize from the outside.
Look, you're feeling an understandable loss of control since
you abdicated in favor of Valdisa. Couple that with the last
several contracts you've worked and your, ahh, irritation . . ."

"Forget the last contracts. Just—*shh,* be still."

Ulthane Gyll and Cranmer were in the outer caverns of
Underasgard, with the moon Sleipnir throwing cold light
past the jagged mouth of the Hoorka-lair. Gyll, sitting
slump-shouldered on a boulder, suddenly lurched erect and
stared intently at a cave-rodent moving slowly across the
broken floor. Cranmer, wrapped in a thick nightcloak,
curled his lips, wrinkling his nose in distaste.

The rodent, a stalkpest—a furred body with patches of

open sores (it had evidently been in a recent fight), a small head from which the thin whip of its eye-sensor sprouted, a lithe quickness when it moved—stopped, started, and crept forward again, always closer to Gyll. Underneath his night-cloak, Gyll fingered the hilt of his vibro as Cranmer glanced from stalkpest to assassin.

The stalkpest stood on its hind legs, the eye-sensor slash-ing like the tail of a nervous cat, then inched forward. Gyll lunged, the vibro hissing from its sheath already activated, the arm plunging down. The stalkpest keened in surprise and terror, the body convulsing against the weapon that pinned it to the ground, the claws skittering helplessly. Gyll flicked off his vibro and sheathed it. He prodded the body with a boot tip.

"One less to get into the stores," he said.

Cranmer, from his boulder seat, shivered. "The damn things give me chills. How can you stand to get near it?"

"A Neweden axiom, scholar—to kill with honor, you must always be near. Our Ulthane taught us that." The voice came from the darkness of the corridor leading back into the caverns. Gyll and Cranmer both turned to see Ald-helm regarding them. His nightcloak melded with the cav-ern's eternal gloom, but Sleipnir's glow played on his face—light eyes above the furrow of a scarred cheek. "Good evening, Ulthane, Sirrah Cranmer," Aldhelm said, nodding to each in turn. His gaze went to the bloody stalk-pest. "Practicing, Ulthane?" A faint smile seemed to twist the ridge of the scar. "A pity our victims are rarely so easy."

Gyll felt a rising anger, fueled by the sarcasm he sensed in Aldhelm's voice. The last three contracts he had worked, the victim had escaped: Cranmer had mentioned it already this evening, and Gyll had been soured by the Hoorka Council earlier. Gyll had heard the whispers of his guild-kin. *Ulthane Gyll doesn't seem to care for the hunt any more—I was with him, and he didn't seem concerned, didn't have the sharpness he once had. He looks like he's brooding, lost. He's gotten out of shape—he doesn't work enough with long-vibro and foil. He thinks about the victims, wonders about their lives. He's depressed, moody. Ever since he named Valdisa as Thane . . .* By the code—Gyll's code—the victim must escape from time to time, but for the Hag to go hungry on three consecutive attempts: it could simply be

Dame Fate's will, but the whispers and the well-meant jests from his kin hurt, made him narrow his eyes in irritation.

"You think I need the practice, Aldhelm? Is that your intimation? Because of the contracts?"

Aldhelm moved in darkness, frowning. Rock scraped rock under his feet. "I didn't say that, Ulthane."

"You didn't have to." Gyll swept his nightcloak over his shoulder. Moonlight glinted from the vibrohilt at his belt.

"Ulthane," Cranmer began from his seat, his voice uncertain. The short, thin man cleared his throat. "I think—"

"I was speaking to Aldhelm, scholar." Gyll did not look at Cranmer, but at the other Hoorka.

Aldhelm stared back. "When I failed *one* contract—yah, it was the Li-Gallant's and thus important, but you teach us that each contract is as important as the next—you gave me this." Aldhelm touched his cheek and the high ridge of the scar. "We all fail contracts, Ulthane. You set us up that way when you created Hoorka. It's what sets us apart. If your failures bother *you*, well, I think you need to shrive yourself, not be angry with kin." Aldhelm's face was set in careful stoicism, neither smile nor frown.

With the words, Gyll felt his anger cool. *Of all Hoorka-kin, he has the most right to taunt you, and he doesn't. You called him a friend once, after all.* But Aldhelm had opposed Gyll on the two contracts the Hoorka had worked for the Li-Gallant Vingi, both intended to kill the Li-Gallant's political rival, Gunnar. Aldhelm had twice felt the touch of Gyll's vibro, and whatever affection they had shared had gone with the blood. Gyll didn't apologize to Aldhelm, but nodded down at the stalkpest.

"Cranmer and I came out here to see if d'Mannberg and Iduna were back, and I happened to see the 'pest. It'll feed my bumblewort instead of raiding our grain." Gyll stopped, noticing the bulging pack under Aldhelm's nightcloak for the first time. "You're going out?"

Aldhelm stared at Gyll, defiance ready in his eyes. "Yah." For a moment, it seemed that he was not going to say more, but then he hefted the pack, adjusting it around his shoulders. "There's an Irastian smith in Sterka, visiting. He's reputed to be very good with blades. I'm taking a few things to show him, and I'm also going to see what he might have for sale." Aldhelm's affection for edged weapons was well known among Hoorka.

"You've gotten Thane Valdisa's permission?"

"After the uproar during Council last night? We both saw the blood from Bachier's wound, Ulthane—and I'm not saying it wasn't what he deserved for arguing with the Thane. But I'm not going to risk my own skin by leaving Underasgard without telling her first."

"I thought she had sufficient reasons for making the ruling," Cranmer said. He had wrapped the cloak more tightly around him; the offworld scholar had never gotten used to the cooler Neweden climate. "With the reports of lassari attacks on lone guilded kin, and Eorl being killed in an unprovoked assault, it makes sense to know where all Hoorka are."

Aldhelm nodded. "I realize that. You don't have to lecture me, scholar."

Though the man's reproof was gentle, Gyll's irritation rose once more; he was silent a moment, forcing it down with an effort. *So quick to anger of late—calm down, old man.* "Go on, then. But be careful, Aldhelm. The kin can't afford to lose you."

"I'm always careful, Ulthane. And I'm also very good with my weapons—I'd worry about the lassari, not me."

Gyll watched as Aldhelm strode past him to the cavern mouth. Gulltopp had risen—its crescent grinned below that of Sleipnir. Aldhelm was briefly a silhouette against the backdrop of night sky (twinned shadow dark on the jumbled rocks of Underasgard), and then he moved on into the night.

Carefully, Gyll picked up the stalkpest in a fold of his nightcloak. "For the wort," he told Cranmer.

"Aldhelm seemed angry." Underneath cloth, Cranmer hugged himself.

"He's always angry," Gyll said. He stared past the cavern mouth to the dawnrock standing lonesome in the clearing and the newly clothed fingers of the trees beyond. "It hasn't killed him yet."

The grounds outside Gunnar's window lay hushed in twilight, which was quickly arranging itself in the darker shades of full night. Sleipnir was up, Gulltopp was rising. Gunnar stood before his window for a long minute, staring at the landscape that surrounded his guildhouse, then he touched the contact that opaqued the glass. A wash of purplish black swirled in the panes; then the tendrils met, snaking about each other, swelling until all was black. Gunnar turned back into his room.

He was not feeling well tonight. A vague boiling churned in his gut and a sour taste lurked in the back of his throat — though, he mused, one might expect such reaction after the evening's dinner. De Vegnes had been the cook for the night; his tastes ran to the unusual, the exotic, the highly spiced. Such fare tended to unsettle the stomachs of guild-kin used to a blander and more provincial menu. But if he wanted Potok to be able to speak before the Assembly next week, he would have to ignore the moaning of his stomach and work. Gunnar shook his head: Potok was an excellent speaker and a charismatic personality, but he needed to be fed the words he regurgitated. He was never able to create them himself.

The Muse of Speech was resting this evening. Even Gunnar, usually quick and facile, couldn't find the words he needed — every phrase that appeared in the terminal of his desk seemed clumsy, falling over itself with pretentiousness. Gunnar clutched his complaining stomach, grimacing. He finally sighed in resignation and reached for the wooden box that sat on one corner of the desk. He opened the mala-wood lid, taking out the black silk that held his Tarot. He toyed with the cards, turning them in his thin hands and leaning back in his floater. He riffled the deck, though his mind was still entangled in the forest of Potok's speech. He thought — as he did every time he handled the cards — that he would have to have them reproduced soon. They were simply too old and fragile for his constant handling. The trader from whom he'd purchased the cards claimed that they came from Terra herself. Extravagant tales of their lineage aside, the cards were ancient in appearance if not in fact: they were printed on cardboard, the image inked on the surface, two-dimensional. The corners were soft, bent, dog-eared with use, and one of the cards — the knight of swords — had once been folded in half.

Abandoning all hope of finding an opening for Potok's

speech, Gunnar spread the cards face down on his desk and plucked a card from the array.

The Tower: an edifice crumbled to dust in the midst of a storm, while figures plunged to their deaths from the ramparts. An eye veiled in clouds watched impassively from above. Gunnar shook his head once more, his narrow face pinched in irritation. The card was ill-omened, not that Gunnar professed a belief in the card's ability to predict events. His attitude was more that of an interested skeptic, though he did feel that a person of some power had once possessed the cards, and that this imagined person had been able to use them to peer murkily into the many possible branches of the future. For his own part, he doubted that Dame Fate would be willing to reveal Her whims so easily. There were times: more than once he had thought he could discern a pattern to the cards that had fallen into a reading, some cohesiveness that suggested a single course of events.

The Tower, then: danger, destruction of plans, ruin. Gunnar tossed aside the card and pulled another from the pile without looking at its face. He held the card in his hand for a long moment, his eyebrows lowered in concentration, studying the intricate scrollwork on the back. The Sun, he guessed.

The Devil. Fate, blind impulse, a secret plan about to be executed: from the card's face, a horned goat stared at him balefully, a scepter before it, and figures below the animal joined in mystic symbols.

"Well, then I'm to be damned and double-damned," he muttered. He threw the card down.

"Light," he said, and the room brightened in response to his command, the hoverlamps in each corner irising open. "Enough." Gunnar leaned forward, gently moved the cards to one side, and touched the metal circle of a contact on the desk's surface.

He leaned back once more, hands behind his head, eyes closed.

"Some notes for you, Potok. Though I think I might end this by telling you not to listen—I think de Vegnes's supper has ruined my sense of composition.

"Point One: that Oldin woman insists that our guild will figure prominently in her plans, though she's yet to give me any indication of what that might mean. She smiles when she says it, and she has a predatory smile. And she's also as closemouthed about her 'plans' as a puffindle. I think we might do well to find out more about her and the Families—she's only been here a few months, but there's been more disruption around Sterka in those months than in the last five standards. There might be a file on the Family Oldin in the Alliance Center. An offworlder isn't going to react as will those of us born to Neweden, and we can't expect her to have our best interests in mind. We need to know which way she'll jump if we push. By all means, bear in mind that you can't trust her—she's an avaricious bitch and she'll go whichever way promises her the most, and I know she's had meetings with the Li-Gallant as well. We have to be in a good position to promise her more, or she may start dealing with the other side. Butter up that tongue of yours, kin-brother. I expect miracles of it."

(His eyes shut, his back to the window, Gunnar did not see the darkness swirl or the stars become visible through the now clear pane. Nor did he see the apparition that appeared there: the head and shoulders of a person wearing a light-shunter. His/her features were torn and scrambled, waves of pulsing shadow moving erratically. Dark against blackness, the head turned and fixed upon Gunnar.)

"I'm going to work on your speech tomorrow." Gunnar stretched his legs out beneath his desk—a joint cracked loudly. "We have to stress the fact that our guild has gained in strength in the last several months. I actually think that I have the Hoorka to thank for that, having failed to kill me twice. It certainly put us in a good light with the other guilds. We'll cite all the economic woes that Vingi's rule-guild is causing. And I'll hit hard on the ippicator smuggling and the lassari troubles—that's Neweden's lifeblood. I expect you to have them shouting by the finish, so we can call for a vote of confidence in the Assembly. We'll lose, but it'll give an indication of the rate of erosion in support for the Li-Gallant, and it might just throw a scare into Vingi. If we can force him into an open election . . ." Gunnar's voice trailed off. His eyes opened, questioningly. He sensed something *wrong* with his room, though he could see nothing out of place. He started to turn in his floater, to rise.

He had only a brief second to glimpse the night-veiled face at the window before the soundless blast of a render tore the substance of the glass into dust and then struck him. His face contorted in agony so intense it did not truly register as pain. The render shredded the fabric of his chest, the living cells ruptured and smashed. Gunnar fell backwards over his desk, his flailing arms scattering the cards of his Tarot. The body, unwilling to admit the reality of its death, jerked spasmodically, then finally lay still.

The face at the window (an elusive and vague outline, a monstrosity of fluid shape) stared into the room for a few long seconds before dropping from sight.

Alarms, far too late to help Gunnar, wailed through the house.

Morning.

The sunstar lathed the Kotta Plain with heat and light. The silent call of dawn woke the small encampment of Dead. Drowsily, they rose at the light's beckoning, gathering their chimes and censers and bells. Someone—an emaciated young man, the filth of the five-day journey across the plain on his body and a scraggled, matted beard of indeterminate age masking lips cracked bloody with heat—began a plainchant, a dirge of greetings to the Hag. The morning offering to their patron rose from the several throats to be snatched away by a westerly breeze.

They readied for the day's march. Though no one spoke to another—conversation was also a thing of life—they knew that they would reach Remeale before the sunstar set again, and perhaps the Hag awaited some of them there. If not, they would seek Her beyond. It was a simple axiom: the encounter with the Hag was inevitable. Until that time, the Dead paid no attention to those that still sought their living dreams on Neweden.

Even the living would one day find the Hag waiting for them.

They were standing now, waiting for one of their number to take the initiative and begin the march. A fume of incense wafted ahead of them, and they were now assembled in ragged order. The chant wavered, then altered itself. It had been noticed that one of their number lay still and unmoving in the grass—a woman, dressed in a soiled, torn tunic. She had been with them for some time, and the Hag had come to her during the long night. They chanted their praise to the Hag. Still singing, the Dead began the slow, inexorable parade to nowhere, leaving the body on the grass of Kotta Plain.

When the noise of their passage had subsided into a faint treble chiming (the Dead now dark specks wavering in the heat of the horizon), the carrion eaters came. They padded toward the abandoned campsite and the burnt circle of grass, moving with habitual caution, stopping every few seconds to sniff the air which reeked of human spoor.

They found the gift that had been left them. If they praised any god for the bounty, they did not say.

They merely feasted.

Chapter 2

Excerpt from the acousidots of Sondall-Cadhurst Cran-mer, taken from the notes of his stay with the Hoorka assassins of Neweden. The access to these notes are with the kind permission of the Niffleheim University Archives and the Family Cranmer.

EXCERPT FROM THE DOT OF 2.27.216:

"I'd thought that the Thane—no, dammit, Gyll isn't Thane anymore; I'll learn that one day soon—I'd thought that Ulthane Gyll had managed to stagger toward some even keel with the Hoorka, but that optimism might have been premature. It's partially his own fault, I admit, and he'd probably admit it also: his ambitions for Hoorka, to see them implanted offworld and escape the bounds of Neweden, are likely to lead to problems. And despite his resignation and the conferral of power to Valdisa, I suspect that Gyll still tries to guide the Hoorka through her, thus removing the guilt of failure by one place.

"No, that's unfair as hell to Valdisa . . . Gyll is proba-bly learning that if he wanted to use her as a figurehead, she will not play that game with him. She's a strong-willed person in her own right; I hope I'm wrong, but I expect the two to come to some confrontation over that.

"The Hoorka are still not politically stable. Certainly the Li-Gallant Vingi holds a grudge against them, as it's an ill-kept secret that it was *his* contract for Gunnar's death that was twice failed. Or, as Gyll would probably say: 'Gunnar was blessed by Dame Fate.' Since the Li-

Gallant holds the reins of power on Neweden, the Hoorka are not going to be given any concessions in their quest to become independent of Neweden, though Gunnar's rule-guild is gaining in support, by all indications I've seen. The problem that's making all that significant is the caste-bound social system of this world. In time, there might have been a slow, natural progression away from the idea of guild-kinship, but the Alliance has put too great a strain on the structure—cracks are beginning to appear, for Neweden finds itself no longer alone. In particular, the lassari are responding to this and becoming militant, no longer content to accept their role as the dregs of Neweden society.

"Now if I can remember to correlate and substantiate all this in the eventual paper ..."

(Here there is the sound of glass against glass and liquid being poured. The transcriber was turned off; when the recording resumes, the time-tone indicates that it is a few hours later. Cranmer's speech is noticeably slower and muffled.)

"The, ahh, social structure here hasn't been subjected to outside influences in centuries: the planet was only on the outer fringes of the Huardian Empire and never knew the yoke of that Tyrant's oppressions; before that is the long darkness of the Interregnum, with only a modicum of contact from the Trading Families. And Neweden was settled only after the First Empire fell apart—that's *your* area of expertise, Bursarius—yah, I know you'll listen to this when I ship it back to Niffleheim, and I'm not going to meddle with that pot of history.

"A point. Is there any significance to the fact that Neweden was settled not by a normal outward push of humanity, but by a group of exiled bondsmen?

"Wandering again ... I'm glad I'm the only one that has to listen to these dots, and I apologize to my future self for all the maunderings. And of course to you, Bursarius. You still there?

"Umm ... I know I wanted to say something else. Oh—the Hoorka code still bothers me, despite all of Gyll's rationalizing. It sets them apart from the common criminals and makes them viable in Neweden society, but it also makes them susceptible to damage from outside change. When Neweden society eventually shifts, as it's going to, I'm afraid the Hoorka will find themselves just one of the corpses in the pile.

"By all the gods, that's a gory image there. Too much binda juice again . . ."

(Here there is the sound of Cranmer drinking, followed by another refilling of his glass. At that point, the transcriber was shut off once more.)

M'Dame Tha. d'Embry, Alliance Regent for the world Neweden, was not pleased with the way the day had gone thus far. She'd awakened to a dismal rain that left the sky a uniform, wan gray. There was also a constriction in her chest that made breathing difficult until she grudgingly let the autodoc in her room minister to her for a few minutes. Her left arm still felt the prick of the unit's sensors, and the constriction, while lessened, was still there, a faint shallowness of breath when she exerted herself. And the rain had not stopped when she'd reached her austere offices in Diplo Center. Outside her window, the ranks of clouds sat unbroken across the sky, and water pooled on the flat expanse of Sterka Port.

The news, when she'd asked Stanee for her report of the night, had not been encouraging: Gunnar had been killed, assassinated by an unknown assailant in his own guildhouse. She'd drawn back from her viewer in genuine shock. Murder, the cowardly slaying of someone without declaration of bloodfeud, was a very rare occurrence on this world. It was far too easy to gain satisfaction through duel. And Gunnar's rule-guild was second in power only to that of the Li-Gallant Vingi. It had been reputed that Gunnar would one day wear the robe of the Li-Gallant; it could not happen now. D'Embry decided she would not like to see this morning's Assembly meeting.

A dim suspicion formed in her mind. "Stanee, is there any indication that the Li-Gallant might have been involved in the murder?"

The face in the viewscreen—amber hair short at the sides and cascading unshorn down the back, lips and earlobes and eyelids touched with shimmering lapis lazuli; all the latest fashion done correctly but without dimming the counter-impact of a plain face—frowned below d'Embry's field of view. "No, m'Dame, though let me check with Intelligence." A moment's pause, then Stanee looked up once more. "By all reports, all of the Li-Gallant's guard force is accounted for last evening; the Domoraj had some festivity. Unless Vingi used a hireling, maybe a lassari . . ."

D'Embry cut off her speculations with a wave of her veined hand. "No, I doubt it. Let it go, let it go."

"Will there be anything else, m'Dame?"

D'Embry ran a hand through dry, whitened hair, glancing sourly out the window to the damp morning. "No. You may return to your other duties."

"Thank you, m'Dame. Oh, Karl's asked me to remind you that Kaethe Oldin of the Trading Families has entered the Center. You'd asked to see her today. Did you want her sent up immediately?"

"Shit," d'Embry said, loudly, then smiled at the shock Stanee tried unsuccessfully to mask. "Surely, child, you didn't think we relics lack the words to utter a curse?"

A tentative grin.

"Send her in, Stanee. I wish I could avoid it today, but why ruin a perfectly awful morning." She sighed, then frowned as a twinge of pain accompanied her next inhalation. "That's all." She reached out with a quick gesture. The screen flickered and went dark, receding into the floor. D'Embry sat back, gingerly testing her breathing and awaiting Oldin's entrance.

Kaethe Oldin was tall and rather too heavy for the standards of Alliance beauty—the legacy of low-gravity life. Yet she carried it well. Her demeanor spoke of confidence in her appearance. The face was angular, a denial of the body's weight. Above high cheekbones, her eyes were large, dark, and impressive. The woman evidently knew the impression they made, for her eyebrows were gilt, drawing immediate attention to the walnut pupils below. The stamp of Fitz-Evard Oldin, head of the Oldin conglomerate, was in his granddaughter. Her attitude told d'Embry more than she wished to know—Oldin strode into the Regent's office with no hint of timidity, nor did her gaze move from the Regent to the soundsculpture in a corner of the room or the animo-painting on one wall; her entire presence exuded purpose. When she stood before d'Embry's desk, it was with one hand on her hip, the other thrust into the pocket of her pants.

"M'Dame Oldin, the Alliance is always pleased to welcome a member of the Trading Families." The words came fluidly from her, but the Regent's intonation was deliberately cold and removed. *It's so easy to fall into after all the standards of practice—that aloof Diplo manner. It's been so long that it sometimes becomes the reality and not the mask. And it's far too late for me to change.* "I once knew your grandfather. You remind me of him."

Oldin flicked her gaze over d'Embry, and the Regent felt as if she'd been dissected, judged, and dismissed: yes, her grandfather's legacy. He'd had the same disdain for the Alliance, the same subliminal declaration of challenge. D'Embry didn't find the realization particularly satisfying.

"Yah, he'd mentioned that you had banned him from Crowley's World after a disagreement over trading rights. He said to give you his regards, Regent." Oldin's voice was bitter honey; a slow, pleasant alto that hid all the meaning behind her words. With her attitude, with her tone, Oldin reminded d'Embry that the Trading Families were not part of the Alliance, that, at best, the two factions enjoyed an uneasy truce.

"I hope you didn't find my request inconvenient."

"It wasn't particularly convenient, Regent—I've duties aboard *Peregrine*. But the Alliance rules here, doesn't it?" Oldin smiled.

"Rule is a poor word, m'Dame. The Alliance is more flexible than that. We oversee, advise, or leave a world as it wishes." D'Embry folded her hands on her desk—fingers tinted yellow-orange with bodypaint—and allowed herself to sit back in her floater. "Would you like to sit?" She touched a stud on her desk, and a hump-chair extruded itself from the carpet.

"I'll stand if you don't mind, Regent." Oldin glanced at the chair, then back to the older woman. Again a slight smile touched the edges of her mouth.

Bitch. Like FitzEvard, yah. "As you wish." D'Embry shrugged. "And since this *is* an inconvenience to you, I'll be brief and frank." Deliberately, she stared at Oldin, meeting her dark eyes. "As a matter of course, I receive all Hoorka contracts here, since they've applied for and been granted temporary offworld visas. Your name was on the contract the assassins worked last night."

"Everyone knows that, Regent. The body of Gies was given to me at my shuttle on the Port. The Hoorka made no secret of that—it's part of their code, is it not?" Her gilt eyebrows flashed reflected light, but she did not blink or look away.

"Cade Gies was an Alliance citizen and an offworlder to Neweden." D'Embry's voice held a cold edge; she pulled her gaze away in anger, glancing at her window. Rain sheeted down the glass. When she looked back, Oldin was examining her hands, unconcernedly; long, thick fingers, broken nails.

"Gies *was* an Alliance citizen," Oldin replied, emphasizing the past tense with a nod. She shoved a hand back in her pocket, put the other on her hip. "And I'm of the Families, and *your* allegiance is to Niffleheim. But we're all on Neweden. It seemed fitting that I, ahh, deal with our conflict, Gies and I, in Neweden manner. That's the Trader way, Regent. When I've dealt with aliens, I've tried to adopt at least a superficial gloss of their customs. The Alliance would not understand that." D'Embry opened her mouth at the unsubtle hint of Alliance xenophobia, but let the woman finish. "I wanted to see the Hoorka work, in any case. They're an interesting group, don't you think?" Oldin's voice was casual, lazy.

"On other worlds of the Alliance, a 'conflict' doesn't have to end in death. Gies wasn't a physical man nor was he easily given to entering arguments. I knew the man slightly, m'Dame Oldin, and I'd be curious as to the nature of your altercation."

D'Embry's voice had risen and she found herself sitting forward in her chair, her back erect. The chest pain of the morning returned, suddenly, and she found it difficult to take a deep breath. She forced herself to relax. *Be calm, old woman. You're giving her exactly the reaction she wants.*

Oldin watched the Regent. She shifted her weight from one foot to another, staring as the Regent made an effort to control her pique. "There's nothing you can do about it, Regent. I violated no laws, and Cade Gies was given every opportunity that would have been given any Neweden kin—or that *you're* going to give other Alliance citizens by allowing the Hoorka offworld work. Are you going to inquire into the disputes for every Hoorka contract? The argument between Gies and myself is my own business—I won't bother you in your areas of authority; please give me the same consideration. I'm here to sell my stock, nothing else." Oldin paused. "With all due respect, Regent."

"All of Neweden falls under my authority, m'Dame."

"It must be a heavy burden." Oldin's voice was just shy of open sarcasm, but her eyes danced under the golden eyebrows. "If there's nothing else to discuss, Regent, I do have work on *Peregrine.*"

As Oldin began to turn (the stocky body eclipsing the rain-smeared window), d'Embry stopped her with a tapping of fingers on wood. "Trader, Neweden is not an open port. You'll abide by all the regulations and restrictions here. I can assure you that I'll be watching you."

Oldin spoke over her shoulder without looking back at the Regent. "That's as Grandsire Oldin said it would be. I can quote verbatim the text of the Families-Alliance Pact— all of the Oldins can. It was drummed into our heads very early. I *know* the rules of this game, Regent." And she walked away with a casual, quick stride, barely giving the door time to dilate.

D'Embry, after the door had shut once again, thumped her fist against the desk. *"Games!"* she shouted. "The woman speaks of *games!"*

"This is no longer a game, Li-Gallant—it has happened too often for us to remain complacent. The facts are known to all of you: a Hoorka contract was signed for the death of Gunnar. Twice, he escaped the assassins. Ricia Cuscratti, the betrothed of Gunnar, was slain by as-yet unknown assailants. Now Gunnar himself has been shamelessly murdered, a deed without honor done in a most cowardly manner. Is there anyone here that wonders why all my kin cry out for the blood that is our due?"

Potok stood in the Assembly Hall, resplendent in the shimmering turquoise robe of the rule-guild. The sleeves of the robe were ripped and tattered: the sign of his grief. The seven windows of the dome above him, each rendered by a rival artisan's guild, were dull with rain, the colored, shifting glasses wavering with collected water. The sunstar hid behind shifting clouds, unwilling to illuminate the murals. Potok flung his arms wide, displaying his raveled, savaged robe.

The Assembly was unusually quiet. Normally the representatives of the various rule-guilds heckled and insulted one another, interrupting the order of business. But now the echoes of Potok's stentorian voice died unchallenged in the vast chamber as the representatives stared at him, afraid to break that silence: the death of Gunnar had shaken them all, for it violated the foundations of Neweden. If Gunnar could be killed in this manner, what protected their own selves?—the thought, uneasy, ran through all their minds.

"There is a vile cancer gnawing at the vitals of our society." Potok let his voice drop into a rasping half-whisper. It pulled the Assembly forward in their seats, made their eyes squint in concentration as they strained to hear him. Again, Potok found himself wishing he had Gunnar's gift for words—this speech had been written by de Vegnes, and Potok could sense that, cliché ridden, it lacked the fury the subject should have possessed. *My voice of fire and steel,* Gunnar had once said, referring to Potok. But now that voice was deprived of the mind behind the words, shorn of substance.

Still, it could have its effect.

"There are those among us that would drag Neweden down into chaos, would destroy all that guilded kin have striven to create. My fellows, Neweden has at its core the idea of honor and truth. We do not hide behind our hatreds or our loves. Yet Gunnar has been taken from us, taken by a dishonorable act. It insults us, it laughs at us. No matter how high or powerful, if we wish to keep Neweden as it should be, we must find that diseased part and *cast it out!*"

His voice had risen to a thundering crescendo. He spoke with a grimace of rage; a fisted hand struck his palm with fury. He waited, but no one dared to mar the quiet. To the rear of the hall, someone muffled a cough with a hand.

"My guild-kin mourn. We weep. We are lost in sorrow. Our sadness is greater than any words I can speak. Gunnar was guild-father to us all. He cannot be replaced. But he may rest in the assurance that he will be revenged. I vow now that he will be given a companion for Hag Death. My guild declares bloodfeud. When this coward's name is known, we demand our satisfaction. Give him to us, as you would a common lassari.

"We cannot be comforted, we cannot be placated. We demand" — a pause — "that the government of Neweden extend all its powers to find the killer of Gunnar. This unknown person struck not only at Gunnar, but at each and every one of us. He struck at the heart of Neweden, and Neweden must show her anger." Potok slumped forward suddenly, as if weary. His voice was a harsh whisper. "I can say no more to you."

Now he sat, his arms dropping to his sides as the sunstar slid from behind a cloud momentarily, lighting the dome with brief shafts of colored light. The first tentative waves of applause broke, then became a flood as the rest of the Assembly, in a rare showing of mutual support, acted as one.

(De Vegnes leaned forward toward Potok, sitting stolid and solemn as the ovation continued. "That was a nice touch, waiting for that rift in the clouds," he whispered. "I noticed you watching for it. Good timing, Potok." Potok did not reply, but the faint hint of a smile raised the corner of his mouth.)

The applause cheered him. Even the Li-Gallant, who had little affection for Potok and his rule-guild, found it politically advisable to force his massive bulk from his floater on the dais and add to the storming of hands. When the clamor began to show signs of abating, he sat quickly and gaveled for attention, the amplified thud of wood on wood sharp in their ears.

"The Assembly is grateful for your words and sympathetic to your feelings, as you must know, Representative Potok." Vingi's voice was ponderous, as heavy as the frame from which it emerged. Corpulent, huge, the Li-Gallant fingered his several chins as his rings flashed light. "You may rest assured that my guard force will do everything in its power to find this person. I will command the Domoraj to begin immediately. Gunnar will not go to Hag Death unattended. We've always had the greatest respect for him." Vingi folded his thick hands on the desk before him, staring down at the Assembly.

Potok exhaled noisily, a sarcasm that only de Vegnes, beside Potok, could hear. Nodding at the Li-Gallant, Potok whispered sidewise to his kin-brother: "They'll probably be just as effective in this as they were when he vowed to find Ricia's killers." The murderers, who had slain her when Gunnar was first involved in a Hoorka contract, had never been apprehended. "I suppose I have to be polite, though."

Potok stood once more, bowing slightly to the Li-Gallant as etiquette required. "We extend our thanks, Li-Gallant. The skills of your Domoraj and his force are well documented." *Let him chew on that and see if it adds up to a compliment.* "My kin and I will endeavor to find this dung-heap of a person as well. The formal declaration of blood-feud will be posted before the Assembly tomorrow—a blank certificate until we have a name. We ask also that a formal day of mourning be declared for all Neweden, an official recognition of all that Gunnar has done for this world. It seems appropriate."

Now, for the first time since Potok had begun speaking, Vingi's face revealed his quick irritation, his mask of sympathetic attention slipping. A scowl bared his teeth. His fingers clenched once and he moved back in his floater, the chair dipping in the holding field as his bulk shifted. It was only a moment, then his face took on once more the aspect of intent seriousness. His voice, when he replied, was as soft as fur.

"It's unfortunate that such an action is not within this Assembly's province. We've no machinery to set such a day aside—we can ask that all guilded kin abide by our wish, but it is a matter of their own discretion. Beyond that"—he raised his arms in a shrug—"we have no power."

Potok flashed anger. His voice, a whip, lashed at the Li-Gallant. "Do you say, Li-Gallant, that you simply don't wish the Assembly to make such a motion? All we ask for is the gesture. The guilds will always act as they wish."

"We'll give all that's within our power." Vingi nodded to Potok, his trebled chin waggling.

"And that is nothing."

"This is an Assembly of the rule-guilds of Neweden, man. I understand your grief and sympathize with your great loss, but we have other duties here. Would Gunnar have wished us to stay idle?"

"You will not make the motion?"

"We can't walk away from the responsibilities we have for the death of one man."

"And what is more important than *your* life, Li-Gallant?"

Vingi smiled. In him, it was not a gesture of mirth. "We ignore a great many insults when in session, Representative, and your sorrow must be taken into account. But I won't ignore covert threats. Withdraw your words."

"Will you make the motion?"

Potok stood defiant, hands on hips, the tattered sleeves visible to all. Vingi stared at the man. Neither moved, neither spoke.

The Vingi sighed. "With the understanding that this will be entirely voluntary to all guilds, I make the motion. I'll have the cleric draw up a proclamation and have it posted. It will be by order of the Li-Gallant, and I'll not call for a vote on this. Are there objections?"

Silence.

"And for your part, Potok?" Vingi scowled down at the man.

Potok, hiding his satisfaction, bowed deeply to the Li-Gallant. "I spoke far too hastily, I'm afraid. I hope that you realize that my mind is addled by grief, and forgive me." Then, under his breath: "You slimy bastard."

Only de Vegnes heard.

Valdisa was a warm softness beside him. Gyll still breathed heavily from their lovemaking, sweat cool on his chest. She cuddled into the curve of his arm, resting a moment, then — with a low growl of mock anger — turned to nip the flesh of his shoulder with strong teeth.

"By the Hag's left teat —" Gyll slid away from her, rubbing his shoulder as the bedfield rippled around them. On his flesh, the impression of her teeth showed white, fading slowly to a dull red. "That *hurt*. What did I do — or didn't I do — to deserve that?" His face was creased in overdone bemusement, the lines about his eyes deepening.

He was answered by an unrepentant giggle. *"That,"* she said, very deliberately, "was for your lack of support during the council meeting last night. A little help from you" — she held thumb and forefinger a centimeter apart — "and Bachier wouldn't have made that firm a challenge. You know as well as I do that he was just testing me."

"You have to pass such tests yourself."

"This one wasn't necessary."

She knelt on the bed, her head slightly tilted, her short hair tousled. Gyll could see the yellow-brown mark of a bruise on her left thigh, a reminder of the fight with Bachier.

"Is this what you think of when we're making love?" Gyll tried to turn the subject, discomfited by her sudden seriousness.

If he expected an apology, he was disappointed. "Yes," she said. Then, as if to take the sting away, she shook her head, grimacing. "No, not entirely. I'm sorry, Gyll. But if I can't expect support from my favorite lover ..." She shrugged, turning her head away.

"I didn't agree with you. It was that simple. Why should the guild-kin need the Thane's permission to go into Sterka when they have no other duties to perform in Underasgard? I never requested—"

"Perhaps you should have," she interrupted, turning back to him. She uncrossed muscular legs, sitting with hands on knees. Her dark eyes challenged him, her chin held upward defiantly.

He reached out for her with a hand. "Valdisa," he began.

She backed away, swiveling from the bedfield with a lithe movement. She went across the room to the floater that held the disorganized pile of their clothing, pulling her tunic from underneath the tangled heap. As Gyll watched silently, she straightened the garment, pulling the sleeves out.

"Gyll," she said, "there wasn't any resentment of the Hoorka until we failed to kill Gunnar. That made us look as if we'd allied ourselves with his rule-guild. That's when all this started."

"Neweden knows the code—" he began as she raised her arms, pulling the tunic over her head. Then she stopped, her head just emerging from the cloth.

"Yah, by the code, some of the victims must escape. But Gunnar was important, a rival to the Li-Gallant. I can understand the reasoning the guilded kin followed. If I were outside the Hoorka, I might wonder myself. Certainly Aldhelm thinks we acted wrong." She tugged the cloth down, pulling it over her small breasts and shaking her head to free her hair from the high collar. "And then Eorl was killed by lassari, or so we both think. We've yet to avenge his death. He still stands alone before the Hag. The Hoorka can't afford any more Eorls."

"And your ruling will prevent that?"

One corner of her mouth lifted: irritation. "Must we argue this again?"

No. How many mistakes did you make as Thane yourself, how many arbitrary decisions made simply because something had to be done, right or wrong! You made yourself resign because of those uncertainties ... But his pride had already spoken for him. "You began the argument." He didn't like his voice. It sounded petulant, weak.

She turned away from him with a raising of thick eyebrows. She pulled the loose trousers of the guild uniform from the clothing (the rest going haphazardly to the stones of the floor) and sat on the floater. From across the room, Gyll could feel the chill of her displeasure.

"If I began it, then let me continue a bit," she said finally. "There are other things that hurt Hoorka, more than any ruling I've ever made. You, Gyll, as an example. You've been involved in three consecutive failed contracts, you who created the Hoorka, who should be a model to them. Your partners in all the cases have indicated that you lacked spirit, that you were slow and seemed uncomfortable."

She could see that her words hurt him. He closed his eyes, as if to deny her existence, but the words still bludgeoned him. With an abrupt movement, a grunt of effort, he sat on the edge of the bedfield. He made a conscious effort to pull his stomach taut, and the unbidden vanity made him angry with himself and, more, disturbed that it was necessary.

"Valdisa," he said. "I think —"

She glanced toward him, her trousers halfway up her thighs, hiding the mottled bruise. She stopped, glaring at him. "You're getting flabby, Gyll. Your muscle tone is deteriorating, and you don't seem to care. You move about as if half somewhere else. You spend too much time inside your head. What's the matter with you?"

He ignored her. "This all started playfully, Valdisa. We were joking with one another, laughing. I didn't mean to hurt you, and I didn't want us to start sniping at one another."

"It was you as much as me."

"I'm sorry for that." He ventured a half-smile. *Please, let's forget this. I don't want to think about it—it haunts me too much already.* "You don't have to leave yet. And besides, these are *your* chambers. I should be the one to depart, tossed aside." He rubbed the gray fur of his chest with one hand. He lowered his head, looking at Valdisa from under the ridges of his eyes. "I'd like you to stay." Softly.

Valdisa shook her head, eyes closed and head raised. She inhaled deeply, through her nose, then let the air escape in a slow sigh. She stood, the pants falling to the ground around her ankles. She kicked them aside, pulling the tunic over her head once more.

"Do I have an apology, Gyll?" She waited by the floater, hands on hips, just out of his reach. Her nakedness taunted him: the darkness between her thighs, the gold-brown areolas of boyish breasts.

"I never meant to hurt you—and I'm always sorry when I do."

"You bastard," she said. But there was a hint of a smile. She came to him; her lips on his, her tongue thrusting into his mouth, and her hands moving low on his body. Gyll tried to respond, but the argument, the recent lovemaking, his tiredness: all defeated him. Valdisa finally rolled away from him, and he reached out to touch her, beginning another apology.

The bell to the room's holotank chimed, a soft insistence. "Damn," Gyll said. Valdisa gave him a glance he could not decipher, then called out loudly into the darkened room. "Yah?"

"Thane Valdisa?"

"Speaking."

"This is McWilms. I was listening to a holocast from Sterka. There's news you should hear."

Valdisa sat, leaving Gyll's side suddenly cold. "I'm listening. What is it, McWilms?"

McWilms said it very simply, and its implications were more intense for the simplicity. "Gunnar's been killed."

Chapter 3

TWO ROOMS, a study in contrasts . . .

. . . Gyll's room, in the labyrinth of Underasgard, was a bare cavern, the walls unadorned dry rock—brown-gray with runneled streaks of some orangish mineral. His few furnishings were scattered about it in no discernible pattern: a bedfield, a floater sitting before a small metal desk at an oblique angle to the wall, a privacy screen in one corner that hid his rack of clothing, and a small wooden table on which sat a cage. The cage shimmered—scarlet lines indicating the perimeters of the field that enclosed a small animal. Gyll stood before the cage, looking down at the bumblewort. It mewled up to him with its small, triangular head and limped to the side of the cage, the large soft pads of its feet still cracked and lined with dark brown—dried blood where the rocks of the hills had torn its tender, unprotected skin. The fur on its soft shell was matted and dull. The wort moved slowly, breathing too quickly, illness showing in its dull gray eyes and the cough as it stopped—half-falling—to sit and stare up at him. Gyll shook his head, reaching down to scratch behind the large oval ears. The wort had been moving better yesterday.

"Why don't you get over this?" he asked it softly, with just the slightest hint of an echo from the bare walls. "If you want to die, you little bastard, you're going to have to do it yourself. I won't help you."

He stood there for long minutes, staring down at the wort without seeing it, petting the animal absently.

. . . Vingi's room echoed wealth. It was large, the walls soft and pliant with hangings that varied their patterns, the warp and woof fluid. His long desk dominated the room,

placed carefully where a visitor would see it first. Its high
polish mirrored the room in reverse. Only the inset screens
of the Li-Gallant's com-link interrupted that brilliance: no
papers cluttered the surface, no stray verticals stopped the
eye. The shape of the room—a parallelogram—the arrangement of the furniture, even the programmed movements of
the hangings, all channeled the gaze to the Li-Gallant.

He sat and watched his com-link, a wash of green from
the unit casting its hue over his face, illuminating it from
beneath. Vingi grinned his corpulent grin. The screen flickered with the evening's news bulletins, all full of Gunnar's
death and its import to Neweden.

The Li-Gallant sighed, sinking back into the pliant grasp
of his floater. "Nisa," he said.

The light from the 'link went green to blue. "Li-Gallant?"

"Have the kitchens send me a small glass of brandy—the
bottle of Neasonier from Longago."

"As you wish."

"And make damned sure the lackey doesn't sample it
himself. Tell him I *know* the level of that bottle and I expect
to find it lower only by my glassful. Have him bring it immediately. Off."

The glow from the 'link died. The Li-Gallant put thick
hands behind his head. He closed his eyes.

Gyll was both hot and uncomfortable. The Hoorka had
gathered in the cavern they used for meetings, and the coolness of Underasgard was tempered by the warmth of their
bodies. The nightcloak Gyll wore chafed his neck. He cursed
the impulse that had caused him to choose the new one
over the bedraggled but soft old cloak. Nor could he seem
to find a comfortable position in his chair. Even the mead
set before him by a dutiful apprentice was warmer than he
liked it. Gyll wanted nothing more than the oblivious comfort of sleep.

It didn't appear that sleep was something he would gain
soon.

The Hoorka had been called together by Thane Valdisa.
The several elders of the guild sat around a battered
wooden table marred with the rings of forgotten drinks.
Hoverlamps threw erratic shadows over them. In one corner, Cranmer fiddled with his recording gear, a look of dis-

satisfied ire on his thin face. The rest of the guild-kin sat on the broken rock around the room, making themselves as comfortable as they could. Around Gyll, a score of unrelated conversations fought each other. He shook his head but could not blame them—the news had caused a flurry of speculation.

Only Aldhelm seemed solemnly quiet. Unlike the others, seated in rude chairs around the table or slouched about the room, he stood against the rock wall of the entrance, his light eyes glancing from one to the other but always seeming to avoid Gyll. His long arms were crossed before his chest, the taut muscles of his forearms standing out in high relief. A gloomy air hung about him, a pall that ignored the brightness of the hoverlamps.

Thane Valdisa entered last. She nodded to Aldhelm as she entered and strode quickly to her seat at the head of the table—with a smile to Gyll in the process. She waited for the talk to quiet.

"I won't bother with normal procedure here," she said when all faces had turned toward her. "We all have heard the news by now, and Gunnar's death may have problems for Hoorka, if it has the import I believe it will have." She swept her nightcloak over one shoulder, moving in her seat. Her forehead was glossed with perspiration. *Simply the walk, or is she that nervous?* Gyll wondered. "I'll let Aldhelm speak now, as he's been in Sterka and has felt the mood there."

Valdisa waved a hand to Aldhelm, who pushed himself from the wall with his shoulders. His hands dropped to his sides. "It's simple enough, Thane," he said. "I heard the news while in the city, and I stayed there long enough to find out what I could, since it seemed to be important to Hoorka." He paused. Gyll saw his hands clench once, then relax. "I'll tell you what little I've garnered. Gunnar was killed by an unknown assailant. The weapon was, by the description I've heard, probably a render. He or she was also very good—from what I was told, the butler posts around Gunnar's grounds did not sound an intrusion alarm, nor did their equipment have any image of the assassin. There have been no bloodfeuds filed against Gunnar or his guild, and he wasn't given a chance to defend himself honorably. It was a shameful murder. And the rumors have already begun. One of them in particular worries me. It's not a pleasant thought, my kin, but the speculations include the Hoorka."

From the table, the deep voice of d'Mannberg dominated the room. "That only makes sense, since the Hoorka failed twice in the contracts with Gunnar. What did you expect them to think, man?"

Aldhelm's face went stony, his jaw clenching, the scar light on his cheek. When he replied, his voice was cool with careful politeness. "What I think isn't important here. I'm concerned with what these rumors mean for us."

Valdisa spoke. "What do they say, Aldhelm?" Her fingertips drummed the tabletop, an impatient rhythm.

He spread his hands wide. "I heard it said that the Hoorka were embarrassed by Gunnar's double escape and that to redeem our gods' favor, we killed Gunnar. And it was also whispered that perhaps we had done this to regain favor with the Li-Gallant."

Gyll shook his head. "No," he said. "I can't believe New-eden would believe such a thing. The Hoorka code is our shield, and we've never been accused of breaking it—if anyone believes we'd abandon it, how are they to place trust in Hoorka?"

Aldhelm shrugged. "Maybe they don't. Maybe we don't give them enough reason to trust us, and give too much leeway to Dame Fate in our contracts."

"If we guaranteed success, we'd be no better than common lassari. I made the code to give us kinship, Aldhelm."

"Gunnar is not the only failed contract we've had recently, Ulthane Gyll. *You*"—with just the faintest emphasis on the word—"should be aware of that."

A frigid rage stabbed through Gyll's composure. The hand went unbidden to his vibrohilt while the other grasped the arm of his chair with knuckles gone white. *You're a failed kin. Three times; not the victim's doing, but your own incompetence.* His own guilt echoed Aldhelm's words, amplifying them and feeding his anger. He spat out his words. "We've had this argument before, Aldhelm, when I was Thane. We're *not* mere assassins—we're instruments in the hands of Dame Fate. Anyone can kill, anyone can do the dishonorable and hire a lassari to do the cowardly deed. We give the option of death *with* honor to both victim and signer. Some must escape, those lucky or fit enough to survive. It will stay that way."

Aldhelm stared down at Gyll, looking significantly at the Ulthane's knife hand. "Survival cuts both ways, Ulthane Gyll. Sometimes to survive, one must change. I'm not afraid of change, and I suspect that the Li-Gallant will now be less likely to harass us."

"We *do not* change, Aldhelm!" Gyll shouted.

"Kin-brothers, please . . ." Valdisa began to speak, softly, but Gyll interrupted her.

"I'll not have the Hoorka a guild that alters itself at a whim. By all the gods, I've finally got us offworld, made d'Embry and her damned Alliance acknowledge us."

"Be silent!" Valdisa pushed herself away from the table with her hands, standing abruptly. Her chair overturned behind her—the clatter of wood on rock was loud in the cavern. "Children," she hissed, her eyes narrowed, "the Hoorka have more important business to discuss than your Hag-damned differences. The practice floor is open—afterward—for a duel, if that's the only satisfaction the two of you will take. But, by She of the Five, we'll keep this discussion germane to Gunnar's death or I'll have both of you doing apprentice work tomorrow. Gyll, *I am Thane*. Remember that, and let me run this meeting."

Silence. Before her anger-sparked gaze, both Gyll and Aldhelm bowed, first to Thane Valdisa, then, with a certain stiffness, to each other.

"Better," Valdisa said. "Better." Behind her, an apprentice moved from the shadows to pick up her chair from the ground and replace it at the table. Valdisa sat, her hands folded in front of her. "Aldhelm, what's the mood in Sterka?"

Gyll watched, still angry, as Aldhelm strode to the end of the long table and leaned down, supporting himself, his fists on the rough top. "Bad. Confused. Angry. Very ugly for Hoorka. I could feel the hostility and hear the murmuring behind my back. I stopped in at a tavern to hear more, and only hesitantly did I get served, with the barest politeness due to a guilded kin."

"Were you threatened?"

A look of scorn. "Not by the barkeep. The guilded kin won't risk a bloodfeud with Hoorka, not yet. And lassari give me a wide berth."

Valdisa frowned. "I'd remind you that Eorl was Hoorka, and lassari killed him, neh?" She cocked her head in question, one eyebrow raised.

Aldhelm straightened, his nightcloak falling around his body. He nodded to Valdisa. "You've made your point, Thane. Forgive me for my presumption."

Gyll watched as Aldhelm went back to his station by the entrance, his movements precise and easy. *Is that why we could never stay close? He's so stoic, so graceful, so confident and self-assured—what I've always pretended to be. Is it envy that causes me to dislike him, or is he truly as dangerous to Hoorka as I think?*

From farther down the table, another of the Hoorka— Sartas— spoke. "My bet is that the Li-Gallant is ultimately responsible for this. That man's a shameless coward, a disgrace to guilded kin." A murmur of agreement came from the others. "Who has better reason to want Gunnar dead?"

"I don't know that even the Li-Gallant would be that foolish, Sartas," Valdisa said.

Gyll nodded his agreement. "Gunnar's rule-guild may well benefit from Gunnar's death in this matter, Thane. I don't credit the Li-Gallant with great intelligence, but he has the craftiness and the sense to have kept most of his power for years. He wouldn't undermine his own position. It's possible, I suppose, but . . ."

Sartas drank from the mug in front of him. Then he thumped the drink back down. "Still, you have to admit that Gunnar's death would give him great pleasure. He's attempted this three times before, twice with us and once on his own. Vingi wanted Gunnar dead." His long olive-tan face turned from Gyll to Valdisa.

Gyll shook his head. He glanced back at Aldhelm. The man stood, leaning back against the wall, arms akimbo under his cloak and his attention on Gyll. Yet—Gyll didn't know why, perhaps something in the man's easy stance, his seeming nonchalance—the glimmering of a faint suspicion came to Gyll: it had been Aldhelm who had advocated the alteration of the code during the last contract on Gunnar, and it had been on that contract that Aldhelm and Gyll had experienced the filial confrontation which had driven a wedge between their friendship. And it had been Aldhelm that had failed in that first contract— and he had felt Gyll's knife for that failure. Aldhelm was a good assassin, good enough to have evaded any safeguards that Gunnar could have set around his guildhouse.

Gyll remembered the pack Aldhelm had when he'd gone out the night before. It was easily large enough to have held a render, and there was one in the Hoorka armory.

No, you old fool, you're letting your paranoia and dislike play games with your common sense. Surely Aldhelm wouldn't do such a thing. But he fell silent, and he looked at Aldhelm with a new intensity.

Valdisa had begun speaking during his musings. " . . . This is all the more reason to continue with the ruling made last meeting. No kin will go into Sterka without my knowledge and permission. And you might do well to be sure that you have a companion, since all the attacks have been on lone Hoorka. You're all well trained, but training means nothing to ambush or overwhelming numbers." Valdisa glanced at Aldhelm. "We keep the code strictly. We perform as we're supposed to. And we should make every attempt to do well—that would do the most to allay suspicions." She waited; a breath. Someone coughed in shadow. Cloth rustled against stone.

"We have a contract for tonight," she continued. Gyll, torn from his inward contemplation, sat up sharply: he was next in the rotation. "It will begin, at least, in Sterka, so Vingi and those that speak against Hoorka will be watching. I can't stress its importance enough, in light of what Aldhelm has told us."

Gyll knew that she was well aware of the rotation schedule, but she would not look at him. He fidgeted, wondering why she wouldn't meet his eyes.

"Who works tonight?" d'Mannberg asked.

"I." Sartas, from his seat, his dark eyes alight.

"And I," Gyll said softly.

"Ulthane Gyll." Valdisa turned to him now, one hand stroking her forehead as if in concentration. Her hand threw deep shadows over her eyes. "I have need of someone to meet Kaethe Oldin tonight. The woman owes us payment for last night's contract. I'd like you to go. She's an offworlder and of the Families, and I'd like to represent us with someone more than an apprentice." She spoke too hurriedly, as if anticipating his anger.

There was silence when she finished. Gyll looked down
at his mug, his hands around it, the fingers stroking the ce-
ramic smoothness. "I work tonight, Thane," he said. His
voice was low, his eyes still fixed on the mug. He waited.
Don't force this, Valdisa.

"Gyll," she began.

He broke in, glaring at her. "Thane, don't say it. I will
work tonight."

She did not look away. Her words were suddenly cold
with distance. "I'll consider your feelings, Ulthane."

He allowed himself to relax slightly. "I thank you for
that."

"Beyond that, I make no promises."

That was all she would say.

The radiance of a captured sun blazed about her, cloaking
her naked body in bronze. She stretched out her arms to
embrace the glow, basking in its warmth and feeling it, a
thousand fingers, on her skin. She sighed, she squirmed in
immodest delight.

"You keep using that and your skin'll look like a liz-
ard's."

Kaethe laughed from within her bath of light. She
reached out and touched one of the four metallic posts that
surrounded her. The throbbing aura began to die as the
posts receded into the carpeting of the floor. "You're too
sour, Helgin. You make up in foulness what you lack in
height."

"Wisdom from the bitch?" Helgin, a Motsognir Dwarf,
scowled up at Oldin, staring at her with eyes the color of
smoke, his gaze unremittingly critical as it moved from
crown to feet. She endured his inspection, smiling. "You're
ten kilos too fat for Neweden—if you didn't choose your
clothes carefully, you'd never get a second glance. And the
Battier Radiance hasn't made a damned bit of difference.
It's a passing fad for the stupid and gullible. That skin's destined to get old just like the rest of you."

"I'll shrivel up and look like a Motsognir?"

"I'm as human as you."

"So you claim." She laughed. Bending at the waist, she
touched the Motsognir's head with cool lips. "Where would
I be without your pessimism, Helgin?"

Helgin backed away from Oldin, two quick steps. She grinned down at him, and he turned his head to spit on the rug of the compartment. "You'd still be your grandsire's whore, spreading your legs for his captains."

Kaethe pursed her lips. "So touchy," she said, as if to an unseen observer. She walked away with her long-legged stride; in the reduced gravity, she seemed to glide. The room was large, by ship standards, as comfortable as her rooms at OldinHome. Deep, soft rugs covered the plating of the floor in subtle earth hues, the deck itself sculpted into irregular hills and valleys— there was no need for other furniture here. The only reminder that Kaethe was on a ship rather than planetbound was a circular viewport that covered most of the ceiling. There, in a sea of darkness flecked with star-foam, Neweden floated, attended by its two moons, Sleipnir and Gulltopp. In this, her refuge, music would come at Kaethe's bidding, the walls would shift, the lighting would respond to her moods; here, she had no pretensions, and here she allowed few visitors. The crew, most of her staff, prospective buyers of the goods stored in *Peregrine's* vast holds: these she would see in the ostentatiously gothic office, two decks below.

Kaethe stretched, yawning, and turned. Abruptly, she sat, lounging back against a carpeted hillock. Helgin followed her graceful movements, glowering at her. He had the typical build of the Motsognir Dwarves, that half-mythical race wandering the frontiers of human space (and, it is rumored, far beyond) since the Interregnum, when the First Empire died and left humanity in darkness. An experiment in genetic manipulation, they had been bred for the heavy planets. The Motsognir were nearly as broad as they were tall, standing about a meter in height, with thick-bunched muscles. Their strength was legendary, as was their vile temperament. The Motsognir, by preference, tended to stay with their own; to see one was something to tell one's children.

"Your trouble is that you're too sure of yourself. What are you going to do when you fail?" Helgin was as hirsute as the rest of his kind. He tugged on the full beard that masked his large mouth.

"I don't plan on failing." Kaethe closed her eyes, relaxing. Stretching out her legs, she hugged herself, then let her arms go to her sides. "I don't care how much you scoff,

Helgin—the Battier makes me feel regenerated and alive,
and you saw that it worked for the Nassaie."

"The Nassaie are avian, not human. You heard what
Nest-Tender said. He didn't think the Battier would work
for us, and wouldn't guarantee there'd be no side effects."

"But we've sold 'em."

"Fools will buy anything," Helgin grumbled, a voice like
rock scraping rock.

"Don't be so damned tiresome, Motsognir. Maybe the
Battier could give you a little height—then you wouldn't
have to worry about knocking your teeth out on somebody's knee," she said sweetly.

"I'd bet on my teeth before your knee, Oldin."

A smile. Eyes still closed, she waved a lazy hand toward
him. "Did you send someone to get the geological reports
Gies left with Renard?"

"I did."

"Good. I'll want to see it in a few hours. Now that Gunnar is dead, we make the shift toward Vingi—and the
Hoorka still intrigue me." She rolled to her side. Kaethe
glanced at the Motsognir, standing—thick legs well apart,
arms folded across his broad chest—near the door. "I read
the profiles on their leaders. You might commend whoever
got them for you—quite good. Gyll Hermond is no longer
Thane?"

"No, but I suspect that he's still their guiding force. They
are his creation."

"I want to meet him then. Get him here."

"You have the most gentle way of making a request."

"Yah. But you'll do it, won't you." The last was a statement, not a question. Her face, for all its smiling, held little
amusement. She seemed more tired than anything. "And
soon, Helgin." Kaethe lay again on her back. *"And* have
Renard told that I want another report soon. He's had
enough time to give us an update."

In self-imposed darkness, she listened to the Motsognir:
a harsh breath, the beginning of another retort, then a guttural obscenity. Helgin's heavy stride hushed on carpet—
even in the light gravity, he sounded ponderous—and the
door slid open with a hiss.

"Helgin."

She could feel his eyes on her.

"When you've made the calls, find me a lover," she said. "And make sure he's tall."

Helgin snorted derision. "You need to become more self-reliant." The door shut behind him with the sound of serpents. Kaethe laughed.

She opened her eyes. Above her, Neweden basked in the radiance of the sunstar. She stared at the world.

The Domoraj Sucai could barely hear Vingi's whining mumble. He scowled in irritation, trying to pierce the auditory murk that fouled his ears. Snatches of song clutched at the Li-Gallant's words; his own thoughts, thundering, drowned them.

Vingi himself seemed to be encapsuled in a shifting cage of sapphire flame that, gelatinous, moved about him slowly. The Li-Gallant's desk rolled like the open sea, but Vingi did not seem to notice. The Domoraj thought that peculiar but decided not to mention it. *Why bother? The Li-Gallant, dear bastard that he is and putting bread in all the kin's mouths, should be allowed his whims. Quiet, quiet; what is he saying?*

Ignoring the muted orchestrion that insisted on playing in the back of his skull, the Domoraj—head of Vingi's guard—cocked his head with intense concentration.

". . . to my attention that you've, well, taken up some odious habits, Sucai," Vingi said. "I've been told you've used lujisa, other drugs—man, how do you expect to guide my guards in this state?"

I don't. I don't want to. Then: *Did I speak that aloud? No, he's still talking. The flames around him are larger now. How can he not feel the heat?*

". . . understand why this sudden sloth, this abuse. What's going on inside your head, kin-brother? You were my most trusted captain, one with whom I could be honest . . ."

Inside my head? Listen: There is a trumpet sounding like green-white shards of ice, and a crystalline note that smells of spices. You hear velvet or taste fire. I don't have to think of the disgrace you—no, there is the smell of silken cloth against my skin.

". . . since the lassari I had you hire to kill Gunnar a half-standard ago failed. I've grieved over that decision a hundred times, Sucai, believe me. I know it caused you considerable pain to send a shameful lassari rather than declaring bloodfeud. But the Li-Gallant must always hold a larger view. It was for the good of Neweden—it gives you no disgrace. Believe that, Domoraj—you should feel no shame."

Shame is a ruby spear. It slices through you and you can't see the lifeblood on the stone. It stays, gigging you whenever you move, and you can't tear it out.

". . . and any dishonor should fall to me. Not you. You were following your kin-lord's orders, as any dutiful kin-brother would. When you reported the failure, I was *glad* the attempt had failed. Do you wish time to think this through, Sucai? Do you wish my help? I could set up an erasal at Diplo Center—d'Embry would do that for me, and the Alliance has an excellent psych unit. Answer me, Domoraj, please."

Sucai struggled to pierce the fog in his head, the hues and tints that chased each other behind his eyes. He spoke, hesitantly, his voice a harsh whisper, his fingers knotting and moving in his lap as he sat before the Li-Gallant.

"I . . . forgive me, Li-Gallant, but I feel . . . disgraced. You've brought shame to me . . . I'm sorry, I wasn't ready when you called for me today . . . I was the instrument of shame." *The ruby spear.* "I've tried . . . a few times since, to talk with . . . our gods. They—" Sucai stumbled over the words, his tongue moving, his face contorted as if he were about to weep. "They . . . don't answer me."

Vingi was speaking again, but the Domoraj could not hear him. A wind like emeralds whispered in his ears, twisting around the ruby spear that impaled his chest and pulling so that the weapon wrenched inside him. He shook his head and the storm abated, moving away. Sucai stared at Vingi and saw that a forest of dark towers had sprung up around the Li-Gallant, each with a scarlet light on its craggy summit. ". . . an erasal whether you wish it or not. As the kin-lord, I command it. You're of no use to me in this state, Domoraj. That, above all, should bring you the most shame."

The spear . . .

"Go and rest. Tell Domo d'Meila to come here at once. He'll be in charge during your absence."

Sucai sat for a moment as the slow realization that he had been dismissed filtered into his consciousness. Vingi, his face like melted ire, gazed back at him. The baleful, laughing eyes of the dark towers about the Li-Gallant surged, flaming about Vingi without harming him, cold. The Domoraj lurched to his feet, nodding in salutation and wonder. He turned to leave, as Vingi, fluid, became tall, thinner.

The carpet whispered quiet insults under Sucai's feet. The door showered him with warm mockings. The air, shrieking, bit into him with a thousand small teeth.

Chapter 4

An excerpt from the acousidots of Sondall-Cadhurst Cranmer. This is an early transcription, dating from the time well before Valdisa became Thane, long before the term "Hoorka" would become a curse throughout the Alliance. It is best to remember that Cranmer was neither a technician nor a fighter, that his views on things military were those of a sheltered layman. Cranmer had never taken a life.

EXCERPT FROM THE DOT OF 8.19.214:

A rustling of paper.

"Here, Valdisa. These are the specifications I was talking about—I had the Diplo librarian dig them out of the Center files. The holocube'll give you an indication of what the damn thing looks like—that's somebody's hand by the stock, so you'll get the sense of scale."

"Sond, did you see how *heavy* this is?" (Her voice holds an obvious amusement—laughter is near the surface of her words.)

"It's no heavier than a long-maser, Valdisa; I checked. The Alliance uses LMs as standard equipment."

"And they also use powered suits. This would weigh down a Hoorka."

"Perhaps, but look at the advantages. You sight through this, and when the trigger is depressed, the weapon uses a range-finder coupled with the heat-seeker to determine distance—you can also override the automatics if you need to. A beam's generated in both spire-chambers—here—and the two beams fuse at the indicated distance. All the destructive power is generated there, since each of the beams by itself is harmless. You can fire directly through your own people and not worry. The range is good, too, and a bodyshield won't keep this one out if it's tuned finely enough."

"Sond—"

"No, let me finish, m'Dame. I may be a scrawny little aesthete to your eyes, but damn it, I can see applications here. If you were within sight of your victim, you could use this and be certain of a kill."

"Sond, that's just the point. The whole thrust of the Thane's code is that the victim is always given a proper chance to escape—we never overbalance the odds. This gadget might be as effective as you claim; if it is, it's *too* effective. You misunderstand Neweden ethics, but then you haven't been here long. There's too much honor involved in a bloodfeud—it's a very personal thing."

"That's just what you Hoorka circumvent: the personal contact of a person with the one he wants to kill."

"That's why you see us using a variant on a blade so often. To Neweden, killing is, as I said, a thing of honor, an individual matter. To be truly honorable, you have to be closely involved in the other's death: you never strike without warning, and your enemy must have the same chance as you. You have to understand the finality of death, how much pain is involved. This toy of yours— well, the more impersonal and distant the call to Hag Death is, the more unlikely you are to hold back. Killing becomes too common and easy a solution. You have to see the blood, Sond, watch the blade sink into flesh, hear the grunt of pain, and feel the life flow away into the Hag's claws. Many people won't do that, and that's good."

"Yah, I understand that point—mind you, I don't necessarily *agree* with it, but I understand what you're saying. That's still exactly what you Hoorka allow. You're a means of depersonalizing combat, of making killing distant and secondhand."

"Which is why we won't guarantee the death of a contracted victim. It *would* make it too easy, and we'd insult both the honor of the signer and their gods. It's also why we give the body of the victim—if there is one—to the contractor and make his name a matter of public record.

Then he sees the results of his actions and receives the consequences. We're not murderers, just weapons."

"Yah, yah, I've talked to the Thane and received the same lecture."

(Valdisa laughs again.) "Well, if you show him these plans, you'll hear it one more time."

(Here there is the sound of paper being torn.) "Then I'll save my ears."

The last three times you have not killed—the thought nagged at him as Gyll stared at the panting bumblewort. He'd come back from the meeting to find the wort on its side, moving feebly, the fog-gray eyes moving dully as it stared up at him. He'd forced it to drink some water, watched it lap halfheartedly at the offering.

"You should put the poor thing out of its misery, Gyll."

Startled, he turned from the wort to see Valdisa leaning against the doorjamb, her nightcloak swept over one shoulder. He found that her presence made the tension return, and he made an effort to appear relaxed, stroking the wort. He wondered if he fooled her.

"You surprised me," he said. "I thought I'd let the door shut." Under his hand, the wort chirruped plaintively; he made his caress softer, slower. The snub nose came up and nuzzled his hand wetly. From the mouth, the slender whip of its tongue rasped around his forefinger, tugged once, then released.

Gyll shook his head. "Come in, Valdisa." He still looked down at the wort. "I assume you've come about the contract."

"Yah." She nodded, pushing herself erect with a quick motion. She went to the floater that sat by his bed.

Gyll was silent, observing her. In the months since he'd given her the title of Hoorka-thane, she'd changed. She smiled less, she laughed less; an aura of moodiness enveloped her in a smoky embrace. He felt responsible and slightly guilty—it was his burden that she'd assumed, because he no longer wanted the problems of leadership. He'd given it to her, and it had sunk its talons deep in her soul.

He stroked the wort a last time, scratching under the delicate skin of the earflaps, and sat on the bed. Valdisa watched him with dark, veiled eyes, her face carefully arranged and neutral.

That hurt worse than anything she might have said.

"How's the wort?" she asked at last. They both knew it for the avoidance it was, and Gyll found it difficult not to lash out at her circumspection. He began to speak, harshly, then swallowed his irritation with a visible effort.

"No better. I doubt that it'll live much longer—its ancestors may have been able to fend for themselves, but we've bred the worts into something that can't be undomesticated and wild. I'm surprised this one's lived as long as it has, since it had to have been abandoned in Sterka. It keeps fighting." He stared at her, waiting.

Valdisa nodded. Her lips tightened once, parting with an intake of breath as she started to speak. She glanced at the wort's cage, as if unwilling to meet Gyll's eyes. He made no effort to make it easier for her. He waited, belligerently silent.

"You know what I'm going to say." Eyes the color of old, much-polished wood: they accused him.

"I suspect—but you're going to have to say it, Valdisa." He shrugged. "I'll tell you that your logic is wrong, though. Yah, I've failed on the last three contracts I've worked. It happens—it *has* to happen. By the code—*my* code—the Hoorka must give the victim a chance to live. If they stay alive, then the Dame wants them to do so. They deserve life. If not—then let them join the ippicators in death and dance with the five-legged beasts before the Hag."

"That's very poetic, love, but it's not all of it." She shook her head, the short, dark hair moving.

Gyll raised an eyebrow in question, making the creases in his lined forehead deeper, and running a hand through his graying hair. He looked down at himself and pulled his stomach in.

She was still not looking at him. Her fingers plucked imaginary lint from the black and gray cloth of her sleeve. "I've talked to the kin that worked those contracts with you, Gyll. They all told me that you seemed listless, unenthusiastic. You seemed to be going through the motions. And they said you complained of tiredness . . ." She glanced up, her mouth a grimace of censure. "I think that you're questioning yourself—whether you still believe in Hoorka."

"I *made* Hoorka." He felt his voice rising with emotion, but it was not anger—his cry was more that of denial than ire. "By She of the Five, Valdisa, I've given more to Hoorka than anyone. How can you question me?"

"You gave up the title of Thane—because you felt yourself to be no longer effective in that role. You can't deny that; you've admitted it to me." Her gaze held him, a vise of accusation. "Now you've failed your last contracts in a sluggish manner. I have to wonder at that, Gyll, and make some kind of judgment."

Now her voice softened. Her back, which had been rigidly straight, relaxed, and she slouched back in the floater. "There's nothing wrong in that, Gyll. I can understand, and there's much you can teach the apprentices, if you don't desire more. You don't have to stay in the rotation if you don't wish to do so. Hoorka have retired: Felling, Brugal, Hrolf . . ."

"No," he said. Very simply. Quietly.

"Is that your pride speaking, or do you really feel that strongly about this?"

"*Damn* your implications, Valdisa!" Gyll shouted. The wort cried in sudden fright, and Gyll rose to his feet, stalking over to the animal's cage. "I was trained to this from the beginning by my true-father, who didn't have the sense to see what those skills could mean to Neweden *if* tempered with discipline, and it was *me* that set up those disciplines and gave the training. You've no right to question my abilities, not even as Thane. I'm as good as any of the Hoorka, my age or mental state regardless. I'll prove that on the practice floor if you insist. I'll challenge you or any of the kin—first blood."

Valdisa was calm, staring at Gyll as if his rage rendered his soul transparent. "Your abilities are not in question."

Gyll shook his head in mute denial, muttering an inward oath but not knowing whom he cursed. "I demand, as kin, to take my place tonight," he said. "I'll consider it an insult to be replaced." His stance was as much a challenge as his words: feet well apart, hands on hips.

There was silence as Valdisa regarded him. They locked gazes.

Valdisa glanced away, shaking her head once more.

"As you wish, Gyll. I won't fight you in *this*"—with a

slight accentuation—"but . . ." She caught her lower lip between her teeth, breathing once. "I am Thane, Gyll. I love Hoorka as much as you, and you've made it my duty to see to our kin's welfare. If that means going against you, I will. I won't enjoy it . . ." She stood, stretching. "I'd do this much for any of the kin. Come to the entrance in an hour. Your gear will be waiting."

She walked over to where Gyll stood, staying a careful handsbreadth from him, and glanced down at the sickly wort. "You shouldn't let it suffer like that, Gyll. You should kill it."

She began to move toward the door. Gyll called after her. "Valdisa."

She turned.

"Thank you," he said.

She didn't smile. "I knew you'd say what you did. I've talked to Sartas. He's grudgingly let me change the rotation. I've given you a new partner for tonight. You'll work with Aldhelm."

And she was gone.

He would have chosen another partner for the contract, had the choice been his and not Valdisa's.

Aldhelm was waiting with bland patience when Gyll finally arrived at the entrance to Underasgard, the Hoorka-lair. A small group of the kin were standing with him, jesting with the apprentices, their voices a loud echoing in the vast spaces of the first cavern. Hoverlamps dolefully lit the scene, throwing huge, distorted shadows on the jagged roof. Gyll forced a smile to his craggy face, knowing what would come.

"It's an easy one tonight, Ulthane. The apprentices have him placed and he's not running too quickly. Isn't that right, McWilms?" D'Mannberg tousled the apprentice's hair with a large, careless hand, his laughter booming from the stones.

McWilms ducked aside from the mistreatment, bowing sketchily to Gyll while casting a dour glance at d'Mannberg. "It's true, sirrah. I gave him the warning and let Ferdin follow. I'll be taking you in the flitter."

"Lose this one, Ulthane, and Valdisa'll have you switching places with McWilms here." Serita Iduna, her olive face laughing, touched Gyll's shoulder with an affection that eased the pain of her words. Gyll, knowing, expecting all the gruff humor, stared out to the darkness outside Underasgard. He endured the unpolished wit, the unsubtle humor, though only the full kin dared speak to him in such a manner, the apprentices watched, grinning uneasily, exchanging glances among themselves.

"You've made sure the blade is sharp this time, Ulthane?"

"Look, just follow Aldhelm—he rarely gets lost."

Grin like a fool, old man. You've no one to blame but yourself. Gyll smiled lopsided amusement.

Only Aldhelm remained quiet. He stood in deep shadow near the torn mouth of the cavern, already wearing the wide belt of a bodyshield under his nightcloak. His eyes caught the green-gold light of the lamps; he stared at Gyll. He nodded.

"Ulthane," he said. His voice was dark.

Gyll nodded in return, buckling on the bodyshield that an apprentice handed him. "How do you feel tonight, Aldhelm? We haven't worked together—" He hesitated, damning himself. *We haven't worked together since the failed contract for Gunnar, since I was forced to use my blade on you to stop you from abandoning the code. Fool, learn to think before you wag your tongue so carelessly.*

"It's been a while." A sad smile flickered across Aldhelm's scarred face—the track of Gyll's vibro. "I remember it very well, though."

His words brought back the memories, and they held all the rancor that existed between them. *Valdisa, of all the kin, why did you choose Aldhelm? He'd be the least willing to understand my feelings.* Gyll was suddenly tired, very tired, as if the contract were already over, a long run finished.

Aldhelm moved into the light, checking the Khaelian dagger scabbarded to his belt and letting the nightcloak fall around his tall, muscular figure. "You needn't worry, Ulthane Gyll. I've no intention of letting us fail this contract." A pause. "And we'll do it by the code."

Gyll couldn't read his face, couldn't dredge deeper meanings from the blandly spoken words—it was the problem he always had with Aldhelm: he couldn't pierce the man's emotional armor. Aldhelm turned away, moving with a determined stride to the cavern mouth and beckoning McWilms ahead of him. Gulltopp, the larger of Neweden's two moons, was now rising beyond the trees, silvering the higher branches and silhouetting Aldhelm as he moved into the night, out from the domain of stone.

Gyll, staring, waved the apprentices back to their work and nodded a brief farewell to d'Mannberg and the other Hoorka. He hurried after Aldhelm and McWilms, the well-wishes of his kin following.

Aldhelm had gone to the dawnrock and stopped, McWilms moving on to the flitter that waited near the clearing's edge. The slender tapering pillar of the dawnrock scratched at the sky, the glass receptor at its summit catching the light of Gulltopp. Aldhelm, seeing Gyll approach, touched the dawnrock with his right hand, stroking where the rock was worn to a glossy sheen from the touch of a thousand Hoorka hands: the last ritual upon leaving Underasgard.

Gyll, with a gesture that seemed almost angry, touched the dawnrock in turn—he could feel the warm smoothness of the stone underneath his fingers. The whine of the flitter's engines moved from purr to roar, rebounding from the cliff-face in which the mouth of Underasgard loomed black and empty.

"What did you mean back there, Aldhelm?" Gyll's voice was a harsh whisper, as if the dawnrock were listening.

Aldhelm shrugged. His nightcloak, dark against darkness, swirled about him. "I know what you're feeling, Gyll, whether you want to believe that or not. I know you've grown tired of killing, whatever your reasons, in the past several months. I've watched you, and you wonder too much about the victims. You always did that to an extent, but the tendency is more pronounced now. You think of them far too much for your own good as Hoorka-kin."

Gyll felt the sting of wounded pride: it flared his anger, and he felt the blood rush to his face, felt his nails dig into his palms. "I *made* Hoorka, kin-brother. And I've killed more than you. Over the standards—"

"Over the standards you've done less and less of it. You want to see their faces, you ponder their lives. You empathize. Do they haunt your sleep, too? All those ghosts you've sent to the Hag . . ."

"*Damn* you, man. Hoorka is *my* creation, all the kin follow *my* code, and the code tells us how to feel. You act as if you understand how I feel better than I do."

"I've always understood you, Ulthane. Ever since you wounded me in the last contract for Gunnar—and I hope the Hag's minions gnaw at Gunnar's soul for eternity. He cost me too much, and I wasn't at all unhappy to see him die. I understood your feelings back then. I understood, and I wasn't angry with you. Did I ever say or do anything to make you think that?"

"It doesn't matter. My feelings aren't within the realm of your concern, Aldhelm." The man's patient calm fueled Gyll's anger. He could feel control slipping, knew he had to break off the conversation or risk saying too much. He fiddled with the shoulders of his nightcloak, tightened the strap of the bodyshield with too much concentration.

"I was merely giving you my observations, Gyll." Aldhelm's face was still a careful mask.

"Then observe tonight." Gyll's head snapped up, his eyes narrowed. "Watch me, Aldhelm." Filled with a fury he longed to vent, Gyll stalked away, slapping the dawnrock once more in passing. His booted feet crackled through dead leaves underfoot with a sound like dry fire. He did not look back to see if Aldhelm followed.

Bondhe Amari, kin of the Guild of Petroleum Refiners, was a man whose mouth was too often ahead of his brain. He was also a poor conspirator.

That much the Hoorka gleaned from their conversation with Sirrah Dramian, kin-lord of Amari's guild and the signer of the contract for the man. Dramian, his white hair a proud sign of a long and successful life, had no sympathy for Amari. "Kill him," he'd said to Valdisa upon signature. "I've no cause to begrudge a man scheming to make his way in the guild—the gods know I've done it myself. But this fool is clumsy. The rumors are just too loud for me to ignore. He offends my honor, and I'm too old to challenge him myself. I can afford your damned high price. Kill him." He'd coughed, twisted one of the rings about his finger, gathered his expensive robes about him, and left the caverns, trailing a spoor of perfume.

McWilms brought the flitter down near Undercity. Here, in the oldest sector of Sterka, the buildings massed above on metal stalks that held them above the floods and the mud of the early rains. The air was filled with the foul odor of rotting vegetation. The flitter squelched to a landing in the mud, settling uneasily in the ooze. Gyll and Aldhelm peered out to the clustering of lights reflecting dully from the wetness below.

"Undercity." Gyll exhaled nasal disgust. "It'll take hours to clean the mud from our boots."

Aldhelm was silent.

McWilms shifted in his seat, glancing over his shoulder to the Hoorka. "Sirrahs, it's not quite that bad, if Amari hasn't shifted positions. Ferdin said to go up the lift there"—he pointed to a diagonal of hoverlamps moving from the river muck to the buildings—"and into Oversector. He's holed up in an abandoned house there. Save your pity for Ferdin. She had to chase Amari through that gunk for a good hour." McWilms grinned at the assassins.

Neither returned his amusement.

The Hoorka flitter had been observed in its landing. Eyes watched from the porches of Oversector as Gyll and Aldhelm stepped out, the mud sucking greedily at their soles. A small crowd had gathered at the terminus to the lift (the mud smeared everywhere, dried into confused footprints). For the most part, they were lassari, though a few wore the insignia of the less-profitable guilds. The spectators eased back from the lift's exit as the grim-faced Hoorka walked out, kicking the clinging filth from their boots. Oddly silent, yet somehow expectant, they backed into shadow, staring.

Gyll leaned toward Aldhelm to whisper as the hungry eyes plucked at them. "This happens more and more. They watch, as if the Hoorka were some damned street entertainers." Aldhelm nodded—sour agreement.

Gyll flicked the cowl of his nightcloak up, shrouding himself. The assassins moved in a pathway ringed with shadows and wraiths. The watchers moved with them, gelid, as the Hoorka moved into the streets of Oversector. Oversector was perhaps the poorest area of Sterka—squalid, far too crowded, and filled with the stench of the river beneath and the poverty above, a subjective fog that was tangible enough to cause Gyll to draw his lips back from his teeth in a snarl of disgust. A woman near him, seeing the rictus, drew quickly back in a rustling of cloth.

"To the right, Aldhelm—that's where Ferdin's to be

waiting." Gyll swept cold eyes about him. "Carrion birds," he muttered.

The way was ill-lit, for most of the hoverlamps that had been placed here were missing, shattered, or simply not functioning. Gulltopp had not yet risen high enough to light the area. Night was triumphant. A hoverlamp thirty meters away showed the open maw of a cross street and a night-cloaked figure waiting there. The figure held up a hand, the fingers moving in the identification code. Ferdin.

The apprentice was slight, boyish. She shivered as if cold as the two approached. "Sirrahs," she said, bowing. "I see you've brought an audience with you." She scowled at the watchers. "They make you almost afraid to speak. I could always feel them staring, as soon as we moved into Over-sector."

"Where's Amari?" Aldhelm's voice brooked no sympathy—a chill reproof, it caused Ferdin to draw herself erect, to stare at the man with eyes gone flat and emotion-less. "In a house two doors down on your right, sirrah. I sealed and placed alarms on the other entrances and windows—he has to come out there." A thin index finger impaled darkness, indicating an archway where a hover-lamp bobbed in a portable holding field. It threw knife-edged light at the door. "I set the lamp."

"Did he give you a long chase?" Gyll could see the mud of Undercity caking Ferdin from feet to mid-thigh. The apprentice caught Gyll's glance and smiled tentatively.

"I'm going to spend the rest of the night cleaning myself, as you can see, Ulthane. But no, he hasn't moved in two hours. He has a sting, but other than that he should be easy. McWilms and I could have taken him a hundred times over. If it weren't for the damned watchers . . ."

"Go on then. McWilms is waiting for you in the flitter."

Ferdin nodded her thanks. She let her nightcloak—with the red slash of the apprentice—fall about her and moved into the night.

"You need to talk with the apprentices, Ulthane. They shouldn't be so easily spooked." Aldhelm watched Ferdin's retreating back, glanced with irritation at the watchers along the street.

"You were never bothered?"

"You have to ignore the lassari fools, neh? I concentrate

on my task—that's what you taught me as an apprentice, Gyll. I simply follow your teachings." He stared at Gyll.

And I should follow them myself: is that what you tell me, Aldhelm? Once I did, to the exclusion of everything and everyone else. I wish it were that easy now.

"Then let's see if I taught you well," he said.

The doorway to the building was grimed in an irregular semicircle about the handle, the legacy of many unwashed hands. Gyll unsheathed his Khaelian dagger, grimacing at the weight (he preferred his vibro, but the Khaelian weapon had other advantages), and prodded at the entrance plate. The door slid into its niche with a rumble. The Hoorka flattened themselves to either side of the archway.

Aldhelm's fingers moved in the hand code: *I'll go first.*

A quick downward flick of the wrist: *No. Wait.*

The interior darkness remained silent, quiescent. Several curious lassari moved nearer, staring at the Hoorka and peering into the open doorway. Aldhelm feinted toward them with the dagger and they fled.

Now. First Aldhelm then Gyll moved into the room, Aldhelm rolling a flare ahead of them. Night fled to the far corners of the space, startled. Shadows reared and died as the ovoid flare wobbled, bounced from one wall, and came to a shuddering halt.

"Amari?" Gyll called. There was no answer.

The light stabilized. The Hoorka stood in a shabby reception hall that had once been grand. Three archways led out—one directly ahead, one to either side. Two floaters lay keeled over in their holder units, their fabric coverings torn and shredded. A broken holotank sat in a small mound of glassine shards. The floor gritted underfoot. From one corner, a stalkpest went about its foraging, unconcerned.

"Aldhelm, do you see the formal warning? Amari's supposed to have a sting, so there should be—"

"Gyll!"

Gyll turned at Aldhelm's shout, the dagger up and ready. He had only a moment's glimpse of a gaunt apparition in the far archway (frightened dark eyes under a shock of brown hair; a , defiant stance) and a fleeting impression of the sting the man held.

The blast struck them.

Gyll's ears ached with the roar, there was a sudden constriction about his body, and he could not move. A dark hail swept around him, and the world slammed him from his feet. His body toppled, stiff.

When the bodyshield released him from its iron grip a second later, the figure was gone. Aldhelm was picking himself up beside him. Slugs from the sting clunked dully to the floor from their nightcloaks; the wall behind them was pitted and torn.

"That cowardly, filthy lassari-sucker," Aldhelm muttered, softly and without inflection. "Without so much as a word to us, without a warning or a thought to his honor and kinship. . . . I can understand the contract for this piece of dung. If it weren't for the shields . . ."

"The bastard," Gyll agreed. He was filled with a sudden rage. All hint of his listlessness was gone, kindled to ash by the rush of adrenaline in the attack's aftermath. He brushed unnecessarily at his nightcloak. He felt as he once had felt—a cool, methodical killer in the service of Dame Fate, a hunter seeking death for the Hag.

"Stay here, Aldhelm—Amari can't escape the house if one of us guards the door. I'll go find him or flush him toward you." Gyll's voice was clipped, high.

"All things considered, Ulthane . . ."

"Neh!" Gyll spat out the word. "His life suddenly offends me, Aldhelm. He's mine. Stay here and be ready."

"He may attempt another lassari stunt, and if we're together . . ."

"We can't talk Amari to the Hag, man." Gyll hefted the dagger in his hand, tapping the floor with an impatient foot. "I insist on this, Aldhelm."

Something in Gyll's demeanor took the fire from Aldhelm's protest. He began to speak but stopped, staring at the older man. He shrugged and moved to the left archway. "I'll wait here for your call, then. If you find him, if you need help . . ."

Gyll shushed Aldhelm with a raised finger. They listened. From the floor above, they heard the sound of furtive movement, a scraping of wood, then silence.

"I won't need your help." Gyll—a dark-clothed wraith—moved into the corridor.

Amari's path was easy to follow: he left behind the detritus of fear and panic. The sting, empty, lay abandoned against the wall a few paces down the corridor, and the dust of the hall was visibly disturbed by his flight. From the end of the corridor, a lift-shaft beckoned. Gyll did not waste time with stealth; he moved quickly to the shaft and peered up.

Nothing.

He tossed the vibro on his belt up the shaft; listened to it clatter on the flooring above. Again, there was no reaction. Gyll let the field take him up.

The second floor was much like the first, a morass of decayed technology and filth. That much he could see in the weary light drifting in from the street's hoverlamp. Amari's retreat had left a scarred track through the dirt. Gyll shook his head. *So easy, so stupid. The bastard acts as no honorable kin, nor does he have the wit to escape the Hag. He panics, and She smiles. Valdisa need not have worried. The apprentices could have taken him.* Gyll picked up his vibro from the floor and sheathed it again.

There was a scuffling sound from a room down the hall: Gyll stiffened, ready to move, to dodge or attack. A moment later, the sound was repeated; a scratching of fabric or leather against something hard, or a tentative scrabbling of hands.

"Amari, you bastard, you're Hoorka's now." Gyll clenched the dagger, ready to throw. He squinted into the darkness webbing the hallways, searching for movement. "The Hag waits for you, coward. Come meet Her messenger." His voice was a loud taunt, a deliberate insulting that no kin would tolerate. He called down the shaft to Aldhelm. "I've found him."

Gyll took another flare from his beltpouch and rolled it down the corridor. Shadows chased along the walls—the scrabbling was loud for a second. Gyll smiled: it came from the first door to the right. Hefting his weapon, letting his anger propel him, he moved toward the room.

"Amari, it's hopeless. Come and fight like kin—go to the Hag with that much honor, not like a lassari." He wanted it, wanted the confrontation, the fight; he could feel his heartbeat quicken in anticipation.

He was not answered. He glanced inside the room.

A grimy window smeared light across the floor and halfway up one wall. The interior was dappled, paint hanging in long strips from the walls. Amari crouched in the furthest corner of the room, cocooned in shadow, his back pressed tightly against the wall as if by sheer will he could force his way through. Gyll could see the eyes, frightened, moving nervously. A tongue licked dry, cracked lips.

With two swift steps, Gyll moved to the center of the room. Amari now could not run without going past the assassin. The polished blade of the Khaelian dagger flicked window light across the walls.

"Bondhe Amari, your life is claimed by Hag Death." Gyll began the ritual for a trapped victim, watching the man. Already, he could feel the anger leeching away, cooled by the man's obvious fear, his helplessness. He tried to kindle it again, keeping in his mind the vision of the ambush, Aldhelm's mocking words, Valdisa's galling concern. The effort was only partially successful. Amari sagged against the wall as Gyll spoke; he seemed craven, exhausted, all resistance and pride gone from him. With the Hoorka's words, Amari moaned, shifting his weight, trying to back away from the dark presence.

Gyll couldn't keep the contempt from showing on his face. "Amari, you disgust me. You don't deserve a clean death."

Amari shook his head, a rapid back and forth. Sweat-darkened hair lashed his cheeks. "Hoorka, I'm sorry for the sting. It—" Amari stopped, snagged Gyll's stare with his manic eyes, and then looked away. His right hand brushed hair back from his forehead. "It was desperation. I . . . didn't know what else to do. It shamed me before all kin."

"You can settle your guilt with your gods, then." Gyll forced a harsh edge in his voice, but he could feel that the anger was entirely lost now; it was pretense. Amari disgusted him, repelled him, but there was also an undercurrent of pity. He would kill him, yes, but it was not a deed he would do gladly. "Prepare yourself, Amari kin-less. How do you want to meet the Hag?"

A fractional step forward—Gyll's boots scritched on the grime of the floor. Amari shivered as if cold, pulled upright. "No . . ." The word forced its way past clenched mouth.

"It needn't be this way, Amari. I can use the dagger, yah, but I can also give you a capsule. A lassari's death, but what is that small shame in addition to the rest you bear? It's painless, even enjoyable, I'm told ..."

A small shaking of his head.

"You can't delay any longer, man. The capsule?" Gyll fumbled in his beltpouch with his free hand, found the capsule and held it out to Amari. *Why do you torture the wretch, old man? Why drag out this farce? It should be over now, the body bundled and given to the contractor. You hesitate, you wait.*

Amari looked sidewise at the capsule, his head half-turned from the Hoorka. His head came around slowly, the gaze always on the palm and the capsule it held. Then something seemed to snap in Amari's eyes. He jerked upright, his hand clapped Gyll's hand away, and he screamed. As the agonized wail jerked Gyll's head back, Amari pushed himself from the wall. Gyll reacted, powered by instinct and training, without thought. He stepped in front of the man, countered with a forearm the wild fist Amari threw. Gyll's dagger slashed forward, sheathing itself deep in Amari's midriff.

Warm, dark, and sluggish blood flooded from the long wound— the low-molecular edge of the Khaelian weapon slicing effortlessly through flesh. Amari gasped, a sound that turned to liquid gurgling. Pink foam flecked his lips. His knees buckled and Gyll stepped back to let the body drop to the floor.

The Hoorka stared down at his hand. Amari's lifeblood stained him to the wrist. Hag Death had come.

"He deserved the slowness, Ulthane."

Gyll turned slowly. Aldhelm stood in the doorway, a silhouette against the guttering brilliance of the flare. The dusty air sparked around him.

"You tell the new kin that they must kill quickly," Aldhelm continued. "You tell them to avoid conversation with the victims. But all rules must be broken, neh?"

Gyll said nothing. He stared at Aldhelm, eyes narrowed.

Aldhelm stepped into the room with unconscious grace. He reached into his pack and handed Gyll the victim's nightcloak. "Let's finish this," he said.

Chapter 5

THE DAY PRETENDED SUMMER.

Those that could find any excuse to be outdoors took the opportunity. Keep Square was crowded and loud. The Li-Gallant's keep itself was opulent in noon. The sunstar deluged the walls with lemon brilliance and spat aching-bright reflections from the windows.

The main gate of the keep swung back with a resounding clash of metal, the intricate designs wrought there shivering with the violence of the motion. Passersby murmured and paused to watch two people stride from the entrance: the Domoraj, resplendent in his dress uniform, and an older, bearded man who also wore the insignia of Vingi's guard. The latter was speaking loudly to the Domoraj, his arms waving in protest as he half-ran behind him.

"By all the gods, think of your kin, Sucai. You can't abandon them like this, can't leave the guard without its Domoraj. You dishonor yourself, dishonor the Li-Gallant, dishonor your kin. And the Li-Gallant has promised you an erasal tomorrow—" The man seemed suddenly to realize where they were. He brought himself to a quick halt, eyes narrowing as he glanced around at the frankly curious on-lookers. He rubbed gray-white hair, muttered an expletive, then resumed his pursuit of the Domoraj. Sucai was now standing in the center of Keep Square, arms at his sides, staring without seeing the buildings and people around him.

"Domoraj," hissed the man in an agonized whisper. "Come with me, please. I've been your aide for standards, man. You know you can trust Arnor, neh? Let's talk this out. Perhaps too much lujisa..." He grasped at the Domoraj's arm, pulling.

Sucai jerked free of Arnor's grasp, his lips drawn back in a snarl. He spoke for the first time, too loudly for Arnor's taste.

"Leave me alone, you damn fool. I'm no longer your kin."

Arnor stood back, uncertain. His brow furrowed, and he turned about—*Too many people. I can't avoid making a scene that'll be the talk of Sterka by nightfall.*

Sucai was plucking at his guild insignia, a small hologram on his right shoulder. He pulled the crest from the fabric savagely, tearing the pin loose. He held it in his hand for a long moment, the sunstar catching the facets of tiny inset jewels. He inhaled—loudly, nasally—filling his chest. His head came up; he stared at the crowd that had gathered around Arnor and himself.

"The person who was once Domoraj of the Li-Gallant Vingi's guild, who is also known as Sucai d'Ancia, declares himself unguilded. He does not deserve kinship." Sucai spoke slowly, using the impersonal mode, insulting himself. He closed his eyes as if in pain. "He is lassari, the former Domoraj. He is Dead . . ." With the last word, Sucai jammed the pin of the hologram into the palm of his left hand. The first rank of the crowd jumped involuntarily. Arnor started to move forward, then—sensing that the onlookers would brook no interference with a private matter of honor— stood back again, gnawing unconsciously at his forefinger.

Sucai yanked the pin from his flesh. Blood welled out. He smeared the lifeblood across the face of the insignia, then flung it to the tiles of the square. The glassine hologram shattered with a treble finality.

"Domoraj," Arnor said softly.

"There is no Domoraj. He is Dead."

"Sucai, you must know me."

"Sucai is Dead. He sees none of the living." His voice was scratchy, pained, as if shaped from agony.

Sucai began to shed himself of his uniform. The crowd drew closer around him, drawn to the hurt etched on the face. It was a rare sight to come across kin at the moment of their commitment to the Dead. Speculation raced: Why would the Domoraj be so shamed, so full of dishonor that he'd be compelled to seek the solace of the Hag? Yet their mood was also solemn, for there was a redemption of honor

in joining the Dead. The Domoraj was now beyond Neweden's laws. He was kin of the Hag.

Arnor began backing away, making his way through the
press of people to the gate. He could do nothing. The
Domoraj stood naked in the square.

Someone threw him a worn cloak. Sucai accepted it
without a word, though his glance conveyed gratefulness.
"The Dead?" he asked.

Several voices answered, one louder than the rest. "I saw
a procession this morning by Niffengate."

Sucai nodded his thanks and began a slow walk to the
west, toward Niffengate. The throngs parted silently before
him, watching, whispering.

Sucai looked neither to right nor left. His lips moved in
a silent chant. The sunstar pooled blue shadow at his bare
feet.

Arnor, shaking his grizzled head, dreading what he
would have to tell Vingi, closed the keep gates.

The morning had not gone well. He and Aldhelm had returned to Underasgard early (Gyll plunging his bloodied
blade into the earth beside the dawnrock to feed She of the
Five Limbs, nodding to the congratulations of his kin), and
he had gone back to his rooms. He'd expected to find
Valdisa there, or at least a note for him to call. He'd had no
reason to expect this from her; it had simply been a pleasant
hunch that had grown without volition on their trip back, a
daydream to take the edge from the unpleasantness of the
contract. Expectation had increased, and he'd been surprised to find how tangible his disappointment could be.
His room had been empty but for the wort; it had whimpered softly at him. He'd scratched its ear, feeling dull frustration.

Valdisa had gone to bed with Serita Iduna.

When he saw her that afternoon, she'd spoken to him,
smiling and joking, and asking if he would see Oldin. She
touched him with gruff affection. Yet he seemed to sense a
forced manner in her friendliness. He wanted to talk to her
and lance the boil of his paranoia, but she'd put him off,
pleading that Hoorka business called her.

"I know you'll understand, Gyll," she'd said. "You were
Thane once."

That had hurt more than his suspicions.

It had driven him into a mild depression that even the unique experience of his flight to the Trader's craft could not dilute. Nor did the pilot of the shuttle help: Gyll had never seen a Motsognir Dwarf before, but if Helgin Hillburrower was representative of his race, they were a gruff and sour lot. He grunted his hello, looked the assassin up and down as if he were a specimen, and grinned savagely. "Like your outfit," he'd said. Gyll could not tell if he was being insulted or not.

Peregrine was huge, massive, looking like a pair of gothic cathedrals glued bottom to bottom and set loose. The Motsognir had whipped the shuttle into a port that was not much smaller than the whole of Underasgard. Around them, the ship was alive with activity: the crew milled in the corridors, nodding to Helgin and staring frankly at the nightcloaked stranger. Gyll could not see enough; he felt the depression leave, shattered by newness. He was inundated with alienness: Down the hall hobbled a bio-pilot, a reengineered human whose nervous system was not set for walking but for guiding ships through the voids between worlds; two people (men? Gyll could not be sure, but both had prominent mammaries) with arms of bare polished metal butted smoothly to flesh; a furred thing like a mating of owl and bear growled at them as they passed. The corridors themselves were set in no sane fashion—seemingly laid out by a deranged architect with a pathological need for misdirection. Gyll was hopelessly lost before they reached Oldin's quarters.

Oldin's rooms were stunning. The place was huge. A thick grass-carpet wandered over hillocks and protrusions—evidently the seating arrangements. Colors, vivid and saturated, swirled restless on the walls, and a large port in the ceiling gave a view of Neweden herself. And set here and there were . . . *things* Gyll could not identify. The arrangement of white globes and blue rods, what was it? Not a sculpture, since it had an obvious control panel affixed. The vial of greasy, rolling smoke; the tank holding what seemed to be only moss-covered rocks; the holos—winged creatures, a neo-dolphin in ceremonial robes, an eerie landscape of storm in which a lightning-creature stalked: all these spoke of the philosophical differences between the Trading

Families and the Alliance, which held all alien things apart from itself.

With a glance of smug contempt, the Motsognir seated himself on a low rise in the carpet as Oldin came into the room. Her face had the delicate hardness of a porcelain doll, the skin silky with an ivory sheen. Her startling eyes were caught in subtle blue, trapped below gilt eyebrows. Here the gravity was heavier than it had been in the rest of *Peregrine*—Gyll decided it was for his benefit—and Oldin moved with a ponderous grace, seemingly uncomfortable in the Neweden-like pull. But it was what she wore that compelled Gyll's attention: it moved, sluggishly. An eye (veined like a bad hangover, a dead black pupil the size of a thumbnail in which Gyll saw himself dimly reflected) gazed back blandly at him from her thick waist. As Gyll stared, it blinked, slowly. A dull black skin covered Oldin's body from ankle to neck, the edges quivering slightly: the amoebic clothing flattered her, thinned the weight that a lower normal gravity and a variant standard of beauty had allowed her to keep. Gyll doubted that she was comfortable. *For effect,* he thought. He stared at the eye.

"Ulthane Gyll, please make yourself comfortable. I've been wanting to meet you for some time now." Her smile dazzled. She noted the direction of his gaze, and the smile widened.

The Motsognir cracked his knuckles, one by one, loudly.

"Helgin," she said, still staring at Gyll, her voice warm, "does not approve of this meeting. You'll quickly learn that Motsognir don't mask their feelings."

"Helgin also does not appreciate being referred to as if he weren't here." The dwarf looked at them, thick eyebrows lowered over deep-set eyes, beard scraggling down his chest. "You'll quickly learn, Ulthane Gyll, that Trader Oldin masks her feelings all too well."

Gyll glanced from one to the other. Oldin didn't appear disturbed by the dwarf's manner, and Gyll, for his part, felt a sudden liking for the Motsognir—something in the gruff manner appealed to him.

A light touch—*by She of the Five, her hands are smooth. Has she ever done manual labor?*—directed him into the room. Gyll pulled away, not wanting to have her clothing contact him.

"You may sit where you like, or have a floater if you prefer." She watched as Gyll chose a spot near but not too near her on the carpeted hills. "I've had refreshments sent up."

As if on cue, the door to her chambers opened and a hover-tray slid in. It came to a halt before Gyll. He looked down at a dish of lustrous, silver ovals, like a nut encased in mother-of-pearl.

"Rhetanseeds," Oldin explained as Gyll reached for one. "They come from well out in the Cygnus sector, well beyond Alliance boundaries. Take one, it will be sufficient."

"Sufficient for what?"

Her smile shone at him. "You don't trust me, Ulthane?"

"M'Dame Oldin, the Hoorka trust only their own kin."

To their right, the dwarf chuckled. "A good trait, Hoorka."

Still smiling, Oldin shook her head. "Nevertheless ... First, Ulthane, please call me Kaethe. I'm of the Trading Families, and we don't follow Alliance mores, or any other of their rulings. And as for the rhetanseeds—ask the Motsognir. Helgin will tell you that they're harmless."

"I'll tell you, Hoorka, that—so far—no one has ever experienced any ill effects. And I enjoy them myself." Helgin whistled (lips pursed behind the forest of beard), and the tray came toward him, leaving Gyll staring at the seed in his fingers.

Gyll waited, watching as the Motsognir plucked a seed from the tray with a delicate touch made almost humorous by the squat thickness of his fingers, and dropped it into his mouth. Eyes glinting, he stared at Gyll as he chewed. He swallowed, overnoisily, and sighed in satisfaction.

Gyll placed the seed in his mouth, letting it roll on his tongue. It didn't taste—it simply felt smooth. He bit, gingerly.

A welter of taste and smell assaulted him: *cina ... no, now it's anis ... too astringent, like lemon, no ... mint and cloves;* then there was a stimulation behind his eyes—*light!* that burst and faded through the spectrum; finally, a surfeit. It was as if he'd finished a fine, long meal. He was not unpleasantly stuffed, but satiated.

"Shit," he said. Quite eloquently.

Oldin clapped her hands in delight. Her attire, responsive, changed to a webbing of scarlet veins in a field of black. The eye blinked massively. "The aliens—I can't pronounce their name . . ."

"Kaarkg—*whistle*—seer*grumble.*" Helgin. "And I *know* your mouth. It's more than pliant enough to wrap your lips around the name."

"Eater of dung," Oldin said pleasantly.

"Ravisher of month-old corpses," Helgin answered, unperturbed.

Gyll stared. When Oldin turned back to him, the smile was still fixed on her lips. "As I was saying, Ulthane, the creatures used the seeds on extended trips, a form of quick sustenance. We've had great success with them as trade items."

"She neglects to tell you that the seeds are nonnutritious to the human metabolism. That's what you need to listen for, Ulthane, her unvoiced words." Helgin grinned at Gyll from his hillock.

Gyll did not know how to react, whether to be angry or amused. He was caught up in a playlet for which he had no lines, snared in a net of words, all of which seemed important and none of which he understood. He did what he could: he slipped on the mask of his old self—the young Hoorka-thane—and let the cool aloofness of the Hoorka-way guide him.

"I came only to collect payment, m'Dame Oldin."

"Kaethe."

"M'Dame Oldin."

Her mouth turned down, but her eyes danced. Her clothing stared.

"One for the Hoorka," said Helgin.

Damn these people, what are they playing at? "The tales of aliens are quite interesting, but I'm here to collect payment for the contract on Cade Gies. You have the check, I'm sure." The last sentence was a cold statement.

"Are the Hoorka always so mercenary and unsociable? You've not smiled since you came, and the lines of your face don't fall naturally into the expression you're wearing." She gazed at him, the guileless eyes wide. Her hand brushed clothing-skin; lines of blue radiated out from the touch.

"M'Dame Oldin . . ."

A raised forefinger, languid. "Kaethe."

He didn't dispute the correction or acquiesce to it. "We

were hired to perform an assassination. Thanks to Dame Fate, it was done. What else do we need speak of?"

"You'll have your payment. Gratefully." As if tired, the eye at her waist closed. "I was simply interested in *you,* Ulthane. You made the Hoorka from lassari criminals, and I'm aware that you've been attempting to advance the Hoorka beyond the domain of Neweden. The Alliance resists, does it not?"

"We've had a few offworld contracts."

"But not many. Not to your potential. The Alliance is too cautious of you, too fearful, too parochial in outlook, Ulthane. That's why the Alliance won't let its citizens have much contact with the other races that dwell outside their sphere of influence. They're intolerant of change and new ideas, and social systems that vary too far from their norm. That's why Neweden has had so many problems with the Diplos."

"But the Trading Families . . ."

Her smile shone, her eyes invited. "The Trading Families are far more open-minded about such things. We seek out the unusual and alien, after all. We're more like you, Ulthane. Like Neweden-kin, we're fiercely loyal to our families; we understand the concept of kinship, though we don't segregate along occupational lines. We've no taboos with experimentation and new ideas—such things tend to be self-controlling. An unviable concept will extinguish itself or be extinguished. That's not far from the manner in which Hoorka view their assassinations, is it not? You say that what's meant to survive *will* survive. You've reason to be proud of yourself, Ulthane. The code is ingenious in the way it fits Neweden."

Her praise warmed him, and he knew he shouldn't let it do so. It was most likely that the flattery was false. Gyll tore his gaze away from her and found Helgin. The Motsognir frowned at him, though the eyes seemed to laugh. Helgin shrugged.

"Don't look at me, Hoorka. I haven't dressed like an expensive clown."

Again, Gyll did not know how to reply. Neither of the two seemed to take offense at anything said, while to him and all Neweden, insult was a deadly game to play. "What are you after?" he asked finally. He kept the shreds of

Hoorka composure around him—distant, always haughty—but he knew Oldin could read the bewilderment he tried to keep from his voice.

"You want Hoorka offworld." Her voice soothed. "You want a chance to expand the opportunities of your kin." The clothing-eye opened once more; in it, a too-thin Gyll reclined. "Fine. I believe that the leading Families can offer Hoorka more than the Alliance and d'Embry. We have our feuds, also, and we're concerned with the concept of honor, and we offer a much larger arena than the Alliance, one virtually without boundaries."

"D'Embry and the Alliance hold Neweden, and Neweden is our home."

"They hold it for the moment, I'll grant." A pause. "Solutions can be found for that. You should at least consider us."

"It's not my choice, even if I were interested. I'm no longer Thane."

"Ahh." Oldin steepled her hands. She gazed at him over ivory fingertips. "Does that bother you?"

Damn, is it so obvious to all? Am I so transparent? "No," he said, knowing he lied. "It's simply a fact. I still have some small say in the affairs of Hoorka—they *are* my creation. But the old guard must give way sometimes." He tried for half-jovial, felt it come out morose.

"You're not old, Ulthane. The hair is graying, yes, and I'm sure you might find your reflexes a touch slower than they once were, but you're far from old. Experience too, that has its advantages."

His sudden irritation surprised Gyll. It was a complex compound, that ire, full of his own frustration at the night before, the wort, his inability to control the conversation with the Trader, Oldin's teasing. Gyll stood, the veins in his neck standing out, his lined face ruddy. His hand went unbidden to his vibrohilt. "The woman talks incessantly and says nothing." He spoke loudly, using the impersonal mode with bitter relish, knowing that it would spark kin to full anger.

But Oldin was not of Neweden. She didn't move, didn't appear in the least alarmed. "I'm sorry, Ulthane. I simply felt that I'd prefer to make the offer to the creator of Hoorka, no matter who has the titular leadership. It's your training and your guidelines they follow. Therefore it's *you* that interests me. Perhaps I should have approached this another way. Tell the Thane, then; tell her I'd like to speak with her."

Her gaze dropped to his vibro hand. Slowly, he let himself relax, let the arm fall to his side. He came as near to apology as he would allow himself. "All Neweden is quick to anger, m'Dame Oldin."

"Kaethe." — Helgin's basso rumbling. The dwarf looked at Oldin and shrugged. "You would have corrected him, yah?"

"You anticipate me so well."

"You're not given to complexity. It was easy."

A nod to the dwarf and she turned back to Gyll. "Kaethe," she said.

"Kaethe." Gyll gave in. "Irritability is a bad habit of mine."

"No apology is necessary. She of the Five . . . Limbs, is it not? The goddess of ippicators?" She changed the subject without transition. It took Gyll a moment to recover, then he nodded.

"She is the patron of ippicators, and of the Hoorka."

"It's struck me as odd since we've been in Neweden orbit—why hasn't your world made some effort to restore the beast of five legs? Its bones are one of your most valuable resources and surely enough genetic information has been recovered. I've seen the polished bones, and there's nothing more enchanting. With a small stable of the beasts, you could continue to export them without worrying. Cloning."

"I know of no cloning techniques which don't require live tissue. The ippicator have been extinct for centuries."

"Surely the vast resources of the Alliance . . ." There was a faint mocking tone in her voice. "Though perhaps they refuse to help you."

"As far as I'm aware, they could do nothing. And besides, a live ippicator would upset Neweden's theology."

"Ahh." Oldin rose to her feet, a quick and graceful motion that startled him. The dark fabric about her moved, the eye blinking in dull surprise. "I'll let you go, Ulthane. I'm sure you've much to do. Helgin will get you the check for the Gies contract. And please talk to the Thane. The Trading Families might have much to offer you, the Oldins in particular."

She came up to him. He could smell a faint musk. It was pleasant, but he didn't know if it was a cologne or the clothing-creature. She smiled, grasping his thick-veined hand in hers. "Come back if you wish, Ulthane. I find the Hoorka fascinating. I'd welcome your company."

He could only nod.

On the way down . . .

"Well, Hoorka, how do you like the enchanting Oldin?"

"How can you speak of her that way, Helgin? I'm surprised she keeps you in her employ."

"You misunderstand our relationship. The Motsognir have their own means of support. I stay with her simply because I find her interesting, because we like each other."

"You've an odd way of indicating affection."

"She offers me adventure. New sights. A thrill of uncertainty. We never stay in one place too long. The Motsognir lust for that. We've never been a part of man's empires. A Motsognir'd die of boredom in the Alliance. In that, Oldin's right. The Alliance can't like the Hoorka, Ulthane. Give them time, and they'll start looking for ways to keep your people contained, safe and ineffective. The Alliance is just a gigantic inertia-machine seeking to preserve itself. Its vision is inward; it's satisfied with the status quo. And the more it tries to preserve itself, the larger the cracks that are going to appear."

"You talk like a philosopher, Helgin."

The dwarf turned a yellow-laced eye toward Gyll. "You just have no ear for sophistry, Ulthane. You're too used to people telling you the truth."

They entered Neweden's atmosphere. The planet welcomed them back with a roaring of mock thunder.

Outside the caverns, the sunstar had settled below the horizon. The night denizens prowled the hills. Deep in Underasgard, Gyll had gone to a spot far from the usual Hoorka lairs. He'd not expected to be disturbed there. He was mistaken in that assumption.

Gyll watched as Cranmer placed a bottle and two glasses on the rock beside him. The clink of glass against stone was loud in the stillness. To one side, a dimmed hoverlamp oscillated golden-green inside the barred cage of a headless ippicator skeleton. Light alternated with shadow on the walls of the cavern. On the rock, the bottle tilted dangerously. "What's that?" Gyll asked.

"Lubricant."

Gyll's eyebrows rose quizzically. He cocked his head.

"You're too literal sometimes, Gyll." The smile did not leave that mouth. It seemed permanently affixed. "It's wine. I thought it'd be a nice gesture. I haven't seen much of you recently."

"A lot going on."

"And you haven't talked to me about any of it. I thought I'd track you down and just talk—the wine'll ease a dry throat."

Cranmer sat. Gyll could see a slight wince as the coldness of the stones made itself felt through the fabric of Cranmer's pants. "You people have to move this planet closer to the sunstar," Cranmer said, noticing Gyll's attention. "I'm always freezing." Despite the heavy jacket he wore, Cranmer hugged himself.

"It keeps the wines chilled."

"Was that a joke?" Cranmer asked with too much surprise in his voice. "Ulthane, you're a constant revelation."

"Cranmer, you're a constant nuisance. If you're going to stay, at least pour the wine." Gyll's voice was dull, as if with fatigue or disgust. He had turned away from Cranmer, staring at the ippicator's skeleton, mesmerized. Cranmer pursed his lips appraisingly. He tugged the sleeves of his jacket down over his wrists, then began talking as if he'd noticed nothing.

"I was in Sterka earlier today," he said, reaching for the bottle and pouring a goodly amount into each glass. "I've a few things you might be interested in hearing."

He placed a glass beside Gyll. The Hoorka glanced at it, then returned to his preoccupied stance. Cranmer sipped his wine, watching, waiting, then shrugged. He settled himself on the rock. "D'Embry's got Diplo security checking out Cade Gies. Seems she doesn't like the thought that Oldin could have an Alliance citizen killed and not inform her as to the reasons. I don't think it's because of any affection for Gies or revulsion because of his death. D'Embry just doesn't care to be left in the dark."

Gyll grunted a reply. Cranmer glanced up to where the shadows of the ippicator's ribs flickered on the jagged roof. He set his glass down. "I also heard that Potok is supposedly considering a truth duel. The gossip all over Sterka is that the Li-Gallant is responsible for Gunnar's murder. The Domoraj joined the Dead yesterday, and that's supposedly an indication of his shame with the Li-Gallant. Everyone expects the challenge to be given within a few days of the funeral."

Gyll had slowly turned to face Cranmer. His face was in light, but a rib-shadow striped him from shoulder to chest. His head seemed to float in air. "Vingi and Potok would be the combatants?"

"Isn't that the basis of truth-duel—the opponents have to be highly placed in the guilds, and the stakes enormous?"

"Yah." A smile came and went. "That'd be a travesty."

"Would it serve justice?"

Gyll shrugged. "Dame Fate is supposed to guide the hands and rule the outcome—that way the assertion is proved true or false. If you believe that the Dame does so, then yah, justice is served."

"What about you, Ulthane? Do *you* believe?"

Gyll turned away again. "I believe it's probably a well-calculated political move on Potok's part. If he thinks he can best Vingi at truth-duel—and Vingi *can't* refuse—he stands to gain quite a bit. I imagine a large monetary fine would be levied, maybe seats in the Assembly given up. It could ruin either guild. A risk, but a calculated one. And the people will be entertained, whether they believe or not." He stared into shadow, into the arch of bone.

"Cynical, Gyll."

"I feel that way." Once more he turned. Light raked across his lined face. "I saw Oldin this morning—she made me think about other possibilities. And afterward, I went into Sterka." Gyll paused. His eyes narrowed. "If you're recording this, Cranmer, turn it off. What I have to say isn't for anyone else's ears."

Cranmer spread his hands in innocence. "You don't trust my discretion?"

"No."

A small grin. "Ah, well. I've not been recording, Ulthane."

"Good. Cranmer, do you remember the night of Gunnar's death? We were in the outer caves. I'd just killed a stalkpest."

"Aldhelm came out—he was leaving the caverns."

Gyll nodded. "He told us he was going to see an Irastian smith who was visiting Sterka. I checked all the local smiths, on a whim. I don't know why I was so suspicious. None of the smiths had seen Aldhelm that night. None had kin visiting from Irast."

"Aldhelm gave you no names. Maybe it was someone you missed. Maybe the smith was visiting true-family. That's uncommon, but it happens."

"Maybe Aldhelm lied. In which case, what was it he wanted to do in Sterka that he didn't want to discuss with kin?"

Cranmer had no answer. He drank from his glass. "Have you talked with Valdisa about this?"

Gyll's laugh was a short exhalation. "It's always the same thing: 'Have you talked with Valdisa?' I sometimes even ask that myself. Once, once, Cranmer, that wouldn't have been needed to be asked." Gyll shook his head slowly. "I haven't seen her since I returned. I was supposed to meet with her after seeing Oldin, but she wasn't in Underasgard—some business with a kin-lord in Illicatta. I won't see her until Gunnar's funeral tomorrow."

"Then confront Aldhelm. Talk to him."

"No. It's not my place." There was an edge of bitterness in Gyll's voice. "I'm not Thane, after all. And I'm not sure it's something I really want to do. Aldhelm is kin; he knows what honor is, and we have to trust our kin to uphold that honor, neh?" Gyll—habitual—moved fingers through graying hair. "I don't know, Sond. I don't know. I'm not sure what I feel this moment. I'm of two minds. One part of me wants to leap in, take over the active role again, even if it means a confrontation with Valdisa. Egotistically, I think I'm the only one who truly understands Hoorka, what I meant it to be, what it should do. And the rest . . . Maybe I'm just being bitter. I keep thinking it's all Valdisa's problem now. Let her work it out. I can't even say too much to her for fear that she'll think I'm interfering, usurping her authority. We've already fought over that. And she *is* my friend, my lover. I don't want to ruin that. She's the closest to me of the kin. So what would *you* do, scholar?"

Cranmer waited a long moment before replying. "I think I might drink my wine."

Slowly, Gyll smiled. He glanced down as if seeing the glass for the first time. "You know," he said, "that may just be the right solution."

Chapter 6

An excerpt from the acousidots of Sondall-Cadhurst Cranmer. The following excerpt is from a conversation between Ulthane Gyll and Cranmer. The lack of background noise and the echoing resonance indicate that the conversation took place in a secluded area of the caverns. The dating of the segment is only approximate. It is included among several other undated recordings, all evidently clandestine.

EXCERPT FROM THE DOT OF 5.15.217:

"I think I might drink my wine." (Cranmer)

"You know, that may just be the right solution. You'll have to excuse my mood, Sond. It's everything taken all together, not just one thing. I let myself get into these depressions, and then I have to come here and think myself out of it. It goes away in time." (Here there is the sound of drinking, a clatter of glass on stone.) "But then you know all that already."

"Still, I'm glad that you don't mind talking about it."

"I don't mind because I trust you to go no further with it. And I have to admit that it's sometimes nice to have someone listen, to talk out loud and hear myself try to explain—you can see the flaws in your logic. It wouldn't work with everyone, though; you won't let this get beyond the two of us."

(Cranmer laughs with an edge of nervousness. After a moment, Ulthane Gyll joins in.)

"Gyll, your trouble is that you're an idealist. Everyone else around you is a pragmatist."

"Is that so bad?"

"It is when you constantly assume that they all think the same way you do."

The two Hoorka were seated in the stands of the guilded kin, a part of the crowd filling Tri-Guild Church square. The lassari, gawking at the expensive display of mourning, huddled at the southern edge while the guilded kin were comfortable beneath a large weathershield near the church. It was not a pleasant day for Gunnar's funeral. The sunstar shrouded itself in clouds and the sky wept, a constant drizzle. The lassari shifted restlessly under improvised shelters.

The censers, borne by a troop of young boys representing all the guilds sworn to Gunnar-Potok's rule-guild, had just passed in golden splendor. The acrid fumes still hung in the air, a pall the rain was dissipating rapidly. The youths had looked frankly miserable. Their gilt finery had been soaked and clung to their skin, their breaths steaming in the chill air. The procession was moving slowly down the lane between the lassari crowds and the bleachers of the kin: a trio of pipes, followed by a phalanx of musicians with krumhorns and tabors; then the beast-dancers from Irast acting out for the fifth time that day—they were becoming rather bored—the death of the Great Ippicator, twirling with awkward arabesques in their five-legged costumes.

Gyll shifted in his seat, restless. "We need to talk, Valdisa. Oldin had an offer—I think we should hear it."

"Yah?" Her gaze was on the beast-dancers. "It will wait until we get back to Underasgard. This isn't the place for business. Besides, my butt's gone to sleep."

Following the beast-dancers, a large floater passed bearing the dignitaries of local guilds, a score of kin-lords. Those absent were most conspicuous. The Li-Gallant's guards, as the policing force for Neweden, were present, but Vingi himself was not. Instead, the Li-Gallant had sent his recording secretary, pleading government business as an excuse. The Hoorka had also been asked to join the group on the floater, but Valdisa had cited their code's insistence on strict neutrality and had instead sat with the mass of guilded kin in the stands.

A smaller floater followed, preceding the bier. In it, the Regent d'Embry stared dourly at the crowds. Her face, under the weathershield, reflected bland sympathy, a public mask. Rigid, she neither moved nor glanced about.

"Do you think we can really trust her, Valdisa?" Gyll nodded toward d'Embry. "Look at her, so stiff—and yet we let her hold the future of Hoorka."

"We haven't a choice in that, Gyll. That's what you always told me."

"Yah, but I don't like it. If there were an alternative ... I'll bet she has to peel off that face every night."

And last, the bier. It was flanked by all Gunnar's kin, their faces chalky with white funeral paint. The rain, in their long march, had streaked and splattered the paint. They looked sufficiently mournful, the turquoise guild-robes tattered and rent, the shoulders dotted with random blotches and smears from the thick paste on their faces. The bier moved slowly, majestically. It was a floating cloudlet, pulsing a deep sapphire from somewhere in the fog that surrounded it. On the mist lay Gunnar, atop a pyre of scented wood. Grotesques, small imps, raced about the edges of the cloud, their miniature faces wracked with pain and grief. As the bier approached Tri-Guild Church, a hidden choir began the descant to the dead; the sapphire glow went amber, the Hag's color. The choir reached a crescendo as Potok came forward toward the cloud-wrapped floater, bearing a torch. It hissed in the drizzle.

Suddenly, a flare arced out from the midst of the lassari. Screeching and wailing as it climbed, the projectile exploded high above the square, a false sun. Heads turned in shock, Potok stood in uncertain surprise, the choir faltered to a ragged halt.

The flare's appearance was answered by a shout from the lassari. "Renard!" was the cry. The ranks of lassari seemed to boil, some trying to back away from the square, others surging forward. With the rest of the guilded kin, Gyll and Valdisa came to their feet in the stands as several lassari rushed the bier. They bore crude weapons. Rough hands shoved aside the startled Potok. A group of the lassari grasped through the clouds of the bier, pulling and tearing. The mist faded, revealing a bare skeletal framework of steel and wiring. The grotesques became mournfully immobile. The lassari pushed, the bier tilted.

A cry of anguish came from the guilded kin, now beginning to recover their senses. But they had no leader and hampered each other more than helped: the rush from the stands was slow, tangled. The lassari pushed again as Potok's kin tried to stop them. The bier toppled in its field, canting over. The pyre broke loose, spilling wood and Gunnar's body to the wet pavement. A roar of triumph came from the insurgents—"Renard!"—a howl of outrage from the kin.

Gyll watched the confusion in the stands, the chaos in the square. "Let's go, Valdisa—we can't do anything here."

"But the damned lassari . . ."

"Vingi's guards are coming. There's enough confusion already. We'd only add to it."

The guards moved, belatedly, attacking with crowd-prods and tanglefeet webs. But they were too far from the bier to get to the locus of turmoil; the lassari made use of the confusion to dart back into the mob. The crowd screamed as one—guilded kin and lassari—as the guards forced their way in pursuit, using their weapons indiscriminately.

The lassari (and some of the kin), angered now, began to resist, fighting back as well as they could. Someone—a plant-pet wrapped about his shoulders—shouted and lassari moved away to harry the guards. People milled in the square, seeking escape, seeking an outlet for anger, seeking someone to strike.

Chaos held sway. The drizzle became a downpour.

M'Dame Tha. d'Embry was furious. A thundercloud of emotion preceded her into Diplo Center. The staff glanced up from terminals and desks as she rumbled through: they quickly decided that to pretend ignorance was the best course. The sight was tragicomic, though a glance at the enraged face forbade laughter. D'Embry's dress tunic was disheveled, soiled, and wet. Her weathershield belt was broken, the casing cracked. Her white hair hung in limp strands, the mouth was cemented with deep wrinkles. Her eyes arced fire.

Heads stayed down, attentive to their tasks.

She stormed into her office, leaving behind a wet legacy of her passage, and barked at the com-unit on the desk. "Karl, get in here. Bring a warm towel. Several of them. Now."

D'Embry turned and glared out her window. A shiny-wet Sterka Port stared back, blanketed in thick clouds. The skull of a large ippicator gazed blindly through the rain, a gift from the Hoorka. A symbol of this world, it seemed to laugh at her. "A damned barbarian place," she muttered. "Gods, I'm sick of it."

Karl entered, towels in hand. He gave one to d'Embry with a carefully expressionless face.

"Don't stare, Karl. It's not polite. And I know you saw the procession on the holotank." She fixed him with a sour gaze.

"Yah, m'Dame."

D'Embry scowled. Karl made no elaboration. She glanced down; Karl held a flimsy in one hand. "What's that?"

"A contract proposal for the Hoorka," he answered, holding it out to her. "It came over the relay from Niffleheim while . . ." He hesitated. "While you were out."

D'Embry glared. She toweled her hair, ignoring the flimsy, then saw that the towel was stained with her pinkish bodytint. "Damn." She threw the towel to a corner and snatched the flimsy with a wiry hand.

"It could be important, m'Dame. A Moache Mining official is the signator."

"Screw Moache Mining—and don't look at me that way. I know the meaning of the word." She tossed the paper to her desk, shaking her head. "The frigging Hoorka keep nagging me, and the whole structure of Neweden seems to be cracking around me. You saw that lassari outburst, Karl. Someone—some *one*—orchestrated that. It wasn't just a spontaneous upwelling. That was a person's name the lassari were yelling. It was *planned,* by this Renard, to hit right where Neweden would feel it the most. The incident will enrage the guilded kin and harden their attitude toward the lassari, and it'll inflame the kinless. It couldn't have been better designed to cause this world grief."

She suddenly slumped into her floater with a sigh, as if all energy had deserted her. Seated, she cupped her chin in her hands, shaking her damp head. "The damned contract can wait a few hours—I'm not so sure that I want the Hoorka to work this. I don't want to see or hear anything having to do with Neweden or any of its idiotic people for the next two hours. See to it, Karl."

"M'Dame . . ."

"*Do* it." She didn't look at him. She stared at the replica of d'Vellia's *Gehennah* standing in one corner of the room. The door hushed shut behind Karl.

"You could've retired to that estate on Arlin. Remember that, you fool old lady. You *asked* for this assignment. You couldn't trust it to anyone else, could you? You had to go and *ask* for it."

It was normal and customary for Hoorka to engage in practice bouts. There was, in fact, an unofficial ranking among the kin as to who was the most proficient with vibrofoils. Gyll and, later, Valdisa, had done nothing to stop this covert hierarchy despite the fact that it was not covered in the Hoorka code. Their silence on the matter promulgated its continuation.

Normally, a match drew little attention. Even Cranmer, after recording diligently the first several that followed his arrival, had stopped dropping by the practice room. The kin who happened to lie in the area might stop to throw in a comment and the results certainly traveled quickly in the gossip of the kin, but few set aside other activities to become a spectator.

The bout between Aldhelm and d'Mannberg was the exception. Aldhelm was generally acknowledged to be one of the best Hoorka with vibrofoil and he was the unofficial leader of the duelists. The kin would seek out his matches to stare and search for weaknesses to exploit. D'Mannberg's presence amplified the interest: Aldhelm and d'Mannberg had for some time been at odds. The last time they had fought, it had gone strangely. Aldhelm, to the surprise and shame of his kin, had put a display of his prowess ahead of adherence to the etiquette of kin-dueling. Before Thane Gyll, Aldhelm had hurt and angered d'Mannberg unjustifiably. Since that time, the rancor had lain between him and d'Mannberg.

The sympathy was with d'Mannberg. The betting favored Aldhelm.

Cranmer was fiddling with his equipment, watched by a skeptical McWilms. The apprentice grimaced at the tangle of holocameras and controls. "Have you placed the cameras correctly?"

Cranmer glanced back over his shoulder. "I've been doing this for a decade. Since before you joined the Hoorka."

"You told me that last time, but the 'cube was all jumbled. Poor placement."

"For an apprentice, you're damned impertinent. Are you gonna help or just offer your expert advice?"

"I'll help. You're going to need it to get set up in time. Aldhelm's just come in."

D'Mannberg was already present, stripped to the waist. He was simply huge—a tall and massive man, his hair and beard shining red in the glow of the light-fungi that lined the room. To the casual eye, he appeared obese—his kin knew better. D'Mannberg was surprisingly fast for his weight, and the flesh masked muscle rather than fat. Aldhelm, readying himself to one side, was more traditionally muscular with a wedged torso. He slid his vibrofoil from its sheath; it whined through the air. The light-fungi tinged his skin, perspiration sheened his back.

D'Mannberg readied his own weapon, clicking it on. The orange-tipped marker shot from the hilt to its full extension, defining the length of the nearly invisible wire. The blade thrummed its power. He deactivated the blade, watching Aldhelm loosen up. "You still want the match, Aldhelm?"

Aldhelm glanced at d'Mannberg, the scar standing out on his face. He gave a noncommittal smile. "Who have you gotten to judge it, kin-brother?"

D'Mannberg turned, surveying the kin who were beginning to crowd the perimeter of the strip. "I'd have asked Ulthane Gyll or Thane Valdisa, but neither is here. Sartas?"

Sartas nodded his willingness, stepping forward. Both Hoorka handed their weapons to Sartas. He examined each blade, locking them on the practice setting—the vibro would sting enormously, but would not cut flesh. The desire to avoid a touch was quite real; painful welts would still form. Sartas touched the foils together: sparks hissed and flared, dying on the earth of the cavern floor. He handed the weapons back and strode over to a rack of vibrofoils, taking one out and activating it.

"Take your places, kin-brothers," he said, standing in mid-strip. His olive face moved from Aldhelm to d'Mannberg. "The match is five touches. All code strictures apply—a lost weapon may be recovered without penalty and the entire body is a valid target. The two of you will disengage when I call halt, or you'll face my blade. Remember that it's not on the lower setting." He paused. "Ready?"

They nodded, assuming the *en garde* position.

Sartas lowered his vibro and stepped from the strip. "Begin."

Beat, beat: a wailing shook the cavern, sparks rained to the ground. D'Mannberg, seeing Aldhelm's foil in the fourth guard, attacked in the high outside line to be met by a beat parry. Riposte, parry, and counter-riposte: there was a whining slap, loud in the room, as Ric's blade found Aldhelm's bicep.

"Halt!" Sartas stepped forward, knocking away the foils. "Touch for d'Mannberg."

Aldhelm stood back, his face sullen, a hand kneading his arm. Ric grinned. "That's payment for the last time we met, neh? I'm not as slow as you might think, and you've given me a fair amount of incentive. She of the Five doesn't care for those who ignore the etiquette."

Aldhelm's face was emotionless. "One touch doesn't make a match, either. And you're a large target." Then, too slowly, "Kin-brother."

A mumbling from the spectators: those Hoorka as yet unsure of the depth of ill-feeling between the two were quickly convinced. Cranmer, behind the shelter of his equipment, pursed thin lips. "What'd you think, McWilms?"

The youth's eyes were alight. "Aldhelm looked lethargic, sleepy. That was very sloppy work on his part. But keep recording, Sond, keep recording. This looks like it might be good."

"You're a bloodthirsty bastard."

"Yah, ain't I." He grinned.

Sartas scowled at the verbal exchange between Aldhelm and d'Mannberg. He slapped his vibro at the floor, kicking up dirt. "Sirrahs, please return to your positions. And watch your tongues. We're kin here, and while I'm judge, you'll act it." His dark eyes moved from man to man. Slowly, they both bowed to him.

"Take your positions again, then." He waited, then stepped back once more. "Begin."

This time Aldhelm was more cautious and less sleepily overconfident. He seemed to be awakening to full arousal, more aware of the match. His vibrotip danced now, flickering as he probed d'Mannberg's defense, backing the larger man slowly down the strip with short, frantic attacks that never let d'Mannberg regain the initiative. Still, all the attacks were successfully met. Aldhelm moved forward, then lunged into the open line, his body extended. D'Mannberg, swiftness belying his bulk, leapt backward and the vibrotip missed. He grinned at Aldhelm.

Now Ric counter-parried and riposted, taking the right of way. Bare feet hushed against the earth, sweat varnished their skin and made dark strands of their hair. Foils slapped and wailed.

"D'Mannberg's improved. A lot."

"Ulthane Gyll's been working with him. That, and he has a revenge to seek here. And Aldhelm still doesn't seem to be fully alert."

D'Mannberg let the tip of his vibro dip slightly away from the high line, as if his arm were becoming tired. Aldhelm took the proffered opening without hesitation, responding with a thrust. D'Mannberg was waiting; his foil screeched along the length of Aldhelm's, bringing them briefly closer, and he kicked out underneath Aldhelm's vibro hand. Aldhelm's hand opened with the impact and his vibrofoil slithered to the ground. D'Mannberg stepped away immediately, before Sartas could move to intervene.

D'Mannberg spread his arms wide. "Pick up your vibro, Aldhelm. We both know the etiquette, neh?" The sarcasm in his voice was obvious.

"D'Mannberg—" Sartas began, threateningly, but Aldhelm waved him silent. Scowling, he bent at the waist and recovered his weapon, checking the setting on the ring control once more. He did not look at d'Mannberg. He was too calm, too reserved. The smile left d'Mannberg's face; he crouched and rose quickly, exercising his legs.

"Gods, McWilms, look at Aldhelm's face." In the monitor holocube, Aldhelm's visage came into focus. "He looks like a killer I once interviewed. He has the same tautness to him. . . . Hell, I can't explain it, but I see it."

"Don't have to explain, Sond. D'Mannberg had better see to his defense. Aldhelm's awake now."

They began: a quick flickering of vibros as Aldhelm went into a furious compound attack, feinting low and coming high, getting the strong of his blade to the weak of d'Mannberg's. D'Mannberg kicked again, but found Aldhelm's thigh rather than his knee. Thrust, beat parry, and a riposte to the inside low line—Aldhelm's vibro slipped over the guard of d'Mannberg's foil but stopped a millimeter short of a touch. D'Mannberg hesitated, open, but Aldhelm didn't take the advantage; d'Mannberg knocked away Aldhelm's blade with a beat. D'Mannberg's sweat-beaded face registered puzzlement. He disengaged, and Aldhelm did not follow.

"You had me." D'Mannberg's vibro was still up, waiting, in the fourth guard. Sweat dripped from his beard.

Aldhelm shrugged.

"My leg isn't a good enough touch? Is that it, Aldhelm? You want something more painful?" His face was flushed with anger. Above the heart, on the face, near the genitals— there the lash of vibrofoil was excruciating.

Aldhelm's face was set in stone. Cold, the eyes; white on red, the scar twitched. "I missed you, that's all."

"What would my pain prove to you? I'm your kin, not some lassari you can toy with."

"Kin believe kin, don't they? Then believe me. I missed you."

"By the Hag, Aldhelm, all the rest saw it too . . ."

"Sirrahs!" Sartas's foil whipped down between them. "If you wish to duel, I'll referee. If you want to argue rather than meet blades, go to the common room. It's all one to me, but you're wasting my time. Assume a ready position or deactivate your foils."

Aldhelm turned to Sartas. "D'Mannberg's eyes are as blind as an ippicator's."

D'Mannberg reacted as most guilded kin would to an insult in the impersonal mode. His ruddy face flared with rage. He spat out a response in the same mode. "Aldhelm has the voice of a lassari. He can speak no truth."

The words cracked Aldhelm's icy calm. With a guttural shout, he flung his foil aside and lunged for d'Mannberg. But Sartas moved too quickly. His strong hands grasped Aldhelm's arm, slipping on sweat, then clamping down. D'Mannberg had begun to move in defense, but other kin restrained him, arms around neck and waist. Both men strained to be released.

D'Mannberg spat on the ground. In his fury, he spoke the question that many kin had thought but none had voiced. "At least I know where I was the night Gunnar was killed. Aldhelm, alone of the kin, wasn't in Underasgard. Did Aldhelm kill him, sneaking like a cowardly lassari?" D'Mannberg stared directly at Aldhelm, waiting.

"Let me go, Sartas. Please." Aldhelm slumped in Sartas's grasp. His voice was dull. "Let me go. I won't dishonor myself." Sartas, slowly, loosed his hold. Aldhelm shrugged once, shaking his head, while the kin watched him warily. Aldhelm nodded to d'Mannberg.

"You can think what you want, kin-brother," Aldhelm said. "It doesn't matter when Hag Death breathes in your direction. And you were right. I wanted the most painful touch—I was angry, angry with myself *and* you. Still, I shouldn't treat kin so badly. And I did *not* kill Gunnar." He stood, hands on hips. "Believe it if you will."

Then he turned and walked from the room. His kin, surprised and (perhaps) disappointed that a bloodfeud had not been declared, watched him go.

"Damn." Cranmer exhaled shakily.

"Yah," McWilms agreed. "An interesting recording you have there, scholar."

D'Mannberg, released from the restraining hands of his kin, clicked off his vibrofoil, sheathing it forcefully.

"Bastard," he muttered.

Valdisa cuddled the wort in her arms, stroking the serrated ear flaps gently. Orangish fur floated about her, clinging to the fabric of her nightcloak; she shook her head, sending hair flying. She could see scaly skin showing through bare patches on the wort's shell. "When did it get this way?" she asked. "Have you named it yet?"

Gyll smiled at the multiple questions. "It's been getting worse in the last few days, and Renier's given me a salve that might help. The poor thing doesn't seem to be in pain otherwise, though it's still too weak to stand for long, and it doesn't eat much. I don't know . . . And I'm not going to name it yet—I don't want to get attached to it just to have the Hag take it for Her own pet."

Gyll sat on the edge of his bedfield, uniform shirt off, boots on the floor beside him, nightcloak thrown in one corner. He shrugged.

"You don't like making commitments unless you're certain of the outcome? Is that what you're saying, Gyll? That doesn't sound like the philosophy of the person that would have created Hoorka, not an idealist. After all, the Hag might have taken all Hoorka for pets, too." A smile; she patted the wort.

"Yah." He nodded in submission. "Let's just say I haven't found a name I like yet—it's got nothing to do with being attached to the damn thing. Will you spend the night with me?"

"Make a commitment without being sure of the outcome? Never." She stroked the wort a final time, sneezing as she did so, wrinkling her nose at Gyll's sudden laughter. She placed the creature back in its cage. The wort growled once in protest, then lay on its side, panting. "So ... We never had a chance to talk this morning, not with all the commotion. You wanted to tell me about Oldin?"

"Yah. I found her interesting. Very much so."

A raising of eyebrows.

"Oh, yes," Gyll continued. "She finds men with graying hair very sensual. She seduced me almost before I could walk in the door ..." He stopped, grinning. "I was never very good at that type of fantasy, huh? She *is* striking in her own way, though that's not what I wanted to talk to you about. And you needn't look so innocent—you've gone to bed with people on a whim."

"Hah. You've been spying."

Gyll didn't respond to her teasing. "It was all business. And she said a few things that we need to explore."

"We?"

"Hoorka." He leaned back on the bedfield. "You and I."

"Mmm." Valdisa crossed the room and sat next to Gyll, one leg up, facing him. She reached down to touch his thigh. "Then talk. You got payment?"

"Yah." He shook his head. "That's unimportant. What Oldin *did* hint at was an offer for a more challenging and open field for the Hoorka. She didn't give any specifics, but the suggestion was there, if we wish to check it further." He shifted position and Valdisa's hand slipped from his leg. She made no move to put it back. "I think we should find out more, Valdisa."

"Work with the Trading Families? The Alliance wouldn't allow it, Gyll. D'Embry'd ban us from offworld work again."

"I know she'd try."

"Then why do you even think of considering it? Neweden's ruled by the Alliance—if d'Embry wants Oldin gone, she just has to order it. If the Alliance bitch doesn't want us to work Trader contracts—and she won't—she'd have no difficulty stopping us."

"You didn't see what I saw on the ship, Valdisa. It was like . . . like having my eyes opened after being blind. Gods, that's a common metaphor. Still . . . Listen, a long time ago I saw what I could do with a gang of common lassari, and I was satisfied with what I'd made for a while. Then I managed to get the Alliance interested in the Hoorka, thinking about the new vistas that would open before us if we could move beyond this one world—I thought *that* was my life-goal. You know I've been moody for some time: I think I was simply dissatisfied. That ship—the Trading Families dwell in a larger world than the Alliance, Valdisa. I saw a Motsognir—you know how rare they are. I encountered new spices, new smells, new sounds—*alien* things, from cultures totally unlike any the Alliance knows. And Oldin, in her own way, seems as if she might actually *care* about the Hoorka, to understand what I've set up. The way she describes the Families . . ."

"The way she describes the Families is probably the way she thinks you'll like best. And the Alliance holds Neweden, not the Families."

"For now."

Valdisa laughed, but her laughter had little amusement in it. "Gyll, the Trading Families aren't going to come and take Neweden from the Alliance. They have agreements, and the Alliance is too strong." She rose, shaking her head. Gyll watched her, watched her turn and face him again. "I just received a contract from d'Embry this evening. Offworld—a place called Heritage. You see, Gyll, we *are* beginning to make real progress, to see the completion of what you set out to make. Vingi can't really oppose us any longer—he has no leverage anymore. Gods, it's all you worked for, and you're still willing to consider this intangible offer of Oldin's?"

"You didn't see the ship."

"I don't need to."

"Valdisa, Hoorka must—"

She severed his words with a violent movement of her hand. *"I'm* Thane, Gyll. Don't tell me that Hoorka 'must' do anything." As Gyll stared, startled by her sudden vehemence, she softened her tone, the lines of her face gentling. "You gave me the responsibility of leadership, neh? Because you didn't want it. Has that changed?"

"I'm simply trying to give you some information."

"But you insist that I act upon it, the way you want me to. No," she said as Gyll began a protest, "you expect Hoorka to follow your lead, as it once did."

"Were I still Thane," he answered, choosing his words carefully, "I'd still listen."

"Gyll"—wearily—"you gave up the title."

"I was . . ." His voice trailed off.

"You're feeling sorry for yourself."

"Don't tell me what I'm feeling, Valdisa!" Gyll's anger flared as quickly as had Valdisa's. He sat, abruptly, a forefinger pointing in warning.

"Then don't tell me what I have to do as Thane." She wasn't infected by Gyll's quick rage. Her lips twitched with the beginning of a word, then pursed in concentration. "It has nothing to do with Oldin, does it, Gyll? You know it. It's because I'm Thane. I *can* guess at how you feel. If you made a mistake in giving up the leadership, I'm sorry that you feel that way. But it's not a mistake that can be rectified now. It all adds up to that, Gyll—your boredom with Hoorka matters, your moodiness, your lackluster performance on your contracts . . ."

"Aldhelm?"

"I don't understand."

"Has Aldhelm been talking to you, giving you tales about the Amari contract? Remember, Valdisa, Aldhelm was the one that counseled me to abandon the code in the Gunnar contracts; it was Aldhelm who was in Sterka the night Gunnar was murdered."

"Gyll, that's an outrageous accusation." Her face echoed inner distaste. "I'm ashamed that you'd say that. Don't you trust kin? How does the code-line go? 'All Hoorka are kin.

You must trust kin implicitly, above all else. Kin do not lie to kin, kin do not conceal their inner feelings from kin.'"

"I know the code." Gyll swept an arm through the air as if waving away her words. "I wrote it, neh? I don't need a recital." Gyll struggled with his temper, wrestled it into grudging quiet. "Valdisa," he continued, more reasonably, "I apologize for that. Let's get back to the question of Oldin. I do find her offer tantalizing. The possibilities might be good for us."

Valdisa's stance was rigid, legs well apart, hands at her waist. "No, Gyll, I don't think so. Neweden belongs to the Alliance. We have to work with them or they'll confine us here, take away all we've worked for. Don't you remember your own arguments with Aldhelm a half-standard ago? He wanted Hoorka to shift away from the Alliance too, even if his view was inward rather than outward. You refused to consider it—because of what the Alliance might do. We don't know that the Trading Families can truly offer us anything. Oldin doesn't run them, isn't necessarily speaking for her grandsire, as far as we know. D'Embry has *real* power here, not just in words."

"But if the offer is tangible, if it could give more power to Hoorka . . ."

"I don't see how that could be, Gyll. Stay away from her. The Traders are devious. They're also centered a long way from Neweden."

"Is that an order?"

"Does it need to be?"

Stalemate. Gyll stared at Valdisa, willing her to yield as she once would have, to defer to his wishes and sit beside him again. He knew himself too well; the words of apology he should utter were chained. They couldn't break loose of his pride. One of them had to give, Valdisa or Gyll—she to yield or he to nod his head in acceptance.

She didn't. He wouldn't.

Gyll glanced away, looking down at the thick-knuckled hands, at the too-paunchy waist beginning to creep over his belt. *Have I just lost her as friend and lover? Is this what I bequeathed her?—by She of the Five, she's much as I was, as I still am. I* am *right, I* am *right this time, and I can't get her to listen.* He glanced up; Valdisa had not moved. "If we can't talk about it, we won't, then. I'd still like you to stay with me tonight." He already knew the answer.

Her eyes were suddenly very bright, very moist. She shook her head, the barest of motions, her lower lip caught between small teeth. "I don't think so, Gyll. Part of me would like to, very much, but—" A pause. She hugged herself, staring at the ceiling, the wort, and finally back to Gyll.

"I don't think so," she said. "No."

Chapter 7

"WHO HAVE YOU been contracted to kill?"

"The rumors are that you've been retained by Moache Mining."

"Can you tell us who contacted your organization on Neweden?"

"Why do you feel that the Alliance is willing to let the Hoorka work in social structures other than your own?"

The questions echoed in the steel vastness of Home Port. The three Hoorka, two full kin and an apprentice, did not answer. They watched a nervous Alliance official check their baggage and examine the traveling visas issued by Regent d'Embry, ignoring the cluster of reporters that had accosted them on their arrival on Heritage.

"Please, sirrahs—this isn't a vacation world. We know it's not that."

"If it's Moache Mining, then you have to be working for Guillene, and your victim has to be de Sezimbra. Why deny it?"

"Do you enjoy the killing, sirrahs?"

Sartas glanced up quickly. He swept his nightcloak over his shoulder, baring the much-used vibro that hung on his belt. Behind him, Renier and McWilms stood away from the Alliance official, their stance suddenly wary and erect. Sartas glowered at the gaggle of reporters. "I only enjoy," he said, enunciating very slowly and clearly, "killing those who insult me and my kin." His flat stare held the eyes of the man who had made the last remark. His right hand touched the hilt of his weapon.

The reporters were suddenly mute but for a nervous coughing and the shuffling of feet.

"Have you finished with us, sirrah?" Sartas turned back to the official. His manner was curt but polite: the Hoorka aloofness.

"You're free to go. I hope you enjoy your stay." The man's last words trailed off into silence. He half-smiled, half-shrugged. "Habit," he said.

Picking up their duffels, the Hoorka began moving toward the arched entrance of the port terminal. The reporters stood aside to let them pass. Except for one, they didn't follow.

He was a short and stout man wearing a luminescent jacket and knee-length pants—Niffleheim fashion. He pursued the Hoorka, matching strides with Sartas. The assassin glanced at the man once but kept walking.

"Wieglin, with the *Longago Journal*," the man said in identification. "Listen, there aren't many secrets on Heritage. It's a poor, lousy world. There aren't but a handful here that I could even think of affording your services. It has to be someone with Moache, eh? Why deny it?" He panted in the effort to keep abreast of the longer-legged Hoorka.

"We haven't denied *or* acknowledged it. The contract's signer will be revealed if the attempt is successful." Sartas spoke without looking at Wieglin. Renier, to his right, broached the entrance, the doorshields dilating.

"Ahh, the *attempt...*" The hot and dry air of Heritage assaulted them, billowing out the nightcloaks and sucking hungrily at the sweat that appeared on their brows. Harsh sunlight cast sharp-edged shadows at their feet. Sartas motioned and McWilms went to procure a flitter from a stand. Wieglin persisted, wheezing.

"You only attempt to kill the victim, like it's a mystical game. Well, it won't work here. Moache—Guillene—demands results, not sophistry. If they thought they could kill de Sezimbra and get away with it legally, they'd do it. Even Moache Mining has to play within some of the laws, and de Sezimbra's too smart to have an accident. It's only because the Alliance let you people out of your cloister. Death is too easy an answer to problems."

"Leave us be." Sartas tried to ignore the man, hooding his face with the nightcloak and staring out at the sun-baked landscape. Already, he missed the coolness of Neweden's day.

"I'll leave in a minute, after I say my piece. I've been on

this world for the last three months because I know there's a story here in what de Sezimbra's been doing, because I know that Guillene's hand is bearing down too much on these people. He bleeds them as dry as the sands. Yah, it's all legal since they're indentured laborers, and all of 'em signed the documents. That doesn't—or shouldn't—make them chattel. De Sezimbra's working to change all that. The money you get from this job is going to be tainted with the blood of every man and woman on Heritage. Guillene is a foul bastard."

"If the victim—*whoever* he or she is—is meant to live, Dame Fate will see to the preservation of life."

"I'm sure that's comforting to all involved. Those who de Sezimbra was helping will hug their children and tell them 'Don't worry, he was destined to die.' That's a real balm."

The flow of words came to a halt as Sartas and Renier, without a word, strode toward their flitter, now stopped a few meters away. The Hoorka threw their luggage in the compartment and swung into the blessed air conditioning of the car. The flitter, in a swirling of dust, left Wieglin behind, hands on hips.

"Welcome to Heritage, eh?" Among themselves, they could finally relax. Renier grinned at Sartas.

"I always thought other worlds'd be exotic, beautiful places. So much for that fantasy. I'm already looking forward to the return. The heat's going to kill me."

They rode through the streets of Home, Heritage's only city. The rest of that world's settlements were the metal expanses of the mining platforms, rumbling colossi moving inexorably across the landscape and leaving behind a trail of pits and broken rock. Home was a collection of small, squat buildings, sitting in the eternal dust, squalid and hot and noisy. Children playing in the bare yards turned to watch the flitter pass; curious eyes stared at them from shuttered windows. Once, a rock flung by an unseen hand cracked off the windshield; a few blocks farther on, garbage rained down on them from a second story window. The people they saw were mostly sullen, unsmiling, as drab as the buildings around them. Their unspoken dislike was palpable. Only the rich rode flitters, and the rich had to be somehow connected with Moache Mining. The tension burned at the Hoorka like the noon sun.

But when the flitter passed the columns of a high, black shield-wall surrounding Park Hill, the vista changed: desert to tropical oasis. Here, hedged by lush greenery and verdant lawns, lived the upper echelon of Heritage. The severity of the sun was masked by foliage as the dreariness of the indentured workers was hidden from the officials of Moache and the offworld visitors. The Hoorka drove past a grove of bubble trees and onto the grounds of the hostel. Sartas, already disturbed by the world, concluded their business with the clerk brusquely, grabbing the keys to their rooms.

"Let's get this over with." He scowled. "Quickly."

De Sezimbra's house stood in the lee of small brown hills a few kilometers from the outskirts of Home. The building was a low, small affair, a few outbuildings as attendants. Shabbily constructed, as well, McWilms noted as he approached. McWilms was both hot and tired after the walk from Park Hill. Sartas had not allowed him use of a flitter, an annoyance he'd nursed from irritation to exasperation on the walk. His nightcloak stifled him, his undertunic was wetly irritating with circles of perspiration, and his patience was at a low ebb. He wanted nothing more than to complete his task and get back to the comfortable and dark rooms at the hostel. He kicked at road dust.

He was certain that he was being watched as he turned from the road onto the path leading to the house. He could feel the pressure of a stare from the outbuildings, from the polarized windows of the house. He forced himself into the role of the aloof, disdainful Hoorka. *Like Aldhelm or the old man himself. Don't let them know how you feel; become an instrument in the hands of She of the Five Limbs.* He tried on Sartas's scowl, found that it fit, and went to the door.

A flat viewscreen was set in the metal of the door. It had already been activated by the time he stood before it: swirling tongues of abstract color were tangled there. A voice came from the screen. "Your business?" it asked curtly, a basso query.

McWilms stared at the screen with narrowed eyes, the scowl a mask. "My business is only with Sirrah Marco de Sezimbra. I would speak with him, and in the flesh." He found himself lowering his voice to compete with the dark tones of the doorwarden; he cracked only slightly.

"And if he doesn't wish to see you?"

"It would be to his advantage not to refuse."

Silence. The screen went to a bland gray-blue. A few seconds later, the door irised open, jerking into its slots. Mc-Wilms recognized the man who stood behind it, but checked the bio-monitor on his belt as a matter of course. The light on the monitor glowed emerald—the man was de Sezimbra. McWilms made a deep obeisance. "Sirrah de Sezimbra."

"You have the advantage of me, I'm afraid." Marco de Sezimbra was tall, dark-skinned, and handsome. He half-smiled at McWilms, his eyes gentle and puzzled. "I apologize for my ward. He tends to be rather surly with strangers—Heritage being what it is."

"I'm Apprentice McWilms of the Hoorka, and the apology isn't necessary, sirrah," McWilms said without the smile that would have made his words friendly. He found himself liking the man, a quick affection. Not, he told himself, that it would affect his performance. And if de Sezimbra appeared overtly amiable, those around him were more cautious. A man and a woman stood behind and to either side of de Sezimbra, holding stings with the muzzles pointed unwaveringly at McWilms. The apprentice nodded inwardly. "My own task is small and I stress"—with a glance at the man's armed companions—"that I intend no harm. Marco de Sezimbra, your life has been placed in the hands of the Hoorka and our patron, She of the Five Limbs."

A quizzical stare, a furtive glance at his companions—de Sezimbra clenched and unclenched his hands. "I don't understand."

"A contract has been signed for an attempt on your life." McWilms was patient but dourly serious. *It's easier on Neweden. What I've already said would have been more than enough. The man doesn't yet realize* ... "The contract will begin at 14:17 local time and end at 23:10; that's the local equivalent of twelve Neweden hours. Your life lies with the whims of Dame Fate. Should you still be alive at 23:10, Hoorka will pursue you no longer."

"Your organization means to kill me?" He seemed on the verge of astonished amusement, as if he still weren't certain that this wasn't a cruel jest.

"The Hoorka have no personal interest in your death. We work for others. We're simply instruments in the hands of another person."

From behind de Sezimbra, the woman spoke. "And if we kill you now, you with the small task?"

"Rowenna—" de Sezimbra began, but McWilms interrupted.

"I'm but an apprentice, m'Dame, a messenger. My fate is always in the hands of the Dame. But my death won't affect the contract. I've nothing to do with it—that's the task of full kin. And there are other options. You may still buy out the contract."

"How much is it?"

"Ten thousand—that's what the signer paid."

De Sezimbra smiled sadly. "He's obviously richer than me."

"Then you must trust Dame Fate."

"What of my friends, the others living here?" De Sezimbra indicated the area with a nod. He didn't seem overly upset or surprised. It was as if he'd been expecting something of the sort; now that it had happened, he could remain calm.

McWilms knew now that he truly liked the man. Most of the victims were quivering and fearful when told of the contract. He found himself hoping that the Dame would be kind. "The contract is only for *your* life, sirrah. If you're protected, we'll attempt to kill only you, but no promises can be made. Other people have been killed before, when they interfere with the Dame. Even Hoorka have died—and we expect you to defend yourself. It's your choice. We adjust our strategy to the situation, for the victim must always retain his chance."

"If I run? By myself?"

"Then none of those here will be harmed, and my kin will carry less."

A nod. De Sezimbra's gaze had an inward look. Rowenna, the sting still directed at McWilms, shook her head vehemently. "You can't do it, Marco. I won't let you." Her voice was quiet, the face haggard. "It's Guillene," she said, looking at McWilms as if she expected confirmation. "It's that frigging Moache bastard. The coward can't even do his own dirty work . . ."

His lover, then. Or she wants to be. The way she stands near him, the possessiveness in her gaze . . . "If the contract is successful, the signer will be made known." *Calm, always calm.* "If Sirrah de Sezimbra lives, then, by the code, we'll reveal nothing and simply leave Heritage. It's not a person's destiny to know beforehand by whose hand he'll die." The last sentence was stiff, a quotation.

De Sezimbra was caught in an icy peace. He nodded to McWilms as pleasantly as he might to a dinner companion. "I should be grateful, I suppose," he said, speaking to all of them. "We knew the danger of coming here and trying to stop the injustice. I thought we'd simply be deported on some trumped-up charge. This . . ." A mournful shaking of his head. "It could've been a simple, brutal murder, as well. At least this way I seem to retain some chance. I don't understand why Guillene would do it this way, but I'm glad."

He seemed to come back to himself then. The eyes flicked back into focus, the melancholy half-smile returned to his mahogany face. He nodded to McWilms. "Is that all you have to tell me?"

"Just one thing more." McWilms reached under his nightcloak, watching the two with the stings. Then his hand came out, proffered toward de Sezimbra as if for a handshake. De Sezimbra took the hand, then suddenly drew back — his palm was wet. The muzzles of the stings came up. Rowenna seemed on the verge of firing, but de Sezimbra shook his head. "No, I'm not harmed." He glanced at the hand; the moisture was rapidly drying. "At least I don't think so. A tracer?" he asked.

McWilms nodded.

"I could wash the hand."

"It's not that easily removed." McWilms glanced at Rowenna, her face a rictus of anger and concern. "We don't wish accidental deaths. In our own way, we Hoorka are very reverent of life." He moved back a step, squinting against the sun. "My task is done. I wish you luck, Sirrah de Sezimbra."

"And I wish your people none, Apprentice McWilms." De Sezimbra almost smiled. "I'd like to talk with you again, though. At 23:11, perhaps?"

McWilms made another, deeper obeisance. "May She of the Five Limbs watch you." With that, he turned and walked down the dusty path, retracing his steps. He heard the door creak shut behind him, heard the beginning of Rowenna's protest.

He didn't go far. He'd scouted the terrain earlier, finding a hidden niche between two boulders on a hill that gave him a view of the house. Cursing the sun and the heat, he settled down to wait.

He did not wait too long. Almost an hour later, the door to the house opened and de Sezimbra stepped out, a pack on his back. McWilms smiled. *I knew he'd be alone. He's too proud and sensitive to let the others aid him—and he's an effective enough leader to make his word stand against all the arguments. Good. Sartas and Renier can have the hunt of knives, since he isn't carrying a bodyshield. They'll be pleased.*

Unaware of McWilms's surveillance, de Sezimbra settled the pack on his shoulders and walked west, toward the wind-swept foothills and the falling sun.

It was 14:33.

16:51. Sartas and Renier readied themselves in their rooms. McWilms had been reporting back to them at fifteen-minute intervals. The preparations had been minimal, since McWilms had informed them that de Sezimbra was both alone and carrying no bodyshield: an extra nightcloak for the possible body, the tracker for the dye on the victim's body, a tachyon relay (the purchase of which had depleted the Hoorka treasury, but which Valdisa insisted was necessary by the code)—it transmitted the arrival of dawn at Underasgard. No stings, no bodyshields, nothing but the vibros. Both of the Hoorka were satisfied with that. It was one of Ulthane Gyll's tenets that killing should be a personal matter, an intimate deed. It's only then that one understands the responsibility involved. A sting, an aast, even to some extent the Khaelian daggers, all allowed the wielder to stand back from the moment of death, to cloak the Hag with distance.

Not tonight. They would face Her at handsbreadth.

They were waiting for the flitter. Heritage seemed to sense the beginning of the contract, the nearness of the Hag. When Sartas and Renier had come into the lobby, everyone had turned to look—a group of people staring over a game of vari-resolve, a couple playing a hologame, those simply reading on the floaters.

"The rumors must have spread. Now we're the vicious, nasty Hoorka," whispered Renier.

"Yah. And we'll eat the flesh of the victim afterward." A scowl. "Just simple, bloodthirsty monsters."

They moved from shade into the bright heat. A man stood near the entrance to the hostel, one hand shielding his eyes. In the lushness of Park Hill, he was an anomaly, dressed in clean but plain and cheap clothing, his feet bare rather than sandalled, his hair cropped close in the fashion of the miners. He saw the Hoorka, blinking against the furnace of the sky.

"Sirrahs," he called out.

Sartas paused, Renier behind. "We've no time for chatter, sirrah." Sartas began to turn away to wave to the approaching flitter, but the man moved a step toward the Hoorka, still speaking.

"You can't do this." The tenor voice quavered, and the man took another tentative step, within an arm's reach of their nightcloaks. "De Sezimbra is a good man."

"Good men die as easily as bad ones. That's not our concern, and we haven't time to argue philosophy." Renier was gentler with the intruder than Sartas would have been. He and Sartas turned to move toward the flitter, but the man stepped in front of them; nervously, but deliberately. "In the name of humanity, you can't do this." His voice was quiet; it was more effective because of that. "They won't say it, most of 'em, 'cause they're afraid of Moache and Guillene. But de Sezimbra is someone who helped us. We don't want to see this happen."

The Hoorka had halted, each gauging the man. "Out of the way, sirrah." Sartas made as if to push his way forward, but the man stepped back and held up his hand. It held a sting.

"I'm sorry, but I can't let it happen." The voice trembled, the apology was ludicrous, but the finger was steady on the trigger. Sartas watched the hand, breathing shallowly. "Better that I be killed than Marco. He's worth more to us — let Guillene do what he wants with me."

The finger went white with sudden pressure . . .

. . . but the Hoorka were already moving, Sartas to the

right, Renier dropping left and rolling. The sting cracked
and bucked; pellets chipped paint from the hostel's wall.
The man did not have time for a second shot. Sartas lunged,
grasping the man's forearm and twisting violently. Bone
cracked, loud in the sudden stillness, and the sting fell to the
grass. Sartas pushed and the man stumbled, moaning in
pain. Renier had already recovered the sting. He pointed it
at the fallen man.

"Death," Renier said, his voice gentle, "isn't an easy gift.
Dame Fate must want the victim, and you must remember
that the victim will always be willing to trade your life for
his. In that, you're lucky that we're Hoorka. We don't kill
when it's not needed."

With a practiced motion, Renier detached the clip from
the sting and slipped it into a pouch of his nightcloak. He
tossed the weapon into a clump of shrubbery. "Get the arm
seen to soon," he said. "It shouldn't be a bad break."

The Hoorka left him, kneeling in shock, as the hostel
denizens emerged, blinking, to view the excitement.

Sartas said nothing until they were in the flitter. Then he
touched Renier on the shoulder, a squeeze of affection.
"This looks like one of the contracts we're going to hate,
one that gets in your dreams. I'll be glad when we get back
to Neweden, kin-brother."

Renier nodded in agreement.

18:41. They'd left McWilms behind nearly an hour ago, pant-
ing-tired and liberally coated with the dust of Heritage.
They'd had to leave the flitter at the outskirts of Home,
where the broadcast power faded. From there, they'd rented
a local groundcar, a decrepit device burning a noisome and
smoky liquid fuel. Sartas had been dubious, but the machine had proved durable enough to climb the rough terrain.

McWilms had had little to report: de Sezimbra was moving slowly but steadily to the west, into higher and more
broken country. They told the apprentice to stay with the
vehicle until he heard from them. Then they began the real
pursuit—on foot, facing the same difficulties as their quarry.

The dye-detector placed de Sezimbra a kilometer and a
half from them. They could follow that trace until they
came too close: the detector would cease functioning when

the victim was within two hundred meters, another example of the code's insistence that the victim be given a chance of escape. And the detector gave them only a modicum of aid. It indicated only direction and distance. In the twisted, rock-strewn landscape of steep hills, they could not travel for long in a straight path. They had to turn and backtrack more than once, their way blocked, moving back and forth among the brown-red stones and gritty earth. The land was torn, dry, and nearly barren, though not lifeless. Now and then they'd glimpse a shadowed form staring at them; the assassins would grasp their vibrohilts, not knowing which creatures were dangerous or what form an attack might take.

In his familiarity with Heritage, de Sezimbra had a decided edge.

They found the first sign of him as the sun eased itself down on the spikes of nearby mountains. A scrabbling of pebbles lay at the bottom of an incline, and there was a mark higher up where weathered rock had broken loose to leave lighter stone exposed. Looking further, they found a scrap of bloodstained cloth. The blood was still wet.

"He fell, then. Scraped himself fairly well too—the cloth's saturated. Think it'll slow him down?"

Renier shrugged, pulling his nightcloak tighter about him. Already the oppressive heat of the day was waning; the chill of night hung in the shadows. "Maybe, if he cut his leg or side. In any case, he'll probably be more careful now— that in itself'll hold him back."

They scrambled up the slope, sure now of their path and alert for small signs of the man's passage. Twilight shaded the sky. A few minutes later, the orb of the sun entirely gone, Renier pulled from his pouch a pair of light-enhancers. A sallow moon hoisted itself in the east. The rocks hid deep shadows, but the landscape was bright enough for them to continue at the same pace. They were gaining quickly on de Sezimbra.

"Renier . . ."

The assassin turned, his eyes goggled with the enhancers. "Yah?"

"The detector went off a few minutes ago. I thought he was just on the edge of the range and it'd come back on, but it hasn't. We're near him."

Their vibros hissed from sheaths, thrumming as if glad to be released from confinement.

The Hoorka followed the man's trail: a scuffling of dirt, displaced rocks, the marks of boot heels. The going was rough, always west and upward. A cliff scarred with vertical slashes like the wounds of a giant claw walled them to the right. On their left, the path fell off steeply into a deep ravine—they could hear the sound of running water in the darkness. The ledge narrowed as they went higher and they were forced to move single file for a time, until the gouged cliff shattered itself into a small plateau littered with large boulders. Hiding places abounded. Sartas muttered a curse.

"We'll have to search here, damn him. Looks as if the cliff begins again just ahead. You start there—see if you can tell whether he's gone on. If not, start working back toward me. If we've got him trapped here, we can go home."

Renier nodded, already moving. Sartas began a slow examination of the area, vibro always at ready, feeling a tension in the muscles of his back. He'd felt the thrill of that tension before—it had always betokened the presence of the victim.

Sartas heard the commotion first: a muffled cry of "Hoorka!" followed by a fleshy thud and the dopplering whine of a vibro moving through air. Sartas ran toward the sounds, dodging between boulders, and suddenly getting a clear view.

Near the edge of the ravine, Renier was grappling with de Sezimbra. Somehow, the assassin had been stripped of his vibro; it buzzed on the ground nearby. De Sezimbra seemed to know the art of hand-to-hand combat. As Sartas watched (still running, wondering whether a thrown vibro would be accurate enough and rejecting the idea) de Sezimbra twisted out of Renier's grasp, kicking with a surprisingly agile movement. With a wailing cry of frustration, Renier stumbled and fell, slipping over the ravine's edge. His fingers scrabbled for a hold as de Sezimbra turned to see Sartas, still meters away, striding toward him. Sartas cursed inwardly: by the time Renier could scramble up again, de Sezimbra would be gone. Again he fought the impulse to throw his weapon—too far, and a twirling vibro was as likely to hit with hilt as well as edge. De Sezimbra scooped up Renier's weapon and ran.

The victim was gone; Renier had yet to reappear. The code was explicit on the point: if kin might be in danger, the victim was to be ignored until the kin's status was determined. Sartas peered over the edge of the depression, thumbing the enhancers to full power. He thought he could make out the figure of a man, but it could well be a trick of shadows. "Renier," he called softly, then more loudly.

The only reply was a faint echo. "By the frigging Hag—" Sartas glanced about—no, de Sezimbra was too far away by now. He could always find the trail again. He decided Renier must be unconscious, must have struck his head on a rock. The code and his own emotions tallied; he made his way carefully down the steep incline, grasping at rocks, slipping, sliding. He cursed de Sezimbra, cursed the Dame, cursed Renier.

It had to have been a freak, a whim of the Dame. When Sartas saw Renier, he halted his descent suddenly, grabbing for a handhold as rocks slid from under his feet. There was no mistaking the angle at which Renier's head rested against his shoulder or the stiff arms that seemed to hug the earth. Sartas had seen death enough, had heard the Hag's cackling at close quarters. He knew, knew from the stillness, from the feel of it.

Renier was dead.

He came down more slowly now. No reason to hurry. Renier might have been asleep from the appearance of the body. Sartas, his hands gentle, turned Renier on his side, rocks cascading below them. The left temple was a jellied depression, the skull crushed with blood trickling sluggishly over the open wound. With no hope, Sartas felt for a pulse and found none. He hunkered down beside the body, bracing himself. Sighing, he invoked She of the Five, performing a quick rite for the dead kin. His words were quick, his gaze restless and always avoiding the body.

He fumbled in the pocket of his uniform, pulling out a small beacon. He touched one face of the device and set it beside Renier. Then he thumbed on his relay.

"McWilms?" He waited a moment, then spoke more harshly. "Damn you, boy, you'd better answer."

"Here, sirrah." The words were tinny and distant, surprised and questioning. "You got de Sezimbra?"

"No," Sartas spat. "Renier is dead. I've set the beacon for

you to follow. Trace it and take care of the body—I did the short rites, but I want you to give him the longer code-rite. Get the car as near as you can—we'll need it." He spoke flatly, almost tonelessly; it was not a voice to interrupt. "Do you understand all that?"

"Yah, sirrah." A pause and a crackling of electronic thunder. "What of de Sezimbra?"

"If he was important to you, I'd have said so, ass." Sartas let go the transmission button and breathed deeply, in and out. Then: "I'm after the man now. Hurry yourself. I don't know what carrion eaters live here, but if that body is touched, I'll take it out of your hide. Understood?"

"I've already left."

Sartas crouched, feeling the loose stones moving underfoot. His legs ached with the night's run. "Hag-kin," he muttered to himself, glancing down at the corpse. "He was luckier than we thought, neh? A worthy opponent. He'll be a fit companion for you, Renier, one to be proud of. I admire him. He's got fire and determination." The assassin reached down to touch the broken face. "You were a fine kin. All Hoorka will miss you."

He straightened, leaning against the slope. He glanced up at the jagged, moon-glazed summit of the ravine.

He began climbing.

21:45. It had been easy to find de Sezimbra's trail. The detector had shown him an image for only a quarter of an hour and had then gone quiet. The fight with Renier—the brush with the Hag's talons—had evidently frightened the man. He left the spoor of panic and fear, no attempt at stealth. Upward, westward, climbing toward the cold, hard sky, pushed by the adrenaline of death-fright . . .

But Sartas knew that his energy would only be a temporary ally. He'd seen it in other contracts. De Sezimbra had had the longer run, and the Hoorka were conditioned for the punishment. Time was still on Sartas's side, if he could get closer.

He found himself filled with a grudging admiration for de Sezimbra. He'd expected the man to be easy prey, but he'd seriously underestimated his resources. That might have cost Renier his life. Hoorka had died on contracts before—not many, but it was something that was expected at times. The Hoorka knew victims would strike back, would struggle against death; for some kin, Sartas was aware, that implicit danger was exciting, titillating. Renier had not been one of those, however. Sartas wished him peace in the afterlife. His kin's death drove him, made him ache for revenge, but the anger was tempered with respect for de Sezimbra. He felt curiously remote from the sadness, holding it back from his consciousness for the time being. Later, he'd mourn and weep with the rest of his kin, would feel emptied as Renier's body went back to ash in the soot-smeared Cavern of the Dead.

In de Sezimbra's place, Sartas would have done the same. He approved of de Sezimbra for that, but he could kill that which he admired. He forced himself to concentrate on his task; all the rest could wait.

He'd seen that de Sezimbra was tiring: the marks were now fresh on the dirt and stone, and the sparse vegetation that the man trampled had yet to spring back up. Close. Sartas pressed himself, moved a bit faster. Soon.

It was not a prepossessing scene: Sartas slipped into a narrow cleft in the cliff wall, following the tracks. The crevice opened out suddenly into a natural amphitheater, a hollow perhaps thirty meters across surrounded by dour gray walls of stone. There was little cover but the moon-shadow. The light-enhancer pierced the murk easily enough. Sartas could see de Sezimbra crouched opposite the entrance, his clothing torn, his side bloody with scratches, his dark skin shiny with perspiration. Panting, he still held Renier's vibro in his hand, but it was not activated. He'd trapped himself.

Sartas, his nightcloak swirling about him as he halted, stared at de Sezimbra. The man was still, not certain that he'd been seen. "Marco de Sezimbra, your life has been claimed by Hag Death."

The assassin's voice, stentorian in the night stillness, startled de Sezimbra. He shook himself, disbelieving, then stood, his breath ragged. "I'm not yet dead, sirrah. And for whom other than this Hag Death do you want me?"

"That information's not for you." Curtly, but not unwillingly, Sartas answered. The man could go nowhere, there was still enough time. If he wanted to talk, let him.

"Ahh." De Sezimbra nodded. "It doesn't matter, really. I know it's Guillene and Moache. He's the only one that would think that he has enough reason. You'll really let me go at 23:10?"

"I *would* have." The emphasis was pronounced.

The ghost of a smile played at the corners of de Sezimbra's mouth. "You still might need to. You won't throw your vibro—that's a low probability attack. You have to come and get me, and I could conceivably get past you."

"Or you could use the vibro."

This time he did smile. "I'm afraid it's not my forte. I'd rather be sneaky."

"You won't get past. Try and you'll feel my blade. I've more pleasant means of death, if you're willing to concede the inevitable. You won't get past." Sartas spoke with confidence, but he remembered Renier; he could not afford to underestimate the man again.

De Sezimbra was almost amiable. He stepped forward into the wash of moonlight, letting his pack drop from his shoulders. He limped slightly, favoring his left leg. "I've been on other worlds that didn't want me, sirrah. I've learned how to defend myself to an extent. Had to. I might not be the easy target you suppose. And I never concede inevitabilities. That's too complacent an attitude. It allows you to let injustices continue. I fight back, instead. Ask your friend—he's waiting on the other side of the cleft, isn't he?"

A spasm of pain twisted Sartas's face, a shadow. "You don't know? You killed him, de Sezimbra." A pause. "He waits for you, but it's not here."

"No." Shock and surprise were loud in the denial. "I wasn't intending that . . . I didn't hold back, that's true, but he was going to kill me if I didn't get away. I thought the fall would give me time . . . I checked with Niffleheim. They said the Hoorka were scrupulous, would follow their code. All I wanted was the time." His eyes pleaded. *A man who's never killed,* Sartas thought, *and who hadn't really contemplated the possibility of having to do so.* "I'm sorry," de Sezimbra said. "I didn't want that to happen. Believe me." He seemed genuinely perturbed, concerned.

"A victim that doesn't resist the Hag deserves his fate. And our apprentice must have told you—we don't take a person's fate out of the hands of their gods. I congratulate you on your skill," he remarked stonily. "Dame Fate was with you. It wasn't your time yet. It is now."

"Dame Fate may still be with me."

"If She is, you'll know soon enough."

Sartas said no more. He moved slowly into the open, watching de Sezimbra, waiting for the man to move, to commit himself. Back, to the left: de Sezimbra retreated, eyes glancing from side to side wildly, looking for an avenue of escape. The Hoorka moved inexorably toward him.

De Sezimbra flicked on his vibro.

It happened quickly. De Sezimbra suddenly leapt straight forward, far more agilely than Sartas expected—the limp was gone, a deception. The man's vibro thrust at Sartas, but the Hoorka, despite his surprise, was already countering. He turned, evading the blade, and slashed with his own weapon, hearing the whine of the vibro and the tearing of cloth. De Sezimbra groaned with pain as the vibro raked his side, and he kicked at Sartas's groin. Sartas deflected the blow harmlessly, lunging. This time he found his target. De Sezimbra staggered back wordlessly, dropping his weapon, hands clenched to his stomach. Blood, bright arterial blood, was slick around his fingers. He moaned, looking up at Sartas. He seemed about to speak; his mouth worked, but no words came. He nodded, almost a salutation, and slipped to his knees. Grunting, de Sezimbra tried to rise again and found he could not. He looked up at the sky, at the watching moon.

He fell to his side on the rocks.

"If I could've denied the Dame's whim, I would have, de Sezimbra," Sartas whispered. "If a man deserved to live . . . I wish you'd been luckier."

The Hag came to Heritage for a second time that night.

Sheathing his vibro (he would not clean it again until he returned to Neweden and could feed She of the Five), Sartas called McWilms, giving the apprentice his position. While he waited, he gave de Sezimbra the rite of the dead and wrapped the body in the spare nightcloak.

In time, McWilms arrived, and they took the body back to the car. On their way to Home, the tachyon relay on Sartas's belt suddenly shrilled, startling them both.

At Underasgard, morning light had touched the dawn-rock.

They could not help but attract attention as they entered the boundaries of Home. The throaty rumble of the groundcar shook the sleepy ones from their beds and turned the heads of those on the streets. All stared at the death-apparitions: the dust-lathered Hoorka in the open car, dark in the fluttering nightcloaks; the silent bundles in the back, wrapped in black and gray cloth.

They knew, the inhabitants of Home. The Hoorka could sense the news spreading through the city, welling outward.

Guillene's home was set well back from the street that wandered through Park Hill. It was further held aloof by a high wall and a wrought-steel gate flanked by two guards. The Hoorka rode toward it through a scurrying of people. Already a crowd had formed before the gates, standing silent across the lane, moving with a quiet restlessness. The guards, dour-faced, perhaps a little frightened, uneasily watched the mob grow, crowd-prods in hand. One whispered into a relay button on his lapel as the Hoorka rode up, shattering the night stillness.

The groundcar shuddered to a halt, the roar of the engine died. Sartas and McWilms, the cowls up on their night-cloaks, dismounted and picked up the bundle behind Sartas, handling it with a curious gentleness. They laid it before the gate as Guillene's men watched, as the mute faces across the street stared. The crowd swayed, murmured. "Is Sirrah Guillene here?" Sartas asked.

The guard to whom he spoke didn't have a chance to reply. From the darkness beyond the gate, a figure moved into sight The muttering of the crowd increased. "I'm Phillipe Guillene, Hoorka." He was tall and slight, his hair a crescent of silver around the dome of his head, and the robe he wore spoke of silken wealth. The voice was smooth, aristocratic. Gray eyes glanced down at the wrapped body outside the gate. "Is that de Sezimbra?"

"It is. Your contract has been fulfilled. Do you need to see the face?"

He glanced up. Sartas could see quick horror in the man's eyes. *So that's why he would pay Hoorka, then. He doesn't want to be near death.* "No," Guillene said, his voice rushed. "I believe you."

There was a concerted whispering in the ranks of people across the way. Guillene looked, seemed to see the spectators for the first time. He looked at them rather than Sartas.

"De Sezimbra was to be an example to them," he said. "The man was a troublemaker and a fool."

"I found him to be a brave and honorable opponent." Beneath the shadowed hood, Sartas's eyes glittered. He defied Guillene to gainsay him.

Guillene's face flushed with irritation, visible even in the dim light of the gate-lamps and the moon. He tugged at the belt of his robe, drawing it tighter around his waist. "You needn't speak your opinions here, Hoorka. I paid you—and well—for your work. It's now done. You may return to Neweden. I want nothing more to do with you."

"And the body?"

"My people will throw it on the slagheaps with the rest of the filth."

Sartas said nothing, but his stance altered subtly. Behind him, McWilms sensed the shift in attitude; he moved back and to one side, in a better position to support Sartas if trouble developed. The crowd-murmurs grew louder, though none of them made a move to cross the street, and none spoke loudly enough for Guillene to understand words. If they were angry with Guillene's treatment of de Sezimbra, they were also cowed.

"De Sezimbra deserves better rites." Sartas spoke slowly, loudly. "As I said, I found him to be courageous and honorable."

Like steel striking steel, his words drew sparks from Guillene. The man reared back as if struck. His eyebrows lowered, his lips parted, and the noble face was suddenly ugly. "*I* decide what is to happen on Heritage, Hoorka. If I say that the body is to be given to the slagheap, then that will be done." He gestured curtly to his guards. "Take it," he said.

Sartas stepped forward, an arm sweeping aside his nightcloak, his hand pulling the brown-stained vibro from its sheath. It whined eagerly; behind him, Sartas could hear the harmony of McWilms's own weapon. The guards, suddenly uncertain, stopped, caught between obedience and fear. They looked back at Guillene.

"Marco de Sezimbra faced Hag Death with honor," Sartas hissed, poised over the body. "I won't have him dishonored now. You'll lose your lives if you try. Sirrah Guillene, unless you want bloodfeud declared against you, tell them to stay away."

Guillene's face was taut, his neck corded with unvented anger. "This isn't your little backward world, Hoorka. There's no bloodfeud here, no kin. The man died because I willed it so. He's to be an example to my employees—I *warned* him to leave Heritage, to go before I was forced to take stronger measures. He stayed. He chose his fate. You stop me now, and you give an unwanted meaning to his death. That's not what I paid for. I won't have it."

"You paid for death. Nothing else." Sartas spoke to Guillene, but he watched the guards, who backed away one step. "The meaning and results of a person's death aren't in your hands but the gods'. You aren't able to pay for that. De Sezimbra will be given the proper rites or more than one person will join him in the Hag's dance. You can summon enough people to overcome us, true, but that'll only give more emphasis to de Sezimbra's death, neh?" Adamantine, that voice, with no hue of weakness. His vibro hummed threateningly, the luminous tip unwavering.

"We'll take the body back to his people." The voice came from the front ranks of the watching crowd; as Sartas glanced that way, a woman stepped out into the light of the gate-lamps. She was plain, heavy, clothed like a miner or lassari laborer. Behind her two men as nondescript as she stepped forward, heads down. "De Sezimbra helped my family once. We'll take the body and do what's proper, sirrah." Her voice was an odd mixture of servility and determination.

Sartas glared, uncertain. He didn't trust these people, so much like lassari, so used to doing Guillene's bidding. Lassari could not be trusted. It was a bitter lesson all guilded kin learned. Turn your back on them, and you'd better be prepared for the thrust of the knife.

Guillene raged behind his ornate barrier. "I'll have your shift masters cut your wages—your family will never leave Heritage. That's the cost of touching that body."

"Sirrah Guillene, I'm sorry, but the assassin is right. De Sezimbra deserves to be treated better than a common thief." She could not defy Guillene for long; her gaze dropped at his scowl. Behind her, the men shuffled their feet.

"You'll do this properly, woman?" Sartas asked.

She glanced at the angry Guillene. A nod, tentative at first, then stronger . . . "Might never leave Heritage anyway. I'll take the body back to his cabin and his people. If we may?"

Sartas, slowly, stood aside, still unsure but swayed by the look on Guillene's face. "You *will* do it," he said again.

"By my word," she replied. Sartas nodded and watched the two men lift the body and turn back into the crowd. The mass of people parted wordlessly, flowing back around them. Guillene, with a broken cry of frustration and rage, turned and strode back toward his house. "I won't forget this, Hoorka." The words came from the night.

Sartas and McWilms, a wary eye on the silent guards, sheathed their weapons. The groundcar roared as they made their way back to the hostel.

The following day was as pastoral as Heritage seemed capable of being. The sky was sooty blue, tinged with orange on the horizon where the metallic cross-hatching of a mining platform gnawed the distant hills. The sun was unrelenting: too hot, too bright, too oppressive.

Sartas and McWilms were pleased. They would be gone soon.

The flitter held the day's warmth in abeyance, circulating cool air through the glassed compartment in which they sat. The windows were polarized to cut the glare, and the scenery passed—ten meters below them—at a tolerable speed. The flitter purred along its predetermined course. The Hoorka relaxed, heads back on the cushioned seats, eyes half-closed.

"Gorgeous view, neh?" McWilms was half-turned, looking down at the orangish landscape.

"I'll be damned glad to leave it. Underasgard'll be very pleasant, even with having to tell Thane Valdisa that we need to prepare a wake for Renier." He glanced back. A heavy, oblong case was secured to the back of the flitter.

"When do we reach the Port?"

"An hour. Just lie back. Relax."

McWilms sighed and closed his eyes. Thus it was that he didn't see the grove of trees to their right nor the gout of fire that blackened the leaves there with sudden fury. Both

Hoorka were only momentarily conscious of the wrenching lurch as something tore into the shell of the flitter, shredding the plasti-steel, ripping off the guiding power vanes. The canopy sheltering them flew apart in crystalline shards; the next lurch of the flitter threw them both from the craft, blessedly oblivious.

Orange and black: flame and smoke tore at the craft and flung it to the ground.

The wreckage plowed into earth a hundred meters from the still bodies, carving a blackened gouge in the gritty dust, burning. Neither Hoorka saw the figures that came from the grove and stood over them, silent and grim-faced.

"They're dead?"

"This one is. The other'll be soon enough. No, don't bother to kill him—let 'im suffer."

It was nearly thirty minutes before the nonarrival of the flitter caused a puzzled Diplo at the Port terminal to send an investigating team out after the tardy vehicle. Neither Sartas nor McWilms heard the exclamations of surprise and concern as the Diplo crew arrived at the still-smoldering mass of twisted metal.

Hag Death, grinning eternally, returned again to Heritage.

Chapter 8

An excerpt from the acousidots of Sondall-Cadhurst Cranmer. This transcript is one of the rarities. In the Family Cranmer Archives there is a dot with what seems to be a live recording of the following scene, but the fidelity is terrible and much of the dot is indecipherable. Evidently Cranmer felt the conversation to be of some import, for he immediately did a dictation of the conversation as he remembered it. It was a method to which he had to resort on other occasions. The concealed microphones sometimes failed. It was, in his own words, "a penance one pays for being dishonest."

EXCERPT FROM THE DOT OF 5.28.217:

"Gyll was not much in a mood to see me. 'Don't even bother, Cranmer,' was all he said when I knocked at his door. I persisted noisily, though, and eventually he had to answer. He looked angry and tired. His eyes were red-veined and he moved with a jerky sullenness.

"'Don't you ever listen?' he growled. 'I'm not interested in talking to anyone.'

"I put on the jolly-old-Cranmer face that Gyll seems to consider the real me. 'Talking can be a catharsis of sorts, you know. You'll feel better afterward; it's guaranteed. I always find that . . .' I went on like that for a time, until through weariness or self-defense, Gyll stepped back to let me in. He'd evidently been cleaning his weapon—the tools were spread out on his bed and the vibrowire was extended. The wort sat quietly in its cage, its head turning to watch us. Gyll sat on the bed, pretending to be absorbed in his task. I took the one floater in the room, asking if he'd heard anything new about the Heritage foul-up.

"Gyll has an interesting face. For all his talk of the code and Hoorka aloofness, anyone that knows his habitual ticks and grimaces can read him. He's virtually without guile. I love playing cards against him: he can't bluff. When he's mad, he looks at you from slightly under his eyebrows, his lower lip sticks out a little, and the mouth turns down. All the wrinkles on his face get a little deeper. All those things happened then. 'I don't know anything,' he said. 'Valdisa insisted on going to see d'Embry alone. She should have let me go in her place, Cranmer. I know that cold bitch of a regent, Valdisa doesn't. She's likely to get some placating story . . .' He stopped and began to polish the vibrowire vigorously.

"I grunted and *hmmmed* a few times in sympathy. 'What interests me is the contract itself,' I told him. I let him know that I'd checked with the Center files and from what I could glean, de Sezimbra was exactly what the miners thought him to be—a good man, a gadfly (and a needed one) to the Alliance. And Moache Mining'd been involved in questionable practices before. 'Does it bother you that the Hoorka have killed an honorable man in the service of a dishonorable bastard, a man who has no sense of moral right or wrong, at least in the way Neweden views such things?'

"That brought his head up. He set the vibro aside too gently. The way he looked at me, I could see that the question was one that was already nagging at him. 'What the Dame wills to happen, happens. And if Hoorka hadn't killed the man, someone else would have, without giving de Sezimbra his proper chance.' But he said it without fire, without conviction.

"I replied that no doubt the fact that it was all the Dame's will was very comforting. 'And no doubt she meant for the flitter to be ambushed, too.'

"Gyll gave me the aggravated look—the one that comes right before anger. 'Because something is fated doesn't mean that it's also right. You know that. What happened with Renier; that was understandable, even expected in its own way. But what Guillene did to the other two ... If that man were on Neweden, bloodfeud would be declared without a thought, and it'd be a slow death if I found him.'

"I figured I had one more push before Gyll got angry and I had to shut up for a while. That's Gyll's way: you have to dig at the man to get him to talk, and all the prodding makes him irritable. 'Guillene's offworld,' I reminded him. 'You can't do a damned thing to him. And in any case, Valdisa's handling it, not you.'

"He didn't say anything at all, which was unlike him. He picked up the vibro again, reeled the wire back into the hilt and attached the holding plate. Then he jammed the weapon back into the sheath and stood up. He stared down at me. 'Cranmer, one day the looseness of your tongue is going to cause it to be cut out,' he said, and then he walked out of the room.

"The wort whimpered at his retreating back. And I sat there wishing that there was another way to get Gyll to react—jabbing holes in a person's dreams is depressing.

"And in any case, I *like* my tongue."

Thane Valdisa was possessed by rage. It sat, an indigestible and bitter lump in her gut. Frustration gnawed at her stomach; sorrow battered at her, demanding release.

Two Hoorka dead, Renier by a contracted victim, but Sartas slain by a cowardly ambush. And McWilms—she'd just left his rooms in the Center Hospital. The surgeon had said that the boy would recover, but Valdisa had seen the misshapen face under the med-pad and the empty socket of his shoulder where they were preparing the arm bud. He might attend his initiation as full kin, but it would be many months before he could take his place in the rotation. The condition of McWilms, his mute helplessness and pain, made her the most angry. Death, *that* she could understand, could cope with, but the boy's mutilation ...

She strode into the brilliant lobby of Diplo Center, the sunstar a mockery at her back, and demanded to see Regent d'Embry. The startled Diplo she accosted mumbled nervously and whispered into her com-unit. The Diplo's eyes spoke of contempt, but her voice was blandly polite. "The Regent is able to see you now."

"She didn't have a choice." Valdisa strode away.

D'Embry's office was awash with lemon sunlight. It glared from the holocube of d'Vellia's *Gehennah* in the corner, a wedge of light shimmered across the carpet and over her desk, slashing across the Regent's thin body but leaving the face in shadow. D'Embry herself was a mobile sunbeam, her hands, shoulders, and earlobes dashed with yellow skin tint. Only her much-lined face was at odds with the day. Her mouth was down-turned, the icy-blue eyes serious.

"Come in, Thane Valdisa. I have to admit that I was expecting to see someone from the Hoorka today. I was sorry to hear about the problems with the Heritage contract."

"*Problems? . . .*" Valdisa glared at the woman. *So frigging secure behind that desk. She doesn't care about Renier, Sartas, or McWilms. If she feels any sorrow, it's only because of the trouble she'll have over Heritage.* "You have an interesting way of phrasing things, m'Dame."

D'Embry toyed with an ippicator bone on her desk. The polished surface caught the light, held it and amplified it, lustrous. Thin fingers, yellow against the bone's subtle ivory, turned the piece and set it down again. "You think I haven't any feelings for your kin in your loss. Believe me, Thane Valdisa, I do." She looked up, and Valdisa was caught in her young-old eyes. "When you've lived as long as I have, you've had to lose those that were close to you. I *do* understand how you have to feel, the anger. The Alliance will pay the cost of McWilms's hospitalization. Consider it a gesture of our concern for your feelings—I shouldn't have let you work that contract. The situation was far too volatile."

"Have you seen him?"

"Apprentice McWilms? No."

"I have." Valdisa tore herself away from d'Embry's steady regard, going to the window. The lawn of the Center stretched out to the flat expanse of Sterka Port. In sunlight, the head of the large ippicator before the Center stared sightlessly at distant port workers. "They told me that half his face had been torn away, like someone had scrubbed at it with a file," she said, staring outward. "He was just a mass of bleeding, shredded tissue. The right arm had been crushed, flattened, the bones shattered. He'd nearly bled to death. Both legs broken, severe internal injuries. Maybe here on Neweden he'd've died, unconscious. Now he gets to live with the agony—and I'll have to tell him that it's the better option. Sartas's injuries had been worse. I think in some ways he's luckier."

She turned back into the room. D'Embry was watching her, silent, hands folded on her desktop. "And *you,* damn you, sit back there and talk about *problems* on Heritage," Valdisa shouted. "Well, they were people, and my kin, and I feel their hurt." She paused, breathing heavily once, and when she continued, the voice was more controlled. "My people are going to want to declare bloodfeud. I can't say that I disagree with that."

"Bloodfeud's not possible."

"Your own report says that Sartas argued with Guillene, went against Guillene's orders. Guillene threatened Sartas, publicly."

"There's no proof that Guillene was responsible for the attack."

"Who the hell else?" Valdisa laughed in exasperation and disgust.

D'Embry shrugged, but her gaze was sympathetic. "De Sezimbra was popular among the miners—it could have been a group of them, or perhaps even de Sezimbra's associates. It didn't have to be Guillene."

"None of the others have any reason to harm Hoorka. We're simply the weapon, not the hand that wields it. Would you destroy a vibro and let the man go that used it?"

"I'd be tempted to destroy both." Then d'Embry sighed, leaning back in her floater. "Heritage isn't Neweden, Thane. They've a different governing structure, a different set of laws. Believe me, I understand your anger and frustration, but there's very little I can do about it."

"Because Moache Mining is involved? Is that it? I'll wager that the word reached you from Niffleheim before the bodies were even loaded on the ship, neh? Leave Heritage alone, ignore the murder of Hoorka." Valdisa's fury boiled; she fought to hold it back, knowing it would either make her cry or rage and knowing that d'Embry would just sit there and watch, unmoved. She stood opposite the Regent, leaning down, her hands on the polished surface of the desk.

D'Embry hesitated before answering, and Valdisa wondered what emotion clouded those clear eyes for a breath. "Moache Mining *is* powerful," d'Embry admitted. "I can't answer for Diplo Center on Heritage. But *I've* had no instruction from Niffleheim or Moache. And even if I had, my actions would be my own."

There was a fierce pride on the Regent's face.

Valdisa glanced at the ippicator bone on the desk, with an inward prayer to She of the Five. "But you still won't let Hoorka act as we wish."

"Only because I don't want Hoorka getting involved in something too big for them. I'll do everything I can. It's an offworld matter, Thane." Reaching out, d'Embry touched Valdisa's callused hand with her softer, vein-webbed one, yellow against tanned flesh. Valdisa began to pull away from the contact, but d'Embry held her with gentle pressure. "No matter what you want done," the Regent continued, "it'll have to be handled through Diplo channels and in accordance with Heritage's own laws, which are the laws of the Alliance. We'll try to find the people responsible, I promise you that. I'll push them if I have to, and I'm a very good, experienced pusher. It was just this kind of situation that worried me when I allowed the Hoorka to work offworld, Thane. Don't make my fears become reality, or I'll have little choice." A quick squeeze of fingers, and a surprising warmth in d'Embry's eyes: Valdisa found herself listening, the anger momentarily background.

The Regent moved her hand back. Valdisa pulled herself erect. "I understand you, Regent. I do. But you'd better get results and a punishment that's satisfactory to Hoorka. I've only so much power to sway my kin, and they're enraged and bitter."

"You're the Thane. They *have* to understand, or at least obey."

Valdisa smiled, lopsided. "I'm Thane, yah. But obedience is another matter, sometimes ... Ulthane Gyll could do it, but Ulthane Gyll also doesn't *take* orders well, nor do some of the others." She glanced away, slowly looking about the uncluttered room. When she looked back, she had again become the arrogant Hoorka-thane.

"You'd better see that something is done quickly, m'Dame," Valdisa said. "You might find that it benefits both you and Neweden."

* * *

The Li-Gallant Vingi found his new Domoraj to be rather less intelligent and less given to moody introspection than the former holder of that title. The combination was more to his liking.

The Domoraj faced Vingi from the corner of his room, which held the rods of the Battier Radiance. Vingi was naked in the glare of the Battier, rolls of fat girdling his body. Seeing the Domoraj enter the room, he reached out and turned off the device, putting on a worn blue robe that hung from one of the posts. This Domoraj is a buffoon, he decided as the light began to fade. He'd keep him for a while, but already the thought of a successor concerned him. Someone younger, more pliable to Vingi's whims. The Li-Gallant moved to his desk, folding thick hands over the scattered flimsies there, his rings flicking particolored light about the room.

"You may sit, Domoraj." Vingi watched the man. The new leader of his guard force was older, paunchier, and Vingi found that the man's smile seemed cruelly superficial—it touched only his mouth. The eyes sat too close to the prominent nose; the uniform he wore was too tight, meant for a younger version of the man. "I hope my lack of proper attire didn't upset you too much."

"Not at all, Li-Gallant."

Vingi had seen the Domoraj's face when he entered the office. "You don't lie well, Domoraj."

The man's smile wavered, like a flame guttering in wind. "Li-Gallant . . ."

"It's not that awful, man, but you should learn to be more careful. I don't like pretension with my staff, Domoraj. You needn't feel threatened." Vingi waited, but the Domoraj said nothing more. He patted his ample stomach. "I've had a most interesting communication from Sirrah Potok," Vingi continued. "It seems that he was most perturbed by the slowness of your security forces during the lassari attack on Gunnar's bier."

A slow nod. "Li-Gallant, the attack was so sudden, so unexpected, and with the discomfort of the rain—"

Vingi halted the litany of excuses with an abrupt hand movement. He'd discovered enough—the Domoraj had fear of him. "I can understand your problems, Domoraj.

Your much-lamented predecessor could have done no better."

The Domoraj relaxed perceptibly. He tugged at his uniform, settling it more comfortably around his shoulders. "I'm impressed by your assessment of the situation, Li-Gallant." He smiled.

"I'm sure you are." Vingi returned the smile. "However, I think you misunderstand me. I see your difficulties, yah, but I do *not* excuse you for them. That was a very sloppy example of your ability to control my forces, a ground for severe reprimand if not an outright dismissal. Do you understand me now, Domoraj?"

Vingi watched the smugness evaporate from the Domoraj, saw the beads of nervous sweat pearl on the forehead. "Li-Gallant—" the Domoraj began.

Vingi ignored the burgeoning plea, knowing what the man would say. "It *would* be sufficient for punishment if it didn't fit well with my own plans. Potok's guild has been shown, publicly, to be weak, lassari-prey. Your incompetence worked well, unintentionally, for you did manage to quell the attack when you finally moved. What worries me is whether Dame Fate will allow such a coincidence twice. If I need a disciplined force and can't have one . . ."

"Li-Gallant, I assure you that it can't happen again. I was just beginning my command then. My methods are just now having effect. In a few months, you'll have an exceptionally well-trained and eager force."

Vingi's lips curled in a half-smile, half-sneer. "Yet I have to have a scapegoat for the Assembly, Domoraj. I can't entirely let the incident go by. Your people were slow. I want you to choose one of your lieutenants—he will be made responsible for the tardiness, and publicly reprimanded."

"Li-Gallant . . ."

"You will do it, Domoraj." Vingi nodded. "And you'll continue to work on the discipline, won't you?"

The Domoraj bowed his head in acceptance.

"Good. You see, Domoraj, I might have some small use for your vaunted training. Potok has challenged me to truth-duel. The Magistrate's Guild has accepted the proposal, and I need to reply by this evening. Potok accuses me of the death of Gunnar."

"You'll not accept it?"

"Oh, but I will. Gods, man, all guilded kin think me guilty already. If I decline, it will be certain to them. Dame Fate will guide my hand, and I believe that Potok will find me in better condition than he suspects. You *do* think me innocent, don't you, Domoraj?" Vingi cocked his head, his several chins jiggling.

"Yes, sirrah. Of course." The Domoraj did his best to appear shocked by the implication that he would not believe his kin-lord. Vingi was not particularly impressed by the acting. *Look at him—those eyes can hide nothing; all his acting is in the mouth. He knows that I tried to slay Gunnar with the Hoorka, knows that I once had Domoraj Sucai send someone after him, and he knows that the Domoraj was recently plagued by guilt. The whispers have been heard—he thinks that the Domoraj joined the Dead because I forced him to dishonor once too often, that I killed Gunnar through him.*

Vingi looked down at immaculately groomed fingernails. "I'm pleased that you're so sure of my innocence."

"Sirrah, what penalties have been demanded?"

"For Potok's guild: loss of five seats in the Assembly; Potok will step down as kin-lord, exiling himself in Irast. Also, we'll receive a large tithe for reparation of the harm that the false accusation has done us. Should we lose (and I know you'll not let that occur, Domoraj), the Assembly will be dissolved and a new election held at once. Our guild must pay the election expenses. I will also retire as kin-lord to an exile of my own choosing so long as it is not within fifteen hundred kilometers of Sterka. We'd be ruined, financially and politically."

"Yet you'll risk that?" Fear showed in the Domoraj; in his stiffness, in the restlessly clenching hands. If the guild were gone, so was his own stature. Vingi gambled with all of them.

"I prefer a quick death to a slow one, Domoraj. My kin-father would have felt the same. If I were to refuse, within five standards all the penalties set out against us would have occurred anyway. The rumors would have done Potok's work for him—I know he hopes for refusal. And I don't intend to lose. Potok isn't young, and if he's not as . . . ahh, large as myself, I doubt that he's any more used to labor. You'll train me, Domoraj; Potok has no one in his guild as well versed in fighting skills."

"Li-Gallant, I can only do so much in a short time—when is the duel?"

"In three days."

"Potok will also be preparing."

"Then you'd best do the better job, neh?"

To that, the Domoraj had no answer.

"But what does it do?" the dwarf kept insisting.

"You can see it and hear it as well as anyone," Oldin replied, sounding exasperated. *"That's* what it does."

"Things have to do something. You can't sell them if they don't."

"Now that's your typical bullshit, Helgin."

The instrument sat in the middle of Oldin's rooms, an ovoid a half-meter across impaled on the tip of a four-sided pyramid. The facets of the pyramid gleamed like cut crystal; from the milky depths a light pulsed, always an aching purple-black that seemed to be just on the edge of the visible spectrum. The device emitted discordant squeals and grunts like a mortally sounded trombone. It was not pleasant to see or hear. Helgin was damned if he could find a pattern in the timing or melody in the pitch. He said as much to Oldin.

"So it wasn't meant for Motsognir sensibilities, Helgin. I won't try selling them to the dwarves, then. Or maybe you're just tone-deaf."

Helgin scowled behind his ruddy beard. He walked up to the object with his rolling gait and reached out to touch. Slick, smooth, cold—far colder than the room. He looked at his fingertip. "Who got you this damned piece of junk?"

"Siljun—he bought three hundred of them on speculation. Said the race that manufactures them puts them around all their buildings. He also said that the noise kept him up all night."

"I can imagine. By Huard's cock, I don't know what you're going to do with them."

"I've got fifty of them. Siljun kept the rest. I thought I might try selling them as some kind of rejuvenation device. Just make 'em expensive enough, give a little tale about how they're important in the natives' ritual orgies . . . They'll sell. And they'll work because people want them to work— the placebo effect."

"Yah." Helgin stared at the woman. Oldin was swathed

in layers of cloth, an iridescent wrap that wandered about her body in complicated windings. It complimented Oldin's stocky physique—enticing, but promised endless troubles with removal. Helgin decided that it fit her well. "You're a dishonest bitch, Kaethe."

"Only when I need to be. At other times I can be quite nice, as you know." She smiled sweetly down at the Motsognir. "I'm going to try selling a few of these with the next load down to Neweden. And speaking of that world—how is Renard? Have you talked with him since the funeral?"

The alien artifact burbled and wheezed through the last part of her question. Helgin was close enough—he kicked out with a sandalled foot. The device rocked heavily and subsided into penitent hisses. Helgin grinned. "I talked to him. He said things are proceeding fairly well. Said to mention to Grandsire FitzEvard that he was right—all Neweden needed was a few pushes in the right places. If the Li-Gallant can retain his power and his viciousness, you'll get what you're after, eventually." Hands on squat, wide hips, he regarded her from under the shadowed ledge of eyebrows. "You should at least express a modicum of remorse, Kaethe-dear. We're discussing the sabotage of an entire society for your grandsire's whims."

She nodded distractedly. "Remorse isn't something taught to the Oldins."

"Too bad. Otherwise, you're almost human. I could almost come to like you." He spoke gruffly, but Oldin smiled at him. From the ovoid came a whimpering in melancholy violet.

"I'm just doing what Grandsire's asked—he doesn't tell me why. I hope the altered Neweden is what Grandsire wants. I wonder if there'll be anything left of the caste system?"

"Like the lassari? He might want them—a built-in servile class. Or are you thinking of other things?" He scowled, twisting his beard. "Anytime you induce change, you destroy something good. The Motsognir found that out when we took Naglfar as home—we gave up much of our culture that was sound and viable when we became wanderers. But we'd lose just as much by settling again. Neweden was changing anyway. I think that's what your grandsire knew. He decided to hasten the change—that's something more easily done than destroying an ongoing and vital society. But I'll be damned if I know what he wants from Neweden."

Helgin shrugged and sat on the grass-carpet, leaning back against the now-quiet artifact. Where his back touched the device, a purplish nimbus welled outward.

"Did Renard say he needed anything?"

"Neh. He's been here long enough to feel comfortable. He said he'd wait for the next ship before he left. Wants to make sure that everything goes well, that he doesn't need to make adjustments."

A nod. "Have you seen Gyll—the Hoorka?"

Helgin—mouth pursed, eyes wincing—pulled a hair from his beard. He regarded the red-flecked, coarse strand. "Why? Is he something your grandsire wants you to save?"

"He said nothing about them."

"That's why I wondered at your talk about an 'offer' to them. Are you playing at a whim yourself, Kaethe?"

Again, a shrug. Her gilded eyebrows rose, fell. She looked up at the viewport in the ceiling. "Grandsire rewards all those who follow his orders. But he rewards best the ones that show initiative. The Hoorka are ... interesting. And Gyll's ideals are close enough to that of the Families to be potentially useful. The Hoorka could conceivably work with us. I wasn't entirely false about the possibility of transplanting the Hoorka. The Oldins could use Gyll's skills, his dedication, and I think he'd be more happy with us than the Alliance." She looked down at him, a speculative gleam in her eyes. "And you seemed to take a liking to him, dwarf."

"I did." He stared flatly back. "He resembles the Motsognir in temperament—he could be as stubbornly disagreeable as me. And I don't like to see people I like get hurt. So if you're just lying to yourself again, why don't you forget the Hoorka?"

"He could be useful." She was looking at the viewport again. Neweden was a bright curve at the lower edge. Sleipnir was a pockmarked face set in black.

For no apparent reason, the ovoid suddenly gurgled and screamed—a high-pitched discord at loud volume. Helgin, leaning back against it, catapulted himself across the room, rolling up against the far wall. Kaethe, hands over ears, laughed at him.

Helgin shot a venomous glance at her amusement, picked himself off the floor, and strode back across the room to the wailing machine. Grunting, he pushed at the ovoid. It moved, then settled heavily back into place. Helgin pushed again, and this time it toppled, striking the floor with a sharp crack. The banshee howl died—leaving only Kaethe's giggling—and the lights on the base flickered once before fading.

"Damn you, you might have warned me about that." Helgin spat on the broken machine. "Now you only have to sell forty-nine."

Chapter 9

DINNER IN UNDERASGARD. The long cavern (calcite deposits stained a pale tan—though where Felling's apprentices had been set to scrubbing, they were milky white) was filled with rude tables and the loud talk of kin. The full Hoorka had gathered to one end of the cavern, which was fragrant with Felling's stew; from the kitchen entrance, the pale faces of the youngest apprentices looked out, sweat-slick, at the doings of their elders.

"The Thane won't do as Sartas's honor deserves. She's just sitting back and letting d'Embry make excuses." Aldhelm slapped the table in front of him for emphasis. "The Hag gnaws at his soul, and we've done nothing to stop Her."

"If that's your feeling, why don't you complain to the Thane when she's here to defend herself?" retorted d'Mannberg from down the length of the table. A susurration of agreement came from those around him. "She's doing what she feels is best for Hoorka, and you've sworn allegiance to her. Unless your word's no better than a lassari's, save your complaints for Council. She'll listen to you, and answer."

"Would that do any good, kin-brother?" Aldhelm stood, one foot up on his stool, arms crossed over his knees. The scar on his cheek was glazed with lamplight. Before any of the kin could reply, he continued. "It's not just Sartas. McWilms is in the Center Hospital. And remember that Eorl was killed by lassari, and we've never found his murderer. We're losing our honor— and we'll lose more if Sartas and McWilms aren't avenged. The tale's already common gossip, and the guilded kin are still muttering about us. Ask Ulthane Gyll—he hasn't said anything about Thane Valdisa's decision, and I'd wager that he's not in agreement with her on this."

"You didn't follow the Ulthane's lead when he was Thane. Why are you suddenly claiming him as an ally?" Serita Iduna, sitting beside Ric, cocked her head at Aldhelm. She leaned forward, her elbows smearing moisture across the wood. "We've suffered no worse than the other guilded kin, at least those around Sterka. We're all involved with the lassari problems—look at Gunnar's funeral."

"Sartas and McWilms weren't attacked by lassari." Bachier spoke in defense of Aldhelm.

"That's true, but the guilded kin talk about Hoorka because it's known that Gunnar escaped us twice. They think a Hoorka might have been involved in his death. I almost don't blame them." D'Mannberg had been looking at Serita; now his gaze moved to Aldhelm. The significance of his glance wasn't lost on the other kin, but Aldhelm did not seem to notice. "If you hadn't asked for permission to visit Sterka that night, Aldhelm, Hoorka couldn't be suspect."

"I'm sorry, but I wasn't aware at that time that Gunnar was going to be killed."

The air between the two of them was charged. Bachier hurried to fill the silence. "We have problems—no one disputes that," he said, glancing from one to the other. "But internal bickering isn't going to solve anything. Yah, I don't like the fact that the Thane is willing to wait for d'Embry to act, but she also said that she wouldn't wait forever. We followed Ulthane Gyll's rulings—"

"Thane Valdisa isn't Ulthane Gyll," said Aldhelm.

"She *is* Thane," Bachier insisted. "And she was the Ulthane's choice."

"Choices aren't always good," Aldhelm retorted. "Mark my words. Valdisa won't do anything for Sartas because *d'Embry* won't do anything. I'm sick of the Alliance and their games."

"So we should limit ourselves to Neweden?" D'Mannberg shifted his massive bulk on the stool. Wood creaked under him. "Maybe we should even make a bid for power and kill a few of the kin-lords, neh?"

Aldhelm glared. "And why not just Neweden? It's our culture and our society. That's what killed Sartas. And why don't you just say all that's on your mind, d'Mannberg? You think I killed Gunnar without giving him proper warning and a chance to defend himself? I live by the code, even when I feel it's wrong."

"Is that why you felt Ulthane Gyll's vibro, because you followed the code? We all know better, Aldhelm. You almost ignored it once, and that was with Gunnar, too."

"I'd still never slay a person in shameful ambush, without letting Dame Fate have Her chance."

"You can say that," d'Mannberg said with some heat. "You talk a good defense, but words are just words." Deliberately, he turned away from Aldhelm, looking at the other kin around him. "You see, Aldhelm is always right. The rest of us are just too stupid to see it."

"Talk *to* me if you've something to say, man." Aldhelm trembled with interior rage.

D'Mannberg ignored him, continuing to speak to the others. "He'd ignore the code on the practice strip, but expects us to believe him in all other things. If Aldhelm thinks I'm that stupid, he's an ass."

Aldhelm's face went scarlet, his hand moving to his vibrohilt. His stool clattered backward, his boots stamped packed earth. Aldhelm pulled the hilt from the sheath and flung it down in front of d'Mannberg. It skidded across the table's surface, stopping hilt foremost half off the wooden planks. D'Mannberg looked up at Aldhelm, a long slow smile forming behind the russet beard. "First blood, kinbrother?"

Aldhelm, tight-lipped, nodded.

Serita, behind d'Mannberg, gestured to the wide-eyed apprentices staring from the door to the kitchens. "Get Thane Valdisa and Ulthane Gyll," she said, gesturing harshly. "Move, you fools!"

They stood before the Thane, Aldhelm and d'Mannberg. Aldhelm seemed tense, on edge, his arms akimbo. His weight shifted from foot to foot, impatient, and he watched Valdisa with a grimace of pride. D'Mannberg seemed eagerly confident, legs wide like a surly dwarf given stature. He seemed almost happy—his blue eyes danced from the Thane to Ulthane Gyll.

Valdisa liked neither one's attitude. She also did not like the way Gyll sat behind her, silent, one hip up on the edge of her desk like some critical overseer. Valdisa paced, back and forth between the desk and the two antagonistic Hoorka, trying to find some way to discharge the tension in the room, trying to ignore her own feeling of pessimistic inevitability. She seemed tiny against d'Mannberg's height and girth, sour when placed next to Aldhelm's masked sto-icism. *Much the way d'Embry seems to me. Too damn much like d'Embry.*

"The two of you do nothing but argue. I'm sick of hear-ing about it—you can't settle it talking, can't fight it out on the practice strips. Now you demand first blood—what was it this time?" She could hear the irritation in her voice, melded with fear of her inadequacy—sharp, petty, nasal.

D'Mannberg glanced at Aldhelm and shrugged. "Does it matter, Thane?" he asked. "We seem to be able to reach no better solution. My honor would like the blood he demands."

"Your honor also demands that you do what's best for Hoorka-kin. Fighting among ourselves only weakens Hoorka. We've enough problems at the moment without risking injury to appease somebody's wounded pride." All the time walking—to the desk, back again.

"You fought Bachier, Thane." Despite his restlessness, Aldhelm's voice was calm. His eyes seemed to mock her. "That was no doubt a great help to our kin."

In the midst of a step, Valdisa whirled about, her night-cloak billowing out like a dark wing. "I *had* to fight Bachier—he insulted me during Council. Every decision I make seems to be grounds for open discussion among the elder kin; I had to prove myself worthy to be Thane, and I had no wish to hurt Bachier. I've seen the two of you, watched you both. You circle each other like tiger cubs, con-stantly seeing how far you can go before the other lashes out with claws. You want to hurt each other too much."

"We only want first blood. Thane. Nothing more. It's our right, under the code, to be allowed to have it," Aldhelm said.

Valdisa nodded. She inhaled, held it, then let the breath go with a sigh. "Can't you wait a few nights, see if it's still this important to you then? If your blood cools, maybe you'll be able to talk out your misunderstanding. I'd be happy to arbitrate, to help the two of you sift out the prob-lems."

"You can't stop them, Thane." Gyll spoke from behind her, his voice natural, unstressed: a simple, factual statement. She turned to him, accusing.

"How can you be so certain of that?"

"Look at them." He nodded to the two assassins. "Neither of them wants to give in. Give it up, Thane. Let them have first blood."

Valdisa blinked in surprised anger at Gyll's indiscreet candor. Feeling the boil of temper rising, she turned back to d'Mannberg and Aldhelm. "You won't wait? You insist on immediate satisfaction?"

D'Mannberg nodded, echoed by Aldhelm.

"Then you can have it." Her voice was clipped, curt, official. She cloaked her feelings in the mask of distant authority. "Ulthane Gyll will judge the match. Call my apprentice as you leave, Aldhelm. Have her inform the kin of the match. Then prepare yourselves. You may go."

She watched them leave, stonily, wrapping her nightcloak around her as if cold. As the door crashed shut behind them, she looked back to Gyll.

"*Don't*"—heavily—"*ever* advise me in that manner again, Gyll."

"You've told me you want my advice."

"As a friend advises a friend. Not like a god advises his worshipers."

"Valdisa—"

"You can leave too, Gyll."

He was suddenly contrite. "Valdisa, I'm sorry . . . I was way too brusque and you deserve to be angry. It just seemed so obvious that they wouldn't have it any other way. I know what d'Mannberg thinks about Aldhelm—you must have heard what he said during their last practice."

Valdisa suddenly lost her anger. Her shoulders slumped beneath the dark cloth of the nightcloak. "I've heard you voice the same suspicion—that Aldhelm might have murdered Gunnar. I still don't believe that, Gyll. And it's not worth shedding blood over."

"If it's true?"

"I believe my kin."

Gyll hesitated. The rest of the tale was on his tongue— his suspicion that Aldhelm had lied that night, his subsequent failure at finding the supposed Irastian smith. It was, after all, the Thane's business—if kin had done the dishonorable deed, then it was the Thane's right to be aware of that and to mete out the punishment. Yet he couldn't say it. He told himself that it was because it was still uncertain—Gyll might have missed the smith, or perhaps Aldhelm had some other task in Sterka that night, and Gyll had also not had the opportunity to confront Aldhelm directly. Whatever the reason, he said nothing; just nodded at Valdisa's statement, wondering at his own arrogance in keeping this from her.

Valdisa smiled, touching his hand. "Hey, you have to judge this, neh? Go on, Gyll. I'll be there in a few minutes." A pause. She almost smiled. "Yah?"

Gyll squeezed her hand. He left.

Valdisa slumped back against her desk. "Damn," she muttered to the walls.

The practice room, noisy with conversation, was crowded. The Hoorka-kin found what room they could, jostling good-naturedly. All other activity in Underasgard had stopped. A few Hoorka, vibrofoils in hand, stood about with sweat-slicked skin, breaths quick and loud, their own practice abandoned. Even Felling, with his stained apron over the swell of his paunch, was present. The blood-duel was not to be missed.

It would be quick. All of them knew that. First blood only (though it was whispered by some who had seen the two before that Aldhelm would not be contented with a simple scratch), and Ulthane Gyll was notorious for being a quick hand with his own foil in judging such matches. A nick would end it, if Gyll had his way. Cranmer, an apprentice towing his hoverholos, was hastily setting up his recording equipment, casting appealing glances at Gyll. The Ulthane strode back and forth along the chosen strip as Aldhelm and d'Mannberg feinted with shadows at either end.

Gyll glanced at Valdisa as she entered the cavern. She moved forward as the ranks gave way before her, leaving her standing in a small, clear circle of ground. Gyll didn't know if that was deference or an indication of some uneasiness in her presence. He did know that the kin had never treated him so, and he could see from her stance that

she was uncomfortable with the distancing. Valdisa nodded/
shrugged to him.

Gyll stepped to center strip. "Kin-brothers, are you both
ready?"

His clear baritone sent the muttering of the kin into silence. Aldhelm and d'Mannberg came to the middle of the
strip.

"Your weapons, please." Gyll quickly examined the vibrofoils (pull the control ring down, twist it sideways three
clicks, let it snap back into position, locked), then he
plunged the foils into dirt alongside the strip. Both went in
easily, earth kicking up around the tips and the shivering
vibrowire. He handed back the weapons and pulled his own
foil from the rack. As the growl of vibros grew loud, he
checked his own blade. "You will remember that this is first
blood only," Gyll said. "If either of you try to go beyond
that, you'll also be fighting my blade. Neither the Thane nor
I wish kin to fight in this way—when it's necessary you'll do
it by the code." He glanced from one to the other.

Ric d'Mannberg was tense—his nervousness showed in
the banded swirl of muscles in the back of his hands, thick
fingers flexing over the foil's grip. The polished guard threw
back the underwater light of the nearest light-fungi; a slash
of emerald crawled his arm. He rubbed his beard with a forefinger, scuffed the packed, resilient earth with bare feet.

Aldhelm was an enigma. The vibrofoil was held casually,
the luminous tip down and swaying a few centimeters
above the lined dirt. He glanced at d'Mannberg with a curious lethargy, as if the anger had cooled to a dispassionate
dislike, as if he no longer viewed d'Mannberg as a person,
but as a problem to be studied for the best method of exe-
cution. He simply nodded at Gyll's admonition.

"This is the last chance," Gyll continued. "I'd prefer that
you reconsider. A disagreement, as Thane Valdisa told
you"—he glanced at her; yes, she'd noticed the contrition in
his voice—"needn't be settled by blood."

"On Neweden, that seems to be the way of things,
Ulthane. Everyone supposes that you must seek blood to
redeem yourself." Aldhelm didn't look at Gyll, but at
d'Mannberg. The tip of his foil swayed. A muscle in his jaw
twitched the scarred cheek. "I assume d'Mannberg still
stands by his words to me?"

"Did I say any untruths, Aldhelm?" asked d'Mannberg.

The scar flicked again, fungi-light staining the flesh. "It doesn't really matter, does it?"

"We'll let the Dame decide." D'Mannberg let the tip of his vibrofoil graze Aldhelm's weapon. Metal whined and clashed; the foils bucked in their hands.

Gyll whipped his foil up, knocking the weapons aside. "You'll begin when I start you, not before." His eyes warned. *Watch this one carefully,* he told himself. *There's been too much hurting of kin.* "Salute each other and begin," he said. He stepped back from the strip.

Vibrofoils came up, met high with a clashing that sent quick sparks cascading to the earth. Their vibrations thrilled the air. Then the foils moved in a sudden dance, d'Mannberg stepping forward with an audible grunt, taking the high inside line. Parry and riposte—Aldhelm's weapon moved with a lithe grace, and the meeting of foils gave birth to a bright, dying rain as vibrowire hissed in anger. Aldhelm moved his blade in a quick circle, a counter-parry of quarte, then lunged to the high inside line. D'Mannberg knocked the foil away with a beat, stepping back, but Aldhelm's foil pursued. D'Mannberg kicked at Aldhelm's foil hand, suddenly, but his foot found only air and as he wavered off-balance, Aldhelm thrust. Vibros screamed, whining as the foils scraped along each other's length. The kin could see d'Mannberg's foil held too low, the guard allowing access to shoulder and bicep. The larger man desperately lifted the weapon as Aldhelm's foil slithered toward him. An intake of breath—those beside the strip were certain of a touch. Gyll moved forward, ready to halt them; Valdisa, in her inviolate circle, frowned.

But Aldhelm moved back, two quick steps, disengaging. D'Mannberg didn't pursue. The cavern was suddenly quiet without the clashing of vibrofoils. The two Hoorka stared at one another. A droplet of sweat ran from d'Mannberg's temple into his matted beard. Some inner communication seemed to leap from man to man. Then d'Mannberg took a step, sweeping his foil in a wide, looping arc like a saber. Aldhelm batted it aside easily. The foils barked metallically.

A breath.

Then Aldhelm took the initiative once more, quickly backing d'Mannberg down the strip. His foil beat d'Mannberg's aside; he kicked out, his foot nearly finding d'Mannberg's knee, slamming into the thick muscle of the thigh. The huge assassin stumbled backward and Aldhelm lunged.

But d'Mannberg was powered by instinct, going with the motion and half-falling to one side. His own counter-thrust was made in desperation, blind, trying to find Aldhelm before he himself was touched. His foil came under Aldhelm's foil, past the flailing arm (even as he felt the agony of Aldhelm's blade in his shoulder), and into Aldhelm's unprotected stomach. The weight of Aldhelm's lunge added force to d'Mannberg's foil. The weapon, slicing upward, parted diaphragm from stomach, slid into lung tissue, the vibro tearing at flesh. Aldhelm, a look of astonishment on his scarred face, fell even as Gyll cried "Halt!" and strode forward. D'Mannberg—eyes wide, his breath halting—had already snapped off his vibro. Blood-slick wire hissed into the hilt. Aldhelm was prone, hands clutched over his belly, his foil kicking dust beside him. Thick blood flowed around his fingers, ran down his hands and arms. Gyll tossed his weapon aside and crouched beside the man. D'Mannberg knelt, bewildered, as the stasis holding the Hoorka broke.

"Aldhelm . . ." Gyll could feel dread twisting his bowels. He could almost smell the Hag's breath in the odor of stale sweat and bitter steel, the faint tang of lifeblood. Aldhelm grimaced in agony.

"By the Hag—" he muttered through clenched teeth. He looked up at Gyll, pain clouding his eyes. "Ulthane . . ."

"Don't talk, man. Rest. We'll get you to the Center Hospital." Gyll glanced up as Valdisa thrust her way through the kin around the fallen assassin. She took a quick look at Aldhelm—her mouth a line of concern—and snapped orders to the kin. "Iduna, get the flitter ready. Cranmer, get on your Center link and tell them we're coming. You three—get a floater for Aldhelm. Move!" She knelt beside Gyll, touching Aldhelm's hands lightly and moving them aside. She winced as she saw the wound.

"Ulthane, Thane . . ." Aldhelm's voice was weak; it brought their heads down. "I didn't kill Gunnar. I've no reason to lie, now. Believe me, I didn't kill him."

"Nobody thinks you did," Valdisa said. She looked at Gyll, her glance angry. "Now be still. Let Bachier take care of the bleeding."

Gyll and Valdisa moved aside as Bachier—now in charge of the healing for the guild since Renier's death—began to minister to Aldhelm. They went to d'Mannberg.

His wound was surface. It bled profusely, but the damage was slight. "Is he—" d'Mannberg began.

Gyll shook his head. "It's an ugly wound, Ric."

D'Mannberg threw the hilt of his foil to the ground. It bounced among the kin's feet. "Thane, Ulthane, I didn't mean for that to happen. It was just a blind thrust, and if he hadn't been moving . . ." A lode of pain thinned his mouth, furrowed his brow. He blinked away sweat. "We've lost too many kin. I didn't care for Aldhelm, I admit; we fought all the time of late. But I wouldn't have deliberately . . ."

"We know." Valdisa laid a hand on his shoulder—the flesh was cool, wet. "Get the rest of them out of here, Ric, and get your shoulder looked at," she said. "And make sure Cranmer's stopped filming."

"It's not enough to lose Eorl and Sartas," she said as d'Mannberg began moving the Hoorka from the cavern, as Aldhelm, moaning, was placed on a floater and rushed away. "We have to find ways of killing ourselves. He's not going to make it, is he?"

"I don't think so." He couldn't think of a gentler way of saying it, and he didn't feel like lying.

Valdisa swore. "Damn it, Gyll," she said at last. "Why did you give me all this?"

"Would you want me to take it back?"

Her chin trembled for a moment, flesh puckering. He thought she might cry, but she shook her head again. "I don't think so, Gyll. But do you want it?"

When he didn't answer, she moved away from him, watching as the last of the kin left the cavern. Then, the room silent and empty, she did cry. Gyll, stricken, didn't know how to comfort her. He could only hold her, hand snared in her hair, pulling her to him.

Tri-Guild Church was a blaze of pageantry. The immense space held within its fluted walls was a welter of light from drifting hoverlamps in field-holders high above the crowds. A phalanx of stained-glass windows (ippicators rampant, Dame Fate with Her enigmatic smile, the Hag leering down) threw wide shafts of colored brilliance down on the massed kin; a scurrying montage of brightly dyed cloth and stain-altered sunlight. Peddlers of refreshments called their wares as they shoved passage through the throngs on the floor and in the temporary stands along the walls. The cries were loud above the murmur of conversation.

Only guilded kin were present. For the rest, the spectacle was being broadcast to a huge holotank set in Tri-Guild Square. Lassari or kin unfortunate enough to be unable to afford seats inside — they milled in the square.

Truth-duel: when between the Li-Gallant and his largest rival, it was an event to fascinate Neweden. It would be seen in Mi, in the Northern Waste, along the Sundered Sea, in Remeale on Kotta Plain. Even the Diplos were present, high on the tiered decks, conspicuous in the bright clothing of the Alliance and gathered around the aged, slight figure of Regent d'Embry.

Truth-duel: on Neweden, it was a venerable but rare institution, invoked only in cases of extreme suspicion where normal judicial procedure could not be followed or guilt proven by evidence. It was avoided because the Guild of Magistrates put the heaviest of penalties upon it. The loss of truth-duel was considered irrevocable admission of guilt. There was no appeal from the judgment of the five deities of truth.

Already the Revelate of Tri-Guild Church had invoked the Five, whose images stood at the points of a star-shaped stage. His orange robes ablaze — tongues of unsearing flame licking up and down the seams; as the hoverlamps faded into dimness and opaque covers slid over the stained-glass panels, he was quite impressive — he named them. One by one, the deities burned with a gout of crimson flame, then threw a tight yellow beam across to its neighbors. The perimeter of the stage was then laced with intersecting lines that would repel unprotected flesh. Only the two combatants would be allowed egress to the interior. The Revelate, invocation complete, led the assembly in a brief prayer as his flaming robes flickered. He raised his hands in a gesture of religious ecstasy — the church, plunged into sudden darkness, was then assaulted by aching white brilliance slicing from above and below the star-stage. An involuntary gasp came from the onlookers. Now, somber in their green vestments (the color of justice), each with a priceless chain of ippicator bone-beads, the elder magistrates moved slowly into the sun-blaze, their slaveboys (naked except for jeweled collars) supporting them. They moved to the corners of the stage, each to a deity's right hand.

And finally, greeted by a sea-roar of anticipation, Vingi and Potok walked onto the dais. Each wore only a simple white cloth around his loins and a wrist bracelet of some dull metal. They were flooded in the fury of a nova. Vingi was a hillock of flesh, his gross folds puckered with cellulite, his breasts almost like a woman's but for the hairiness of his chest. Yet he moved with a strange grace despite his grotesque appearance. He did not provoke laughter, but a strange silence. Potok seemed only out of shape, his bald head shining, the body of an overweight man given to little or no exercise. He was small beside Vingi, but appeared to be far more mobile. Neither looked the part of fighter.

The beams from the truth-deities parted as they approached, falling back into place behind them. The magistrate at the head of the star-stage tottered a step forward, leaning heavily on the shoulder of his slaveboy.

"Your bracelets, please," he said. Hidden amplifiers gave his voice deific proportions. "Place them at the edge of the arena."

Vingi and Potok did as requested, removing the iron circlets from their wrists. A nod from the magistrate, and his attendant darted forward (beams breaking around him), grasped the bracelets, and came back to his station. The magistrate touched the panting head with affection, a small smile on his lips. "Your weapons, sirrahs," he said, looking up again.

Rising slowly from the center of the star-stage, a platform held two crowd-prods. A simple rubber grip, a stubby metal cylinder, a thumb contact: they were simple weapons, but capable of delivering a jarring shock to the nervous system. Applied in the right area or to the body in general a number of times, they could reduce a person to gibbering, slack-jawed shock or unconsciousness. Vingi and Potok picked up their prods, holding them in uncertain hands. The platform sank and became flush with the floor again.

"The truth-duel is now initiated," the magistrate said as his fellows nodded. "If one of you asks to yield or is unable to continue the duel, the other will be adjudged the victor

and the penalties previously decided upon will be given.
There will be no rest periods, no pauses, no particular rules.
You cannot leave the star-stage until the gods have ruled—
the gods will guide your hands and destinies, for one of you
lies."

The magistrate stepped back, leaning on his slaveboy. He
nodded in the shadow of his truth-deity. "Begin."

Prod-metal flicked light over the expectant faces in the
crowd: Vingi swung his weapon up and back. Potok hefted
his prod, feeling its weight. The guild-kin of each rule-guild
shouted their support.

The Li-Gallant took a ponderous step forward. His flesh
jiggled about his waist, on his thighs. Potok was obviously
much quicker, he moved forward and to the side, swinging
his prod. A clatter of steel: Vingi, arms moving, blocked Potok's intended blow with his prod. Potok, moving as Vingi
turned slowly to attack, swung again and touched the Li-
Gallant. A shrill buzzing came from the prod, a choked-off
moan escaped Vingi's lips. The touch was above the kidneys,
just under the ribcage. Vingi's face went red, his eyes watered.

But he still followed Potok, if slowly, who had stopped to
see what effect the prod had on his opponent. The Li-
Gallant's arm swept out (light-glare shimmering the prod's
length); Potok, startled, beat at the weapon. Vingi, for all his
girth, masked muscle beneath the continents of flesh. His
prod bullied past Potok's flailing defense to touch the man
on the right side of the chest. Potok groaned as the prod
crackled like a lightning stroke. He stumbled backward as
Vingi thrust at him again. Once more, Potok's greater agility saved him.

Both were now more cautious, having been hit once. As
the crowd settled back into noisy restlessness, as the parti-
san kin cheered, the two played a game of patience. Potok
would lunge and dart back, Vingi would attempt to maneuver Potok into a corner where the Li-Gallant's greater
reach and strength gave him the advantage. To the connois-
seur of finesse and grace, the match was a dismal farce. It
was far too slow. The cheering waned. A few more touches
were scored, but the duel dragged on: fifteen minutes, half
an hour. Both men were now obviously tired; sweat dappled
the star-stage, darkening the cloth about their waists and

shining on their backs. Slowly, the eventual outcome was becoming apparent to the spectators. Vingi's kin began to become noisy; Potok's guild was watchful, quiet, afraid.

Vingi was stronger, in better shape, and more able to bear the stinging bruises of the crowd-prod. Potok, fish-mouthed and gasping, struggled to stay one step beyond Vingi's reach. His attacks had become little but desultory feints that did nothing to drive the Li-Gallant back. Vingi stalked his prey, moving slowly, but always moving.

Vingi stepped, and his bearlike arms pummeled air, his prod clacked as he struck Potok's weapon. The prod shivered in Potok's grasp, and Vingi struck at it again. The prod slithered away from Potok, clattering across the floor. Potok, his eyes frightened, moved to recover his weapon (his kin moaning as one), and Vingi lunged.

The Li-Gallant's prod found its mark.

Potok screamed, a wailing cry that echoed in the hall, now lost in the joyous whistling from Vingi's kin. Potok rolled, reaching out for his prod with desperate, wide-spread fingers. Vingi's huge foot came down on the hand, hard. The cracking of bones could be heard in the nearest rows, and Vingi's prod ran the length of Potok's spine. The squeal of agony choked off suddenly. Potok's head lolled against the floor.

It was over.

The yellow beams from the deities faded, the aching glare of the star-stage altered to sapphire as Vingi stepped away from Potok. He smiled. The magistrate moved forward to declare him victor.

To declare him truthful and innocent.

It was much later when Gyll finally returned to his rooms. The wort mewled at him—he'd missed its feeding. He stared at the animal, wondering. *How can you be alive, so improbably, when Hag Death snatches at everything else around me? You damn thing, you weren't built for survival, yet you continue to fight* ... He reached down over the cage to stroke the furred hardness of the shell.

It had all gone wrong so quickly—so needlessly. Aldhelm had not survived the trip to the hospital. Yet the death was still an unreality, a dream—*he wasn't meant to go that way, not by the hands of his own kin, accidentally. That was how it was in the early days of Hoorka, before I disciplined them, before the code was set.* He sat on the edge of the bedfield, staring at his hands knotted on his lap. The hands were a network of tiny cracks, whitely dry, the light reflecting satin on the surface, golden-shadowed in the wrinkles.

Why did you give me all this, Gyll? Valdisa's words kept coming back, insistent. *But do you want it?*

He could feel a sense of change, like a faint spice-smell in the chill dark air of Underasgard. And for the first time, he welcomed change. He thought he knew the answer to Valdisa's questions. He didn't care for that answer, knowing what it might mean. But more and more he was certain.

Chapter 10

An excerpt from the acousidots of Sondall-Cadhurst Cranmer. The following is part of several interviews Cranmer recorded outside the context of the Hoorka. It is perhaps more interesting in how it reflects Cranmer's own shift in attitude over the standards he spent on Neweden. As Cranmer remarks in his Wanderer's Musings *(Niffleheim University Press, 252), it took him quite some time to readjust to our society after living in that society. Certainly the Cranmer I knew before the Hoorka study would never have been so patronizing. He began, afterward, to wonder if the attitude of the elite toward those below them wasn't something lying dormant in all people, and to question whether his humanistic views weren't merely a civilized veneer far too easily scratched away. Cranmer, ever afterward, was active in social reform, perhaps to the detriment of his status in his field; it is not good for one engaged in the study of societies to be active in endeavoring to change the one in which he lives.*

The lassari of this interview has never been identified—another indication of the odd and uncharacteristic contempt that exudes from Cranmer in this dot.

EXCERPT FROM THE DOT OF 9.26.215:

"You're a lassari?"

(A moment's silence.)

"Speak up, woman, and show some wit. This is an audio recording. Your nods don't register. And please don't look so frightened of me. Now, you're a lassari?"

"Yes, sirrah." (The voice trembles a bit; contralto, a bit rough.)

"And you live . . . ?"

"In Brentwood. My true-father has a place there, sirrah. He doesn't mind my staying."

"Do you work?"

"How'ya mean, sirrah? I do what I have to do, certainly."

"You needn't take offense. I'm interested purely as a scholar. What do you charge for your, ahh, services?"

"Are'ya interested, sirrah? For you, I could—"

"Have you looked at yourself? No, this is simply for my notes. If I need comfort, I can find the Courtesan's Guild."

(She laughs, then stops quickly as if afraid of offending Cranmer.) "The guild-women are far too expensive for the likes of what I get, sirrah. I'm not skilled or pretty enough to join 'em. And I'm cheap."

"But that allows you to survive."

"Like the rest of lassari. You do what you can, as long as you want. After, there's always the Dead. You can find 'em if you need."

"You don't sound as if you enjoy your life."

"Neweden's fine for the guilded kin, sirrah. If you ain't kin, then maybe next time Dame Fate'll be kinder— I went to a seeress once, and she told me that I'd been kin in earlier lives, that I'd be kin again. It feels right. So you accept it—if you kick back now, then maybe the Dame'll kick *you* when She steals you from the Hag again, send you back lassari again. Or maybe She'll just leave you there as one of the Hag's handservants."

"Don't you ever get angry? You people act like complacent cows."

"When you're jussar, you're angry. You forget to get angry when you become lassari, when no guild wants you. You live better and longer that way."

"A complacent attitude."

"Hmm?"

"Damn . . . ahh, never mind."

"I'd like to see someone pull the lassari together, demand something better for us and make it stick. If that person ever comes along, maybe I'll join 'im. Until that happens, I'll stay quiet."

*   *   *

Gyll tried to strike a balance between unabashed staring and nonchalance. He didn't succeed.

Kaethe Oldin reclined on a grassy hillock in her chambers between four metal pillars that radiated a golden light. It made every centimeter of exposed flesh glisten; being nude, she glistened quite a bit. Ulthane Gyll, on whose cool and strict world casual nudity was uncommon, felt rather provincial and uncomfortable. He didn't know where to put his gaze. Beside and below him, Helgin—who had ushered him into Kaethe's rooms—chuckled.

Kaethe sat up on one elbow. A gilt eyebrow winked light at him; she smiled. "Ulthane Gyll. I'm glad to see you again. A moment—let me get rid of the Battier." She reached out, languid, to touch one of the posts. The glow dimmed, the Battier receded into the floor. All the light in the room now came from the panels on the walls and Neweden, floating beyond the viewport.

"Kaethe thinks that an angelic glow can be achieved from the outside, rather than requiring a saintly interior," Helgin commented. Grunting, he seated himself on the carpet, crossing his stubby legs underneath himself.

Gyll nodded, not knowing how else to reply. Helgin disconcerted him. Gyll knew that he wouldn't tolerate such casual insult from guilded kin. On Neweden, the Motsognir would either prove himself to be an excellent foilsman or die. But, as she had the last time, Oldin reacted as if she'd expected his sourness. She nodded sweetly to the dwarf.

"If saintliness were required, you wouldn't light the darkness either." She stopped, laughing suddenly. Her laugh was crystalline; Gyll found himself smiling in response. "I've embarrassed you, haven't I?" she said, looking at Gyll. "I'm sorry, I just forgot where"—she tapped at a wall. It opened, revealing a closet, and she plucked a robe from its fasteners, slipping it about her shoulders—"I was for a moment. I hope I haven't . . ."

"You haven't." Gyll paused, searching for something else to say. "The view was . . . interesting."

A smile rewarded his effort.

"And if you think the exposure wasn't deliberate—despite the fact that Kaethe could use some exercise—you're a fool, Ulthane." Helgin; gruff, scowling. He plucked at the grass-carpet.

Gyll started involuntarily, smile evaporating into frown. His eyes narrowed, folding the crow's-feet at their corners deeper. "I think what I please, Motsognir, and I'm *not* a fool."

The dwarf snorted laughter and slapped the carpet with his hand. "You Newedeners antagonize too easily. It's no fun baiting you. I tell you, Hoorka—I'm good with any weapon you can name, even better with my hands, and I'm a damned small target to hit."

The wizened, beard-hidden face was comically furious.

Despite himself, Gyll found his irritation gone. He shook his head into the dwarf's red-veined stare. Helgin's lips drew back from teeth: he leered. "Try me sometime, Ulthane."

"Keep talking like you do, and I probably will."

Oldin had lain back down on the hillock again, upper body supported on elbows behind her, legs crossed at ankles. "The two of you complement each other. The Family Oldin could use both Motsognir and Hoorka." She glanced questioningly at Gyll. "The reason I asked to see you again, Ulthane, was to find out whether you had talked with Thane Valdisa."

A shrug. The port view shifted as *Peregrine* made an orbital adjustment. Ocean-blue light swept across the floor toward Gyll, moving with his shrug. "I've talked with Thane Valdisa, and I'm sorry I haven't responded before now— much has been happening." He thought of Valdisa; when he'd left Underasgard, she'd been making arrangements for the construction of Aldhelm's pyre. "She doesn't appear interested."

"But *you* are?"

Gyll wondered if he were that easy to read, but decided not to deny his interest—if it was a game she played, he'd go along for now. "To an extent, I am."

"Good. The Family Oldin can offer Hoorka far more than the Alliance. The Oldins are quite strong among the Trading Families, and we could use your skills to enhance that—the exact manner in which the Hoorka might operate would of course be up to you." She sat up, smiling. "My offer, then, is this. Come with me when I return to Oldin-Home—as soon as my business is done here. Spend time among the Family societies, see what you need to see, and determine how you can devise a code to allow you to work with and for us. I think you could fashion the code to work within our context."

"Trader Oldin—"

She shook her head. "I won't try to correct you this time, Ulthane. But 'Kaethe' would be preferable to 'Trader Oldin.' This is hardly a formal meeting, neh?"

Gyll hesitated, began a "Kaethe" and ended elsewhere. "I once used a vibro on a kin-brother who insisted that I change the code to fit a situation. I feel that strongly about it—if you think that the Hoorka-code must be changed to work within your society, then perhaps I should leave now and waste no more of our time." The remembrance of Aldhelm conjured by his words brought back the dull ache of his death. Gyll choked down the ghost, forcing his mind to stay on the subject.

"I didn't mean to suggest anything distasteful to you," Kaethe said. "I know you created the code, managed to bring order out of chaos, and the code fits Neweden's society ingeniously. I expect that you could devise a Hoorka-guild under another similar culture. I compliment you by saying that you could change the code, believe me. In any case, your coming with me to OldinHome binds you to nothing. I'd pay you as an adviser—ten thousand, in Alliance currency if that's what you want, for a third-standard of your time. No restrictions beyond that. Just come and see the Families' society, perhaps give a suggestion or two to our fighting masters to enhance their training, and make your decision later."

"Your words still say the same, even under the sugar-coating. The code works, m'Dame," he said, stubbornly.

"On *Neweden* it works, Ulthane," she answered, lifting her hands as if in supplication. "You've never been off-world, never seen the varieties of structures I have. No one code can work for them all. I know about Heritage, about the killing of your kin—it's part of the same problem, Ulthane. You're a Neweden native, born here. What works for Neweden *might not*"—he could see her watching his face carefully for reaction—"work elsewhere. I can understand your reluctance to abandon what's taken you so far, but I'd be silly not to warn you about inflexibility. It's not a survival trait, Ulthane. Not even in a society as static as that here. And I think you're a survivor."

"You talk a lot like Aldhelm."

"Aldhelm?"

"He is . . ." Gyll's lips tightened, his brow furrowed. The pain and anger and sorrow nagged at him again. *Down. Stay down.* "He was one of my advisers. A good friend at one time. He told me much the same thing once—we never could agree on it, and it drove us apart."

"Did you reconcile yourselves?"

Down. "No. I followed the code and insisted that he do the same." For a moment he thought of telling her everything, of the struggle that ended with Aldhelm feeling the bite of Gyll's vibro as Gunnar fled before them. But something held him back, as if by saying nothing he apologized to Aldhelm. "He did as I said, and it worked."

Kaethe sat forward, hugging legs to breasts, looking at him with her chin set on knees. "Nothing in this universe is in stasis."

"Perhaps not, but Neweden hasn't changed significantly in two centuries."

She stared at him, unblinking; the intensity of her gaze made Gyll uncomfortable. The gilt eyebrows shivered with reflected planet-light. "It will. Believe me, Ulthane, Neweden will change. When it does, and it might be sooner than you believe, nothing will be the same here. The Hoorka will have to change with Neweden or your guild will die."

Her certainty worried Gyll. He wondered at her fervor. "I was Thane for a few decades. The code has always managed to bring us through crises. It's the only thing that allows us to work on Neweden—if the Li-Gallant thought we'd ever break our ways, he'd have us hunted down. The code is the one thing that sets us apart from lassari and jussar . . ."

"You're not Thane anymore. And if the society on which the code is based changes, then you needn't worry about the Li-Gallant. He'll be facing his own problems. The code would be outmoded, a confining set of useless rules which'll bring you death."

Gyll scowled. "Everything brings death. Just living brings the Hag closer every day. Perhaps we needn't talk further, m'Dame."

Kaethe suddenly uncurled herself, standing. She tugged at her robe's belt, stretched. "I want to show you something, Ulthane." She turned to Helgin. He was picking at his toenails, seemingly oblivious to the conversation. "Helgin, you know what I want. Would you get it?"

The Motsognir rose to his feet slowly, joints cracking. "At your service, oh master . . ." he said with too much joviality. He glanced at Gyll. "Ulthane, in this she might be right. The Motsognir have seen many ways of life in our exile on Naglfar. Some things change very slowly. It may take centuries to see the flow, but all things do change." He left the room.

Helgin returned a few minutes later, a large hover-tray bobbing behind him on a tether-line. On the tray, inside a nutrient tank scaled with bubbles, floated a creature the size of a wort. Eyes closed, the embryonic head large and the limbs but half-formed, it was still recognizable. Gyll had seen it in a hundred renderings.

Ippicator.

Helgin grinned enigmatically, Kaethe sank down on the carpet again as if weary of standing in the Neweden-like gravity. They both watched as Gyll went up to the hover-tray and stared. He thought for a moment that it might be a replica, but it moved, a faint quivering that had nothing of the mechanical in it. The head turned slightly, the limbs twitched. Gyll marveled at it, at the smoothness of the orangish skin (in the replicas he'd seen, they had always been slate-gray). He touched the tank—it was warm. "It's real," he said, and immediately felt foolish. Emotions twisted at him—ones he'd thought safely removed. *It goes deep; Neweden training, Neweden religions. Even for one who doesn't entirely believe, it's hard to shake off the ties. An ippicator, the gods' pet . . .* "I thought . . ."

"That I said it was impossible. I know." She looked at him over steepled hands. "It *is* impossible, if live tissue isn't present. The Trading Families are *old*, Ulthane, older than the Alliance or even Huard. Our roots lie back with the First Empire. We've been to many places, sometimes before anyone else. I checked with Oldin Archives. They had a specimen of tissue, a frozen sample—evidently the Oldin captain who came here first found the five-legged beasts fascinating too, enough to have taken the sample against future cloning. I had it sent here."

"It sounds like a damned expensive way to impress Hoorka." Gyll watched the embryo turning slowly in the tides of the tank, still trying to decide what he felt.

"She's spent more on other failures—it's a family trait, I think," Helgin rumbled. "Throw enough money at something, and it solves everything."

"I bought your services, didn't I, Motsognir?" Kaethe smiled at the dwarf, then turned back to Gyll. "The fifth leg, incidentally, is a sensing device—the beast fed on the tender roots of certain grasses that were also the favorite of a local burrowing insect. The 'leg' extends a small horny spike into the soil, and the ippicator can hear the grubs moving. Where there are grubs, there are roots—the poor creatures are virtually blind. You know, the Archives didn't even know they possessed the sample. We could've been breeding them for the bones. It'd have to be in small quantities, of course, or we'd drive down the prices, but . . ." Again, that slow smile. "You see, it wasn't necessarily just to impress Hoorka."

"Yah, don't expect altruism of Traders, Ulthane. They threw the word out of their dictionaries." Helgin scratched at his dense growth of beard.

Gyll frowned. He forced his gaze away from the ippicator. "She of the Five Limbs . . . All of Neweden would curse you for a heretic for this, m'Dame Oldin. The ippicator is sacred in some way to nearly all guilded kin. This fetus is an abomination."

"To you, also?"

"I was brought up to believe in Neweden's gods. My true-mother was devout. She worshiped every day, praying that her jussar son would become guilded kin. My true-father—he didn't believe; he was an offworlder. He'd scoff, and then they'd fight. . . Me, I sometimes believe, and I always must seem to do so. I believe mostly in myself and the code. But I look at this thing, and I feel disgust. Ippicators belong to the gods and the dead."

His hands plunged into the pockets of his nightcloak. He shifted from foot to foot. "I guess it's not easy to escape your conditioning."

"I'll have it destroyed, Ulthane. Helgin—"

"*No!*" His own vehemence startled Gyll. He shook his head. *Calm, always calm. That's the way of the code.* "Yes, destroy it, but wait until I've left. I want to look at it some more, fix it in my mind. Then send it to the Hag."

"As you wish."

"Trader Oldin, I had thought only to tell you that Thane Valdisa had no interest in your offer. She speaks for Hoorka."

Kaethe leaned back. Neweden light bathed her. "And you?"

"I've made my life Hoorka's." He stared at her, suddenly the aloof Hoorka again.

"I'm much less interested in Hoorka as a whole than in the person who created them." A muscle tugged at the edges of her mouth. "I'll ask one thing of you, Ulthane. Repeat what I've said to Thane Valdisa. Ten thousand—simply for you to look at the Trading Families. We can see a time coming when we might need Hoorka. There are movements in human space, Ulthane, tides that are swelling. When these movements end, the Alliance will no longer be the way of the future."

Helgin laughed into the silence that followed her statement. Both Kaethe and Gyll looked at the dwarf. "Nor might be the way of the Families, Kaethe. The safest way is to be a Motsognir and hide on Naglfar. But, Ulthane, you'll find more Motsognir on Trader ships than on Alliance planets. That may tell you something."

"Are the Traders threatening the Alliance?" Gyll asked.

"We always have, implicitly." Oldin shrugged. "And that's all I can say. But I'll make you another offer, to make the original one more tangible. I'd hoped that the gift of an ippicator would please you, but I've misjudged Neweden on that. No matter, it will die." Kaethe waved a hand in dismissal. "Ulthane, the tale I've heard is that the Hoorka lost two men on Heritage, and that another lies in Center hospital. I've also heard that the Regent d'Embry has refused to allow you to pursue bloodfeud."

"That's true enough."

Kaethe nodded. "I will provide—as a gesture of goodwill—one Hoorka free passage to and from Heritage. What you do there is entirely up to you. The Alliance won't know unless Hoorka tells them, or you're not as adept as I've been led to believe. If you're not, then perhaps I should reconsider the offer anyway."

"Hoorka don't kill without warning."

"I know that transmissions have gone back and forth

from Diplo Center here to Heritage. Guillene knows that
Hoorka wanted the declaration, believe me. Bloodfeud is a
Neweden custom, Ulthane. If Moache Mining thought
Guillene in any real trouble, they'd pull him offworld, give
him a new name and face. The man has no respect for you,
or your kin wouldn't have been slain. Moache Mining has
no respect for you, or Guillene would be gone. You know
what to do on Neweden—you can't say the same anywhere
else."

Quiet. The ippicator's tank burbled. Helgin dug at his
bearded chin. Neweden performed a slow somersault in the
port.

"Guillene knows what you'd like to do," Kaethe continued. "He just doesn't believe you capable of it."

"I'll tell Thane Valdisa," Gyll replied. But he knew what
he wanted. He knew that if the decision were his, he'd make
the pact now. He'd never liked or trusted d'Embry and the
Alliance, but they'd offered the only path for Hoorka's
growth. If he were Thane again . . .

Gyll said no more to Kaethe.

When he'd gone, Helgin came back to Kaethe's rooms,
shading his eyes against the reborn radiance of the Battier,
relishing the lowered gravity. The ippicator's tray was gone.

"He was quiet on the way down," Helgin grumbled.
"Pensive and withdrawn. You've confused him, Kaethe."

"Only for a bit. He'll do it, Helgin. If he has the will I
think he has, he'll find a way."

"No matter what it costs him? Kaethe-dear, you sound
as if you're gaining respect for the man—that's unlike you.
I don't think you enjoy the idea of what Renard is doing to
Neweden, either. Gods, woman, are you growing a conscience?"

Kaethe smiled benignly. "If I am, Grandsire'll rip it out
by the roots when we get back."

Gyll could see the tension in Valdisa from the moment he
entered her room. She stood before her desk, a pile of flimsies behind her, an apprentice in front. She dismissed the
boy with uncharacteristic gruffness as Gyll came in; when
she looked at him, he saw that her face was drawn and haggard, the skin pale.

"You haven't slept," he said.

"It shows, neh?" Valdisa managed a wan smile and collapsed onto her bedfield with a sigh. Sitting, legs dangling, she rubbed at her eyes with the heels of her hands. "I couldn't seem to rest much last night. I kept seeing Aldhelm, that terrible wound; Sartas, too. I didn't want to take a pill, so I just kept tossing until I got up and went to the Cavern of the Dead—made sure the apprentices were doing everything right. Looked at the body for a while. Then I came back here and went over the records—we're not broke yet. You?"

"I managed to sleep. Not too well, though, and not long."

"You don't look so bad. Did you talk with Oldin?"

"Kaethe? Yah."

"Kaethe?" Valdisa repeated. "So you're on a first name basis with her. Is she attractive, Gyll?"

"The Traders like their women chunkier than Neweden."

"You've never had an offworlder, have you? Have you asked her yet?" Valdisa seemed to find his discomfiture amusing. Her eyes—drawn in lines of blood—laughed at him. Gyll leaned against the wall, watching. "I'm sorry, Gyll," she said at last. "I couldn't resist teasing you a bit. What did Oldin have to say?"

"I told her that you weren't interested in her offer. She asked us to reconsider. She wants one of us to go with her for a third-standard, and she said she'd pay ten thousand for that, with no other obligations." Gyll was careful, slow. Cloth whispered against stone as he shifted.

"Ten thousand just to see the Trader society?"

"To see them, decide whether Hoorka could work with them, and to give them advice on their training."

Valdisa lay back slowly, sighing. She closed her eyes. "Ten thousand is a lot. But there's nothing to reconsider, Gyll. Not in my opinion. Neweden belongs to the Alliance, and Hoorka to Neweden. It's *your* dream we're chasing, after all. You should be more vehement about it than me." The eyes opened, found him. "You should know better than any of us that we can't go with the Traders, no matter what they offer."

"She'll ferry a Hoorka to Heritage. With no restrictions, without the Alliance knowing."

"Gyll"—wearily.

"No, Valdisa." He levered himself away from the wall,

striding over to the bedfield and sitting beside her. He took
her hand in his, forcing enthusiasm into his voice. He was
surprised at how easily it came. "The Alliance won't know.
The Hoorka can go to Heritage, do what's necessary to
avenge Sartas and McWilms, and return. The Alliance won't
be able to prove that it was us, and we send company to Hag
Death for Sartas. The kin already talk, Valdisa. You've heard
them, and I've been told that it was partially the source of
contention between Aldhelm and d'Mannberg. You can
settle the dispute. You can also enhance your standing with
the kin, especially if *you* are the one that goes."

"If I go?" Her hand moved away from Gyll's, touched his
shoulder and trailed down his back. "Gyll, they all know
that you were the one talking to Oldin. It'll simply say to
them that Ulthane Gyll is still guiding the Hoorka, making
sure that Thane Valdisa does what's right."

Gyll could hear the pleading in her voice, the cry for his
understanding. She wanted him to drop the subject before
it created a rift between them. But he couldn't. It had in-
flamed him since he'd left Oldin. He wanted, and he
wouldn't let Hoorka go without it.

"She had an ippicator," he said. "Alive."

"What?" Surprise lanced her voice, dragged her upright
on the bedfield. "No ippicators have been seen—"

"A clone, Valdisa. Oldin brought it out to show me that
the leading Families were on Neweden long before our ancestors. Some subtle point in her argument, yah? She thinks
it demonstrates how the Alliance is just a fleeting organization in comparison to the Families."

Valdisa moved on the bedfield, leaning away from Gyll
and his fervor. "If Neweden learns that an ippicator has
been cloned, then by all our gods, there'll be a jihad—both
among the guilds who hold it sacred and toward all offworlders. That's a rank insult to our beliefs, a vile
desecration—the ippicators belong to the afterlife. How
could Oldin think—"

"She had it killed, after. I watched them put it in the
vaporizing field. She also promised that the tissue sample
would be destroyed."

"And you trust her?"

"Would it do any good if I didn't?"

"Still . . ."

"She simply wanted it as an example. Something to shock us out of complacency. You have to admit that it does that. She meant no insult."

Valdisa stood, the bedfield rippling behind her. Gyll got to his feet a moment later. He reached out to touch her, but she drew back, shaking her head.

"Gyll, I love you," she said, "because I like the way you've pursued your dreams and tried to turn them into reality. Because you were so damned sure of yourself. And because when you thought you might have hurt Hoorka, when Aldhelm failed the contract on Gunnar and you had to stop him from breaking the code—well, then you took yourself away from leadership rather than risk harming your dream, your organization. Now you scare me, Gyll."

Light from the room's hoverlamp threw shadows over her face as she looked down at the floor, then up to Gyll. "Why are you suddenly so insistent? Don't you trust me to follow the guild's code? Don't you think that I want what you want—for Hoorka to become stronger and grow? You want to see Hoorka move offworld; it was *your* idea to contact the Alliance to pursue that goal. This damned Trader woman comes, fills your head with more dreams, and suddenly you want to abandon the route you've taken. Gyll, why in hell do you think you can trust her? Why do you think it's worth losing the ground we've gained?"

"I know it is, that's all." He frowned, angered by her anger. "Valdisa, she's extending an offer, nothing more. It doesn't interfere with what we have with the Alliance, not yet. We lost nothing. All she asks now is for someone to look at the Trader structure, to bring information back to Hoorka so we can make a judgment. As for the Heritage offer, that's just to indicate the seriousness of her interest, and it's a better offer than you've gotten from d'Embry. The Alliance has done nothing to Guillene. What makes you think we can trust *them?*"

Valdisa looked as if she were about to retort. Then the fire seemed to die in her. Her shoulders slumped; she stared down at the hard-packed dirt of the floor.

"Valdisa," Gyll said. "I don't want to fight with you." He reached out to pull her to him, but she pushed aside his hands.

She went to her desk and fiddled with the flimsies there before swiveling in her floater to look back at him.

Her chin was up, defiant. Her mouth was a slash of tight lips.

"I'm Thane, Gyll. That tide's supposed to give me the authority to control Hoorka's actions." Down, the chin. The lips flexed in a frown. "But the kin still see you as the real leader, despite that. You could undermine my authority in a moment. The kin would back you, almost every one of them—especially now that Sartas and Aldhelm are gone. Do this thing on Heritage if you must, Gyll. I won't try to use the shadow-thanedom you gave me to stop you. I can see the uselessness of that gesture."

She stopped, leaning back. She rubbed her eyes with thumb and forefinger, wearily. "Gyll, you're a frigging self-ish person. You only care about yourself. You—made—Hoorka." Valdisa lowered her voice in a parody of Gyll's tone. "That's your cry whenever something threatens. You may even be right in this. But I think you're just tired of the inactivity, maybe even tired of being Hoorka and all the killing and death that it brings with it—surely your last con-tracts have indicated that." She stopped and almost smiled. "You'd rather nurse that damned wort back to health than kill on contract, wouldn't you? You're tired of the slowness of the Alliance, and bored because you've removed yourself from the thaneship."

"That's not true, Valdisa." Even to himself, the statement lacked conviction. He said it too softly, too slowly.

"It's not?" Valdisa cocked her head. An idle hand rustled sheets on her desk. "This Trader woman's offered you a new challenge, and you're eager to take it—it's something new, another creation for you, neh?"

"I want to avenge Sartas. That's as far ahead as I'm thinking."

"You're sure of that? Then go ahead and do it, because I can't stop you."

"Valdisa, if you don't want this, I won't go."

"Maybe you wouldn't, Gyll. Not this time, at least." She yawned suddenly, stretching. "Gods, I'm tired. Gyll, the day would come when you'd find another thing so important to you that you'd do it over my objections. It might as well be now. Go and tell Oldin that you'll go to Heritage. The rest . . . I'll think about it. But remember, Gyll, *you're* the one that will kill Guillene. I'll send no one else. If you don't want to kill, then tell Oldin no."

"You think I don't want the revenge?"

"I think you want the revenge. I'm just not so sure you'll like it." Valdisa reached over the desk to press a contact on the wall. Her door opened. Beyond, the dark corridors of Underasgard were loud with kin.

"You're angry with me," Gyll said, but he could find no anger in her face.

"No," she said. Her voice sounded only weary. "But please go now, Gyll. I don't feel like arguing anymore, and I want to try to sleep."

Gyll didn't move. "I could stay . . ."

Valdisa rubbed her temple with a hand; she smiled. "Later, perhaps. Gyll, I don't know how you feel right now, but I know I'm not in the mood."

"I won't go to Heritage. All you have to do is say it."

She shook her head. "You say you want it. Just remember this, Gyll. I'm selfish, too. If you try to fight me again, try to go over my authority—"

"I wasn't doing that now."

"Maybe you don't think so. But I'm still warning you, kin to kin, as a friend—I'll fight back next time. Hard, and as nasty as I need to be. Hoorka's been my life—I may not be its creator, like you, but to me, Hoorka is all. I'm Thane, and I intend to be Thane in more than words."

Gyll could find nothing more to say. Valdisa leaned back once more, closing her eyes. Gyll walked into the corridor. The door closed behind him with a sinister finality.

The Regent d'Embry was relaxing in her office. A cup of tea steamed aromatically on her desk. The window was polarized black, the room lights were off but for a spotlight on the replica of d'Vellia's soundsculpture. The office was twilight, silent. D'Embry reclined on her floater, eyes closed, trying to forget the tedious drudgery of her day.

A bell chimed in the room. D'Embry groaned, muttering a curse that would have ensured a session with the morality-whip on her long-ago home world. "Leave me alone, Karl," she said to the room. "Handle it yourself. Show some initiative." She kept her eyes firmly and defiantly closed.

Again: a shivering of bright sound.

"Huard's cock—"

Her eyes opened. D'Embry groaned upright, took a sip of the cooling tea, and touched a contact that brought her com-unit down from the ceiling niche. The flat screen stared at her.

Another chiming, louder now.

Lips pursed in a scowl, she activated the screen. A wash of greenish illumination flooded the room. "This had better be good, Karl."

A whorling of light-motes resolved itself into a sallow and thin face. "I'm not so sure 'good' describes it, m'Dame, but it's something you'll want to see. Just a moment, and I'll switch you." His voice was high, excited. The screen dissolved into momentary chaos, then settled.

She saw.

Men and women in the uniform of Vingi's guards were moving through Dasta Burrough, a lassari sector. The view was jerky, dim, as if the camera operator was trying to keep his hoverholos near the center of the action but out of sight. The scene horrified d'Embry. The guards were working with quick and brutal efficiency, dragging lassari from their houses and taking them to a waiting flitter bearing the insignia of the Magistrate's Guild. Brutal: the guards used their crowd-prods liberally, without need, for the lassari were unarmed and sleep-confused. Screams punctuated the scenes. One guard (the camera zooming in) used his prod like a club. He swung, striking the head of the man he held by a twist of shirt-cloth. The lassari staggered from the blow, eyes rolling, hands up in futile defense. Blood streamed down the side of his face, soaking into the shirt.

The view suddenly shifted away.

"Karl, what in hell's going on?" D'Embry's voice was taut, her stomach coiled in a knot.

Karl's voice came over the scenes of carnage. "Dasta Burrough, m'Dame. From what I've been able to learn, the Li-Gallant sent his guards in to arrest suspected dissident lassari. He heard that this Renard was living in Dasta. It all happened suddenly—one of the monitor probes just happened to pick it up."

"Get me the Li-Gallant."

"I'm already trying, m'Dame."

A woman came stumbling from a darkened doorway into the street. There, a guardsman was using his crowd-prod on an unresisting man. The woman leapt on the back of the guardsman, beating with balled fists. The guard twisted, throwing the woman to the ground; she fell hard, and the sound of an activated vibroblade hissed in the speakers of the com-unit. The guardsman's arm—luminous vibrotip gleaming in the dark—rose and fell. The woman screamed.

D'Embry, stonily, watched.

Shift. An alley. In a pile of debris, a naked lassari lay. A guardswoman kicked him in the ribs, and the lassari's body shuddered from the impact. He did not otherwise move. A second guard watched, his crowd-prod bolstered. Another kick . . .

Shift. A woman, lassari by the clothing, ran down a narrow lane. Her face was frightened, her disheveled hair hung in sweat-damp strands. Two guards ran after her. Then, around the corner ahead of her, three more guards appeared. The woman stopped, trapped, glancing about frantically. The guards laughed as they closed in around her.

Shift. The Li-Gallant. His thick face peered soberly out at d'Embry, a head-and-shoulder view. He wore a robe with metallic ribbons woven into it—they sparkled in the cloth. Behind him, an animo-painting swirled lazily. "Ahh, Regent d'Embry." He nodded. "I was surprised to receive the call from your staff—you keep late hours, m'Dame."

She had no patience for his amenities. "Li-Gallant"—her voice was trembling with reined anger, she strove to control it—"call off your guards."

His lower lip stuck out, the eyes narrowed. "You've been snooping, m'Dame. But I credit you—your sources are quick."

His uncaring banter drove her to fury. "*Damn* you, man!" she shouted. Her fist struck the desk. China rattled, tea sloshed. "What you're doing is violent and unnecessary. Call them off."

A slow shaking of his head. "What they're doing is *entirely* necessary for the good of all Neweden, Regent. We have a different set of rules here, after all. It demands an approach that varies from the one—"

She wanted to pick up the cup and throw it at the screen.

His smugness mocked her. "I'm not calling you to discuss differences between Alliance worlds, Li-Gallant. As representative of Niffleheim, I'm telling you to stop this brutality."

"And I'm telling you"—the Li-Gallant seemed to lean back, as if reclining in a chair. The background focus shifted as the camera kept the face sharp—"that the Alliance has no authority in this. It's purely internal. It affects only Neweden and her people. As Li-Gallant, they are under my authority. This action is condoned by vote of the Assembly. I warn *you,* Regent. If you interfere, I'll lodge a very loud protest with Niffleheim Center. I'll also call for the Neweden Assembly to revoke our agreement with the Alliance. You know I now control the Assembly. I wonder who Niffleheim would back, Regent? You—an old woman obviously exceeding her authority and interfering in the affairs of this little world? Or me—the governor of that little world, merely doing as his society dictates?"

Vingi grinned. "I've nothing more to say to you, Regent d'Embry. Good night. Enjoy your pictures."

His face dissolved in a flurry of light.

With a cry of inarticulate frustration, d'Embry picked up her teacup. She held it in her hand, arm back, then paused. It took more control than she thought she had, but she brought the arm back down.

She drank.

The tea was cold.

Chapter 11

THE CRAFT SPREAD vaned fingers to the stars. Neweden wheeled below, then suddenly behind, a fading ghost.

The bio-pilot chortled, a dribbling of spittle flying from his lips, and craned his neck to glance at his passengers. "Shit," he said, noticing the chain of globules floating about him. He closed his eyes a moment and an exhaust fan began to purr, pulling the droplets away. The BP leaned back in the skeletal chair, the umbilical cord of the ship's nervous system trailing from his spinal sockets. He floated in free fall against the restraint of his harness, one leg twitching spasmodically.

"Away and gone," he said. "We're home again, Helgin."

Gyll was impressed by the way Helgin interacted with the BP. The Hoorka found the jerky, ungainly mannerisms embarrassing; he did not like looking at the man, and yet he had to force himself to avoid staring. Before they'd left Oldin's ship, the BP had turned to find Gyll regarding him with an expression of distaste; the man had merely smiled, as if used to that reaction. Now, without the comfort of gravity, Gyll found that *he* was the bumbler, the one with little coordination, and it bothered him that the BP seemed to be understanding of Gyll's discomfiture. Helgin, at least, had not seemed to be distressed by the spastic motions of the BP. He was at ease, joking, acting much as normal. Now, with Neweden hidden behind the cowl of their engines, Helgin loosened his harness and shot across the cabin, evidently luxuriating in the feel of weightlessness.

"By damn, Illtun, that was a cute maneuver past the Alliance station. You're sure we weren't monitored? We could still do a feint toward Longago and give them some misdirection. Siljun's there; he'd back up our story."

"Shit. You friggin' dwarves don't trust nobody." Illtun's head jerked to one side, his left arm moved up, hand clenching, then down again. "I promise you we weren't seen. Promise. I know this ship and I know the mass-blinder. We were absolutely transparent to their detectors."

"You're the pilot." Helgin bounced from a wall (Gyll wondered how the circuits fixed there managed to continue working after the abuse) and twisted in mid-cabin to face Gyll. "You like this, Ulthane?"

Gyll vacillated between politeness and honesty, decided on compromise. "I'm not sure," he said. He was fighting nausea that had swept over him when an evasive move had put an unusual amount of g-stress on the ship and its occupants. Gyll didn't care for the grin on the dwarf's face — the Motsognir must know what he felt like.

"I don't think Ulthane Gyll likes me, Helgin," Illtun said. Gyll, startled, began a quick denial, but Illtun continued over his protest. "It doesn't really matter, Ulthane. We BPs get fairly thick skins from all the eye tracks. The ones I *do* mind are the ones that decide to reshape your face because of their displeasure."

Illtun's face spasmed, a quick blinking of eyes. Gyll decided that it was another symptom of the restructured nervous system. He could not understand it any other way.

Helgin, now upside down to Gyll's orientation, frowned a denial. "Neh, Illtun. The Hoorka isn't scowling at you — he's just trying to control his stomach. Gods, Gyll, if you can stand killing, you should be able to take this."

The banter bothered Gyll. He could feel his face redden in response. Neweden reflexes: his hand strayed closer to the hilt of his vibro, lost in the folds of his freely floating nightcloak and further encumbered by the seat harness. "You joke too much, Helgin," he said darkly, but the dwarf only burst into sudden laughter.

"Gyll," Helgin said, his voice booming in the small cabin, "you're a mudballer, a dirt-eater. Your training's been very good, but it needs altering out here. The nightcloak — it's more hindrance than help now, isn't it? I could take your weapon from you, disable you with ease, if you wanted to fight. You have to learn to quit responding with that damned

Neweden pride, at least in situations where you're at a disadvantage. It's only because I like you and think you're intelligent enough to change that I say anything. Most world-bound asses aren't worth the effort. Up here, even Illtun—who looks so slow and ungainly under gravity—could do things beyond your abilities."

Illtun smiled, almost shyly, at Gyll. "It's not that tragic, sirrah. I'm quite used to the first-time stares, and I'm used to mudballers. If a BP goes out of the port on most worlds, he risks getting the shit beat out of him. Or worse. There's a lot of prejudice in the Alliance, a lot of blank adherence to their social structure. If you're on the bottom of that structure, it can be difficult."

"The Hoorka were once on the bottom. I changed that."

Illtun shrugged. His foot tapped the deck in erratic rhythm. "It's nice to be able to change things. Me, I work for the Oldins." He reached behind him to touch the umbilical of the ship. "I *am* the ship, out here. I can close my eyes and *be* the ship. No mudballer can match me with that. I kick, and the engines boot us along; flex my fingers, and the vanes swivel to catch the solars. I can be graceful with that metal body, if not my own. Watch," he said.

He closed his eyes—suddenly the port opposite Gyll was dizzy with star-trails, then all settled back again. "The Alliance made me from a nonfunctional being, a neurotic precatatonic, into something that works offworld. I'm grateful to 'em for that. But when they changed the brain stem and flipped the neural responses and fidgeted with my spine, they didn't make us acceptable to the mudballers. We're *still* mental defectives to them; cripples, half-humans. We ain't liked. You get used to it, but you never like it." Then he smiled again and seemed to laugh inwardly. "And I'm sorry for the lecture—it surfaces every once in a while, and you just have to suffer through it. Helgin knows."

Gyll didn't know how to respond. "Hoorka get stares, too. Every time we walk in Sterka."

"Still, your stares are at least veiled in respect," Illtun answered.

"Only because I strove to make it so."

Illtun smiled again. "So you tell me that the BPs need to do something to gain respect, to force it? No, Ulthane, sometimes there is no way to find a niche for yourself, and

you have to go search for another place. You were lucky on
Neweden. That might not happen anywhere else."

Illtun's good humor took the sting from his words. Gyll
could not find it in himself to be angry with the man. As he
tried to find a reply, Helgin spoke. The dwarf had one hand
around an exposed pipe, his legs dangling in air. He seemed
to recline on an invisible cushion. "The Hoorka didn't do
well on Heritage."

That brought back the bright spot of anger in Gyll's
mind—Guillene. Guillene had insulted Hoorka, and by insulting the guild, had insulted Gyll. The weapon that had
killed Sartas had been aimed at all of them. "Hoorka will
amend that mistake."

Helgin frowned. "Killing Guillene isn't going to solve
anything."

"It will send a companion for Sartas to Hag Death. It
will comfort his soul. It will calm my kin's rage."

"It will kill one man and do nothing to change the reasons Sartas was killed. You're too caught up in mythology
and fate, Gyll, or at least you play that game."

"It's not a game to Neweden."

"And you'll never learn that Neweden isn't the universe."

Gyll spat his disgust, a guttural oath. "You think words
can change—" he began, but a bell chimed on Illtun's console. The BP's head snapped up and he motioned to Helgin
to take his seat. "No more useless arguing," Illtun said. "It's
jumptime. Settle yourselves. I'll wake you on the other
side."

He turned away from them. Deep in the bowels of the
ship, thunder began to growl.

Frustration filled Gyll. He wanted to turn to Helgin and
give vent to his resentment, to ask why—if Helgin felt this
way—he would let Oldin send Hoorka to Heritage. But his
head began to spin, as if he were suddenly dizzy. His eyes
seemed to no longer work. He was being flailed by strands
of pure color, torn by subsonic bellowing that grew ever
louder. Gyll moaned, and as a yellow wash of tendrils
snaked through the stars outside the port, all went dark.

He was still angry, but his ire had nothing to do with Guillene.

Gyll had needed all his skills at silentstalk. There had
been only one way into the confines of Park Hill—through

the streets of Home. Even in the darkness of early morning, the avenues had not been deserted. He'd kept to the back ways, staying in shadow and simultaneously cursing his nightcloak for adding to the tropical heat and appreciating its dark cover. He was another fragment of night, moving through the grime and squalor of the outer sector. Helgin had urged him to use a light-shunter as additional camouflage or to at least dress like the rest of the populace, but Gyll had declined both options curtly. Dressing as a Heritage native would cause him difficulty once inside Park Hill, and the light-shunter would simply weigh him down. He'd gruffly reminded the Motsognir that Oldin had been willing to trust Hoorka expertise, and that the twentieth code-line stated that all cannot be anticipated: always take what is needed for the known hazards and trust skill and ingenuity for the rest. Extra equipment is extra hazard. Helgin had nodded in slow agreement, and Gyll had taken pleasure in reminding the dwarf that this was one of the code-lines that he and Oldin seemed so intent on having the Hoorka abandon. Helgin had merely bared his teeth in an unamused smile. "They catch you, Gyll, and the Diplos'll throw the Oldins from Alliance trade. Kaethe will find Grandsire FitzEvard manifestly not pleased, and his displeasure is never forgotten."

"It seems a terrible chance to take, then, on something that doesn't directly concern her."

"Don't worry," Helgin had replied. "She thinks she'll get something out of it, or she wouldn't have offered."

He made the transition from Home to Park Hill; filth to ornate cleanliness. He kept near the side of the road, ready to seek a hiding place if threatened, but Park Hill seemed caught in slumber. He pressed on, moving in the shadows.

He thought of Sartas and the torn body that had lain in the Cavern of the Dead: it had not even been recognizable as his kin-brother. And McWilms, still and silent in the antiseptic womb of the med-pad, covered with the crusted scabs of lacerations, the sheets empty where an arm should have been. *Guillene.* If he could keep the fury kindled, if he could see Sartas and McWilms when he stood in front of the man, it would be an easy kill, then. He'd do it gladly. *Another one to the Hag, another to join the dance that you began . . .*

The guards at Guillene's gates were simple: a hypodart of tranquilizer shot from the cover of nearby bushes—though Gyll garnered a few scratches even through his nightcloak; the thorns were sharp. Gyll hurried across the lane to the fallen men. There was a sharp buzzing in his ear, and he checked the snooper at his belt. A diode burned red—the gate was alarmed, and (swinging the snooper in an arc) the top of the fence. It took several seconds for the random field generator of the snooper to find a setting to blind the alarms. Finally, the diode went green and Gyll slipped inside, dragging the guards after him one by one. The gate closed behind him. *Soon, Sartas. Soon.*

Heritage's groundcover was pleasure, quiet and soft, hushing under his slippered feet. There were parts of Neweden where snagglegrass, crackling underfoot, was nearly as effective an alarm system as any electronic device. The snooper remained quiet, and Gyll could sense no other guards on the grounds as he crossed the lawn. It seemed ludicrously easy to him—the rich on Neweden swathed themselves in protection.

The house was dark but for a few windows on the third floor. The structure was built of native stone; it felt warm to his touch, still radiating the fierce heat of the day. Gyll slipped around the house, looking for a side entrance. A door: the snooper shrilled in his ear, and once again Gyll paused to let it find the combination of signals to open the door quietly. He heard the soft click of an inner lock and touched the door's contact. It yawned open. Gyll waited, sheltered in darkness, dartsling ready. No one came to investigate. He slipped inside.

It was quiet and cool. A sweet, smoky aroma hung in the air. He seemed to be in the kitchen; dishes were piled on a sonic washer, ovens lined the wall, a cup of mocha sat on the sideboard. Gyll looked closer at the cup. It steamed, still very hot. Someone was very near, then, or would be returning shortly. Either way, he had to move.

The third floor—he knew that must be the bedrooms. He needed to find the way up. The tense excitement of the hunt gripped him again. His mind clutched at the feeling, willing it to stay.

Gyll moved through a plush landscape. The house was filled with evidence of the company's money. The walls were friezed with animo-screens, all still and quiet now; the furniture was massive and glittering. He could see the umber gloss of malawood, the more expensive red-brown of teak. An old pipichord filled one wall with keyboards, pull-stops, and brass foliage. Lifianstone statues stood in static poses along a hall, a monstrous holotank filled the center of another room, chairs in disarray around it.

He found trouble only once—as he came to the top of the ramp leading to the second floor, he heard a voice just down the hall and the click of an opening door. He had no time—he froze, ready to fire a dart. A man—muscles in Gyll's belly relaxed as he saw that it was not Guillene—chuckled to himself as he entered the hallway. The man didn't look in Gyll's direction. Gyll watched him walk away, entering another door farther along. The door shut behind him.

It seemed that Dame Fate was watching Gyll. Nothing could go wrong. The feeling bothered Gyll. It all was too easy, too pat. At any moment he expected to be set upon; the back of his neck prickled under the collar of his night-cloak, but when he looked back, he saw nothing.

The snooper shrilled at him as he set foot on the third-floor ramp: someone above. Gyll barely had time to move back before he heard footsteps and off-key whistling. Gyll put his back to the wall, dartsling readied. He watched the floor—*he'd told them a hundred times in practice sessions: if you're around a corner, the first part of a person you're likely to see is the foot or a hand. Watch the floor, watch the wall at about waist level—it will give you an extra half-second to react, and it may keep you alive.*

He saw the worn tip of a leather boot and stepped forward, already firing. The man had no chance. The hypodart spat, the man crumpled, and Gyll caught him before he reached the floor, lowering him quietly. He glanced at the face—not Guillene. He moved the man away from the ramp and his escape route, then darted cautiously up the ramp, listening.

Still nothing. This floor was smaller than the others—one large chamber in which he now stood, the far wall glimmering with ice-colors from which a cool breeze emanated. In the middle of the room, floaters were arranged around a large table. Two doors led off the room. The place looked

and felt empty, but Gyll had the snooper survey it. Nothing.
He went to the nearest door and thumbed the contact. It
hissed open.

A kitchen. Gyll left the door open, moving to the next.
He touched the contact, feeling the tenseness grip his stomach again. He knew already, before the door opened.

Yes. He looked into a bedroom dimly lit by a shuttered
hoverlamp. On a bedfield of rumpled sheets, a man and a
woman slept. As Gyll stepped into the room, the woman
woke, staring at him with startled, sleep-rimmed eyes, her
mouth just opening in the beginning of a query. She
knuckled at her eyes, sitting up, pulling the sheet over her
breasts.

The dart hit her then. The mouth closed, suddenly, and
she fell back. Gyll let the door shut behind him and moved
to the bed, but the man didn't awaken. He opened the shutters on the hoverlamp, letting the light fall on the man's
face. A smear of wetness trailed from the mouth; he smiled
in his dreams.

Guillene.

Gyll stared at him, assessing the man who had killed Sartas. *About my age, and that body hasn't seen much work. If
he's cruel, it's a mental cruelty, and others do the work for
him. Sartas, I hope you enjoy his company. Make him your
slave before the Hag.*

He let the snooper check the room, found two alarms
and deactivated them. Then he pocketed the dartsling and
slid his vibro from its sheath. He activated the weapon; the
luminous tip darted out, trailing the wire. Its growl filled the
room and woke Guillene.

The man turned in his sleep, moaning, and his eyes
opened—blue-green, with flecks of brown. He saw Gyll.
Guillene bolted upright, the bedfield rippling. The woman
jounced with it, oblivious.

"Who the hell are you? Where is Cianta? I told him
to . . ." Guillene seemed to see the vibro in Gyll's hand for
the first time, and his voice faded to a whisper. He glanced
at the drugged woman slack-jawed beside him. "Mara?" he
said. He did not touch her.

"She won't wake."

"You killed her?" For the first time, genuine fright
showed in him; he looked as if he were about to scream. He

slid away from the woman, as if the fact that she might be dead and that close to him frightened him more than the rest. Gyll knew then that he'd never had to see the results of his orders, never had to deal with the mess.

"She's done nothing to Hoorka," Gyll answered. "She's not dead. We don't kill the innocent if it can be helped." When Gyll named the Hoorka, Guillene had gasped, an involuntary intake of breath. He looked as if he were about to shout. Gyll put the vibro near his throat. "Don't yell, man. No one in the house will hear you; they're all like her."

"If you want valuables . . ."

"I simply wanted for you to be awake, so you can tell the Hag who was responsible." The vibro moved, menacing. Guillene leaned as far back from Gyll as the bedfield allowed. The sour odor of urine suddenly filled Gyll's nostrils. He looked down to see the sheets wet at Guillene's waist. His nose wrinkled in disgust.

"I can give you money, Hoorka. Far more than the contract." Guillene seemed not to notice that he had fouled himself. His voice was pitched high, he spoke too fast. "I'm worth nothing to you dead. Let me live, and I'll enrich your organization. It will do you more good in the long ran."

Gyll didn't want to argue with the man. He tried to force himself into anger, and found that it had gone. "You're a poor trade for Sartas, man," he said. "You don't deserve the quick death of the knife." *And words make a poor substitute for action. Remember Sartas; remember McWilms's face, the empty sleeve.* "Dame Fate must want you. She made it easy for me."

"Kill me, and nothing changes, Hoorka. It doesn't alter this world in the least. Moache will send someone else."

"I don't care about this world."

"They'll know who did this, Hoorka. The Alliance will seek your people out, because Moache will want them to do it. You can't hide your presence, and you'll just destroy your guild—that's the price of using your weapon." Guillene pressed his back against the wall. The dampened sheets dragged at him. He looked down at the vibro, not at Gyll, his chin pressing against his neck.

"Sartas's honor demands it." The scarlet rage had not left entirely. It was still there, masked by his disgust/pity for Guillene. He nurtured it in his mind as he would nurse a spark on tinder, willing it to grow, to leap into burning—to make the vibro move. *Stop the talk, man. Do what you wanted to do, what you told Valdisa you must do.* "This is for the Hoorka you killed and the apprentice you maimed. Tell Hag Death that Ulthane Gyll sent you to Her."

"You don't even know that I did this."

The man's bravado took Gyll aback. He let the vibro move away and heard the trembling breath of Guillene. "Who else?" Gyll spat. "You'd go to the gods with a lie on your tongue?"

"Hoorka," Guillene said. His voice trembled. "Your people killed de Sezimbra. His people would have had more reason for revenge."

"*You* killed de Sezimbra. Not Hoorka." But the vibro didn't move.

Guillene seemed to take hope. The chin rose, the eyes met Gyll's for an instant, as if in a plea, but the voice was stronger. "Hoorka, I give you my word. I'll spend what I have to and find the guilty ones, drag them to you with their confessions."

Gyll knew the man lied. He could feel it in the words. He summoned up the image of Sartas's body. *That's what those lies bring,* he told himself.

Guillene still spoke, as if the voice could stop the thrust of vibro. "Hoorka, things don't work the same on other worlds. You can't expect us to do as you would. Gods, man, if you Hoorka haven't learned that, then you're all fo—" Guillene stopped. His eyes widened.

"*Fools!*" Rage flared, finally. "Is that what you say, man?" The vibrotip circled before Guillene's face.

"Hoorka, please, you can't—"

"Insult Hoorka, and you insult me."

"You must understand—"

"Strike at Hoorka, and you've struck at me."

The vibro keened hungrily. Gyll's hand lunged forward, slashing across the throat.

The body fell sidewise, hung on the edge of the bedfield for a moment, then slid softly to the floor.

Staring down at Guillene, Gyll searched for the satisfaction he should feel in the death, the gratification. He felt very little. He went to the bed, grasped the woman under shoulders and knees and took her into the larger room. She would wake there—away from the blood-spattered bedroom and the stiffening corpse.

Then, frowning, he made his way from the house.

Aldhelm's body had lain the proscribed ten days in the Cavern of the Dead. Each day, as the sunstar touched the dawnrock with morning, an apprentice had added a scented log to the pile of wood that held the body, first anointing the log with the blood of kin. Ulthane Gyll, Thane Valdisa, d'Mannberg, Bachier, and Serita had done the blood service—the first five days from a cut on the left hand, the second from the right. Chips of ippicator bone had been placed over the open eyes. Aldhelm's nightcloak had been pressed, the hem rewoven with gilt.

Now, as the dawnrock noted the passing of light, the Hoorka gathered. First came the jussar applicants with cloaks of red, then the apprentices with the normal black and gray uniform adorned by a scarlet sleeve, and finally the full kin. Their footsteps echoed among the stones. Glowtorches guttered fitfully in the hands of every tenth Hoorka, the erratic light throwing mad shadows to the roof. All passed once around the pyre, intoning the kin's chant to Hag Death. Cranmer, on a ledge above and to one side, busied himself recording the ceremony. The Hoorka rustled to a halt, arrayed before the pyre.

Gyll was moody, tired. He'd arrived at Sterka Port only a few hours before, with time only to plunge his vibro into the ground near the dawnrock and then ready himself for Aldhelm's funeral. He had not been able to talk to Valdisa, to tell her that Guillene was dead. Now he sat on the ground next to her, staring at the pyre and its silent burden, feeling the chill of Underasgard against his flesh. The scent of oil was heavy in the cavern, mingling with the pungency of spices. Flame crackled beside him as an apprentice came up and handed Valdisa a torch. Gyll glanced at Valdisa. She seemed to feel the pressure of his gaze and turned, smiling wanly. He touched her hand, almost as cool as the rock it rested on. Her fingers interlaced his and pressed gently. "I'm glad you're back in time," she said.

"It took longer than Helgin had thought. It wouldn't have mattered. You're Thane. It's your task to see Aldhelm's rite done property."

"Still, this is better." The erratic torchlight made her face waver, as if crossed by some unguessed emotion. She moved her hand away, staring again at the pyre. "It's done, then?"

"Guillene's with the Hag."

"Have you told the kin?"

"Tomorrow. Tonight is for Aldhelm."

She only nodded, solemn. Smoke from her torch watered Gyll's eyes. He leaned away from her.

The torch Inglis held stank in Gyll's nostrils—or perhaps it was Inglis himself. Gyll had found the cave system after an old and drunken lassari had babbled of it in Sterka. He'd taken Inglis with him to explore it. The caves, in Gyll's mind, might make an excellent base for the group of lassari and jussar he'd joined: thieves and murderers hiding from the wrath of the Li-Gallant Perrin. Gyll had ideas for them— they had begun to listen, grudgingly. Now Inglis stumbled over the broken floor of the cavern and the torch came dangerously near Gyll's clothing.

"Damn it, man. Watch where you're stepping."

Inglis reared about, the torch whuffing through air. "Shut your friggin' mouth, Gyll. Just because you've managed to get the rest of 'em to listen don't mean you can order me around. Try that again, and I'll shove this friggin' torch down your throat."

Gyll knew that the confrontation between him and Inglis had been coming. The man had been undermining Gyll's growing influence with the lassari band. Inglis had been one of the leaders, ruling by grace of his size and feared brutality. Gyll preferred to lead through discipline and intelligence, but these were not traits Inglis understood or appreciated. The lassari had been waiting to see which was the way of the future. Gyll could think of no better place to settle it—the dark caverns, the rest of the band waiting by the jagged mouth.

"Inglis," he said, wearily. "You've seen me fight—if you still think you're better, then you're nothing but a fool."

Inglis cursed and charged. The caverns echoed with their conflict—it was short. Inglis knew only one tactic—a bear-like charge, a straightforward attack. Gyll dodged the first blow of Inglis's large fist, kicking the man as he lunged. As Inglis bent over in sudden agony, Gyll hammered at his neck with coupled hands. Inglis moaned, but did not go down.

Gyll hit him again, and the man crumpled to the stones. Rock clunked dully under him, the torch guttered nearby.

In a few moments, Inglis groaned to his knees, as Gyll watched.

"Enough?" Gyll asked.

For his reply, Inglis yanked the dagger from his belt and charged once more. This time, Gyll had to break his arm. He picked up the dagger from the stones, held it at Inglis's throat from behind, one hand holding the chin up. The others of the band had by this time heard the fighting and entered. They stood around them like shadows, watching in silence.

"Enough?" Gyll asked again.

"You can beat me now, bastard, but I'll find you sometime," Inglis muttered through his teeth. He reached behind for Gyll, unwilling to yield.

Gyll pulled the dagger deep. Lifeblood splashed on the stones.

It was the first conflict in Underasgard between the lassari that would become the Hoorka.

Valdisa had risen, handing the torch to Serita Iduna, who stood beside the pyre. From under her nightcloak, Valdisa took out a dagger in a jeweled sheath—the Hoorka death-blade. It had once been a plain weapon, but now the blade was silvered, the hilt shone. She ascended the pyre—a rude stairway had been made in the logs—finally kneeling beside the body. Torchlight shone in her eyes; Gyll could see the tears gathered at the corners. He envied Valdisa her grief. Searching inside himself, he felt very little. He could make excuses—he was still buoyed by the adrenaline of the Heritage trip, tired from the long day, but no . . . He'd tried to summon up the sorrow that he should feel, that he knew he *must* feel somewhere inside, but it had hidden itself. Yes, he felt emptiness, but that was an intellectual sensation. Valdisa's bereavement was genuine. Gyll wondered what was wrong with him.

Valdisa lifted the dagger and kissed the blade, tears shining behind the bright metal. She touched the flat of the blade to Aldhelm's lips, then (her mouth taut, eyes half-closed and forcing the tears from under the lids) she plunged the dagger into Aldhelm's breast.

A sigh came from the massed kin.

Still kneeling, she let go of the weapon. Hands at her sides, she began the invocation of She of the Five Limbs. The yellow-white hilt caught the torchlight. It shone, lustrous.

The sunstar was in Gyll's eyes—a bad position, but he couldn't move without making it obvious that he expected a fight. Kryll spat on the ground at Gyll's feet. "You can't do this, boy. I won't let you."

Gyll widened his stance, waiting. "No one can tell me what I can or can't do. If you people don't listen to me, we're going to stay lassari shit. I can make us guilded kin, but you're going to have to do things by my code."

Kryll laughed—yellowed teeth, cracked lips. "Man, you're a frigging idiot. Oh, a good fighter, I'll admit that, but you're a dreamer first. I've killed five men, two of 'em guilded kin. It may not have made me rich, but I'm better off than those idiots just dying in Dasta. We're comfortable out here, away from Sterka. Keep your damned stupidities to yourself."

"Kryll, if I have to kill you to get what I want, I'll do it. The Li-Gallant's guards'll even pay me for the body, neh?"

Kryll laughed again. He pulled an ugly, battered crowd-prod from the belt-loop at his waist. Gyll had seen him use it before. The prod had been altered, the limiting circuits taken out. It used the full charge of the battery with a touch. It charred the flesh, perhaps even killed. Kryll waved the weapon at Gyll. "You bother me too much, boy. C'mere, and I'll teach you what happens to lassari with dreams."

But quite another lesson was taught, and Kryll was not the professor but the student.

Valdisa took the dagger from Aldhelm's breast and sheathed it again. She reached over the body and took the bone chips from the eyes. Though the body was too high-placed for him to see, Gyll knew that the eyes would be open, allowing the *j'nath*, the essence of the soul that is left behind when breath departs, to exit when the flames released it. Summoned by the invocation, She of the Five would take the *j'nath* and incorporate it into Herself. The ippicator chips were placed in Aldhelm's hands, an offering. Valdisa bowed her head, rising to her feet. Spreading her arms wide, she intoned the benediction.

"Our brother Aldhelm goes to join She of the Five Limbs. Let all kin give praise."

With the others, Gyll repeated the response. "Let all give praise." The phrase echoed through the cavern.

"He will give Her the love of kin."

"Let all give praise."

"He will intercede with Her for Hoorka."

"Let all give praise."

The litany continued, phrase and response, for several minutes. Then Valdisa lowered her hands. She bowed deeply to the body of Aldhelm and descended the pyre.

That kind of conversation always seemed to happen after lovemaking.

Darnell had cradled her head in his shoulder, sighing. Tangled, faintly damp hair spread over his chest; the chill air of Underasgard cooled the sweat on his body. Gyll touched the headboard—covers obediently slid over them. "Thank you," Darnell said. She snuggled closer. "That's much better."

Gyll hmmmed agreement.

"I saw the uniforms. They're dark and somber." Her voice was sleepy, lazy. "You think they'll make much difference, Thane?"

"Yes." He was emphatic. His fingers kneaded her smooth-muscled back. "They'll give us an identity, a unity. I think it'll draw us closer, probably closer than the kin of most guilds."

"Some of the others don't like the fact that you didn't consult the rest before you made the decision."

"It was my decision to make. You have to grasp for what you think is right—whether it actually is or not—or you'll lose the leadership."

"And if the decision's wrong?"

"It doesn't matter. It's all in the act itself. You have to do what you think is right, regardless of consequences. Otherwise, you lose the respect of the rest; more importantly, you'll probably lose your respect for yourself. And that's worse."

"You sound as if you've thought out all the answers."

"I have. I'm Thane. I intend to stay Thane." He lay back, hand under head, relaxing. It was all going so well. Li-Gallant Perrin hadn't been able to ignore their application for guild status: the future of Hoorka would come to a vote in the Assembly within one phase of Sleipnir, and Gyll had talked with several of the rule-guild heads. It looked hopeful. He pulled Darnell closer, smiling. Yah, very well. He rested, content.

Serita handed the torch back to Valdisa. The flame dimmed, then flared. Shadows slid over Valdisa's face. She looked at Gyll. "Ulthane," she said, "will you send Aldhelm on? I think he would prefer it."

Gyll nodded, rising to his feet. He shook sooty dirt from his nightcloak and walked over to Valdisa, taking the torch from her. He wanted to hug her—the face was so tragic, so hurt. Tears had left faint tracks on her cheeks. Valdisa stepped away from him, going to join the silent kin; Gyll turned to the pyre. The aroma of sandalwood and oil was heavy. He looked up at the body. "Aldhelm"—a whisper— "I wouldn't have it this way. I'm sorry. I wish we could have remained friends, kin-brother."

He touched the flame to the base of the pyre. Nothing happened for a moment, then a small flame appeared, wavered, and surged. Crackling, hissing; the fire leaped from log to log, climbing. The buffeting heat drove Gyll back while the eternal night of Underasgard was banished from the cavern. The smell of smoke and oil filled the room. Gyll knew that the dark cloud of Aldhelm's funeral would now be rising from the vents of natural chimneys in the room, a fuming from the slopes above Underasgard's mouth. The wind would smear the soot and ash across the sky.

In reverse order of their entrance, the Hoorka filed from the room. Gyll, standing beside Valdisa, touched her arm. She smiled sadly at him; Gyll pulled her to him with one arm. She touched her head to his shoulder. Through the pall of smoke, Gyll could see Cranmer—coughing and sneezing—getting ready to vacate his perch.

Their turn came. Gyll squeezed Valdisa, then walked ahead of her from the Cavern of the Dead. At their backs, logs collapsed in on each other. A frantic gathering of sparks danced their way to the roof.

Chapter 12

An excerpt from the acousidots of Sondall-Cadhurst Cranmer. The following transcript is from one of the earliest recordings of the Hoorka dots. The subject, Redac Allin, was one of the original Hoorka, a member of the lassari thugs taken by the young Gyll Hermond. The dot was quoted by Cranmer in the first treatise on the Hoorka, Social Homogenization: The Hoorka in Neweden Society. (Niffleheim Journal of Archaeo-Sociology, Marcus 245, pp.1389-1457.) Cranmer, in his notes, recorded that he wished to do a later full-holo interview with Allin, but the man was slain a few weeks later during a contract. His passing was not particularly mourned, even by the Hoorka-kin.

EXCERPT FROM THE DOT OF 11.16.211:

"Sirrah Allin, you were one of the original Hoorka."

"Yah. I can remember when Gyll—the Thane—came to us."

"What did the band do before the Thane organized you as a guild?"

"I did the same's I did after. I killed. Only difference was that I didn't take the person's money. Sometimes the old way was better—we didn't need no contract."

"But you were lassari then. Isn't the kinship better?"

"Yah, I suppose. Ain't much choice when you're lassari: steal, do the shitwork kin throw at you, or starve. Good choices, neh? I stole. Got more that way, got to stick knives in kin."

"You didn't have to kill, did you? I mean, there was no compelling reason for you to do so. From what I un-

derstand, most of your band refrained from that, if for no
other reason than the fact that the guilded kin pursue
murderers far more than thieves. You were an exception."

"The ones the Hag eats don't talk. That's how half the
suckers get caught and lose their hands. Killing keeps
'em quiet. It's safer to kill."

"Did you enjoy it, find it pleasurable?"

(A longish pause.) "You look at me like I'm some
kind of specimen, scholar."

"I meant no offense. I'm interested in your feelings.
I've heard it said that you don't find your task as Hoorka
at all, ahh, distasteful."

"You could find out. I'd arrange a demonstration for
you. The Thane could get other scholars later."

(There is a nervous rustlng of flimsies. Cranmer clears
his throat.) "Ahh, that won't be necessary."

"Too bad. I tell you, scholar, I don't mind the killing.
Not at all. People will go to the Hag anyway—maybe
she'll like me better when my time comes, neh? After all,
I send her so many . . . It's better now, with the run. It
gives it a thrill, like a hunt. The bastards might get away
from you unless you're careful, if you ain't good. The killing, the last part—I don't mind it at all. Does that bother
you, little man?"

"No." *(A remark that might be made here—Cranmer
was never known as a man given to foolish bravery. Given
that, his following remarks can only be attributed to errant imprudence.)*

"But some might think that it's an indication of some,
ahh, mental misalignment. The Alliance—well, if you
were on Niffleheim, you'd've been wiped."

"Ain't on Niffleheim, are we? And on Neweden, you
can't insult kin and expect to be untouched."

"It wasn't an insult. It was just a statement."

"So I'm not even smart enough to know the difference? Scholar, you wag your tongue too much. Let me
take it out for you."

(The next few minutes on the dot are quite confused.
There is a scuffling of feet, chairs clatter to stone, and
Cranmer shouts for the Thane. There is the sound of a
struggle, a yelp in pain in Cranmer's voice, and a muffled

exclamation. The recorder is — possibly — knocked to the ground, for the next sound is Cranmer.)

"Hello? Oh, good. It still works. Thank you, Thane. I . . . well . . ."

"You're not much of a fighter, Sond. You'd better get that cut seen to. Allin, you'll apologize to Cranmer, and you'll keep your temper in Underasgard."

"Your scholar insulted me, Thane. I had the right —"

"The scholar's not from Neweden. He doesn't yet understand us. Man, do I have to treat you like a child? Go to my rooms and wait for me." (The sound of the door opening and closing.)

"Thane, I didn't mean to cause trouble. I should have been more careful in what I said to him."

"We all have to learn, Sond. But I'd suggest you learn Neweden ways or learn to fight. Preferably both."

"Karl, get Oldin. Now."

"Surely, m'Dame, but it will take a few minutes."

"Just do it."

D'Embry quivered with fury. She could not stop the trembling of the thin hand she held out in front of her. Muttering a curse, she gave up the effort.

Damn that scheming bitch!

She wanted no more calls like the last. It had come from Diplo Center on Heritage. Heritage's Regent, Kav Long (she remembered him as a vaguely competent secretary doing menial tasks when she'd last visited Niffleheim) had been curt and scornful.

"I thought you had Neweden under control, d'Embry," Long had said, with no preamble.

"I do." She'd been puzzled and irritated with the morning's interruption.

Long had laughed without amusement, his face creased by static — the transmission was none too good; something in the Einsteinian jump always did that. "Guillene was killed last night, d'Embry. It couldn't have been more than one or two assassins. They entered Moache grounds, disabled several guards and the household staff, and killed the man in his bed. Very neatly: the throat was slit. He was dead too damn long before we got there, too — the brain'd deteriorated beyond the point of saving. Some of your frigging assassins got loose." The blond face quavered, lost in electronic storming.

She had protested, but the vague suspicion that Long was right already had formed in her mind. "That's impossible. Listen, you young fool, the Hoorka haven't any craft capable of it, and Sterka Port is tight—I can guarantee that. Guillene wasn't exactly loved by the Moache employees or by de Sezimbra's associates, was he? I'd suggest you look closer to home, Long. You can get assassins on any world."

He'd exhaled in disgust. "I'll admit that. I'll admit that vibros are common enough, too, but let's be realistic. It wasn't anybody here—none of them would be that good. That leaves your black and gray wonders. Moache Mining is upset." He laughed nervously, and d'Embry realized at that instant where his anger originated. "Hell, they're a lot more than just upset. They've already bypassed the Center here and gone straight to Niffleheim. You know they're going to listen there. Moache's got the money to make 'em do it. You goofed, m'Dame. Niffleheim'll have your head." A pause, a snarling of static. "Mine, too."

Kav Long cut the contact.

Oldin. It had to be through Oldin.

"M'Dame, I have Oldin."

"Good," she snapped. "Karl, I want you to go through the records of all the satellite net stations. See if you can find the slightest indication that a Trader craft might have left Neweden space. And do it quickly."

"Yah, m'Dame."

D'Embry took a deep breath, running her hands through her thin, white hair. She settled herself in her floater, arranged the ippicator necklace on her blouse. A vein-laced hand reached out, touched the contact on her desk.

The screen of the com-link pulsed light and settled. Kaethe Oldin smiled beatifically out at her. Oldin's eyebrows were today slivers of platinum, shimmering. Half the face was in cosmetic shadow. The glossed-mouth moved. "M'Dame d'Embry, what can I do for you?"

"You sent a Hoorka to Heritage, Trader Oldin. You allowed Guillene to be killed."

Eyebrows, glittering, rose in surprise. Her head half-turned, but the gaze was fixed on d'Embry. "That would be a violation of the Trader-Alliance pact, Regent. Certainly you don't think me stupid enough to ruin my business here by running a ferry service for assassins? The Hoorka can hire Alliance vessels, and Grandsire FitzEvard would have my head if I lost revenue."

"Let's not play games, Trader Oldin." *She's good at it— Just the right expressions, the correct stance between indignant surprise and amusement. If I didn't know it had to be her . . .* "I'm awfully tired of games."

"Games, Regent? Are you making a formal accusation, then? If so, I demand my right to refute the proof of misconduct." Again, the smile, infuriating. "If you're not making the accusation, then I think you're mistaken as to who's playing a game."

D'Embry forced down a retort: she breathed once, slowly, knotting her hands together. "Trader Oldin, the Hoorka have no interstellar craft. No Alliance-registered ships have gone to Heritage in the last few days—I've checked. You are the only possibility left."

"Has the orbital net noted one of the boats from *Peregrine* leaving for anywhere but Sterka Port?"

"No," d'Embry admitted ruefully. "But what one person can design, another can find a way around. Believe me, Trader, I've no delusions as to your capabilities."

"I thank you for the compliment, m'Dame, but I still suggest you owe me an apology." Oldin said it sweetly, a sugared voice.

"Ulthane Gyll has been to *Peregrine,* Trader. The first time was only for a few hours. He went again two days ago; he didn't return until yesterday evening."

"That constitutes no crime, Regent. As you know, I've used the Hoorka myself. I wanted Ulthane Gyll to see the ship, to see the goods we had. Then I asked him to stay overnight. He was kind enough to accept my offer. I find him quite charming, actually."

"Trader Oldin, this is a serious matter." D'Embry's voice was rising. She forced herself back into the icy demeanor she affected before her staff. *Calm, calm. You're falling right into the bitch's hands. That's exactly what she wants from you—anger and the loss of control. She's most likely recording the conversation.*

"I realize that you consider the situation serious, Regent. Is Moache Mining putting pressure on you? I would wager that Niffleheim called and wanted a scapegoat produced to drag before the Directors, and it's your job to find one or be used yourself. I can understand your anxiety to place the blame on the Trading Families, m'Dame. I'd be doing the same were I in your position. People have spat on us for centuries: the Alliance, the Free Worlds, Huard. Why change now—we're convenient gypsies, there and gone again."

"You plead your case eloquently, Trader. One would think you've given it much thought. Did you know you'd need to defend yourself?" She wanted Oldin, wanted that ship out of Neweden space.

"What of the other guilds, m'Dame?" Oldin continued as if she hadn't heard d'Embry. "Some of them are rich enough to have bought or hired the needed ship—silence can be bought, too. Maybe they ferried Hoorka in hopes of future favors. Or maybe one of your Alliance ships logged a false destination code. Or maybe Guillene was killed by one of his own." Behind Oldin, some out-of-focus person bustled past, carrying something that looked halfway between snail and dog. Oldin glanced at him, snapped an unheard order, then turned back to d'Embry. "My log is available to you, Regent. Call and ask for our pilot or the Motsognir Helgin. We can send it to you within a day or so."

"I *do* want that log, Trader. I can tell you that now. I want it by noon."

"Regent, it will take—"

"Noon, Trader. A failure to comply will indicate that you are not willing to cooperate with the local authority. That can result in your expulsion from Neweden space. That's in the pact, too." D'Embry allowed herself to enjoy the look of irritation that crossed Oldin's face, wiping away the smug half-smile. The Regent was certain that the log would show exactly what Oldin intended it to say, even with the lack of notice: there would be no record of a *Peregrine* boat leaving Neweden orbit. D'Embry wouldn't prove anything, but if it caused Oldin *any* discomfiture, she found it worthwhile. Somewhere inside, a small voice chastised her—*you're getting petty, old woman, hurting back because you've been hurt.* And the answer *yah, doesn't it feel good?*

Oldin seemed to begin a statement, then swallowed the word with a twitch of her mouth. She stared at d'Embry. "Regent, I protest—"

"You may protest as much as you like," d'Embry said. "As Regent, I'll give your protestations the attention they deserve. Just be sure that your log reaches me in the next few hours. By noon. That's all, Trader Oldin."

With a sense of childish enjoyment, d'Embry snapped the contact. The petulant face of Oldin disappeared in static. The screen went black.

Ulthane Gyll looked at the silent, expectant faces around him and put a foot up on the stool's seat. Most of the full kin were there, seated or standing around the table. Only Thane Valdisa was absent. That caused him pain. She'd said that she would not come — *this is your show,* she'd told him, *not mine. It's not pettiness on my part, Gyll. But I didn't want it. Not the way it was done.* He had tried to convince himself that her absence would not make a difference.

"Guillene is dead," he said simply, without preamble. "I killed him. She of the Five has fed on his blood."

Gyll was surprised at the amount of satisfaction he heard in his voice. He'd not thought he would feel that way; it had taken him so much effort to will the blade to move. But now that it was done ...

The kin said nothing for a long moment, though Gyll could see smiles on some of the faces, nods of pleased relief. The debt to a kin-brother was settled. Serita said it for them all, a throaty few words, half-whispered. "Good. Then it's over."

"Did he die easily, Ulthane?" d'Mannberg asked.

Gyll shrugged. "He died," he said.

D'Mannberg's thick hands clenched. "He knew it was Hoorka?"

"I knew that he'd been informed of the bloodfeud, and I didn't kill from hiding. He was awake. He knew."

"And who gave you the ride?" Bachier, down the table. "Certainly not the Regent?"

"Neh." *Certainly not, and it's why Valdisa was wrong in this. The Regent would never have let her do it.* "I talked to Trader Oldin — it was due to her generosity. And that's not information to go outside the kin, either. Nor is this: I've talked to Oldin about other possibilities for Hoorka." He didn't know why he said that; he'd not intended to discuss Oldin's offering publicly, not until he and Valdisa had arrived at a decision. He pulled his nightcloak around him, wondering if it hadn't been a mistake.

"Offworld?" Serita's voice held a cautious note, a negative query that puzzled Gyll. "The offworld contracts have caused us nothing but trouble, Ulthane. Maybe Hoorka should stay on Neweden, where we're understood." She looked at him with steady green eyes.

Her words doubly startled Gyll; they were identical to the argument Aldhelm had given him. *Is Aldhelm coming back to haunt me, like the rest of the dead ones that get in my dreams?* "Hoorka must expand," he began, automatically. "That had always been my intent. Neweden was to be our beginning, our home, but never the totality of our existence. That's Thane Valdisa's feelings, too."

"We know that, Ulthane. Most of us agreed with you." Bachier again. He shifted in his seat, nervously. "We probably still do, to an extent. But Sartas and McWilms . . . The situation has made *me* think it over again, I know. We've enough problems right here on Neweden: the Li-Gallant and Gunnar, the lassari killing Eorl and bothering all guilded kin." Bachier shook his head. "I'm not saying anything definite, Ulthane. But *maybe* we should ask ourselves whether Neweden should be enough for us. Maybe we should postpone our dreams for a while and make sure we're stable here."

Others about the room nodded. A murmur of agreement rumbled around the table.

Gyll pulled back suddenly, the boot that had been on the stool stamping earth. The nightcloak swirled. He could feel anger building inside him and he wanted to leave, before it burst out in front of kin. "That's a damned poor way of thinking." As he watched, Bachier's face went scarlet. *Careful, you fool.* "I'm sorry, Bachier, but I can't agree with that at all. *I* would not be satisfied with Neweden. I expected us to go offworld one day, even though the code was designed for this world. Opportunities await us—we shouldn't be afraid to grasp at them."

"It's not that we're being fearful laggards." D'Mannberg's booming voice pulled Gyll's head around. "And we're not trying to change Hoorka policy. We're just asking if maybe the time isn't right."

"To the Hag with time!" Gyll shouted the words. He

strode to the far wall of the cavern, turning on his toes to face them again. "If we do that, Sartas has died for nothing, and McWilms is suffering for a whim. Are you all so afraid of the Hag that you'd cocoon yourselves on this one world?"

"Ulthane—" d'Mannberg began.

"No! Listen to me." Gyll halted the protest with a raised forefinger. "We have to be able to admit mistakes. That much I can agree with. The Alliance may not be the best way for us to pursue our goals. Maybe we need to examine client worlds more carefully. But Hoorka *will* go offworld. Through the Regent or some other way. We aspire, or we die. I won't see the Hoorka become like the ippicator."

"We can understand how you feel," Serita said.

"Can you? Damn it, I *made* Hoorka. I killed to be sure it was molded the way I wanted it to be. I fought the prejudices of Neweden for it. I gave up the thaneship, but Hoorka is still my creation. I won't see it die. And to stay on Neweden is to accept a slow death."

Gyll strode to the mouth of the cavern. He looked back at the assassins. "I won't have it," he said.

Chapter 13

GYLL COULDN'T DECIPHER Valdisa's mood. She seemed caught on some intangible interface between frantic gaiety and quiet moodiness. Something worked at the muscles of her drawn face—a pensiveness he couldn't understand.

She was sitting at her desk floater when he entered the room, intent on the flimsies there, a hoverlamp casting a dark image of her head on the cavern wall. She looked up at the sound of the door. Seeing Gyll, she smiled with an odd enthusiasm. She rose and went to him, taking his hands. "Well, Gyll?"

"I told them," he said. He didn't return the pressure of her hands. She held them a moment longer, then went to the bedfield and sat. She patted the covers. "Here. Sit with me."

It was the opening he needed, he thought as he sat beside her. A chance to explain his feelings, to vent all the uncertainties and come to a final understanding. He no longer wanted to go on the way they had, always circling each other and never settling anything. He sat, trying to find a beginning. "The reaction was odd, Valdisa. They didn't say what I thought would be said."

"McWilms is coming back to the caverns," she said, interrupting him. Her eyes were wide, too wide, as if she were frightened. Still, the voice was calm and steady. "They'll release him tomorrow. I talked with him over the com. He'll still need a portable med-pack, and it'll be some time before the arm bud grows well enough for him to begin using it, but he's anxious to be in Underasgard again. He wanted to talk to you, Gyll. He wants to know about Guillene, how it happened, everything."

"He knows the man's dead, doesn't he?"

"Yah, but he wants it told to him, in all the detail. He's very bitter, Gyll, very angry." She picked at the cloth of the bedsheet, then smoothed it down again.

"Does he blame Hoorka, like the rest? Does he think it was all a tragic mistake?" He couldn't keep his own spite from his voice.

"No." Her eyes questioned him. "He's very anxious for his initiation into full kinship, if that's what you mean. He doesn't blame Hoorka for what happened. What he is angry about is the Alliance, the way they handled it."

"Oldin told me that they wouldn't handle it well."

Valdisa broke in hurriedly, before he could say more. Gyll could see the nervous smile, the restless eyes, the quick movements of her hands. Though he let her talk, he knew it to be an avoidance. *Oldin's the key—that's the subject she's steering you around. She doesn't want to argue. But it will just be harder later.* "Well, McWilms doesn't want us to abandon the work we've done," she said. She faced him, one leg on the bed, one on the floor. Her hands sought his once more, clasped them to her knee. "That's the good part. He doesn't feel that Hoorka should stay on Neweden. I thought that the kin might react that way—and your face is too open to have hidden it from me. I can guess at what they told you. But they all admire you, Gyll. You're the creator. McWilms is still sure of Hoorka's goals. The rest of them will return to that way of thinking, in a few days or weeks. Ahh, Gyll, don't look so damned hurt."

She pulled him to her—he didn't resist, didn't help. Arms around chest, she hugged him; after a moment, Gyll put his arms around her and returned the embrace. They kissed, softly, then she laid her head on his shoulder. "Gyll, I don't want to fight. Not tonight. I've hated it, every time." Her voice was a rough whisper in his ear.

"You don't want to be Thane?" He spoke into the fragrance of her hair.

He could feel her head shake—a short movement. "I'm not giving that up, Gyll; neh. But I also don't want it to drive a wedge between the two of us."

"Valdisa—" he began. Emotions waned: to tell her that he had already made a decision in his own mind, to hold it back lest he ruin the moment—the intimacy had become rarer between them of late. "Valdisa," he said again.

"Hush, love. Not now." Her mouth sought his, open. She leaned back, pulling him down on her. He felt her hands slip under the folds of his nightcloak, tug at his shin. Warm, her fingers kneaded his back and ran the hills of his spine. She hugged him fiercely.

Aroused despite himself, he responded. He kissed her, as if that gave denial to his doubts. The interior debate dissolved in heat. He fumbled with the clasps of her blouse, and she laughed under his mouth at his clumsiness. "Here, let me help."

"Quiet," he told her. "I can manage."

Cloth fell away, whispering.

Afterward, they lay in each other's arms. Valdisa's breath was cool on his face as he lazily stroked the damp smoothness of her side, fingers tracing the lines of her body. As he reached her waist, she quickly rolled away, muscles rippling under his hand. "That tickles," she said, grinning.

"You didn't think so a few minutes ago." He touched her again; she moved farther back, then rolled into him, nipping at his shoulder.

"Hey! That hurts, woman."

"You didn't think so a few minutes ago."

Gyll laughed, rubbing his shoulder. "Consider the point made." He stroked her again, this time with more pressure. "Better?" he asked.

She snuggled against him in answer.

They lay that way for several minutes, simply enjoying the closeness, the dark, cool silence around them. Gyll's hand moved. They kissed—long, slow, gentle—then lay back again. Gyll found himself more aware than ever of the separation their clashing prides had caused. He found himself wishing that they could have returned to this long ago.

"You're thinking," Valdisa said, a contralto accusation.

"I'm not allowed? And how did you know?"

"Your hand stopped. You're lying there with your eyes focused on the ceiling, open. You've entirely ceased to notice me, yet nothing's intruded on us—the distraction has to be inside. Now, what are you thinking?"

He thought of delaying, of temporizing, then knew that

even that hesitation had spoken for him. "I wanted to tell you before," he said. "So you'll have to forgive my waiting."

On her side, head on hand, she waited.

"I think—I *know,* rather—what I want to do, for both your sake and mine," he continued. The words were slow at first, hesitant, but came faster and more definite as he went on. Valdisa watched him as he spoke, her gaze never letting his eyes wander. "That's what I've been ruminating over for the past several days. You need time, love, time without my interference so that the kin accept you wholly as Thane. I know you've felt it—a slowness when they take orders from you, a belligerence from some of them; Aldhelm was certainly that way."

Sorrow tugged at the corners of her mouth at his mention of Aldhelm, then she frowned. "All you're doing with this preamble is giving your words a sugarcoating, Gyll. I'm all grown up. If it's going to be bitter, just say it." Her stare challenged him. He couldn't evade it. He said nothing for a moment, gathering the words in his mind. Then he nodded, sighed.

"Yah, you're right." He took a breath, touching her, as if by contact he could make her take the phrases as he wished them to be taken. "I want to go with Oldin. They'll be leaving in a few weeks. I want to spend a few months investigating the Trading Families; see what FitzEvard Oldin is holding for the Hoorka, see if we can be mutually helpful to each other. And that will leave you as the only authority here. It'll get me out of your way so that the kin don't go past you to me."

"The kin have never 'gone past me.'" Her voice mocked him. "It's just you and me, Gyll. We fight more than any of the rest of the kin." She glanced back at his hand, atop her waist. Slowly, he removed it.

"If that's the case, Valdisa, then maybe we just need the time apart."

"If you feel that way, all you have to do is say so. You don't have to go running off with this Oldin woman. Underasgard is big enough."

So quickly from affection to argument: she had not moved, but Gyll could feel a growing distance between them. He chastised himself. *You knew it, you knew it . . .*

"Valdisa, you're my friend, my lover, my only real confidant among the kin. Do you think I'd give that up so lightly?"

"I don't think you want to give anything up, Gyll. Not me, not Neweden, not Oldin, not the Alliance, not—especially not—your leadership of Hoorka. I think you've found that you've made a mistake, giving up the thaneship."

He didn't try to deny it. "All I want to do is explore a possible new avenue for Hoorka, for my—*our*—kin. It doesn't violate any of our present agreements with the Li-Gallant or the Alliance, and it may give us a new avenue for expansion. It's just me and a few months, Valdisa; that's all we're talking about. The Hoorka can spare that much."

Her laughter scraped at his composure. "With Aldhelm, Renier, Sartas, and Eorl dead? With McWilms hurt? With the kin's morale at low ebb? Gods, Gyll . . . The rotation's already too tight."

"Then one more out of it won't matter. And my work's been mediocre of late—that was everyone's complaint, even yours. I'll admit it." He could hear the bitterness creeping into his voice, the pitch moving higher and louder. He forced himself into calmness again; he tried to sound rational. "The kin can spare me. Both you and d'Mannberg are better teachers than I for the apprentices, and a quicker rotation will only hone the skills of Hoorka. We can use the practice room less."

"It's amazing how convincing you can be when you want something, Gyll." Valdisa growled in disgust, deep in her throat. She rolled off the bedfield to her feet, whistling on a hoverlamp. Golden light threw harsh shadows across her body—under the disheveled hair, under the small breasts, across one leg. She half-turned from him, gazing into nether space. Her head shook, then she turned back to him. Her eyes were narrowed, hard; her face was pinched and somehow ugly.

"No," she said. "No. I don't like the idea. And Gyll . . . I want you to leave me now. Don't talk anymore. Just take your clothes and go back to your room. Go pet your wort."

"Valdisa—"

"No!" She turned her back to him, facing the desk, the cold stone of the wall. "Just go."

She would say nothing else.

*   *   *

Helgin lounged against the side of the shuttle's landing gear. The gear was both dirty and oily; it smudged the sleeve of the tunic he wore. He scratched at his beard with a crooked forefinger and glanced at Gyll. Around them, the port made busy noises.

"She's not on *Peregrine*, Hoorka. She had business in Sterka, someone to see. I don't know when she'll be back, and I doubt that she'll be in the mood for visitors. Oh, she'll pretend it, but she's a poor actress."

Gyll didn't let his disappointment show. He nodded. "There wasn't anything specific . . . I just wanted to talk with her . . ." He felt vaguely foolish. He hadn't wanted to stay in Underasgard after the argument with Valdisa and had come to the port on a whim. He'd gone to his rooms after leaving her, fed and cuddled the wort for a time, then left. It hadn't been until he reached Sterka that he realized where he was going. He'd gone through port security and out onto the field after seeing the shuttle in its dock.

"Well, she talks well enough. I'll grant that." Helgin moved against the gear. Grime smeared his back. "And she'd probably not mind talking with you, usually. But her real weakness is for short men with beards." He leered under the lush foliage of facial hair.

"Helgin, I don't know how to take you. I tell you again: You'd die on Neweden."

"You can pretend that if you like." The dwarf lurched upright. He stretched out his arms, seemed to see the dirt marbling the fabric for the first time, and grimaced. He rubbed at it. "You want to come inside? It's warmer."

Gyll shrugged. They entered the shuttle, went to the small lounge. Helgin walked over to an ornate chest sitting on the room's table and opened it. In a bed of bluish velvet, glass clinked. "Want a drink, Gyll? I've some brandy from Desolate that is better than fair."

Gyll stood, hesitant, but Helgin had already begun pouring. He handed one of the glasses to Gyll. The pungent odor wrinkled Gyll's nose; he sniffed, swirled the liquor. Helgin watched.

"Yah, that's the proper way—it doesn't do you a damn bit of good, but it looks nice," Helgin said. "Have a seat. You look distressed."

Gyll frowned, not sure whether he should be annoyed or

flattered at the dwarf's concern. He watched the brandy move in the glass. "You talk too openly, Motsognir."

"Are you going to be stuffy again, Hoorka? You need to learn that people who have an affection for you aren't likely to jump behind your defenses and leave your ego in rubble. Either that, or you need to conceal your face better. And if that insults you, then so be it. Gods, I get tired of you New-edeners."

"I'm sure they're none too pleased with you," Gyll replied.

Helgin grinned. It was infectious. After a moment, Gyll could only smile back. Shaking his head, he sat in the nearest floater. Helgin sat across from him. "I don't understand you, Helgin. If you were one of my people, if you were guilded kin, then we'd have been in more than one fight over your atrocious lack of manners."

"And I'd've won most of them, which wouldn't have proved anything or have bettered those manners." Helgin drained his glass in a gulp. He grimaced, then smacked his lips and reached for the bottle.

"Is that the way you were taught to drink a brandy?" Gyll shuddered in sympathy.

"Ahh, you see, that's where you're wrong again. That *is* the way to drink a brandy on Desolate—quickly, before the sun takes it or dust settles on it or somebody tries to take it away. It's all in your cultural set." He poured. "Why'd you want to see Oldin?"

Gyll rotated the stem of the glass between thumb and forefinger; he took a sip. The brandy warmed its way down his throat. "Valdisa and I talked again," he said at last. "Actually, we had a bit of a disagreement. She doesn't see any value in having Hoorka go with the Trading Families."

Helgin downed the second glass with an abrupt motion. He wiped at his lips with the back of his hand. "And where does that leave you?"

"I don't know," Gyll admitted. He sipped again, relishing the fiery tartness of the liquor.

"Do *you* see a value in it?"

"Yah." He said it easily, surprising himself.

"Then there's no problem. You go." The dwarf leaned back, then reached forward again for the bottle. Gyll could see a streak of oily filth on the floater's back. Helgin looked at the remainder of the brandy appraisingly, then set it down again.

"You don't understand, Helgin. It's not that easy. She *is* Thane. I've no authority over her; I gave all that up. She's the leader of my kin. She's also my lover, my friend. I risk losing all that. And she may well be right—it could all be a waste of time. Kaethe's simply vague about the possibilities, and in any event it's not her but her grandsire that would make any decision."

"Gods, you people make everything so complicated for yourselves." Helgin rose from his floater. He paced the room, pulling at his beard. "Everyone makes their decisions based on their fears. You're afraid of Valdisa, so you chain yourself to Neweden. Your Li-Gallant's afraid to lose his power, so he raids the helpless lassari to demonstrate his capabilities. D'Embry's afraid of Niffleheim, and Kaethe— she's afraid of FitzEvard. All the choices predicated on fear, never on hope."

"What are you afraid of, Motsognir?" Gyll tugged at his nightcloak; he set the brandy glass on the arm of the floater. "All you do is talk."

"Nothing here frightens me."

"Then you don't know Neweden very well."

Helgin nodded. He halted his aimless wandering of the room and stood in front of Gyll. Gyll couldn't decide whether the dwarf was irritated; he glowered under the bristling of eyebrows, but he seemed to always glower.

"I know Neweden better than you might think, Gyll," Helgin said. "Better than maybe yourself. What event has occupied the minds of guilded kin for the last several months?"

"The killing of Gunnar, I suppose." Gyll could not fathom where Helgin was heading.

"Do you know who killed him?"

Lines deepened in Gyll's forehead. He leaned forward in his floater, feeling his stomach tensing. "You claim to have that knowledge, Motsognir?"

Helgin nodded; his beard moved on his soiled tunic. "Beyond any doubt."

Gyll could only think of Aldhelm, of the way he'd looked, transfixed on d'Mannberg's foil, the pain etched on his face. *Leave the Hag-kin alone. Let him rest.* "I've no interest in that."

"I couldn't tell you, in any case. And knowing wouldn't change any of the results. I'm pleased you don't ask. That's an advance in your perceptions."

"And all you've done is brag again, without having proved a thing." Gyll snorted in disgust. "And you spout sophistry like a university professor. You're a deep man, Helgin, for one so short."

"Then let me tell you something else." Helgin reached for the brandy with deliberate nonchalance. He poured himself another glassful, watching Gyll. Gyll sat in what he hoped was an attitude of stolid unconcern. He was growing tired of the Motsognir's posturing. Helgin looked as if he were about to drink, then lowered the glass slightly. His dark eyes regarded Gyll over the rim. "You *need* to go with Kaethe, Gyll. She makes noises like she's very interested in whether you do so or not, but in reality I tell you that it doesn't really much matter to her. It can't, because she has to do what FitzEvard wishes. But you *need* the Trading Families, if you really are concerned with the survival of Hoorka. Neweden doesn't yet realize it, but Gunnar's death is a watershed. Neweden was slowly changing, but his death has tipped the balance. With Gunnar gone, with Potok in exile and his rule-guild in disgrace, Vingi has a free hand, and he's not clever enough to use it well. Neweden is going to undergo a wracking change and the Hoorka—if they want survival—are going to need as many options as they can gather."

"That may or may not be, but Valdisa doesn't want it. And I only have your word that this 'change' will occur. That doesn't mean much, does it?"

There was silence for a moment. Gyll stroked the bowl of his brandy glass. He glanced up, but Helgin was peering into the depths of his own dark liquid as if some answer were hidden there. Then, with that same casual toss, the dwarf drank. His eyes closed for a second, then he threw the glass aside. It shattered in a corner.

"Get up," he said.

Gyll hesitated, uncertain as to the Motsognir's intention. The knot of tension in his stomach returned. He rose, slowly, looking down at the dwarf.

"Get out your vibro."

"Helgin—"

"Get it out," Helgin growled, hands on hips. A sandalled foot scuffed at the floor impatiently.

Gyll moved his nightcloak aside with a practiced swing, unsheathing the vibro in the same movement. He held it before the dwarf, unactivated. The Motsognir nodded, then stepped back. He spread his hands apart, crouching.

"Turn it on and come at me."

"Helgin, I don't—"

"Do it."

Nearly, he did not. Almost, he turned and walked away. But the dwarf started a mirthless laugh as Gyll's hand dropped, and that brought the vibro back up. Gyll touched the stud on the hilt and the vibrowire slicked out to dagger length: threatening, for unlike the foils, the dagger could not be adjusted to a lesser setting. Its low murmur shivered in his hand. Gyll saw that Helgin's attention was now focused on the weapon. "It's not going to prove anything, Helgin."

"Don't worry, Hoorka. You're not going to touch me. You're too old and too fat for that. Look at your waist— you're out of shape. Try it."

"You're a fool."

"Then let me be one. I'll prove it otherwise. Come at me, or does even this kind of challenge frighten you?"

Gyll wasn't angry. The taunts were too transparent for that. He was only puzzled. Yet he did move forward, letting his instincts guide him but still holding back: he did not want to harm the dwarf. Helgin backed away as Gyll advanced, then suddenly rolled and kicked in one gliding motion. Gyll winced as Helgin's foot caught his wrist, moving the vibro aside and nearly tearing it from his hand. Instinct ruled: he jabbed at the Motsognir, but the dwarf was too quick. The vibro sliced air, and Helgin was past and on his feet again before Gyll could turn.

"You see, Hoorka. You're not nearly as good as you like to think." Still in that low crouch, Helgin sneered. His teeth gleamed in lamplight, mocking.

Gyll said nothing, but now he too set his balance lower, the vibro moving before him in a small, tight circle. He closed cautiously, backing the dwarf to the wall, not letting him slip past. Helgin swept out an arm, cuffing at Gyll's knife hand. Gyll cut at the hand, and Helgin came at him, a blur of motion, shouting. Gyll felt pain lance his forearm as

Helgin struck him; grunting, he slashed, felt the vibro touch, and then Helgin hit him again. He couldn't hold the vibro this time—he heard it clatter away from him.

They faced each other, breathing heavily. Beneath torn cloth, a jagged line of blood showed on Helgin's arm. Gyll stared at it, and in that hesitation, Helgin could have attacked or dove for the vibro. He did neither. The Motsognir abruptly straightened. He began the usual grin, but midway it was inverted into grimace. He touched his injured arm gingerly, looked at the blood on his finger as if he could deny its existence. "Well," he growled.

"I'm sorry, Helgin." Gyll shook his head. "You . . . goaded me. I didn't mean . . ."

"Yah. Don't worry, Hoorka. I'll live. And I could have still taken you. You gave me too much time, and you've a lot to learn about using your hands and feet as weapons. If you want proof . . ." Again, Helgin went into that crouch, but Gyll shook his head once more.

"I don't want to fight you."

Helgin stared at Gyll.

"Let's call it even," Gyll continued. "You disarmed me, and, yah, I'll even admit you're far better than I would have thought, and I wouldn't want to face you on even terms. I don't consider you a braggart any longer."

Helgin nodded, pursing his thick lips. He scratched at his beard. "You don't like killing, do you?"

Gyll forced down irritation. "I don't like unnecessary bloodletting. That's all."

"Ahh." Helgin said nothing more. Rubbing his arm, he strode past Gyll back to his floater. Gyll went to where the vibro lay, picked it up, and sheathed it again. He sat.

"If both you and I were fools," Helgin said, "that little exhibition would prove that I've always spoken the truth to you. But I don't consider you a fool—you can think what you want about the rest. But . . . I repeat, Gyll, you need to go with Oldin."

Gyll did not want to return to that subject. "You need your arm attended to."

Helgin glanced down. Blood had soaked into the raveled edges of cloth. "It's a scratch. And you're avoiding the statement."

"I can't do much about it. You say it's for the sake of

Hoorka. Fine. But if I go against Valdisa, then I've done quite a bit to harm Hoorka myself, just by that act. Either way, I seem to lose. And if I'm here, at least I have a chance to give her advice."

Helgin made a disgusted sound. "You need to learn another lesson, Gyll. Worlds and politics don't matter. It's the individuals involved in them. You need to worry about yourself first. A little healthy selfishness never hurt anyone."

"I'm done talking about it."

A dour head shake; Helgin leaned forward, poured Gyll more brandy, then sat back holding the bottle. "Then we'll talk about something else. Have you ever seen rockfoam from Karm's Hole? It puts a polished ippicator bone to shame . . ."

They were still talking about nothing when Kaethe returned to the shuttle a few hours later.

Chapter 14

An excerpt from the acousidots of Sondall-Cadhurst Cranmer. The following was a very informal recording—much like some of the others, it was most likely done without Gyll Hermond's knowledge or consent. The "Ramulf" spoken of appears in the Neweden Chronicles as a minor thief executed on 9.19.214—evidently some discussion of this was used by Cranmer as a device to probe Hermond.

EXCERPT FROM THE DOT OF 9.20.214:

". . . but you have to realize, Sond, that Ramulf is—eh, *was*—just a friggin' lassari. Man, you can't expect better from the kinless."

"They're just people like the rest. Thane. The fact that you're part of a guild doesn't alter your basic personality."

"You say that, but I notice that you tend to avoid lassari, too."

"I would have thought you'd be more sympathetic toward them."

"Hmm? Explain yourself, scholar."

"As I understand it, your family was lassari. Your father . . ."

"My *true-father*—" (Here Gyll pauses, as if pressing home a point) "—was lassari, yah. But that relationship, true-father to biological son, doesn't have much importance on Neweden. Once you've reached puberty, you're jussar and free to find guild-kin. My true-father and my true-mother died lassari—I don't hide that fact from anyone because it doesn't bring any shame to me. If he'd had even a spark of creativity ... but his mind didn't work that way. Understand: he was an offworlder, trained to kill, yah, but narrow-minded and stupid. He didn't have the cultural set for Neweden. I grew up here—Neweden is ingrained in me. My true-father was dirt, a common thief. I'm glad he bothered to train me as he did, but I'd still spit in his face if he were alive. He's lassari. I could synthesize his training, his skills, and I saw that I could devise something out of it that would be viable here."

"Your true-father was executed?"

"Sent to the Hag unguilded and without honor, as he deserved. It doesn't hurt to say that, Cranmer. Neweden isn't and shouldn't be kind to murderers—it's the foulest thing to do when you can declare bloodfeud and retain your honor and your vengeance. Man, I'm not kidding you—if I met my true-father tomorrow I'd prick him with my blade, and it wouldn't be a fast death."

"Hell, Thane, the Hoorka slay, what—fifty, sixty people a standard? I know your objection, too, so don't say it. You've no personal grudge against those people; you don't even know them. Even I might be able to kill someone who'd provoked me a great deal, but I doubt that I could go out and kill without provocation—do it for pay."

"In a war you'd be killing, and doing it for pay. Cranmer, you ought to think before you talk."

"Still, I have to persist. The Hoorka aren't at war."

"Hag's ass, Cranmer. Then why do you bother with us? You can find an assassin on a hundred worlds, but you chose to look at the Hoorka—if you didn't think us different, you wouldn't bother."

"Do you enjoy your work?"

(Here there is a long pause. Hermond seems to be about to reply, then stops in mid-syllable.) "I don't enjoy it, scholar. I also don't necessarily dislike it. It's what I've been trained for, and it's all subject to the gods' wishes."

"That's all? Thane, I think I know you better."

(A breath-sigh.) "And you won't rest until I say more ..."

(Laughter. But it is only Cranmer's gaiety that is heard.)

"Fine, Sond. I'll tell you something, then, but if it ever goes past this room, if it's ever whispered to anyone else, I'll have you given to the Hag in pieces. At times, every once in a while, I wonder if I'd do this again, if I'd create the Hoorka. And I ask myself if all the souls I've sent to the Hag aren't going to be waiting for me when it's my turn."

Long before they could be seen, the presence of the Dead was announced. First, a faint and distant chant like the sound of a muffled chorus; then, as the soughing chant became louder and more distinct, the acrid smell of the too-sweet incense invaded the air. Nostrils wrinkled, heads began to turn . . .

The procession of the Dead snaked through the outer streets of Sterka toward the ornate arch that signified the boundary of Neweden's capital. They ignored the fine, soaking mist the morning had brought.

There, near the Avenue of Taverns, a band of jussar had gathered under the weathershield of the Inn of Seven Ogres. This was the group's daily ritual, however confined by the weather—the flaunting of their carefree status, neither kin nor kinless, a loud display of self. They wore little despite the chill drizzle; the day had the promise of summer's heat and the clouds near the horizon looked broken, a possible herald of late sun. Fluoro-patterns swirled on bare chests, around the nexus of nipples; chains of heavy, dull links draped over the right shoulders and wrapped twice around the waists. On their wide belts, sheathed vibros were prominent. The jussar jostled one another (the inn-master looking out in disgust but not having the heart to cast the youths out into the rain) and annoyed the passersby. They made their comments with a caution native to them: jussar were tolerated past the point of other guild-kin—and certainly beyond the constricted limits of lassari—but they were by no means inviolate. Despite the patience shown them, jussar died as often as kin in insult-born arguments.

The slow tidal swell of the Hag's chant came to them, mixed with the subsonic drone of the port's machinery and the assorted waking-sounds of Sterka. They laughed. The Dead were easy prey on a miserable day, a harmless butt for jest and gibe. As the procession came into view down the long expanse of the avenue, the jussar strolled out onto the wet pavement, splashing each other, cursing, laughing. They arranged themselves in a ragged double line, a gauntlet through which the Dead would have to pass. The Dead paid them no attention, continuing the march with eyes focused ahead or half-shut, their mouths moving in the endless mantra. The jussar harried them, shouting insults, pushing against them, the boys fondling obscenely the female Dead, the girls taunting the men with bare breasts and suggestive touches.

They received little reaction, but it was a pleasant enough diversion.

Until . . .

One of the jussar, mouth open in a giggling shout, stumbled up against a Dead One—a burly man who looked as if he might once have been a laborer or mercenary. The man's torn shirt revealed the squared firmness of taut musculature. He staggered back as the jussar shoved against him to regain his balance, but the Dead One retained his footing with a deft movement. The jussar, still giggling, pushed at the man again, easily, half-turning away as he did so, obviously expecting no resistance.

The Dead One did as none of the Dead had done before: he reached out with a meaty hand, clamped fingers on the jussar's shoulder, pulling him back. "Hey!" the jussar said, angrily, as he turned, but the Dead One's fist stopped his words. The boy held his nose in pain and surprise, blood trickling from one nostril and over the fingers. For a moment, the tableau held, the jussar sniffing in consternation, the Dead One with his hand still fisted at his side, his composure shattered and his mouth slack with surprise. The chant-bell the Dead One held in his other hand dropped to the pavement with a dull clunking.

The jussar, with a scream of rage, hauled the man from the Dead's procession. The rest of the Dead walked on, seemingly uninterested in their fellow's plight. The group of youths surrounded him, leering; he made no further resistance, head down, hands at sides. The jussar closed about him. Fists rose and fell, the whine of a vibro shrilled. They beat him bloody and senseless, leaving him in the puddles of the street.

The Dead, uncaring, went through the arch and away from Sterka. They would seek Hag Death elsewhere.

The Regent d'Embry laced her fingers together on her bare desktop. The fingers were alternately blue and red—bodytint shimmered at the interface of color.

"I'm glad all of you were able to be here on such short notice," she said. "This business could have been conducted over com-units, but I prefer the more personal contact."

The two Hoorka seated across from her looked everywhere but at the Regent. Kaethe Oldin, cloaked in a heavy and glaring-orange cape, had her back to the rest of them, intent on the d'Vellia soundsculpture in the corner of the room. D'Embry was slightly puzzled by the attitude of the Hoorka. All her reports had said that Gyll and Valdisa were quite close, lovers, yet the two were seemingly at odds: it showed in the way the Ulthane leaned away from Valdisa, in the covert glances the woman sent toward him. D'Embry shrugged mentally. She felt *good,* for once; she would allow none of this to bother her, not a tiff between the Hoorka, not the presence of Oldin, not the dreary rain that pattered on her window. She'd not realized just how much the annoyance of Oldin had permeated her moods.

"You're kicking me off Neweden." Kaethe spoke without turning from the sculpture. As the others glanced at her—d'Embry with a sudden, unbidden scowl—Kaethe touched the artwork with an appreciative forefinger. She took a step toward the desk. Under the metallic arch of her eyebrows, her face revealed no distress. "It doesn't matter greatly to me, Regent. I've been thrown out before. You're by no means the first to do so; the Families are quite used to it. How long do I have?"

D'Embry determined once more that she would not let Oldin antagonize her. She regarded the woman blandly—no one noticed the whitening of flesh under the bodytint as her hands clenched together more firmly. "Since you've anticipated me so well, I won't bother with niceties, Trader Oldin. I want *Peregrine* and you and all your paraphernalia out of orbit and heading away tomorrow."

Oldin glanced toward Gyll. D'Embry saw the contact and wondered at it. Valdisa too looked at Gyll. "By the terms of the pact"—Kaethe returned her attention to d'Embry—"I've a right to know why you're taking this action." She stepped forward again, so that the full cape touched the edge of d'Embry's desk. The cloth was distressingly bright; d'Embry found the color hideous and most unflattering to Oldin's skin.

"For our part, I wonder why you've asked the Hoorka here," Valdisa said.

"Your guild is peripherally involved in this, and I've other business to discuss after Trader Oldin has left. However, if you want to leave until we've concluded this . . ."

"No, Thane Valdisa, by all means stay. It'll be an education for you." Oldin smiled, but there was little friendliness in the gesture. Still, of the four, she alone appeared relaxed, neither uncomfortable nor impatient. Oldin glanced about, reached down to extrude a hump-chair from the floor, and seated herself heavily and too quickly. "I'll never accustom myself to this much gravity," she said. She arranged the cape loosely around her. "Set out your case, Regent."

"Very well." D'Embry turned cold gray eyes to Oldin. "First, there is the matter of two voided guarantees on items purchased by Neweden citizens."

"That's petty, Regent." Oldin dismissed the point with a wave of her hand. "That can easily be rectified."

"I don't doubt that, Trader. But there is also the Hoorka contract you signed against Cade Gies. In itself, I can do nothing about that, as much as I find it distasteful. But . . . in his work for the Alliance, Gies had access to the Center terminals. We've discovered that he had abused that privilege, having illegally obtained records from the archives. There was some attempt at deception, but the man was rather clumsy, and his access-code has been traced. We've searched his office and rooms thoroughly, but have been unable to find the printouts of that information he acquired. We also have found that Gies 'purchased' several expensive Trader items—they were in his rooms. He could not possibly have afforded them on his salary."

"I see your implications, Regent—you needn't go any further with this. I have heard no proof that I'm in any degree responsible for the alleged espionage."

Oldin leaned forward in her seat. Elbow on thigh, she cupped her chin in her hand. With the same faint mocking smile, she waited. "And what else, Regent?" she asked.

"There's another matter, which may or may not be directly related to the first: the death of Sirrah Guillene on Heritage."

D'Embry, anticipating, saw the glance between the two Hoorka. It confirmed her suspicions—the Hoorka were involved in Guillene's murder. She felt no anger. From what she had heard of Heritage and Moache's practices there, Guillene was not someone that would be greatly mourned. Still, it irritated her that Valdisa and Gyll would have circumvented her authority in that manner.

Oldin slouched back in the chair. "That's just rancor on your part, Regent. I know Niffleheim's been screaming about that one, and I think you've been listening to your own paranoia."

Damn the woman. So frigging smug... The thoughts surged, and d'Embry choked them down, trying to retain the good humor, the anticipation of success. "Ulthane Gyll was ferried up to *Peregrine* the day Guillene died. He was there for quite some time."

"That's not exactly an offense." Oldin glanced at Gyll, the smile widened. D'Embry watched Valdisa watching Gyll.

"Yet you have to admit that it arouses suspicions," she said. "I've no delusions about the Families' wiles—you could have easily slipped past our monitors."

"Proof, Regent?"

D'Embry shrugged. "I'll admit that I have very little at the moment. Still, I've forwarded a record of my order to Niffleheim. I asked you here so that you're legally informed and to see if you wish to have a court examination to determine the justification of the eviction order. By the pact. Do you want it, Trader? I assure you that if you say yes, I'll have my people begin digging, very hard. I think we both know what will be found."

"There's nothing to find, Regent. Believe me. I guarantee it." For a brief second, their eyes met, locked in interior battle. Then Oldin's lips lifted in her mocking smirk, and she leaned back "But *Peregrine* was leaving soon in any event. Our sales have slowed, and your port charges aren't cheap. I'd already told Ulthane Gyll of that intention. Having you bring together the courtmasters and arranging for my defense would take up more time than I'd planned to spend on Neweden. It's simply not worth the trouble, Regent. I'll obey your damned order." With a groan of exertion, she stood. The cape settled around her knees "Which means that I've much to arrange. Is that all, then Regent?"

"Almost, Trader Oldin. I've heard that you may have extended an invitation to Hoorka, some offer."

Oldin pursed her lips, nodding. "Good, good. Your sources are excellent, and I compliment you, Regent. I'll have to check the tongues of some of my crew. But . . . any agreement between the Hoorka and Family Oldin is only my business and theirs."

D'Embry looked from Oldin to the Hoorka. Valdisa stared into a blank corner of the office. Gyll examined his callused hands. "Oldin's right," he said. "It's not the concern of the Alliance."

"As long as the Hoorka are based on Neweden, *everything* the Hoorka do affects the Alliance." D'Embry's voice had the inflections of a teacher scolding a child. It snapped Gyll's head up. His mouth was a tight line, but he said nothing.

"You see, Ulthane—the Alliance always works on bluster and force." Oldin, near the door, grinned back at them. "They try so hard to make you fear them, so that you do what they say and don't upset their nice, safe, little boundaries."

"Trader Oldin, if you wish to see force, keep *Peregrine* in orbit after tomorrow." Softly.

Oldin shook her head. A brief coruscation, her eyebrows caught light. "It's not worth it, Regent. I'd love to be the one to teach you a lesson about overestimation of abilities, but it'll have to be postponed for now. Grandsire would be upset if I endangered the pact without his permission. You played out the scenario nicely, though, timed it just right. It will look like you succeeded in getting rid of me, when all you had to do was wait a few more weeks. I'm certain it'll look good on your record. Niffleheim can say to Moache, see, we got rid of the nasty troublemakers."

"For a woman with much to get ready, you talk a lot."

Again, that eternal smile. "I'll be going now. Ulthane, Thane; whatever she says to you, remember that what we've spoken about is still valid. Don't make a decision just because you're scared of jeopardizing your standing with the

Alliance. They're a lying breed. They'll soon join the ippicators and the Hag like all he rest."

Oldin slapped at the door control, swept through, and strode into the corridors of Center.

D'Embry watched the door sigh closed. She'd not moved from her position. The hands were still in an attitude of reverence on the desk, the spine was erect against the straight-backed floater. "That wasn't a scene I wished the two of you to see."

Valdisa shrugged. She brushed at the shoulder of her nightcloak. "How does it affect Hoorka? That's all I care about."

"Did you send someone to Heritage?"

"We'd declared bloodfeud against Guillene, m'Dame. All we wanted was his death, in any manner it could be accomplished. If someone else did the deed before us, it really doesn't matter. Guillene's Hag-kin now, and we don't speak of him."

"You haven't answered the question."

Silence.

After a moment, d'Embry exhaled heavily, closing her eyes. She unclenched her hands, her posture sagged. The movement aged her. She tapped at the desk with a finger the color of ice. "I don't know where this leaves us, Thane, Ulthane. Niffleheim was upset with the entire Heritage affair—the Hoorka work well enough for Neweden, but Heritage . . ."

"Which means what, Regent?" Valdisa asked the question

"It means that there has to be some reevaluation, an examination of Hoorka and the Alliance."

"But you're not restricting us to Neweden again?"

"I didn't say that, Thane."

"What *are* you saying?" Gyll broke in. He was tired, tired of the evasion, tired of the semantic games he'd seen played here this morning. He'd rather be out in the drizzle and clouds, or back in Underasgard—to have time to think.

D'Embry smiled faintly. "I'm sorry, Ulthane. You'll have to forgive an old woman her whims. I'll try to be more direct. I do feel that the Hoorka can still find a place in the Alliance. But I think we—you and Thane Valdisa and I—need to examine the offworld contracts more carefully, with

an eye toward the compatibility of social structures. For the
time being, I'm going to hold all contracts in abeyance, until
I've had the opportunity to study this more."

"But we'll eventually have offworld work?" Valdisa.

"I would think so."

Valdisa looked at Gyll. He was unable to decipher her
expression. It seemed to waver between triumph and uncertainty.

"In that case, you may consider the Hoorka to have
dropped any thought of working with the Trading Families."

D'Embry nodded. "That's good, Thane. I wouldn't have
liked the other options open to me."

Gyll could only seethe, silent, in frustration.

The thin, cold drizzle glazed the expanse of Sterka Fort. The
rain-slicked surface darkly mirrored the ships on their pads,
the spires and conveyors that fed and relieved them. Farther back were the huddled buildings of the city, looking
miserable under the mist and low clouds.

Gyll turned from the window and handed his identification to the impassive gate-ward. "I'm boarding the *Peregrine* shuttle," he said.

The ward nodded, glancing at Gyll, the full pack over the
Hoorka's shoulder, the bumblewort in its traveling cage. He
rustled the flimsies in pretended scrutiny. "You know *Peregrine's* asked for clearance to leave orbit." The sentence
fell halfway between declaration and query.

"I know," Gyll replied. He gave his attention to the view
outside the window again.

It had not been a pleasant day. He and Valdisa had begun arguing from the moment they'd left d'Embry's offices.
It was a quiet disagreement, marked by an exaggerated politeness that bothered him more than any violent confrontation. The apprentice driving their flitter had kept his eyes
discreetly averted, but Gyll knew that the ears had been
busy. The gossip would spread through Underasgard as
soon as his shift was done. Valdisa had left him at Tri-Guild
Square, saying that she had errands to run. Gyll knew the
excuse was to avoid continuing the discussion in her rooms
where the civilized pretense could be dropped. And he
knew that her position was now set in stone, hardened by
her fear of losing authority as Thane. She would not bend.

He'd begun packing as soon as he'd returned to his rooms. He took very little beyond a few essentials, amazed at what he felt he could do without for the few months he would be with Oldin. He could have given the wort to Cranmer for the duration, but he indulged a whim and shrank the field-cage down to traveling size. A few months . . . and then he would know whether the Families were worth further expenditure of energy. He told himself that Valdisa's anger would be softened by time.

And he told himself that he wasn't simply avoiding Valdisa by doing it in this manner. He left a short note for her in her com-unit; it would have to be enough.

The ward snapped shut the paper-case with a grunt. "You'll need to be quick, then. You'll only have a few hours before she leaves."

He nodded—the ward did not have to know that he didn't intend to return before *Peregrine* left. Gyll started toward the field entrance.

"Gyll!"

The shout turned him. Down the corridor stood Valdisa, breathing rapidly as if after a long run. Port workers and passengers moved aside, away from the Hoorka woman with anger on her face, her nightcloak back to reveal the dagger at her belt. Gyll watched her approach, waiting, willing himself to stay calm. The wort moved in the cage, curling itself in a corner. Valdisa stopped a few meters away, hands on hips, frowning. The gate-ward began to come forward and demand her papers, but Valdisa quelled him with a look.

"Ulthane," she said. Her voice was dangerously quiet. "I hope you're not taking the shuttle. I hope it was just an airing for the wort." Over her dark eyes, lines deepened.

He shrugged helplessly. "I'm sorry, Valdisa."

"*Thane* Valdisa, Ulthane. You left Underasgard without my permission. You break your own code—obedience to the Thane is paramount."

"I told you what I intended." Then, after a pause: "Thane. We've gone over it too many times. I'm doing this for the good of your own authority and for Hoorka. That's not exactly deserving of censure."

"You're doing it for yourself first. I know you that well, Gyll." For a moment, the harshness softened, the lines of her face smoothing. Gyll thought she might smile, that they might hug and depart still friends. But her stance had not altered, and if her fingers clenched uneasily, they still strayed near the hilt of her dagger. Her eyebrows lowered, the corners of her mouth twisted down. "I didn't want it to come to a confrontation, Gyll, but you seem to want to force it. Fine. As Thane, as kin-lord of your guild, I'm telling you to return to Underasgard. We'll talk there, try to settle our differences—maybe we need to split the guild, start another guildhome on Illi or the Waste, with you Thane of one. I don't know, but we can find some way to assuage your boredom, your ennui. But first you have to come back."

Almost, he stepped toward her. He swayed. Then his resolution hardened. "I can't."

"You mean you won't."

Again, he shrugged. There seemed to be nothing else to do. He stared at Valdisa, willing her to back down, but she would not—she returned his gaze flatly. Gyll shifted the pack on his shoulder, hefted the wort's cage in his right hand, wiped at the sweat on his forehead. The gate-ward examined papers to one side. Passersby stared curiously at the two, sidling past and giving the Hoorka as much space as possible in the corridor.

"Valdisa, you know how I feel about you. I really don't want to hurt you. That's partly why I want to go with the Families."

Her face spoke disbelief.

"I don't want to hurt myself, either," he continued. "It's better this way. When I come back, much of the pain'll be gone. We'll both be surer of ourselves, more confident of our positions." He waited for her to answer, half-wanting her to say something to convince him to stay, half-impatient to leave. His fingers drummed the strap of the pack. When she said nothing, he finally turned away. Through the windows of the port, he could see the Trader shuttle. Under the spidery bulk, a figure lounged near the lift: Helgin.

"You can't go as Hoorka, Gyll."

He stopped.

"I mean that, Gyll." Her voice wavered on the edge of breaking. Her defiance was brittle; he knew he could break it with a word. Her gaze fluttered, away and back. "If you go, you do so unguilded. Lassari, not Hoorka-kin. And you won't be welcome to return."

"You can't mean that."

"I do, Gyll. I mean it more than anything else I've ever said to you."

He could see a trembling in her lower lip, but he knew her better than to think it vulnerability. Emotion, yes; she might give in to tears when this was over and she was alone, but he could sense no weakness in her resolve now. He wanted to touch her, to pull her to him, but he knew he could not—she wouldn't allow it. *It would make you look silly, old fool. It's over between you.*

"You'll change your mind," he said. "When I come back."

"No." Chin lifting, she defied him. "Stay or go; it's your decision, Gyll. I'm long past thinking I can change your mind or force you into acceptance with logic or bribes or love. You insist on doing everything alone. Fine. But you're not going as Hoorka, and if you step on that ship, you may as well stay with the Families forever. You've Hoorka property on you. I've come to reclaim it."

"What!" Surprise lashed him into irritation. He nearly bellowed the word. People nearby halted in mid-stride. "I *made* the guild, woman. I got us everything we share."

"And now you've cast yourself from the kin. Your night-cloak, the guild holoclasp, that vibro: they all belong to Hoorka. I'll let you have the wort's cage, but I want the rest, Gyll." Her fingers caressed the dagger's hilt. "I'm as stubborn as you. Or is the Ulthane a thief as well as lassari?"

Her eyes were suddenly arid, the verging tears gone. Even the gate-ward, an offworlder, could sense the head of the conflict. He put his back to a wall, eyes wide. Muttering, those watching skittered away. Gyll was startled by Valdisa's quick vehemence, the casual use of the impersonal mode to insult him. He grimaced, lips drawn back. He set the wort's cage on the floor, let the pack fall unheeded. He set his legs apart, a fighting stance. For a long moment, they regarded each other, balanced between fury and defiance.

That's Valdisa, not some contracted victim, not an enemy. Gyll's restless hand touched the smooth leather of his vibro sheath. *You've not liked taking blood—do you want hers so badly?*

"I mean it, Gyll."

The rage left him. He couldn't do this, couldn't let the conflict become physical. *You forced it, old man. Be satisfied with it.* Slowly, Gyll forced himself to calmness. He unclasped the nightcloak from his shoulders, swinging the heavy cloth around and letting it drop around his feet. Then, hurrying as if he wanted the task done, he unbuckled the sheath-belt with the Hoorka insignia and let vibro and belt drop on top of the cloak. He stared down at the pile.

He felt very naked.

"Is this the way you want it?" he asked.

She shook her head, slowly, sadly. She let her nightcloak fall around her shoulder, reached back to pull the hood up so that her face was shadowed. All he could see was the glinting of her pupils. "No, Gyll. It's the way *you* wanted it."

"That's very facile." He could not stop the words from sounding bitter.

A shrug.

"Your feelings will change, Valdisa. You'll miss me, miss the advice and help I can give you. You'll need it, when the Li-Gallant tries to control the guild's way, when d'Embry procrastinates on her promises." He bent down to retrieve the pack; it slid over his shoulder easily without the encumbrance of the nightcloak. He picked up the wort's cage. Outside the window, above its rain-image, the shuttle still waited.

To the side, the ward began rustling paper once more.

"I won't say that you're wrong, Gyll. But there's a lot of scars that have to heal. I don't think I'll change my decision." Valdisa stepped forward, bent to take the cloak and vibro. Holding them in her arm, she looked at Gyll. He could not guess at what she might be feeling under the mask of gray and black cloth. They were close enough to touch, but then she pivoted and began walking away. Gyll watched her leave, thinking with every step that she would stop for another word, another chance at reconciliation.

She reached an intersecting hallway and turned left.

Gyll was suddenly aware of the gaggle of people, offworlders and Newedeners, staring at him. He forced himself into aloofness. *Feel the emotions, yes, but keep them hidden.*

You have to feel, but don't let the others see it unless they are your kin. The old code. The Hoorka lore he'd created.

Except that now he had no kin.

Gyll moved away from the onlookers and Neweden. He walked out into the damp embrace of the sky.

Helgin, seeing his approach, waved.

A QUIET OF STONE

TO THE FAMILY:

—Walter and Betty Leigh, for more than can possibly be expressed here. They are ultimately responsible.

—Eva Kohnle. Gigi, for gentle and uncritical encouragement.

—Sharon and Pam, because they insisted.

With much love to all.

Chapter 1

MCWILMS NEVER LET HIS HAND stray far from the sheathed dagger's hilt. He knew the gesture for the nervous habit it was, but he'd long ago convinced himself that the feeling of proximity gave him confidence.

"How many are there, and what have they got?" he asked the apprentice brusquely, staring at the building before him. In the wan light of Gulltopp, it looked formidable enough. He was willing to bet that they'd need a disruptor to batter down that doorshield.

McWilms hated this contract, this night.

The apprentice was nervous. It showed in his skittering eyes, the restless shifting of weight. "We're not sure . . ."

"Then stand still, boy, and think. Your frigging uncertainty could cost us kin, and I'm not going to lose someone because you didn't do your job. I'll toss you back in there first." Moon-shadow hid his gaze, but the apprentice could feel the anger in McWilms's voice. "Now tell me what you saw, and do it quickly. It's getting late."

The boy nodded. "We trailed Vasella here, and there were at least two others already inside—we saw them, a man and a woman, when they opened the door to let Vasella in." The apprentice grimaced and swallowed hard. "That's when they used the sting on us. I ducked and rolled, like in the lessons, but when I looked up again, Elzbet was still lying there in the street. There was a lot of blood. A lot."

The boy stopped again, sniffing. McWilms made no move to hurry him, but waited as the apprentice wiped at his nose with the sleeve of his nightcloak. "I didn't know whether to try to get to Elzbet or stay behind cover. It was like I was frozen there . . ."

There was more than a hint of hysteria in the boy's voice. It softened McWilms's anger. "She'll live, Steban," he said. "The Hag won't have her yet." She'd been badly hurt, though; seeing Elzbet had made McWilms recall the months he'd spent recovering from a cowardly assault after an offworld contract. Eight standards ago, now, yet he could still feel the weakness in his right arm, the budded one, and the skin of his chest was hairless and glossy with scars he hadn't bothered to have removed. Elzbet would be a long time regaining her health, and the pain would never entirely leave. He knew that too well. "Don't worry about her," he said to Steban. "Worry about your kin that are here now. What else did you do?"

Steban inhaled deeply, let the breath out in a trembling sigh. "I used my relay to call Thane Valdisa and get the full kin here early. Then I went out and pulled Elzbet back here. I tried to stop the bleeding; there were people around—lassari—but none of them would help," he said, bitterness tingeing his voice. "I may have missed someone coming in or out of the building then. I don't think so, but I can't be sure."

"But there are at least three of them, and they're armed with projectile weapons?"

Steban nodded. "I'm sorry I don't know more . . ."

"It will do. I doubt that anyone could have done much better." McWilms's gaze had gone back to the blank darkness of the house. The uproar in the street had caused the curious of the neighborhood to assemble. Around the Hoorka assassins, intent faces peered from windows, and a crowd jostled elbows on a streetcorner a judicious distance away. Not too near, for the Hoorka were known to be less than gentle with those daring to interfere with their contracts, but close enough to see the blood if there was to be any. Their faces were strained with an almost happy anticipation. McWilms cursed the morbidity of the onlookers. "I want you to do one last thing, Steban. Go and bring d'Mannberg here—he's to the back of the building. Then you can head for the flitter; Felling's put a good meal in there for you."

"I don't know that I'm hungry."

McWilms pulled Steban to him, hugging the boy firmly. "I can understand, believe me. Get d'Mannberg here, then tell the flitter pilot to take you directly to med-center. Go see Elzbet."

Steban smiled. "Thank you, sirrah." Then he was gone, his nightcloak (with the red slash of the apprentice) blending into the night's shadows.

McWilms paced restlessly as he waited for d'Mannberg. His fingers tapped an erratic rhythm on the dagger's hilt. He hated nights when the victim barricaded himself in with companions and weapons. It was dishonorable, an insult to the demands of Dame Fate, and wasteful of life. And it was becoming far too common. A *shame to their honor, but the lassari and low kin don't care. And these cows will be here watching, counting the bodies as they come out. Smiling and talking.* The fact that the contract was another of the Li-Gallant Vingi's didn't help his mood. Politics again: Mc-Wilms knew that without reading the sealed contract in his pouch. The crowd knew whose house the Hoorka had surrounded, and he could hear the whispers from the spectators. *The Hoorka are doing the Li-Gallant's dirty work again. He points, and they kill, and only those with power benefit.* Vasella was reputed to be one of the leaders of the insurrectionist group known as the Hag's Legion, a group of low kin and lassari—those unguilded and without kin. If rumor were true, the Legion was responsible for the sabotage of the transport *Five Winds.* The ship had gone down over the Dagorta Mountains. Its cargo of ippicator bones had been ruined or lost, and the crew had all died in the crash. The kin demanded revenge, the kin-lord calling for bloodfeud, but there had been no answer to her challenge.

Cowards, all of them, with no honor.

McWilms shook his head. Bloodfeud was the accepted custom of settling affairs of honor between guilds, but the Hag's Legion ignored custom, turning their backs on the gods of Neweden. McWilms didn't care for the Hoorka to appear as vassals of the Li-Gallant, but if a man deserved to be sent to Hag Death, Vasella was that man. He hoped Dame Fate and She of the Five would not allow Vasella's escape at dawn, when the contract ended.

The situation made his stomach sour.

The whispering throng parted abruptly, and d'Mannberg strode through the cleft. The Hoorka was a huge man, both tall and massive, and the crowd gave him wide berth, as if

his touch might contaminate them. A scowl lurked in
d'Mannberg's reddish beard. He came up to McWilms and
spat toward the house. "Shields," he said. "I *hate* wearing a
shield, especially the worn-out things we have. They're too
frigging stiff and constricting. And too damn hot, as well."
His voice boomed in the night, heedless of anyone over-
hearing. "Well, Jeriad m'boy, there's not a way around it, is
there? Damn; we always seem to get the nasty ones." He
shrugged. "If that's what the Dame wants, I'm just as glad
the rotation paired me with you."

"I'm glad that makes you happy."

"Don't go patting yourself on the back, now. There's still
things I can teach you on the practice floor, youngster."
D'Mannberg grinned at his companion. "One lesson I can
think of is humility, Jeriad."

McWilms smiled briefly. D'Mannberg was his kin-father,
the one who had sponsored his transition from apprentice
to full kin, and McWilms enjoyed the man's gruff good humor. It did a little to alleviate his feelings of foreboding, that
bad luck seemed to haunt this contract. "Thane Valdisa's
sent over another of the kin—Serita, she said. The com-unit
at Underasgard said that'll even up the odds."

"The bastards inside should be so honorable."
D'Mannberg's voice held disgust. "I swear, sometimes following the code can be galling, when it seems only to benefit the victims."

"The victim must always have his chance to escape."

"I can quote the code better than you. I've lived with it
longer." D'Mannberg flashed a grin. An oddly dainty hand
prowled his beard; delicate fingers twisted hair. "I want
nothing more than to take a long, hot shower, Jeriad. And
Vasella's holed up in there so tight we probably won't get
near him until dawn, if at all. They're going to wait until
light, then laugh at us. Damn them." He spat again.

"I don't think they're going to be that lucky, Ric. She of
the Five isn't going to be kindly disposed to them after what
happened to Elzbet and Steban. That was on the far borders
of honor, though I'm sure they'll claim that they didn't see
the apprentice-slash, and that they shouted a warning first."

D'Mannberg grunted. "Shit. That's what that is." He let
out a deep breath. "Well, are you ready?"

"As soon as we see Serita's flare."

The signal came a few minutes later. A hissing, spluttering gout of blue-white arced into the sky; Gulltopp, startled, had hidden its face behind the roof of a nearby building. Long, dark shadows moved in the street as the flare rose, fluttered at zenith, and fell. The watchers in the street murmured. "Now," d'Mannberg said.

They moved toward the house, swiftly and quietly, like shards of night themselves in the gray-and-black Hoorka nightcloaks. McWilms expected at any moment that the sting would bark again from one of the shuttered windows, but the house remained silent. The two assassins pressed themselves against the wall on either side of the doorshield. With little hope, d'Mannberg touched the contact for the shield. A bell chimed inside, distantly, but the shield remained up. D'Mannberg shook his head, McWilms grinned. D'Mannberg's hands moved in the silent code. *Disruptor?*

Yah. Quickly.

D'Mannberg reached behind him for the device, an ugly, plain box strapped under his nightcloak. He pressed a switch, and a rank of lights shivered from scarlet to emerald. They pulsed. D'Mannberg pointed the smaller end of the disruptor toward the shield. Sparks—violent, sputtering—danced from the doorway to the pavement as erratic light played over the Hoorkas' features. The empty darkness between the doorframe began to glow an alarming orange-white. It throbbed like an uncertain heart, then—suddenly—was gone. The disruptor wailed, its serried lights gone amber. D'Mannberg touched the end of the device, winced silently as it burned his forefinger. He set it down. The air smelled of ozone.

McWilms went to his knees and leaned forward to peer into the interior of the house. He could see nothing of import: some furniture too small to hide behind, a carpet that looked half-dead, all lit by a hoverlamp near the ceiling. Everything looked well-used and rather shabby. He nodded to his companion. *In. Fast.*

D'Mannberg unsheathed his vibro, McWilms his dagger. They entered.

A corridor led off the room through an open archway. There was no other exit. McWilms glanced about, looking for the formal warning required by Neweden law that a weapon other than one requiring proximity was being used.

There was none. McWilms knew that d'Mannberg had noticed that lack as well—a scowl creased the larger man's face.

The corridor (narrow, paint falling from the walls in long strips) was empty. A few doors led off its length, another was set at the end. McWilms didn't like it: the place had the smell of a trap. Too many possibilities for ambush, and these people were too dishonorable to ignore any possibilities.

D'Mannberg signed to him: *bodyshield.* McWilms touched his belt and felt the sudden rigidity as the shield snapped into place around him. The shield would repel slugs from a sting or similar weapons, though it still left them vulnerable to slower attacks, such as a vibrofoil or dagger. The borders of the field slowly exchanged outside air for that trapped behind it, but the shields, overused and much in need of expensive repairs that the Hoorka guild could not afford, were both hot and uncomfortable. Once supple, they now constricted movement. McWilms could sympathize with d'Mannberg's often-voiced distaste for them; still, they were needed protection if Vasella decided to use the sting again. Neither Hoorka was foolish.

The assassins moved slowly down the corridor, one to each side, hugging the walls. McWilms nudged the first door with a foot. It swung open, revealing a stairway leading down into darkness. He listened, heard nothing, and shrugged to d'Mannberg. Too many choices: *separate?*

Neh. D'Mannberg pointed with his chin. *Keep going.*

McWilms clenched the hilt of his dagger. D'Mannberg had yet to activate his vibro—the whine of the weapon would have screamed of their presence. They continued down the hall, McWilms now slightly ahead of the other Hoorka. He couldn't shake the feeling of wrongness that had afflicted him from the moment he'd seen Elzbet. Dame Fate was looking away, She of the Five was somewhere distant, attending to Her own affairs with the ippicators. Hag Death cackled softly nearby. His muscles ached, fighting the gelatinous resistance of the bodyshield. His breath was too quick, and the air about him was tainted with his exhalations.

It happened quickly.

A woman burst from the door at the end of the hall. McWilms saw little of her but the sting she held. She shouted, her face a rictus, but he could make out no words. She fired twice, rapidly. McWilms felt his shield go rigid, locking up his body as the pellets ricocheted about the corridor, gouging the walls, tearing loose chunks of masonry. He strained toward the woman (the sting down now, unprotected, yet her flat, plain face was curiously triumphant) but the shield held him, slow to release. In the second before he could move again, he heard footsteps and the characteristic high keening of vibros.

Behind. Behind.

McWilms could even admire the plan while abhorring the dishonor in it: force the Hoorka to use shields, fire the sting, and then attack in the instant before the shields became flexible again—a small advantage, made larger by the condition of the equipment the Hoorka used. The skin of his back crawled in anticipation of the blade, then the shield relaxed and he let himself fall with it. A vibro whined over his head (moving in the slow-time thrust of shield-fighting— his assailant knew the technique) as McWilms rolled and kicked blindly up. He was lucky: the man—it was Vasella, he saw—howled in pain, clutching his groin. McWilms slashed with his dagger, and the howl became a wail. Vasella looked surprised and almost sad as McWilms thrust again, the edge of his weapon going deep. Vasella went to his knees, a dark stain spreading out on his clothing. He gasped, fish-mouthed, a hand grasping for the vibro he'd let fall. McWilms, on his feet again, kicked the weapon aside.

A clatter behind him: McWilms, cursing the slowness forced on him by the shield, turned to face the new attack, grateful only that the shield forced his opponent to move a touch slower with his thrust. A vibrofoil slapped ribbons of paint from the wall as McWilms ducked aside. The foil, backhanded, gashed his leg. McWilms could feel the warmth of blood, and he had time to wonder whether the leg would support him as he moved to defend himself. It was all instinct—Ric's training, Ulthane Gyll's training. Everything had happened too quickly for a measured plan; he could only react. There was a blur of a face, an intricate pattern of blue and white on a shirt, a grimy wall and something dark and mounded lying on the floor a few meters away. McWilms parried the foil with his dagger—wishing now that he'd chosen a vibro himself. The man (he had a twisted nose,

a frown on thin lips) beat the dagger aside easily and thrust
for McWilms's chest. The man was too eager this time. The
shield deflected the foil slightly, the blade scoring his side.
McWilms grimaced, twisting aside. He touched his belt control, felt the shield go.

(Somewhere, a shout in a voice he knew, the cough of the
sting, and a shrill cry of pain.)

McWilms forced himself to move as if the shield still
constricted him, waiting for the man's next thrust. When it
came, the Hoorka suddenly leapt aside and around the lethargic attack, moving at his opponent. Echoes of Ulthane
Gyll's old teachings: *In a real fight, don't go for half-
measures or worry about etiquette or technique. Do what
you need to do and worry about style later. And kill, don't
wound.* McWilms felt the cut in his side tear further, felt the
throbbing of his leg as he bowled into the man. Grunting,
he slammed the dagger into the man's chest. He wrenched
it back out, sheathed it again under the ribcage, thrusting
up. The vibrofoil slid from nerveless fingers, the body went
slack under him. McWilms let him crumple to the floor.

"Jeriad?"

At the sound of his name, McWilms glanced back at the
doorway. Serita Iduna stood there, the sting now in her
hands, the other woman—moaning—sitting against the
wall, holding an arm that dangled at a wrong angle. "Ric,"
she said. With the sting, she gestured behind McWilms. He
did not like the look of her face.

He turned. D'Mannberg was on the floor, the nightcloak
tangled around his large frame. There was a stillness about
him that made McWilms's throat constrict, his breath catch.
He hurried over to him, glancing at Vasella. The victim was
still alive. Dark eyes stared back at McWilms. "I'll deal with
you in a moment, bastard," the Hoorka said, and went to his
kin-father.

He grasped d'Mannberg's shoulder, turning him. The vibrofoil had come from behind, cleanly. There was very little
blood. "Ric?" he said, knowing there would be no answer.
D'Mannberg's light eyes stared at nothing. With a guttural
curse, McWilms brought the eyelids down. He made the
star of She of the Five over him.

"How is he, Jeriad? I've the relay for the flitter. It can be here in two minutes. Less." Serita's voice was full of her concern.

He glanced at her, still kneeling. His face was stony, his voice did not sound like his own. "Call the flitter, but tell them they don't need to rush." Then: "Oh, *damn!*" His voice caught on the word, almost breaking.

Serita's shoulders sagged with sudden grief, the sting wavering in her hands. McWilms shook his head at her. "Later, kin-sister. We'll mourn him later." There was a wavering in his sight. He felt weak, fatigued. He nearly stumbled when he rose to go to Vasella. He cleared his throat, blinked quickly.

"You don't deserve the quickness I'm code-bound to give you, Vasella. You're lassari shit that doesn't deserve the rights of guild-kin, and I hope the Hag gnaws at your soul for the rest of eternity."

"Do you talk all your victims to death, Hoorka?" The man's eyes were clouded with pain, his fingers knotted into fists against the hurt. Blood had pooled beneath him, seeping into the wooden floor. "Tell your master Vingi that I'll be waiting for him."

"The Li-Gallant isn't Hoorka's master." McWilms didn't bother to deny that it was Vingi's contract they worked—it would have fooled no one, and he was too tired. He wanted to sit down, wanted to weep. "We'll be the weapons in anyone's hands."

Vasella laughed. It was a hoarse, phlegm-loud rasp of sound. "Tell that to the lassari and low kin the Li-Gallant beats down." The man paused, coughed once more, bringing up bile. "Tell it to the ones he kills with your blades."

A sudden heat of anger filled McWilms, turning his sorrow to ash. Ric's death, Elzbet's wounds, the cowardly attack, and Vasella's taunts: all goaded him. *"Bastard!"* He kicked the prone man, nearly falling as he did so. The soft thud of his boot was surprisingly loud. Vasella howled, the lassari woman sobbed in sympathy.

"Jeriad!" Serita shouted. "Stop it, man! Kill him and end this Hag-damned contract, but don't torture him. You're Hoorka, kin-brother. Remember our code."

"Damn the code," he replied. "The code and our frigging broken equipment killed Ric, didn't it?" He swung around

to face her. The hall seemed to sway slowly around him. "Look what it's gotten us. Insults from scum like Vasella."

"You just feed the misconceptions of those like him, Jeriad." Her voice was soft, pleading. "I know how you feel, Jeriad. Ric was *my* friend, too, and a lover as well. And he wouldn't want this from you. You foul his memory."

McWilms wanted to shout back at her, but the weariness had returned, worse this time. His leg seemed to be on fire, his side gigged him whenever he breathed. The hallway wouldn't stay still. His hand threatened to lose its grip on his dagger, and he clenched harder, closing his eyes for a moment. He took a breath; pain lanced him. Serita was staring at him, concerned. He shook his head, glancing down at Vasella again.

"Sirrah Vasella, your life is claimed by Hag Death. I can make your way easy, if you prefer. The blade or a capsule: the choice is yours." McWilms forced himself into the role of the aloof Hoorka once more, a distillation of cold neutrality caring only for the contract and guild-kin. His voice was stiff with ritual. Vasella, huddled in a fetal position below him, simply grimaced.

"Do it however you want, Hoorka. Whichever way gives you the most pleasure." Vasella coughed again. His eyes closed. "Just end it." He spat, bright red.

McWilms nodded. He knelt before the man, but his leg betrayed him. He staggered, bracing himself with his right hand. Serita came over to him, but he shrugged her hands away from him. Scowling, he steadied himself. His dagger flicked out, came back running blood. Vasella gasped, then was still. McWilms let his weapon drop. He sagged.

"Jeriad, you're hurt." Serita's strong hands gave him support.

"I'll be fine. Get the flitter here, let the woman go, and take Vasella's body to the Li-Gallant. Just let me rest a moment first."

He blinked. The hallway danced about him. It seemed to be getting darker, but he could keep his eyes open no longer to see why.

"They all look good from here, Gyll. That's the trouble. You can't see the filth until you get close and stick your nose in it."

Gyll turned from the port where Neweden's reflected glare snuffed out stars. One of the world's two moons, Gulltopp, leered around the curve of the world like a small child over the shoulder of its mother. Sleipnir, Gulltopp's companion, rode between Neweden and *Goshawk*, Gyll's ship. Its curve filled the bottom of his view. Gyll found the scene entrancing enough, but he smiled back at Helgin. "And you smell the stench already, neh?"

The Motsognir Dwarf was perched on the leather seat of Gyll's floater, petting Gyll's bumblewort. The animal purred satisfaction as Helgin leaned back and put bare feet on the desk in front of him. The ship's gravity was set to Oldin-Home norm—the movement stirred flimsies set there. The paper moved sluggishly, as if under water, rising and settling slowly. One of Helgin's hands stroked the bumblewort's furred shell, the other played in his thick, long beard. "If you could open the port, stick your head outside, and take a good whiff, you'd lose that delightful dinner we just had. And I'd have to assign someone to clean the side."

"If I could do all that, they'd have to rewrite all the physics texts in existence, Helgin. That scenario's utterly impossible."

"What's impossible is the thought that I've been crazy enough to be talked into coming back to Neweden. I didn't like it here the first time, and I doubt that eight standards have improved the place at all."

Gyll laughed, Helgin frowned. The dwarf's thick fingers pressed too hard on the wort's shell. It mewled a protest. Gyll turned back to his contemplation. "It's my homeworld, Helgin. FitzEvard Oldin is interested enough in it, and so am I." Gyll stared at the planet, giving names to the places he could glimpse below the ragged cloud cover. Neweden's main continent faced them, and he searched for the once-familiar landmarks, following the path of the largest river through haze to where he knew the city of Sterka lay, then south to the mountains. There: that was where the caverns of Underasgard hollowed the earth. Hoorka-lair.

"Lots of memories?"

"Yah, a few." Gyll spoke to the port.

"Sentimentality is a disease, Gyll," Helgin grumbled behind him. The Motsognir shifted to move the wort from his lap and scratched at his beard. "It eats into you and turns your mind to cold oatmeal. It can make you think that a shrieking harridan is the woman of your dreams just because she once let you into her pants. I never let sentiment interfere with my feelings."

"You keep telling me you don't *have* feelings," Gyll replied mildly. He gazed at the slow ballet of planet and moons.

Helgin's feet thumped the deck. "I lied." It seemed he was going to expound at length, drawing himself up to his full height of a little over a meter and striding toward Gyll, but the holotank chimed. Both men turned. "Yah?" Gyll said.

The holotank sparked into life—the figure of Gyll's aide, Fischer, bowed to them through greenish sparks that gradually faded. The aide was dressed in the plain, loose clothing of the Oldin-Hoorka. "Sula," he said, addressing Gyll by his title, "there's a transmission from Diplo Center. The Regent d'Embry would like to speak with you."

"In a moment, Fischer. I'll call you. Give her the stall while I settle myself first. Off."

The holotank darkened once more. Gyll glanced down at Helgin; the Motsognir was grinning under his beard. His rough voice sounded gleeful. "You see, the unpleasant memories make their first appearance. There you were, getting all misty-eyed about Good Old Neweden, and—poof! Welcome, the bitch woman of the Alliance. Might've thought she'd be dead by now."

"Helgin . . ." Warningly.

The grin would not go away. "Just don't go telling me that I didn't warn you, Gyll. I'm going to take great pleasure in giving you the 'I told you so' routine. Now, I'll simply stroll down to the pharmacy and get a Nopain tab ready for you. You'll need it for the headache." Helgin reached down and picked up the wort again. Then, with the rolling gait of the dwarves, he went to the door. He punched the contact on the floor with his big toe, stepped through. "Give her a kiss for me," he said as the door shut behind him. Gyll could hear Helgin's roar of self-amusement as the Motsognir walked away. He was singing in an off-key bass.

Gyll sat at his desk. His smile faded as he shuffled flimsies into a neat stack, swept stray acousidots into the drawer, and set the com-unit terminal to one side. He sighed deeply, closing his eyes, willing himself to relax. He straightened the sleeves of the simple cotton tunic he wore, the Family Oldin crest sewn at the breast dragging at his skin. *You're more nervous than you should let yourself be, old man. She's just another one of the bureaucrats that keep nagging at the Oldins, another obstacle. Look at the challenge and be calm. Calm.* Finally Gyll checked the view of the transmitter, made sure that the impression was one he wished d'Embry to see. He nodded to his camera-self in the monitor: a gray-haired, rather thin and chiseled head inclined in answer.

Not bad. Ascetic, but not too stern. "Fischer," he said aloud.

"Yes, Sula?"

"I'm ready now."

The holotank seethed with aquamarine interference, then cleared. For a moment Gyll and d'Embry stared at one another, looking for the changes wrought by nearly a decade. D'Embry was still thin, still tinted at earlobes and eyelids and mouth with the bodytints (a vivid scarlet, this time) that had gone out of fashion well before Gyll ever left Neweden. She'd acquired, somehow, a dowager's hump: it took a moment before Gyll realized that the bulge behind her shoulders was a symbiote. She was in ill health, then. The symbiote would have taken over most of the automatic functions of the body, its well-being dependent on hers; the symbiotes were stupid creatures, but possessed of a high instinct for self-preservation. Gyll wondered what it would be like—the bloodroot lancing her spine and connecting her to the parasite, always feeling just below the surface of her thoughts the presence of the creature. He'd seen symbiotes before, knew what they could do medically, but the sluglike appearance had always made him shiver with distaste. If he had to choose between the parasite and death, he wasn't sure the symbiote would be his choice. He didn't envy d'Embry her decision, and he wondered idly how Neweden had reacted to the blatant evasion of Hag Death. *No, that's the old religions. Let them go, those gods infecting this world. And don't judge so quickly, fool. You've made choices you'd never thought you would make, when they became necessary.*

D'Embry had finished her own inspection of Gyll. She nodded as if what she saw confirmed her expectations. Her voice was as reedy as he'd remembered, but softer. "Ulthane Gyll," she said.

He knew, he *knew* that she used his shorn title deliberately to goad him. He tried to control his expression, but the words jabbed inside. He'd walled up the pain of the day he'd left this world and Valdisa and the Hoorka, all his past, but the old title gouged a hole in that wall. It hurt.

Helgin was right. He was beginning to remember why he disliked the woman. "You told me so," he muttered.

"Hmmm?"

"Nothing. Regent. And I'm *not* Ulthane Gyll," he said carefully. *Tread lightly, and don't show anger—she may only want an excuse to rescind the trade agreement.* "'Trader,' perhaps. Or 'Sula.' That's my title among the Families." *The bitch knows it damned well, too. That was the way I signed the request for* Goshawk *to enter Neweden orbit.*

D'Embry smiled. It was a slow, surface movement of the lips and nothing else. Her voice was slow as well, careful. She seemed tired. "My apologies, Sula. My seneschal—not merely an aide, mind you; he's to be my eventual replacement as regent..." She hesitated an instant, the faintest hint of a scowl crossing her mouth. Gyll wondered what in that last statement irritated her so, and how he might use it. Then she took a breath and continued. "...told me that you'd prefer 'Sula,' but we ancients sometimes slip into old habits."

The self-mockery was unlike her. Gyll began to see that there had been changes in her beyond the mere physical. "The apology is unnecessary, Regent."

"I give it to you anyway. You've changed, Sula, but not as much as I might have thought. Grayer, thinner, but you look healthy and fit. Better than when you were Hoorka-thane."

Again, the chipping at the wall. "Thank you, Regent. The life with Family Oldin is better for me than Neweden was. You've changed also, m'Dame."

When he said nothing more, her smile became genuine for the first time. The heavy-lidded eyes brightened, and she nodded. "And you aren't about to say whether it's for the better or worse. Good, a point to you. You've gotten other things than health from the Oldins, it would seem. And you needn't be so superficially polite. I know all too well how I look. I know what the symbiote does for my figure." She half-turned in her seat, so that he could see the ridge trailing halfway down her back. "It's not been a good time for me, but I'd advise you not to mistake physical frailty for anything else."

"I wouldn't make that blunder with you, Regent."

"That's intelligent of you." She sat back in her floater with a sigh. A thick-veined hand came up to brush at dry, wispy hair. "When I received your request to enter Neweden space, I was sorely tempted to refuse it. My seneschal—Sirrah Santos McClannan—was adamant about doing so. Were he in my place, you'd be off to Longago or some other world with your cargo. He may even be right. The Trading Families have brought nothing but trouble, in my experience."

"We sometimes bring benefits, as well."

"What? Devices that glow and sing, all bound with promises of health and well-being, but which do nothing?"

"You have a symbiote sharing your blood. Regent. That came from the Families. Two decades ago, the Family MacGuire brought them to Niffleheim."

She hadn't known that—Gyll could see it in the deepening of the creases between her eyes. Then she shrugged. "And I dislike the monster intensely. It's a parasite; it uses me, and I'm always aware of its presence. I'd almost rather have the bulky machinery and the tedious drugs, Sula, but my doctor insisted that the symbiote would be better. I'm not sure I can believe someone who's lived far less than me, but I let him convince me. Had I known who brought the symbiotes to the Alliance, I might have been less gullible." She paused, and closed her eyes for a moment. Gyll began to speak, but she cut him off in mid-word. "I gambled with the parasite, though. I'm gambling with you, as well."

"That's kind of you, Regent."

"It has nothing to do with kindness," she barked suddenly. The effort cost her. She coughed violently, a spasm that bent her over. Her body shook, racked, and the symbiote shivered beneath the glowcloth tunic. Then, still hunched over, she cleared her throat, dabbed at her mouth with a tissue. Slowly she sat up again. Her gaze was angry, as if she dared him to comment on her weakness. "I know you damned Traders, and especially the Oldins. You'd have started spouting the fine clauses of the Alliance-Families

Pact, then cried 'foul' to Niffleheim Center. You'd've caused me more trouble than I want to think about, and in the end I still might have had to endure your presence. I'm a realist, *Sula.*" She put more emphasis on the title than was needed. "I don't believe in giving myself the aggravation, not at my age, not in my situation. You're here, and that's bad enough. But I can deal with you."

"Regent—"

"No, please indulge me. I don't know why you've come back to Neweden. I'd like to think that it was merely to see your old homeworld again, but I don't believe that. You're with the Oldins, and they don't work that way. I *do* know that I won't tolerate disruption here. There's enough of it already, with Renard and his Hag's Legion. This isn't the same Neweden you left. Be very careful, *Sula.*" Again, that strange inflection, as if d'Embry mocked him.

She allowed Gyll no chance to retort. With a harsh gesture, she broke the contact. The holotank swirled with jagged color, then collapsed into darkness. With the dimming of the room, the globe of Neweden pulled at Gyll's attention. He contemplated it for a long time in reverie, leaning back in his floater. He shook his head.

"Welcome home," he told himself.

Chapter 2

THE LI-GALLANT VINGI'S OFFICE was as Gyll remembered it: large, shaped so as to channel the eye to the Li-Gallant's desk and the massive floater behind it, the walls crawling with ambulatory colors of mobile tapestries. Ostentatious, and too rich for the world. The expansive window to one side gave a view of the keep's gardens, a landscape of topiaries and intricate beds of flowers. The grounds were a buffer separating the Li-Gallant from the tiresome sight of his lessers, a vista of fertile soil, none of the products of which were at all anything but decorative.

A waste on a world where people sometimes starved.

The Li-Gallant reminded Gyll of those gardens. Bloated like a puffindle, and ornamental. Flesh, only thinly concealed, hung from his ponderous frame. His body shook with each movement; he wheezed, his chin was trebled. Rings adorned each of his thick fingers, his manicure was immaculate. The eyes, small and almost lost, were clear and alert, and the tiny mouth was set in what might have been a smile, might have been a smirk.

The Li-Gallant didn't rise from his floater behind the desk as he would have been compelled to do if Gyll had been guilded kin—as he had done before when Gyll was kin-lord of the Hoorka. Vingi remained seated, hands steepled just below his mouth. "My secretary gave your title as 'Sula,' Sirrah Hermond. Is that correct?" Vingi asked the question without preliminaries, without the amenities that, on Neweden, marked the beginning of a conversation between equals. It was, Gyll realized, another small statement. Not quite insult, not quite blatant enough to give cause (to

another Newedener) for bloodfeud, but fixing the parameters and giving notice to Gyll of his status.

As familiar as he was with the tactic, a spark of anger
began to grow inside Gyll. *As antagonistic, as predictable as
ever, the Li-Gallant. The man has damned few attacks, but
he's not loath to use them.* "The title's correct, Li-Gallant,"
Gyll answered. "It marks me as head of the Oldin military
arm." Gyll smiled back at the Li-Gallant and, with a trace
of satisfaction he could not help feeling, pulled a floater
from near the wall and sat without invitation before Vingi's
desk. He crossed his legs, laced his fingers around his knee.

The Li-Gallant's reaction was pleasing. Gyll knew what
buttons to push in this society—it was one of the few advantages of living in a static and formalized system; emotions
were easier to manipulate. Vingi's face reddened, his flabby
arms pushed his bulk back from the desk, the mouth began
to open. Gyll, still in his relaxed pose, shook his head into
the beginning threat. "Li-Gallant, remember who I am and
what I do. And who I was. We're both past our physical
primes, but I've kept in training. No matter how fast you
think you can call your guards, you'd be dead before they
arrived. I've made that threat here before to you, Li-
Gallant. You know I meant it then. Do you want to take the
chance that I'm bluffing now?"

Gyll spoke blandly, slowly, while Vingi stared. The Li-
Gallant's hands made a short convulsive movement. He
swallowed. Then he sat back once more and pulled his
floater to the desk. He smiled a predatory smile.

"You still know the Neweden mentality, Sula, but you
speak like an offworlder. No guilded kin would be that
blunt, not to me."

"I'm not guilded kin."

"True. You're lassari, unguilded. I remember Thane
Valdisa appearing in council to announce your ouster from
the ranks of kin. She spat on the floor when she spoke your
name." A pause. "She seemed very angry."

"She had reason to be," Gyll replied. *He's trying to provoke his own reactions, searching for a weakness to exploit.
Don't let him see it.* "Li-Gallant, let's start over again. I think
we can both respect one another's positions, even if we're
no longer part of the same culture. You're much more intelligent than you pretend to be at times; you know as well as

I that Neweden's ways are not the ways of the rest of humanity."

Vingi nodded. He twisted a ring around a finger, watching reflected light flare in the gemstone. "And that was spoken like the Oldin woman, not the old Hoorka-thane. Which are you, Sula: kin or trader?"

"Both," Gyll said. "And neither. But more trader than kin. I've renounced citizenship in the Alliance, and Thane Valdisa left me no alternative but to leave Hoorka. I'm of the Family Oldin, Li-Gallant. They have my allegiance."

Vingi seemed not to have heard Gyll's reply. He was still staring at his ring, as if lost in the facets of the stone. "I use the Hoorka quite a bit, Sula. I've heard it whispered that the lassari consider your old assassins to be my hirelings, my own elite guard. And of course that feeling has its roots back when you were Thane, when you failed twice to kill my rival Gunnar on my contracts—the guilded kin thought then that you'd allied yourself with Gunnar. When Gunnar was killed in a cowardly murder, *then* they thought I'd finally paid you enough to join with me. Now your Thane Valdisa fights against the image, trying to prove that the Hoorka are indeed neutral, but it's more and more difficult, since the Hoorka are poor, except when I furnish them funds via contracts."

"I've heard those rumors as well, Li-Gallant. The part of me that was kin hates them." *He's still looking for your sore points—tell him some of the truth, but not all of it.*

"You hate it, neh? And do you intend to do something about it? I wouldn't like opposition, Sula." His tone was almost jovial as he said the words.

Gyll said nothing for a moment. He wondered if it would be this way for the rest of his stay on Neweden. First d'Embry, now the Li-Gallant. *Always chipping at the wall, always trying to provoke a reaction, always trying to hurt.* "That's all past, Li-Gallant. History. One can't change that."

"Well, Sula, because of Hoorka's history, the guilded kin view your old assassins with much suspicion; because of the whispers that Hoorka—under your direction as well as Valdisa's—from time to time ignored the code of neutrality you built for them, has led to a decline in their status and wealth. They may be feared; they're no longer respected."

"As I said, Li-Gallant, my loyalty is now to the Oldins, not the guild Hoorka. Not anymore."

"Not even though they're your own creation?"

Despite himself, Gyll felt irritation roughen his voice, pull his mouth into a frown. "Li-Gallant, if I felt that Hoorka were a corruption of all that I'd set out to create with them, I'd be happy to destroy the guild, or let them be destroyed by you. I don't know that such is the case—I haven't been on Neweden for some standards, and I haven't kept in contact with Hoorka." He'd unlaced his fingers and put both feet on the floor, leaning forward slightly from the waist. *Fool, you're giving yourself away. You're showing him just how much you* are *interested in Hoorka, in Neweden.* He made an effort to calm himself, to put his back against the floater's cushions.

The Li-Gallant looked pleased with himself. "So you've returned to meddle in Neweden's affairs."

Calm. Gyll made himself smile. "No. The Family Oldin survives by selling our goods, and I know Neweden. I came to see you because it's only good policy to speak with those in charge of the worlds we service—it smooths potential problems. Kaethe Oldin told me of the, ahh, arrangements she made while she was here. I'm prepared to double that fee—and the exact amount of the stipend will not be disclosed to the council. Your guild, and you as kin-lord, will be the prime benefactors."

That had been Kaethe's suggestion. She'd gauged the man well. The Li-Gallant's eyebrows rose slightly, the lips pursed, contemplative. He made no attempt to conceal his satisfaction. His greed was almost palpable. *That bastard's more avaricious than you'd imagine, Gyll. I knew him better than you in that sense, and his drive for wealth overrides the rest. That's the key to him.*

"When Kaethe Oldin was here," Vingi said, "she sold me an alien trinket: the Battier Radiance. It's broken."

"And it will be repaired without charge," Gyll replied. "The Family Oldin honors their commitments, Li-Gallant. If you recall, it wasn't by choice that we left here the last time."

"Nor will it be this time, neh?"

Gyll shrugged. Vingi laughed.

"Ah, well. The Oldins brought me luck—I rule Neweden

unhampered now, Sula, except for a few paltry groups of malcontents, and I have the Hoorka to take care of them, neh?" He laughed again. Gyll smiled, hoping that he looked convincing. He didn't enjoy deceit, wasn't particularly good at it when he tried, no matter what d'Embry might think he'd learned from the Oldins. Kaethe used to laugh when he tried to hide anything from her—*Gods, you're so transparent, Gyll,* she'd said. It took all of his effort not to rise and leave this corpulent vulture. The thought of Helgin's mocking taunts stopped him more than the surety of FitzEvard Oldin's displeasure.

"Fix the Battier, Sula, and have the funds you've spoken of transferred to my account. My secretary can handle the arrangements." Vingi shifted position in his floater as if restless. Gyll, taking that as a sign that the interview was at an end, rose. The Li-Gallant's gaze stayed with him, speculative. Gyll inclined his head. "Yah, Li-Gallant?"

"I'm not given to intrigue and circumspection, Sula. You know me well enough to expect bluntness. In fact, you probably consider me too direct, too readable. To an extent, you're right. I'm not overly devious. Even my enemies give me credit for that." Pause. The Li-Gallant put his fingertips together under the swell of chins. Reflections stuttered on his rings, shivered on the walls. "Why are you really here, Hermond? I'm not a fool. You're a hell of a lousy salesman—Kaethe Oldin had a much better patter and was better-looking, as well. You're too dour and agreeable. I doubt that you're on Neweden entirely to sell Trader junk. Why, then?"

"You're mistaken, Li-Gallant."

"You're the Sula, head of the military, by your own admission. Why send *you* on a simple trading mission?"

"You misunderstand the structure of the Families. Yah, I'm Sula, but the Families don't segregate along occupational lines as strictly as we"—Gyll smiled at his unintentional slip—"as *you* here on Neweden. There are no guilds as we know them. Everyone, even the soldiers, even the leaders such as FitzEvard, take their turns on the ships. I was sent to Neweden because I knew the planet, knew the society. And, as FitzEvard told me, there's not a whole lot for me to foul up here."

"That was almost plausible, Sula." Vingi nodded. "It was

even fairly well said, well rehearsed. But Kaethe Oldin hinted to me of plans that the Family Oldin had for Neweden, and she said that I might well fit into them."

"Then she's neglected to tell me of them. I seek only trading opportunities, Li-Gallant."

"I think not."

"Li-Gallant, all I can say is that the Family Oldin finds Neweden quite satisfactory. For trade. Or they wouldn't have sent me here."

Gyll smiled at the Li-Gallant and bowed in salutation— the bow of equals, of kin. Vingi slowly rose, with a groan of exertion. He stared at Gyll, measuring him for a long moment, then returned the bow.

"You *will* keep me informed of your progress here, Sula. And we'll talk further, I'm sure." There was no interrogative in his voice.

"Certainly, Li-Gallant. I can assure you that you stand very high in the estimation of Family Oldin."

"As you are in mine, Sula. Just remember who it is that controls this world."

The Regent d'Embry wished that Santos McClannan would shut up. Too many things about her seneschal annoyed her. His voice was mellifluous and pleasant—that annoyed her. He was handsome in a superficial, cosmetic manner despite (she told herself that she wasn't simply being petty) an odd asymmetry to his long face. That annoyed her as well. He was efficient, if somewhat prone to overstepping his limits of authority, and he was invariably polite, no matter what he was saying to her.

That annoyed her most of all.

"I know it's not my place to criticize, Regent, but I think you're going to find that allowing the Traders, *especially* the Family Oldin, back on Neweden was a tragic mistake." McClannan had been staring out the window toward the port, where a *Goshawk* shuttle was unloading cargo. Now he turned back to d'Embry, a smile of inoffensive apology touching the corners of his full lips. She returned the smile— if he wanted to play the game of excessive politeness, let him; she wasn't inexpert herself—and sipped from the cup of mocha on her desk. The dark liquid shivered with the involuntary tremor of her hand. She wished she could lean back in the floater, but the chair's back was high and contacted the hump of the symbiote. She was afraid of hurting it, fearful that she might dislodge the bloodroot despite the doctor's assurance that the symbiote was quite unfragile.

"There's the slight problem of legality," she answered. Her voice was soft; she didn't seem to have the energy to speak more forcefully anymore. "By the Alliance-Families Pact, the only captain I can refuse is Kaethe Oldin. Not unless I have due cause."

McClannan's smile widened, showing white and perfect teeth. He sat on the edge of her desk — another annoyance — and beamed down at her. "Ahh, but that's an easy thing to acquire, that due cause. We both know that — a little money spread in the right places, a violation of the Pact swiftly enters the records, and this Sula Hermond is gone. And so are our troubles."

"But it still wouldn't be right, and it wouldn't be that easy, despite all your assurances. The Li-Gallant, for one, would scream in rage. I know that the Oldins bribe him with a percentage of their profits, and FitzEvard would never allow Sula Hermond to leave until every legal and illegal channel had been pursued. We'd only give ourselves more aggravation." She looked at him, blinked slowly. "There *are* chairs in the room, Seneschal."

"Pardon me, Regent." He stood slowly, seemed to hesitate, then extruded a hump-chair from the floor. He sat again, crossing his legs. Over steepled hands, he regarded her. "M'Dame, what's better, pragmatically? To follow the regulations blindly, or, by a bit of selective blindness, avoid larger potentials for trouble? The Oldins are interfering bastards. Despite the Pact, they stick their noses in the politics of every world they visit. They undermine our influence, subvert the locals, and do us no good whatsoever."

"Damn it, McGlannan, I know the Oldins better than anyone!" D'Embry's breathing stuttered with her outburst. The symbiote squirmed on her back in response. She covered her discomfort by picking up her cup and pretending to study the contrast of her fingers (tinted lime green today) against the delicate porcelain. "And are such quasi-legal questions the things they ask in the Academy nowadays? Seneschal, I know the Oldins, and, believe me, you underestimate them."

"Yet you've allowed them to return." McClannan shook his handsome head carefully, his hair staying delicately in place. "When the Oldins came here last, they helped the Hoorka assassins kill a head official of Moache Mining. Gunnar, Vingi's rival, was killed, and Vingi was able to seize dictatorial powers. The lassari organized under the unknown person Renard—whom we still haven't captured—and lassari attacks on the guilded kin increased tenfold." He continued to gaze at her, still without much expression, as if talking to himself. She sniffed, set the cup down, and tapped her fingers near the switch for her com-unit, hoping he would take the hint.

He didn't. "Niffleheim Center had to explain to Moache Mining why nothing was done to catch the persons responsible for slaying their man, and this whole planet's social system was rocked. It's still rocking. You were nearly removed from this post. You had to call in every last political favor you've earned over the decades to keep this regency—and if the Legat Gioneferra weren't your friend, it *still* wouldn't have been enough. I *know* that, Regent. You were the talk of Niffleheim that standard. Now tell me about legalities, about why we should let Sula Hermond and the Oldins back here."

He looked as nearly smug as he ever allowed himself to look.

"There are these things called ideals, Seneschal. Did you talk about them in between gossiping about me?" She really did not feel well. She told herself that it was the company and not just her body. "I pledged myself to follow the laws of the Alliance because I felt that, even if not perfect, they were for the most part just. I don't intend to follow that oath only when it's convenient for me, nor do I think myself wise enough to alter the laws I follow because I might not be comfortable with the results. Now, that's an old woman talking, mind you; I haven't your sophistication or education, Santos. But I *am* Regent. As long as I am, we'll do things according to my wishes."

"Some of your accomplishments are in the textbooks at the Academy, Regent; your work on Thule, for instance. But"—he smiled again, as d'Embry thought that, somehow, she'd known that particular word was coming—"everyone, even the best, can sometimes make a mistake in judgment."

"We should both remember that, shouldn't we?" She'd raised her voice to say that, and the weakness of her lungs betrayed her. She doubled over in a paroxysm of coughing. Dull, insistent pain throbbed in her stomach and chest, the symbiote moving uneasily. The attack subsided slowly. D'Embry reached for a tissue, spat into it and folded it in her fist, wishing she hadn't given in to anger. It made her look weak, feeding the pity she sensed McClannan felt for her.

"Have you heard from your daughter lately?" Had he said it in anything but the carefully neutral voice he used, she might have been provoked again, sensing in his indelicate change of subject a placation for an old used-up woman and a none-too-subtle suggestion that she should retire.

"No, I haven't," she replied tartly. And just as well. Every time, Anne would try to get her to come back to the estate on Aris, to give up the Diplos. The last time d'Embry had been to Aris, it had taken only a week of sitting, surrounded by four generations of offspring, to become bored and surly. Anne hadn't enjoyed the visit, nor had d'Embry. She wondered how Anne contrived to forget the horrors of each visit and invite her again.

"Aris is a beautiful world," McClannan ventured.

"They spent several fortunes taking everything dangerous or unsightly out of it."

"You have a lot to look forward to when you go there." The prodding in his voice almost made her laugh scornfully.

"It's an antiseptic, artificial place. It's like living in a museum with all the exhibits chosen by someone else. After the first enthusiasm wears off, it's dreadfully stultifying. I'm never comfortable there."

McClannan pursed his lips, almost—but not quite—looking disappointed. He shook his head slightly. "Have you ever told your daughter that?"

"Many times. Every visit." She felt a quick shudder of pain in her abdomen. She willed herself not to show it. The symbiote twitched; d'Embry felt a flooding of relief as it released some chemical of its own into her bloodstream. Her discomfort passed, but a faint fogginess remained, calming her but dulling her senses. She could not seem to care much about McClannan's slick criticisms. They still irritated her, but she didn't want to do anything about them. *Damn it, you parasite! Don't do this to me. Leave me my feelings even if it means pain.* "You'd like Anne," she said. "She resembles you. She listens to what's told her, then selectively ignores what she doesn't want to hear."

It pleased her to see a hint of peevishness in McClannan. His fingers tightened, a faint redness touched his cheeks, and his lips pressed together, whitening. Another time, that would have been enough to make her feel childishly gleeful at having broken his facade. But this victory wasn't as sweet as it should be. She couldn't summon enough energy to care.

"Well, Regent, I really didn't think I had much chance of persuading you to change your mind, and I see you're in a bit of pain today. I doubt that you want to be bothered with Neweden affairs or idle chatter."

Meaning that I ignore my responsibilities as Regent, you son of a bitch. Even as she thought it, the lethargy slid back over her, making everything seem distant. She fought the tiredness, forced herself to smile.

"I probably shouldn't be bothered with useless and stupid second thoughts on decisions already made," she said. She waited a moment, watching the flash of anger behind his eyes. "Let me get some work done here, Seneschal. I'm sure you have duties to attend to as well. Duties other than mine."

He rose primly and bowed slightly to her. "Always, Regent, always. If I can help you, though, please let me know. I won't hide what I feel—I believe that you've made a mistake in this. Sula Hermond is an enemy of the Alliance, as are all the Oldins."

"I knew the Sula when he was Thane of the Hoorka, Seneschal. He might have been proud, arrogant, and stubbornly blind, but he was a man whose word you could trust. He tells me he's only here to trade."

"He's been eight standards with the Oldins. What if he's changed, or what if they're using him as a dupe? I saw the record of your talk with him—I don't like the man, Regent."

"I wouldn't think you would, Seneschal. Sula Hermond speaks his mind freely, without guile, and I've always found that he keeps to the spirit, not just the letter, of his own morals." She stared at him, he looked steadily back. "We disagree on most things, the Sula and I, but I find that I like the man."

"Then I pray that you don't discover your affection for him to be your downfall, Regent."

"I'll manage, Seneschal," she said.

"I'm certain you will," he replied, with absolutely no conviction in his voice. "Are you certain you don't wish me to pursue this further? A thorough check of a ship's log inevitably unearths some discrepancy . . ."

"I think you know my answer."

McClannan nodded. He strolled leisurely to the door, stroking the replica of a d'Vellia soundsculpture as he went by—it moaned in the wind of his passage. He waited patiently for the door to open. He went through.

D'Embry sighed, leaning back gingerly in her floater. She closed her eyes. After a few minutes, her breathing deepened and became more regular. The head lolled back.

She slept.

He'd taken a flitter from Sterka Port to Vingi's keep. Stepping from the gate of Vingi's grounds into the overcast day, Gyll indulged a whim. He waved away the flitter's pilot, deciding impulsively to walk and see Sterka again.

For the most part, the city seemed the same: cluttered, narrow streets made for pedestrian traffic and not groundcars, rich and poor dwellings separated only by a street of small shops, residences and businesses mixed hodgepodge. Chaotic. It brought a smile to his face, born of memory and amusement at what he now saw as archaic and haphazard planning. Sterka was nothing like the sleek and clean lines of OldinHome, the ordered beauty of the buildings and parks there. The scenes gave him hope that he could accomplish his mission on Neweden, the true reason that he'd kept from d'Embry.

He would take Hoorka away from Neweden, away from the Alliance. He would lead them again, under the Oldin flag.

(And as he walked, something nagged at him, some vague feeling of unease, a prickling at the back of his neck: *danger*. He stopped, turning this way and that, but he could see nothing out of the ordinary. Just a street crowded with people, that was all; a noisy conglomeration, most of whom seemed to be kin intent on their own thoughts. Gyll continued walking.)

He'd badgered and cajoled Grandsire FitzEvard, telling the wily old man that he could not give the Oldins a viable military force without a nucleus of trained people—his own old kin. Oldin wanted them too fast to start from scratch. Oh, yes, the Trader-Hoorka he had already were good people, but the Neweden Hoorka would serve as a larger training force, and the work would go that much faster. Let me go back to Neweden, Gyll had said. Let me go back and get them.

It had taken time and much argument, but FitzEvard, under pressure from Gyll, Helgin, and Kaethe Oldin—Gyll's lover and FitzEvard's granddaughter—had at last relented. Kaethe was banned; she could not go, but Gyll and Helgin would return to Neweden. FitzEvard had even smiled when he told them. Gyll would be in charge of the ship, and it would operate as any Oldin trading mission—except that Gyll would seek to recruit his old guild as well.

Gyll knew what he had to offer—far, far more than squalid Neweden, the world Gyll had once thought as all. Far more than the Alliance offered. Gyll could see now why all the Trading Families disliked the Alliance. If the Alliance died, Gyll would not grieve. If what Gyll did here helped to negate its influence, he would be pleased.

Gyll had found several truths about himself in the time since he'd left Neweden. Paramount among them was that he enjoyed being a leader. *The* leader, the one who commanded, who created. He'd given that up when the guild of Hoorka had faced political problems on Neweden, when it seemed that he had dealt with them poorly—and he had found that he was bored and restless, and that he could not keep his hands away from the reins of leadership. That had led to his conflict with Valdisa, to whom he'd given the Thane-ship. It had driven them apart, driven Gyll from his kin, and the troubles of Neweden had given the Hoorka less and less work.

He would amend that all now, if he could.

He could not change Neweden, but he could change Hoorka. It would have to be slow, have to be careful, but he was confident. He was Sula now, not Thane, and the title suited him better.

If d'Embry knew, *Goshawk* would swiftly be seeking some other port. Meddling, she would call it, interference with Alliance business. Gyll did not enjoy lying, but he was slowly finding that it was sometimes necessary. If he had to lie to get Hoorka, he would do it.

As he walked, Gyll let the impressions soak into him, comparing them with remembrances of standards past. He strolled slowly (though the small uneasiness he had felt earlier would not go away), observing. It seemed to Gyll that it was the people as well as the city that had changed. Yes, much was still similar: lassari still drew back from him, as they were supposed to do, the guilded kin nodded politely even as they stared at his clothing and the strange emblem on his belt where the holo of the guild insignia should have been. It seemed that there were perhaps more lassari now, more low kin whose shabby clothing proclaimed the poorness of their guild. And the churches—Neweden had always been haunted by piety and a multitude of gods from which to choose; that trait seemed to have become more pronounced in the time he'd been gone. Neweden was, as the scholar Cranmer had written, "surprisingly rich in gods for a damned poor place; it must be the cheap rent." Gyll was most surprised at the number dedicated to She of the Five Limbs, goddess of the extinct ippicators and also patron of the Hoorka. It seemed that a cult had sprung up around Her. Whatever, every block he walked had its church, of one god or another.

Gyll could only speculate on what that might mean, whether it was due to the solace provided by religion in bad times and the promise it gave of eventual reward, or because, by becoming a member of the clergy, a person became something between guilded kin and lassari. To become a minister of the gods had always been one way of improving your lot if you were lassari, and that was why the regulations regarding the establishment of churches were strict here: high taxes, an avalanche of paperwork, and constant proof of a sufficient congregation.

He knew FitzEvard Oldin would be pleased either way. It meant that things were not all well on Neweden.

There was something odd in the way Gyll was regarded by those he passed, something subliminal. He could sense hostility from the lassari even as they stepped out of his

direct path, and the guilded kin seemed wary rather than
strictly polite. Twice, he saw the green-robed Magistrates of
Justice judging a duel, a crowd gathered around the conflict — that had always been a rare scene when he'd last been
here. And though kin had always gone armed on the street,
the weapons were now more prominent, placed boldly at
the hip as if in defiance and challenge. Guild-kin walked
together in bands, as well, traveling with companions rather
than alone. The sense of worry came back to him, stronger
now. He stopped and glanced behind him: guilded kin went
in and out of the door of a bakery, a pack of jussar youths
lolled against a wall, two women argued prices with a vendor of sweetmeats, a group of kin (the Sterka Jewelers'
Guild, by their buckles) scowled their way around the obstacle of his body. Nothing there to feed his paranoia. Gyll
shrugged and continued his aimless strolling.

A building he did not remember blocked his path. He
turned left, found that the street died after a few blocks,
forcing him to go right, down an alley to another street. He
knew where he was, roughly if not precisely; somewhere on
the edges of Dasta Burrough, one of the lassari sectors. Gyll
didn't care for the sights or the smells, and that nagging feeling of being pursued still insinuated itself. The street was
less crowded now. He stepped around a sated wirehead
sprawled near the central gutter, moved into shadow and
out again, now making his way up a series of wide steps. He
kept his hand near his dagger even as he cursed his uneasiness, then justified it by recalling what he had taught his
new Hoorka. *To an extent, fear is good. Only a fool is truly
unafraid, and fools tend to die quickly in a crisis. Don't allow
fear to cripple you or make you change your tactics, but don't
shut it out, either. Listen to it.*

He turned left at a crossing street, then left again, trying
to find his way back to the street of shops without admitting
defeat and retracing his steps. He came to the mouth of an
alley. The houses near him were empty and dark, ruinous,
and the street was oddly deserted. Something about the
scene, something in his fear and the net of shadows around
him made him hesitate. Maybe the scent of rotting garbage
and dampness welling from the alleyway: Gyll took a false
step forward, waited, thinking that in a moment he would
feel rather foolish.

The feint saved him.

A hand holding a crowd-prod stabbed air where he should have been—that first glimpse of the prod showed Gyll that the weapon had been altered, and the ugly blue-bronze scorch marks at the tip indicated that the alteration was likely to be deadly. Gyll caught sight of his attacker; a thin, sallow face, a gray bodysuit with a tear at one shoulder. The man took a quick step from the alley. A dagger held in the left hand followed the prod, slicing at Gyll. He side-stepped, feeling cloth tearing as the dagger's edge slid along his side; in the same motion, Gyll grasped the man's dagger hand at the wrist. He twisted, hard, and brought the hand down and his knee up. The weapon went clattering away as the man yelped in pain. Another lunge with the prod; Gyll went with the move, falling backward and bringing up his legs sharply into the man's midsection, propelling him back over Gyll's head. Gyll lurched to his feet, sliding his own dagger from its sheath, crouching, watching as his assailant groggily regained his footing. It took the man several seconds, but Gyll did not move toward him. He waited, breathing quickly but easily.

There was no guild holo on the man's buckle, no identifying insignia anywhere on him. The ripped bodysuit seemed to be plain dress available anywhere. "Back off now and this won't go further, lassari," Gyll said. "Think about it, man; if I'd wanted you dead, I had plenty of time."

The lassari grimaced, whether in pain or answer, Gyll could not tell. He shuffled his feet, his fingers loosening and tightening on the prod's handle. "You're bleeding, off-worlder."

"Don't mistake a scratch for anything else."

The lassari straightened, the crowd-prod now held down at his side. He nearly smiled—the edges of his mouth curved upward. "You were almost Hag-kin. You're quicker than you look to be, old man."

"For a frigging coward who'd attack without warning, you don't move nearly as quickly as you need to. With your skills, you'll be Hag-kin yourself soon enough."

The smile vanished. Thin shoulders shrugged under frayed cloth. "Give me another chance, offworlder. I'll be glad to show you the ways of Neweden. A personal introduction to our gods, neh?" The man spat on the pavement between them. In another time, that would have sent Gyll into a rage: Neweden reflexes. Now it almost amused him, a futile, empty insult. It didn't touch him, didn't mean anything. "You're blocking my way, lassari," he said simply. "I'm not really interested in proving to you that I'm good with this blade, but I am. Very. It's your choice."

The lassari shifted weight from one foot to the other. He seemed to turn the decision over in his mind; thought twisted the narrow face into a mask, a snarl. Gyll braced himself, certain that he'd be attacked once more—*when you were Thane, you wouldn't have hesitated when the man was done. You'd have finished it, and not had to worry.* He hoped the man would back down, was afraid he wouldn't. He had no real fear of the man—he was inept and clumsy—but he didn't want to begin his stay on Neweden with another death. He'd killed too many here already. On the bad nights, they crowded his sleep.

The lassari took a step away from Gyll. Then, as if that movement broke the stasis of confrontation, the man fled, turning and running. The sound of his flight echoed from the buildings.

Gyll straightened. The muscles of his back were sore, and he tried to convince himself that it was a result of the unaccustomed drag of Neweden's gravity that made him ache. He examined his side—the dagger had barely broken the skin, though now that the adrenaline surge was gone, he could feel the pain. He frowned. The dagger the lassari had lost was stuck halfway in a pile of garbage the wind had gathered against the curb. Gyll picked it up—a cheap thing, the blade filed from some stock metal, the hilt just tape over the bare steel. Rough, but effective enough; a lassari weapon like a thousand he'd seen before. Gyll stuck it in his belt. He began walking.

There were people around him before he'd gone two blocks. He mused on the attack. Once before, such a thing had happened after leaving the Li-Gallant. Coincidence? Gyll shrugged back the phantoms of speculation and looked about him. He could see the spire of Tri-Guild Church transfixing clouds. He moved toward it, ignoring the stares his torn, bloody tunic caused.

He wasn't really aware that he'd slipped back into the

old Hoorka aloofness. It didn't matter what others might think: let them stare if it pleased them.

McWilms was noticeably bursting with some news. He smiled, his eyes danced, and though he feigned nonchalance by leaning up against the cool rock of Valdisa's chambers in Underasgard, his body didn't seem to be at rest. His hands fidgeted with the clasp of his nightcloak, his boots scuffed the packed earth of the floor. Valdisa, pushing the hover-lamp away from her desk, looked up at him with a quizzical smile.

"Fine, Jeriad. I'll bite. Has the Li-Gallant overpaid his last contract and not noticed? Or did Nisa finally agree to go to bed with you?"

"Gods, Thane, she did *that* weeks ago. You're not very observant." He laughed, and Valdisa could not help but join his amusement. McWilms hadn't been smiling much in the past few days, since the death of d'Mannberg. He'd limped about the caverns in dour silence, keeping to himself, accepting solace from no one. She was glad to see the sorrow beginning to come to some proper perspective. Hag Death was a harsh god—She struck often here, and Dame Fate wouldn't interfere. Grief was good, a needed release, but she didn't care to see one of her best kin-brothers disabled by it.

"Weeks ago, was it?" she said. "Really? And was the reality better than the fantasy?—everyone saw you lusting after her."

He simply grinned. "I didn't come in here to tell you about my love life—but she didn't complain."

"That's hardly a tribute, simply discretion. So, what's got you so bouncy? Come, Jeriad, you can't wait to tell me—I see it in your eyes."

"Hah, you're just jealous because I got to Nisa first." McWilms shouldered himself from the wall and came over to the desk. He still favored his wounded leg. He picked up a crystalline ball with a piece of polished ivory set inside—an ippicator's bone—and hefted it from hand to hand. "The Trading Families have sent another ship here. It's in orbit, and their shuttle's docked at the port."

The depth of her reaction to his announcement shocked

Valdisa. The words brought back unwilled, unwelcome memories, none of them pleasant. She ran a hand through dark hair cropped close to her head and tried to keep her expression in some semblance of normalcy. *The frigging Families. I haven't thought of them for ages, haven't thought of what they did to Gyll and me.* She attempted a smile that felt tentative and false.

And which did not fool McWilms. His own buoyant satisfaction dissipated instantly. He frowned, set the ball down. "Thane, I'm sorry. Damn, I didn't think . . ."

She waved a deprecating hand. "Don't worry about it, Jeriad." She affected unconcern. "What about this Trader's ship? It's not the *Peregrine*, is it; Kaethe Oldin's craft?"

Suddenly she could see that he was reticent to continue. He slipped back into the hesitant lethargy that had followed the Vasella contract. It was more than simply Ric's death; all the Hoorka were experiencing it to some degree—the hardly veiled intimations that the Hoorka-kin were the Li-Gallant's minions in all but name was at the root of the depression. The other contracts with guilded kin had slowed. Vingi's name was on most of their work, and their treasury was pitifully low. The fact that their code of neutrality—Gyll's code—forced them to these straits didn't reduce the gall. Valdisa nodded to McWilms. Her dark eyes encouraged him. "Out with it, Jeriad. You were aglow with the news a moment ago. It can't be just the arrival of a Trader ship. What's the rest of it?"

"No, Thane." He gathered his nightcloak around him as if the cool air of Underasgard chilled him. The cloak was bulky around the bandages lacing his side. "And if I wasn't such a damned idiot, I'd've realized how you'd feel about it."

He grimaced and sat on the edge of the desk.

"You going to tell me or just keep going around it awhile longer?" She smiled again; slow, gentle. "I don't have all day, Jeriad. And I'm a big girl. What are you holding back?"

He sighed. "Yah. Well, I thought it was interesting enough that the Family Oldin owns the ship. Not *Peregrine*, though. *Goshawk*. When I heard, I checked with Diplo Center, and learned two more interesting items about the ship. First, there are paramilitary people aboard her, ostensibly the ship's guard. At least that's the rumor."

"I doubt that's so unusual. The Families don't trust the Alliance. They'd keep their own guards."

He didn't look at her. He examined his hands closely. "They call themselves Hoorka, these guards," he said.

McWilms heard the intake of breath, but when he looked at Valdisa, her face was emotionless. She returned his gaze flatly, with little emotion in her voice. "That's indeed one interesting item, kin-brother. What's two?"

He took a breath, looking away from her again. "Ulthane Gyll is in charge of the ship. He calls himself Sula now, but it has to be the same person—Gyll Hermond."

Valdisa looked down at her desktop, feeling McWilms's gaze on her again. She fiddled with an acousidot holder and sat back in her floater. She looked up at him from under her eyebrows. Her eyes had an unusual sheen. "Damn," she said huskily. "He's back."

"I thought," McWilms ventured, "that maybe you'd be glad to hear that."

"Hag's *teats,* Jeriad!" Valdisa slapped the desk with an open hand. "I had to strip him of his kinship when he left. He didn't leave me any choice. Why should I be happy to see him again?" Abruptly she laughed, a quick breath, and glanced at McWilms bemusedly. "I'm a fine example to you, neh, losing my temper like that. I'm sorry, Jeriad. I guess I wasn't ready for it."

"I understand. And I didn't bother to think about how you might feel. I'll take half of the blame, anyway—easier to share it, neh?"

Valdisa smiled at him, and phrased a question even as her lips turned down again. "Are *you* glad he's returned?"

"He created Hoorka, even if he later left us. And he was always fair with me. He taught us all a lot, and I'm grateful for that at least."

"But do you want him back?"

McWilms shrugged. "It's not my decision, is it?"

"He'll cause trouble, that's all." Then she laughed once more, fully this time. "Listen to me, talking about my old lover as if he were an enemy, as if he weren't once kin." She shook her head. "Leave me alone for a while, will you, Jeriad? I want to think about this, so I won't be so startled when someone brings it up next time."

"Whatever you wish, Thane." McWilms rose. His nightcloak fell around him, swirling. "I have to do the blood-duty for Ric, anyway." He faltered a little on the last words. He swallowed too hard. Valdisa looked up at him.

"We all miss Ric, Jeriad."

"Yah." Sharp, quick. "It's the damned Li-Gallant and his contracts. He enjoys making us appear to be his hirelings. Ric hated that."

"He feeds the Hoorka. How many other contracts do we get?"

"He makes us look like his lackeys. Ulthane Gyll hated Vingi."

"Enough, Jeriad," Valdisa said warningly. She softened her tone. "Do the blood-duty for your kin-father." She stared at him, at the shadows the hoverlamp threw on his lean face. "If you're not too busy with Nisa, would you want to keep your Thane company tonight? I know it's been some time, but I . . ." She stopped, wondering why she felt that she had to explain it to him.

"Yah," he said before she could speak again. "I'd like that."

"You're sure you're well enough?"

"If you don't mind a slow lover." He indicated his chest, his leg. "I can't support myself very well."

"A slow lover sounds preferable, and there are ways around having to have you support yourself." She rubbed at the back of her neck, smiling faintly, stretching in her floater. "Thank you, Jeriad."

"You don't have to thank me. I don't expect the pleasure to be quite that one-sided."

His grin made her laugh despite herself. "Get out of here."

She was still smiling when the door slid shut behind him. Slowly the smile slid into frown. She closed her eyes, forehead propped on hand.

"Damn that man," she whispered. "He would come back."

Helgin glared at Gyll from under thick-ridged brows. Pupils shot with yellow regarded the Sula, taking in the grimy pants, the slashed tunic, the stain of dried blood at his side. "For a person with a hole in him," the dwarf growled, "you're damned cheerful."

"Just a scratch, Motsognir. You've given me worse in practice." Gyll glanced back at the prickly skyline of Sterka. Around them, the port was busy in a thin drizzle. A tram clattered past full of trader goods from the hold of their shuttle. "How's business?"

"That's what you're supposed to be worrying about, rather than looking for ways to kill yourself." Gyll started to speak, but Helgin interrupted. "I know. We've received an invitation to a costume ball, and you're going as a corpse."

"Helgin . . ."

"Business is well enough, I suppose." Helgin squatted on the tarmac in the shadow of their craft. Rain was spotting the pavement around them. "Is the Li-Gallant responsible for the scratch, or did you just stumble into thornbushes?"

"You don't give me enough options. It was a lassari attack."

Helgin raised his eyebrows in mock surprise. "A damned strange thing to have happen, your first day back here." The dwarf picked a pebble loose from the field, flicked it away with a stubby forefinger. "Of course, it's probably just coincidence — they *do* have a god here for coincidences, don't they?"

"Don't make more of it than it is, Helgin." By his tone, it was obvious that Gyll didn't care to elaborate on the incident any further. Helgin chuckled.

"Which means that you're worried about it, too." The roar of his amusement was blunted by the shriek of a transport leaving the field. Helgin raised his voice to carry over the tumult, shouting. "Face it, Gyll. Neweden's not going to look upon you with a friendly eye; not the Regent, not Vingi, not your precious Hoorka-kin. Nobody. All those too many gods you have here are going to be pissing their bedsheets, worried about what you mean to do here. They ain't gonna like you." The Motsognir chuckled again as a frown deepened the lines of Gyll's face.

"I don't particularly like the idea, either, Helgin."

"But you're willing to go along with it because you know that Oldin, despite his personality flaws, is right."

"I suppose."

"Then sharpen your knives, Sula." Helgin spat on the ground. He stared at the result critically. "You're gonna need 'em."

Chapter 3

THE LIGHT OF GULLTOPP, like some silvered liquid, flowed over the figure of a man moving in the forest near Underasgard. The nocturnal creatures were making their nightly chorus of chirps and howls; the intruder added little noise to the concert. He moved swiftly, quietly, sure of his ground. He halted once near the end of the broadleaves. Staying to the whispering darkness of the shade, he peered into a clearing beyond. There, a tall, slender column of stone stabbed the sky, a cluster of glass-eyed receptors at its summit: the dawnrock of the Hoorka assassins, the announcer of life and death. Beyond the dawnrock, the opening of Underasgard loomed like a gaping mouth half-hidden in a fold of hills. From the darkness of the caves, he could sense watchfulness, eyes regarding the night. The man crouched under the broadleaves for long minutes, breathing softly, staring at the maw of Underasgard, rubbing a pliant leaf between thumb and forefinger. After a time, he let the leaf, torn and broken, fall to the ground. The faint scent of the foliage clung to his hand.

He stood, dappled with Gulltopp's brilliance. His clothing echoed the night, and a hood left his face in eternal shadow.

In time (always carefully, always with deliberate slowness), he moved to the western side of the clearing, staying just inside the cover of the trees. There, he spent a few minutes arranging a small pile of dead leaves and twigs, leaving it sitting inside a circle of bare earth. Turning his back to Underasgard, he puffed a thin cigar alight—he'd found them offworld; the tobacco addiction wasn't well-known on Neweden—and placed it carefully in the twigs. He took a small pouch from his belt and added a pinch of dark powder near the cigar. A thin coil of smoke was already curling upward. As carefully as before, he made his way back to the other side of the clearing. Once more, he crouched, waiting. A ruddy light flickered among the trees where he'd left the cigar. It faded, then pulsed again before becoming a steady, wavering glow. He could smell the sweet smoke. He watched the entrance of Underasgard.

Someone stepped from the tumble of rocks into the clearing, wearing the black-and-gray nightcloak of the Hoorka. The man could hear the faint whine of an activated vibro; moonlight shuddered on the vibrowire. The Hoorka stared at the fire, turned and said something toward the cavern mouth, then ran quickly across the clearing into the broadleaves' shadow.

The man smiled, rising to his feet. Still in a half-crouch, he ran toward the entrance. He paused momentarily, in a listening attitude, then vaulted over a boulder into Underasgard.

The Hoorka on duty—an apprentice—reacted far too slowly. The intruder kicked aside a vibrofoil that, belatedly, the apprentice drew from its sheath. Unactivated, the hilt clattered away into darkness. A swift hand movement followed the kick, without delay, and the apprentice slumped, wobble-kneed. The intruder caught him, laid the boy down gently. His thin, gnarled hands pulled up an eyelid, felt the flutter of heart underneath the cloak. Then he stood. Under the cowl of his hood, his eyes stared, watching for movement in the twisting corridor leading back into the caves where the Hoorka lived.

Nothing. Empty, silent night lay there. With a glance back at the apprentice, he moved deeper into the Hoorka-lair.

Twice, he had to disable lone assassins walking the maze of tunnels; each time, luck was with him. He had no difficulty, and his attacks were as silent as he could have wished. He skirted the brilliance of the common room, with its sounds of many voices. Finally he came to a doorshield with the Hoorka-Thane's insignia set above it. He stood there a second, contemplative, as if suddenly unsure of himself. It was at odds with his previous demeanor.

And at that moment, the alarm sounded, a hooting ululation like Hag Death's wail. The intruder bounded into shadow—thankful that Underasgard was always shadowed—not waiting to see the woman that rushed from the Thane's room. Instead, he moved deeper into the labyrinthian system of caves, away from the areas frequented by the assassins, away from the welling uproar.

He smiled, as if with some secret amusement.

"You're sure no one saw you?"

Helgin took off his cloak with a sweeping motion that stirred a small breeze in the dankness, and threw the garment into a corner of the room. He glared at the speaker and the two people sitting in shadow behind the man. "What do you take me for, Renard? When I don't care to be seen, I can be much more elusive than you—after all, who did Kaethe send to do her dirty work here? It wasn't you, was it? She knows your abilities."

Renard grimaced. His skin was the color of tea; he was stockily built, but rather tall. In the wan glow of a half-shuttered hoverlamp, the outline of his figure was indistinct, but Helgin could see the thorny spines and thick coil of a plant-pet around his shoulders. Renard stroked the thing as he talked.

"Keep your voice down, Motsognir."

"Are you worried, Renard?" The dwarf grinned lopsidedly at him. If anything, Helgin's voice was a trifle louder, raspy as always. It carried well. "I saw the people you had hidden outside. One on the roof across the street, another down the way pretending to be casually leaning from a window. Right? You need to teach them better, but they'll keep away any of Vingi's guards. And I lost the two others that trailed me from the port, lost them way back on the outskirts of Dasta."

"Vingi's people?" It was the woman behind Renard. She stepped up into the light. Helgin looked at her appreciatively—then decided she looked too serious.

"No," he said curtly. "Diplos. The Regent's lackeys."

He could see the relief pull at the woman's face. "Good."

"Don't deceive yourself, m'Dame. What the Diplos know, Vingi will eventually find out. He has a better intelligence network than you might think." Helgin turned back to Renard. "Do these two have to be here?"

"They're part of my cell."

"Tell them to wait outside."

Renard stared at the Motsognir, one hand idly petting the beast around his neck, smoothing down the fleshy spines. Helgin looked back at him blandly, one hand on his hip. The tableau held; then Renard jerked his head in the direction of the door. "Micha, Alex. Please."

The two gave Helgin appraising glances as they passed him. The dwarf waited until the door had shut behind them, then went over, opened it again, glanced outside, and latched it. He pulled a chair from the side of the room to the table behind which Renard stood. He sat.

"How long have you been here this time, Renard?"

The man's eyes narrowed. "Three standards, almost. I was gone for nearly five. Why?"

"FitzEvard worries about his hirelings, that's all. Doesn't want them to become too involved in their work and forget who's ultimately the benefactor of all you've been doing."

"Are you making an accusation, or just noise? I don't frighten that easily, man."

Helgin's eyes widened in mock surprise. "Frighten you, Renard? Me try a silly tactic like that?"

"Just tell FitzEvard I haven't forgotten."

"I understand you lost Vasella."

Renard grimaced. His hand left off its stroking; a tremor ran the length of his living collar. "Yah, the damned Hoorka . . ."

Helgin shook his head in exaggerated sadness. "Now, you see, that's just the problem—you shouldn't let yourself get so perturbed. Your job is to see that the low kin and lassari stay angry. What's going to anger them more than losing a folk hero? You *want* Vingi to do exactly what he's doing. And you could certainly stand to have a martyr to play with, especially when it's not you."

"I understand that, Motsognir. You needn't lecture me. But I could have used Vasella—alive—a while longer."

Helgin nodded into Renard's irritation. He crossed his legs underneath him on the seat. "The woman's your lover, or the man?"

"*Damn* you and your frigging useless questions!" Renard slapped the table; the plant-pet quivered. "Dwarf, did you come here deliberately to irritate me? I tell you—I know what I'm doing."

"I don't mean to irritate you, Renard. That's just my outgoing personality shining through my dour exterior. I came to find out how things are progressing for you here in the dregs of Neweden society. You haven't sent reports lately; FitzEvard's slightly curious. I can't say I really blame him, considering what he's paying you."

"I haven't had the time for paperwork." Renard didn't bother to disguise his growing anger. "Nor the chance. I can't very well send them by the legitimate routes, now can I? In any case, why should *you* be the one so concerned? — you've a Sula in charge of *Goshawk*."

Helgin frowned. He tugged at his beard. "The Sula Hermond doesn't know everything. He knows what FitzEvard Oldin wants him to know. He's not here for the same reasons you are." Helgin glanced critically at a hair plucked from his beard, then let it drop to the floor. "FitzEvard wants the reports to go only to me, not the Sula."

"So he's just another pawn in the game."

"One metaphor's as good as another."

"Pawns are cheap, easily lost, and sometimes it pays to sacrifice them."

"I hope not. I like this one."

"I could use him, Motsognir." Renard looked thoughtful. His hand had gone back to stroking the plant-pet. He paced to the rear wall and back. "Think of the conflict it would create if your Sula were to die in the right manner — say, by lassari rebels. Vingi would be furious at the loss of potential profit, and embarrassed because of the way it happened. The Diplos wouldn't raise a finger, and old d'Embry might just get thrown out of her job because of the backlash . . ."

Helgin had risen, standing on the seat of his chair. In another, the posture would have been ludicrous, but the wrath twisting the dwarf's face forbade amusement. "You'll leave him alone, Renard." His voice was uncharacteristically low; it seemed more sinister because of that.

Renard only smiled. *"Now* who's emotionally involved? You like him, Motsognir, neh? Is he *your* lover?"

Helgin spat. His hands curled into fists. "I'm telling you to work with what you have here. Do you understand that?"

"Are you giving me a choice?"

"No."

Renard shrugged. He waved a lazy hand in acquiescence.

Slowly, his face still ruddy with anger, Helgin sat again. "So long as we understand each other, Renard."

"I understand what I need to do. I know who pays me, and that's all I need to know."

Helgin nodded. His expression relaxed in stages. The grin returned; he cracked his knuckles loudly. "Good. Then let's get your friends back in here and tell me what you've been doing and what you plan to do."

As Renard moved toward the door, Helgin put his bare feet up on the table and leaned back dangerously in the chair. "And get rid of that damned thing around your neck," he said. "It's ugly and it stinks."

She could see him sitting before the headless skeleton of the ippicator. Light from a handflare barred the walls and ceiling of the cavern with beast-shadow. He didn't turn to look at her, though she knew that her approach, over the broken, treacherous stones of the empty caves far from the normal haunts of Hoorka, had hardly been silent. She stopped, hand near the hilt of her dagger, her nightcloak thrown back over her shoulder, out of the way.

"Hello, Gyll," she said. It was not what she'd been rehearsing in her mind.

Now he turned. A hand swept the hood back from his head, revealing hair well-laced with gray. Gyll half-smiled, nodded. "Valdisa, it's good to see you again. I knew you'd figure that it was me, and that you'd know where to look."

"You take a damned lot for granted, then," she replied gruffly. She'd thought she'd known how she felt; now, seeing him, she was no longer certain. Emotions warred inside. She kept her hand near the leather hilt—Hoorka's comfort, she thought, like Jeriad. "I have three kin being attended to for your bruises, and Underasgard is in an uproar. I'll have to take disciplinary action that none of the kin—including me—is going to like. I could have sent kin back here to kill you for an intruder."

"You didn't." His attitude conveyed a studied relaxation: one arm propping up the body, the other across the knee of a flexed leg. "Hell, Valdisa, none of the kin were really hurt beyond their pride and a bruise that'll be gone in a week. I'm good enough to have made sure of that. It'll be a good lesson, especially to the apprentices you had guarding the entrance. It was too damned easy, m'Dame. Way too easy."

She continued staring at him, but her weapon hand relaxed, fisted on her hip. "Once, you were good enough to have made it look that easy. You're telling me you're back to that shape?"

Gyll laughed, a full-throated amusement that rolled across the folded walls of stone. Valdisa didn't share the laughter, didn't move at all. *I should hate him. I should hate him for what he did to me, did to his kin, did to Hoorka—for abandoning us as if his own damn restlessness were more important than the welfare of guild-kin. I should be angry with him. So why is what you're feeling closer to jealousy?* Her flat gaze watched him as Gyll leaned back to vent his pleasure, watched as the laughter slowly faded to a chuckle, watched as he stretched and rose. His loose clothing had the look of a uniform, but she saw no weapons. His face was as craggy as ever, etched with yet more time-lines, but the eyes were alight and restless, gleaming in the harsh light of the flare.

"It's good to hear you say that, Valdisa," he said. "It must show a little, then. Yah, I feel much better now. You always told me that I was losing my tone. I was horribly out of shape those last few standards here."

"You could have managed to get back in trim," she answered. Without leaving, she almost added.

He knew. "Leaving was one of the best things I could have done."

"Not for Hoorka." A pause. "Not for me."

"You did miss me, then." His voice was very soft.

"I've never taken lovers or made friends easily. You were both."

A look of something akin to sympathy came to his eyes—Valdisa knew only that she didn't like the expression. Its very empathy repelled her. Gyll took a step toward her, holding out his arms in the welcoming attitude of kin to kin. The gesture rekindled Valdisa's anger. She glared at the proffered hands. After a few moments, Gyll let them fall to his sides. "But you still harbor the grudge, neh?"

"What the *hell* do you *think?*" Fury goaded her into shouting, the patronizing tones of his voice fueling the emotion. Gyll watched her, that cool sympathy/pity on his face, not saying anything, not reacting much at all. Valdisa forced herself into calm again. *Hoorka show their inner faces only to kin—that's how the code-line goes. Remember, he's not kin. Not any longer.* Her face became blank, neutral, a mask of flesh. With it, Gyll's expression altered as well. The shoulders fell slightly, his lips clenched, and he seemed to sigh.

"So that's the way you're going to play this?" he said. "As Thane to a dishonored kin-brother?"

"Gyll Hermond is not a kin-brother, dishonored or otherwise. Gyll is nothing. He's lassari, kinless. I do not hear him." Valdisa spoke scathingly in the impersonal mode. Such a callous and deliberate insult would provoke a Neweden native to rage, and Valdisa readied herself, widening her stance for his attack.

When he didn't react at all, she knew just how much he'd changed in the intervening standards.

"You needn't speak that way, Valdisa," he said mildly. "I wanted to see you again, sit in the quiet of the caverns with my old friend the ippicator, to see if the beast still made me feel close to She of the Five."

"Do you?" she asked, despite her anger.

"I don't know. I think maybe I do. The ippicators were always sacred to us, inviolate relics and not something to be sold as the rest of Neweden would do. I feel something looking at it." His head turned back to regard the great ribs, the sheen of the bones, the five legs sprawled in collapse. "I think about how they were the pets of the gods and how the gods took them away from Neweden to live with them. And I look at the Great One here and I think about how much those bones would be worth, cut and polished." He looked back at her. "You didn't have to speak that way to me, Valdisa. I wanted to see you again most of all. I didn't want us to scratch open all our old wounds."

"You could have communicated with me in the time since you left, but you didn't."

"You could have initiated it just as easily."

"It wasn't *me* that came back to see if he still felt Her presence in the bones of the ippicator."

Gyll exhaled loudly. He shifted his weight, and rock clunked dully under his feet. The sound was loud in the cavern's stillness. "We're both damned stubborn, aren't we? Neither of us was ever willing to bend much."

"I don't know that I'll ever bend in this, Gyll. What are you here for? I hope you didn't think to begin our relationship again." Saying it stirred memory. The ghost of their affection and love was still there, underneath, battered and broken. It nagged at her. She glanced from Gyll to the five-legged ippicator's skeleton, not wanting to look at him. *She of the Five, why did You bring him back here? Why couldn't you have kept him away?*

"Valdisa, there was a lot of feeling between us. That's never really altered for me."

So careful he is. He makes it sound so easy, as if the rift were simply a crack easily plastered. "You've a hell of a durable set of feelings, then. You disobeyed a direct order from me as Thane, you made me declare you unguilded. You left me. You chose the Oldins over the Hoorka, Gyll. What's the matter, don't your Trader-Hoorka satisfy you? Doesn't Kaethe Oldin open her legs for you, or don't you have a pretty underling there you can seduce?"

His smile was unsure. It flickered across his lips. "Valdisa, let's be fair. I know I hurt you, I know I hurt the kin, but it seemed to be something I had to do. And I'm glad I did, in most ways. The Oldins are good people, Valdisa, and the Trader-Hoorka is an organization with great potential, not constricted like we were becoming here." His eyes narrowed suddenly, and his gaze traveled her body. "Your nightcloak is tattered, the uniform is thin in places . . . I've heard tales since I arrived, Valdisa—they say that Hoorka is poor, that you don't get many contracts anymore, and those you do work are always from the Li-Gallant."

"Nobody's starved yet, Gyll. But, yah, we don't get the contracts, and d'Embry won't allow us offworld. What of it? It means we have to wear our clothes longer, means we don't eat as well, means that some of the equipment can't be fixed as soon as it breaks. You going to blame that on me, too? It wouldn't have been different if you'd stayed Thane."

He didn't believe that. She could see it in his eyes, in the way his mouth tightened. "The rumors have truth, then," he said.

She knew what she wanted, suddenly. "I don't think talking with you is what Hoorka needs, Gyll. I want you gone."

"Valdisa, I left Neweden because—whatever you might believe—I thought I could do something for Hoorka. For us. I think I do have a future to offer, having seen the Families' society." He spoke with a fervor she remembered all too well. It engendered the same reaction in her that it always had. She shook her head into his words, and he began to speak rapidly, as if speed could alter her denial. "They can offer Hoorka much, far more than Neweden or the Alliance. Gods, Valdisa, you don't know how suffocating the Alliance really is, don't know how much they keep out from paranoia or some false elitism. Hoorka could be . . ."

He stopped, realizing that she wasn't listening to him. "Valdisa—" he began.

"Gone," she said. "And don't talk to my kin, Gyll. Stay away from me, stay away from Hoorka."

"Talking isn't going to harm anyone, Valdisa. There's so much I wanted to tell you, so much I want to hear from you; how the kin are . . ."

"Kin have died. You weren't here to mourn them, weren't here to give blood-duty."

The words hurt him. Seeing the pain in his eyes made her feel simultaneously pleased and repentant. She didn't enjoy the ambiguity.

Still, he persisted. "I don't want us to be enemies, Valdisa. Maybe talking will change things, at least vent some of the bitterness you seem to feel."

She forced herself back into the Hoorka aloofness. "Maybe that's exactly why I'm telling you to stay away, neh?" She turned her back on him, strode into the darkness of the corridor leading back to the Hoorka caverns. Her voice, disembodied, came back to him. "I'll have my people away from the entrance in ten minutes, Gyll. I want you to leave. If you're still here in half an hour, you'll be considered an unwelcome and dangerous threat, and I'll make sure you're treated accordingly."

He could hear her footsteps moving away.

The endless, mocking silence of earth and stone returned.

The next day the confrontation was still in the forefront of his thoughts. He mused on Valdisa and the Hoorka as he helped one of his crews unload crates from the shuttle hold, his shirt off like the rest of the laborers despite the Neweden chill.

"Sula?"

Gyll turned. The woman who'd addressed him was of moderate height, rather plain of face, and her clothing was that of a lassari. Yet she stared at him without the humility that should mark a lassari addressing a social superior. Her hands were on her hips, her head cocked at an angle in challenge. "I'm Sula Hermond," he said, wiping his hands on his pants. "And you?"

"My name's unimportant," she answered. She seemed nervous despite her air of arrogance. Her gaze moved about, and she licked her dry lips. "Can we move over by the other end of the shuttle, Sula? I would like to speak with you privately."

Gyll was tempted to refuse her, this no-name lassari. Yet his curiosity prodded him. *You're reacting with the vestiges of Neweden mores. This reluctance to talk to her is only because she's lassari. Remember that you're not a Newedener anymore, but an Oldin.* "All right," he said finally. "Marko, take charge here for a few minutes, will you?" The man grinned back at Gyll, glancing knowingly at the lassari.

"Certainly, Sula. My pleasure."

Gyll smiled at Marko, shaking his head. He picked up his shirt, then walked with the woman toward the nose of the shuttle, putting on his shirt against the cool breeze. When they stood in the shadow of the nose, the thick strut of the landing gear beside them, he spoke to her. "Well, m'Dame? They can't hear us here."

She glanced about once more. "I don't like being here," she said. "It's too open. Too many people could be watching." She looked back at Gyll and shrugged. "But I needed to contact you, Sula. From everything I've heard, everyone's attention is centered on you: the Li-Gallant's, the Regent's. They want to know what you're doing here."

"Just what it appears I'm doing—trading." He could not keep a faint hint of condescension from his voice. "And which of those watchers do *you* represent?"

"The Hag's Legion and Renard."

Gyll knew that she watched his face for a reaction. He didn't know if he was successful in keeping the shock and disgust hidden, but then, he did not particularly try. "What does the Hag's Legion care about the Family Oldin?" His voice had turned colder, more distant. It hardened her face, made her step back away from him.

"You were guilded kin once, Sula. We know that. You were Thane of the Hoorka, the scum that kill lassari for the Li-Gallant. They cast you out, Sula, those Hoorka. Thane Valdisa had you banned from the company of all guilded kin; she made you lassari—no better than me as far as Neweden society's concerned." She paused, glancing about once more. Two people were walking toward the shuttle from the Sterka gates of the port. The woman kept her gaze on them, speaking faster now. "We need to know where you stand, Sula. Do you support the guilded kin who spat on your name and discarded you, or will you help the truly needy ones of this world, the lassari that look to the Hag's Legion for support? You could aid us greatly."

"I'm a Trader, m'Dame. I don't dabble in politics."

"You can't avoid that here, Sula. If you deal with the Li-Gallant, you tread on the backs of all lassari. All we ask is that you consider that. There are things that the Hag's Legion could use that wouldn't involve your visible support: money, material, perhaps arms . . ."

The two were still approaching, and Gyll could see that both wore uniforms—one that of Vingi's guard, the other that of a Diplo staff member. The woman saw them as well. Her nervousness increased. She shifted her weight from side to side uneasily. "Sula?" she said. "I need an answer to take back to Renard."

"Then tell him no."

The woman scowled, baring her teeth—they were not good teeth; discolored, broken. "Sula, you're not kin, you're lassari. One of us."

"No."

She hissed, drawing her breath in between snaggled incisors. "Very well, then. You've made a mistake, Sula. I hope you don't regret it later." She looked at the guards, then back to Gyll. "I can't argue with you any longer."

"I understand, m'Dame," Gyll said. His voice had softened despite himself—he felt empathy for her, for the risk she had taken to come here openly, for the obvious passion of her convictions. "M'Dame, I bear no grudge at all against lassari, believe me, but I don't intend to endanger my trading mission here."

"Then you've made your choice, Sula. As I told you, all the forces here look to you as a part of the solution to

Neweden's problems. You can't avoid the politics: whether there's a reason or not, those in power all look to you. Their thoughts center around you. You're involved, Sula, despite your protests."

The two guards had increased their pace. One pointed to them. The woman slid around the bulk of the landing strut and ran. Gyll heard her footsteps, watched as Vingi's guard took flight after her. The Diplo waited for a moment until pursuer and pursued had disappeared into a maze of idle machinery, then sauntered over to Gyll. The Diplo nodded to Gyll pleasantly. The badge on his tunic had the name Vorman inscribed on it—a miniature Vorman leered up at him from the holo ID. "Think he'll catch her?" he asked.

"I don't know," Gyll answered. "She seemed fast and agile. Bet she has better wind, too."

"Who was she?"

"She didn't say," Gyll said flatly. He'd already decided that he did not like this Vorman. "She was looking for a handout." Gyll elaborated no further. Vorman nodded, staring at Gyll.

"My friend from the Li-Gallant seemed to think she might be Hag's Legion."

"I know the woman was lassari. She might have been involved with the Legion, I suppose. It *is* largely lassari."

"Ahh." Vorman nodded again. He smiled; it touched only his lips. "I don't know how the woman got out here, Sula—as you know, all Neweden natives are restricted to the public area of the port."

"Then shouldn't you be chasing her as well?"

The smile became wider and still did not reach his eyes. Gyll's dislike for the man's false camaraderie increased. "It's a purely internal problem for Neweden, isn't it, Sula?" Vorman said. "At least as long as she was just here to ask for charity. Perhaps we'll find out more if she's caught."

Gyll glanced back the way she'd gone. "My money's on the woman," he said. "Care to wager?"

"I think not." Vorman shrugged. "I'll have to make a report, though. The Regent insists on knowing what happens inside the port." He glanced at Gyll and the smile vanished. "Especially where it concerns you, Sula."

"It's nice to know she cares."

The smile returned. "And I'd been told that you had very little humor in you, Sula. Well, I'll leave you to your work."

Vorman walked away, moving toward the gates of Diplo Center. Gyll watched him leave. "Gods damn all officious assholes like you, Vorman," Gyll muttered.

Then, puzzling over the incident, he went back to his crew.

Chapter 4

THE FUNERAL OF VASELLA was held in one of the hundred or so small churches dotting Dasta Burrough — the Church of the Vengeful Ippicator. Renard had chosen it, whimsically, for its name; certainly not for its grandeur. It was an uncomfortable choice in most ways, though that made Renard feel pleased rather than the opposite. Too many people were crammed into too small a space. The interior was hot despite the autumnal temperatures outside, and it was crowded. Renard's clothes were sticky and damp. He'd left behind the plant-pet as rendering him too conspicuous, but was glad now that the creature's burdensome weight didn't add to his discomfort. Micha and Alex pressed beside him, too close. Still, the scene made him smile. Little annoyances bred anger, and the child of anger is violence.

Only the corpse of Vasella had room. Shrouded in plain glowcloth, it lay on a bier between the congregation and the altar, bedecked with flowers and small burial gifts. The mourners were almost entirely lassari and low kin, the residents of Dasta Burrough and Oversector and the wretched areas like them in all of Neweden's cities. Squirming in his seat in the front pew, Renard could see them, filling the ranks of seats, lining the walls and clogging the aisles, seemingly about to overflow the balcony. *Good, good. They're already edgy and bitter, and this poor excuse for a church feeds their irritations. Good.* The mourners shifted, fanned themselves, shouted across to friends, all under the cartoonish glare of a rendering of She of the Five that filled the rear wall. Behind the poorly drawn goddess, a simplistic sky tossed thunderheads jerkily from left to right. Renard smiled up at the visage, mockingly. He fingered the rough cloth of the hood on his lap—he'd brought the Hag's Legion here with their faces concealed, for a squadron of Vingi's guards had been just outside the church, filming all those who entered. There had been muttering and covert insults, but no trouble. Not yet.

The Li-Gallant plays into my hands. Again. As always.

The crowd quieted as the Revelate Brotsge walked slowly from the sacristy to the bier. Brotsge was old, frail of body, and foul-tempered, an old-line lassari who preached of eventual rebirth and reward for those who followed the mores of Neweden society. The revelate had been absurdly happy at receiving the overlarge tithing for the funeral service. Seeing the church, Renard could understand: it needed repair. It seemed to be held together with erratic strips of paint and prayer. Whatever the revelate's usual congregation, they were neither large nor generous with what little money they had.

The revelate shuffled forward and put a trembling right hand on Vasella's shroud. At his gesture, the lights in the church dimmed—haphazardly, for some went entirely dark and others stayed nearly full—while the sky behind She of the Five became twilight with a flickering of scratchy lightning. The Revelate Brotsge's voice was as palsied as his hands. It reverberated tinnily through the church.

"We have gathered to send the soul of Urbana Vasella to our gods and their mercy." He leered out to the people in what Renard assumed was Brotsge's interpretation of a sympathetic smile. Renard frowned back, properly respectful and sad at this death of a friend. Micha leaned toward him slightly, speaking in a whisper. "I wish we could have done this outside. My pants are itching from all the heat." Renard nodded back, still looking at Brotsge.

The revelate took his hand away from the bier and made the sign of the star over the body. "Sirrah Vasella prepares to meet She of the Five, who will snatch him away from Hag Death and prepare him for his next life here. She will take his *j'nath,* his essence, and mold it in a new form, one that mirrors the worthiness of his past lives. We should not grieve here, my friends, for Urbana is dead only for a little time, as the Gods count such things."

"He's dead! That's all that matters, Revelate!"

The shout came from the packed rear of the hall, followed by scattered shouts of agreement. Restless, the congregation mumbled to itself. Heads craned to view the source of the interruption. Renard sat, silent and still, hands folded on his hood, ignoring the sweat and the heat and the closeness, watching the consternation in the face of the revelate. The man peered myopically out into the crowd, seeking the taunter. Brotsge blustered, scowling, the sound system amplifying his spluttering ire. As the gathering settled once more into restive, uneasy quiet, Brotsge gathered together the shreds of his composure once more, drawing himself up and glaring down at the assembled, his chin high. Renard leaned back, not letting the band of wetness down his spine bother him. This would be interesting.

Brotsge had motioned to his acolyte—a boy that could have been no more than ten. Obviously hot and uncomfortable in his voluminous, heavy surplice, the boy came over to the revelate, bearing a tray on which sat censer and spices, a flask of holy water. The boy kept glancing at the crowd, especially at the solemn rank of the Hag's Legion. Brotsge cleared his throat, said something to the acolyte in a whisper. The child blanched, blinked heavily. The tray shook, but his attention was now entirely on the revelate. Brotsge took the flask and walked once around the corpse, now and then sprinkling the liquid inside over the shroud, all the while intoning the litany of She of the Five. Renard watched, impassive, biding his time and listening more to the whispers of the people behind him than to the ritualistic mutterings of the revelate. He wiped sweat from his forehead with his sleeve, folded his muscular arms at his chest.

Revelate Brotsge faced the congregation once more. Sweat had made ragged strands of his white, thin hair. Dark circles of perspiration were visible under the sleeves of his outer garment. He bowed his head: Renard watched a droplet of sweat fall from the revelate's head to the floor.

"We send Urbana on with our prayers and the blessing of She of the Five. We pray he will return soon, his *j'nath* purged by his passage." His head still bowed, Brotsge waited for the traditional response: "All praise Her." It came only from his acolyte. The crowd began the refrain, but came to a ragged halt as Micha—at a nudge from Renard—rose from her seat and spoke loudly.

"You're quite mistaken, Revelate." She had a strong, firm voice. It carried well in the mugginess of the church.

The revelate gaped at her, his mouth open comically. At his side, the acolyte giggled nervously. Brotsge flung a hand sidewise; it struck the boy on the cheek, silencing him and rocking the utensils on the tray. The revelate shut his mouth, straightened. He fixed Micha with a squinting glare. "M'Dame—" he began severely.

"Revelate," Micha interrupted. Her audacity snapped shut his mouth again. In his seat, Renard grinned to himself. *Good.* The church was utterly silent, everyone's attention drawn to the conflict. Even the swishing of improvised fans had stopped, forgotten. Micha's words fell into the quiet like stones. "Vasella was a lassari, like most of us in the Legion, like most of those here today." She swept her hands wide to include the gathering. "He had no wish to return to this miserable life on the vague *chance"*—she paused, as Renard had taught her—"that in this mythical next life he might return as guilded kin."

"M'Dame—"

"No, Revelate. Vasella will return to us when the ippicators return, as all our lore tells us they will do, when the time has come to destroy this society the guilded kin have built to serve their own needs." Another pause, and as Brotsge began to make some comment, Micha shouted over him. "Vasella would not *want* to be kin, not when it would mean defiling all he believed in. He would not turn around and spit in the faces of the lassari and low kin, who were as a family to him."

At that, there were scattered applause and sounds of agreement from around the church. Only the row of the Hag's Legion sat silent, unperturbed. Renard was pleased with the response. *A little heavy-handed with the words, but she's doing it well. Good and better.*

Brotsge clapped his hands together. The sound, amplified, rang through the hall. Slowly the crowd settled before his obvious anger: a revelate, after all, was a person touched by the gods, an institution they had all been taught to respect. Only Micha stood, defiant, with the presence of the Legion behind her.

"Woman," the old man said, "why do you persist in this blasphemy?" His use of casual address caused Micha's face to tighten into a scowl. At Renard's side, Alex started to rise, and Renard quieted him with a harsh gesture. He didn't like having to do that—it showed his power over the Legion to a careful observer, and his safety lay in anonymity.

"Is it blasphemy to speak truth, Revelate?" Micha trembled, but she held herself. Renard leaned forward in his seat, ready to interrupt if he had to, but hoping it would not be necessary—it was not his intention to have the lassari anger vented here, in private.

"I speak the truths of She of the Five." Revelate Brotsge nodded to her. "And I apologize for speaking to you so rudely, m'Dame. I only wanted you to listen."

Renard sighed in relief. He slouched back.

Micha bowed to the revelate, the deep bow of equals. "Your apology is accepted, Revelate. Vasella was a devout man in his own way, and we of the Legion knew he would want the blessing of She of the Five. But he also believed that She meant for us to be more than chattel, that She didn't want the lassari to vanish like Her ippicators. The guilded kin would like us to be content with the belief that we will someday be kin ourselves. They hope that will keep us in line, underneath them. And we *will* be kin, Revelate: we of the Hag's Legion have pledged that. But we won't receive recognition by being docile and waiting for that eventual reward."

"My dear child," Brotsge began—not an insult, but merely the perception of the elderly toward the younger.

Still, it caused Micha to toss her head back. She laughed, loudly, almost joyously.

"We're not children, Revelate. None of us. We lost our innocence a long time ago, in the blood the Li-Gallant, the Hoorka, and all the kin have taken from us."

"I know that this man's death"—Brotsge indicated the bier with a grandiose gesture—"has bereaved you greatly."

Micha smiled. "You'll never suspect what his death means to us, Revelate."

"Let us mourn him, then, m'Dame. Calmly, and without rage, as She of the Five would wish it."

"His whole life was rage, Revelate," Micha persisted. "He wanted a revelate's blessing to take with him to the Hag. That's all."

"He has that," Brotsge growled. He gripped the flask of

holy water tightly, then seemed to realize for the first time that he was still holding it. He placed it back on the acolyte's tray. "I've given him that blessing."

"Then," Micha said, "we will take him."

At her signal, the Hag's Legion stood and came forward, ignoring Brotsge's protests. They took hold of the bier, lifting it to their shoulders. Petals of flowers littered the floor in a slow, bright rain. Brotsge, shouting, grasped at Alex's arm, next to Renard. Alex grinned at the revelate as if amused and, with a shrugging motion, flung Brotsge aside. The acolyte, with a cry, abandoned his tray and clutched at the falling revelate's robes. He did little good. Brotsge struck the floor hard, his head thudding against tile. The boy shrieked in fear; Brotsge—echoed by the sound system— howled in pain. "You can't do this," he screamed, holding his head. Bright, thick blood welled between his fingers. "You make a mockery of my church."

Renard, adjusting the weight of the bier on his shoulder, glanced down at the man, at the boy holding him and attempting to stanch the flow of blood with his surplice. "You're exactly right, Revelate Brotsge." With his free hand, he placed the hood over his head. His voice muffled, he continued. "And we'll continue to do so as long as the churches serve the guilded kin and not those who need comfort the most." Renard's eyes, cold and unsympathetic, stared from the ragged holes in the hood. "You've given Urbana his blessing. That was all we required of you."

The bier lurched forward, Renard moving with it, his attention leaving the plight of the old man. Moving slowly, they stepped down into the main aisle and were immediately surrounded. The church was noisy and chaotic now; shouting faces, sweat-slick brows, raised hands. A rock arced over Renard's head and the bier; behind him, he heard a crack as the missile struck the animo of She of the Five, then the bright clatter of shattered glass striking the floor. Around him, people cheered, jostling him. He grinned, the dangerous excitement of the crowd filling him with energy. A man near him shouted: "Down with kin!" Renard shouted back in kind, gleeful. The bier seemed very light; those nearest were reaching out to aid the Legion bearers. Above Renard, the bier rode like a raft on an uneasy, living sea. Someone ahead of them thrust open the doors to the church—they slammed back against their supports, askew; behind, to the side, there were more sounds of destruction, glass breaking, wood splintering. Renard could feel the chill touch of outside air.

Clamorous, moving; the crowd spilled from the church, down the wide steps to the street. As they came out into the night, into the soft illumination of the hoverlamps, Renard could see the squad of guards, still watching from across the way. They looked worried. Their hands stayed close to the handles of their crowd-prods, and one fidgeted nervously with a relay button on his lapel. The bier tilted dangerously as they came down the steps, and Renard had to give all his attention to the unseen footing beneath him. When he could look up again, he could see very little above the bobbing, restless sea of heads on every side of him. It didn't matter. Events had, so for, gone the way he'd planned. He knew what would happen, knew what *must* happen.

He waited for the first sounds of chaos.

Afterward, descriptions of the events (and, of course, the official assignment of the blame for the incident) would vary according to the sources consulted. The Hag's Legion would hold that one of Vingi's guards struck the actual first blow. The Li-Gallant's Domoraj, before the interrogators of the Neweden press, would just as vehemently contend that it was a vile lassari who first made the confrontation a physical one.

Neither side would deny that what precipitated the fray was a photodot. One of the guards raised a camera to record the scene—all agreed on that point. Certainly the lassari were quite sensitive toward Vingi's interest in Vasella and the Hag's Legion, and especially the mysterious figure of their leader, Renard, who was rumored to have attended the funeral. Certainly (as well), the lassari were in a foul, bitter, and angry mood, especially concerning full kin. And (certainly) they felt the security of numbers, the pressure of their peers, no matter how well-armed the guards. There were a few hundred of the lassari mob, only twenty of the guards: ten-to-one odds tend to make even the most cowardly people brave.

Whatever.

Within a few moments of the photodot being taken, a

melee had begun between the guards and the mourners around the bier. The guards reacted with the ingrained ferocity of guilded kin toward the social canaille: they fought viciously, with all the power at their command, and without restraint. That only incited the lassari further, fueling their anger.

The first sound Renard heard was the cough of a sting at close range, followed by a mass wailing as the crowd-creature of lassari shouted alarm and pain. People bucked back against the Legion members, the bier tossing alarmingly. Renard screamed at them to back away. "Put the bier down! Gently, gently—and get the hoods off. They only mark you now."

Micha was shoved up against him. He grabbed at her sleeve, and she twisted to hug him quickly, her face a mixture of fear and pleasure. "It's going as you said it would." Someone ran past them, yelling wordlessly, blundering into the bier. Alex, cursing, pulled the man free.

"We have to get ourselves out now," Renard answered Micha. He could not keep a quick smile from his face. The night was loud around them, alive with pain and fright. "Tell the others to leave. Go separately, then stay in hiding for the next few days. I'm going to stay here for a few minutes, then go myself. Move!"

"Not without a kiss."

"If this excites you, m'Dame, then you're a disgusting creature." But he smiled again as he said it.

"I'm disgusting."

He kissed her, quickly, roughly, then thrust her away. "Now, get moving."

"I'm gone." She laughed back at him, her eyes crinkling in delight. "I hope Vasella doesn't mind being left here."

"He's being comforted by the Hag. He doesn't care. Now, will you *go.*"

She left him without another word, slipping her way through the pushing, milling throngs. Vasella's flowers were being trampled underneath; the shroud had slipped to reveal the face of the corpse, shining with the funeral oils for the cremation. Renard nodded to Vasella's body and moved away, back to the steps of the church where he could survey the scene.

The fighting had spread, the nucleus of the conflict still

in the streets. At least two of the guards were down, dozens of lassari lay still on the pavement. It was no longer simply lassari against kin—it was riot. On the opposite side of the street, Renard could see a knot of people around a storefront. The holo-display had been shattered, looters moved through the wreckage. A sting spat once, then again—screams came from around a corner of the church. Renard ducked behind a pillar. A group of lassari came running up the steps toward him. They flung some noisome, pungent liquid in a bottle at the broken doors of the church. Glass splintered, the liquid splashed. Renard, suddenly frightened, ran, as a crude torch, flame guttering, was tossed into the spreading pool. The front of the building exploded with light and heat, bright searing flame. Smoke roiled up, billowing, hiding the moons. Over the roofs of the nearest houses, Renard could see the flashing strobes of approaching cruisers. Reinforcements had been summoned.

Renard wiped at his pants—some of the oil had splashed onto him. He no longer wanted to stay: this mess would continue just as well without him. He made his way around the church and into the warren of dark streets.

The mob howled at his back. Sirens shrilled in answer.

"Damn you, Santos, I can't believe you just sat here and watched this without waking me."

D'Embry was furious, and fury made her weak. The symbiote wriggled on her back, restless, no doubt pumping sympathetic chemicals into her to leech that rage, and she wanted none of the parasite's solace. Not now, not when the screen of the com-unit showed her Dasta Burrough in flames, not when she could look out her office window and see the smudge of smoke in the sky and the distant smear of erratic light.

McClannan was at the window now, gazing out. He turned to face d'Embry, who sat in her usual floater. "Regent," he said far too calmly, "I contacted the Li-Gallant's office. No one there wanted our assistance in any way, not even our fire-fighting apparatus. That ties our hands—we aren't allowed to interfere in local affairs without the Li-Gallant's explicit permission. We didn't have it, so I saw no reason to rouse you from a comfortable bed."

He seemed eminently logical. He looked handsomely innocent. He even smiled, an offer of reconciliation. She despised his easy manner. "I don't believe this," she said again. Yellow fire spat at the viewscreen, and glowing sparks coiled heavenward. "Death and destruction on this scale hasn't been seen here since that typhoon six standards ago. There's a small-scale battle being fought between lassari and kin, and *you* didn't think it warranted awakening me." She let sarcastic amusement lash at him, a bitter marveling at his stupidity. "McClannan, my dear Seneschal, what *would* impel you to get me out of bed? Does Diplo Center have to burn first? And wherever did you get the idea that you were competent to make *any* kind of decision?"

McClannan's face took on a pained expression. It still looked like a regal mask. "I'm sorry you feel that way, Regent. Believe me, I only had your comfort and well-being in mind."

"I don't want comfort!" She shouted the words, and the effort reminded her that, indeed, she was still tired and that it was early in the morning. She sagged back in her seat, mindful of the hump of the symbiote on her shoulders. She put her hand on her forehead, her elbows on the padded arms of the chair. She closed her eyes and concentrated on breathing.

"Get me the Li-Gallant," she said wearily. "Not his office, not some damn underling, but Vingi himself."

"Regent—"

"Do it." She didn't have the strength to do more than whisper the words. *Come on, parasite. Do your job and give me some help.* She could feel its faint movements, could—somewhere under the surface of her consciousness—feel its presence, tandem with her own. A soothing coolness spread through her chest; she could breathe without pain. She kept her eyes closed. In the background, she could hear McClannan fidgeting with her com-unit, then his low, too-pleasant voice speaking. Someone replied, he spoke again. D'Embry stopped listening, her attention on her body, on her breathing, on all the small pains that added up to a nagging uneasiness.

"Regent?"

Maybe it is getting to be time. Maybe this next visit, Aris wouldn't be just a pleasurable prison but a home.

"Regent?"

She started. The hands came slowly down to rest on her desk; she opened her eyes. "Yes?"

McClannan was staring at her quizzically. "The Li-Gallant will be on in a moment."

"How do I look, Santos?"

"Perhaps you'd want me to talk with him," he ventured softly. "You *do* look as if you've been awakened in a rush."

"Good. I'm ready, then, Seneschal."

The Li-Gallant looked almost jolly. He nodded at the screen and pursed thick lips at d'Embry. "You look tired, Regent. Surely a small problem such as a fire in Dasta hasn't kept you up? It's a task for the local government, neh?"

"Frankly, Li-Gallant, I slept through the beginning of it." —with a glance at McClannan— "I assume the initial problem was Vasella's funeral?"

Ponderously Vingi nodded. Behind him, d'Embry could see his office and the shadowy figures of his guild-kin bustling about. "That's not exactly a difficult supposition to make. Yah, it was Vasella's funeral. The lassari—unprovoked, I might add—attacked the guards I'd sent there to protect those very same lassari from any harassment. But then, you can't teach gratitude to the lassari, Regent; they'll just turn and bite you."

"How many of them did you have to kill for their ingratitude, Li-Gallant?"

Vingi nearly smiled. "I see that your lack of sleep hasn't blunted your tongue, Regent. There *has* been some loss of life, I regret to say. Two of them were my kin." The Li-Gallant, abruptly, looked quickly and impossibly sad. It nearly made d'Embry laugh. For once, she was glad of the numbing effect of the symbiote.

"I'm sorry for your loss," she said. "But I pray that you haven't let it affect your judgment. You *are* dealing with the problem calmly, I trust."

"I want the people responsible for this outrage, Regent. The Hag's Legion, as you must know, are the ones to blame, not me."

"Still—"

"Your humanitarianism is well-known, Regent, if perhaps a trifle misplaced in this situation." A hand bright with rings came up to brush the Li-Gallant's hair back from his forehead. "And, in any case, at this moment my people are doing very little."

"You can't just let Dasta burn, Li-Gallant." Anger and dread rose in d'Embry's throat. Adrenaline banished fatigue. "I won't let you do that. We have both the equipment and the people to work it here in the Center. I'll send them down."

"That won't be necessary, Regent." Again, Vingi smiled. "I've already received another offer of assistance, and I've accepted it."

"And whose might that be?"

"Sula Hermond of the Traders, Regent. He and his Trader-Hoorka. They've offered to secure the area, snare any of the rioters they find, and be certain that the fires are contained."

"Traders? Gods, Li-Gallant, Hermond was *kin.* He'll kill them . . ."

"Just as I would?" Vingi finished the sentence for her. "You forget, Regent, that I've decided that I like the New-eden Hoorka. Maybe Hermond's people will be just as helpful to me, neh?"

A vague burning knotted d'Embry's stomach. She clenched her teeth against it. Her breath was shallow and unsatisfying again. "Li-Gallant—"

"M'Dame, why do you persist in trying to do my job as well as your own? I've given Sula Hermond the task, not your Diplos; we'll see how well he does. Without interference."

"You're indeed right, Li-Gallant. We *will* see. I hope for his sake that I enjoy the scene. Good morning to you, Li-Gallant."

With a feeling of childish glee, she slapped the disconnect contact. The Li-Gallant's startled face faded into darkness. D'Embry rose slowly and walked hesitantly over to the window. She leaned there, hands against the sill. Smoke was light against the backdrop of the night sky. It threw a pall over the city-glow of Sterka. "Santos, get a flitter readied. We're going to Dasta."

"Now, Regent?"

"Now."

"Regent, please, the exertion . . ."

"It won't kill me, Santos. And if it does, you can bungle the regency to the best of your ability. Get the flitter, Seneschal."

"I just don't see—"

"I know you don't. Get the flitter."

She remained silent to the rest of his protestations. Finally, with a sigh of resignation, he called for the vehicle.

"Hey, Gyll! Enemy approaching behind us."

Helgin shouted loudly enough that d'Embry and McClannan heard the bellow. The Motsognir swung off his perch on an overturned flitter and strode toward the bank of screens where Gyll stood. Gyll glanced up, startled, then laughed when he saw the Regent and her Seneschal making their way toward him, flanked by Trader-Hoorka guards. "Damn it, dwarf," he said. "You had me thinking there was a horde of lassari bearing down on us."

"Lassari you could handle. The Regent's more trouble than that." Then the Motsognir bowed low to the approaching d'Embry. "Good morning, Regent. Out for a stroll? A little too warm for Neweden, don't you think?"

D'Embry didn't appear to be amused. Her face was pinched, drawn. She frowned, and her walk was stooped and halting. Gyll stepped forward to greet her, dismissing the escorts with a hand signal. The Hoorka nodded to him and walked away. "Regent, Seneschal," he said, bowing. "I can only assume that you've talked to the Li-Gallant."

"You're quite right, Sula." D'Embry's voice was husky. Gyll had never heard her sound so weak or tired. "It worried me enough that I felt I had to come here."

"What would you like to see first?" Helgin had taken a seat on one of the consoles. LEDs flickered angrily under him. "The torturing of the prisoners, the maiming of children, or the despoiling of the dead?" He grinned.

Gyll glared at the Motsognir, who shrugged, then turned back to the Regent. "You're welcome to look, as long as you stay out of the way of my people." He gestured widely to indicate the area. They were set up in the middle of Charing Cross, a main intersection just outside Dasta. A bank of five large screens stood in an arc before them, each displaying a different scene. Before the screens was a maze of wiring and the bulwarks of the consoles. Several people in the uniform of the Trader-Hoorka sat before them, intent. Hoverlamps, full open, bathed the area in brilliance, making the darkness around them dense in contrast. Traders moved about, shouting, talking, rushing, but all with a sense of order, of studied calm. The stench of smoke was in the air, heavy and suffocating. Flames flailed at the sky far down the street. Just overhead, a firebus shrilled past; the wind of its passage buffeted them. Gyll did not speak until it had passed.

"What can I show you, Regent?"

"How many lassari have been killed?" If her voice was weak, her eyes were not. At her side, McClannan shifted uneasily. He seemed uncomfortable.

"Forty, possibly more," Gyll answered. "It's difficult to keep an accurate count in all this confusion, and there may well be bodies in some of the buildings that have burned and collapsed. We won't have any kind of accurate count until the fires are out and my people can get in there safely."

"How many will you kill before then?"

Gyll took a deep, hissing breath. Behind him, he heard the slap of Helgin's feet on the pavement as the dwarf jumped down from the console. "How many innocents has your Alliance killed, old woman?" the Motsognir thundered. "On Longago, on Heritage . . ." McClannan looked as if he were about to step up between d'Embry and the Traders. "Oh, good," Helgin said, now standing alongside Gyll. "That's it, McClannan. I'd love to splatter that noble beak all over your face."

"Helgin!" Gyll shouted. He placed a hand on the dwarf's shoulder. Helgin glowered, but subsided into low muttering. "Regent, before you start making remarks that make you sound like an idiot, please let me show you what we're doing. Make your judgments after you're aware of the facts."

D'Embry's face was more sour than before. She coughed suddenly, and Gyll realized that some of her evident irritation stemmed from the environment, that she was uncomfortable. The symbiote shivered under her tunic—the sight made Gyll slightly ill-at-ease himself. He wondered, again, how that would feel, to be linked with the parasite. D'Embry cleared her throat liquidly. "My pardon, Sula. Please conduct your tour—it seems that the Li-Gallant wants you in charge here."

"With good reason," Helgin commented.

If d'Embry heard, she made no answer. Gyll led them forward into the glare of the hoverlamps. "The fire's starting to come under control," he said, gesturing at one of the screens. A firebus hovered in the midst of flame and smoke, a demon from hell; as they watched, it loosed a cloud of its own that fell into the inferno. The fire gouted, then began to subside. "A flame inhibitor we've developed, Regent. We've sold it to several of the Alliance governments. We could have stopped a lot of this destruction if the Li-Gallant had called us in earlier. Several blocks of Dasta will be leveled, but it won't spread further. My Hoorka made a sweep of the critical areas first—we've set up aid stations for those burnt out of their homes. We're not killing *them,* Regent."

He didn't give her time to reply. He swiveled, pointed at another of the displays. "There's still some minor skirmishing going on with lassari rioters, but it's all disorganized and scattered now." The screen looked down on a filthy, wreckage-strewn lane. Several men and women, lassari or low kin by their clothing, were running from a phalanx of Trader-Hoorka. The group halted suddenly in mid-flight as another squad of the Hoorka turned a corner before them. Tangle-foot bombs went off; the lassari fell in a writhing, fouled heap. Gyll's people, using neutralizing sprays carefully, separated them one at a time and led the lassari away. "We'll be taking them to the building just to your left. Some of the Li-Gallant's guards are there, and the captives are checked against a master file of known insurgents. If they aren't matched, and if we've no actual evidence of any unlawful acts, they're taken to one of the aid stations. If they *do* match . . ." Gyll shrugged. "Vingi's people are in charge past there. They take them, and if you've a quarrel with that, talk to the Li-Gallant. Neweden has its own legal codes, after all. But no one's being killed here, and none of the Trader personnel are doing harm to anyone unless we're attacked first. I'm not going to lose *any* of my people if it can be avoided, Regent, but I'm also not starting a vendetta against the lassari."

Gyll turned away from the screens. A woman hurried over to him, said something to Gyll in a low tone. He answered her, slowly, quietly. She left. Gyll stared at d'Embry.

"And unless I'm mistaken, Regent, I'm owed an apology."

D'Embry gazed at the bank of screens, at the rush of

people, at the dwindling shroud of smoke. She seemed to breathe too quickly, but she nodded. "You have it, Sula. I spoke far too hastily. All I can say is that Neweden does that to a person."

"Oh, hooray," Helgin said without inflection or excitement. D'Embry's sharp stare flickered over the dwarf. "That's a *good* look," Helgin remarked, hands on hips. "I'd be quaking in my boots if I were wearing them. Keep working on it." He flexed his toes on the pavement. They cracked.

Unexpectedly, d'Embry smiled, even as McClannan scowled. She laughed. "Sula, Motsognir, you don't know how *relieved* I am to see this. I expected . . . Well, let it go. You're going to cause me royal headaches with the Li-Gallant because of your damned efficiency, but at the moment I don't care." She laughed again. McClannan stared at her in amazement. "I really don't care," she repeated, shaking her head.

"Regent, perhaps we'd better leave. The Sula is busy here, and tomorrow's schedule's rather hectic." McClannan came out of his stunned silence, bending over d'Embry like a solicitous nursemaid. Gyll thought for a moment that she would snarl at him, but she glanced at the man with an odd tolerance. *The symbiote, some sedative it put in her? Everyone knows she can't stand McClannan. Or is she truly pleased with what she sees here?*

"All right, Santos," she said. "We'll leave the Sula to his duties. But let me first ask if you, Sula (and Sirrah Motsognir as well), would dine with me. I'll be having a supper with the Li-Gallant in a few weeks."

Startled, Gyll still managed to smile and bow. "Certainly, Regent."

"Well, then, we'll leave you to your tasks." She turned to go, always slowly, stooped under the hump of the symbiote. Two Oldin guards materialized to escort them back to their flitter. Gyll watched them disappear in the smoky night.

He turned back to find Helgin grinning up at him. "I'm really a charmer, neh?" the dwarf said. "She didn't know what hit her."

It was nearly dawn before they'd finished. The sunstar's rising made Gyll feel strange, as he'd not felt since returning to Neweden. False dawn chased the stars, and memories came with the light. They were not all pleasant.

The streets were empty. Most of the onlookers had left far earlier, after the worst of the fires had been dealt with — there is only so much crowd appeal in ash and soot. Only the Trader-Hoorka were left, disassembling the portable screens, coiling wires, packing equipment into padded boxes. Only one screen was left untouched, a small one with a privacy shield set to either side. Gyll stood before it. The view was not of Dasta Burrough, not desolate ruins and scorched rubble, but a green-cloaked peak, the sunstar just now touching the summit. As Gyll watched, a fume of dark smoke came from a hidden vent near the peak's jagged top. It rose straight in the air, spiraling, puffing; then a breeze snatched it, smearing it eastward. There was nothing else to see: no people, no wildlife, no flame. Just the slow pulsing of the dark cloud from the trees. Gyll sighed.

"That's near Underasgard." The voice came from behind him. Helgin.

Gyll turned. The Motsognir stood between the privacy shields. He looked tired; his broad shoulders slumped and he rubbed at one bloodshot eye. "Yah," Gyll replied. "The peak is Caladriel, above the Chamber of the Dead. There's a natural chimney leading down into the caverns. That's where we burned our kin."

"There's smoke now."

"I know." Gyll shook his head. "I almost feel like I should be there."

"Why? Because you're on Neweden again? Come on, Gyll; you've missed a lot of funerals since you left."

A smile touched Gyll's lips, and left quickly. "I know that, too. Valdisa reminded me of it. Not very gently, either. And you're right, Helgin. It's been a long night, neh? Let's get back to *Goshawk* and get rid of the stench. Fischer can finish up here."

"Sounds fine. We smell like the guests of honor at a barbecue, and it's going to take more than one drink to get rid of the smoke in my throat."

They walked away. At the opening of the shields, just before they went out into sunlight, Gyll glanced back at the screen.

Snagged in trees, a fume of woodsmoke sagged against the sunrise.

Chapter 5

THE VICTIM WAS KIRLLIA MECHEM, temple harlot for the Church of Bazlot in Henima, halfway across Neweden from Underasgard. Bazlot was a minor demigod in the Neweden pantheon; most of the Hoorka knew little about Him except for His existence, though Steban ventured that he thought Bazlot was the god of cloth-dyers. None of the kin knew why a god of cloth-dyers would need a temple harlot, but the speculation was varied and amusing. It seemed that Kirllia had somehow contrived to blackmail one of the priests of the temple. She'd been clumsy; the revelate was not inclined to take the punishment into his own hands or to go through the authorities. "Let Bazlot decide through Dame Fate," he'd said. "She's not worth the money for your contract, but the church has it and it saves me trouble. If she lives, she'll be more docile, and, who knows, it may be good sport."

Valdisa had found that she did not care for the man at all, but that was not a matter for Hoorka. They needed the money. She'd taken the money and swallowed her misgivings. She sent the apprentices.

The alternatives had been offered—Kirllia had no wealth of her own, and Bazlot's revelate forbade any church member to lend her funds. She would run. Watch was set, and the full kin readied.

Serita Iduna did not care for her partner. Meka Joh was new to full kinship; he'd been a low apprentice when Ulthane Gyll had left the Hoorka. Joh was competent enough, Serita admitted, but there was an eagerness to him when he was working a contract, an enthusiasm that bothered her deeply. It wasn't present when he practiced—he was rather far down on the unofficial rankings of practice matches—but Joh became animated and excited with a contract. There were others in the Hoorka like him: blood excited them, the thrill of the hunt coupled with a modicum of danger gave them a pleasure akin to sexual arousal. Serita avoided Joh and those kin he emulated, and she disliked being paired with him. Serita looked across at Joh's sharp profile as they circled Henima, preparatory to landing. He was leaning forward, his nose just touching the flitter's window, peering down at the small city anxiously. He seemed to notice Serita's stare; he pulled back and smiled as the craft banked and descended. "Should be fun, Serita. I've never run anyone in Henima before. Have you?"

"No," she said, simply. She moved her gaze away, glancing at the windshield as they landed near the Church of Bazlot. The overhead rotors churned air.

"I took a glance at the maps before we left. There's quite a large lassari sector here. The revelate and his people are half-lassari anyway. My bet is she'll hole up with someone from the church."

"Could be." *Shut up, shut up. Why couldn't it have been McWilms or Bachier, somebody I like?*

"You're awfully quiet. Not feeling well? We could still call Underasgard and tell the Thane—"

"No," Serita interrupted. "I'm fine. Let's just get this over with, Meka."

His face brightened slightly at that. He swung his door open; the cool air of Henima, far north of the equator, lashed at them. Serita pulled up the hood of her nightcloak. Even the presence of the sunstar, high in a thin net of clouds, didn't seem to affect the chill. Serita shivered.

An apprentice met them before they reached the church. "Easy one, this woman," the apprentice—a boy by the name of Relka—said. He was a tall and lanky youth, cocky and sure of himself; too much like Meka Joh, to Serita's mind. He laughed. "She's unarmed, unshielded, and running. You'll have the hunt of the knives; a quick one, at that. She's slow and she's stupid. Go down this street to the first corner, turn left. Mala should be there to meet you and point out the victim. When I left her, the idiot was in a market, trying to pretend that she was just one of the locals, shopping."

"Good job, Relka," Meka said. He slapped the boy on the shoulder. "Head for the flitter, then. Felling's got a stew packed in for you."

Serita merely nodded to the apprentice as he passed her. He shrugged at her silence and left them. The two Hoorka followed his direction. In the daylight, the city was dingy and active; mostly low houses huddled close together as if for warmth against the northern breezes. The Church of Baz-lot stooped over them like a stern parent. A persistent wind shuffled papers in the gutters. The people milling about gave the Hoorka their customary wide berth, caution due them for their reputation. There were unguarded sour stares from the men huddled around small fires on the porch steps; long assessing glares from women leaning, elbows on sills, from the grimy windows. It was like any poor district they'd seen before, but there was nothing to balance the image. They saw the busy, noisy filth, and they saw the whole of Henima. "Worse than Dasta before it burned," Meka commented as they walked. "And damned colder."

Mala waved at them as the Hoorka entered an open square crowded with shoppers and tiny stalls crammed with produce. The open market was loud, chaotic, and filled with smells. The Hoorka went to the apprentice, and found themselves standing in an inviolate circle around which all passersby moved, scowling but unwilling to risk the anger of Hoorka. Mala shook her head. "They hate us," she said, holding out her cloak so both Hoorka could see the purple stain spreading over the cloth. "A rotten sweetrind—someone threw it at my back. Just be glad you'll get out of here quickly. The woman's down this row, the second one over. She's wearing a blue scarf on her head, and a dragon-patterned tunic. Can't miss her; she looks absolutely terrified. She'd never have made it as an actress."

"It's really going to be that easy?" Meka Joh looked disappointed; that disturbed Serita more than her kin-brother's previous eagerness.

"Let me take her, then, if it's not interesting enough for you," she said, more sharply than she'd intended. Joh glanced at her strangely.

"You're the elder, Serita. You rule the contract, not me. Tell me how you want it done."

Serita shrugged. A gust of wind made her squint, threw

dust from the street into her eyes and flapped the canvas tops of the stalls. She stared at the passing crowds—*they know we're on a contract, and they wonder who we hunt. And they hate, even if they say nothing and are careful not to offend.* "Go around to the end of the row she's in—I'll give you a minute or so to get there, and then we'll work in toward her. You know the woman's face?"

"I'll recognize her. There won't be a mistake."

"Good. Mala, you can go back to the flitter. You've done well, girl. Our thanks." Mala nodded to the Hoorka and moved away. Joh, after another glance at Serita's noncommittal face, swiveled on his toes and strode off. People bumped and shoved each other to get out of his path.

Serita was left alone in the circle of fear. Now they stared at her, the hateful eyes; wondering, cautious. She tugged at the collar of her nightcloak, trying to bring the hood farther over her face. Only her eyes could be seen. She reached for her belt, felt the comforting, worn hilt of her vibro. The gesture made the watchers stumble back, and when she strode forward, a path cleared for her. No one spoke; her silence was herald enough. All would leave off haggling to watch her pass, holding a forgotten melon or swatch of cloth. The strident cries of the vendors trailed off in mid-pitch. *Hoorka.* Serita heard the word: a curse, a whisper. They crowded again behind her, spectators now at this deadly amusement. She could feel them pressing at her back, filling the lane between the stalls. *Hoorka.* They might hate, but they would watch, would feed on the death.

Serita returned their hate.

The crowd parted before her. Serita saw the woman a fraction of a second before the victim noticed the Hoorka. She was indeed painfully obvious, her gaze never resting, never stopping to examine the wares around her. When that wandering glance found the assassins and saw Serita staring, her face paled, and Serita could hear the intake of breath. Far too late, Kirllia noticed that everyone had stepped back from her, leaving her and the Hoorka in the center of the lane. She tried to follow the crowd's example belatedly, clumsily, half-stumbling. Serita halted, waiting. She pulled again at the nightcloak's collar.

"Kirllia Mechem, your life is claimed by Hag Death and

She of the Five," Serita said, her voice low and soft. Kirllia's eyes closed; she moaned. Serita thought she might fall.

Then, abruptly, Kirllia slashed out at those next to her with hands curled into claws. She ran, but she did not go far. A few meters down the way stood Joh. Kirllia was trapped in a narrow tunnel walled with people, death at either end. A high wailing escaped her clenched lips.

"That's it, woman. Run right to me." Joh's vibro flickered from its sheath, its throaty growling loud. "Let's see if you can get past me."

"Meka!" Serita took a step toward the woman. She glared at Joh, then back to Kirllia. "There are other ways of death," she said. "We have a capsule that will bring you laughter and sleep. This doesn't need to be painful if you don't resist. But my kin-brother is right; you can't escape us." Closer, always closer. One step, another. The crowd watched, rapt, silent.

"No . . ."

Step. "You can't deny the Hag with words, Kirllia." Step. "She won't listen, or She'll make it more difficult for you."

"Let her run to me, Serita," Joh said loudly. "Why waste an expensive capsule on *this?*"

The sneer in his voice was entirely too audible. With Joh's words, several things happened at once. Serita began to speak—angry words—but someone in the crowd acted first. A frozen puffindle from the fishmonger's stand arced toward Joh's back. The Hoorka, with preternatural awareness, seemed to sense the missile; he ducked, and the puffindle struck ground. Kirllia was already moving, trying to make her way past the crouching Joh into the mass of people. It was a foolish move. Joh tripped her with an outthrust leg and, in nearly the same motion, brought his vibro down and over in a slicing motion. Kirllia died with the sudden screams of the crowd. Blood splashed and seeped into the dirt between the stalls.

Joh ignored the body. As Serita ran toward him, he picked up the puffindle and brandished it before the faces near him. "Who's the coward that threw this? Will he stand up and admit it, or is he the typical lassari?" Joh used the impersonal mode scathingly, his gaze raking the spectators. His vibro gleamed red; a droplet shivered on its tip.

"Meka . . ." Serita said warningly. She knelt beside Kirllia; the woman was dead. She made the sign of the star over the body.

"I didn't throw it, Hoorka," a man said. He pushed his way to the front of the crowd, a burly, tall lassari with close-cropped hair and an ugly, pocked face. "But I might've, if it had been closer to me. What of it, neh? What's wrong with giving the woman a chance?"

"You interfere with Hoorka, man, and you risk your own life."

"Insult lassari as you do, and you risk yours, as well. Look around you, assassin; how many of us are there? And there's only two of you, and all you have are vibros—a stick might serve as well, neh? I mean no insult"—the man's voice bordered on sarcasm—"but you might consider where you are before you open that stinking mouth of yours again."

Serita did not let Joh reply. She felt suddenly cold and frightened. *"Meka,"* she said, sharply. The Hoorka stared at the lassari. His hand twitched around the vibro hilt; Serita could see muscles bunching in his forearm, and she thought he would cut at the man. *"Meka,"* she shouted again. "I need your help wrapping the body."

Joh stood motionless; then, angrily, he flung the puffindle back to the ground. His vibro flicked off and he shoved it into his sheath. He stalked over to Serita as the crowd watched, as the tall lassari chuckled deep in his throat. The Hoorka began wrapping the body in a spare nightcloak.

"If you *ever* behave like that on a contract again, I'll see you flayed before all the kin, Meka," Serita whispered harshly as they worked. "Believe me, kin-brother, the Thane will be told of this. Your silly theatrics could get us both killed. I won't have it. Not again. You insult the victim, her people, and Hoorka with your attitude."

His eyes narrowed dangerously, but his voice was soft. "Why, kin-sister, one might almost think you *like* these scum."

"They're people. Like you or I might have been. Give it a thought, Meka. Maybe She of the Five will see that you come back as the lowest lassari scum yourself."

"I'd still like to knock that bastard's laughter down his throat, along with his teeth. He's still there, still watching us."

"All it would prove is that you're a stupid fool who courts the Hag."

"I won't take *your* insults either, Serita." His voice was still soft. "I'll call for first blood on the practice floor in satisfaction."

"You've got it, then. First blood, Meka, when we get back. And I hope you enjoy being cut." Serita stood, wiping her hands together. The crowd had thinned, going back to the day's tasks, but the lassari man still watched, leaning against a corner of a nearby stall. He smiled, gap-toothed, at Serita. She gave him the barest of nods in acknowledgment. "Let's get this body back to the revelate, then," she said. "Afterward, we'll settle our differences."

Gyll thought he recognized him. Taller, yes; a man, not a boy anymore, changed. But the face, the walk . . . "McWilms?" he called. "Jeriad?"

The man across the street, in the sable-and-gray night-cloak of the Hoorka, turned at the sound of the name. The face went from aloof neutrality to a shocked smile. "Ulthane? I'll be damned . . ."

Laughing, they embraced in the middle of the street. Those around them stared curiously: the Hoorka never show affection, never smile except at death; conversations that night would be preceded by "You'd never believe what I saw today . . ." Gyll held McWilms at arm's length, studying him and shaking his head. "Look at you, boy. When I saw you last, your face was a wreck, and this arm was gone. They did a fine job on you. Gods, that's good to see."

"And you, Ulthane. The standards haven't touched you. In fact, you look better than my memory of you. I'll bet you could still show me some tricks with the vibrofoil."

They grinned at each other, hugging once again. For a moment, there was some awkwardness. Gyll did not know what to say, or rather, there were too many topics from which to choose; McWilms seemed to revert to the shyness of his apprenticehood. Finally Gyll pointed at a tavern just down the street. "A drink, Jeriad?" Gyll shrugged away the remembrance of Valdisa's warning—*stay away from the kin, Gyll.* He'd not sought out McWilms; it was simply chance. Dame Fate laughing. And if the Dame wanted them to meet, who was he to gainsay Her? Jeriad, for his part, seemed to be at ease. If Valdisa didn't want Gyll consorting with his former kin, she evidently hadn't told the Hoorka. Jeriad nodded at Gyll's suggestion, and glanced up at the sunstar, just rising above the spires of Tri-Guild Church, a few blocks away.

"I've some time," he said. "Why not? A good cup of mulled wine would take the chill out of me."

The inn was one of the fancier ones in Sterka, holding an eternal twilight behind cut-glass doors and maroon curtains. They took a booth toward the back, both pretending to ignore the gawking of the patrons. Gyll eased himself behind a plastic table masquerading as malawood; Jeriad sat across from him. Gyll shook his head at the man. "I can't believe it, Jeriad. You look *good,* my friend. It must have been a rough few standards after the accident."

McWilms shrugged. He toyed with a napkin. "It took some time, yah. But it wasn't that difficult or painful. The kin could afford the treatments then, even if the Regent hadn't picked up the bills. It wouldn't be so lucky for an apprentice now." He looked up, and his smoky eyes were troubled.

Gyll frowned. "I've heard rumors to that effect, and Valdisa hinted at it when I talked to her in Underasgard."

"That *was* you, then, that caused all the commotion. Valdisa wouldn't talk about it afterward, but all the older kin said it had to be you, or the Thane wouldn't have been so upset. She really laid into the entrance guards." Jeriad smiled.

"Are things really that bad, Jeriad?"

McWilms's smile faded as quickly as it had come. His gaze dropped back to the napkin wrapped in his fingers. "I shouldn't complain, I suppose. But, yah, the contracts have gotten scarce, and most of them we do get are the Li-Gallant's. We haven't been offworld since Heritage. Our equipment suffers most of all. The flitters are old and eating into the treasury with repairs—we only have two that are at all reliable. The bodyshields"—Gyll saw a shadow of pain cross McWilms's face—"are in poor shape. I'm convinced they cost Ric's life on our last contract."

"I saw the smoke of the funeral. I didn't know who … D'Mannberg's gone to the Hag?" Gyll asked softly. "I'm very sorry to hear that."

"He was my kin-father. I guess you wouldn't have known that; my initiation came after you left. He gave me the rites, sponsored me." He'd dropped the mangled napkin. He rubbed at his right arm—the budded one—as if it pained him, as if some vestige of the former hurt lurked there.

"I'm sorry, Jeriad." Gyll reached out to touch McWilms's right hand, still on the table.

McWilms gave him a wan smile. "We all knew about the shields, Ulthane. It's no one's fault really; we knew their limitations, and Ric and I should have been more careful, neh? Thane Valdisa would have had them repaired if she could. It's ironic; with the money from that contract, she *did* have two of them fixed." With a visible effort, McWilms shook off his mood. He pulled his hand back, sat back against the wall of the booth. "How about the drink, neh? On me."

"After that tale? I've got all of the Oldins' money to spend, Jeriad. I'll waste some of it here."

Gyll looked up—the innkeeper seemed to be engrossed in a conversation at the bar, but he was not looking at the woman with whom he talked. His attention wandered everywhere but in their direction. He would not look at Gyll. The woman placed money on the bar and left, following another couple out the ornate doors. Gyll noticed for the first time that most of the patrons seemed to have departed—the inn was nearly empty now. The innkeeper finally glanced their way, an unhappy look in his eyes. Gyll waggled a finger to attract his attention. "Two mulled wines, if you please, sirrah." The innkeeper nodded.

The wine arrived a few minutes later. The innkeeper was ill-at-ease, serving them. Sweat dappled his generous brow. He wiped meaty hands on his apron. "We don't often see Hoorka in here," he said. His smile slipped in and out, uncertain, a false sun behind quickly moving clouds. "Can we expect to see more of your excellent kin in here in the future, sirrah?" He glanced from Gyll to Jeriad.

McWilms stared at Gyll for a long moment, but Gyll could not read his expression. Then the Hoorka glanced up at the innkeeper. "I doubt it, sirrah," he said with the exaggerated politeness of guilded kin. "I simply happened to see my friend here on the street. Your fine establishment was convenient and attracted us."

"Ahh, that's sad news." It hadn't seemed to make him excessively unhappy. The tentative smile almost broke into a full grin, and there was relief in his voice. "I'm glad you chose us for a quick refreshment, though." There was perhaps too much emphasis on the word "quick." Gyll would have spoken, but a glance from McWilms made him sit silently.

"We just wished to warm ourselves for a few minutes."

"Well, enjoy it, sirrahs." The man sauntered back to the bar. Halfway there, he began whistling.

They didn't say anything for a moment, hands around the warmth of the mugs. Gyll was taken aback by the innkeeper's unsubtle hints; McWilms seemed simply bemused.

"That sort of thing happen often?" Gyll asked.

McWilms nodded. "It was always there, Ulthane. Even when you were on Neweden last."

"Call me Gyll. I'm not Ulthane anymore."

"Gyll, then. You remember it—that vague hostility from the guilded kin. It's gotten worse. A lot worse, sometimes. Nobody's particularly overt, because the Hoorka are still feared, but they all know that we can barely lay claim to being high kin with our finances so tight. We couldn't afford the tithing for the last election, so no rule-guild represents us on Council this session. Not that that matters; most kin look on us as allied with the Li-Gallant's rule-guild. They won't do anything to disturb Vingi, but they don't like us." McWilms sipped his wine. "Try it, Gyll. It's pretty good."

"You don't want to talk about this?"

"*None* of the Hoorka would want to talk about it." He sipped again. "Sometimes I feel like we're on the down side of our evolution, like the Hoorka are going to be the lassari we once were."

"Because of your Thane and the way she's handling the guild?"

That brought up McWilms's head. He started to speak, then shook his head and started again. "Is that what you'd like to think, Gyll?"

"I'm trying not to think anything."

"It's not her fault. It's Neweden, and the way it's changed."

"Then maybe Hoorka should change."

"That's not what you used to say, is it?" Then McWilms gave a short chuckle. "Can we change the subject?—it depresses me. Tell me about the Family Oldin, Gyll. How do they function, what are you doing there, and who are these Trader-Hoorka I keep seeing around the port?"

"Thane Valdisa wouldn't want me to talk about them."

"She doesn't have to know." A pause. "Please, Gyll. I'm curious. It's been ages since I've heard from you, and you know about the kin. How about *you?*"

"All right," Gyll said. And he spoke.

"That was pretty good, Renard. Do you always burn down half a district to make your points? If so, remind me to stay out of the fire-insurance racket."

"How was I to know that the Li-Gallant'd respond so frigging slow? I know you, dwarf; you're not worried about all the innocent lives, are you?"

It was a squalid and dingy room hidden in a warren of dark streets and buildings deserted by all but the poorest. Of the two men, only Helgin could stand upright. The illumination was a candle set precariously on a rickety table. A mattress festooned with snarled bedsheets was in one corner. Helgin's bare feet scratched against the gritty dust of the floor. "Nice place you got here," the Motsognir said. "How much is the rent?"

"I'm only here for a few days—then we'll go back to the old place. I'd be interested to know how you found it, though."

"I followed my nose. That plant-pet of yours stinks, remember?"

Renard fondled the thick coil of the creature around his shoulders. He was sitting across the table from Helgin. Candlelight wavered across his face, glinting in his dark eyes. "Don't hide behind insults, Helgin. What's on your mind that you'd take the effort to find me? As I said, I doubt that you've been stricken with a conscience this late in your life."

Helgin shrugged. "You can't effect change without some harm. I just don't like seeing it done wholesale. You could have been more subtle, Renard."

"Is that you speaking, or FitzEvard Oldin?"

"Me." A throaty grumble.

"Then don't whine about my tactics, dwarf. I do what I feel I need to do. No more, no less, and *Oldin* pays me, not you."

"I'm FitzEvard's representative here."

"And that pet Sula of yours isn't, neh? Don't be upset; I know you have to show off for the Li-Gallant, don't you? You even got some of my people the other night—the ones I wanted you to get, of course, but enough to satisfy Vingi. I didn't mean for Dasta to burn, but I don't have a hell of a lot of control over a riot, do I?"

Helgin laughed. Renard continued to stroke his plant-pet, but slowly he smiled. "Oh, you deserve congratulations," Helgin said. "You've put the Sula in a good light. I just don't want you to overstep your bounds, to forget your role in this little drama. Don't get the feeling that you've got the leading part, Renard. Don't start thinking of yourself as powerful."

"You're too damned ugly for the star role yourself, Motsognir."

Helgin grinned. He got to his feet. "Don't make me angry, Renard. You *can* be replaced or eliminated altogether. It might even give me pleasure, if you goad me too much."

"I don't worry about your threats."

"I think you'd better." Helgin went to the door. Hand on the latch, he turned to look at Renard again. "Why is it we don't get along? It'd be a lot easier if we did. You could try being properly subservient."

"Get out of here, dwarf."

"No answer, then?"

"Out."

Helgin pulled the door open. Down a short corridor, sunlight gleamed through the uneven boards of another door. "Don't be too zealous, Renard. Oldin wants something left of Neweden."

"Don't trouble your tiny brain about it, Motsognir. Just get me the things I need."

"They're being prepared. You'll get them soon."

"See that I do. And if you're done giving me your shit, I'd appreciate the privacy."

Helgin looked about the room. "You could always raise mushrooms. They need a lot of shit, too." He laughed. Still chuckling, he went out.

*   *   *

"Well, Helgin? How did your meeting with that distributor go?"

They were back aboard *Goshawk,* in Gyll's cabin. Neweden wheeled below them, half-shadowed. Gyll cuddled his bumblewort in his lap, scratching its ear flaps gently. It hissed in contentment.

Helgin was staring at the dark world outside the port. "Well enough, I suppose," he said. "The man's a penurious sort, but I managed to get some business done. You want the details?"

"No," Gyll replied. "Just put them on the com-unit, and I'll go over it later." He glanced at the broad back of the Motsognir. "You seem distracted tonight, Helgin."

"Just tired. The gravity here pulls on me too much."

"You haven't insulted anyone in hours. You've been almost civil."

"Not funny, Gyll." Helgin turned. The dwarf, with the side-to-side walk of the Motsognir, came over to Gyll's chair. He reached out to pet the wort. It chirruped in ecstasy at the attention, rolling over heavily onto its back. Helgin kneaded the soft fur of its underbelly. "You took care of the tariffs for the last shipments?"

"Yah. And I met someone as well—Jeriad McWilms. You remember him? One of the apprentices—the one that was almost killed on Heritage."

"Not really."

Gyll glanced at the dwarf. He'd been joking, but there was a moodiness to the Motsognir that he'd never seen before. Helgin was quiet, laconic. He looked up at Gyll, noticing his stare, and his eyes were almost angry, the walnut pupils darkened almost to black. "Well, did you talk to him? Is that what you're waiting for me to ask? You want to brag because you were brave enough to ignore Valdisa's warning? How can I show you how impressed I am?"

Helgin pulled his hand away from the wort angrily. The animal screeched in protest at the roughness of the motion and jumped from Gyll's lap. It went to a corner of the room and curled up, keening softly to itself.

"Hey, Motsognir. Easy."

Helgin glowered at Gyll for a moment, unrepentant; then the rage seemed to leave him. He sighed deeply, rum-

bling an apology. "Sorry. I really am tired, Gyll. That's all.
Still not used to Neweden yet, neh?" He knuckled his eyes,
yawned widely. "What'd McWilms have to say? Evidently it
bothers you, or you wouldn't have brought it up."

"Are you just impressing me with your perception, or do
you really want to hear it?"

Despite his mood, Helgin grinned. "That sounds like one
of my lines. You've been working with me too long. Reverse
the two clauses, though; it works better."

Gyll smiled. "Yah?"

"You have to polish your insults. They don't just happen.
So . . . what did McWilms tell you?"

Gyll leaned back in his floater. He put his feet up on his
desk, clasped his hands behind his head. "What caught my
attention wasn't really anything he said, specifically. It was
the whole tone behind his words, coupled with what I've
seen and heard so far. I think I might hate the Hoorka, what
they've become. It bothers me to see them regarded as
Vingi's private assassins, to see them treated like low kin, to
see how poor they've become."

"Does that mean you'll be able to convince them to go
with us easily?"

Gyll frowned. "If it were just that, probably yes. But
Valdisa. . . she doesn't want me to get close to them—or
her—again. Today was just an accident, not a defiance. But
maybe that's what I should be: defiant. I don't know, Helgin.
I hate what I see."

"You can't do a damn thing about it," the dwarf grumbled. "You ain't Hoorka; not that kind, anyway."

"But I created them."

"And you feel responsible."

"I feel like I might want to destroy them."

"And who the hell are you, one of the gods? I think
you're being a trifle melodramatic, Gyll. Besides, you're
here to recruit the Hoorka. They might be a little irritated
if you start undermining them, and then FitzEvard would
be angry with *you*, and he can act like a god a damned sight
better than you." Helgin shook his head. "Better just to be
unemotional about it. Be silent and unmoved, like a rock.
Like me."

Gyll laughed, and his laughter had an edge. "You're no

rock, Motsognir. You just hide your sensitivity and pretend it doesn't exist. That rock of yours is only a stage prop."

Helgin snorted derision. The wort looked up, curious, from the corner. "I still wouldn't try kicking it, Gyll. You might break your foot."

Chapter 6

T HE STATE DINNER was held in an ornate hall near the main entrance of Diplo Center. The high walls displayed a shifting landscape of arid beauty, melding imperceptibly at the corners. Above, the ceiling was masked by blue-gray streaks of cloud behind which lurked an orange sun. The clouds moved with the wall landscape, entering and leaving the room left to right. The people in the room could well believe that they sat on a small plateau high up in new and jagged peaks. Boulders sat here and there; the floor was earthen and except where the long table stood, was not level. One could see to the horizon in every direction; there, a long finger of topaz ocean, or a scintillating line of river snaking across windblown plain, and to the left the line of majestic and austere mountains marched into the haze.

Gyll did not envy the people that had to clean this up afterward.

Helgin walked to where the plateau, at the juncture of wall and floor, seemed to drop in a sheer, knife-edged peak. He leaned carefully forward, looking down. "Shit," he said. He backed up a step and bent at the waist again, reaching out with a forefinger. He touched nothing, and—badly overbalanced—rocked back on his feet once more. He took a tentative step toward the cliff and repeated the process. This time his probing finger was halted by the invisible wall.

"Hah," he announced. "If anyone here has vertigo problems, their supper's going to be all over the floor. Good thing it's dirt."

Gyll held back a laugh. McClannan, standing beside d'Embry, looked annoyed. The Regent herself seemed politely amused while nearby waiters (actually some of the lower-echelon Diplo staffers recruited for the evening) smiled but kept a discreet silence. Helgin moved to the door, which stood without visible support at one end of the plateau. He leaned as close to the wall as he could without touching it, peering around the back of the door.

"Good," he said. "You wrapped the diorama around the back as well. The thing even throws a shadow. Very good." He tapped the wall with a fingernail. It gave off a sound like crystal. "Too damned good for Neweden." The dwarf glanced from McClannan to d'Embry. "Who's supposed to be impressed?"

Gyll began to speak, but McClannan was quicker. "It obviously impressed *you*, did it not, though I can see where a much-traveled Trader might be jaded—"

"*Seneschal*," d'Embry interrupted. McClannan glanced at her; she smiled up at him too sweetly. "I'm afraid you've fallen into the Motsognir's trap. He deliberately goads you. Do you not, sirrah?" she asked, turning to Helgin.

The dwarf grinned at Gyll, who shook his head. Then he bowed deeply. "You render me transparent, Regent. It's a fault of mine, I'm afraid; I like to see people make asses of themselves."

McClannan scowled. D'Embry, the hump of the symbiote concealed in glittering cloth that flickered uneasily from azure to scarlet, nodded back to the dwarf. "You see, Seneschal," she said, "Traders are wonderful manipulators, and the Motsognir are most likely their teachers. FitzEvard, best of all, has learned his lessons."

Gyll cleared his throat. He was dressed in a close-fitting tunic and pants, white piped with blue. The color flattered him, the fit accentuated the lean hardness of his body. He spoke softly, pleasantly. "I've always found FitzEvard Oldin to be a man of his word, Regent."

"I don't doubt that he is, Sula. If, for instance, he said that he would never kill you, he'd send somebody else to do the job."

Gyll bridled at that. His eyes narrowed, and the polite smile he'd worn as part of his costume dissolved. "You play the same games as the Motsognir, Regent. At least *he* doesn't pretend to have the veneer of civility."

Gyll expected anger, expected d'Embry to turn cold and

ask them—civilly—to leave. Certainly the expression on
McClannan's face was that of unmasked venom. But
d'Embry simply waved a hand (glinting silver) in dismissal.
"Sula," she said, "the Motsognir insults simply because he
enjoys getting the reactions; whether he says the truth or
not doesn't matter to him. I was Regent when FitzEvard
Oldin came to Printemps. There was another Trader on that
world as well, of the Family Shannon. They argued, and I
was forced to intervene. FitzEvard vowed to me that he
would do nothing to harm this man. *He* didn't. In fact,
FitzEvard was with me when an intruder killed the Trader
Shannon. I could never prove anything, but both FitzEvard
and I knew what had happened." She paused a moment,
and her face took on an aspect of sternness. She seemed to
stand straighter. "Up to that time, I thought I liked Oldin
well enough myself. We'd even flirted, and I'd considered
letting it go further. He was handsome enough then—he
probably still is; his type seems to age gracefully. He was
slick, and he looked straight at me and lied with a smile on
his face and we both knew he was lying. It didn't bother him
that I knew, as long as nothing could be proved." She
stopped and regarded Gyll. "I only tell you this to warn you
about your employer, Sula."

"I think I know him well enough already. And I also
think your bias shows, Regent."

The discussion went no further. The doorward chimed,
and the Li-Gallant Vingi entered. He moved, as always,
heavily, ponderously, each step deliberate and certain. Rolls
of flesh jiggled under a wide and ornate belt; his multitude
of rings flashed light. Behind him came the kin-lords of the
other rule-guilds. Gyll searched the crowd for familiar faces
as d'Embry nodded to the waiters to begin circulating with
trays of hors d'oeuvres and wine. Gyll recognized only one
of them: Sirrah d'Vegnes, who had been one of the under-
lings in Gunnar's rule-guild standards ago, once one of the
challengers to Vingi's dictatorship. D'Vegnes wore the belt-
holo of kin-lord now, and he was not at all the match of his
slain predecessor. He fawned over the Li-Gallant, posturing.
Gyll took a glass from one of the waiters, watching as
d'Embry and McClannan moved among their guests. There
were polite compliments on the setting of the room.

"You know what gives it away, Gyll?" Helgin startled

Gyll out of his reverie. He looked down at the Motsognir. Helgin held two glasses of wine; as Gyll watched, the dwarf drained one and set it firmly upside down in the dirt.

"What gives what away?"

"The illusion of this room. The acoustics foul the pretense. This still sounds like a room, not outdoors. Too much presence, too much quick echo and reverberation. Once you notice it, you can't be taken in again."

Gyll made a face. "Thanks. I was rather enjoying it."

"Well, that's the trouble with illusions. They fall through too quickly."

"Some people simply can't appreciate beauty when they see it."

"Some people just like being fooled," Helgin retorted.

They stared at each other, half-smiling. Then Gyll shook his head. Helgin slapped him on the rump. They laughed.

"Well, it's good to see that Traders, unlike our two Alliance hosts, get along well." The voice was a low purr: the Li-Gallant approached them. Helgin nodded to Vingi, Gyll gave the low bow of kin. After a hesitation, the Li-Gallant bowed in return—though less fully—to Gyll. "What gives the two of you so much amusement?'

"We were just discussing the room."

Vingi nodded massively, glancing slowly about. "It's rather effective, isn't it? It would be nice to have something on this scale in the keep. Could the Families do this?"

"We could do it easily enough," Gyll replied. "I've seen Oldin dens that had much the same, if not quite so elaborate a scale—mainly, we simply project holos beyond false windows. But I'm certain it could be duplicated without trouble."

"Ah." Vingi twisted a ring around a finger. He plucked a meatrind from a passing tray. "Perhaps I should price your equipment in comparison with that of the Alliance." Daintily he placed the meatrind in his mouth.

"The Oldins will be cheaper," Helgin said.

The Li-Gallant rolled the meatrind around his tongue appreciatively. He swallowed. "Yah, but will it continue to work after the ship has gone?"

"Simply make certain that we stay, Li-Gallant."

"Perhaps I could. If it were worth my effort." Vingi looked from Helgin to Gyll.

"We've no doubts as to your abilities, Li-Gallant," Gyll said.

"Very polite of you to mention it, Sula." A bell chimed. "But I think we're being called to dinner. Maybe we can continue this conversation there."

They had no chance. Vingi was seated next to d'Embry, at the head of the table. Gyll and Helgin flanked McClannan at the other end. Only Helgin relished that arrangement. He picked up a fork, examined the silver critically. "Not bad, Seneschal," he said, polishing the tines on his sleeve. "It's even clean."

McClannan did not seem disposed to comment. He smiled, weakly, tiredly. He looked resigned to a trying evening.

The dinner was long and varied, a sampling of cuisine from many worlds of the Alliance. Portions were small but multitudinous. Gyll more than once found himself glancing quizzically at Helgin after a plate of unidentifiable something was set before him. Several others he recognized, though he'd tasted few of them before: cockatrice from Thule, spineballs, unijells, Terran beef, and even a puffindle from Neweden's cold seas. Gyll was sated well before the last course—a pastry of questionable origin that tasted too sweet—but found that he could not resist sampling. Helgin ate everything placed before him, quickly, as if it might be taken away if he tarried.

McClannan talked with Gyll as they ate the pastry. "You know, Sula, what strikes me as the worst fault of the Families is their lack of a central government. We Diplos, for instance, answer to Diplo Center on Niffleheim, which in turn is under the leadership of the Legatus Primus and thence the entire Alliance structure. There is accountability for all our actions."

"Which doesn't prevent mistakes, but simply breeds cautious, slow, and mediocre Diplos." Gyll toyed with his pastry, not looking at the Seneschal; crumbs flaked delicately away from his fork. "It's my feeling that the looseness of Family society is its virtue, not the opposite."

"I can't agree." McClannan leaned forward, pushing his plate away. His handsome face was eager. "It's been proved time and time again that anarchy is no answer. Our entire history tells us that: all the times of a strong central government are the times of expansion. When there is none, human space is in shambles."

"Every time of strong government, from the Reduxtors of the First Empire through Huard, has also ended in chaos. Everyone grabs for the power—spread it out, and there's less chance of losing everything."

"Still, you can't blame the Interregnums on anything but Dame Fate. And it has always been a centralized government, one unified entity, that has brought us back out of those times."

Gyll shrugged. "But in all that scrambling, we've yet to match the technologies of the First Empire . . ."

Gyll found that McClannan bothered him less as he began to know the man. That facile, easy handsomeness must have actually been a burden to him; Gyll suspected that McClannan had always been expected to be successful and had often fallen short of that mark. He was ambitious but not overly gifted with talents to aid that ambition. Gyll would not have wanted the Seneschal on his staff or anywhere in a position of importance, but if the man ever managed to make a friend, he would probably not be a bad companion: facile, and not deep. The polar opposite of d'Embry . . . Gyll made his disagreements in the discussion milder than he might have. "I might also point out, Seneschal," Gyll continued, "that it was only the Trading Families that kept any glimmer of civilization alive during those dark times. Could the Alliance have formed at all without our work having given them the chance?"

"You speak as a convert, Sula. All converts are more zealous and less objective."

"Then let a nonconvert speak, man," Helgin broke in. He dabbed at his plate with a forefinger, picking up stray crumbs. "The Motsognir have no allegiance to either the Families or the Alliance. For myself, having seen both, I far prefer the Families' society." He licked his finger.

McClannan made a poor attempt to mask his revulsion. "Without meaning offense, what do the dwarves know of human civilization? The Motsognir fled human space centuries ago after you stole the ship *Naglfar* from the Reduxtor Pieter III—you made your choice, then."

"The Motsognir are as human as you, McClannan—and a hell of a lot smarter. *We* had no choice about being reengineered—that was an experiment of one of your precious strong central governments," Helgin said darkly. His mouth twitched under the growth of beard. Gyll began to interrupt, hoping to head off the too-fragile temper of the dwarf, but the doorward chimed. Everyone at the table looked about. At the table's head, a puzzled d'Embry gestured to one of the waiters. The man began to move toward the door, but it burst open in a gout of sparks, wrecked. Amidst shouts, a group of several lassari entered the room, holding crowd-prods and stings. Gyll jerked to his feet as, around the table, people frantically tried to scramble from their seats. The foremost of the lassari lifted her sting and fired at the ceiling. There was a crystalline explosion; a shower of broken sky rained down on the table. Someone screamed.

"Sit down, all of you!" the woman shouted. "Sit *down!*"

Most of the guests did so. Gyll hesitated, glancing at Helgin. "After-dinner entertainment, I suppose," the Motsognir muttered, and shrugged. He sat, as did Gyll. McClannan had not moved; he stared at the lassari, stricken. Pieces of the ceiling littered the table in front of them.

"Better, better," the woman said. She lowered the sting and looked slowly around the room. The sun was flickering, the clouds had vanished, there was a hole in the sky that revealed piping and wooden beams. "Isn't this nice. Well, Li-Gallant, was it a good dinner? Was there enough food for that gross stomach of yours?"

D'Embry rose to her feet; Vingi remained silent. "I'm the Regent d'Embry," she said coldly. "Who are you?"

"Does that matter to you, Regent? Well, I am Micha, and those behind me are part of the Hag's Legion. Somehow, our invitations didn't arrive for the dinner tonight. We're sorry we're late, but your guards were rather unfriendly."

"I want all of you out of here."

There was laughter from the lassari. "That's not a request you can enforce, Regent. Your guards are all asleep in the corridor—try to call them."

"If you've hurt any of them . . ."

"Hurt *them* like the Li-Gallant and his pack of pet killers hurt us?" She paused, and then she smiled. "We're not barbarians, Regent, despite our image."

Listening, Gyll felt helpless. Weaponless, outnumbered, there was little he or Helgin could do. If he could reach one of them before he was shot, get a sting, if Helgin could get to one as well ... No. He squirmed in his seat, restless, a little frightened. The movement caused Micha to glance at him.

"Ahh, Sula," she said. "How does it feel to know that your Hoorka are now nothing but the hired thugs of that pig down the table? Does it bother you? I hope so. And I hope it bothers you to have to sit there, helpless, wondering what we intend to do with you." She glanced around the table. "I hope it bothers all of you."

Gyll could see panic and shock in some of the guests now. The Li-Gallant, especially, seemed touched by fear. He was breathing too quickly, his bulk pressed back against his chair as if to be as far as possible from the threatening woman. His face was pale, his eyes wide. Gyll knew that the Li-Gallant did not expect to live. For himself, Gyll knew only that he would try to take someone to the Hag with him, should it come to that. Ransom for his soul.

"What do you want?" d'Embry asked. She alone had a voice; she, of all of them, was calm, had the shreds of her presence around her despite the situation.

"Perhaps we're going to cut the hump from your back and see how long it takes you to die, Regent." Micha grinned at d'Embry's sudden intake of breath. "Or maybe we'll give the Li-Gallant an immediate diet, remove some of that excess weight he carries. It would be simple, and even just, as well." She shrugged, one-shouldered. "Oh, that's lassari methods, isn't it?—without honor. Your gods must weep for us."

"You'd never get away with it," Vingi stuttered.

"Resorting to *clichés*, Li-Gallant? Words—especially old, worn-out ones—are a poor shield against a sting. Well, unfortunately, you're nearly right. Killing any of you in this way would only increase our difficulties. We're not ready yet to take full advantage of your absence, Li-Gallant. I'd fear for the existence of all lassari if someone worse than you were ruler. We simply want to make a point. We want to be heard."

Micha gestured harshly, scowling now, all pretense of her sarcastic good humor banished. Two lassari stepped from the mob behind her, carrying a long object wrapped in cloth. It was an awkward burden, for they staggered as they

moved. Gyll recognized it—he'd seen it too many times. But
before he could speak, the lassari cast it down on the floor,
holding the ends of the cloth. A body rolled out onto the
dirt—a thin, gaunt woman with sunken cheeks and a
bloated belly. Her arms were empty bags of flesh, the muscles slack in a pouch of flesh. Those at the table were in an
uproar, most standing now, their faces horrified.

"She died of starvation. We don't know her name—no
one does," Micha said. "She's lassari, so no kin cared about
her. Her death was lonely and long. That's what we wanted
you to see." She stared at them with somber and furious
eyes. "I hope all of you enjoyed your meal."

Again, she gestured. The lassari began to leave the room,
Micha in their midst; the body, accusing, was left behind.
Someone down the table was vomiting noisily. Gyll watched
the lassari leave, the muscles in his stomach slowly unknot-
ting. He glanced at d'Embry, her face reflecting a cool inner
rage, and back to the departing intruders.

And he caught a glimpse of steel.

"*Down!*" he shouted, flinging himself to one side. A
throwing knife hissed through the air. He heard the *tchunk*
as the blade struck the wall, and he rolled to his feet, certain
that the weapon had been intended for the Li-Gallant.

But it was Helgin who sat in his chair, head turned to
contemplate the knife just centimeters from his head. The
weapon seemed to hover, shorn of its point, motionless, in
the landscape of mountains.

Helgin wrenched the knife from the wall. His bearded
face unreadable, he examined the blade, then tossed it onto
the table. China clattered and broke.

"Wasn't close enough to bother moving," he said.

The best that could be said for Felling's stew was that it was
hot and took away some of the chill of Underasgard. It
wasn't particularly Felling's fault that the Hoorka found it
unappetizing: it was plain fare, but savory enough. He'd simply served the stew or something akin to it too often. But
stew made use of meats and odd ends—it was the most eco-
nomical way to cook, and Thane Valdisa insisted on economy.

McWilms toyed with the conglomeration on his plate
like the rest. The bread, at least, was newly baked, and the

mead was satisfactory, if slightly diluted. McWilms broke off a piece from the loaf and chewed enthusiastically, trying to convince his palate that this was an amazingly subtle combination of tastes.

His palate was not fooled.

The Hoorka were gathered in the common room off the kitchens. Apprentices, who would eat later, stood waiting along the walls, which were studded with glittering nodules of calcite deposits. From the kitchen could be heard the noise of the jussar applicants, doing their drudge work under Felling's baleful eye.

McWilms sat at the Thane's table with most of the elder kin: Serita, Bachier, Kristagon, Sholla, and others. Valdisa ate with them, and she seemed no happier than the rest with their menu. "Smile, Serita," she said. "I told Felling to buy some groceries tomorrow with part of the money from your contract. Supper should be much better." She stabbed at a piece of meat with her fork, and contemplated the gristle marbling it. "It should be better than this, certainly, with no offense to Felling, who's doing the best he can."

"Well, I'm glad to hear it," Serita said. Her face was mottled with a bruise on one cheek, a remnant of her fight with Meka Joh after their return from the contract. Joh, his arm in a sling and a wrapping around a leg, sat elsewhere. "I was beginning to think we needed to expand into the thieving business and hit the food stalls at Market Square." She mused on that for a moment. "Ric would have volunteered," she added, a sadness in her voice. D'Mannberg had been one of her lovers, and his appetite had been the source of many well-intentioned comments among the kin.

The mention of his kin-father blunted what little remained of McWilms's own hunger. He pushed the half-finished plate of stew away and laid down his bread. He glanced at the table: rough, gaps between some of the planks, scarred with gouges from idle knives, and stained with spilled food. It made him think of his apprentice days, when Felling would set them all to scrubbing down the tables. When Gyll had been Thane.

As if in counterpoint to his own thoughts, Bachier spoke wistfully from down the table. "Do you remember the feast we had when we first had a contract from the Diplos, under old Regent Vogel? Ulthane Gyll had Felling buy ice-steak for all the full kin. By She of the Five, *that* was a meal. I remember how the apprentices all looked forlorn when it was gone—no scraps left, just a few well-gnawed bones."

McWilms laughed. "I was one of those apprentices, Bachier. And if you think we didn't get to sample that dinner, you're wrong. Old Felling's eyes have never been fast enough to stop us from lifting a few choice pieces. Remember, Kris?—you were an apprentice then as well."

"Tender and incredibly rich—and of course we took only the choicest morsels," Kristagon elaborated. "We'd send the dregs out to the kin."

The laughter rippled around the table, but McWilms noticed that Valdisa didn't seem to share the amusement. He wondered at that. "What do you think, Thane?" he asked. "Are good times like those still waiting for us?"

She smiled back at him, but the gesture touched only her lips. Her eyes, with the fine time-wrinkles at the corners, seemed to be almost hurt. "You never know, Jeriad."

"The Ulthane loved his food as well as the rest of us," Bachier said. "Began to show on him a little toward the end, though—still, he always did well enough on the practice strips. Wonder how he looks now? Can't have lost his skills too much, considering how he snuck in here recently." Then, to Valdisa's accusing stare: "We all know it had to be him, Thane. Who else would you have let leave peacefully after that?"

"The Ulthane looks very good," McWilms said without thinking. He could feel Valdisa's gaze on him now, and he didn't dare look at her. He berated himself. *Fool, does such little mead go to your head so quickly that you can't control your mouth?* "I saw him on a street in Sterka, going the other way," he added as casually as he could. He picked up his bread again, broke off another chunk.

"Did he speak to you?" Valdisa asked sharply. Her voice was acid, stern.

"You told us to avoid the Traders," he answered. It seemed to satisfy her, though she still looked at McWilms appraisingly.

"If *I'd* been one of the kin the Ulthane met on his way in, it would have been different," Bachier said. "He wouldn't have put *me* on the floor."

Valdisa's head snapped around to him. "Don't be so

damned sure," she said. "You're strong enough, Bachier, but the *Sula*"—she used Gyll's new title with heavy emphasis—"has always been one quite able to counter strength with a move."

"Thane—"

"No," she interrupted. "I don't know why the Sula returned here just to sit in the back caverns, but my orders still stand. I want all of you to leave him alone, and to tell me if he tries to contact any of you. And I hate this subject," she added. "Let's find another."

"Thane," McWilms said. He kept his voice gentle, casual. "The Ulthane isn't Hoorka's enemy, after all. He *did* create the guild, made us kin. We shouldn't pretend that he doesn't exist. Some of us had great affection for him . . ." His voice trailed off as he glanced at her.

He knew he'd gone too far, said too much. He could see it in the way Valdisa drew back, in the flush that crept up her neck, in the way her fingers curled around the arm of her chair. She hovered on the edge of anger, and he could see her fighting it. There was silence around the table. Slowly, Valdisa relaxed, the creases in her face softening. McWilms regretted, far too many times at this supper, his words.

"Thane, I'm very sorry," he said. "Sometimes there's an idiot working my mouth."

She shook her head tightly. Her voice played with nonchalance and failed. "It's all right, Jeriad. What you say is true. We shouldn't forget our past or what the Sula has meant to us." She nodded to the kin. "If you'll excuse me, I need to get the money ready for Felling."

Deliberately, Valdisa pushed her chair back from the table and rose. She bowed slightly to the kin and, walking a shade too quickly, left the room.

"Stuck your feet in it that time, didn't you?" Serita said to McWilms when she had gone.

He didn't answer. He stared into the darkness after the Thane.

The night was uneasy for Gyll. The dream at first was gentle and erotic. Kaethe was with him, as she had been the night he'd left with Helgin for Neweden. She was on top of him, moving, her eyes closed, lost in their passion. He reached up to touch her swaying breasts, and they were suddenly Valdisa's; smaller, the texture of the skin rougher under his hands, and it was not Kaethe's face that loomed over him but some strange melding of Kaethe and Valdisa—his two lovers, his two lives. In his dream, he did not care, but lunged with her as they sought release, and when they finally found it, he cried out as Kaethe/Valdisa laughed.

He woke, sweat-drenched, and oddly frightened of the dream. He forced himself to stay awake long hours after that, watching Neweden move beneath his ship. In time, he could not keep his eyes open, his tired body forcing him to return to his bed.

When he dreamed again, it was of lassari and dead women and knives of bright, sharp steel.

Chapter 7

THE NOTE HAD COME to Gyll in a most roundabout fashion, handed to a Diplo guard at Sterka Port by an apprentice Hoorka, and then given to one of the Family Oldin crew on their shuttle. When the shuttle returned to *Goshawk*, it was placed on Fischer's desk, who gave it to Sula Hermond.

It said, simply: "Ten a.m., the river below the falls. Valdisa."

The note did not seem to require an answer, and evidently Valdisa did not expect him to miss the appointment; she knew him that well. Gyll took the next shuttle down, wondering, memories of his odd dream and the fiasco of d'Embry's dinner occupying his thoughts.

The falls spread cold mist over the morning. The wind shifted, and curtains of water spread across the river. The falls were pretty but unspectacular—some worlds were blessed with a hundred better scenes. The cascade clambered down the worn steps of the bluffs well outside Sterka. There was the normal amount of litter scattered about, remnants of old rendezvous. Gyll shrugged his jacket tighter around him. The mists beaded his hair. He ran a hand through the wetness, shook his head. He reached down and picked up a flat rock. He skimmed it across the roiling water.

"Hello, Gyll."

He'd not heard her approach in the clamor of the falls. She wore the Hoorka nightcloak, the hood up. "Chilly out here," he said.

"Sorry."

"Your note didn't give a reason for this . . ." He didn't know what to call it.

"You talked to McWilms."

There was a flat and curiously dispassionate accusation in her voice. Gyll could sense her body under the cover of the nightcloak; muscles flexed, ready to move at need, as if the confrontation would of necessity be physical. All he could see of her were her eyes and a strand of hair curling down over her forehead.

He didn't bother to deny her charge — he didn't lie easily; Helgin had told him many times how transparent he was when he tried. "Did Jeriad tell you?"

"He didn't have to."

"Don't blame him," Gyll said. "We really didn't seek each other out. It was just a chance meeting on the street, and I invited him to have a drink. I know you asked me to stay away from the kin, but I don't find anything horrible in talking to Jeriad. Have some compassion, Valdisa. He's an old friend."

The wind blew mist back into their faces. Valdisa turned away before he could see if there was a reaction to his words in her eyes. When she finally looked back, there was a troubled hardness to her stare. "I've as much compassion as any of the kin, Gyll," she said. "At least that's what I tell myself. But the Thane sometimes isn't allowed to show it or respond to it. She has to be a bitch." Now she swept the hood back, turned down the collar. Mist swept down eagerly. "I don't like it, but it's necessary. You should know that." Slowly, faintly, she smiled. "I *do* understand, Gyll. I don't really mind."

Gyll smiled tentatively back. "Good. I'd hate to have you angry with me. We've done that to each other too often in the past."

"I'm not angry."

"Then can we move out of this damned mist?"

She laughed, her face sheened with water. "Certainly."

Down the riverbank, they found a sheltering wall of cliff. There was a small hollow where the wind could not find them. Narrow, it brought them close together of necessity, and each of them pressed their back to stone to lessen the intimacy. Gyll stared out at the river, not at her face, suddenly too near his own. "I assume you had some other purpose with the note than just giving me a shower?"

"I want to know more. I want to know why you've come back, what you intend to do."

"I thought I'd told you."

"Maybe. I'm not sure *you* know. From what I gathered from Jeriad, he seems to think that you're rather perturbed by Hoorka, by what you've seen since you got here." She said it carefully, neutral. Her gaze sought his, but she seemed only attentive, waiting for his answer.

"Yah. I don't like it. I especially don't like what people keep telling me." Her eyes would not let him go.

"What is that?"

"That the Hoorka belong to Vingi."

Lines creased her forehead, her lips tightened into a scowl. "You've been listening to the wrong sources, then. Give me some credit, Gyll. I've followed your code, strictly. If that gives Hoorka the appearance of being Vingi's, then it's the code's fault, not mine." The timbre of her voice changed, tinged with spite. "You weren't around to see how that might come about."

Gyll reached out a hand, touched her shoulder through the nightcloak, amazed at the texture of the material—he'd remembered it as softer. Valdisa flinched away from his touch, and he let his hand drop back. "No, I wasn't around," he said softly. "And I've learned quite a bit since then—about myself, mostly. For one, I've learned that you shouldn't let pride speak before necessity. I know I would never have said this before, but maybe the code needs to be changed."

The mildness of his answer only seemed to feed her ire. She made a sound of disgust deep in her throat, taking a step out of the hollow and back. She glared at him. "Gods, the Family Oldin's done wonders for you, hasn't it? The bitch Kaethe feeds you her dreams, and FitzEvard substitutes his own vision for yours. What's happened to you, Gyll? You're not the person I made love with, the proud Hoorka-Thane. Do the Oldins unman all their employees?"

Fury raced through Gyll, a blind, white heat. But he did not move, didn't instinctively reach for the sheathed blade at his side as he once would have done. He willed himself into some semblance of control—the same rules he'd imposed on his Trader-Hoorka. *Think before action. There's*

*usually more time than you believe, and deeds aren't easily
undone*. He tore his gaze away from Valdisa's challenging
eyes. He breathed deeply, listening to the rushing dance of
the river. "I don't understand this, Valdisa," he said at last.
"I don't understand why we insist on making each other
angry." Bleak, he turned to face her. "And, by the Dame,
you succeed in it. You succeed admirably. But I don't kill
anymore, and I only fight when there's no other recourse. If
you're trying to goad me to that extent, it won't work. I
won't let it."

She didn't believe him; he could see it. Her stance
mocked him, her face scoffed. "You're Sula, head of a military force. You tell me that you don't fight, don't kill?"

"I teach."

"You send others to do your dirty work, then, like the
Li-Gallant."

He visibly recoiled from that accusation, sagging against
the rock of the cliff as if wounded. A jagged finger of stone
dug into his back. Wearily he shook his head. "I still believe
much of what Neweden taught me, Valdisa. The blame for
any death rests with the person that ordered that killing, no
matter who held the weapon. But I avoid such a final decision if I can avoid it, and the Oldins seem to prefer that
approach."

"It's more devious."

"It's more effective."

"Then why in the hell do you want my Hoorka? What
good can we do you? We kill, Gyll. That's what you set us
up to do, trained us to be—assassins. Nothing more."

"I'd like to retrain you, use your skills in other ways . . ."
He shrugged, thrusting away from the wall with his shoulders. They were very close. He could smell the spice of
Valdisa's breath. "And, in any case, killing is still a needed
skill."

Her gaze searched his face, curiously soft. He began to
wonder if her anger had merely been a sham devised to
destroy the vestiges of their old affection. "Gyll . . ." she began; then her lashes came down to shield those eyes, drawing deep lines at the corners. "Just what is it that you're
offering?"

"Comfort, challenge, a new meaning to our kinship."
He paused, wondering how to phrase what he wanted to

say. "Maybe even to see if we can be friends—or more— again."

"Those are just words, Gyll. They don't mean anything."

He smiled. "You're right. You want specifics: the Hoorka here would be the nucleus of a special-forces division within my current group, for use when one or two people are needed—for subversive work, perhaps even assassinations, though I would prefer not. We'd move you from Neweden to a planet near OldinHome that I've made my base. You'd be in charge of the kin, Valdisa."

"But subject to your orders."

"To FitzEvard Oldin, through me."

"Or just you, if you decide something needs to be done. The Oldins would back you, wouldn't they?"

"I suppose that's possible," he admitted.

"And we'd be back to where we were eight standards ago."

"Was it so bad?"

She sighed, and he knew that she was finally beyond the reflexive Neweden anger. A melancholy smile drifted over her face and she cocked her head, listening to the distant thunder of the falls. "I've changed a lot too, Gyll, if not in the same ways you have. For me to do this would be the same as admitting I've ruined Hoorka, and I simply don't believe that. We've had bad times recently—I'd admit that to anyone—hell, *Neweden's* had bad times, but the kin are still together. I've talked with d'Embry about new offworld contracts and I'm hopeful that she'll consider them. We've had two contracts in the last half-standard that weren't Vingi's. I'm not going to admit defeat, Gyll, and that's what you're asking." She passed her hand through her hair, raining droplets on the ground. "No, it wasn't all bad between us, Gyll. I enjoyed being with you, learning from you, being your lover. It was a good time. But we also had our differences; they drove us apart then. I figure the same thing would happen now, and I'm getting too old to want to take that kind of chance."

"You sound like I did," he said. "Eight standards ago."

She grinned. "Maybe."

"And I've found that I was wrong in that thinking. Valdisa, the Oldins are what Hoorka needs to grow. The Alliance is only a dead end, Neweden is just a blind alley.

We suit the Families, they suit us. From everything I've seen and heard here, the Hoorka will be lassari shit in another few standards, dead like the ippicators. Let me at least make my offer to the kin, let them decide."

The grin had fallen from her face. "No," she answered; then again, softer. "No."

"Why?"

"Because I don't trust the Family Oldin."

"Then you don't trust me. Gods, you sound like d'Embry."

"Maybe she's right."

Gyll scuffed a heel against rock. He sighed, a long exhalation. Valdisa waited as he looked upward at the mist-driven sky. Then she did something that surprised him. She took a step, pressing against him, her arms around him in a firm hug. A moment, and then he responded, clasping her against him. The sudden affection brought back a flooding of memory. He bent his head down to kiss her, but she had moved back again. "Why did you do that?" he asked.

"I wanted to do it while I still could," she answered. Gyll didn't know what to say to that. He stood there, shifting his weight uncertainly until she spoke again. "You were a fine lover, Gyll, but you never were very easy with affection. You'd always say nothing, or the wrong thing."

"You could give me another chance at it. You could let me talk with the kin."

"With *my* kin," she emphasized. "It's not their decision to make, Gyll. I'm Thane, and I've said no."

"Valdisa, I don't like what Hoorka has become. It makes me sick to think of the guilded kin reviling my creation. I want that to end, one way or the other."

Her anger was back before he'd finished speaking. A minute ago, he'd thought there was a chance. But all that vanished, riven, with the rage that twisted her face. She clambered away from the hollow, into the wind and mist, her hair tousled, the heavy fabric of the nightcloak swirling. *"Damn* you, Hermond. You've no more sensitivity than a frigging stone. All you can think about is how things affect you."

"And what are you doing?" he asked mildly.

"You believe I'm just as selfish, neh?" She put her hood up against the wind. "Maybe I am. Maybe I can't stand the thought of losing my little tithing of power. If it is, so be it. No, Gyll. That's going to remain my answer to you. No. If I find that you're trying to go around me, I'll take actions. We were friends and more—I'd hate to see us become enemies."

"Valdisa," he persisted. "Everything I see of Hoorka here makes me angry."

"And what bothers you most is that you have no power over it. Well, you gave that up voluntarily, Gyll. You understood Neweden and Hoorka fit it very well, but you went looking for power elsewhere. It's a shame, because I don't think you understand the Families and the Alliance much at all, and I'm afraid they're going to swallow you whole."

"Then come with me and help me understand."

"Stay away from us, Gyll."

"Hoorka was my creation."

"And we're past you now. Sula Hermond is not kin, and he has nothing to do with us."

He ignored her tone, her use of the impersonal mode. "I'm not certain of that."

"Stay away, Sula." Her lips narrowed. She spat out the words as if they burned her tongue. "Or I'll kill you. I swear it, Gyll, I'll use my knife."

She turned in the middle of his reply, the nightcloak moving around her with finality. He made no effort to go after her. He listened to the sound of her boots against rock, his head leaning back against the cold stone. Finally, he could hear nothing but the soughing of the river; still, he did not move. It was only when the sunstar, climbing, found him that he kicked himself away from the cliff and began the walk back to Sterka.

"Li-Gallant, I want to apologize." The words tasted like gall. D'Embry didn't care for Vingi's office, didn't like the discomfort in her chest and the headache with which she'd awakened, didn't enjoy the half-smirk on the Li-Gallant's face. "I don't know how that disturbance happened last night, but I'm damned well going to find out."

"There is an old adage on Neweden about closing the cage after the moonwailer has gotten out."

D'Embry watched as the Li-Gallant laced thick fingers together. All of his face frowned except for the eyes: they openly laughed at her. She tried to find a comfortable position in her floater; the movement threatened to split her head. A hammer thudded behind her skull. *Damn it, symbiote, do something.* "Li-Gallant, we thought that the security arrangements we had were more than sufficient, and we were on the Center grounds, as well. That's Alliance territory."

"Evidently your captains were wrong about the security, and lassari don't care for territorial semantics."

Fine, be difficult about this, you bastard. You're enjoying it. Gods, symbiote, aren't you going to ease this throbbing? "What can I say, Li-Gallant? From what we've reconstructed so far, the lassari knew the layout and location of the guards perfectly. We've made the assumption that one of the guards—or one of the guests—was sympathetic to the Hag's Legion or was bribed. All of the Diplo staff are undergoing psych evaluation—we'll get our subversive and punish him to the full extent of Alliance law. They couldn't have gotten in and out without help."

"That fact worries me more than the rest, Regent." His slow regard moved down to the sea-wash illumination of his desk terminal. Green light swirled the lines of his face. Then he looked at her again. "You look pale this morning. I trust that the excitement and apprehension haven't been too much for your, ahh, condition." He arrayed himself in comic concern.

Bastard. She forced herself to ignore the ache in her head, the catch in her breathing. "I'm not that delicate an individual," she said, unsmiling. "I never have been. I don't allow infirmities to rule me."

"Ahh, but sometimes we have to realize that they limit us."

You're so obvious with your baiting, fat man. Stuff your limitations. She forced a smile that was as false as his solicitations. "It's the mind that matters, not the body, as you must know, Li-Gallant." *There, mull on that for a bit.*

He did. He didn't seem to enjoy it. He peered back into the terminal, idly touching a contact. "I understand the symbiote puts its own natural drugs into your bloodstream. It must dull the pain considerably, Regent."

And the mind; right, Li-Gallant? "Not as much as the available treatments would. You misunderstand the purpose of the symbiote. It's a regulator, not something to debilitate me. A regent, a li-gallant, *anyone* in a position of power, can't afford to have a fogged mind."

"In Neweden culture, one is supposed to submit to the inevitable. I'm afraid your symbiote is useless for me, should I ever be in a position to need such a thing. I would lose all respect from guilded kin for my avoidance of the commands of Dame Fate. I would be ousted, and the parasite taken from me. One should not hide from Hag Death, Regent."

"Are you telling me that you fail to respect *me*, Li-Gallant?"

He smiled. "I'm a product of my culture, inescapably, Regent. But I *do* understand that your mores are not Neweden's, that different rules apply to you. Perhaps other guilded kin cannot make that distinction, but I can."

D'Embry's brows tightened with pain; she hoped it resembled concentration. The headache was making her sick to her stomach, as well. She promised herself an hour's nap—*later this afternoon. Just let me get through this. Damn, if Niffleheim would have sent me someone competent for seneschal* . . . "Li-Gallant, I can only offer my apologies again for the dinner, and my assurance that we will do everything we can to apprehend those responsible. It won't happen again."

Vingi nodded. "Your apology is accepted, Regent." Again, he stared down at the terminal, lips pursed. "But you must admit that a question might cross the minds of the guilded kin here: if the Regent can't protect us, maybe her Seneschal could have. Or, if there's nothing at all the Alliance could have changed, then possibly the Family Oldin would be more effective."

His smile was that of a predator. "An interesting speculation, isn't it?" he said.

Helgin threw the knife down on the floor before Renard. It stuck there, quivering. Micha, flanking the larger man, stared down at the blade. Renard raised an eyebrow quizzically. His left hand slowly stroked the plant-pet around his shoulders.

"You seem angry, Motsognir," he commented.

"You'd *damned* well better believe it," Helgin roared. His fury contorted his bearded face. Legs widespread, hands on hips, he glared up at Renard, eyes flaring under thick brows. "I got Micha and her bunch of goons in, and it was perfect—until someone decided to throw *that.*" He pointed at the knife. "Renard, we'd agreed that an entirely peaceful demonstration was what we needed to impress them. What the hell did you have in mind with that damned knife, and who was supposed to be hit?"

"An accident, Motsognir," Renard purred, his deep voice resonant. "A mistake."

"Then I want the man that threw it. I want to know why he aimed at me, and I want to see how he'll look with that knife sticking up his ass."

"Micha's already talked with him. He threw at the Li-Gallant."

"Then he's as blind as a cave-fish. The fat man's a big target, and he was halfway down the table." Helgin spat on the floor; Renard looked from spittle to dwarf. "Don't play me for a fool, Renard," Helgin growled. "Let me talk to this myopic knife-flinger."

"He's dead," Micha said. She could not keep her gaze from the knife-hilt protruding from the floorboards. It seemed to fascinate her. "An argument with someone in Dasta. Yesterday."

"Awfully convenient."

She shrugged. "True."

Helgin rumbled disgust. A bare foot stamped the floor.

Renard smiled over to Micha. "I don't think our little co-conspirator believes us, Micha."

"Your little co-conspirator is wondering whether he should beat the truth out of the two of you," Helgin answered.

Renard's eyes went hard. His hand ceased caressing the plant-pet and went to his side. He drew in a long breath, filling his chest. "I wouldn't make a threat you can't keep, dwarf."

"Oh, I never do." Helgin smiled into Renard's stare. He flexed powerful arms, folding them across his chest. "Never."

For a moment, the confrontation held on edge, caught by tension. Micha held her breath, waiting. Then Renard's stiff posture relaxed. He bellowed a rich laugh, and his hand sought the beast around his neck once more. "Maybe next time I'll ask you to prove that boast, Motsognir."

"Why delay my pleasure? I haven't had a good fight in days."

"As you've pointed out to me before, FitzEvard has his own interests, and he doesn't care to see his agents at each other's throats."

"Then remember who's in charge here."

"On *Goshawk* and with the Alliance, you rule, Motsognir. Here, on Neweden territory, I have the final say. Oldin has given me his orders, and, curious as I might find them, I carry them out."

"The same way your people end a simple demonstration? With a thrown knife — treachery?"

Micha started to speak again, but Renard's upraised hand stopped her. "Dwarf, you begin to sound like that Sula of yours — everything words with no action. Are you afraid of blades, like your pet Hoorka? Does the stench of blood bother you, as it bothers Hermond?"

The smile seemed cemented beneath the cover of Helgin's beard. His feet rasped against floor, and he crouched lower, tensing. "One more word, Renard, that's all it will take. Leave Gyll out of this — he's an honest and admirable man, better than either one of us."

Renard spread his hands wide. He shook his head. "So you keep telling me."

"Believe it, or I'll teach you to say it — ungently."

"FitzEvard wouldn't like your tone."

"Then let's talk about something he would like."

Renard nodded agreement. In slow stages, Helgin relaxed. He strode over to the knife in the floor and pulled it loose from the boards. He touched the tip to his forefinger; flesh cratered around it. Looking at the weapon, he spoke to Renard. "A pity we're both so loyal. I'd enjoy being your enemy."

"Maybe later." Renard smiled back. "You might yet get your chance, neh? But until then, let me tell you what else we have planned . . ."

Chapter 8

THERE WERE TWENTY-THREE of them, and they were the Dead, a group of lassari who, hopeless, had given themselves entirely to the vagaries of Dame Fate and the claws of Hag Death. They were walking in their endless march to nowhere, far from any of the cities of Neweden. Sterka was three hundred kilometers to the south—they were moving vaguely in its direction. The rolling hills of the Preada Valley spread around them; a river coursed to their right, swelling with more speed and purpose toward the distant city. In a few days more, the small towns that clustered around Sterka like anxious children around a parent would appear. For now, they could be striding through the long grass of Neweden's primal past. The landscape was gently soothing and, except for themselves (who were, by their own reckoning, already outside the ken of the living), barren of the intruder humanity.

They did not care. The Dead care only for the Hag. They chanted the sibilant phrases of the eternal mantra; they tolled their bells and swung their censers.

The carcass lay in their path—a fairly large animal. It had been dead a few days. The stench of decay hung around it like a foul cloak, and some local carrion-eaters had torn at it. The vanguard of the Dead chanted their way around it, perhaps with an involuntary wrinkling of noses and rolling of eyes. Perhaps some of them even noticed that it was not any beast with which they were familiar; it was not until the midpoint of the line that an older man dressed in the tatters of a cloak stumbled to a halt, eyes wide. Those behind him stopped as well, bumping him. He stared at the dead animal, his filthy head shaking slowly from side to side. The censer he held dropped unheeded to the ground with a soft thud, coals smoldering in the grass.

He breathed a word which rustled like a paean through the ranks of the Dead, spoken louder and louder until it became a shout.

The beast of fable, the long-extinct god-creature of Neweden. Omen, pet of the gods. Symbol, whose very bones meant power.

Ippicator.

"Well, Thane. Did you meet with him?"

"Yah, Jeriad. I did."

"And?"

"No. I'm sorry, Jeriad, but I told him no."

Chapter 9

HE'D BEEN SULLENLY QUIET during the flight to the village of Malcala. She endured his sullenness, his monosyllabic replies to questions until the flitter landed and they clambered out. They could both see the apprentice waiting for them at the edge of the park in which they'd set down, but she held him back.

"What is it, Jeriad?" she demanded.

"What, Thane?" Under the hood of his nightcloak, Mc-Wilms looked back at her. His voice was heavy with some emotion, short and clipped.

Valdisa dropped her voice to match his. Her fingers gripped his shoulder tightly. "Listen, Jeriad. I won't take that tone from you. Not in private, and most certainly not on a contract. Spit it out, kin-brother, if something's troubling you. I don't want to play the nasty kin-lord, but I'll do it if I have to." She paused. "Well?"

She thought for a moment that McWilms wasn't going to answer, that she'd have to send him back to Underasgard and finish the contract with the apprentices, for she wasn't about to go further with his unspilled rancor fouling their teamwork. Too many kin lost their lives that way.

But his mouth worked, though his steady regard remained a challenge. His cerulean eyes watched her. "It's another contract for the Li-Gallant, isn't it?"

So that's it. He's guessed it, like the rest. She did not deny or acknowledge the charge. "Remember the code, Jeriad. We're just weapons. It doesn't matter to us who signed the contracts."

He shook himself away from her grasp. In the darkness, she heard more than saw his movement. Behind her, the flitter's engines moaned into silence—she knew that the apprentice piloting it would be watching them, curious; the tale would get back to Underasgard, no doubt well-embroidered.

"It didn't really matter, once," McWilms said. "I think you know that, sometimes, who we're working for *does* make a difference—when it's always the Li-Gallant's signature. It bothers all the Hoorka, especially the older kin."

"What do you want me to do, Jeriad? The Hoorka would starve without those contracts. And I notice that you're willing to eat the food we get from those same contracts."

McWilms rubbed at his right hand, as if a memory of pain troubled him. "Thane, I'm sorry if what I say bothers you, but surely you realize how this troubles all the kin. None of us like the whispered gossip we hear every time you go to Vingi's keep to collect our money. I do what I have to do, but it leaves a bitter taste."

"If it's making you act the way you do now, Jeriad, then I don't feel safe. If the rest of the kin are the same, then I'm surprised we haven't lost more kin than d'Mannberg recently."

McWilms's face took on a strange aspect between sorrow and anger. "Thane, I hope you don't place the blame of my kin-father's death on me. If you do, then we have more to settle than just a few contracts."

Valdisa could hear the pain in his voice. She softened her words. "No, Jeriad, I don't. That was Dame Fate's whim and a cowardly ambush from that Hag-kin Vasella. Still, we have to hunt tonight, and I don't want you slow to react because it's the Li-Gallant's enemy we look for."

"Then it is Vingi's contract?"

She shrugged. "Does it matter?"

"I suppose not." The answer was a second too slow.

"Then let's go meet the apprentices, or the dawnrock will call us too early."

They moved away from the flitter into a fragrant night. Boots shushed against sandy grass. Malcala was a collection of a few houses and buildings on the eastern edge of the Sterkian continent. They could smell the tang of salt water and rotting fish, hear the boom of surf. The sea was Malcala's life. Everyone here was tied to its moods, its tides. A quiet place with homes where people retired early and woke with the sunstar.

Usually.

The long, gangly form of the apprentice Ritti waited for them at the edge of the village. A crowd stood behind him at a short distance. The lights of Malcala threw their shadows at the Hoorka. Valdisa glanced from the onlookers to Ritti. "Trouble?" she asked.

The boy's voice wavered between tenor and baritone. "Not yet, Thane, Sirrah McWilms. But the Shipmaster would like to speak with you." Ritti sounded uncertain, vacillating between hilarity and fear as his voice did between child and man.

One of the spectators stepped forward. Even in the dimness, the Hoorka could see his weathered skin, the thick muscles of his shoulders and chest. The scent of salt was on his clothes. "I'm Shipmaster Le Plath," he said. The voice matched the frame: thick, ponderous.

Valdisa bowed, kin to kin. Beside her, McWilms did the same. "Shipmaster, I can't wait here. Forgive my abruptness, which is not worthy of you as kin-lord, but what is your reason for delaying us on our contract?" Valdisa's words were polite but laden with the Hoorka aloofness. Le Plath didn't quail, as she had seen others do. He simply planted his large feet in the sand and scratched at his armpit through his tunic.

"We have a problem," he said.

"We?"

"The Hoorka and Malcala," he answered. His hands plunged into his pockets; at her side, she felt McWilms suddenly tense at the gesture, his hand going for his vibro hilt. Le Plath noticed, as well. His thick eyebrows knotted over his splayed nose. "You got to tell the Li-Gallant he can't have Pauli."

"Pauli Shroyer? Shipmaster, he's our victim, and the Hag will have him or not as Dame Fate and She of the Five will. It's not up to you or me."

"Ain't talking about you or me. I'm talking about the Li-Gallant; I want you to tell him."

"You misunderstand the Hoorka, Shipmaster," McWilms broke in. He shot a strange glance at Valdisa. "We've no communications with the Li-Gallant other than any contract we might have, nor, in any case, do we reveal the signer of a contract until after the hunt."

"That ain't what people say," Le Plath continued doggedly.

"Then people are wrong," Valdisa declared harshly, all attempts at kin-politeness gone. "And you're delaying us too much, Shipmaster."

Le Plath did not move, did not react. The Hoorka began to see the crowd as something more than just a passive irritation. If these onlookers chose to resist, neither McWilms nor Valdisa nor the apprentices could really stop them, not without better weapons and more kin—the apprentice's report had told them that Shroyer had armed himself only with vibrofoil, and the Hoorka had given themselves the same weapons. Enough determination from these people and they would go down; with an entourage to parade before the Hag, but they would die. Valdisa wondered whether they shouldn't retreat to the flitter and call Underasgard.

Le Plath sniffed and swallowed.

"Pauli Shroyer has a mouth that speaks the truth too much," he said. Stolid, slow, plodding, the words came. "Pauli knows that the Li-Gallant taxes us too much. He said that to the wrong people. That's his crime, Hoorka. Would you kill him for that, leave all his kin weeping? He's a good man. I need him."

"You may still have him—if the Dame wishes."

Le Plath's smile was as slow as his speech. "The Dame is like the sea, always changing. I don't trust Her."

"It's your only way, Shipmaster." Valdisa glanced at McWilms. His face told her nothing. He seemed impatient, yet at the same time almost gleeful, as if this reception vindicated his feelings about the contract. "If you try to stop us," she continued, "more than Shroyer might die. The Hoorka don't want that; we've no interest in killing anyone but our victim. Come between us and him, and you endanger yourself. How valuable can one man be, set against the potential loss of many others?"

Le Plath mulled that over, one large hand stroking a thick-stubbled chin. "I understand what you say, Hoorka, but we had wanted the Li-Gallant to know that we would have paid the fine for Pauli's insolence."

"The victim was offered that alternative," McWilms said. "That's our code."

"Then Pauli never spoke of it to me. He's that way." His

gaze rolled back and forth between them. "What's the price of Pauli's life?"

McWilms looked at Valdisa. "Two thousand," she said.

"A small cost for a life, isn't it? It would seem that the Li-Gallant only wanted a lesson taught."

Valdisa shrugged. *"Whoever* signed the contract set the price, not Hoorka," she said. "And only he knows his reasons."

"Well, let me see." Le Plath turned. Hands on hips, he faced the ranks of spectators. "You heard the Hoorka-kin. We need two thousand to save Pauli. He's done things for most of you; now you do something for him. I've a hundred here myself — what about the rest of you?"

They dug into pockets. Others went to nearby houses to return with their offerings. Le Plath counted it all in his deliberate, methodical manner; cajoling, pleading, threatening until, by small increments, the entire amount was collected. He handed the thick wad of scrip to Valdisa. "Two thousand," he said, simply. "Do you wish to count it?"

Valdisa took the money silently. She held it a moment, then thrust it into a pocket of her nightcloak. "Ritti," she said.

The apprentice jerked into alertness. "Thane?" His voice broke on the word.

"Is Steban watching Sirrah Shroyer?"

"Yah, Thane."

"Then go find him. Both of you will tell Sirrah Shroyer that the contract can be voided due to Shipmaster Le Plath's intercession. See if that is acceptable to him." Turning to the Shipmaster, she bowed. She spoke with unaltered, uncaring aloofness. "We'll wait for our apprentices in our flitter, Shipmaster, then return to Underasgard. Good night, Sirrah."

His smile was wry and twisted. "The Li-Gallant bleeds us dry whether Pauli lives or not, it would appear. We're poor here, m'Dame, and that two thousand is more than the taxes we might have paid — that we'll have to pay anyway. Either way, you've hurt us."

"You've given the man back his life. That's what you wanted, that's what you've accomplished. If that doesn't please you, Shipmaster, then there's nothing the Hoorka can do for you." Distant, always distant, as the Hoorka must be.

"We just continue to feed the Li-Gallant's hunger."

Valdisa allowed a hint of anger to color her voice. Her eyes danced warningly, her hand near her weapon's hilt. "Do not mistake the Hoorka for the Li-Gallant's guild, Shipmaster. The *Hoorka* will keep your money, and return the signer's fee. And remember that this signer is always unknown unless the victim is killed. You may make what assumptions you will, but keep them to yourself. If you have a grievance with the Li-Gallant Vingi, then declare blood-feud against the man."

"I'm not so foolish, m'Dame."

"Then listen to your lack of foolishness and be quiet." She turned to McWilms. "Let's go back to the flitter, kin-brother."

They moved back into the sibilant grasses, toward the flitter in its circle of harsh light. They walked in silence for several strides; then McWilms spoke, a whisper that Valdisa almost did not hear.

"Two thousand?"

Valdisa's mind was still on Le Plath's stubborn insistence on lecturing the Hoorka. She snapped back at McWilms carelessly. "Yah, two thousand," she spat.

"Awfully little money, isn't it?"

"You take what you can get. It puts food on the table."

"The Li-Gallant's food. A mere scrap from his larder."

Valdisa whirled about. Sand scattered beneath her boots. "That's *it,* Jeriad," she hissed. "Say anything more and I'll have you working with the apprentices tomorrow."

"Thane—"

"I mean it, man."

McWilms nodded. He was suddenly very formal, as if talking to guilded kin outside the Hoorka. "I apologize, Thane. I didn't intend to insult you or your leadership. I will admit that I wish you'd decided to let Sula Hermond talk to the kin, but I haven't said so in front of the others. And I won't. I'll keep our disagreements private."

She did not say what she thought: *You'd damned well better, too.* She simply nodded to him in return. "Thank you for that," she said, as stiffly as McWilms.

The wait for the apprentices was long, freighted with a smothering, charged silence.

Gulltopp had slipped below the horizon. Sleipnir was yet to rise. The night was as dark as Neweden ever was under open sky. There were only the distant, aloof stars.

It pleased him. It was necessary.

He could see Vingi's keep just ahead, white stone stark under the glare of floodlamps. The building cast a reflected glow into the surrounding gardens, and he liked that very little. He wished now that he'd used some of the money they'd given him to purchase a light-shunter. *Greed gets me every time—by She of the Five, the scrip's half-gone already.* But no, he rationalized. Vingi's guards will swarm all over Neweden after this, looking for suspicious purchases. There wasn't time to do it right, and he was better off this way.

And if he could do this, his name would be remembered in the annals of Neweden forever. Fame *and* wealth: the ultimate combination. Enil d'Favre, set alongside the greatest names in history. Enil d'Favre, liberator of the lassari (that had a nice alliterative ring to it), hero of the social restructuring, destroyer of the tyrant.

Assassin of Vingi, the last Li-Gallant.

D'Favre moved from shadow to shadow, crouching, his eyes keen for a sign of the guards, his ears preternaturally alert. His sting thumped at his waist, its heavy presence a comforting reassurance. So far it had been easy, slipping over the wall into the garden and avoiding the sleepy guards. He'd seen nothing to worry him, nothing—no sudden flaring of lights, no wail of alarm, no increase in activity around the grounds. Easy. D'Favre wondered how Vingi had managed to live this long, if his security was so lax. He visualized the moment when he'd pull the trigger. That obese body would be torn by the slugs. He'd aim for the head, watch the brains splatter . . . *No, hit him lower, in the stomach. Let him see you, let him feel the pain, then give him the coup de grace.* In his vision, there was very little gore. It was almost sterile and clean—d'Favre had never seen a body struck by the violence of a sting.

Fifty meters, and he would be at the keep's left wall, in shadows between the floodlights. He hunkered down behind a prickly shrub, studying the ground between himself and the wall. No cover at all, just open grass. Still, all the windows there were polarized black or were unlit. Nobody was watching.

Easy.

He thought he heard a noise to his right, a rustling of wind or a footfall. D'Favre went rigid, suddenly frightened, the fear twisting his stomach until he thought he might moan from the pain. He bit his lower lip, trying to breathe softly and slowly, straining to hear more.

Nothing. He relaxed again, the muscles unclenching, his bowels loosening. He smiled to himself. *Fool. You're the one creeping in the night. They should be afraid of you. Enil d'Favre, the night-monster.* He shifted his feet, balancing on his toes, his weight leaning forward for the run.

And then sudden harsh light pinned him. His head came up, he gaped in terror, almost falling. *"Don't move!"* someone shouted at him, too loud, too near. Even as his sphincter relaxed involuntarily and he soiled himself, he fumbled for the sting at his side. He fired wildly in the direction of the voice, his eyes squinting against the revealing glare. The noise of his weapon pounded at him, the recoil bucking the muzzle upward; a voice cursed in darkness.

A blow hammered at him, throwing him to the right, then back to stunned equilibrium as another blast slammed into his chest. He was vaguely aware that two concussions had accompanied the pain. His head lolled down and he saw the ruins of his chest and body. It was not clean, and there was too much gore. He vomited blood as he fell.

It became very dark, the light narrowing into a globe, then a pinpoint like a star. He reached to grasp the tiny sun, but it eluded him and winked out.

Enil d'Favre was lost in night.

"What was his name, Domoraj?"

Vingi did not like being summarily awakened in the middle of the night. He'd thrown on a robe and then grudgingly trudged out to his office, where the Domoraj Kile, head of his security force, waited for him with news of the attempted assassination.

"Enil d'Favre, Li-Gallant. A lassari from Dasta. No previous record of him in the Magistrate's files except for the normal minor lassari offenses. He had a press release—

handwritten—in one pocket, taking credit for your death in the name of the Hag's Legion." The Domoraj held up a paper from a pile of oddments on a cloth draped over Vingi's desk. Vingi frowned at the note in disgust—there were ugly stains on the paper. He made no move to touch it.

"Did you need to bring all this in here?" he asked.

The Domoraj looked visibly disturbed. A tall and too-thin man, when under stress, his Adam's apple bobbed restlessly, and his jaws twitched. The Domoraj ground on a molar before replying. "I'm sorry, Li-Gallant. I thought you might need to see the lassari's effects, and I thought . . ." He stopped abruptly, realizing that Vingi's sleepy stare was fixed on him. He swallowed; the bulge of his throat danced.

"Please don't think, Domoraj. It's too late at night for that. You've done your job splendidly, I'm sure, though a live prisoner might have been a trifle more useful than this collection of artifacts." Vingi paused to ascertain that his criticism had the proper effect on the Domoraj; the Li-Gallant was willing to trade a certain amount of effectiveness for servility in his guards. The Domoraj was the essence of fear when in the presence of his kin-lord, and Vingi knew that the man passed down his shame at being thus treated by employing strict and harsh measures with his own subordinates. The chain of dominance gave Vingi moments of pleasant contemplation.

"He fired on us, Li-Gallant. For the protection of our kin I couldn't afford gentleness." The Domoraj spoke forcefully enough, but his face was woebegone.

At another time, Vingi might have enjoyed playing out the scene, toying with the Domoraj, seeing how the man balanced between fright and confidence; tonight, he was tired. Vingi wanted only his bed and the kin-sister who was warming it. He tugged at the expanse of his robe. "I'm not doubting your judgment, Domoraj, just commenting on the whims of Dame Fate. I assume you've something else to show me in this pile?"

The Domoraj's face took on a feral expression. He slid over to the cloth and stood behind it, like a merchant displaying his wares. "D'Favre had quite a bit of money in his possession, Li-Gallant. Quite a lot."

Vingi glanced wearily at the pouch the Domoraj held. "So he was paid. That's hardly surprising."

The Domoraj's eyes gleamed. He seemed to pounce on the Li-Gallant's words. "Ah, yes. But the money is not Neweden currency, Li-Gallant. It's all new Alliance scrip." His bony chin came up in triumph; he dumped the contents of the pouch on the desk—brightly colored paper fell.

Then Vingi laughed, a full-throated roar that demolished the Domoraj's triumph and set his throat back to quivering. "By all the gods, that's really clumsy. Domoraj, you must see that this ploy's far too obvious. I doubt that the Hag's Legion, *if* they sent poor d'Favre, expected me to truly believe that they were privy to Alliance scrip, in d'Embry's employ. I don't doubt that they *stole* it somewhere, but to have us think that d'Embry . . ." He roared again. "That is good. Well, Domoraj, I'll play the game a bit and see what it gets me. Alliance scrip . . ."

The Domoraj grinned uncertainly into Vingi's hilarity. If the Li-Gallant was happy, he was happy. Or at least he hoped so. The Domoraj ground his incisors softly.

Being a Neweden native and once a kin-lord had its advantages. Gyll heard the news—perhaps—before the Li-Gallant or the Regent d'Embry. Certainly the word came to him before the kin and lassari of Neweden, who awoke to the startling news in the morning.

A newly dead ippicator had been found.

Gyll didn't know what thoughts might run through the minds of those on the ball of mud below *Goshawk*, whether Neweden might turn to piety or destruction. A dark and disquieting suspicion grew in his own head, causing him to push the bumblewort from its comfortable seat on his lap and pace his room. The wort howled thinly at him for the neglect, but Gyll ignored the creature. He stopped before his viewport and glared down at Neweden.

He'd seen an ippicator once before—alive: in a nutrient tank aboard *Peregrine,* Kaethe Oldin's craft. She had told him then that the ippicator, cloned from ancient tissue samples in the Oldin Archives, had been destroyed. Gyll had insisted on that, knowing what the creatures meant to both economy and theology on Neweden. She had promised, and he had witnessed what he'd thought had been the beast's end.

She had promised. Now he wasn't certain that Kaethe's promise had meant anything beyond the bare words. He didn't like the feeling that he might have been duped, that he might not be in control of everything that happened aboard his ship. A slow fury began to build in him; the bumblewort, perhaps sensing this, left off its useless protest and sulked underneath the desk.

"Damn!" Gyll slammed his open hand against the port—a smudge obscured Neweden. Gyll stormed from his cabin, following the tortuous corridors of the ship to the biological section.

"Camden!" Gyll shouted as he entered the small lab. His sharp tone caused the woman there to start and lift puzzled eyes from a com-unit.

"Sula, what can I do for you?" she asked. She wiped her hands on her smock; the Sula made her nervous. She found his presence intimidating. He was always polite but never friendly; the crew whispered that he'd been an assassin for standards, that—though they'd never seen him in a fight— he enjoyed killing. The smell of blood, a bitter tang, always seemed to be about him, although she knew it must be only her imagination. She smoothed her smock over her chunky figure, trying to smile.

Gyll was in no mood for amenities. He was far less polite to Camden than he had been. "Call up your inventory," he said sharply. He strode over to the com-unit, swiveled the terminal so that it faced him. "Get this junk off the screen."

Camden stared at him, then reached out for the keyboard with a stubby finger. The screen flashed emerald and went blank. "What are you looking for, Sula? Maybe I can help."

Gyll brushed her offer aside with a wave of his hand. "I'm not sure. Just get me the inventory files."

He busied himself with the lists for the next hour, occasionally asking Camden to explain an obscure entry to him. She gave him the answers with a growing curiosity. Finally, he rubbed weary eyes and leaned back from the terminal. He slapped at the powering contact, and the unit sank into the desk.

"You look tired, Sula. Tea? Mocha?"

His fury had been dulled by frustration. He'd seen nothing in the inventories to indicate that the ippicator might have been manufactured on *Goshawk,* but he wasn't going to fool himself—if someone had wanted to hide the equipment and supplies in the com files, it could have been done easily enough under another access. Hell, it might not have been entered at all. Gyll wasn't going to find it. "I *am* tired," he said to Camden. "Tea would be nice."

Camden, with a strange glance at him that he couldn't decipher, went to a small plate set on a counter. In a few minutes, water was boiling. "I could help you more if I knew what it was you're looking for, Sula," she said, her back to him. "This *is* my bay, and I know everything that's here."

"I know," he replied. "But I don't want to tell anyone at this point—I don't need gossip." He realized how that must sound to her and tried to apologize. "I'm sorry. It has nothing to do with not trusting you. The only trust I'm worried about is my own, I suppose."

Camden brought back cups. Stains were set in the china, blotches of discoloration. She saw him glance at them. "Don't worry," she said. "They're sterile. You won't get poisoned."

Gyll smiled. He sipped at the tea noisily. "Hot." He set the cup down. "Camden, have you or anyone else used the nutrient tanks lately?"

She thought a moment, the cup steaming in her thick hands. "Just me, and not too recently. Last time was a week or so ago, when that clumsy dockhand—what's his name? . . . ahh, Dani, I think—lost three fingers forgetting to fasten a shield. Before that . . ." She shrugged. Gyll was scowling, and she kept the questions she wanted to ask him inside—the Sula didn't seem to be able to tolerate an interrogation.

"Damn," Gyll muttered. "By the Hag . . ." He glanced at Camden, caught her staring at him. She glanced away hurriedly. "Where else on *Goshawk* could someone clone a large animal, say, three meters long or more?"

Camden shrugged again. "Nowhere. You'd need too much equipment that's only available here. I'd know about it."

Gyll sighed. He tapped fingers on the desk, then abruptly swung to his feet, startling Camden with the motion. Tea sloshed over the rim of her cup. Gyll didn't notice her discomfiture. He nodded to the woman and stalked out of the lab without another word. Openmouthed, she gazed after him. "Thanks for the tea," she said under her breath.

She brushed dampness from her smock. "That damn frigging killer's too spooky for me," she said.

Chapter 10

"REGENT, the Li-Gallant is furious. I've never seen him so angry."

"Santos, the Li-Gallant wanted you to *think* he's furious. The man can be a half-decent actor when he wants to make the attempt. I wonder if he's ever been on the stage."

D'Embry leaned back in her floater with her eyes closed, half-turned on her side so that her full weight wasn't on the hump of the symbiote. She'd had a bad, restless night; her chest had ached, her breath had been shallow and gasping, and nothing the symbiote pumped into her seemed to have much effect. She'd almost thought she could sense the parasite's fear that she might die. Yet she hadn't called the Center's physician. Instead, she sat in her bed, fighting the pain. Eventually, in the early hours of the morning, it had passed. She'd been able to sleep, if not for long, before the almost-simultaneous reports of the finding of the ippicator and the attempt on the Li-Gallant's life.

She knew who had to be responsible for both events. When she found the energy, she was going to be very angry herself.

D'Embry listened to McClannan pacing the room in front of her desk. "Let me guess, Santos," she said. "He made the accusation that someone at Diplo Center—his implication is, of course, that it's me—sent this lassari d'Favre after him. He was righteously indignant, threatening to sever his ties with the Alliance government." Gods, she thought, I'd love a few more hours' sleep. "He's done it before, Seneschal. It's not a new stunt."

"Regent, if you read the report, you know that d'Favre

was carrying Alliance scrip. I can see where that might make the Li-Gallant suspicious."

"The Li-Gallant probably finds that as obvious as I do." She did not open her eyes. "Alliance currency isn't *that* hard to obtain on Neweden."

"In those denominations, Regent? This is a poor world—who'd have that kind of resources?"

She knew, but she said nothing, knowing that if he'd bother to puzzle it out, he'd know as well.

"The Li-Gallant had other questions, as well," McClannan continued. "He was asking if we've made any progress finding the ones responsible for wrecking the dinner party."

"Hinting that we're dragging our heels on it because it's someone here, yah?" Sighing, she sat up, opening her eyes. McClannan was staring at her. He glanced away. "It's raining out," she said.

McClannan's gaze went from d'Embry to the window. An eyebrow raised quizzically. "Yah, it is," he said abstractedly. "Regent, what we're discussing is a trifle more important than the weather. I want to send a full report to Niffleheim Center."

"No!" D'Embry's vehemence widened McClannan's eyes and sent the Regent into a fit of coughing. She reached for a tissue, wiped at her mouth. "No," she repeated, more softly this time. "It's not worth the trouble and expense, Santos. We should deal with it here, unless you want Niffleheim to think we're incompetent." The tension in her chest eased slowly as the symbiote wriggled against her.

"Regent, with all due respect, there's the possibility we may have someone high up in the staff who's deliberately sabotaging us. I think that's worth reporting. Niffleheim could check backgrounds to which we haven't access." His handsome face was intent and serious.

"You believe the Li-Gallant, then?"

"We can't disregard that possibility."

"Do you also suspect me?"

He waited a breath too long before replying. "I didn't say that."

"That's good."

"Then let me send the report, Regent. If nothing else, it will ease the Li-Gallant's suspicions, show him we're actually making an effort to help him."

Once more, d'Embry leaned back gingerly. She looked at her hands—she'd neglected to put on her usual bodytint this morning. Her hands were pale, withered, cracked-skin claws. They mocked her with age and stiffness. She glanced up at McClannan so she would no longer see them.

"No," she said.

He started to stalk away, disgust radiating from him. She let him get nearly to the door before speaking.

"Santos."

He turned, his hand on the door's contact. "Regent?"

"Be reasonable. If *you* wanted the Alliance off Neweden, how would you go about it? You'd do just what is now happening: try to make us seem culpable, try to place the blame for everything on the Diplos. You'd finance the Hag's Legion. You might even fake an ippicator just for the chaos it could create in this society."

"You think the ippicator's faked? The report I saw—"

"Wait until you have more information before you commit yourself to an opinion, Santos. That's what I intend to do, and that's why I don't want you to send a report. All you'll do is cause unnecessary concern and trouble for us here."

"You're just concerned with your own reputation," he said harshly. Then his face smoothed into blandness once more. "I probably shouldn't have said that, Regent, but you'll have to admit that it's one appearance your refusal gives. Either that or you have something to hide."

His accusation stunned her. *Am I really doing that, at the bottom of it all? Is he right?* She shook her head in denial, not trusting words. "Seneschal," she said finally, "Neweden had very little trouble until the Oldins arrived. Now that they're back, it's beginning again."

"It's never stopped, Regent. Neweden's been in upheaval for standards. Things seem to be finally reaching a head, that's all. The Family Oldin is a convenient scapegoat for you."

"If you believe *that,* Seneschal, then you're more a danger to us than anyone." Her voice was dangerously quiet.

He didn't answer her. He slapped at the contact and the door irised open. He went out.

D'Embry closed her eyes again. *Come on, symbiote. Do something so that I don't care what the fool thinks.* But she knew the parasite had no drugs for that. Worry burned at her stomach like acid.

Helgin had been fairly sure that the ploy wouldn't work. He was surprised—Valdisa *would* accept the invitation to dinner aboard *Goshawk*. It nearly forced him out of his composure. "No business will be discussed at all, Thane. That's what Gyll told me to tell you. It's simply a dinner, conversation; a pleasant time."

"Simply being there at all allows you to 'impress' me without speaking a word, doesn't it? It's a little more subtle that way, Sirrah Motsognir, but that's still business," she'd replied, but her tone was soft. Helgin had found that he liked her voice, her wry unwillingness to let him twist words. "Why does Gyll really want to see me?"

"I don't know." He could answer that truthfully. He didn't know, because Gyll had never requested that Valdisa dine with him. Helgin wasn't even sure why he'd decided to fool with such a deception, except that Gyll was increasingly gloomy about his failure to convince Valdisa to tie the Hoorka with the Family Oldin. Helgin suspected that Gyll's moodiness went deeper than that; the Motsognir was certain that Gyll missed Valdisa the lover as well as Valdisa the Thane. Gyll had bedded his share of partners in the standards he'd been gone from Neweden—if nothing else, he'd seemed to be the rising new star in the Oldin firmament, and there were those who threw themselves at him only for that—but Gyll had formed no permanent relationships. He seemed to avoid them, in fact.

Helgin could understand that. The dwarves tended toward solitude as well. But seeing Valdisa again had altered that in Gyll; therefore, Gyll should be given all the opportunities he needed or wanted. That was simple enough. Gyll was a friend, as much of a friend as Helgin had ever had. A bit of deception in personal matters didn't bother him: what was another small lie in the midst of much larger ones?

Valdisa had accepted his statement; Gyll, after all, had been known for his closemouthed secrecy concerning his feelings. "I'll come," she'd said. "But no business, remember. No Family Oldin propaganda."

No business, no propaganda. Helgin had hurried to tell

Gyll what "Gyll" had just done. The Sula tried to scold Helgin halfheartedly, but his delight kept breaking out in a smile. "You little bastard," Gyll had said at last, laughing. Helgin had bowed, grinning. "Someone's gotta run your life for you, Gyll. You do such a lousy job by yourself."

Now Helgin wasn't so sure the idea had been that brilliant. He'd been trying to keep the conversation going for what seemed to be a century. It was tiring work; he'd already drunk half a liter of brandy, and his throat ached. He reached for the decanter again. "Don't let *Goshawk* intimidate you," he said to Valdisa, who sat solemn-faced at one end of the table. "It's just a big hunk of metal that's been made to look confusing to the casual eye—that's just a way to dazzle the visitors."

Valdisa sat stiffly in her nightcloak, the holo clasp of the Hoorka glinting in shiplight. Her gaze kept drifting to Gyll, uncertain; whenever they happened to meet eyes, they'd both look away. "It doesn't intimidate me," she said. "The reaction's quite the opposite. The ship makes me feel claustrophobic, confined."

"But living in a cave doesn't?"

She made a sound that might have been a laugh. "That sounds silly, doesn't it? But Underasgard feels comfortable, natural."

There were uncomfortable moments of silence. Helgin pleaded silently with Gyll to say something. He didn't. The Sula toyed with his food. "Did you ever have that problem, Gyll?" Helgin asked finally, desperate.

"Hmm?" Gyll glanced up at Helgin, who frowned at him. Belatedly, he shrugged. "No, I didn't, I suppose."

Helgin waited for elaboration. There was none. Valdisa had lapsed back into silence as well. Helgin sighed deep in his chest. He inhaled, filling his lungs.

"Hell!" he roared suddenly, slapping the table with an open hand. Liquid sloshed, china clattered; Valdisa's hand, unbidden, went to the hilt of her dagger. Gyll started, half-rising and suddenly alert. "I've *had* it!" the dwarf shouted, standing on the seat of his floater. "I've tried to make this miserable dinner work, but it's no good. You two can sit and converse with your spoons if you want, but *I'm* going to find someone with more conversational skills than your average

stone. Enjoy yourselves." He stormed out in the middle of a stunned silence, with a glare at each of them in turn. The door slid shut behind him.

Valdisa looked at Gyll. "Does he always do that?"

"He's . . . volatile." Gyll settled back into the cushions of his floater. "And, yah, he's like that a lot."

"It almost seemed that this hadn't turned out the way he'd expected, as if he'd been trying to arrange things."

"He likes to think he's in charge of destiny, not Dame Fate." Gyll hedged his answer. *Damn the dwarf for his intrigues, and especially for leaving me with the shambles of them.*

"Was this really your idea, Gyll?"

He would have lied, had she appeared angry or upset. But she merely gazed at him, head propped on chin, elbows on the table, a half-smile flitting at the corners of her mouth. He smiled back at her. "I never could lie to you," he said.

"No, you couldn't. Are you going to try doing it now?"

"No. Helgin planned it all."

Her expression didn't change. That cheered him. "Well, Gyll, *he* lies awfully well. How do you manage to trust him?"

"I don't know always," Gyll admitted, "but I do."

Valdisa nodded. She turned her attention to her food again. Silence settled around them as she took a forkful of meat. Gyll cut his portion into small pieces but made no move to eat.

"You can go ahead," Valdisa said. "You're skinny enough."

That brought back his smile. "Thanks. That wasn't the case eight standards ago, was it?"

"You were out of shape," she said matter-of-factly. "You look much better now."

Valdisa took another bite, Gyll shoved the pieces across his plate. "Is what you said true, Valdisa—*Goshawk* makes you uncomfortable?"

"That sounds like an overture to business, Gyll."

"I'm just curious."

She sighed, glancing at him as if to be certain of his intentions, pushing her floater away from the table. He watched her. "Yah, it makes me uneasy," she said. "That's a better word, I think. I don't like the sense of enclosure. Underasgard never gives me that feeling—and somewhere there's a psychologist waiting to explain all the arcane symbolism behind that. I like knowing that the floor is just earth, not some metal deck with gravity conductors running underneath. I'm sorry, Gyll." She shrugged at him. "I'm sure it's a big, beautiful, wonderful ship you command, but I don't like it."

"You always were candid."

"When I should have been diplomatic?" She smiled. "We were both that way. Maybe things would have been different if we weren't."

"You make it sound so final." He could not keep the wistfulness out of his voice. *You're too damned honest, Gyll. Anyone can read you.* Helgin's words.

Her eyes narrowed, the lips thinned. "It's a little too late for reconciliations, Gyll. Eight standards too late. I thought we both knew that already."

"I don't want to believe that."

"You're joking." Her voice was flat with disbelief. "You can't possibly mean that, Gyll. With all the problems between us, you think we could still be lovers or even friends?"

"Yes."

"It won't work. It can't work."

"You don't want it to work, that's all."

She shook her head, her short hair moving. It was not so much denial as bewilderment. Gyll didn't press her. He waited. He looked for a sign of optimism in her face, her hands, her posture. There was nothing. She sat rigid in her floater, fingertips touching on the table. He remembered those hands—they were rougher, more callused than before, thick with work. Practical, deadly. They had been loving as well; it was easy to forget that they also killed.

"Don't say any more, Gyll. It'll only make this worse."

"I'm not trying to pressure you, Valdisa," he said gently. He raised one shoulder in a desultory half-shrug. "Just trying to understand."

"It's damned obvious, I'd think." Her voice began to rise a little; whether from anger or some other emotion, he couldn't tell. Her eyes had a curious sheen. "Gyll, you left Neweden, you left your kin, and you left me. You can't expect to come back and regain all or any of that simply because that's the way you wish things would happen—there's too much time and too much damage between us. Oh, damn it, I've told you all this before. Didn't you *listen*?" She bowed her head, hand over eyes. "Please drop it, Gyll," she said, her voice almost a whisper. "You made your choice."

"I don't regret my choice," he said slowly, after a long pause. "That's where you're wrong, Valdisa. I find that I prefer most of my present life to my past one. I feel like I've gotten younger, not older. Gods, I used to brood about my age all the time. But there are still parts that I miss: you, the rest of the kin. And I'd like for you to have the opportunities I've had."

Her head came up. "You're back to business."

He waved the objection aside. "On this topic, it's not something I can entirely avoid."

"Then change the subject."

"To what? The finding of the ippicator, Alliance music, Trader fashion, what?"

"Anything at all. I don't care."

"If we could avoid tender subjects, would you think about staying here tonight?"

He didn't really understand what compelled him to ask that; a whim, a sudden boldness. It sounded lame and melodramatically passionate to his ears, like a line in a bad play. In the play, the woman would turn in her seat, tears would brim in her eyes, and a shy smile would touch her lips. "I've been wanting you to say that for so long," she would say.

Valdisa frowned, and her eyes were dry.

"Gods, no," she said.

Then she closed her eyes for a long moment. "I guess you deserve more explanation than that, though. Gyll, part of me would like to stay, the part that remembers Thane Gyll. But I don't know that I love you anymore. I don't even know if I *like* you, because I don't know Sula Hermond at all. And going to bed with him won't tell me much that's important about him."

Gyll felt foolish under her steady regard. He regretted his impulse. *Think before actions, old man. That's what you tell your people.* "I'm sorry, Valdisa," he said at last. "I suppose I was trying to presume upon the past. Too much."

She was becoming aloof again, slipping into the role of Hoorka-Thane. It distressed him. Her back straightened, her gaze became remote. "No apology's necessary, Gyll. I understand."

He knew that any chance for intimacy was gone, destroyed. He knew that she would be Hoorka-Thane and he Sula for the remainder of the evening. He felt sadness for that, and he masked it with a false smile. "Would you like to see the rest of *Goshawk* while you're here?" he asked. "I promise you; no business, just a tour."

Her face told him nothing. Her features might have been a carving. "Just a tour," she said flatly.

Chapter 11

GYLL DID NOT sleep well that night. His thoughts and dreams mingled, contentious. When the bell of his com-unit chimed, he was awake but tired. He knuckled his eyes, yawned. "Yah, Fischer?" he said to the darkness of the bedroom.

"Sula, the Regent d'Embry is calling for you. Line fourteen."

"Tell her I'll call her back in ten minutes."

"She was quite adamant, Sula."

Gyll closed his eyes, opened them again. He brushed hair back from his forehead. "Stall her for a few minutes, then. Off."

He lurched from the bedfield, yawning again. He turned on the lights and dressed. Grimacing at the image in the mirror, he combed his hair perfunctorily. Then he sat at his desk and touched a contact; the screen pulsed into life. "I'm ready now, Fischer."

"Here she is, then. Enjoy yourself, Sula."

The screen flickered with interference and settled into the figure of d'Embry. Immediately, Gyll's mood darkened—her face was skewed with anger. "I thought you to be more subtle and honest, Sula," she said without preface.

"And I thought you more clear, Regent. What *are* you talking about?"

He could see the hump of the symbiote as she shifted in her seat. "Don't be obtuse, Sula. I know you have your contacts on this world. You're well aware of what occurs here: I'm speaking specifically of the attempted assassination of the Li-Gallant, and of the finding of a certain creature thought holy by Neweden—and that may well be more important than the other. There are already reports of small-scale disturbances in some of the cities here."

Gyll punched up a side screen, scanned it. "In Irast, Sterka, and Remeale—a few deaths, a few injuries, some property damaged, mostly in the lassari sectors," he said. "And the attempted assassin was named Enil d'Favre, killed by Vingi's security people." He glanced back at d'Embry. "It seems he had a goodly amount of Alliance scrip."

D'Embry smiled without amusement. "There, you see. I knew you weren't as innocent of the facts as you pretended."

"Helgin gave me most of the news last night, among other items more important to our trading mission here. It didn't mean that much to me, I'm afraid. The man never got close to the Li-Gallant, Regent. It's a cowardly and dishonorable act, but unfortunately that's become less and less important to Neweden. The Alliance's influence, I fear. As for the ippicator, I'll wait until the carcass has been examined before I venture an opinion there."

His tone bordered on the jocular. It soured d'Embry's face further. "Don't go playing games with me, Sula," she said sharply. "You know damned well that someone set us up to be blamed for d'Favre. That leads me to an obvious conclusion."

"Let me tell you how I think on the matter, Regent. I have only your word that this assassin wasn't one of your people. That's all. And it leads me to make no conclusions at all, except that you're upsetting yourself unnecessarily." He said it forcefully enough, but inside the doubts arose to nag at him—the mission to Neweden was beginning to stink in his nostrils, a vague uneasiness that events were proceeding around him over which he had no control.

D'Embry's cheeks flushed. She sat silent for a second, then struck the top of her desk—Gyll saw the motion, heard the slap of her hand below the edge of the screen. "Sula, I'm going to order *Goshawk* out of Neweden space. I know the damned pact, too: you can expect to have notice of a formal hearing before the arbitrators within four local days, as soon as I can get them here. I want you gone."

"Regent, I think you're moving too fast with too little evidence." He spoke quickly, trying to sound calm while wondering why her words disturbed him so much. *What makes you so afraid of that, old man? Are you unwilling to admit that you've failed in your task, or are you frightened that the arbitrators might find that you've been duped?*

"Evidence, man? Dame Fate would laugh at you. Funny how the Hag's Legion springs full-fledged into open defiance just as you arrive; strange how assassins prowl the Li-Gallant's grounds with Alliance scrip in their pockets, or that lassari burst into private gatherings on Alliance territory. Odd that an ippicator appears at a critical moment in the crisis. And the Family Oldin just happens to be there."

"There is such a thing in this universe as coincidence." He did not believe it, not really. He knew she wouldn't, either. It sounded pompous and lame.

She laughed harshly, a syllable of derision. "I don't believe you expect me to credit that."

"It's still true," he persisted. "Consider how the arbitrators might choose. You've no evidence beyond the coincidence of timing. The Hag's Legion call this Renard their leader. Who is he? And would I have aided the Li-Gallant after Vasella's funeral if I intended to kill him a few weeks later? If my sources are as good as you claim them to be, then they've told me correctly that the Li-Gallant has as much as made a formal accusation against the Alliance for the assassination attempt."

That struck her; he could see her go suddenly cold and distant. That was more frightening than her anger, for it was more the d'Embry that he remembered. "As for the ippicators," he continued, "they are the pets of the gods, Regent, and the Family Oldin doesn't claim godhood. Ippicators aren't in our province."

"I've heard rumors that say otherwise, Sula."

Gyll wondered at that, whether she knew more than he thought concerning the samples in the Oldin Archives, or whether she was simply playing with words. He'd told Valdisa of the episode with Kaethe, eight standards ago. If Valdisa had told others of the embryonic ippicator he'd seen, or mentioned it to the Regent herself, then the charade was over—he had implicated himself, a lie of omission. He hated lies, but they seemed to be all around, and untruths were sometimes the easy path.

But he knew he was safe when she spoke. "Sula, you've gained yourself time, but don't fall into delusions. You're right; I haven't enough evidence, and I thought I could frighten you into leaving on your own." She paused. "I *will* get that evidence, Sula, and if you've violated the pact, I'll have you and all the Oldins prosecuted. I'll hound you with legalities and fines and whatever else I can find. Are you certain you don't want to leave now?"

"I haven't finished my work here." *But if last night was an indication, you have.*

D'Embry shook her head. A hand came up to cup her chin; the fingers were tinted aquamarine. "Sula, you puzzle me. You're either totally ignorant of what your people are doing, or you know and don't care."

"I know my ship *and* my people," Gyll said stiffly. "I'll take responsibility for them."

"And you still haven't lost that prickly Neweden pride."

"It offends me to be unjustly accused, yah."

She said nothing to that. He saw her reach out as if to sever the contact, but then her hand drew back. "I wasn't bluffing, Sula. I'm going to dig for that evidence."

"I never thought you were bluffing, Regent. That idea never even occurred to me. You won't find anything."

"You can't believe that."

"I do."

He could tell that she didn't believe *that,* either. The Regent mused for a moment, clearing her throat noisily, as if she suddenly found it difficult to breathe. "As you wish, Sula. I understand that the Li-Gallant intends to display the ippicator in Sterka Square a few days from now."

"Yah, and he's employed me to be in charge of security. It seems he doesn't trust the Diplos. Helgin is already on-planet, making arrangements for the viewing."

"You know that it's simply a political maneuver on his part. It has nothing to do with your expertise."

"You're entitled to that opinion."

She nodded, her face stony. "Then I'll leave you to your tasks, Sula." She peered at him strangely for a moment. "You know, Sula, there are times I can almost believe you."

"I'm glad to hear that," Gyll replied, his voice without inflection.

"And because of that, I feel very sorry for you. FitzEvard doesn't care what happens to those he uses, so long as he gets the results he's after."

"I've often heard the same about you, Regent—with no offense intended."

He had hoped that she would show some reaction to that, show hurt or anger. But she did nothing beyond a slow nod. "Yes, I'm sure you have," she said firmly. He thought that she was finished and began to make his leave, but she continued. "I meant what I said about feeling sorry for you, Sula, and that bothers me. It's not good to have sympathy for your enemy."

"I don't consider us enemies."

"Then that's even worse, Sula."

"You know, Gyll, I've never had anything that could be construed as a religious experience."

"Well, dwarf, all of Neweden gets one of those today."

They were inside the circle of Trader-Hoorka surrounding the body of the ippicator. Behind them, a shield sparked at the four corners of the large hover-plate on which the beast reposed. The ippicator stank; Gyll was glad that the breeze blew in his face and that the day was overcast and cool.

"Did you know that Vingi wanted to restrict the viewing to the guilded kin—the fool. No low kin, even, and certainly not the lassari and jussar."

"I'm glad you talked him out of that notion."

"I'd've *beat* him out of it before I'd have let you put our people out—this place would have been absolute chaos. He would have had a running battle for us to deal with. He'd had his private viewing, and that was all he cared about."

Tri-Guild Square was a static ocean of humanity. In convoluted paths defined by glowing beacon-lines, they trudged slowly up to gaze at the dead beast. Trader-Hoorka moved them along, not letting anyone gaze overlong. "Do we have lights, Helgin? We're going to be here all night."

The dwarf laughed. "All night, and the next day and the next: Vingi now wants it kept out here for three days. The scientists are screaming to get their hands on it, the revelates are spouting contradicting prophecies and doing their own screaming for 'relics.' Gods, I hope the refrigeration units in the plate hold up—if that thing gets any riper, no one will be able to get within fifty meters of it. You could

have reminded me that Neweden law forbids the use of pre-
servatives."

"One gives to Hag Death all She wants—or She comes
after you."

"She wants the ippicator badly, then."

Gyll laughed. "Has there been any trouble yet?"

"Neh. Your setup is working fine. We've vendors all
along the lines, as you suggested, and guards are circulating
prominently. There's been a few skirmishes and more than
one bloody nose, but not much else. It's strange; I expected
worse, especially after the violence just finding the thing
caused."

"I did, too. One would think a Parousia would have a
strong impact. You'd think the Hag's Legion would have
thought of it."

"Maybe they have—we shouldn't get smug yet."

Gyll turned to look at the beast again, the myth made
real. It was ugly—the skin left by the carrion eaters was a
sickly, splotched orange with a dull sheen. The five legs were
stumpy and ungraceful; he could see the probe in the fifth
leg where the animal sensed burrowing insects and
animals—its food. The snout was well-formed for digging; a
hard, thin proboscis complemented the long claws of the
forefeet. It looked dumb, stupid; the eyes were porcine and
small, the braincase narrow. Not an imposing sight, really.
And it was small, no longer than a man, much smaller than
the skeleton that lay in the caverns of Underasgard.

A young specimen, or one just out of the nutrient tank.

The presence still filled Gyll with foreboding. He didn't
like looking at it. He studied instead the faces of those who
stared at the creature. If he was looking for signs there, he
fared no better. He saw shock, awe, fear; a hundred varia-
tions on each. The ippicator might be a portent, yes, but
Neweden seemed unsure exactly what it heralded.

Gyll glanced back at Helgin, who, hands on hips, was
glaring at the crowds. "When I first heard about this ippicator, I scoured *Goshawk,* looking for proof it had been made
there."

Helgin did not turn. He still watched faces: an old woman
weeping, a jussar with a defiant gaze and an open mouth
that belied the angry eyes. "You did, eh? Find anything?"

"No. But then, I didn't expect to."

A revelate shuffled forward, ecstatic, his lips moving in silent prayer, followed by a guilded kin in his finery, his stare contemplative. "Decided you could trust me, then. Is that it?"

"I decided that if you or anyone else had wanted to hide it, FitzEvard could have arranged that easily enough."

Helgin made as if to spit on the pavement, scowling, then seemed to recollect where he was. He swallowed loudly. "Gyll, that sounds oddly like you're making an accusation."

"Don't be angry, Helgin." Gyll put a hand on the dwarf's shoulder. He could feel muscles bunching underneath. "I'm simply letting you know what I'm thinking—trusting you with my paranoias. I'm sure you're willing to share such things with me, as well."

"Hmm," the dwarf grumped, sniffing. "Why don't you just ask me outright: 'Helgin, did you have anything to do with that ugly bag of bones in back of us?' Or shouldn't friends be that direct?"

Gyll ignored the jibe. "D'Embry's sure that it's our doing, somehow. And she's reason to be concerned. There are the riots, and religious zealots left and right proclaiming the end, lassari who look on the ippicators as a sign."

"Sterka's been quiet."

"You sound disappointed, Motsognir, and you're changing the subject."

"I thought you'd gotten your answer."

"I suppose I have. I'm sorry, Helgin. It's just that the creature back there bothers me."

"I thought you were over the god-madness of Neweden. Damn, Gyll, next you'll be getting a revelate to shrive you." The Motsognir kicked at the pavement. He set his hands on his hips again. "Don't give me this crap, Gyll. That thing's just an animal, and a very dead one. It doesn't *mean* a damned thing. If I thought it'd taste good, I'd carve it up for steak."

Gyll's mouth was compressed tightly, his brow was caned with lines. He tried to smile; the effort was a failure. "Most of the people here would say you blaspheme, Helgin. I'd keep my voice soft."

"I don't believe in signs or gods."

"It doesn't matter what *you* believe. What matters is that Neweden does."

"Well, fine, maybe we'll have some excitement. This is damned boring."

"We'll have more than you want, I'd wager."

Gyll's prophecy seemed in error by night. There were skirmishes and scuffles, the usual results of having too many people in a confined space, but no real difficulties. As the sunstar slid behind the spires of Tri-Guild Church, hoverlamps were lit, transforming the square. The crowds had not eased; there were always more to replace those who had left. Floodlamps cast their blue-white glare on the ippicator. Near midnight, Gyll sent Helgin back to *Goshawk*. Gyll stayed, still uneasy, and—though he would not have admitted it to the Motsognir—unwilling to leave the presence of the five-legged beast. He was surprised that he saw none of the Neweden Hoorka among the crowds. She of the Five, goddess of the ippicators, was the patron of the guild, his own choice. The ippicator should have aroused great interest in the devout among the Hoorka, even if Valdisa had been noncommittal about it. He wondered if perhaps, for some reasons of her own, she had ordered the Hoorka to stay away.

Gulltopp was riding at zenith, Sleipnir was hauling itself up toward its brother moon. Everything was doubleshadowed outside the blaze of light around the ippicator. The night chill had caused Gyll to put on a jacket—light but warm, with the emblem of the Oldins blazoned at the chest: a stylized bird of prey clutching at a world with its claw. The crowds, hours into the viewing, showed no signs of declining. Around the square they shuffled, following the beaconlines, waiting for their few seconds of closeness.

"Sula?" She was a woman in the white tunic and pants of the Trader-Hoorka. She held her crowd-prod nervously, twisting it in her hand. Gyll thought he remembered her name.

"You're Alden Hessia?"

"Hestia," she corrected. "Sula, I've been making the perimeter check. We're missing one of the sniffers."

Gyll was immediately concerned; the sniffers were Trader-Hoorka equipped with explosive-detection devices. The equipment was not capable of sensing anything particularly sophisticated, but Gyll had not expected sophisti-

cation of Neweden. Certainly, as Thane, well-versed in
Neweden's offensive weaponry, he had known nothing that
would elude a good sniffer. That one of them was missing
filled him with foreboding—he could see the fear in Hestia's eyes, as well.

"What's the name of the sniffer?" He searched the
crowd near him as if the man might suddenly appear there.
The faces suddenly had an ominous cast. They no longer
pleased or entertained him.

"Culdoon."

"Culdoon . . . Damn, he's been no trouble beforehand.
You know him better, though. He couldn't have gone off by
himself, taken a rest while his officer was somewhere else?"

"He's not that type, Sula. I know him pretty well." Hestia
was confident of her evaluation. Her round face was taut
with earnestness. "I'd have looked more if I'd thought that.
I came here right away."

"How long has he been missing?"

"I'm to check every hour—no longer than that."

Gyll pursed his lips in concentration. "Yah. Hestia . . . get
another sniffer to cover Culdoon's post. Tell Lutana Creption to get her squad and sweep that sector: see if she can
find Culdoon. And tell the Lutana to get her squad's sniffer
moving in the lines—they aren't moving too fast, so our intruder can't be too far in; no more than a quarter of the way.
Neh . . ." Gyll abandoned that thought. "He might be paying
to get closer—best to check all the way from the beast out.
I'll get the people here to slow the lines down—that'll buy
us time, since we can't clear the crowds without starting a
riot." He was thinking out loud, realized it. Adrenaline
made his voice tense and quick. "Move, Hestia—let me
make arrangements. Go!"

The woman saluted and moved off at a run. Gyll went to
the com-net and called *Goshawk*. Quickly he advised Helgin of the situation. "It may just be someone sleeping on
duty, but I've a bad feeling, Helgin."

"I'll be down as soon as I can, Gyll, but it won't be soon
enough, if you're right."

"Then let's not waste time talking. You contact the Li-
Gallant, tell him to be ready to provide medical assistance
and additional guards if we need 'em. Hurry, Motsognir."

Gyll cut the contact and touched the code for Lutana Creption. She answered his call gruffly.

"Creption here."

"Lutana, this is Sula Hermond. Any news?"

Her voice immediately became less irritable. "I've begun the sweeps, Sula. I'll let you know immediately if we find Culdoon. If he's asleep or having fun with some local, he'll wish he *had* been ambushed."

"You have a sniffer in the lines?"

"Yes."

"Our intruder will be halfway in or better—they'll have known how long they had before the sniffer was missed. Get another sniffer off the perimeter and into the lines. Let me know if anything's spotted. And make sure everyone's using a shield."

There was very little he could do beyond that. He could watch the faces that came up to stare at the ippicator and wonder if one of them harbored something other than reverent curiosity. He could worry. What was the intruder— if there was one—planning? Did he take out the sniffer because he had explosives, and if so, what type, where would they be placed or thrown? Could it be a red herring, a diversion to lead them away from the real focus of trouble? Could it, please Dame Fate, be nothing at all?

Gyll felt impotent, helpless. It had been different with the Neweden Hoorka. Then you knew what you were expected to do, knew what your victim might attempt. Everything was open, everything was one-on-one, personal. You and someone else. He hated crowd actions because they were impersonal and confusing. Lutana Creption was probably a better tactician with this situation. *I hate it. Give me the chase, the contract, the hunt.*

The Trader-Hoorka nearest to him knew that something was awry. Gyll could sense it in the covert glances back at him, and he suddenly realized that he was pacing, hands behind his back, near the com-net. He forced himself to stand still, to wait. That was the hardest part of his present job—to delegate the authority and then just await results.

The com-net chimed. "Sula here."

It was Lutana Creption. "We've found Culdoon. He's just about alive; someone used an altered prod on him. He

was behind a stack of crates in an alley a few streets away
from the square."

She said nothing else, waiting. Gyll knew that her
thoughts were running parallel to his own. "Then they've
got someone in the crowd," he said. "Shit."

"I'm sorry, Sula. And since they bothered to go after a
sniffer, I'd worry about explosives first."

"The two sniffers we have checking the lines aren't
enough, then. Send in all the perimeter crews and seal off
the square to anyone trying to enter the lines. If they want
out, fine, let 'em go, but let's not get anyone else in danger."

A brief silence spoke her uncertainty. "We're going to
have problems with that—these people keep coming to see
the beast. They won't like being turned back."

"They'll have to wait."

"We'll have trouble."

"Then we'll have to handle it," Gyll snapped. "Seal off
the square and send the sniffers in. If we need more bodies,
use Vingi's guards until Helgin can get here with more
Hoorka."

"Yes, Sula." She did not sound pleased.

"Lutana, I know these people. I'm one of them. Be firm,
but be very polite. Make sure your people frame everything
with respect—they're touchy about honor and you might
find yourself in a fight by accidentally insulting the wrong
person. But they do understand authority; they'll obey if it's
handled correctly."

He heard her sigh. "Polite but firm. Yes, Sula."

"And gently, Lutana. I don't want any innocents hurt because our people were clumsy."

"As you say."

Gyll cut the switch. The Hoorka nearby were looking at
him again. He ignored them, pretending calm. He beckoned
to one. "I'm taking a net patch. You stay by the com and
relay any calls for me."

"Yes, Sula."

Gyll stuck the patch—a small, sticky pad—in place just
behind his ear. He touched the vibro on his belt, made sure
that it slipped easily in its sheath. Then he moved into the
crowd, sprinkling apologies before him, though all but the
high kin moved back from him without asking, recognizing
the uniform as belonging to those running the spectacle.

Though he had no clear idea of what he intended, it felt better to be moving, to be closer to any potential action.

Rising on his toes to peer above the crowd, he saw one of the sniffers two lines over. Excusing himself to those around him, he made his way over to the man. "Anything yet, Benoit?"

Benoit didn't look up from the display screen of the bulky equipment strapped to his chest. "There's a slight reading, Sula—I'm trying to vector it now." He swiveled in place, his hands moving over knobs. He shook his head, grimacing. "I can't get it isolated—wait! There it is. A hundred-twenty, hundred-thirty meters southeast. Crude stuff, but there's got to be a lot of it if I'm picking it up this far off. Stuff's leaking into the air like homemade. It'll be volatile junk, Sula. Want to move closer?" He was speaking in a whisper now. Gyll had to lean forward to hear him above the crowd's noise.

"Hold a moment." Gyll touched the patch. "Lutana?" he said, subvocalizing. The patch's reception was tinny but clear. Her voice seemed to reverberate in his head.

"Here, Sula."

"Benoit's got the intruder." Gyll leaned over the screen and read coordinates to her. "Got that? I want you to start closing in on that area: shield up. Get as close as you can without alarming him. Benoit and I will start working our way in, and I'll have him work with the other sniffers to get a more precise location. Don't get too close or let him see you. And we could use a volunteer to take off shield and uniform, get close enough to give a visual description."

"Should we still be polite?" He could hear an inflection through the patch that annoyed him—he would have to speak with her after this, and not mildly.

"You'd damned well better be if you don't want a riot. Let me know immediately when your volunteer has that description."

"He" turned out to be a woman. The description was relayed to Gyll: "Dark hair, close-cropped, not too clean. She's wearing a loose leather coat, tan-colored, and she looks to be pregnant—that'll be the bomb, I'm sure. Light blue pants, brown boots. She's in line, looks a little nervous, keeps glancing around."

Lutana Creption broke in. "I've got someone with a

nightscope in a building along the square, Sula. He says it's a bad shot; she's packed in with the rest. Getting her out isn't going to be easy, and the people around her aren't wearing bodyshields. If she gets too nervous, we're going to lose a hell of a lot of locals."

"Let me think a second, Lutana." The people around Gyll stared at the sniffer, at the white-haired Trader-Hoorka beside him. Gyll could feel their sublimated hostility—they were the Li-Gallant's hirelings. "We're the only safe ones out here—if we can surround her with shields, it'll confine the damage."

"Nobody's safe if the blast throws us into something—the shields aren't going to help with that, or the concussion."

"It'll take five or six of us, more if we're not close. I'm one. How about you, Lutana?"

A pause, static-filled. "That's two."

"You got a few more daredevils in the squad?"

After a minute, she replied. "I'm stocked with fools."

Gyll chuckled despite himself, wondering why he suddenly felt good again. "Fine. Is your spotter still there?"

"Yah, Sula," came the voice.

"Your task is to fake a collapse—heart attack, anything that'll give us an excuse to be hurrying in your direction. With that pretext, we should be able to move people aside, out of the way, and maybe even get to her before she does anything stupid. I doubt that she's suicidal; if she can't place the bomb and get away, we should be able to take her safely."

"And if she decides to become a martyr?" Lutana Creption.

"Then we'll hope the shields work. Gods, I wish we had the ship's stores close; a paralyzer, stun-gas—there's a dozen alternatives on the ship."

"You couldn't anticipate all the needs, Sula." Creption's voice was oddly respectful. It made Gyll smile quickly. "If we'd brought an arsenal, there'd still be problems. Your plan's as good as the next."

"That doesn't make me feel better. Well, let's see if it works. Make certain the shields are up and the ears are protected."

The collapse was well-performed; the spotter was a de-

cent actor. From his vantage point, Gyll could see little, but
he heard the welling of loud voices, the sudden heightening
of crowd-awareness as heads craned to see what had caused
the commotion. "Let me through, please!" Gyll shouted as
he began pushing toward the woman. Each person behind
him was one less likely to be injured—the Oldin bodyshields
were far superior to those Gyll had known on Neweden.
They did not hinder a person much at all. For any explosive
he could conceive of this woman having, they would shelter
the fragile body from the initial burst and any shrapnel as
well; though they well might be flung away like sticks, perhaps scorched from the blast, they would in all likelihood
survive. Not the kin and lassari around the woman—they
would be fragile dolls in a hurricane; broken, torn, and
bloody.

Gyll could not get that red-imbued vision from his head.
He struggled forward against the crowd's resistance. Shadows from the hoverlamps threw crazy, erratic shadows over
them; the buildings around the square loomed against
moonlight.

Suddenly, he could see her. She clutched at the expanse
of her belly, wide-eyed, her gaze skittering like that of a
trapped animal. She was pretty in a disheveled way, not at
all the hard, stoic woman he'd expected to see, but a woman-
child, frightened. To his right, a knot of Trader-Hoorka were
bending over a prone figure. Others came in, moving Newedeners aside, crowd-prods out. The woman was becoming
more isolated, and he could sense her desperation, could
see that she now knew that she was discovered and trapped.
More of Gyll's people arrived, shouldering aside those
nearest the woman. He took a step toward her as the ring
began to close.

"No!" she shouted, startling him. She whirled to flee,
only to find Lutana Creption standing there. She swung
about again, arms swinging, her coat flapping open—Gyll
could see something strapped there. He lunged for her—his
hand caught her sleeve, but she wrenched it away, cloth
tearing. "Renard!" she cried, as if to the air. "You
promised—" She said nothing more.

A flash of orange-white, a deafening "thu-*whump.*"
Gyll's shield went rigid in that instant—he felt himself being tossed, striking something, bouncing. The world whirled

about him, dancing, tumbling; the echo of the explosion dinned in his ears through the plugs; his vision was lost in a welter of glaring afterimages. He hit something hard—even through the constriction of the shield his head snapped back.

Amidst a roaring, sight faded.

Someone had used his head for an anvil. He could taste the iron-tang of blood in his mouth, and his legs didn't seem to want to work. Either he couldn't open his eyes or he couldn't see. He could hear vague noises, garbled speech. He hawked, spat up phlegm.

"Shit!" someone said. "I might've known you'd aim for me."

"Helgin?" His throat rasped the word.

"No, your friggin mother. Who the hell do you think it is?"

"I can't see." Each word was a breath, an agony.

"Your eyes are bandaged, fool. Here, feel."

Gyll felt someone take his hand, move it to his face. His fingertips touched soft cloth. Gyll sighed and tried to flex his legs—pain shot through him, but they moved.

"You certainly like to cause yourself unnecessary pain," Helgin commented, "but you probably won't settle down until I give you the details, right?—No, don't answer; I know you. The medics say you'll be fine, no thanks to your little attempt at heroism. Didn't you ever hear about delegating authority? Staying in one piece is one of the advantages of doing that."

"Couldn't ask without . . ." His mouth was dry. He swallowed. ". . . going myself."

"Damned nice of you. That's gotten you flashburns on the face and hands, a small concussion even through your thick skull, assorted bumps and bruises, but nothing broken. You'll have a hearing loss for the next several days—I'm damn near shouting at you now. They want you in the medidoc overnight, but after that you're on your own again."

"The others?" He wanted water, anything.

"All our people are fine—all in much better shape than you. The blast killed nine bystanders and the woman, of course. There's about thirty others in for various injuries; all of them should make it. It could have been a lot worse, Gyll.

A lot worse. The Li-Gallant has managed to praise you and condemn you all at the same time."

"Water?"

"Here."

Something nudged Gyll in the lips—a straw. He sucked on it greedily, feeling the coolness soothe his throat. Helgin pulled it away before he finished. "That's the whole glass, Gyll—you want more?"

"In a moment." He could speak again. "She didn't set it off, Helgin." He licked dry lips, found them cracked and torn. "I saw her hands the whole time. I think she was using a transmitter—she called Renard—the Hag's Legion. Then it went off."

"We found some of the pieces. It was triggered by a remote switch."

"Renard."

Gyll could hear the Motsognir's shrug, a rustling of cloth. "Most likely."

"I want him."

"Thought we weren't going to interfere in Neweden politics?"

Gyll tried to sit up, couldn't. He felt dizzy, and lay back, panting, until the spell passed. "This isn't politics," he said at last. "It's filthy murder. Killing without the redemption of honor. I want that bastard."

"D'Embry might have something to say about it. So might Vingi."

"I want him. I don't give a damn about the rest, Motsognir."

"I don't blame you. I want him too." The dwarf sounded strangely fierce. "He was watching, you can bet. Watching, and waiting for the right moment." He paused. Gyll stared at the darkness before his eyes until the Motsognir spoke again. "I think I can find him, as well. A week, Gyll, then we'll go together, when you're well. I'll find him."

"A week." Gyll repeated the words.

He heard Helgin rise and walk away. More footsteps approached. A hand touched him on the shoulder. "Sula?" It was a gentle voice; a woman. "We're going to move you back to *Goshawk* now." There was a cold swabbing; something pricked his arm. A cold numbness began to spread over his chest. "I've given you a sedative for the trip—just let yourself sleep, Sula. You'll be back on the ship when you wake."

He felt himself being lifted. He swayed. The motion was curiously restful. He was moving—he could feel the breeze on his face.

And somewhere, he slowly drifted into dreamless sleep.

Chapter 12

*I*t was the first time they'd made love.

Afterward, he kissed her and rolled from the bedfield. He came back with a hot washcloth and a soft towel. Gently he cleaned her. She hadn't expected such tenderness from him—it surprised her, touched her. She stroked his face as he used the towel.

"Thank you," she said. "That was nice."

"Good." His voice was husky, a bedroom whisper.

"Part of your code?" she teased.

"A personal part."

"And a good Thane always follows his own rules."

"Rules are made to be obeyed."

She brought his head down, kissed him long and thoroughly. His hands moved on her body, arousing her again. She brought her arms around his shoulders, rolled him on top of her. "Don't ever change that code."

"You don't change what works."

Valdisa sat before the headless skeleton of the ippicator and watched the light of her hoverlamp shift colors along the bars of the ribcage. The cavern walls flickered gold and green. Thoughts raced, directionless, in her mind. She did not resist. She drifted helplessly with them.

Damn Gyll. Damn him for coming back, damn him for leaving. And, most especially, damn him for making her realize that she still cared about him. She thought she'd exorcised that ghost. She missed the intimacy which she hadn't been able to find with any others among the kin, and she wished him gone so that the old pain would settle into dormancy again.

Go away, Gyll. You hurt me too much.

Drifting . . .

An ippicator—not long extinct, but newly dead. She of the Five, what is that supposed to mean? Why do You send Your pet back to this world—in the lore, it says that the world will dissolve into chaos. Is that what You intend?

Drifting . . .

You don't change what works. And if it doesn't *work? The code would kill them, a long and slow strangulation as the society on which it was based changed around it. You have to do something, woman; you even know what it must be, but you don't want to take the step, do you? You're afraid.*

You're damned right I'm afraid. But I'll do it.

"I'll do it." The sound of her voice brought her from her reverie. She was surprised so much time had passed since she'd come here; she was surprised to find that, unknowingly, she'd been crying. Valdisa sniffed, obliterating the wetness on her cheeks with the sleeve of her nightcloak.

She flicked the tether of the hoverlamp and the light obediently bobbed toward her. Letting it ride above her head, she began walking back toward the outer sections of Underasgard. Her contemplation had helped, though the strangely moving events of Neweden still puzzled her. At least it seemed clear to her what Hoorka must at last do.

Abandon the code of Gyll. Ally the guild with Vingi. Only that way would they survive. The Regent would be no help to them, and she did not trust the Oldins. She didn't like the taste of her decision, but she could think of no other solutions.

She was very afraid that there were none.

Chapter 13

HELGIN HAD NOT WANTED Gyll to come with them. He cited the lingering effects of Gyll's injuries: a slight limp, a ruddiness to the skin. Gyll told him curtly that the doctors had released him and he *was* going. They'd glared at each other for a moment, then Helgin had given in to the inevitable. Gyll was Sula, and could halt the entire operation with a word. Helgin bowed to that fact with a Motsognir's normal ill grace, but he bowed.

It just made his intentions much harder to realize.

It was night. Dasta Burrough crawled with life. The five of them, in the dingy, tattered clothing of lassari, moved through the shadowy streets—Gyll, Helgin, and three of the Trader-Hoorka. Despite their guise, there were still stares and whispered comments—there was no disguising the Motsognir build. Dasta was worse than Gyll had remembered. Parts of it were now scarred, blackened rubble from what the populace called Vasella's Fire; the rest was cluttered and filthy. Garbage piled uncollected against the buildings and in the central gutter of the street. Occasionally they would come across a wirehead sprawled unconscious in the pathway, oblivious of his surroundings. Jussar—youths caught between kinship and lassari—prowled in gangs, rowdy and noisy; the lassari and low kin walked the streets with an air of paranoid caution, weapons (for the kin) placed visibly on their belts. Prostitutes of both and indeterminate sexes cajoled and insulted from doorways and windows.

"Gods, I hate this place," Gyll muttered.

"I don't know; in some ways, I rather like it," Helgin replied.

"You would."

"Hey, it has a certain energy, a vivid, crude life."

"Next you'll be talking about the ambience."

Helgin grinned. "I mean it, Gyll. Just because it's dirty and squalid—which it is—doesn't mean that it's not a 'good' place. It has a feeling of secrecy, of adventure."

"It's squalid, yah, and the only things that lurk here are hatred and despair."

"Both are honest emotions."

"They're not ones I care to experience."

"Right," Helgin said. "And which one of us wanted Renard's ass?"

"It's an honest emotion, dwarf."

They turned where a narrow alleyway held darkness between two tall buildings. There, hidden behind a stack of broken crates, they checked their weapons: tanglefeet bombs, crowd-prods, two stun-grenades, vibros. Helgin had an ancient projectile weapon bolstered to his side. Gyll frowned at the sight of it. "You'll only kill someone with that, Helgin. I'd rather have him alive."

Helgin put his hands on his hips, belligerent. "I want something that'll stop someone quick, if I need to. None of this junk'll do that."

Gyll stood, unmoving, for a moment, then shrugged. "Then be damned careful with it. I don't trust revolvers, and they're frigging noisy. They're also not honorable weapons."

"Neither's a bomb."

Gyll nodded. "Your point's taken. Just be careful with it."

"Don't worry—just stay out of my way."

Helgin did not say what he really thought—if all went well tonight, Renard would not be alive to tell his tale of treachery. He would be forever silent, and Gyll would never know of Helgin's involvement in the Hag's Legion. The Motsognir wanted Renard removed from Neweden; if this was the only way, so be it. The relative morality of the situation didn't bother him. He'd long been pragmatic about such things.

Gyll gestured for silence. His hand moved in familiar patterns: the Hoorka assassin's hand-code, the code he'd taught to the Trader-Hoorka as well. *Quiet. Helgin . . . lead.*

They'd traded their lassari disguises for dark, form-fitting clothing. Their faces were darkened as necessary, and the blackened handles of their weapons hung within easy reach. They slipped from shadow to shadow like wraiths: down the alley, across the next street quickly and unnoticed, then into a warren of claustrophobic lanes. Helgin stopped them again just inside the mouth of another alley. *There.* He gestured to a doorway across the street and to their left.

Gyll signaled to one of the others to check the area. The man unslung a snooper, swinging it in an arc—all the monitors remained green. He shook his head.

? Gyll queried Helgin, who frowned.

Something wrong, the dwarf replied.

Pull back?

No. Helgin glanced out at the street once more. No one moved down its short length. Few of the windows of the buildings were lit, and there were no streetlamps. *Traps?* he gestured to the Hoorka with the snooper, who swung it about again. Green. *No.*

Trap? Helgin asked again. The Hoorka, with a grimace of irritation, held out the snooper to the Motsognir. Helgin hesitated, but took the device. He tested all functions, then surveyed the street once more. All LEDs remained emerald. The dwarf's shoulders slumped visibly; he handed the snooper back. The man took it ungently.

Gyll leaned out, glancing left and right himself. The snooper would have detected most alarms or suspicious concentrations of metal, but that left a hundred possibilities. He didn't like the feel of the situation, and he knew that the others felt that unease as well. There was a subtle sense of something being awry: the street was too deserted, the task looking too easy. Gyll hesitated, half-tempted to call off the operation rather than walk into an ambush the snooper had missed. He'd expected *something* in the way of guards for Renard.

Weapons out, he gestured at last. *You*—to Liana, the fastest of them—*go across. Quickly.* The woman nodded; she crouched, leaning, then ran, her footsteps loud in the stillness. Gyll watched the street, the windows, the rooftops. Lightly panting, Liana had flattened herself against a wall. She examined the buildings across from her, then gave a wave of her arm. *Clear.*

Gyll glanced back at Helgin, received a shrug. He signaled to the others. *Let's move.*

The Motsognir, surprising Gyll with his speed, hit the door first—the wood splintered under his foot. Another kick, and it swung crazily open. Helgin was inside with the motion, rolling a hand-flare into the room as he ducked right. The others entered behind him in a rush, ready, but Helgin had already slid his weapon into its holster. The room was neat, shabby furniture set in place, the desk scarred but clean. There was no dust. It looked as if someone had set the room in order before leaving. Helgin kicked at a chair; it clattered to the floor.

The Motsognir turned to Gyll. His dark eyes glinted under thick eyebrows; he pulled at his beard.

"The bastard's gone," he said.

It began as a routine visit to the Li-Gallant's offices. Vingi's signature was needed on a release form for those being treated at the Diplo hospital after the explosion in Tri-Guild Square. Afterward, McClannan and Vingi were to appear at a press conference. But the Li-Gallant steered the Seneschal aside into Vingi's private office, and he had startled McClannan with his first words.

"You strike me as the ambitious sort, Seneschal. Why don't you get rid of d'Embry?"

McClannan found himself momentarily speechless. The Li-Gallant grinned corpulently at him, fingers steepled under his trebled chin. Animo paintings swirled dizzily on the walls. McClannan decided to try for righteous anger. He put the expression on his face like a mask.

"That's not the way the Alliance works, Li-Gallant. And she is my superior."

The order of excuses did not escape the Li-Gallant, nor did McClannan's attempt at judicious irritation fool him. He laughed under his breath, a snort of amusement. "Seneschal, please don't assume that because I'm fat I'm also stupid. I've seen the Alliance work for decades now, and I know that you work much the same as Neweden, once you dig under the surface of your laws. I also know that d'Embry isn't exactly in favor back on Niffleheim—she's offended too many of *her* superiors, neh?" Vingi sat back in his floater; he fiddled with one of his many rings. "You should

take a lesson from that, Seneschal. She's achieved her reputation by defying those in power when she felt they were
wrong. One must be selfish to achieve either reputation or
power, and one must know when to go against those above
you."

McClannan did not disagree. He drew himself up to his
full height and let his eyes narrow slightly as he smiled. It
was one of his favorite poses. "It's a dangerous course of
action, as well."

"One never gets anywhere without taking risks. That's
one of my axioms, Seneschal, as true here as in the Alliance.
The danger may be physical or not, but it's always there. Do
you gamble?"

"I've been known to do so."

"Then you must know that to win you always choose
with an eye to the odds and to your luck. Do you feel
lucky?"

McClannan allowed himself a small laugh. He shifted his
position slightly, a model's turn. Long, well-manicured fingers tapped at his belt. "I've done well enough. I've been
lucky."

Vingi nodded. "You know that there's been continuous
pressure from Niffleheim for d'Embry to resign, especially
after that Hoorka contract on Heritage."

A nod. Vingi studied McClannan—he didn't like the
man, found him to be as superficially intelligent as he was
superficially handsome, but he knew that the man was pliable. His ambition was his weakness, and Vingi prided himself on his ability to exploit weaknesses. "Bring her down
and *you* become Regent—you're already being primed for
that job. A word to the right ear, and the title is yours."

Vingi watched McClannan lean forward as he said the
words. The man could not keep the eagerness from that
face; it made the handsomeness ugly, feral. "And what do I
whisper to that ear, Li-Gallant? What more can I tell them?
They've already heard all the rumors and have done nothing. They know what she does."

The man's vapid willingness to engage in treachery repelled Vingi. *Gods, the bastard doesn't even bother to disguise
it. He doesn't worry about recordings or countertreachery or
blackmail. He either discounts that possibility or chooses to
ignore it. Either way he's a fool, an easy fool. No wonder*

d'Embry despises him. Can he really be this gullible, or is he a trap within a trap? No ... that's not d'Embry's way. Vingi made no attempt to conceal his disgust. He looked up at Mc-Clannan with distaste in his eyes. "Are you always so ready to stab someone in the back, Seneschal? I'm looking for allies, not new enemies."

McClannan looked confused now—why had the Li-Gallant suddenly retreated? "I'm not your enemy, Li-Gallant. Nor is the Alliance."

"D'Embry's help has always come grudgingly to me."

"That will change when I'm Regent, I assure you." There, McClannan thought; back to the subject.

"I get the same assurances from the Family Oldin—if I'm willing to rescind the treaty Neweden has with Niffleheim." He'd expected that statement to have an effect. He was not disappointed. The studied posturing of McClannan gave way to incredulity. "You wouldn't do that."

"I would. All it takes is a vote of the Neweden Assembly. I own that particular institution."

"But that's never ... Gods, the reputations of the Diplos of a world that left—"

Vingi pounced on the phrase. *"Your* reputation, Seneschal? That's your alternative, man. Enhance your reputation or ruin it—it's your choice."

"You're bluffing." McClannan didn't sound convinced. "The Alliance has much more to offer than the Family Oldin."

"You're just spouting the party line, McClannan." Vingi's voice was suddenly harsh and strident. He spoke quickly, as if delivering a lecture to an errant student. "You, like most of the Diplos, know very little about the Trading Families, the Oldins in particular. Your d'Embry is an exception to that, and that's why she fears FitzEvard so much. As for *me*, Seneschal, I'm a pragmatist and an opportunist—I pretend to be nothing else. I plan, and I take what's offered to me. An example; I spoke with Thane Valdisa of the Hoorka yesterday. She's going to ally the assassins with my guild, and I intend to take them. The Hoorka will give me fear, and I can use that fear to enhance my own standing. So if you think I'm bluffing, Seneschal, simply turn around prettily and walk out of this office and I'll see you at the press conference in ten minutes. What I'll have to say to the reporters isn't in the script you've been given."

Vingi waited, staring at the man before him, unsmiling. McClannan grimaced. His eyes squinted, then relaxed. His gaze could not stay with Vingi's steady regard. He studied his hands, turning them over and curling the fingers. But he did not move toward the door.

"I can tell Niffleheim that the only alternative to losing Neweden to the Family Oldin is to replace d'Embry?"

Got him. Vingi nodded slowly. "One should always tell the truth to one's superiors—if it serves him to do so."

Tight-lipped, McClannan nodded in return. "I'll do it," he said, simply.

Vingi smiled. With a groan of effort, he hoisted himself from his floater and arranged the expanse of his clothing. "Then let's go to the damned conference and pretend to be signing papers." A pause. "Regent McClannan."

The day was windy and cool, with spatters of rain from scattered clusters of cloud. Few people braved the weather this afternoon. Tri-Guild Square was nearly empty. Even the Mason's Guild, which had been repairing the jagged hole in the pavement, had retreated before the elements. McWilms walked past a temporary barrier of ropes, ignoring the sign warning him back. He gazed at the last mute remnants of the ippicator's visit—the beast was now under study in a government lab.

McWilms didn't know what he was looking for here—a sign, perhaps, a symbol, something to give him direction.

The last several days had been nothing but arguments in Underasgard. It had begun with the display of the ippicator. Many of the kin had wanted to see the mythical beast, the visible sign of She of the Five. But Valdisa had refused them permission to go. Too many people, she'd said. A potential hazard. Their presence might spark a confrontation. Her arguments had fallen with dull precision, and she had ignored all discussion on the subject.

Hands in the pockets of his nightcloak, McWilms stared down at the hole. Rain had pooled there, and not much work had been done thus far. He tried to imagine the violence of the explosion, how it must have been, bodies flung, blood everywhere. He could not visualize it well—his experience of death had always been closer, with a knife or a hand weapon, individual. As a Newedener, he didn't truly understand this distanced, random killing that the Hag's Legion had employed. It was foreign, alien. No honor was there; they didn't even know who might be sent to the Hag. Who had they been after?

The argument about the ippicator had not been the last. A few days later, she had told the kin that she intended to alter the code—Hoorka would align itself with Vingi's rule-guild. They would still accept contracts on the same terms from anyone, but the Li-Gallant would have the approval of them. A roar of protest had followed—they were then no better than the Li-Gallant's personal assassins, and how soon after this would they no longer give Dame Fate Her chance, but agree to kill anyone contracted, without the victim's chance of escape being given? Valdisa had been cool, logical; she'd opened the guild's books to all of them, shown them how badly Hoorka fared. It would not get better; Neweden was changing. Ulthane Gyll had said you don't change what works, but his code no longer worked here.

Neweden was changing. Had changed.

His ignorance bothered him more and more. Neweden society, after centuries of only slow evolution, had altered drastically. He could feel it. Neweden was more and more an alien place with alien mores, and none of the guilded kin had experience of that. Ulthane Gyll had become one of the outsiders, but *he* knew, McWilms was convinced. Valdisa wanted the Hoorka to remain ignorant; that, to McWilms, led to the death of the guild as certainly as the Thane's alliance with Vingi, as Neweden's contact with the Alliance had dealt a fatal blow to its society.

As the ippicators had died, unable to cope with evolution. But now an ippicator had returned, god-sent. What did it portend? If the gods of Neweden had any control, it meant something. It must.

McWilms couldn't read meanings from shattered tiles and broken ground. The square had been washed clean—nothing except the mute hole remained to show the violence that had erupted there. McWilms scuffed a piece of tile over the crumbling edge—it splashed in the muddy pool.

It began to rain again, cold and hard, beading on the cloth of his nightcloak. McWilms pulled the hood over his head, moving back over the barrier once more. His head down against the wind-driven shower, he went to the center of the square, where the ippicator had been displayed. Blinking water from his eyes, he looked around the square. Tri-Guild Church was lopped off at mid-spire by low clouds. A few uncomfortable-looking kin hurried diagonally across a corner, cloaks flying. Incongruously, a break in the clouds let the sunstar touch a cluster of tall buildings a few blocks away, light sliding quickly up the sides. The gap closed as McWilms watched; Sterka became dreary again.

Suddenly McWilms laughed, loud and long. His amusement echoed from the buildings around the square. "Gods," he said, "I'm looking for signs in the weather, omens in the dirt. Jeriad, you're quite an ass."

Chapter 14

"I WANT TO SEE that frigging son of a bitch McClannan. Now!"

D'Embry slapped the com-unit's contact without waiting for her secretary's answer. She could feel the hot flush of anger on her cheeks. She leaned back, breathing hard and loud. The symbiote squirmed on her back, and slowly she felt her breathing ease again, her face cool. When she felt somewhat normal, she bent forward with a groan and picked up the flimsy on her desk. Her hands trembled as she glared at it, the paper rustling so that she could hardly read the words. She didn't need to see them; they had burned their image into her mind the first time they'd been read.

EFFECTIVE IMMEDIATELY: IN APPRECIATION OF YOUR LONG SERVICE TO THE ALLIANCE AND THE DIPLOMATIC RESOURCES TEAM, AND CONSIDERING YOUR UNCERTAIN HEALTH, YOUR RESIGNATION HAS BEEN ACCEPTED. ALL BENEFITS ACCRUED TO YOU ARE NOW RELEASED PENDING YOUR ARRIVAL AT NIFFLEHEIM CENTER. YOU ARE TO GIVE REGENT MCCLANNAN ACCESS TO ALL DIPLO CODES AND RECORDS, AND FACILITATE THE QUICKEST TRANSFER OF POWER TO HIM. REPORT TO NIFFLEHEIM CENTER ON 6:22:225. PASSAGE ABOARD THE CRUISER MENGELO HAS BEEN ARRANGED, DUE IN NEWEDEN ORBIT 3:5:225. DEAR LADY, SOMETIMES EVEN THE ELDEST HAVE TO GIVE WAY.

It was signed "A. Pettengill, Director," over the stamp of the Legatis Primus de Matraup. The last sentence was Pettengill's, she knew, telling her that this time there was no way around the forced resignation—it had been Arthol who was at the end of many of the strings she'd pulled to keep the Regency after the Heritage fiasco. All debts have been paid, he was saying.

She had a sinking feeling that he might be right.

D'Embry stared at the flimsy as if the intensity of her gaze could alter the words. The symbiote fed her cooling balms that did little to quench her fury.

Santos McClannan entered her office without knocking. He strode over and extruded a chair from the floor before her desk. He sat, watching her. She let the flimsy fall to the desk. A thin forefinger tinted bright orange skidded it across the slick surface toward McClannan. "I assume you've seen this," she said dryly.

Something between smile and frown tugged at his mouth. He picked up the paper with a strange gingerness. One hand ruffled through his hair as he scanned it—as she had somehow known it would, his hair fell back perfectly in place. "I was aware of the decision," he said at last. He was not sure how she was going to respond, and he was also a little frightened—d'Embry could see that in the way he sat, in his fiddling with the edges of the flimsy, in the fact that he could not look at her directly for more than a few seconds. *Damned frigging coward. I wonder where he got the courage to go over my head?*

"I'm not going to make any pretense, McClannan," she said. "You're responsible for this, aren't you?"

His face shifted to shocked innocence an instant too late. "M'Dame, I—"

She shook her head. The motion stopped his protest. "I could still fight this, McClannan. I don't have to accept this forced resignation." She said it merely to see how he would react—she was not disappointed.

He sat back, dumbfounded, hands clenched into fists on her desk. "That would be a waste of time, m'Dame." The fact that he neglected her title didn't escape her. "Surely you know that," he said in his darkest tones, full of gentle sympathy whose falseness burned at her. "You'd simply compound the difficulties here, maybe wreck all that you've worked to gain on Neweden. Simply for spite? I don't believe you're that selfish, m'Dame. I won't believe it."

She didn't answer for long seconds. McClannan looked more and more uncomfortable with her silence. When she did speak, it was to say one word. "Bullshit."

She closed her eyes and felt dizziness. *Make it stop, symbiote. Come on, you damned Trader slug.* And with that came an unbidden afterthought: *Maybe they're right. When you must divide your attention between crises and your health . . .*

McClannan's soft voice interrupted her reverie. "M'Dame—"

"It used to be 'Regent.'" She did not open her eyes.

"M'Dame," he persisted, "all that you'll gain by fighting this decision is dissension, both within the Neweden government and our staff here."

"Our staff?" Her eyes opened, blue-gray eyes blinking. "You mean *your* staff, don't you, *Regent* McClannan?"

"I'd hoped you wouldn't be bitter, m'Dame."

"Just what the hell did you expect me to be, McClannan?" She shouted as loudly as she dared, feeling the raggedness in her throat. She forced down a fit of coughing. *Not now, symbiote. Punish me later.* "Did you think I'd sidle up to you, all sweetness, and kiss your cheeks proudly? Did you want me to tell you how glad I am that you stabbed me in the back?"

"I did nothing."

"Gods, spare me your protestations. I *know* what you did, McClannan, at least some of it—my com-unit logs all calls from this Center, and I know you contacted Niffleheim two days ago. Don't tell me that's coincidence."

This time, at least, he didn't deny the allegation. "M'Dame, didn't you defy those in power when you felt they were wrong?" He seemed to be mouthing someone else's words. She wondered whose they were—Sula Hermond's, the Li-Gallant's, or some other traitor within her staff. "Who told you that trash?" she snapped.

He did not lie well. He almost stuttered his reply "M'Dame, your reputation . . . in the classes at Diplo Center they talked about you, about some of your, ahh, old confrontations with authority. And the teachers, the Diplos who'd known you . . ."

D'Embry waved a hand as if brushing aside a troublesome insect. Multihued flesh broke off McClannan's sentence. "It's not important, I suppose. You've done it, McClannan. You're now the Regent. I hope that Dame Fate sees that you receive what you deserve for it."

He looked relieved, knowing that she would not fight the

resignation. "M'Dame, I think you'll be surprised to find that I'm quite competent."

"You're right, McClannan, I will be. Let me tell you what I think will happen." She leaned forward, elbows on the desk. Her thin, much-lined face was intent with the force of her emotions. "You're a conceited, ineffectual fool—a good toady because you frighten easily. You'd make someone a fine assistant as long as they didn't give you too much responsibility."

He stiffened in his chair. His voice was suddenly formal and distant. "M'Dame, I don't have to sit here and be insulted. As Regent, I have much work facing me. Neweden—*your* old regency—is a mess." He began to rise.

"Sit down," she said. "If you think I'm a toothless old beast, you're wrong. None of the staff knows about your appointment yet. I could have you incarcerated on some trumped-up charge, and how do you think Niffleheim Center would react to that? They'd still replace me, but they'd send someone to replace *you* as well, just to be safe. So sit down and listen, if you really want this job."

"I don't believe you," he said. He did not sit, but neither did he move toward the door.

"Then walk," she replied. Her finger poised over contact on her desk. "I'll have Karl put you under house arrest as soon as you touch the door. Embezzlement should be a good charge—easy to fix, hard to disprove."

Still he hesitated. Then, fists clenched at his side, his mouth a hard line, he sat again.

"You see, McClannan, that's one of your problems. You can't judge the risks properly. If you knew me at all, you'd know that I've given my life to the Diplos, the Alliance. I wouldn't do anything to hurt them because I believe in what we're doing, if not always in how we go about it. And if you knew that, you'd have known that I also realize when I'm beaten. It was a bluff, McClannan, but you took it, so you might as well stay and listen to the rest." She paused, winded. The shortness of breath was returning, and with it the paroxysms of coughing, the bile she would spit up from her ravaged lungs. *A while longer, symbiote. A few minutes more. Please.*

McClannan looked more angry than before. As Vingi

had seen, he was not handsome in his rage. "Get on with your speech, then."

"It'll be short," she said, and the first of the deep coughs struck her. She reached for a tissue as she hacked, hunched over in her floater. When it passed, she spat; folding the tissue, she wiped savagely at her mouth. "You've much to learn, McClannan, and now you've ensured that I won't be here to give the lessons. Let me tell you what I see happening if you don't learn quickly. You'll lose Neweden—violently, most likely—because you'll be the dupe of the Li-Gallant, and for all his subterfuge and wiles, he's no match for FitzEvard Oldin. I'd give you no more than a standard, maybe two, before that happens."

"That's your own paranoia speaking," he said. "You're obsessed with the Family Oldin. You invent plots when there are none."

"I assure you, it's not paranoia. FitzEvard and I go back decades. We've skirmished many times on many worlds."

"I can't agree, m'Dame," he replied, still distant with anger.

"Then there's very little I can teach you in the few months I'll still be here. I don't have the patience to coddle an unwilling student."

"In that case, what good's your proud altruism for the Alliance?" he answered. The words stung her, and she sat in silence, unsure how to reply. McClannan rose again, going to the door this time. "You may keep this room as your office until the *Mengelo* arrives, m'Dame. I'll use my own office for the Regent's business. I expect you to disclose the contents of the letter to your staff this afternoon. Good day, m'Dame."

He left. D'Embry waited, knowing that the punishment would come now. She was amazed at how little she cared. "Maybe you're right, McClannan," she whispered. "But I still only give you six months." Then the attack struck her and she could speak no more.

Valdisa thought that she could gladly kill Gyll at that moment.

Not that it was his fault. Probably not. If anyone should be blamed, it should be Dame Fate. The note's seal had been addressed to Thane Valdisa only—who could have

anticipated that a clumsy courier would have knocked off
the seal in his pouch and, rather than reattaching it, have
stuffed it inside the envelope. And the apprentice who received the note at the entrance to Underasgard gave it to
McWilms first, because the Thane was busy on the practice
strip. McWilms had read it to see if he should interrupt the
Thane at her exercise.

The words were Gyll's typical blend of arrogance and
innocent disbelief that anyone could see the world in a
manner different from the way he viewed it.

Goshawk *will be leaving soon, I'm afraid. With her will
go our last opportunity to get the Hoorka off this dead-end
world. I don't mean to be so unforgiving of my homeworld,
but I've been outside it now for some time, and so can view
it in a more dispassionate light. It is a dead end for Hoorka—
in that, old Aldhelm was right. I'm asking you again to let the
guild come with me. We'll share the leadership, Valdisa, work
it out whatever way we have to. Maybe we can do more than
just settle our differences (or so I can hope). Let me know
when I can talk with the kin and make an offer. Please, make
it soon.*

Valdisa crumpled the paper in a sweaty fist. McWilms,
standing before her in the practice room, said nothing. She
went to one of the benches set around the cavern (greenish
light from the fungi-strips moving over her wet-dark clothing) and angrily pulled a towel from a stack set there. She
began drying her short hair furiously, facing the rough stone
wall. *By She of the Five, now I need another workout to get
rid of this anger.* Her shirt clung to her—down the back,
under the arms and breasts, sweat-cold in the chill of Underasgard. She heard McWilms come up behind her, and
she could also hear the sound of paper being unfolded—
he'd picked up Gyll's message from where she'd dropped it.
The cavern echoed with the clash of steel on steel: other
Hoorka-kin fencing.

"If you want to keep this a secret from the kin, Thane,
you shouldn't leave it lying around."

Valdisa whirled about. McWilms's face was a study in
neutrality. "Don't give me that sarcasm, Jeriad. I'm not exactly in the mood for it."

"You'll never be in the mood for this, will you?"

He said it quietly, matter-of-fact. Valdisa, hands on hips,

stared at him for long seconds. He stared back. Then she took a step away. She stretched, bending over at the waist to touch the ground. "I'll ignore that, Jeriad," she said, grunting with effort. "I've asked you once, now I'm telling you. Drop the subject."

"Thane—"

She came up. Her dark eyes flashed. "I mean it."

"I know you do," McWilms persisted. "I know, too, that Ulthane Gyll's offer would tempt quite a few of us. Is that why you don't bring the matter up before all kin? Are you letting your personal feelings get in the way of what's best for Hoorka?"

Valdisa's eyes narrowed, her head reared back as if slapped. She glanced right and left, surveying the room. When she spoke, her voice was a harsh whisper; only Mc-Wilms could hear it in the noise of practicing kin. "You listen to me, Jeriad. If anyone else had said that to me, I'd have him on the floor now for first blood. Don't you *dare*"—the cords of her neck went taut with the half-shout of the word—"give me that kind of crap as an excuse. You don't deserve an explanation, but let me give it to you again. Sula Gyll made his choice against the Hoorka eight standards ago. If he's sorry for it—and he isn't—then let him apologize to the kin and see if they'll let him rejoin the guild. Maybe then I'll consider the offer."

"You want him to apologize to you, as well."

"Yah, damn it. I deserve it more than any of the rest of the kin, if it comes to that."

"And until you get it, you'll ignore whatever he has to say."

She glanced at him, then sat on the bench, leaning back against the rough wall. "Are you deliberately trying to provoke me, or are you no longer in control of your tongue?" Her voice was as cold as the stone at her spine.

McWilms breathed once; again. He was not looking at Valdisa, but at the rest of the room—pairs of fencers, a knot of laughing kin, a huddle of apprentices around one of the kin-masters, a torn-down vibro in front of them.

"Jeriad, listen," Valdisa said behind him, her voice suddenly gentle. "It's more complicated than simply my relationship with Gyll. It's the Traders, for one: I don't know that we can trust them."

"Gyll trusts them." He spoke without turning to her. Across the cavern, the kin-master adjusted the vibro for the apprentices, the click of the control ring loud and metallic.

"Gyll can be duped. That's one of his weaknesses—he's very trusting. He tends to believe what people tell him until a lie is obvious."

"Many people call that a virtue."

"It's only a virtue in a saint, and Gyll doesn't come close to that status." She waited, but McWilms didn't reply. "It's not just the Traders, either," she continued. "There's a whole pile of objections involved, with the Li-Gallant, with our arrangements with the Alliance, with our holdings on Neweden."

"You don't think those can be worked out?"

"If they can, is it worth the effort, or are we just throwing everything away for a false dream?"

"I think you're wrong," he said. He watched the kin-master snap the haft into the proper slot, reel in the vibro wire.

"You're not the Thane." Valdisa's voice had lost its friendliness again; it walked on the edge of fury. McWilms could hear it.

"Gyll will wish that you weren't when he hears that you've allied us with Vingi."

McWilms heard the movement even as he began to turn to Valdisa: a sharp intake of breath, a half-grunt of effort, the scratch of boots on stone. Instincts took hold. He sidestepped to the left and back, his left hand slipping the vibro from its sheath, his weaker arm up as a shield. Valdisa was on her feet, crouching, ready to attack or defend. Her eyes were on his vibro. She was peripherally aware of the sudden silence in the cavern—they were being watched, and that deepened her anger. "Is this what you want, Jeriad? Fine, let me get my own vibro and I'll give you the satisfaction you're after. First blood, kin-brother? Fine."

McWilms shook his head. "That won't prove a thing. We both know that." But he did not sheath the weapon.

"Is Serita an acceptable choice for referee?"

"Thane—"

"*Answer me!*" she shouted. "Or is Jeriad McWilms afraid?"

Heat flushed his cheeks as she slipped into the impersonal mode, insulting him. His hand, reflexive, tightened around the vibro's hilt. "She's fine," he said tensely.

Valdisa nodded. She straightened, wiped her hands on her pants. "Arioch!" she called. The kin-master looked up from the midst of his apprentices.

"Thane?"

"Send one of the youngsters to get Serita Iduna."

"Thane," McWilms broke in. The anger had left him. "I won't fight, not like this. I'll stand there holding my vibro if you insist, but I won't move, won't defend myself. First blood will be yours."

She stared at him. The tableau held for a second, Valdisa stern, McWilms strangely sad. Then, with a sound of disgust, Valdisa strode away from him, moving toward the entrance of the cavern.

McWilms watched her leave, feeling the stares of his kin.

The connection was damned expensive and not of particularly good quality.

Gyll would never have initiated the call himself. The fact that FitzEvard did so was well in character for Grandsire Oldin, who was well-known for costly extravagances—at the same time, Gyll knew him well enough not to expect the normal social amenities. He and Helgin, sitting before the flat-screen viewer, didn't get them.

FitzEvard had a voice of sandpaper, roughened further by the transmission difficulties. "You've made money, at least," he said without preamble. "I didn't expect you to get the Hoorka, Sula, not with the troubles Neweden is having. I was right, it seems."

Flares of interference gamboled through the face of FitzEvard. The family resemblance was stamped into him as it was in all the Oldins: wide, round faces; large and dark eyes under gilt eyebrows; bodies stocky and a bit too heavy by Alliance standards.

"I've not given up on that yet, sirrah," Gyll answered. He didn't enjoy talking with FitzEvard, never had—the man's gruff curtness made him uncomfortable.

"We'll see, Sula. I'll wager you a month's wages you won't get them."

"And if I fail to take that bet?"

"Then I'll know you're lying about not having given up."

"In that case, I'll take the bet, sirrah."

FitzEvard grinned. It reminded Gyll of Helgin's grin: dark, somehow devoid of much humor, interior. FitzEvard, it was gossiped, smiled only when shown a potential profit. Gyll knew that to be as true as any adage—he'd heard the Neweden saying that the Hoorka smiled only at death. A grain of truth, nothing more. Yet FitzEvard was a driven man and the parameters of his success could be outlined in wealth. "Good, Sula. You'll save me money on the payroll."

Helgin, feet up on the desk next to Gyll, snorted. "He'll make more than that back in the bonus—*Goshawk's* stores are damned near empty."

"Trinkets for a small world," FitzEvard observed. His gaze stayed with Gyll as his image on the screen wavered and split. "Next time, Sula, we'll give you a wealthy world where the captain's bonus will be worth taking."

"Promises, promises," Helgin muttered.

FitzEvard's words came through a spluttering of static. "I didn't hear that, dwarf, but I assume it was an insult."

"You assume correctly."

"How do you like being back on Neweden, Helgin—away from me?"

Helgin grimaced. "I never thought I'd say this of you, but your ugly face looks better all the time. OldinHome will be welcomed."

"We've had some problems with a lassari named Renard," Gyll elaborated for the Motsognir.

"Ahh?" FitzEvard seemed to sit a bit higher in his seat, as if that comment had piqued his interest. "And how does this Renard trouble you?" he asked, glancing from Gyll to Helgin.

Gyll gave FitzEvard an account of the ippicator's display—he half-hoped that mentioning the beast would cause some display from FitzEvard, but the man disappointed him, seeming to be genuinely surprised. Gyll then spoke of the attempt to capture Renard. During the telling, he noticed that FitzEvard looked more to the Motsognir than to Gyll, and he wondered at that. He found himself glancing frequently at the Motsognir, who glumly endured the account. Puzzled, aware that some hidden exchange was occurring, he made his tale brief. "We intend to find him," he concluded.

"You do, eh," FitzEvard said heavily. Again, he was looking at Helgin, not at Gyll. Bands of jagged color scarred his face. "I doubt that it's worth the effort, Sula. Wouldn't you agree, Helgin?"

"Not when he interferes with us," Helgin replied.

"Maybe you're just standing in his way—and in any case, it's an internal Neweden matter; you and the Sula will be leaving soon."

Gyll felt increasingly irritated. He shifted in his seat, starting to say something about the side-conversation that seemed to exclude him, but then FitzEvard turned back to him. "Be careful, Sula. We wouldn't care to see you hurt." Again, that smile, marred and distorted by the transmission—tachyon relays were rarely good; this one seemed to be getting worse. FitzEvard's body swayed, distorted. "Kaethe asks after you, too. She's planning to bring *Peregrine* to OldinHome about the same time you'll be arriving—though what she sees in you, I don't know. You're too skinny."

Normally, that news would have cheered Gyll. He smiled weakly. "That's good news, sirrah."

"It had better be—it's not every whim of Kaethe's that I'll let her indulge." He leaned forward, as if peering through a fog. "This relay is terrible. It's not worth the money I'm spending on it. I'll see you both soon, then."

He gestured to someone offscreen and the relay ended in a blizzard of hues. The static-ridden hiss of the speakers cut off, leaving them in a sudden, aching silence. "What was going on, Helgin?" Gyll stared at the blank flat-screen.

"I'm getting ready to get some mocha. I need it." The dwarf grumbled to his feet, but Gyll, moving quickly, grasped Helgin's arm. He held the dwarf tightly, fingers whitening under the pressure.

"FitzEvard was talking to you, not me, Helgin. Something I didn't understand." His voice was harsh; deliberately, he softened his tone. His grip on Helgin's arm loosened. "I think of you as my friend. Tell me what I'm missing here."

"I don't know what you're talking about."

"You found Renard rather easily."

"I have contacts, just like you. And he wasn't there, was he?" The dwarf pulled away, rubbing at his bicep. "Damn it, Gyll—you do that again and I'll break that hand." It didn't sound to Gyll like the normal surliness of the Motsognir. The words had an edge.

"Would you lie to me?"

"What do you think?"

"I'd like to think you wouldn't."

"Good."

"Then what was going on?"

The Motsognir hesitated. Gyll thought he would speak at length. Then the dwarf grinned and shook his head. "Nothing," he said. "You want some mocha or not?"

"Then all I'm going to get from you is flippancy."

"Mocha, too." Then Helgin shook his head. "Gyll, I can't give you a conspiracy that doesn't exist, can I? Not unless you simply want some false collaboration for your paranoias. You should be glad we're leaving Neweden, my friend. It's making you see things."

Chapter 15

ELGIN CAME TO SEE GYLL the next morning.
"You checked with Camden in the bio section about
the ippicator," he declared without preamble. His feet set
well apart, he stood in front of Gyll's desk like an accusa-
tory statue. Outside the port, Neweden threw the sunstar's
light at *Goshawk*; the glare slashed across the room between Gyll and Helgin.

"Of course I did." Gyll had been standing behind the
desk, reading a cargo manifest. He let the list fall to the
desk. "What would you have done in my place? I was
damned curious, having seen an ippicator on Kaethe's ship.
Helgin, I told you that I looked aboard the ship. I wasn't
hiding anything."

"You were paranoid, you mean. You don't trust me."

"It never occurred to me that you might have something
to do with it, Helgin; I thought it might be someone else
aboard the ship. So who's paranoid: me, or someone who'd
sneak around to see if I'd been checking up on him?" Gyll
paused, then tried to change the subject without segue.
"We're damned low on the power chips we've been selling
the southern continent. Can we divert some from anywhere
else? I've an order from the Irastian Coalition."

"You don't want to talk about it."

"An astute observation, Helgin. We've a business to run."

"I think you're still looking for a conspiracy."

"I think you're the one that's paranoid."

With a growl, Helgin snatched the manifest from the
desk, the white cloth of his tunic flaring as it entered Neweden's reflected light. He scanned it quickly. "We could divert
some of the shipments to Remeale—"

The com-unit chimed. Gyll held up his hand. "Just a moment, Helgin." He touched a contact. "Yah, Fischer, what is it?"

"A call for Helgin from on-planet. The caller's rather insistent, so I thought I'd track him down. Is he there?"

Gyll glanced at the Motsognir, who shrugged his shoulders. "He's here, and he'll take the call from this extension." He activated the wall flat-screen. "I'll leave you to your call, Helgin. We can work with the manifest when you're done."

"You don't have to leave, Gyll. I'm not so paranoid that I worry about you hearing my private calls."

Gyll laughed at the overdone hurt in the dwarf's voice. "Fine. Whenever you're ready, Fischer."

The screen swelled with light, obliterating the planet's illumination. A man stared at them—tall, dark, with the coil of a spiked plant-pet wrapped about his shoulders. The room behind him was nondescript; wooden walls barren of decoration. "Good morning, Helgin, Sula."

Gyll saw Helgin's stance go wide again, defensive, and he wondered at that. "Sirrah d'Vomiis, is it not?" the Motsognir said. His voice was unusually deep and soft. "What do you want?"

The man smiled, slowly. One large hand stroked the plant-pet; it quivered, the thin spikes moving. "I've not seen you for some time, sirrah. I thought perhaps we had further business we could conduct."

The dwarf harrumphed. One foot scuffed the carpeted deck. "I'm afraid I'd written you off as an unreliable source, d'Vomiis."

"I know I missed our last, ahh, meeting," d'Vomiis replied pleasantly. His gaze flickered from the Motsognir to Gyll. "I apologize for that—it might have been mutually productive, in the right circumstances. I was wondering if I could make another appointment with you."

Something about the man's oily good manners bothered Gyll; it seemed to touch the Motsognir as well. The dwarf acted almost angry, as if the call irritated Helgin's already evil mood. For Gyll's part, this d'Vomiis was someone to whom he took an instant dislike, a gut reaction. There was nothing friendly about his smile—it was simply a uniform he put on to conduct business, and the plant-pet seemed a malevolent thing to wear—perhaps that was it.

"Is the meeting to be with the Sula Hermond as well?"

"I'd hate to waste the Sula's time for business that the two of us are quite capable of handling, sirrah. I'm sure his time is quite important, and, in any case, what I have to say is only speculation." The hand slid along the barbed length of the plant-pet, the smile remained fixed in place.

"Where?" Helgin queried, curt and gruff.

"The Street of Singers in Sterka, near Oldman Church. There's a small market square there that I've made my center of trade."

"When?"

"Would eight tonight be convenient, Sterka time? I regret it can't be sooner—I've another meeting."

"I'll be there, but this had better be worth my time, d'Vomiis." He spoke in a growl. Gyll began to speak, swallowed the words.

"I think it will settle all the questions we've had, sirrah." D'Vomiis nodded to the Motsognir, then to Gyll; the half-bow of kin to kin, a Neweden politeness. "My thanks, sirrah. I'll leave you to your tasks. Until eight, then." His hand left the coil of the plant-pet and stabbed at something below the screen. He faded.

Neweden light asserted dominance again, aquamarine.

"The Street of Singers isn't in the best area of Sterka. Mostly low kin." Gyll spoke to Helgin's back; the Motsognir still stared at the screen.

"I know the city well enough."

"He's one of our brokers? I don't recall his name on the lists."

"He wants to set up an arrangement. I've kept putting him off." Helgin turned, and his bearded face was fiercely jovial. "The man doesn't know when he's been bilked. I sold him a lot of faked T'Raith trinkets to see how he'd do. He had to fight to break even on the deal, but he's still interested."

"I'm surprised, after all that."

Helgin grinned. He spread his hands wide. "He thinks he can turn the tables on me, that's all. I'll teach him another lesson entirely. What do you think, Gyll? Am I the teacher type or not?"

"You've taught me a few things."

"Hah, you see."

"And you've always made sure that you still know more than me."

Helgin chuckled. "That keeps me in a job. It's the most important lesson of all."

The Street of Singers might once have been aptly named. That was no longer the case. Helgin heard no songs, and the only images the street would have evoked would have made sad and dreary verses. "Shabby" was the best word for the place; not barren and wrecked like Dasta Burrough, but the melancholy ugliness of riches gone to seed, of beauty neglected until it has turned plain and old. The area had been wealthy enough once — he could see it in the lines of the ill-kept houses, in the spaciousness of the trash-filled yards. A few houses here and there still reflected the pride of their owners, but those were increasingly rare as he approached Oldman Church. That name, at least, seemed appropriate: the old ones sat on porches or stared from windows as he passed: empty, sagging faces.

The street was dark, as well. Many of the hoverlamps lay in shards, vandalized. Others were simply not functioning. The few that were still lit only seemed to accentuate the night, to deepen the shadows.

More and more Helgin was filled with foreboding, more and more Renard's arrangements had the smell of a trap.

He didn't care. An expected trap was not as dangerous as the one tripped unknowingly. He was prepared. It was seven, not eight; early enough to catch them off-guard. He swaggered down the middle of the street. He whistled, off-key, pursing his thick lips, a sound muffled in the tangle of his beard. He nodded to the wrinkled visage of an elderly woman in a window to his left, almost cheerful.

Oldman Church sat at the end of the Street of Singers, blocking the lane. Old, gray-wood, two-storied; it was as dreary as an old matron's face, half its windows gone, though a battered glow-sign proclaimed the times of service. Approaching the building, Helgin moved to the right side of the street, slowing, taking to the cover of the houses nearby. He slid the battered revolver from underneath his tunic, checked the cylinder. He chuckled. From the shadows, he bellowed, "Renard!"

The street seemed startled into silence. From the next

block over, a dog barked at the noise, but there was no reply. Helgin waited a few minutes, then called again.

Nothing.

He grunted as he shoved away from the sheltering wall with his shoulders. He eased out into the street, cautious, his ancient weapon ready. He did not expect the trap to be sprung, not yet. The street was deserted, but too public. Inside, that's where Renard would be, waiting. Helgin wondered what it would be—something mechanical, or an ambush, a person waiting with a sting? One, two, or a multilayer of tricks? The man had all day to prepare the place. Or would there be nothing, just Renard, maybe that woman of his?

You'll find out, won't you, Motsognir?

He examined the door and its frame carefully, using the thin beam of a pocket flash. Rotten wood, mostly, and a rough job of carpentry at that—Oldman Church must have been built later than the rest of the neighborhood. Low on the right there was a strip of wood that had a different grain than the rest. Helgin stood to one side, pushing at the door with the barrel of his gun. It swung open easily, and there was a quiet hiss and a soft *tchunk* as two small darts embedded themselves in the wood to the left of the door. Compressed air, triggered by the opening of the door. Damned clumsy—only a fool would have walked straight in and been caught by that. Helgin knew that if he examined the tips of the tiny slivers of metal, he'd find them poisoned. Renard was outlining the rules of the game. Go back now, and there'd be no further contact between them, and Helgin would be telling Renard that he'd won. Go farther, and there would come a final confrontation.

Helgin hesitated. There were a thousand ways to kill a man with traps, and there was no possibility that, armed and defended as he was, he could find them all. If Oldman Church was a maze of such things, the Motsognir would die. But that wasn't Renard's way, if he knew the man at all. He liked to see his killings, even if he didn't do them himself. He'd be here, to watch, maybe to take a hand.

No, not traps. An ambush.

And it was not a Motsognir trait to be subtle. There is a certain power to a straight overhand thrust when your opponent expects a feint and a jab. Standing to the side of the door, he called into the black interior. "Awfully clumsy, Renard. I want you, my friend, but if you think I'm going to walk into this pit, you're wrong. I'll find you some other time."

Silence; then the sound of someone moving in the darkness beyond the door. "Why wait, dwarf? I'm here now, and you'll be leaving soon. I could hide where you'd never find me in the time you have left. This may be your only chance."

"What, to meet you with all your friends?"

A low, quick laugh was his answer.

Not going in, that's for certain. Now to back out with a whole skin.

A scraping of wood above alerted him. He was almost too late, despite that. He whirled, moving aside, the revolver up. He heard the cough of the silenced sting before he saw the man leaning from the window. He felt a searing pain in his side as the ground next to him erupted in pouts of dust. He fired; the noise was deafening. The man screamed, dropping the sting and falling back inside the building. Helgin wasted no time wondering whether he'd hit the man or simply scared him with the noise. He grabbed the sting from the ground and ran, limping, feeling the wound in his side tear further. His tunic was wet, torn, dark with blood. He dodged between two houses, halted there a moment. He tore the tunic away, shivering in the cold air, probed the wound with tentative fingers—deep, but essentially superficial, he told himself, hoping he could believe it. The loss of blood worried him the most. He wrapped the shreds of the tunic around the worst of it, knotting the fabric viciously. *Best you can do, old son.* He checked the clip of the sting: five shells left. He thrust the revolver into his belt. The sting was a better weapon for this, a bit more comprehensive in its coverage: it didn't require much aiming, as the pellets spread.

He could hear them. Running footsteps, a panting breath. *So much for your damned appraisals, Motsognir. Public or not, he'll kill you here and blame it on the Hag's Legion. You shouldn't have come, shouldn't have come.* The thought thundered in his head.

He turned, began to run again. His side ached, already tightening, making him slow. He ignored the pain. Coming out from between the houses, he checked the next street.

The dog he'd heard before was barking furiously now—he could see the animal in a front yard two doors down. It was facing back, between the houses. He decided to risk the street. Groaning, he bolted across the pavement and back between two buildings. He was halfway down the narrow space before he really saw the fence—board, both high and well-constructed. He made an attempt to scale it from a running start, his fingers scrabbling for the top. He did not make it, didn't come that close, and he felt a stabbing of pain from his wound, a gushing flow of blood. He collapsed, his back to the fence, sting across his knees. He squinted against the pain, fighting the onslaught of unconsciousness and shock. *Superficial, was it? Fool, fool!* When his vision cleared again, he struggled to his feet, blessing the low Motsognir center of balance and cursing the heavy Neweden gravity. He went back toward the street, one hand on the nearest building for support.

The dog was still barking. Suddenly, it went silent. He peered around the corner of the building. Lights were on now in several of the windows, but the residents stayed judiciously inside and hidden. Bloodfeud was a sacred custom on Neweden—you learned not to interfere in others' quarrels lest they become your own. They might watch, but they would not help. Helgin couldn't see the dog; he could only assume that its owner had taken it inside, or that Renard had rendered it permanently quiet. Helgin watched the street. Someone crossed it a hundred meters to his left, running in a crouch—too far for the sting, and the noise of the handgun would point to him like a finger. *Damn, they'll be coming at me from the back as well.* He felt the beginnings of despair and found he did not like the emotion. *Go out in the street again and they'll take you; stay here and you're trapped. A hell of a choice, dwarf.* He backed down the way he'd come, toward the fence.

There were windows. He tried them, one by one; all were locked. If Renard didn't know where he was, the shattering of glass would tell him, and a house was as much of a trap as this place—perhaps worse, for he'd have to deal with those inside. *Better to wait, at least for the moment.* He went to the fence and huddled into a corner of it, both weapons ready now, watching the opening to the street and listening for a sound.

It was the latter. Someone began climbing the fence from the far side. Helgin held his breath, not moving except to bring up the sting. Head tilted backward, he watched the city-glow of the sky. The silhouette of a head and shoulders appeared, with a hand holding a weapon to the right. Helgin aimed, pressed the trigger. The sting bucked, jamming hard into his shoulder, there was a dry cough from the silencer. The head was gone; there was the sound of a body falling to earth.

Amateurs, and a damned good thing—it might keep you alive. He struggled to his feet once again, using the sting as a crutch. *Now the windows; that body'll tell them exactly where I am. Move!*

He didn't have time.

A figure appeared at the street end of his cul-de-sac, hesitating a second and then whirling back. Helgin whipped the sting up and fired; the pellets scored paint, sent chips of masonry flying. He let himself fall to the left as the figure glanced around the corner—a line of brilliance arced across the alley; Helgin could smell paint blistering, the tang of scorched wood. *Oh, fine, he's got a hand-laser, and* you *came with a frigging handgun that can't hit much beyond thirty meters. Good choice, Motsognir, and I hope you live to regret it.* Helgin fired once more from his prone position. He had not thought of hitting the man—he could only hope to keep him back.

Someone was at the fence again: Helgin turned in time to see a head disappear. He aimed at the fence where the climber might have been, groaning as the sting jolted his shoulder once more. He was breathing heavily now; his side was soaked with blood. He could not even feel fear—the certainty that he was going to die was simply there, a cold realization. All he could do was delay the inevitable. He lifted the sting, thinking that it suddenly felt heavier, that the night was dimmer. He aimed for the corner once more, fired, then pointed the muzzle at the fence—this time there was only the click of the trigger striking an empty chamber. *Hell, you can't even count anymore, can you?* He let the sting drop, pulled the revolver from his waistband. *Keep them down; that's all you can do. It won't help you. You're going to find DwarfHome before you expected, Motsognir.*

He lurched along the wall, staggering, his hand against

the bricks, making his way to a window. Without aiming, he
fired at the street end of the space. *Keep them down.* He
thought he heard a sound behind him, and shot at the top
of the fence, splintering wood. He continued his slow progress toward the window.

He didn't see the sting, just heard the scrape of a footstep. Kicking against the wall, he flung himself backward—
the sting spoke; pellets struck him in mid-leap. He rolled,
helpless, the shock of impact knocking the handgun from
his grasp. Through pain-fogged eyes he could see a man
standing near him, bringing up the sting again. Helgin tried
to lever himself to his feet; his legs would not cooperate. He
could only stare at the death awaiting him.

But the man was suddenly down himself, as Helgin
heard the characteristic whine of a vibrofoil. Helgin blinked,
unbelieving. *By the great god Skafidur, not dead! Not dead
yet!*

"Gyll!" he tried to shout. His voice sounded like a
cracked whisper. "The fence . . ." He thought he was going
to go under. He fought the darkness.

Gyll stepped forward between the houses. He had a vibro in one hand, a hand-laser in the other. He wore the
night-clothing of the Trader-Hoorka. A black cap covered
his grayed hair, and his hair and face were grimy with soot.
"It's taken care of," Gyll said. "Fischer's back there." Gyll
whistled—there was an answering call from the far side of
the fence. Gyll went to Helgin, switching off the vibro, hol-
stering the laser. He went to one knee. Helgin grinned up at
Gyll through a face twisted with pain.

"You took your damned time," he said. He tried to laugh,
found that he had to grit his teeth against the pain.

"You went there early." Gyll's hand probed Helgin's
side, his face grim. "How can I have you followed when you
don't follow the only schedule I knew—d'Vomiis had said
eight."

"I was being smart."

"It looks like it was a real good idea, too."

"No thanks to you, I almost died."

"Next time, ask me to come along." He looked up from
his examination of Helgin. "You'll live, I suppose, though
that's a nasty side wound, my friend. You've lost a lot of

blood, and that last shot chewed up your right leg pretty well."

"Don't look at me with that long face, then, or are you lying to me?"

"None of the lies today came from me. You'll live." A groundcar screeched to a halt on the street. Trader-Hoorka leapt out.

"Then why so solemn, Gyll?"

"I killed that man. I haven't taken a life for standards, dwarf." Gyll's voice was gruff, angry. "I find that I don't like the feeling. I don't like it at all."

"Gyll—"

"Shut up, Motsognir." Gyll waved to the Hoorka—they came at a run, bearing a litter. One began attaching a portable med-pack to Helgin's chest, grimacing as she tore away the red-stained remnants of his tunic. They placed the dwarf on the litter. As it began to rise on its hover-tethers, Helgin beckoned to Gyll. "Is one of them Renard?" he asked.

"I wouldn't know. I've never seen him." There was a strange sadness in Gyll's eyes. He looked older.

"Yes, you have." Helgin swallowed with an effort. He tried to turn on his side; one of the Hoorka gently nudged him back. "I talked with him this morning. The man who called. D'Vomiis."

Gyll's eyes went hard. He seemed to withdraw farther into himself. "D'Vomiis," he said, detached, distant. "Neh, he's not one of them. No." He paused a moment. "I think you've a lot to tell me, dwarf."

"You won't like it." Helgin tried to smile. "Why don't we just take a walk instead. Let me hop off this litter—"

"I think you're going to talk to me." Gyll waved a hand at the Hoorka—the litter moved toward the groundcar. Gyll watched them leave. Doors slammed, the engine purred into life, its headlights carving the darkness. The beams swung as the driver turned and drove away.

Gyll walked slowly over to the body of the man he'd killed. He still held the sting, sprawled faceup, the eyes caught in eternal surprise. The man was young, good-looking in a rough way, perhaps still jussar. There was a lot of blood, black in the darkness; vibros were not clean weap-

Stephen Leigh

ons. Gyll reached down, squatting, and gently closed the eyes. "I didn't know you," he said quietly. "Enemies should always know each other." He spoke to himself, his hand still on the man's face. Sighing, he rose to his feet.

"But then," he said, "so should friends."

Chapter 16

GYLL DID NOT GET BACK to *Goshawk* as quickly as he had expected or hoped. One of his aides drove up to him as he entered the field gates of Sterka Port.

"Sula?"

He inclined his head in acknowledgment. "Yah, Levitt? What is it?"

The young woman spoke over the purr of the ground-car's motor. "There's a group here to see you, Sula. They won't talk to any of the rest of us."

"Who are they?"

Her dark face remained noncommittal. "Hoorka," she said. "Neweden Hoorka." Her eyes tracked him up and down, taking in the smudged and bloody uniform, the quickly and inexpertly wiped face. He knew he should change.

"Thane Valdisa?" he asked. He couldn't keep the hope from his voice. The intensity of it surprised him, but the beginning of Levitt's headshake quelled the optimism.

"Others," she replied. "Nine or ten of 'em. The one that does the speaking for the group is called Jeriad McWilms."

"Where'd you put them?"

"Out at the shuttle shelter—it'll be a bit before the shuttle gets back: we took the Motsognir right up to the ship."

"Take me out there, then." He swung into the open cab as Levitt accelerated away. He was tired; he rubbed at his eyes. *Too much happening at once, old man. They don't give you a chance to rest.* Gyll didn't want to face another crisis tonight. All he wished was the oblivion of sleep. He felt sick, sick at having killed a man he didn't know, sick because Helgin was hurt, sick because there seemed to be duplicity all around him, even from the Motsognir, whom he'd trusted most of all. He approached the shelter with little enthusiasm.

The Hoorka-kin smiled as he entered, the smiles going flat as they saw him. McWilms, concern on his face, bowed low to Gyll, who returned the bow sketchily, perfunctorily. "I'm sorry, Ul . . ." McWilms stopped himself. "Sula," he corrected. "I didn't mean to have you disturbed at work. Are you all right? The blood . . ."

"It isn't mine," Gyll said wearily. "I'm just tired. What can I do for you, Jeriad?" He glanced at the others: Serita Iduna, Bachier, others he recognized, apprentices when he'd left the guild.

"We've left Hoorka," McWilms replied simply.

Gyll didn't know how to reply. He felt awkward, slow; all of his reactions, dulled. "Jeriad, you surprise me . . ." He brushed at his clothing.

"Sula, we're here to join you," Serita broke in. "Some new recruits, neh?" She grinned.

"Does Valdisa know?"

The faces registered a varying range of emotions: neutrality, open distaste, hurt. McWilms seemed to be recalling something unpleasant; Serita's olive face still smiled, but the smile was forced now; Bachier frowned. "She knows," Bachier said. "She knows very well."

"The Thane was quite angry," McWilms interjected. "She made threats, she cursed us—and you. There was nearly a confrontation with the rest of the kin. It was rather ugly, Sula."

"Why did you leave?"

McWilms looked at the others. He rubbed his right arm: a nervous habit. "The Hoorka . . ." he said haltingly, "aren't what they once were. You knew that. It's worse now, Sula. Valdisa's made a deal with the Li-Gallant; we're now a part of his rule-guild, under his control. It's not the same now. It's all cracked and changing. Why wait for it to fall apart?" He paused, shrugged. "We'd like to go with you."

"She's abandoned the code," he said, almost a whisper. Anger surged through him; he forced it down.

"At least parts of it, Sula. And who knows how much longer the rest will hold? We'd rather move with the opportunities you offer."

He should have felt some triumph. Instead, Gyll almost laughed, mockingly. This no longer mattered: the bright future he'd thought he was offering his old kin was tarnished now, blighted by the deceptions of Helgin, which in turn threatened further lies, other actions done behind his back by people he'd thought he trusted. If he hated what Valdisa had done to Hoorka, he hated it because it had become something other than what he'd intended. But there was no deliberate deception there; simply a change in the framework in which she operated. It seemed that the Family Oldin might have misrepresented itself from the beginning.

He didn't know which was worse.

Gyll had little enthusiasm to give McWilms and his fellow defectors. He was too tired to think, too exhausted to deal with it.

"I'll tell my chief aide Fischer that you're here," he said at last. "He'll see to you all, make arrangements."

Gyll could see puzzlement and disappointment in McWilms's face, and he forced a wan smile to his lips. "I'm sorry," Gyll said to all of them. "I know you've all taken a huge chance on my recommendation, and now I'm not showing much enthusiasm for your courage." He ran a hand through his hair—it came away sooty. "I'm very glad you're here, but it's been a long, difficult, and strange evening for me."

"We understand," Serita said. "The woman—Levitt—told us some of what had happened. We're sorry that the Motsognir was hurt."

"It's very different, what we have to do for the Oldins," Gyll said. "I had to kill a man tonight, with no warning, with no honor. He was someone who was no personal enemy of mine, for whom I had no contract."

"He was attacking a friend," McWilms said. "That seems reason enough."

"It should be," Gyll answered, "but it wasn't."

Chapter 17

THE ROOM WAS DARK, the port partially shuttered, though in any case it showed only the salt-on-velvet of stars, looking toward the band of spilled light that was galaxy center. The gravity was set very low—Gyll had to watch his step lest he push too hard and flounder in air for an instant. The bedfield was a white mass in the center of the room, over which hovered the spiked bulk of a medi-doc.

Gyll paused at the door, hesitant. He did not look forward to this confrontation. He didn't want to hear the words.

"You look like you're waiting for a funeral, and I'm not planning to die. You want to come in instead? If you've got ale with you, I'll even give you a kiss." Helgin's voice was hoarse and weak. Gyll could see the dwarf, his beard dark against the sheets, eyes gleaming in starlight.

"No ale. Just me."

"Then no kiss."

"How are you feeling?"

Even in the twilight, he could see that familiar, battered face shape itself into a scowl. "I'm just resting a moment before I get up and start dancing. How the hell *should* I feel, Gyll?" Above Helgin, a diode flashed amber on the medi-doc. Gyll watched the light with seeming fascination: amber, a flicker, then again green. "I've got a hole in my side, several smaller companions in the legs," Helgin continued. "I'm scraped up all over and I feel like a vampire's leftovers. And my hair's filthy and my beard itches. I'm feeling like shit, Gyll." Helgin fixed the older man with a sidewise stare. "So . . . when are we going to drop the inanities and talk about what's really bothering you?"

Gyll came fully into the room, letting the door close behind him. He walked all the way around the bedfield, touching the medi-doc tentatively; he lifted the shutters of the port and peered out at the folded curtains of stars. "I'm not feeling so well either, Motsognir."

"I haven't got a lot of sympathy to spare at the moment for simple mental anguish."

His back to the Motsognir, Gyll shrugged to the universe. "I can understand that." He let the shutters fall back with a clatter, turned, and leaned against the wall, hands behind him. "You lied, Helgin. Lied a lot."

"It's the way of the worlds, Gyll."

"It's not the way of friends."

"I suppose telling you that it was for your own good won't appease you either."

"I don't need any more lies."

"That's an excuse, not a lie. There's a difference."

"Who's Renard, Helgin?"

The Motsognir turned his head away at the question, his hair rustling against the pillow. "It matters that much, Gyll? You just can't ignore it, look the other way for a few days, and let me play out my own problems? I heard the news that you got a bunch of your precious Hoorka to take back with us—that wins you your bet with FitzEvard. Why can't you just worry about getting them ready?"

"Who's Renard?"

Gyll thought that Helgin would not answer. He waited; there was no reply but the Motsognir's slow, loud breath and a faint humming from the medi-doc. With a growl of disgust, Gyll thrust himself away from the wall. Helgin's voice halted him.

"He's a frigging bastard, a low-life whose loyalty is measured by the price he's paid. A piece of scum, stuff you'd get on your boot walking through Dasta."

"Who pays him?"

"You already know that answer."

"Tell me anyway," Gyll insisted.

"FitzEvard. Renard's an employee, just like you."

Gyll muttered a curse. The Motsognir heard; he laughed bitterly. "You can't tell me that you haven't known that since last evening, Gyll. It's no big thing—FitzEvard pays a lot of people. You're in good company as well as bad."

"Why'd the two of you fight?—FitzEvard pays *you,* as well."

Helgin sighed. One hand fluttered above the sheets. "We don't like each other, first of all. And we have differing priorities. Renard doesn't care what he does as long as it creates chaos on Neweden. He'd love to kill *you,* Gyll, because of the uproar it would cause if done in the right place, at the right time. I wouldn't let him. And we also had a power conflict—who was in charge. If he killed me, it's almost as good as getting rid of you, because of the stink you'd raise." The long explanation seemed to tax him. The hand fell back to the sheet; the dark eyes closed and his head sank back. Lights shimmered amber above him.

Gyll knew that he should feel guilty, interrogating Helgin when he was in this condition, but he felt little but anger and sadness. "And now?" he asked.

"Now?" Helgin echoed. "Nothing, Gyll. Nothing."

"We could go to d'Embry or the new Regent."

"Why? The damage to Neweden's done. This world's been pushed over the edge of change, and we can't stop that now. And—you may have trouble with this, Gyll—I still wouldn't trade the Oldins for the Alliance. Not at all. I'd gladly kill Renard, but I'd go back to FitzEvard afterward, not d'Embry."

Gyll shook his head. "You're right. That's hard to believe."

"It's the truth. You're the one that desires truth, O Righteous One." His voice was full of scorn.

"You're damned right," Gyll answered heatedly. "I'm frigging tired of this, Helgin. If I'm archaic and stupid, fine, but Neweden shaped me and I still believe in that outmoded concept of honor."

"Neweden lies worse than anyone, man. Look at the Li-Gallant if you want to see a slimy eel." Helgin lay back again. His hand lifted, then fell, as if he wanted to reach for Gyll but was afraid that the gesture might be misinterpreted or rejected. "Gyll, you can't go around bothered because the universe doesn't conform to your idea of morality. It doesn't work that way."

Fury was in Gyll now. A calm, distant part of himself recognized the anger for the catharsis it was; it boiled, driving his open hand against the medi-doc. The device rang with a metallic protest, shivering in its holding field. "Don't give me this philosophical shit, Helgin!" he roared, feeling the words ravage his throat. "I don't give a *damn* who's lying or why, I just need to understand. What are we doing on Neweden, what does FitzEvard want with it?"

Something had changed in Helgin's eyes. Under the hedge of his eyebrows, they had narrowed, gone hard. He twisted a strand of his beard between thumb and forefinger, lips pursed thoughtfully. "Want to know what else I've done, Gyll? It's more than just consorting with Renard. You remember Gunnar, Vingi's old rival, killed in a most un-Neweden-like manner by an unknown assassin? That killer was me, Gyll. Me. Acting on FitzEvard's orders. But then, you Hoorka don't blame the weapons, do you? You're just the weapons in someone else's hands. That was me as well: a weapon in FitzEvard's hands."

Gyll could not speak. He'd told himself that he would not be surprised by anything the dwarf could tell him. But this eight-standard-old confession startled him. "Why did you kill Gunnar?" he said at last.

"Me?" Helgin started to sit up on his elbows, but then grimaced in pain and lay back once more—a flurry of varicolored dots flickered with his motion. "I did it because FitzEvard asked me to do it. Not *told* me, *asked* me—we Motsognir have our pride, after all."

"Then what were FitzEvard's reasons?"

"I forgot to ask him," Helgin muttered, then shook his head. "Gyll, FitzEvard and d'Embry have had a running confrontation for decades. I don't think it insignificant that Oldin would choose to come to Neweden when d'Embry's Regent. Maybe that was entirely it—he wanted to cause d'Embry problems. Or maybe he really *wants* Neweden, for whatever purposes."

"It sounds damned petty."

"To you or me, yah. We ain't FitzEvard, are we?"

"What about the ippicator?"

"I don't know anything about it. Honestly."

Gyll's fist beat a rhythm on his hip, a steady *slap-slap-slap*. Suddenly he stopped and swiveled on his toes. He began to walk toward the door.

"Where are you going, Gyll? You didn't tuck me in."

The door slid open as Gyll touched the contact. The light

of the corridor beyond spilled into the room, falling short of the bedfield and leaving Helgin lost in gloom. "Can't you ever be serious, Helgin?"

"I'm always serious. Where are you going?"

He answered truthfully, "I don't know."

"Shut the door. Please."

Gyll stepped back; the door sighed mechanically and abandoned the room to twilight once more. "Make this quick, Motsognir. I'm suddenly not much in the mood for talking."

"I just want to know what you're planning to do, Gyll. I ask as a friend, because I do care about you."

"I've declared bloodfeud against Renard, and any member of the Hag's Legion. I intend to follow that up."

Helgin nodded. "You're not going to quit Family Oldin, not going to try some heroics that'll just be used by both sides?"

"I don't know what I intend to do. I'll think about it, first. What worries me most isn't you or me or the frigging Oldins. There are ten Hoorka here on the ship, ten of my old guild-kin, who came because they trusted me. I can't leave them, and Valdisa won't take them back from me, not if I know her at all. I trapped them here."

"I wouldn't phrase it quite so pessimistically."

"I would."

There didn't seem to be anything else to say. Gyll waited; Helgin lay still. The medi-doc purred to itself, and Gyll went back to the door.

"You gonna tell them?" asked Helgin, behind him.

"Who?" He did not turn.

"Your Hoorka foundlings. You gonna tell them about all this?"

"No. At least not yet."

"You see, you're learning it too, Gyll—it's better sometimes to lie or omit the truth." There was no triumph in Helgin's observation.

"You might be right." Gyll punched at the contact with a forefinger; the door opened. "But I hope you're not."

He left.

Gyll sat at his desk for a long while, turning the thoughts in his mind like spadefuls of earth. He stroked the bumblewort in his lap, his feet on the desk—orangish fur floated through the room.

"Fischer," he said at last to the empty air.

A click as a speaker activated: "Sula?"

"Get me Thane Valdisa in Underasgard."

"Yes, Sula." The speaker snapped off.

Gyll swung his feet from the desk—the bumblewort chirruped in irritation. He tried to dump the creature off his lap, prodding the soft shell of its back. The wort braced its legs, not wanting to leave. Sighing, Gyll let it remain where it was, scratching its earflaps absently.

Click. "I have Thane Valdisa, Sula."

"Thank you, Fischer." Gyll activated the camera and flatscreen. Valdisa stared out at him, the broken walls of the caverns behind her. The view gave him only head and shoulders—a dark, wrathful woman. "I assume you've called to gloat," she said before he could speak.

He'd expected the bitterness, but had expected it to be encapsuled in the Neweden circumspection. He hadn't thought she'd be so blunt. "Not to gloat," he said. "Just to tell you that they're here. And to give it one last chance with you."

"You still have the bumblewort, I see."

Gyll glanced down—the wort had put its front paws on the desk, peering up at the screen. Gyll rubbed its nose, and the wort ducked away with a shake of its head. "Yah, I still have the wort, and you're evading the question."

She nodded. "You've told me all I need to know. They came to you. If you're not gloating, I don't see where we have anything further to talk about."

"Will you take them back, if they decide to return?"

Her face changed with that. She became suspicious, puzzled, her lips drawing back slightly, her nose wrinkling. "Don't you want them now that they're there? No, I won't take them back. They've made their choice; let them die with it."

"Let's at least be reasonable about this, Valdisa."

"Reasonable?" She laughed, her face twisted. Her eyes seemed large, touched with moisture; the skin under her eyes was dark with a lack of sleep. "You've done the cruelest thing you could do to Hoorka, Gyll. You crippled us—who knows, maybe it's the mortal wound you were after,

but it'll be a while before we die. If you wanted to watch
Hoorka suffer, this'll do it. All I have left are the dregs of
the full kin and the apprentices. I haven't enough people for
a viable rotation; that means we might have trouble with
some contracts. I may lose kin to thievery or lassari-traits—
some of those I have left are damned close to that now. The
new Regent won't even talk with me, much less try to open
offworld options." She seemed to run out of steam, her vehemence collapsing. Her shoulders sagged; the focus of her
camera shifted slightly as she leaned away.

"You're allied with Vingi now. You won't starve."

Her eyes widened. She shrugged. "I had to do it."

"That has destroyed Hoorka more than anything I've
done."

"You're not Hoorka. Don't let it bother you."

Gyll snorted derision. "If I were staying longer, I'd dis-
mantle the Hoorka myself—I could do it; go to the Li-
Gallant, offer him the services of the Trader-Hoorka at a
break-even rate, guarantee the death of a victim. I could
even make it a point of our agreement that he outlaw the
assassins' guild called Hoorka. He'd do it, Valdisa."

"If you've become that vicious, you've changed a lot in
the time you've been gone, Gyll."

"Oh, I've changed, Valdisa. Very much." He looked away
and back. "And I hate the Hoorka, Valdisa. The guild has
outlived its usefulness. The society changed around it, and
it's no longer viable. Give it up."

"And come to you?"

"You'll be nothing but a tool for the Li-Gallant if you
stay." *Neweden is gone,* Helgin had said. *I still wouldn't
trade the Oldins for the Alliance.* The wort mewled at him.
He stroked its shell.

"And whose tool would I be there?" Anger colored her
cheeks. "The Sula isn't content with his small victory," she
said, breaking into the impersonal mode. "He wants everything."

"Valdisa, don't cut me off like this. Let's at least talk."

She had turned away from him. "The Sula is an ass. I
don't hear him anymore."

"Valdisa . . ."

But her hand had already reached out. The screen went
dark.

*   *   *

"Gods, McClannan, certainly you're not serious?" D'Embry was startled into a half-shout. She could not believe what he'd said. "You're talking about a man's life, not some silly game."

McClannan shrugged. They were in her office, now rather bare. The d'Vellia soundsculpture was packed and crated, silent. The animo-paintings swirled unseen in boxes. Only the desk remained. The carpet was dying; she'd let her daily maintenance lapse since McClannan had mentioned in passing that he intended to have it removed after she left. He stood in front of her desk now, immaculate, wearing the robes of office that she'd always eschewed as too ostentatious, the sunburst symbol of the Alliance golden at his throat. He looked the proper image of a regal Diplo—the very type she'd always abhorred. He brushed at his lower lip with a thumb.

"I didn't expect your approval, m'Dame."

"That's good. Then you won't be disappointed. Why even tell me? I can't even fathom your reasoning, man. A Hoorka contract for Sula Hermond's life? It's absurd."

"I don't think so."

A spasm of pain shot through d'Embry's chest. She closed her eyes against the stabbing hurt. These attacks had come more and more frequently over the last week, and the symbiote on her back seemed less quick to cope with them. *Getting old and worn-out, woman, and McClannan's taken away the reason you kept fighting: cause and effect.* She wondered as well if the symbiote wasn't wearing out, thinking that it would be just like a Trader item to do that. D'Embry grimaced, knotting a tiny fist on her lap. She could feel McClannan's gaze on her, definitely less than sympathetic, somehow predatory. She bid her eyes to open, made her hands relax. "What good is this supposed to do, Regent?"

"The Li-Gallant tells me that the Alliance needs to show that it is better for Neweden than the Family Oldin, that we're stronger."

"And this contract is supposed to prove that? Excuse my stupidity, but somehow the logic escapes me." A cold amusement rippled through her; she found it difficult not to laugh, scoffingly. "Not even a fool like Vingi would believe that kind of crap—and in any case, the Sula will simply buy out the contract. It will never be run."

"I don't think he'll pay it off." He seemed too calm. That worried d'Embry, made the pain of her body recede.

"He'd be crazy not to do so. The Oldins are easily rich enough, no matter how expensive you made the price. All you'd prove is that the Oldins are as wealthy as the Alliance."

"I have additional information, m'Dame." Smugness tightened his smile. He waved a negligent hand. "It's a calculated risk, admittedly, but I think he'll run."

D'Embry shook her head. "McClannan, you're talking about murdering a man."

"I'm talking about letting Dame Fate decide. That's the way it works here, isn't it? Let Dame Fate decide if he's to live or die."

"It's still a life."

McClannan adjusted the collar of his robe. He brushed at imaginary lint on the silken sleeve. "How many people will die if the Li-Gallant boots the Alliance off-planet? Given a free hand to deal with the lassari as he sees fit, how many will die? Let the Oldins do what they want, and how many more will go to see the truth of Neweden's afterlife? You've said it yourself, m'Dame: wherever the Oldins go, turmoil and death follow. I'm trading one life against several."

"All your altruistic excuses aside, it's *still* a life." She could feel the beginnings of the pain again. She ignored it, breathing deeply despite the agony that caused her. *Damn you, symbiote, take care of this. Do your frigging job.* "And it still comes down to speculation on your part. You *think* this, you *believe* that. Are you willing to gamble for a life? I wouldn't. I repeat—it's not a game."

"Game or not, it's already done."

"You can still cancel the contract. All that costs you is money; McClannan, I'll pay that out of my pension if the expense worries you."

He hesitated. She saw it in the set of his chin, the slightly open mouth. She attacked before he could answer, sitting forward in her chair. "Do you really want the Sula's body dumped at the gates of Diplo Center?" she asked. "That may work here, but *you've* never had to kill a man, never seen the blood. Hell, man, our whole thrust is that we offer peace and security—civilization. How would Niffleheim view this contract?"

"Niffleheim allowed you to let the Hoorka work off-world."

"Not often, and only with great reluctance. After Heritage, never."

McClannan scoffed, his composure returning and confidence coming back to his voice. "Come, m'Dame. You stopped the offworld Hoorka contracts because of Niffleheim's pressure, not your own altruism. So don't lecture me about ethics and morality. Neither one of us is an expert in those fields."

She knew that she should not be angry, not if she wanted to convince him. She had to remain calm, yet control eluded her. She didn't know why—the influence of the symbiote's chemicals, a lack of patience that had increased as her health deteriorated, whatever . . . She could hear the snappishness in her voice; she immediately regretted it. "What field *is* your area of expertise, McClannan? Lying? Going over your superior's head? Or are you just looking to increase your skill with murder?"

McClannan drew himself up to his full height, glaring down the length of that classic nose at d'Embry. "I told you not to lecture me, old woman," he said, his words clipped. His facade of respect for her was gone; what she saw behind that abandoned facade appalled d'Embry—*Gods, I didn't know he hated me that much.*

She softened her tone, trying to recover some of the ground she'd lost to anger. "I'm sorry, Santos. You're right, that was uncalled for. Let's talk about this rationally."

It did not mollify him. "I've no interest in talking any further, m'Dame. I'm the Regent; please allow me to make my decisions without interference."

She sighed; the pain was arcing through her and she felt nausea boiling in her stomach. "I'm just trying to show you that you're making a decision you'll regret. Santos, I *do* have the experience—it's sometimes worth listening to."

"Tell me you've never made a decision you've regretted."

She kneaded her stomach. "I wouldn't make that claim," she said. "You know that."

"Then don't claim that your advice is so valuable." Mc-

Clannan nodded to her. "I think you've said enough." For an instant, his face showed concern as he looked at her. "You're in pain. Should I call the Center doctor?"

"No, thank you."

"Then I'll be about my business."

He turned and left the room. D'Embry waited until he was gone, then doubled over, "Oh, *damn!*" she muttered through clenched teeth.

Chapter 18

THE APPRENTICE HAD A LOOK of joy as he handed the flimsy to Thane Valdisa. "A contract," he said, smiling.

She didn't look at it. She stared at the apprentice in reproof. "You don't need to be so happy about it," she told him. "The Hag will smile at you one day—those that gloat at death, She keeps. She of the Five will never snatch you back."

The apprentice ducked his head. "Go on, get back to your post," Valdisa told him. As the boy left, she unfolded the flimsy, read the words there. She glanced up, still holding the paper, and seemed to gaze into an unseen distance.

"What is the man thinking of?" she said in a whisper. "Gyll won't run. He won't run."

Chapter 19

STEBAN WAS AWED. The port overwhelmed him with noise and fury—open spaces and huge machines. And his contract was even more unusual: the creator of Hoorka, that figure of the full kins' tales. Steban had never met him; Gyll had gone before the Hoorka had chosen Steban from the ranks of jussar applicants. There was a certain thrill knowing that he would meet the man soon.

It had taken time, longer than any contract he'd initiated before. First he'd had to pass the port's Diplo guards, polite but insistent on knowing his business. He'd had to wait until one of them called Diplo Center and received clearance. Then, with a badge clipped to his nightcloak as a pass, he'd gone to the shelter beside which *Goshawk's* shuttle rested. He contacted the unbelieving people there, insisting that he would speak fully only with the Sula. It was his first view of Traders—they seemed normal enough, burly men and women whose main tasks seemed to be moving boxes and taking inventories. They'd radioed the ship, evidently quite pleased to pass the responsibility upward. Then had followed a long wait; he'd watched the shuttle depart, and spent an hour talking with the Traders—he did not believe half of what they told him, tales of offworld sights and pleasures. He'd nodded politely, but kept a skeptical grin on his face.

And now he stood before Sula Hermond himself. Steban arranged his face in the neutral aloofness Thane Valdisa had taught him, and bowed deeply to the man. Sula Hermond didn't appear overly prepossessing; he was old, to Steban's eyes, his hair gone mostly white. His eyes were more sad than anything else, as if some old mood had settled there, wrapping itself in folds of quiet and sorrow. Still, the body was lean, taut with well-toned muscles, and there were tracks of old knife scars on his hands. Steban felt that he'd probably like the man. He could understand why Thane Valdisa had once been his lover. "Sula Gyll Hermond?" he asked when their gazes met.

"Yes," the old man replied quietly. A strong voice, Steban thought, but I doubt that he raises it often. A man who rules by strength of friendship rather than fear. Steban glanced down at the bio-monitor on his belt—a light glowed green: positive ID.

"Your life has been claimed for Dame Fate and She of the Five, Sula. We of the Hoorka have received a contract naming you as the victim." Steban's voice was dispassionate, made distant by the rote recitation of memorized, well-rehearsed words. His eyes were half-closed, as if he rummaged in his head for the text. "You have several options—"

Sula Hermond had raised one hand, a gentle interruption. Steban wondered—this is the man who created the assassins, gave them their skills, had killed more himself than any of the rest, more even than the famous Aldhelm? Sula Hermond acted like a shy teacher. "I know the routine," he said, and he smiled. "You say it well, too—you've done the lessons properly."

In confusion, Steban smiled back, then immediately replaced the smile with the mask of Hoorka aloofness. He knew that Sula Hermond saw the slip and was amused by it; the man's smile grew larger. "Do you wish to negate the contract, Sula?" Steban asked. Thane Valdisa had told him to expect payment. Steban was already fumbling for the pouch on his belt in anticipation.

"I think not." Softly, always softly.

Steban looked up, bewildered now. He let the flap of the pouch drop. The old man still smiled at him, sad and gentle. "Sula, I thought—"

"—that I would pay," Gyll finished for him. "I know." Steban did not understand. From the tales he had heard, from what he'd seen here today at the port, the Family Oldin was wealthy. Surely the Sula misunderstood him. He shook his head. "Sula, if the contract is paid out, you will not be hunted."

The smile was still there, but harder-edged now, the eyes gone distant. "I realize that, son. Don't forget who wrote the code." The man took a deep breath, straightening and stretching, and Steban realized that, despite the Sula's age, he would be a formidable opponent. He looked quick and devious. "It would be amusing," the Sula continued, "to ask Thane Valdisa what she would do if I were to simply take this shuttle back to *Goshawk* and sit. Would she rent a shuttle herself and come knocking at the door? Do the Hoorka have the powered suits and heavy artillery she'd need to breach the hull? Boy, I tell you, the Hoorka wouldn't have the money, the people, the equipment, or the expertise. *I* could do it, she could not. The sunstar would rise laughing at the guild-kin."

Sula Hermond had become more and more perilous to Steban's eyes as the old man spoke, less the kindly teacher and more the vaunted assassin of Hoorka tales. Now he sighed, a long exhalation, and leaned back against the rough wooden wall of the shed, arms folded at the chest, and he was once more the gentle elder.

"But I won't do that," he said. "You'll tell Valdisa this, boy: I've neglected the gods of Neweden long enough—*my* gods, whether I want them or not—and I intend to do penance for that neglect. I'll put my life in Dame Fate's hands. I will run—tell Valdisa that it will end in the hunt of knives, and that I quite intend to see the sunstar rising tomorrow. Tell her that—you can remember it all?"

Steban nodded. He'd forgotten the Hoorka mask again; his mouth hung open.

"Good. You've done your duty then, boy. I know the rules of this game, if not some of the others I've been forced to play recently. At least I should be good at it. You have some tracer-dye with you. Use it, and you can go."

Sula Hermond extended his hands toward Steban. The apprentice fumbled again under his nightcloak, pulling forth a small vial. He touched the cap—a fine mist covered the hands, a quickly drying dew. "Fine. Now give my words to the Thane."

As Steban turned to leave, Sula Hermond called after him. "Tell her one more thing, apprentice. Tell her that he who creates has leave to destroy, as well. I don't like what Hoorka has become. This will be the last hunt."

"Sula?"

"Just tell her that."

Steban left the shelter. He was confused, his mind a tumult. He could not decide what he had just seen, which Sula Hermond was the true one: the harsh assassin, the gentle old man.

They stayed—a static triangle—as far apart in the room as they could. Gyll was seated behind his desk; Helgin, looking battered and bruised, was in a floater snuggled in the corner nearest the door; McWilms, his attention divided between the other two and the view of Neweden through the port, stood, arms akimbo, leaning against the outside wall.

"It was a good little joke, Gyll," Helgin said. His voice was hoarse, his face—what could be seen of it under the beard—was mottled with a gold-brown bruise. He twisted his beard around a finger. "A wonderful little joke. Hah, hah," he said with leaden precision. "Now please tell me that you weren't serious."

"I am. I'll run the contract."

"Don't push the joke too far, Gyll; I might not think it's funny anymore. I might even start believing that you're telling the truth."

"I know it surprises you when people do that." Gyll glanced at Helgin. The Motsognir stared back, impassive. "It's the truth. I want to go through with it."

"Valdisa will be one of the Hoorka, Sula." McWilms spoke, shrugging away from the wall. He didn't look comfortable to Gyll, as if the fit of the Trader-Hoorka uniform bothered him, or as if he were forced to be privy to a private quarrel in which he had no part. "We, ahh, didn't exactly leave her with many good full kin. She'll be one of those hunting you, almost certainly."

Gyll frowned. He'd suspected that such would be the case, but McWilms's words made him face the truth of that speculation. "I wish that didn't matter to me, Jeriad. But it does. It fails to change the essence of my decision, though."

McWilms looked through the port at the expanse of Neweden, as if fascinated by the cloud patterns. "I wasn't trying to change your mind, Sula, just pointing out something you might not have known. I understand your decision quite well, myself, unlike others."

"I don't," Helgin grumbled. He glanced at McWilms, scowled at his back, and turned to Gyll. "I don't understand at all."

"You're not from Neweden," McWilms commented, staring at the world, "and you're not Gyll. You're not *any-thing* like Gyll."

The dwarf shot a glance of venom at McWilms. Gyll spoke hastily, seeing the irritation in the dwarf—he knew the short-fused Motsognir temperament. "You know how the Hoorka are set up here, Helgin. A victim won't die if it's not his time to do so. Dame Fate rules Hoorka."

"That's superstitious rationalization that you don't believe much more than me. And you also set it up to buy out the contracts."

"There were always some of those who could afford to pay off the contract, and who still chose to run."

"Yah, the idiots with death wishes, or fools who felt themselves invulnerable, like childish heroes."

"Which am I, Helgin? Idiot or fool?" Gyll felt his own temper rising, his voice gaining volume to match the thunder of the Motsognir. McWilms had turned to watch them, his face grave, his left hand very near his vibro hilt.

Helgin gave each of them a look of disgust. "And people complain about *my* temper," he said. "You're neither one, Gyll. You're my friend, whether you let yourself believe that now or not. The Motsognir don't give friendship outside our race easily. I speak to you as I would one of my own: what the hell do you hope to accomplish?" Around and around: his finger toyed with his beard.

"I've no idea, Helgin." Gyll took a deep breath. "It could be a whim, I suppose. But too much has gone on around me lately. You know what I'm referring to. Now someone's gone to the trouble of signing a contract for my life. I want to know who that is—and there's only one way, by my old code, to gain that information, and that's to die. I don't intend to do that, but neither do I want to feed Hoorka's purse. That's not all," he said, raising a hand to silence the protest he saw forming on Helgin's lips. "The reasons are all small and all internal." *Yah, killing that unknown man, finding that I've been splendidly lied to, seeing the manipulation going on behind my back, even the finding of the ippicator.* "I'm not sure I could articulate them very well, but they add up to this—I want to take the chance. I want to see where I stand with Dame Fate."

"It sounds damned silly to me."

"Helgin—"

"I mean it." The Motsognir lurched to his feet. Unsteadily, limping, he strode over to Gyll's desk. "People don't play frigging games with their lives. Not if they're sane."

Gyll rose as well, leaning on the desk, hands on the wood. "And you don't tell me what I can or can't do." He stared at the Motsognir, but he could feel McWilms's gaze on him as well. "I'm well aware that this isn't a game."

"I know what you're after, Gyll—a sign from the gods that you've been doing the right things, that you've done all you could. You're looking for absolution. If the answer's 'yes,' then you live; 'no,' and you die. Very simple."

"And my business."

"No!" The dwarf stamped a bare foot into the rug. "It's not just your business. You've given allegiance to the Family Oldin. You owe them your services as Sula—you owe that to the Neweden Hoorka that have joined you."

McWilms stirred. "Those Neweden Hoorka will, to a person, understand what Gyll is doing, Motsognir. Leave us out of your arguments."

"The Oldins lied," Gyll said stiffly. "That makes me wonder about loyalty."

Helgin shook his head. "You're stubborn, the lot of you. The Oldins didn't so much lie as they did leave you out of their machinations."

"Lies of omission," Gyll half-shouted.

"Kindness to your frigging sensibilities, you mean," Helgin roared back.

For a long minute, no one said anything. McWilms returned to his survey of Neweden. Gyll and Helgin stood in poses of defiance. Then Helgin, with a curse of disgust, spat on the floor and turned. He stalked from the room without looking back. Gyll watched the door close behind the Motsognir, his feelings twisted.

McWilms moved away from the wall. He smiled at Gyll with compassion. "I'll bet he's a real bastard when he's mad."

Gyll's face was still downturned with anger. "You can be

certain of it." Then he forced himself to smile in return—the effort was not entirely successful. "I'm sorry you had to watch this, Jeriad, but I wanted you to know what I intend to do. It doesn't endanger your status here; Helgin will make sure of that, once he calms down."

"I understand, Sula."

"Helgin doesn't." Again, the frown. "He thinks I'm crazy. There're times I'd like to wrap that beard of his around his throat."

"Whenever you want to do it, let me know. I'll give you a hand."

Despite himself, Gyll chuckled. "Did you manage to find out anything in Sterka?"

"I checked around, as you asked, Sula. I think I have good news for you. Let me go and get the map I drew."

Gyll nodded. McWilms reached out, grasped Gyll's bicep with a firm hand. "We could wait until morning to do this, Sula."

"If Dame Fate wills it."

"She does. I'm certain."

Gyll smiled. "I'm glad you think so. But no, we do it now."

Outside her window, the sunstar was setting behind Sterka Port, sinking into a cushion of low clouds and touching the sky with a ruddy orange—not an overly pretty sunset, but adequate. M'Dame Tha. d'Embry stared into the last light of the day, shielding her eyes with a hand tinted the shade of the sunstar itself. She could see that the Trader shuttle had left the port—and she wondered whether it would return.

A spasm hunched her over, her fingers clenching the sill with whitened knuckles. *Falling apart, aren't we, symbiote, just like this world. Falling apart, and all we can do is delay the inevitable.* She felt the release of the symbiote's chemicals into her bloodstream, allowing her to slowly straighten. The sun had dipped lower, wrapping itself in the clouds, its light gone muddy.

Well, go ahead and make the grand gesture. It won't do any good, but you'll be able to tell your conscience that you tried. She sighed, and made her way back to her desk. She was conscious of her walk, that it was stooped and slow—an old woman's walk, an invalid's hobble. She lowered herself down on the floater's cushions, her arms supporting her. The effort made her wheeze asthmatically. She waited, felt her breath come slowly back. *So tired; gods, is it worth it?* And, as always when she had those thoughts, the symbiote—its survival dependent on hers—slipped a mild euphoric into her. So *you can sense the despair, symbiote? Too bad you can't communicate—what a strange existence you must have, a leech listening to the maunderings of a worn-out mind.* She could feel the parasite lurking, just below the threshold of her thoughts, as if she could, in some deep concentration, reach out and speak with it.

She stretched out a tinted hand, touched the contact that activated her com-unit. It swiveled slowly up from the desk. She laid her fingers on the keyboard and stared for a second at the contrast of her wrinkled skin against the smooth and perfect keys. *The machines stay young while we fall apart.* She tapped out the familiar letters of her key entry, then asked for the line to Diplo Center on Niffleheim. She thought for a moment that McClannan had been smart for once and canceled her validation code, but the screen lightened with the menu of access codes for Niffleheim, as well as the local time there: 2:04 p.m. That meant, if she was lucky, that Arthol would be back from lunch. Maybe. It would be safer to wait, but she was afraid that she'd be too tired later.

She was always tired.

502G3486DC: ARTHOL PETTENGILL. She keyed in the code deliberately, one-fingered, pressing needlessly hard. The screen went into a flurry of static as the tachyon relays kicked in, and she heard the ocean roar of interference. A minute. Two. She thought of canceling the call, of trying again later; then there was the distant click of connection. A faint, shrill burring rode in the interference, and then a wavering, static-pocked face stared out at her; mustachioed, balding, but with surprisingly young eyes in the pudgy face.

"Tha! Good to see you . . . well, perhaps not so good, is it? Trouble, it has to be trouble or you wouldn't look so serious, and you wouldn't be wasting good Diplo money on the relay."

She had never been one to mince words—she knew

Pettengill would not expect it now. "Do the Diplos want to be called murderers?" she asked dryly. "If that's trouble, then yes, you're right, Arthol. And you're looking good, young man—a credit to your teacher, I hope."

Pettengill chuckled at the contrast between the two halves of her speech. "You were a tough one to follow, m'Dame, but I try. I try. Now, what's this about a murder?"

"Your little Regent McClannan took out a Hoorka contract on a Trader—and an Oldin at that—Sula Gyll Hermond."

In the welter of interference, Pettengill frowned. "Hermond was the head of your assassins' guild, wasn't he?—the one we think killed Guillene on Heritage?"

"Yah, and he's been with the Oldins for the last eight standards. McClannan, over my protest, bought a contract on the man—a damned ugly way for a Regent to deal with his problems, if you ask me. I want McClannan taken out of here, Arthol. He's not competent. If you have to have him as a Regent, put him somewhere else. Not here. He'll botch it, I guarantee you." She paused for breath, ready to resume her commentary against McClannan, but she waited too long.

"And put yourself back in as Regent, Tha?"

He said it gently. It stopped d'Embry in mid-word.

For a moment, she was silent with shock, both at the soft accusation and at the fact that she'd not anticipated it, when it seemed so logical a conclusion to make. "Arthol, I think you know me better than to sling that particular piece of mud at me," she said carefully. "My interest in this is the image of the Alliance, as damnably altruistic and self-sacrificing and false as that sounds. And in any case, I think . . ." She halted again, realizing that what she was about to say was the truth. *So you've come to that decision at last. Good.* "I think that my health would preclude any reappointment. Hell, Arthol, I'm all done, both with New-eden and the Diplos. All I care about is making it through the next day. I'm an old woman, good for the occasional lecturing and speechifying, the relic you'll drag into your classrooms once a standard for the entertainment of the current batch of bright young hopefuls." A breath, again, and this time Pettengill did not interrupt. "Just let me do one more thing for the good of the Alliance, my friend.

Bounce McClannan out of here. Put him somewhere safe. Make him rescind the frigging contract. It's not the way we should deal with crises, this method of his."

She sat back, waiting. Beneath the view of her screen, his hands would be moving, clasping, unclasping—nervous habits she remembered well. His face shuddered with some vagary of the relays, breaking apart and reforming. "As I understand the Hoorka, Tha, the victim can pay off the contract. The Oldins are rich enough. Why not bleed their pockets a little?"

"McClannan—for some reason or other—thinks Hermond will run. And in any case, that's not the point. We're talking about a moral position, Arthol, not a game of chance. And I wouldn't be surprised if FitzEvard regards the contract as a violation of the Alliance-Trading Families Pact. He may even be right. You're likely to have to fight a long legal battle, whichever decision Hermond makes."

A hand, wavering in the mediocre transmission, came up to run a thumb along the line of his cheek. *That's bad—he's got that frown to his mouth. You've lost, old girl. It's just going to be words from here on unless you can come up with something good.*

"I don't think you've judged the situation correctly, Tha." She strained to hear him against the storm of the background. The friendly warmth seemed to have seeped from his voice, though it might have been only her own perception. "Again, as I recall *your* Hoorka"—he stressed the word—"the signer of a contract is revealed only if the contract is successful, the victim killed. I think we all agree that this is unlikely to go that far, in which case, all FitzEvard has are his suspicions, and he's not going to waste a lawyer's fees on those."

"So you're willing to take the risk as well."

"I think so."

"If we were to lose Neweden, we lose the ippicator bones as well as the other resources of this world."

"We won't lose Neweden."

She sighed. "What if Hermond should die, Arthol? What if it was learned that you'd been informed in advance of the contract? When FitzEvard raises the stink you know he'll raise, your career will go down with McClannan's, and you've got a lot farther to fall. You'll lose everything."

That threat was not a gambit she liked to play, both because it was weak and because it would lose her whatever affection the man might have for her. But she had no more strings to pull, no more favors to call in. All she had were empty bluffs, and a knowledge of a bureaucrat's instinctive fear for his reputation.

Pettengill's eyes had narrowed—in his fleshy face, that looked almost porcine. "I didn't think you'd stoop to threats, m'Dame. It's not like you. Why don't we just forget you said that?"

Arthol, I'm sorry for what I'm going to do. Really I am. "Why don't you worry about your future a bit?" she replied. "Diplo Center has a log of this call—that's automatic. Even if I'm gone when the investigation starts, they'll start checking the texts of all the incoming relays from Neweden in the past few months, and they'll find that I just told you about the whole problem—unless you are going to say that you'll erase the recordings after I sign off. In that case, Arthol, I'd ask you to consider that I could be making a copy here myself."

There was no expression in his eyes; they'd gone distant and unreadable. "That's a disgraceful attempt at blackmail. It shames you."

"It does indeed," she admitted. "Nevertheless, I'm doing it—call it trying to right a larger wrong with a smaller one. What are you going to do about it, Arthol? Are you going to play a game like McClannan, and let your career rest on the chance that Hermond won't run, or that if he does, he isn't killed? Let me remind you of another statistic—only about twenty-five percent of contracted victims escape the Hoorka if they run. That's pretty low, isn't it?"

When he hesitated before answering, she allowed herself a moment of hope, diluted by the manner in which she'd gone about it. But he shook his head at last. "You can't bluff me that way, d'Embry," he said, and even through the static she could hear the coldness in his voice. "Thank you, but I think I'll decline your little scheme. We have to trust the people we put in charge—I think you've used a similar argument when people here have tried to have *you* removed, after the Heritage incident, for example. Listen to your own advice, m'Dame. Let McClannan make his own mistakes."

"He's already made them. You'll find that out. Leave him

installed as Regent, and you'll lose Neweden within a standard."

"That's supposition only, and one that might easily be attributed to jealousy." The speaker in her com-unit hissed and crackled. "And I think that Regent McClannan would be distressed at the cost of this relay. Unless you have further arguments, m'Dame . . ."

She did not. It was over. "You've just made a mistake, Arthol. It will be a big one. Remember that I told you that."

"I'm not likely to forget this conversation at all. And I have a meeting in a few minutes."

D'Embry nodded wearily. She made a curt good-bye and switched off the com-unit. She sighed wearily, sinking back in her floater, her eyes closed. "Well, old girl, you tried. At least you tried."

Chapter 20

HE'D SENT MCWILMS ON BEFORE, following him by a few hours.

When Gyll stepped from the shuttle into the cool Neweden dusk, he scanned the flat expanse of the port. He put himself in the role of the apprentice who would be watching for him, charged with the task of keeping the contract victim in sight until the full kin took up the hunt near midnight. *Remember, it doesn't matter if the victim knows he's being watched, but don't expose yourself to danger. Observe, but stay your distance.*

Gyll saw the apprentice almost at once. The boy leaned against an empty trailer, making no attempt to conceal his presence. Gyll could see the red slash on the nightcloak even through the murk of gathering night. He bowed in the boy's direction; Gyll could not be sure, but he thought he saw an answering inclination of the hooded face. Gyll stretched unnecessarily, letting the boy see that he carried nothing but a sheathed vibrofoil—no suspicious bulges, no pack that might conceal sting or other weapons, not even the thick belt of a bodyshield. The apprentice would convey that information to Underasgard and Thane Valdisa. The full kin would be armed accordingly.

Gyll waved to the shuttle pilot and strode over the tarmac toward the gates nearest Diplo Center. Behind him, he could hear the footsteps of the apprentice. Gyll walked slowly, staying to the middle of the pedestrian lane, making no attempt to elude his shadow. The last glow of evening was in the sky, the first stars trying to overcome the lights of Sterka. The port beacons were on, turning the area into a glittering maze. There had been times when Gyll would have tarried to gaze at the scene, but he had no eye for aesthetics tonight. He gave his identification papers to a sleepy Diplo guard who perused them haphazardly and then waved him through the gates. Gyll went across the way and into Diplo Center, startling a night receptionist who had just come on duty and who seemed to have nothing better to do than to be certain that his hair was arranged satisfactorily.

"I wish to see former Regent d'Embry."

"I'm sorry, she . . ." the receptionist began, and only then looked up. He swallowed his words abruptly and set down his comb. "Excuse me, Sula. I'll ring her." He had a brief, energetic conversation under the security hood of his com-unit, then turned back to Gyll. "She's in her office, Sula. You may go right in." Gyll nodded. He glanced back to the entrance of the Center; the shadowy form of the apprentice stared at him through the glass. Gyll made his way to d'Embry's office.

It had changed since the last time he'd seen it. Only the desk was still uncovered, the remainder packed for shipment. D'Embry was in her floater, the room lights dimmed. Only her eyes moved when he entered.

"Sula Hermond," she said. He was surprised at how weak her voice had become, at how frail she appeared to be in the cushions of her chair. Her skin seemed gray and almost translucent—under her tunic, the hump of the symbiote bulged. It seemed larger than before.

"M'Dame d'Embry."

"I can't help you, you know. I tried, but they wouldn't listen, not McClannan, not Pettengill; no one. Except for McClannan, they all said that you wouldn't run." Her eyes closed slowly.

"Then McClannan was right," he replied softly.

"Which proves that there is a first time for everything." Her eyes opened again. She lifted a hand in a half-wave: flesh tinted ice-blue. "Take a seat, Sula."

Gyll went to the front of the desk, pulled a hump-chair from the floor, and sat. "You seem awfully damned relaxed for a hunted man," d'Embry commented.

"The contract run is something I know, if always experienced from the other side before now." He shrugged. "At least I know the rules of this."

"But not of other things? Such as the role of a Sula?"

"I thought I knew them, m'Dame. It seems I might have been mistaken."

She nodded as if she knew what he meant, or perhaps she was merely indicating that she had heard him; Gyll wasn't certain. This was not the d'Embry who had been Regent. This was a slow old woman who lacked the flash and fury of the Regent. Defeated, he thought. *The fight's left her, and she's given up.* The realization forced Gyll to alter his planned speech—he wondered if he shouldn't just forget this and begin the run now, save his breath for the hunt.

"It's FitzEvard's doing," he said baldly. "All of it; Gunnar's death, Renard, the Hag's Legion, probably the ippicator as well. Oldin's behind all the problems Neweden's had recently. I don't know his reasons—maybe just to spite you, m'Dame, to cause you difficulties."

She smiled at that. "The difficulties I've had aren't Oldin's doing. I managed them myself."

"M'Dame, Renard is in the pay of FitzEvard. The man's been here a decade or more, off and on. Renard organized the Hag's Legion, he's made sure that the lassari stay discontented and angry. As for the killing of Gunnar, that was done by an Oldin assassin. And, m'Dame, when Kaethe Oldin was here, she once showed me an ippicatorian embryo engineered from a tissue sample in the Oldin Archives."

Nothing. Nothing. Gyll had been certain that the revelations would goad her into rage, would rekindle the cold anger he'd seen in her before. It did not; she only nodded and clasped hands underneath her chin. "Why do you tell me all this now?" she asked, too quietly, too softly. "Two weeks ago ... perhaps less ..."

"M'Dame—"

"Sula, my access codes have all been canceled as of four hours ago. I can't contact Niffleheim except through slow-time channels. McClannan wouldn't know what to do with the information you've brought even if he were willing to listen to me. He'd most likely accuse the both of us of concocting the whole tale to discredit him."

The blank hopelessness on her face appalled him. "I'm sorry, m'Dame."

"Oh, so am I," she said tonelessly. "Tell me, Sula, are you leaving the Oldins?"

He shook his head. "No, I don't think so. I came here to repay the Oldins for lies spoken to me; I wanted to hurt them, to show them that I was angry. And I had a question to ask of you—I'd hoped that this would guarantee me the truth."

"And the question?"

He'd been thinking of it since Helgin had told him of the deceptions, since McWilms had arrived with his contingent of Hoorka. Gyll leaned forward, intent. "Do the Hoorka have a future here—on Neweden, with the Alliance?"

She smiled faintly. "It would be simple to lie to you like all the rest, Sula. That lie would hold the satisfaction of hindering the plans of someone who's given his allegiance to FitzEvard. You're so open that you'd believe anything I told you, Sula. You should learn to curb that inclination; it may kill you someday." She started to laugh, coughed once, then with a wracking spasm that drained her face of color. When she had recovered, she shook her head at him. "But I'm not going to lie to you, Sula, and you'll just have to accept that I'm not going to tell you the truth, either. I'm not Regent. I can't answer your question anymore. Nor am I Thane Valdisa, who holds the other half of the answer."

"You know McClannan, know how he'll react."

"Sula, I never thought McClannan would betray me the way he did. So much for thinking that I know the man. All I know is what's happened to me. I've grown old and decrepit in a world that's changed. Maybe Hoorka's done that as well." She looked at him, her gray eyes rheumy. "And maybe not."

"You won't answer."

"I can't."

"I think I knew the answer before I came here." Gyll glanced around the room, not wanting to look at her. "M'Dame, if you could find a way to tell your superiors what I've said, the regency might well be yours again."

"And then you could ask your question. Again."

"I know you didn't step down voluntarily."

She laughed, dry and hoarse. "Still after your revenge, Sula? You do tempt me, but as I told you, I've no authority here, and I find that I'm glad it's gone. Sula, if you're going

to continue with this nonsense of running the contract, then
you'll have your questions answered for you. I just pray that
you'll enjoy the solution. Or you can go to McClannan with
this story of yours, but I think I should tell you that he's the
signer of the contract against you. He's not going to believe
you; he won't want to. He'll shake his head and smile nicely
at you. He'll see nothing but a potential trap, and he'll laugh
you from the Center."

"So it's McClannan's contract." Gyll smiled sadly.
"Thank you for telling me — I would have always wondered.
It makes sense."

"McClannan's a fool. I told him he couldn't win this way.
If you live, you add to the reputation of the Oldins; if you
die, he stands a good chance of being removed by Niffleheim. I told him that; he wouldn't believe me."

"You seem to have good reasons for disliking the man,
m'Dame. I trust your judgment. I won't go to him."

"But you'll run." D'Embry shook her head wonderingly.
There was a slight tremor to the movement, a palsy.

"I'll run."

"You're crazy, Sula." She stared at him. "You come here
with a tale all wrapped up like a present, FitzEvard caught
in the bow. Yet you're going to go back to that same man as
one of his captains, *if* you manage to live through the
night — because of a contract you could void in a moment.
Sula, if you haven't paid off the contract because you don't
want to take Oldin money, take mine. I won't need it."

"M'Dame, it's neither money nor misplaced pride."

"Then what?"

He shrugged. "I'm playing by my old rules once more
before they're no longer valid. I'm letting Dame Fate have
Her way."

D'Embry sighed. She looked down at her hands. "Sula, I
never thought you really believed in that theology, or that,
if you had, your recent standards away from Neweden
would have destroyed your faith."

"I thought the same." He rose, with a groan of effort. His
legs ached, as if already fatigued from the night's run.

Her gaze had not followed him. "I find this foolish and
wasteful."

Gyll didn't answer. He moved toward the door, opening
it. "Sula?" she said behind him.

"Yah?"

"Good luck."

The apprentice still waited by the main doors. Gyll passed the boy, who moved back away from him, then followed behind. The sky was almost fully dark now, the stars at the horizon obscured in skyglow. He moved at an easy pace toward Sterka's busy streets. Gyll made his way toward the Street of Singers as Sterka changed from evening to night around him.

He came to the Street of Singers at an intersection a few blocks above Oldman Church. There, a figure in dark clothing, a bulky pack beside him, waved to Gyll.

"You're late," McWilms said, nodding to Gyll and watching the apprentice dodge into shadow—he knew that the boy would be calling for advice from Underasgard.

"There was something I had to do," Gyll said curtly. He glanced down the street toward the church. "Are they there?"

McWilms nodded. "Four of them, counting Renard—I was lucky; I watched them going in."

"What's our best approach?"

"I don't know, Sula. There's a rear door and two side entrances, plus the windows. They can't watch them all, but there's no way of knowing what they might have in the way of traps or alarms."

"Then we'll find out. You brought the equipment?"

McWilms tapped the pack beside him. "It's all here."

"Good. Follow me, and keep to the shadows as much as you can."

"And your apprentice tag-along?"

"If Valdisa's taught him well, he'll stay out of the way. Let's go, Jeriad."

McWilms shouldered the pack. Gyll in the lead, they made their way back to the avenue paralleling the Street of Singers. The apprentice ducked back between two houses as they passed. Gyll and McWilms moved quickly down the street, ignoring the stares of the residents, watching from porches and steps. "One of them, any of them, might be Hag's Legion, Sula. They could give a warning to Renard."

"It's a chance we take, Jeriad. You can leave if it worries

you too much. This is my bloodfeud—you don't have to be involved."

"It's my quarrel as well, Sula. Renard killed Ric, ultimately; who knows how many other kin have fallen to him? I'm going with you."

At the end of the street, they turned between the buildings into an alley once used by Helgin. Oldman Church sat before them, dark-shuttered and quiet. The structure looked empty, deserted, like the houses nearest it. McWilms set his pack down once more, rummaged through it to find a biometer. He set the controls, checked the range; diodes flashed on the monitor. "I'm getting four readings, Sula," he whispered. "It should be the same ones."

The apprentice turned into the alley behind them, halted in a scraping of gravel. Gyll turned, scowled at him. "Keep out of this, boy," he growled harshly. "It's none of Hoorka's business. Just be quiet." Wide-eyed, the boy nodded, his gaze more on McWilms than Gyll. McWilms nodded to him. "You heard the Sula, Steban," he said. "Do as he says— what we're doing has no effect on your contract." Again the nod; Steban slunk back into shadows.

They turned back to Oldman Church. "I like the nearest side entrance, Jeriad. No windows nearby—if we can get in, we might be able to surprise them."

McWilms raised a shoulder. "One way's as good as another."

"Get out the snooper and bodyshields—leave the rest of the pack here for now."

They buckled on the bodyshields, checked that their vibros were loose in their sheaths. Quickly, with all the skill of silentstalk, they slipped unseen to the side of the church. His back against the paint-peeling wall, Gyll used the handcode. *Snooper.* He gestured at the door.

McWilms aimed the snout of the device at the wooden door. A dot of scarlet showed on its face—he held the monitor toward Gyll, who sighed inwardly. Going to one knee, he examined the door carefully. He found nothing to indicate the alarm detected by the snooper. *It's inside,* he signaled to McWilms.

Other door?

No. Gyll hesitated, weighing his options. The likelihood was that all entrances were guarded or alarmed—it was just as likely that there was no way around it short of sophisticated electronics which would take hours to receive from *Goshawk*. Time was a commodity he did not have. At the same time, those inside would be expecting nothing: Renard, from what Gyll knew of him, was arrogant enough to expect no trouble from Gyll despite the declaration of bloodfeud; the man would not be here otherwise. And his contacts were probably good enough that he knew of the contract against Gyll. He, like the rest, would be expecting Gyll to be sitting safely in his ship. *Other side,* Gyll signaled to McWilms. *Give me a feint, then leave.*

McWilms looked at Gyll askance. *Dangerous.*

Do it. The gesture was harsh. Gyll's eyes brooked no further argument. After a moment, McWilms slid away around the far side of the building. Gyll waited, his vibro now out but unactivated. A minute, two: he heard a crash of splintering wood and the distant burr of the alarm. On the second floor, lights flashed on. He heard the sound of running footsteps, moving away from him. Gyll moved back a step, kicked—the frame gave way, the lock still attached, the door swinging open. Gyll switched on his bodyshield and moved inside.

Adrenaline surged through him, excitement raced in his head. He felt young again, invincible. He felt good.

A set of stairs led upward down a short corridor, light spilling down the steps. Gyll moved toward them, staying close to the wall. There were no shadows on the stairs—no one standing at the top. Gyll moved up them quickly, pausing on the third step to raise on his toes and scan the landing above him. There, the stair opened out onto a balcony that circled the church, a few doors opening off it. Hoverlamps, all lit, were spaced at intervals around the balcony. One of the doors to his right was open; in the light of the room beyond, shadows moved. Two people, he estimated. He moved toward the door.

When he was next to it, he put his back to the wall, reached in his pocket for a coin. He flipped it over the balcony's edge; the coin clattered on the floor below. "Micha?" someone called from the room. It was a deep voice, one that Gyll recognized: Renard. Gyll waited. He could hear the sound of a whispered consultation in the room; if Renard was the type of leader Gyll thought him to be, it would not be Renard that went to investigate the noise.

A man stepped out; a thin, wiry lassari. Gyll moved, hammering at the man's throat with the hilt of his unactivated vibro. The man choked, gasping, his knees buckling as Gyll shoved him aside, switching on his vibro as he moved into the room.

Renard was waiting. The sting fired even as Gyll moved. The Trader-made shield, far more supple than those the old Hoorka had employed, went rigid only for a second as slugs hammered into the walls and tore the life from the man Gyll had disabled. Then Gyll could move again.

He faced Renard.

The man's smile was nearly a grimace, showing teeth white against his skin. The plant-pet was coiled around massive shoulders, the sting held in large hands, its muzzle trailing a thin line of smoke. The man was bearlike, imposing. Renard threw the sting aside.

"The bodyshield indicates a lack of trust, Sula," he said, moving away from Gyll as the Sula advanced. Renard pulled his own vibrofoil from a sheath on his belt; the air was loud with the double howl of the weapons. Renard went into a guard of two—foil down and to the right of center: an unorthodox guard, one designed to throw off an opponent's timing. "You require a warning when such weapons are used on Neweden, don't you? I'm afraid I neglected to post it."

"Distrust works when one deals with a dishonorable opponent, Renard."

"Honor is a manmade virtue, Hermond. It has no existence by itself. I deal with my enemies by whatever method works."

"This method failed, Renard. I intend to settle our bloodfeud now."

Renard circled to the center of the room, Gyll moving to keep him away from the door. The foil was still down, waiting for Gyll's move. Gyll thrust with deliberate slowness; Renard's blade whipped up and slapped the thrust aside with a screeching of metal. Renard immediately riposted, a straight counterthrust. Gyll backed a step, batting Renard's foil aside as sparks flared. They halted, Renard's foil back in guard two, Gyll's up in a more traditional guard of four.

Gyll thrust once more, and this time when Renard parried, Gyll went around the movement in a circular parry,

down and then over as he advanced. Renard backed, his
vibro flailing. The weapons screamed. Gyll did not let Renard rest this time. He went into a compound attack, never
letting the other man take the initiative. Twice he thought
he had the man, his foil piercing Renard in the forearm,
nicking his chest. Blood showed on Renard's shirt, ran
down his arm, slowing his movements. Gyll advanced, confident.

And Renard again did the unexpected. With his free
hand, he snatched the plant-pet from his shoulders and
whipped it into Gyll's face as he stepped forward. Gyll
ducked away too late—the animal's spines lacerated his
cheek and temple, narrowly missing his eyes. Gyll blinked
away blood, trying to watch Renard's weapon.

The plant-pet flailed at Gyll again. Gyll blocked it with
his left arm, barbs digging into his forearm, letting Renard's
momentum carry the man toward him. He brought his foil
up; Renard's blade deflected the thrust and Gyll's vibro
only nicked Renard's side. They were now nearly corps-a-
corps, the vibros thrumming madly. Gyll leaned back,
kicked. His foot found Renard's knee. The man howled in
pain, staggering and dropping the limp body of the plant-
pet. Gyll thrust at the man through Renard's frantic defense. The vibro found Renard's chest; Gyll leaned into the
thrust, pulled back, lunged again.

Renard moaned, spitting a foam of blood. He fell backward, collapsing into a sprawl, his vibrofoil chattering on
the floor. Gyll picked up the weapon, turned it off.

There was a sound behind him; a footfall. Gyll whirled,
vibrofoil moving. Sparks flared with a clattering of blades.
"Sula!"

Gyll stepped away, seeing McWilms. "Damn it, I told you
to leave—you could have gotten yourself hurt."

McWilms flicked his vibro off, sheathed it. Gyll did the
same; the room was suddenly very still. "The two that came
after me were easy," McWilms said. "One was a woman,
who was the better of the two, and a foolish man who kept
getting in her way. I thought I'd see if you needed help. I
notice you don't. That's Renard?"

Gyll wiped at his face with a sleeve—it came away scarlet. Blood dappled his hands. "That's Renard," he acknowledged.

"Your face looks awful—some of the cuts are deep. Should I call the ship?"

"I have other things to do tonight. The cuts can wait."

"All Neweden will thank you for that man's death."

"He didn't die for Neweden." Gyll looked about the room. He found paper, took a stylus from his pocket. *I, Sula Gyll Hermond, did this,* he wrote, as Neweden law required. *My declaration of bloodfeud is over.* He laid the paper on Renard's corpse. "Bastard," he said. "Cowardly, dishonorable offworlder."

Still looking at the body, he spoke to McWilms. "Thank you, Jeriad," he said. "I know you didn't have to help me with this. Go to the Assembly and notify them of the outcome. I'm sure the Li-Gallant will be anxious to hear the news." He turned, wiping a trickle of blood from his eyes. "And do me one more favor. Give me your tunic."

"Sula?"

"There's a homing dot under the collar of mine—I found it before I left *Goshawk.* Tell Helgin for me that this is none of his business."

"As you wish." McWilms pulled his tunic off, handed it to Gyll. "Sula, none of the kin will think less of you if you come back to the ship now."

Gyll did not answer him. He stripped off his tunic, put on McWilms's.

"I'll be back after dawn," he said.

Chapter 21

GYLL SUSPECTED THAT there were now two apprentices—Steban behind, and one other ahead of him with the detector for the dye on his hands: in accordance with the code, the detector would function only when Gyll was more than two hundred meters distant from it. Closer, and the detector ceased functioning, giving him the chance due him by Dame Fate. Fine; they would know in what direction and how far away he was if they lost him—unless he could get beyond the unit's range. As he remembered, they were not exceedingly powerful, perhaps twenty or thirty kilometers at best.

Gyll began to increase his pace; he heard Steban shift abruptly into a trot to stay with him. Gyll swung around the first corner, turning right and breaking into a run. Startled pedestrians stared as he jostled his way around them—a gray-haired man, his face scored and bloody, dressed in dark Trader costume. Gyll turned right again, then settled into a walk once more. That feint should have drawn in the other apprentice—Steban would have relayed the news of the sudden flight. Yes, there she was across the street, peering desperately about in the inviolate circle Newedeners habitually gave Hoorka. She saw him in the same instant; Gyll saw her whisper into the relay button on her collar. A few seconds later, he heard the panting approach and sudden stop of Steban. *Good. Now they'll both stay closer, afraid they'll lose me again.* Gyll resumed his leisurely strolling, moving slowly toward the center of Sterka. He glanced at a time display in a storefront: 9:37. In a little more than two hours, the full kin would take up the hunt.

For the next hour and a half, Gyll made a sauntering tour

of the city, stopping first at a public facility to clean his face and stanch the flow of blood. He bought a flavored ice from a street vendor, sat on a bench and watched a juggler perform, shopped in several stores. Now and then he would turn abruptly, move at a trot for a brief time, darting and turning but always stopping after a few minutes. He faked weariness then, pausing as if short of breath in full sight of the apprentices. They stayed very near him, especially in crowds, sometimes both abreast of him, sometimes behind, but always within a few quick steps. Gyll saw no other Hoorka—he once made a dash when both apprentices were momentarily obstructed, knowing that they would call in any third, unseen watcher. They did not. He wondered what they were thinking, his shadows, of this crazy old man who sometimes seemed to forget that his life was dependent on the whims of Dame Fate, and who did not have the breath to elude them for long.

11:15. By now, the full kin would have been wakened and made ready. A flitter would be sitting near the dawnrock, ready to take them to Sterka and a meeting with the apprentices. He had to make his move now.

A mistake common to most victims was that they, oddly enough, became complacent under the loose and benign surveillance of the apprentices. They would try to elude the shadows at first, but after a few failures, simply stop trying—most of the apprentices were used to that pattern. Gyll had followed it as well; all his runs had been earlier in the night. For the last half-hour or more, he'd simply walked. He knew he could not outrun the girl, who was faster than Steban. Still, Steban most likely had better wind than Gyll. So a straight course was out of the question. Gyll needed to be able to dodge and twist, confuse them, present them with too many variables. The best place for that was in the streets nearest Market Square, bordering on Dasta. Faster now, he began heading in that direction.

Opportunity came early. The apprentices moved closer to him as the streets became narrow and more crowded. Ahead, the avenue rose in a series of long steps, curving to the right and, at the top, passing over another street in a low bridge. Suddenly Gyll broke into a run, heading toward a knot of people around a fruit stall. The apprentices moved behind him halfheartedly, waiting for him to run out of breath as he had every time before. Gyll halted, leaned over as if catching his breath, watching as the apprentices slowed to a walk. Then he pumped into a full run, shouldering his way through the customers around the stall. Shouts of anger pursued him. The apprentices were caught flat-footed, additionally hampered by the annoyed crowd. Gyll saw a side street, ducked into it, and then into a shop where a bemused clerk glanced at his scratched face quizzically. Gyll moved back into the dark recesses of the shop, followed by the gaze of the curious clerk. He pretended to examine merchandise—sexual toys—while keeping the window in the edge of his vision.

"Many of our customers like our stock of masks, sirrah. They can keep an, ahh, overzealous partner from making too visible a mark." The clerk stared at Gyll's face, a smile touching his lips.

"No, thank you." Steban trotted past, glanced quickly through the window of the store, but missed Gyll in the shadows. Gyll moved toward the door. He peered out, up and down the street.

"There's no need for shame, sirrah," the clerk said behind him. "We cater to a natural function. No one here will think less of you whatever your preferences for stimulation."

Gyll laughed. "Then I'll be back," he said, stepping into the street. The apprentices were not in sight. Gyll backtracked, staying close to the buildings in case he needed to hide quickly. He vaulted the low bridge, landing easily on the street below. At a jog now, he made his way back to the wealthier business sectors.

His luck held. He saw no sign of the Hoorka apprentices. Hopefully, they would spend the next several minutes looking for him in Market Square before the tracer told them that he was no longer close. By then, it would be too late.

Forcing himself to move calmly, to meld with the people around him as best he could, he went to a transit stop and boarded a public tram, taking it from central Sterka to its last stop on the southern outskirts of the city. Overhead, he knew, a Hoorka flitter would pass the tram, moving toward Sterka and the apprentices.

Gyll left the tram, moving from the small secluded station that served the farmlands around Sterka. A flitter-

rental outlet stood nearby. Gyll rented one of the
machines—an old flitter well past its prime—and flew south
across the fields toward Underasgard, perhaps five kilometers away in the hills. He put a hand in his pocket, fingering
the small round pellets there that had come from his ship's
armory. *I'm sorry, Valdisa, but it's time to end this farce.* By
now, the full kin would have learned from the chagrined
apprentices that Gyll was gone. The tracer would be used to
find him—if he was very lucky, he was already beyond its
range, and the Hoorka would have to guess which way he'd
gone. Given that, Gyll could, by lying low and continuing to
move, most likely elude the Hoorka without confrontation
and greet the sunstar free and alive. He did not count on
that luck, though; if he was still within the detector's range,
they knew which way he was heading, and he had only a
small time in which to do what he intended to do. He raced
the flitter as fast as it would go, landing finally in a clearing
near Underasgard.

The cavern mouth looked as it always did. The dawnrock
stood impassive under the stars, Gulltopp's light throwing
its shadow across the grass. The cave entrance yawned
darker than night under a wrinkled brow of rock. Gyll knew
that the guards would be there and watching—after his last
visit here, the vigilance would be tighter. He knew that the
old trick he'd employed then would not work again. No—
this time it would have to be a headlong confrontation; Gyll
would need luck. He muttered a brief prayer to Dame Fate,
the old words passing his lips strangely. *Praying again; next
you'll be bowing low to full kin and getting out of their way
like a lassari.*

He made a circuitous approach to the mouth of Underasgard, moving as quickly as he could without making excessive noise. It took all of his standards of expertise in the
skills of silentstalk, but at last he crouched behind a boulder
just outside and to one side of the caves. He took a deep
breath, held it, listening intently: no talking, but he could
hear two shallow breaths, amplified by stone. Gyll reached
into his pocket once more, took out a vial wrapped in cotton. He removed the protective covering and tossed the vial
into the cave mouth. A tinkling of glass, a sharp hissing: Gyll
waited a few minutes, then swung over the boulder and
darted into the cave. Two apprentices lay slumped on the

ground there, breathing deeply in sleep. Gyll smiled and moved deeper into Underasgard.

He knew the ways well. He slipped easily past the inhabited sectors into the less-traveled corridors. He broke the seal on a glow-tube, following its bluish light over the rough trails of broken stone. Slabs tilted beneath his feet, falling back with an echoing, dull clank. The noise did not bother him; there were no listeners here but the cave animals. He passed through a cavern where the light of the glow-tube failed to reach the walls, leaving him surrounded by leering darkness, where a cold wind blew past him like Hag Death's breath. He came, in time, to the cavern of the headless ippicator, and there he stopped, shock and anger welling inside him.

Bones were missing; not many, but a few. Gyll's eyes narrowed, and he walked nearer the skeleton. It was not disturbed or defiled—whoever had removed the bones had been reverent and careful—and by the tracks, the intruder had worn boots, such as those the guild-kin wore.

Abruptly, he knew who it had been, and knowing that, why. "Valdisa," he breathed. "Is it so bad that you'd sell what is sacred to the kin?" A chill not of the cavern went through him. D'Embry had said that he would have his answer if he ran the contract—he knew now. The code was cracked and broken, a vestige that would soon be gone entirely. Dead, like the ippicators themselves. "Valdisa, She of the Five will leave you with the Hag forever for this," he whispered, then straightened, inhaling. *No time, no time— do what you came to do.*

He set the glow-tube down and pulled a handful of dark pellets from his pocket. Frowning, he took each one between thumb and forefinger and twisted. Small, dry clicks accompanied the rotation; he counted them carefully. When each pellet was timed and armed, Gyll took two of the seed-like objects and dropped them carefully near the entrance to the ippicator's cave. "Rest forever, Old One," he whispered. Then he left, going back the way he'd come. As he neared the Hoorka caverns he placed more of the pellets, then—stealthily—set them around the Hoorka lair itself. He used the old apprentice backtrails to move toward the kitchens. There, in the greenish illumination of the glow-fungi, he saw Felling, the Hoorka's cook, sitting in his room off the kitchen, reading.

"Felling," he called softly.

The man looked up, his mouth agape in a rotund face.

His pudgy fingers dropped the reading wand. "Ulthane?" Felling stuttered with nervous laughter. He wiped his hands on his pants, his mouth undecided between smile and frown. "Gods, you startled me. I thought one of the little apprentice bastards . . . Well, you're certainly a surprise. Thane Valdisa's out on a contract tonight, if you wanted her . . ."

Gyll leaned against the wall. He smiled. "I know," he said. "She's hunting me. I'm the victim."

Felling started to smile, changed his mind. His gaze skittered about the room, nervous. "But . . ." he began, then shook his head. "You pick a funny place to hide."

Gyll laughed softly. "I'm not here to hide, old friend. I need you to do something for me."

"Ulthane, if you're being hunted—"

Gyll waved him silent. He moved away from the wall, taking a step toward Felling, who backed away. "Get everyone out of the caverns. You have about ten minutes. The kin are to leave everything and run. Anyone left here will be food for Hag Death."

"You can't mean that."

"Oh, but I do." He still smiled. "Underasgard will be filled with rock in ten minutes, buried and gone. Unless you want the kin to be part of it, get moving." Then, more softly: "I'm sorry, Felling. I truly am. Tell Valdisa this for me—tell her that from here on it will be the hunt of knives. I leave my fate to the Dame." He gestured harshly. "Now *move*, man!"

As Felling fled one way, Gyll went the other, out from the caverns, sowing his pellets and lastly putting one beside the dawnrock. Then he moved away from Underasgard at a run, angling deeper into the folded landscape of hills and forest.

Minutes later, he felt more than heard the explosions. The rumbling added speed to his feet, and he prayed that Felling had gotten all the kin outside.

Gyll knew that they followed.

He could feel it in his stomach, twisting with worry— he'd seen the flitter from a vantage point on a ridge near Underasgard, seen the noisy apparition wheel across the sky with its flickering riding lights, sliding behind the trees below him near the wreckage of Underasgard. The flitter's presence meant that someone in the caverns had the presence of mind to contact Valdisa before his explosives had brought down the rock. Which meant, also, that they would know he was near, that the detector would point toward him like a deadly finger. Gyll rubbed his hands; ill luck, that. Had the Dame been mindful of him, Valdisa might never have known of Underasgard's destruction until the dawnrock failed to chime at the sunstar's arrival. With luck, they'd have been scouring the land around Sterka for him. With luck.

But perhaps the myriad gods of Neweden had wanted to see the excitement of a close chase, the furious, frightened scurrying of the hunted quarry. Perhaps the Dame still intended for him to live.

Gyll was moving through a stand of trees newly shed of their leaves, moving diagonally up a steep slope. His boots were muddy to mid-calf, and he pulled himself up, gripping at branches and the trunks of young trees. The night was fairly bright. Both Sleipnir and Gulltopp were up now, and the woods shimmered in their double glow. Gyll struggled to the top of the rise, panting. *Worn out in truth this time, old man, and Valdisa and her companion will be fresh and anger-driven. Better find your reserves soon.* He crouched, head down, his breath loud and visible in the chill air. Sweat made his spine cold beneath his clothing; the dampness had gotten into his boots, numbing his feet.

Crack!

The sound was sharp in the stillness. It made Gyll draw in and hold his breath, brought his head up sharply, narrowed his eyes. Luck, his luck this time; across the valley he'd just left, two figures in nightcloaks moved. They'd been on the far side of their ridge when he'd made his climb. If he moved quietly now, the noise of his passage would be masked as he moved down into the next valley. The Hoorka—too distant to see who they were—moved slowly, obviously casting about for signs of Gyll's passage. He was within the near limits of the tracer; they knew he was close, knew basically which way he was moving. But the luck was still holding. They were moving at a slight angle to him, away from the obvious tracks he'd made getting down from that last ridge. It had rained recently, and the earth was soaked. Except under the carpet of dead leaves (and sometimes even there), his trail was painfully visible; if they found it, they would not need the tracer any longer. Gyll looked to the moons—it was around three, as near as he could tell. Dawn at Underasgard would be just after six— three hours. Even if they found his trail, he had a chance. His breath had returned. Gyll thought that he could keep the distance between them. To stay close, where their detector would be useless, gave too much to chance; a misstep, a sound, or a moment when he was not hidden, and they would be on him.

Crouching, he slipped over the top of the ridge and started down the far side.

There was a creek at the bottom, thin ice at the edges of noisy water. He stepped carefully across it, hoping that none of the rocks in its course would tilt and shout alarm to his hunters. The next hill was bare except for dry meadow grass; Gyll decided to move down the creekbed toward another stand of trees. The wind picked up a bit, blowing in his face—bad; it would carry sound behind him, but there was nothing he could do about the wind. He was almost to the trees. He glanced back over his shoulder. What he saw froze him for an instant. Against the night sky, a figure stood on the hilltop. It pointed at him. Another figure came up beside it. Together, they half-ran, half-slid down the slope.

A shiver ran the length of Gyll's spine. For a second, he could not move. Then, with a curse for the vagaries of his luck, he turned and fled into the trees, seeking height and shelter. As he ran, he put himself in his pursuers' place, trying to decide what they would do. One would be certain to follow his trail, but the other . . . that one might take the easier route through the tall grass, figuring that Gyll would make for the top of the ridge—a pincer trap, with the quarry between. Gyll pulled his vibro from its sheath but did not yet activate it. He retraced his steps a few meters, trying to stay in his tracks, then swung himself up onto an overhanging branch. Crouching against the bole of the tree, he waited. *Don't let it be Valdisa. Please don't make it be Valdisa. And keep me hidden.*

The Hoorka was a man, alone. Gyll thought he recognized the face, much younger in his memory, as a surly apprentice named Meka Joh. The Hoorka made his way through the stand of trees, his head—despite Hoorka training—down and intent on the trail Gyll had left. *Boy, you should have learned your lessons better. Use all of your vision—keep the trail low in your sight and your head up.* Gyll waited until Meka was underneath him. His muscles tensed for the leap.

He hit Meka just behind the head, flicking his vibro on at the same time. Gyll fell heavier than expected, twisting to face the Hoorka. Meka was slow, stunned, but his weapon—a Khaelian dagger—was out in a defensive position, instinctively. Gyll moved with a grunt of effort, his vibro moving past the dazed man's guard easily, warding off a slash of the dagger. The foil slid easily into Meka's midriff. With a low moan, the Hoorka doubled over. His head up, he stared at Gyll with wide, pain-stabbed eyes. His mouth worked but no words came out.

He fell.

Blood steamed in the cold; from Meka, from the gore covering Gyll's foil.

He felt very little: no guilt, no remorse, just a cold satisfaction that he was still alive, that he'd taken out his enemy. *Would it be the same if Meka were Valdisa, if she were the one I'd given to the Hag?* He shook the thought from his head—he must move. Gyll slipped the vibro back into its sheath, took the Khaelian dagger from Meka's unresisting hand, slipped the homing device for the dagger from the body's waist. Then, grimacing, he stripped Meka of the Hoorka nightcloak. He put the cloak on, feeling the once-familiar weight of the heavy cloth, the old clasps, the fullness of the hood behind his neck. It fit him well. He shrugged the nightcloak into place around his shoulders and made the sign of the star over Meka's body. "Rest well, Meka Joh," he whispered. "May the Dame snatch you back from the Hag soon." He strode away in the direction he'd come, pulling the hood over his head.

Once outside the trees' shelter, he looked for Valdisa. She stood at the top of the ridge, watching him. Against the sky, her hands moved.

? she signed.

Not there, Gyll answered with the hand-code, hoping that the nightcloak and darkness would allow his deception to work. Valdisa was perhaps forty meters away, but her face was hidden in the shadow of her hood. *Go around,* Gyll told her, waving her toward the far side of the stand of trees. *Circle. Surround.*

Valdisa hesitated. She seemed to regard him strangely. Then she moved, down from the summit and toward the trees. When the tangle of limbs finally hid her, Gyll put his back to the trees and ran upstream along the creekbed. *Be with me, Dame, and this will put an end to the night. Another soul's gone to the Hag by my hand, but it's not Valdisa and it's not me. Give me a little more time, and she can't take me.*

Running, he did not see Valdisa come back out from the trees, did not see her watch him and then—swiftly, lithely—begin the chase, keeping to the higher ground, moving parallel with him.

He could not run for long. His wind was low, his side ached with each breath, his legs were sore with fatigue. Gyll had put himself in good condition over the last few standards, but the night had taken its damage, as had age. He simply did not have the stamina of his youth. He forced himself to continue moving, if only at a trot, coming to an area of broken rock. He began to climb, seeking a hollow where he could rest in concealment for a while. He reached for an outcropping of rock with his left hand.

Steel grated against rock—his hand throbbed with stabbing agony. Gyll bit back a shout of pain and surprise. A Khaelian dagger impaled his hand. Like a live thing, it twisted and bucked, tearing flesh, grating against bone, blood spilling down his arm. It pulled loose even as he reached for it, a hissing coming from the tiny jets in the handle. The dagger turned in the air and was gone, spilling droplets of red. Gyll turned to watch it go, cradling his injured hand. Valdisa was there, above and behind him, and the dagger was back in her hand. Her arm went back to cast it once more. Gyll twisted sideways, sliding down the rocks, his hand in torment, sharp outcroppings tearing at his clothing and skin. Valdisa's dagger clattered against rock where he had been, falling and then leaping up again to return to Valdisa. Gyll found his footing and ran, knowing that the range of the Khaelian weapons was very short, aware that the fuel for it was limited. *Run. She won't throw again until she's very sure of her target.* He couldn't move the fingers of his left hand, and the blood poured forth—he put pressure on the wound as he ran, trying to stop the flow, gritting his teeth against the hurt.

He didn't know why he hadn't used the dagger he'd taken from Meka. *Was it because the target would be Valdisa, or did you simply forget with the pain and fear?* For the first time that night, he felt that Hag Death might be able to take him, and panic at that thought filled him with a new energy. He ran, knowing that Valdisa and the Hag were close behind, each pursuing him relentlessly. If he had harbored doubts that Valdisa could finish this task, they were gone now. She would. She would kill him.

The worst realization was that he was not sure if, to stop her, he could kill her first. Certainly he might be capable of it—self-preservation is a powerful motivator—but would he strike first with all his strength? To try to wound her, disable or disarm her, was to limit himself, to lower his odds. He knew he could not run long enough to avoid a confrontation. Already the new rush of adrenaline was gone. His breath was harsh and loud, his lungs cried for surcease. He had to turn, had to become the hunter instead of the hunted.

Damn Neweden, damn all of its gods: She of the Five, Dame Fate, Hag Death. Why did You bring me to this? The night could have gone easily, but You wouldn't permit it. Why, damn You? Why?

Ahead, the valley widened into a meadow dotted with large boulders. The creek meandered through the middle, glinting in moonlight. There was no cover here, but the walls about the valley were steep and high. Valdisa would have to enter as he had, along the creekbed—she would be too easy a target if she attempted to descend the cliffs. Gyll crouched behind a scree of rock, trying to slow his breath. He heard her footstep and rose slightly, Khaelian dagger in his hand.

He threw it, knowing he could not miss. She was too close.

And he knew he had been abandoned by the gods. The dagger tumbled, awkward, like any plain dagger. Broken. It struck her fully in the chest, handle foremost. Valdisa let out a cry and leapt back. The dagger flopped on the ground, the jets moving it spasmodically.

Gyll knew that dawn was close. It might as well have

been hours away. If he ran, she'd use her own dagger again, and this time she would not miss. If he stayed, she would come to him.

"Valdisa?" he said loudly.

He thought at first that she would not reply. Then her voice came from darkness. "You've destroyed the caves, Gyll. I hope it gave you pleasure—there's no home for the guild now. I'll have to go begging to Vingi, and we'll lose what little autonomy we had."

"You won't go begging if you've sold the ippicator's bones."

He heard her grunt of surprise. "So that's why you demolished Underasgard," she said. "Because of a religion you claim you don't believe."

"I would have done it anyway."

"Then you're simply vindictive and you deserve to die, Gyll. As for the bones—they would have staved off the inevitable. You've destroyed us, Gyll. The Hoorka have no future here, and your code and the guild will die together. I'll sell the rest of the bones if I can get to them, and we'll guarantee deaths, for the Li-Gallant at least."

You'll get your answer. I hope you enjoy it. "I'll smash the Hoorka myself, then. I told you that I could do it. Now I will."

"Hoorka wants your life. I'll have it, too."

"It's almost dawn, Valdisa."

"What is dawn, if the code's gone?"

He felt a thrill of fear tightening his back. "You can't mean that," he said.

"Does that scare you, Gyll? Good. But you needn't worry. You'll never see dawn." Then she stepped out, kicking aside the dagger he'd taken from Meka. He could hear the whine of her vibrofoil, could see the glimmering of vibrowire in the moonlight, the luminous tip glowing. "You have a foil, Gyll. Use it, and see if She of the Five will forgive you." Valdisa hefted the Khaelian dagger as well, holding it easily in her right hand. "Come out, or are you going to hide like a lassari?"

He'd finished tending the wound. Dame Fate had made her decree known. Gyll slipped his foil from its sheath, held it in his hand, unactivated. He ducked behind the rocks, moved a few meters to his left, then peered up again.

Valdisa was looking to where he'd been, the dagger ready. Gyll stood in a rush, flicking on his vibro. Valdisa whirled and tossed the blade.

Gyll sidestepped, his vibro in front of him. He was lucky; he managed to touch the quickly thrown weapon; that, plus his motion, deflected it enough. The keen edge nicked his side, tore a hole in Meka's nightcloak. Gyll rushed at Valdisa, who had transferred her foil to her other hand—their weapons met with a clashing. Brilliant sparks arced to the ground. Gyll tried to muscle past her defense; Valdisa parried, riposting. Gyll countered the attack, still advancing. They did not speak. Their feet scraped on rock, their breaths loud and harsh, their gaze always on the other's foil.

Valdisa had been good. She was better now. It took all of Gyll's skill to keep her back, to stop her from reaching him. The Khaelian dagger slashed through the air near him, hissing like an angry dragon, clacking against Valdisa's homing belt. She took the dagger in her left hand as fear hammered at Gyll's chest—he could not watch two weapons at once.

Neither had noticed the rising sound through the clamor of their vibrofoils, but now thunder rushed by overhead: a flitter, low in the sky. Valdisa's foil stopped in mid-attack, though she did not glance up at the craft as it passed them, nor did she let her guard drop to give Gyll an opening. Gyll had seen the insignia on the flitter's side: the taloned world of the Oldins. He lunged at Valdisa, a straight thrust. She hesitated a fraction of a second too long; his foil nicked her shoulder as she knocked his blade aside. He could see her hand, just at the edge of his vision, tightening on the handle of the Khaelian dagger. He knew she was ready to use it, and he did not have enough hands or the two sets of eyes he needed to defend himself.

The flitter wheeled about savagely, dipping, then careened to a halt in the meadow near them.

Valdisa, underhanded, tossed the dagger. The jets spat vapor, speeding the weapon unerringly toward him. Gyll tried to slap it aside with his foil. As he did so, Valdisa thrust, lunging.

The dagger struck him in the stomach, burying itself deep, twisting as it entered. The vibro slid into his chest, striking bone and then slithering between the ribs.

"Valdisa . . ." Gyll began. He could not feel his hands; he

heard rather than felt himself drop his weapon. The vibro
screamed against stone. Valdisa stared at him and he found
that, curiously, she seemed to be crying. He tried to smile to
her, but the night was dimming. Gyll could not be sure, but
he thought he saw Helgin step from the flitter. He would
have spoken, but the ground swirled around him, lumber-
ing, then slammed up at him. Gyll felt cool stone on his
cheek. He knew that he should be hearing the grumbling of
the flitter's engines, the keening of the vibros, but the
sounds were gone. There was only silence and the chill of
the rocks.

Then, nothing at all.

"Back away!" Helgin snarled. The sting he held was pointed
unwaveringly at Valdisa. "Turn the vibro off and toss it gently to one side, and back away from him."

Valdisa turned to face the Motsognir. Helgin could see
the glistening of her eyes; he could also see the blood on her
foil. "The body is mine," she said, her voice steady despite
the obvious emotion she was feeling. "It has to be given to
the signer of the contract."

"And I'm telling you to get away from him, or you won't
be killing anyone else in the future. I haven't got Gyll's
sense of honor, lady, and that's my friend lying there — I'd
love to see you pay for him. Now, move back."

She hesitated a moment, staring at the dwarf and the
weapon he held. Then she switched off her vibro (though
Gyll's still chattered on the ground) and moved away from
the body. Helgin came forward, knelt beside Gyll, one hand
at the sting's trigger, the other probing Gyll's neck for a
pulse.

"Damn," he muttered. "Oh, *damn!*"

"He's dead?"

"What the hell do you think?" Helgin said throatily. The
dagger was still in the body, its fuel exhausted. Helgin took
the weapon out, threw it down on the stones. He picked up
Gyll's vibro, flicked it off, and put the weapon in his belt.
"Help me put the body on the flitter," he said.

"The body's mine, Motsognir. You know the code. Go
against Hoorka, and we'll be hunting you."

"Where? I'm not like Gyll, Thane. I'd sit in *Goshawk* and
laugh at you. And I've got the sting."

"You can't hold it and the body, too."

Helgin scowled. He rose to his feet, legs well apart. He lifted the sting, pointed it at her chest. "I can move him myself if I have to, Thane, but I won't leave you standing there to stab me in the back while I do it. It's your choice. Frankly, I hope you don't decide to help me."

Neither of them moved for long seconds. Then Valdisa sighed. She shrugged. "All right, Motsognir. What's the difference now, neh? The code's junk, and there'll be no more contracts—I'll be killing those pointed to by Vingi. I'll help you." She looked at the body, the nightcloak tangled around it.

As they lifted Gyll's limp body into the passenger seat of the flitter, she leaned over it, feeling for the pulse. Helgin watched her, impassive. "You don't trust me, Thane? Did you think I'd lie to you?"

"I'm surprised you'd want the body, Motsognir, that's all. And it's my duty to see that Gyll's dead. The last duty."

"Gyll was my friend, and friends do what they can for each other. I couldn't get here quicker, but I'll take him back to the Oldins." False dawn touched the eastern sky. Shadows had become more distinct, color had returned to the landscape, the stars had fled.

"He was my lover."

"You certainly have a touching way of showing your affection."

Valdisa hissed, a sharp intake of breath. Her hand went to her vibro sheath, found it empty. She stepped back from Helgin, her hand fisted at her side. "Gyll would have done the same to me," she said.

"Keep telling yourself that. Maybe someday we'll both believe it."

Helgin swung into the pilot's seat. He revved the engines—the rotors whined as a harsh wind sprang up, billowing Valdisa's nightcloak, ruffling her short hair. Helgin leaned from his seat, bellowing against the roar of the engines, his beard flying. "Thane, I'll give you a chance you don't deserve, because *he* would have done it. You can come with me, go back to the ship. We'll make a place for you."

She hesitated only a moment. "No," she shouted back to him. "I can't."

Helgin grunted. "Good." He reached for the flitter's controls and wrenched the craft into a quick ascent, circling the meadow as he rose.

Valdisa watched until the flitter was gone behind the hills, until the morning stillness had returned. She stared for a long time at the blood spilled on the stones.

Then, the clouds touched with light, she made her way back to the ruin of Underasgard and her kin.

RM Meluch
The Tour of the Merrimack

"This is grand old-fashioned space opera, so toss your disbelief out the nearest airlock and dive in."
— *Publishers Weekly* (starred review)

THE MYRIAD	978-0-7564-0320-1
WOLF STAR	978-0-7564-0383-6
THE **SAGITTARIUS** COMMAND	978-0-7564-0490-1
STRENGTH AND HONOR	978-0-7564-0578-6
THE NINTH CIRCLE	978-0-7564-0764-3

*Available October and November 2013
in brand new two-in-one omnibus editions!*

Tour of the Merrimack: Volume One
(The Myriad & Wolf Star)
978-0-7564-0954-8

Tour of the Merrimack: Volume Two
(The Sagittarius Command & Strength and Honor)
978-0-7564-0955-5

To Order Call: 1-800-788-6262
www.dawbooks.com

DAW 48

S.L. Farrell
The Cloudmages

"Besides great, fast-paced fun, full of politicking and betrayal, Farrell's tale is a tragic love story with a surprisingly satisfying ending."
—*Booklist*

"Richly imagined fantasy... Intriguing, fully developed characters abound. This entry can only enhance Farrell's reputation as one of the rising stars of Celtic fantasy."
—*Publishers Weekly*

HOLDER OF LIGHTNING
978-0-7564-0152-8

MAGE OF CLOUDS
978-0-7564-0255-6

HEIR OF STONE
978-0-7564-0321-8

To Order Call: 1-800-788-6262
www.dawbooks.com